The Christmas Chronicles

ALSO BY JEFF GUINN

The Sixteenth Minute: Life in the Aftermath of Fame
(with Douglas Perry)

*Our Land Before We Die: The Proud Story of
the Seminole Negro*

*You Can't Hit the Ball with the Bat on Your Shoulder:
The Baseball Life and Times of Bobby Bragan*
(with Bobby Bragan)

*Sometimes a Fantasy: Midlife Misadventures
with Baseball Heroes*

Dallas Cowboys: Our Story

*When Panthers Roared: The Fort Worth Cats
and Minor League Baseball* (with Bobby Bragan)

JEREMY P. TARCHER/PENGUIN

a member of Penguin Group (USA) Inc.

New York

THE CHRISTMAS CHRONICLES

The Autobiography of Santa Claus

How Mrs. Claus Saved Christmas

The Great Santa Search

JEFF GUINN

JEREMY P. TARCHER/PENGUIN
Published by the Penguin Group
Penguin Group (USA) Inc., 375 Hudson Street, New York, New York 10014, USA •
Penguin Group (Canada), 90 Eglinton Avenue East, Suite 700, Toronto, Ontario M4P 2Y3, Canada
(a division of Pearson Penguin Canada Inc.) • Penguin Books Ltd, 80 Strand, London WC2R 0RL,
England • Penguin Ireland, 25 St Stephen's Green, Dublin 2, Ireland (a division of
Penguin Books Ltd) • Penguin Group (Australia), 250 Camberwell Road, Camberwell,
Victoria 3124, Australia (a division of Pearson Australia Group Pty Ltd) • Penguin Books
India Pvt Ltd, 11 Community Centre, Panchsheel Park, New Delhi–110 017, India •
Penguin Group (NZ), 67 Apollo Drive, Rosedale, North Shore 0632, New Zealand
(a division of Pearson New Zealand Ltd) • Penguin Books (South Africa) (Pty) Ltd,
24 Sturdee Avenue, Rosebank, Johannesburg 2196, South Africa

Penguin Books Ltd, Registered Offices:
80 Strand, London WC2R 0RL, England

The Autobiography of Santa Claus was originally published in 1994 by the Summit Group
First Jeremy P. Tarcher/Penguin edition 2003
First trade paperback edition 2010
Copyright © 1994, 2005, 2006 by Jeff Guinn and 24Words, LLC
All rights reserved. No part of this book may be reproduced, scanned, or distributed in any printed
or electronic form without permission. Please do not participate in or encourage piracy of
copyrighted materials in violation of the author's rights. Purchase only authorized editions.
Published simultaneously in Canada

Most Tarcher/Penguin books are available at special quantity discounts for bulk purchase
for sales promotions, premiums, fund-raising, and educational needs. Special books or book
excerpts also can be created to fit specific needs. For details, write Penguin Group (USA) Inc.
Special Markets, 375 Hudson Street, New York, NY 10014.

The Library of Congress catalogued the hardcover edition as follows:

Guinn, Jeff.
The Christmas chronicles / Jeff Guinn.
p.   cm.
ISBN 978-1-58542-669-0
1. Santa Claus—Fiction. 2. Christmas stories. I. Guinn, Jeff. Autobiography of Santa Claus.
II. Guinn, Jeff. How Mrs. Claus saved Christmas. III. Guinn, Jeff. Great Santa search. IV. Title.
PS3557.U375C48   2008   2008018852
813'.54—dc22

ISBN 978-1-58542-830-4 (paperback edition)

Printed in the United States of America
1 3 5 7 9 10 8 6 4 2

BOOK DESIGN BY AMANDA DEWEY

CONTENTS

THE CHRISTMAS CHRONICLES

The

AUTOBIOGRAPHY

of

SANTA CLAUS

Contents

Editor's Preface

I WROTE A BOOK with Santa Claus. Not too many people can say that. In fact, I'm the only one I know of.

In just a page or two, Santa will begin telling you about his life, and in his words, not mine. But I thought you might want to know how this book came to be written in the first place. It was sort of an accident, but a wonderful one.

A few Decembers ago, my newspaper printed a story I'd written about little-known facts of Christmas—why it's celebrated on that specific date, how the name "Saint Nicholas" was changed to "Santa Claus" in America, and some other things. Most of us take our Christmas traditions for granted. We have no idea about when some of our favorite customs started, or who was responsible. I enjoyed writing the story, but I pretty much forgot about it right after it appeared in print.

A few months later, the receptionist in the newspaper's lobby called my third-floor office and said a man was asking to see me. "He seems very friendly," she explained. "He says his name is Felix."

The fellow was about average height and had an engaging smile. He was dressed in an ordinary gray business suit, wore glasses, and was a bit over-weight. I guessed he was in his early forties.

"You're Felix . . . ?" I asked, expecting him to tell me his last name.

"Just Felix." He grinned as he removed a bit of folded newspaper from his coat pocket. It was a copy of my Christmas story.

"We read this with a lot of interest," Felix said. "It's all right as far as it goes, but it didn't really have much important information. So we took it to him, and he said he believed it was time to tell the real story, all of it."

Not pleased to hear my story criticized, I replied sharply, "Who exactly is 'we,' and who exactly is 'him'?"

Felix's smile grew even wider. "I can't tell you yet. What we hope you'll do is agree to accompany me on a trip. When we get to where we're going, you'll get your answers. Please—don't worry. This isn't a trick. It's just that we're people who value our privacy. You're going to be asked to help with a writing project, but before we leave, you must agree not to tell anyone about who you met, or where—that's if you decide you don't want to get involved."

Like most writers, I'm curious by nature. Besides, there was something about Felix that made me trust him. I agreed to his conditions. We left the next day to meet this mysterious "him."

I can't describe the trip itself. Obviously, we went to see Santa Claus at the North Pole, but part of my agreement with Santa is that I can't reveal how we got there.

When we arrived, you can imagine my shock at being greeted by an instantly familiar figure. In person, Santa is everything you'd want him to be—wise and jolly, white-bearded and thick-bellied, and, above all, genuinely warm and caring.

Before we had our private talk, Santa introduced me to some of his helpers—his "friends," he insisted on calling them. My amazement at actually meeting Santa Claus doubled when I found myself shaking hands with some of the most famous people who ever lived and, apparently, hadn't died. I won't name them here—Santa will do that in his own time.

Once we were finally in Santa's study, seated in front of a warm fire and munching chocolate chip cookies, he explained why he had invited me to the North Pole.

"The true story of Christmas, and my part in it, is as wonderful and complicated as the world itself," Santa said. "Very few people really know much about the holiday at all. For some time, Layla has been urging me to tell the real story, so everyone will understand Christmas and Santa Claus better."

"And Layla is . . . ?" I asked.

"My wife, of course," Santa chuckled. "She's a much more interesting person than the meek little lady people usually picture when they think of Mrs. Santa Claus. Anyway, I'm not a writer myself, so I thought I might find one who'd record my story as I tell it, then turn it into a book for everyone to read. The story you wrote for your newspaper convinces me that you truly love Christmas, although I'm afraid you don't know nearly as much about it as you think you do."

How could I refuse? I called home, told my family I'd be away for a while, and began helping Santa with his book. It seemed more like fun than work. Santa's stories were full of adventure and wonder. Sometimes Layla, Felix, or other friends would join us and add their comments.

Throughout the project, Santa insisted that our book be historically accurate. "We want readers to learn some things about world history as well as the history of Christmas," he constantly repeated. Whenever any date or other fact was in doubt, we consulted history books. So, as amazing as it might seem, just about everyone whose name you read here really did exist. Only a few of the main characters—Phillip, Felix, Layla, Dorothea, and Willie Skokan—can't be found in history books, because they valued their privacy so much.

Well, that's enough from me. Santa's the one whose voice you want and need to hear, so prepare yourself for a unique story that's equal parts history and magic.

In closing, let me assure you doubters—there really is a Santa Claus. I learned from working on this book that you don't need to go to the North Pole to find him. It's only necessary to look into your own heart.

—*Jeff Guinn*
Fort Worth, Texas

Foreword

YOU'RE RIGHT TO BELIEVE IN ME.

Oh, I know it's hard sometimes. There always are people eager to tell you there isn't a Santa Claus, that I'm just a story made up long ago and trotted out every Christmas since. I suppose I should be angry with them, but I feel sorry for them instead. Have you ever noticed that it's always unhappy people who attack the things happy people believe in? That's been my observation, at least, and I suppose I've been around long enough to know.

So let's start with this. I've decided it's time to tell the real story of Santa Claus, and to have it told by the one who knows it best—me. It's a long story, going back the better part of two thousand years. I'll try not to bore you too much with dates and places, but there are important times and people in my life you should know more about—my wife, for one, and Felix, who was my first helper fifteen centuries ago, and others. Without many faithful friends, my role in Christmas wouldn't have been possible, and that's one reason I want to tell my tale. I always get the credit. From the beginning, my philosophy has been, "It's better to give than to receive," and I want to see the credit properly shared among all those who deserve it.

I remember one time, for instance, when the pilgrims maintained it wasn't right to celebrate Christmas at all. They decided anyone caught observing the holiday would be punished, and I found myself telling Felix that I should just give up ever doing my holiday rounds in the new land called America. Felix convinced me otherwise, of course; we'll tell that story in its proper time. But it's a good example of why someone else deserves some of the glory. Probably I was just feeling discouraged when I made that remark to Felix—even Santa Claus gets discouraged sometimes—and almost certainly I would simply have waited the pilgrims out. Still, it's also possible that without Felix's encouraging words, no child in the United States would ever have awakened Christmas morning to find filled stockings and a present from old Santa under the tree.

Another reason I'm writing this book is to clear up some matters that apparently have troubled too many people for too long. On Christmas Eve, for instance, they wonder how Santa can possibly get around to the house of every deserving child in the whole wide world. Why do I have different names in different countries if I'm just one person? Do my helpers and I really live at the North Pole, and do reindeer really know how to fly?

I'll tell what I can, but I must say this right away: There are some answers I don't know, either. This is the difference, the very important difference, between illusion and magic. Illusion is when something happens that seems impossible, but eventually can be figured out. Magic is when something happens that can't be understood. Quite simply, illusion is explained, but magic just *is*. There's some illusion in what I do, but there's a fair share of magic, too. You'll learn about times I couldn't quite understand what was happening to me, and how I finally realized there are some things that can't be understood, just accepted.

But what I hope you'll learn above all else is that the real magic of Christmas involves love, and that the greatest joy is giving rather than getting. Just as this isn't a perfect world, Christmas isn't a perfect holiday, and won't be until all human beings on this beautiful planet can live together in harmony. No single person can make this happen, but if we each do what we can, then there's still hope that one Christmas Day we'll find ourselves enjoying the most wonderful gift possible—complete peace on Earth, and goodwill from everyone to everyone.

Well! That was quite a speech I let myself make! Layla—I suppose she's better known as Mrs. Claus—would point out I was sounding like quite an old windbag! "Get on with the story!" she'd say if she were reading this. And she'd be right; it's time to begin. After all, I don't want to put you to sleep.

Unless, of course, it's Christmas Eve.

X-large

~~De~~ Paris ~~Tru~~ Tack

Derby Originals

Patterned Double

Layer Nylon ~~Ryer~~ figure

8 Cow Halters

ONE

My Earliest Memories

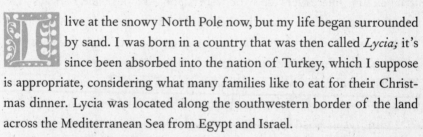 live at the snowy North Pole now, but my life began surrounded by sand. I was born in a country that was then called *Lycia;* it's since been absorbed into the nation of Turkey, which I suppose is appropriate, considering what many families like to eat for their Christmas dinner. Lycia was located along the southwestern border of the land across the Mediterranean Sea from Egypt and Israel.

The year of my birth is recorded as 280 A.D., or two hundred and eighty years after what is now considered the "official" birth year of a much more important baby, whose name was Jesus. Actually, records weren't kept as carefully in those days, so no one is really sure in which year Jesus was born. The main thing is, I was born about three centuries later in the Lycian town of Patara. Sometimes I find it odd, and other times amusing, that I know the exact details of when I came into this world, but have no idea how long I'm going to stay. Patara was a prosperous village as villages went in those days, meaning many of the four hundred people living there got enough to eat and had houses to live in. Today my hometown would seem very primitive—no indoor bathrooms, no video games, no cars roaring up and down its streets. But everybody knew everybody else's name.

My father's name was Epiphaneos and my mother was called Nonna. They were quite old when I was born, probably in their fifties. People didn't live as long then as they do now—maybe to sixty if they were lucky. We didn't have much in the way of medicine, and everybody ate what they wanted without worrying about calories. Anyway, I  arrived long after my parents had given up hope of having a baby. I was quite a surprise to them! They celebrated by naming me Nicholas, which means "victorious." It was a name I liked very much. No one used nicknames in those days, so I was always Nicholas and never Nick or Nicky. I acquired my nicknames much later in life.

We were a Christian family. As I grew up and learned more and more about my religion, one thing Jesus said always stayed with me: that we should treat other people the way we would want them to treat us. That made sense to me even as a little boy. Other parts of being a Christian weren't as much fun. There were days you were supposed to fast, and I always liked to eat. Even goat cheese tasted good to me. One of the sadder things about living now at the North Pole is that I just can't get goat cheese anymore. Maybe a few of you reading this book will leave me some next Christmas Eve instead of the usual cookies, though I'm certainly glad to have the cookies—especially homemade chocolate chip, if anyone's taking notes.

I was given a good education, by which I mean I was taught to read and write Hebrew, Greek, and Latin. There were a lot of languages, because we lived in what was called a "melting pot," or a place through which people of all different countries and races might pass. If by chance someone came to our family inn and spoke only Hebrew, he might go on to the next town and the next inn if we weren't able to answer back in Hebrew.

Being able to read and write in several languages made me something of a scholar. There wasn't any formal schooling then. Boys learned as much as their parents wanted them to. Girls, I'm sorry to say, were seldom allowed to go to school at all. People thought they were only suited to stay home, keep house, and someday raise children of their own. I'm glad people finally learned better, although it took much too long. (I hope my wife, Layla, will be pleased I mentioned this so early in my book; it was always an important point to her, as you'll learn when I get to the part of my story about when I met her. But that's a hundred years after the time we're talking about now.)

My parents guessed they wouldn't live long enough to see me grow up, and they were right. They died peacefully during the year I was nine—my father first and my mother a few months later. I loved them very much and grieved over their loss. I believed in heaven and felt they'd gone to live with Jesus, but I wished they could have gone on living with me. All these centuries later I remember them very well. As long as people are remembered by someone, they're never completely gone. My parents were generous people, and I'm sure that somewhere they've enjoyed watching their son go on to such an unexpected—and long—career.

It was arranged that I would be put in the care of guardians, the priests of the local church. There were five of them, all very busy most days traveling from our village to other smaller towns. These trips could be long ones. Often, there could be forty miles or more of desert between one place and the next. By choice these priests were poor, giving up nice clothes and good food for the privilege of serving others. They didn't even have oxcarts or donkeys to take them where they wanted to go. They walked. I admired them, but I didn't think much of all that walking.

I stayed at the inn where I'd lived with my parents. The priests had papers from my father allowing them to spend the money I inherited as they saw fit. Therefore, they paid the staff of the inn a little extra to make sure I received all my meals and got my clothes washed when they were sufficiently dirty, which usually meant once every few weeks. Lots of sand blew through the air and there were no washing machines. Clothes were washed in big pots of boiling water, and it was a chore to haul buckets of water from the river back to the inn. I didn't mind my clothes staying dirty awhile, since I was always the one told to go fill the buckets.

My life stayed the same for several more years, but as I grew older I noticed that some people in Patara weren't as well-off as I was. It didn't seem right that I ate two or three good meals every day when some of the poorer families were lucky to have a little bread, and perhaps even went hungry once in a while. I found I couldn't enjoy my nice clothes when neighbors had to wear rags. I talked about it with the priests, and they all agreed I was right to feel uncomfortable. But they said <u>I would have to decide for myself</u> how to deal with those feelings.

There was one priest in particular named Phillip. His job was to take care of the church's goats and chickens. He looked rather like a goat himself, right down to his scraggly little white chin-beard. I helped Phillip with the animals sometimes, and he was someone whose opinion I especially respected.

"How can I stop feeling guilty about having so many things when my neighbors have nothing?" I asked him one day. We'd just fed the goats and were standing alongside their smelly stall.

"The answer is already in your heart, Nicholas," he replied, tugging at his beard. "You've heard the words of Jesus. The richest men in heaven will be the ones who gave away the most during their time on Earth."

I knew he meant I should give away most of my things, such as my warm clothes to those wearing rags, my good food to those who were hungry, and so forth. I was willing to do it, but even simple generosity had its problems, the most important of which was other people's pride. Adults would feel ashamed if it became known they'd accepted charity from a twelve-year-old boy. I said good-bye to Phillip and went back to the inn to think about it some more.

That night I was sitting in the inn's dining hall, still feeling troubled. I'd had my usual nice supper of bread and cheese and fat juicy olives, washing it all down with lots of fresh goat's milk. By this time, most of the guests had been fed and were back in their rooms. A few men from my village were sitting in front of the fireplace talking about Shem, another citizen of Patara who'd once been rich, only to fall on hard times. He'd made some money selling camels and then invested the money in two freight ships. Sometime later, the ships were caught in a storm and sank. Shem's fortune sank with them. Now he went from house to house in Patara asking to mend fishing nets for whatever anyone wanted to pay him. His wife had died years earlier, and he was trying to raise three daughters all by himself. And that was really Shem's problem, these men were saying.

"All three girls of marriage age, and no money for even one dowry," one of the men remarked. "It's sadder still because each has a young man who wants to marry her. I think the oldest daughter's fifteen, too."

One of the other men made a clucking noise with his tongue. "Fifteen! Another few years and it'll be much too late for her to ever marry. Oh, well, it makes no difference. Shem will never be able to put aside money for their dowries in a hundred years."

I should explain here that back then people got married at much younger ages. Girls as young as twelve or thirteen were considered ready to be brides. Boys could wait a little longer, maybe until they were fifteen or sixteen. Shem's daughters were fifteen, thirteen, and twelve, meaning all three were old enough to be married.

But the dowry custom complicated things. When a man married a woman, he had to support her for the rest of her life, so the bride's father was expected to give his daughter's new husband some money to help pay these future expenses. I thought the idea was silly when I first heard it, and still do. It was just another way in those unenlightened days that women were treated as though they weren't as good as men.

So these poor girls all had suitors who wanted to marry them, but custom wouldn't allow those marriages to take place as long as Shem didn't have money for dowries. Then I had a wonderful idea. I had money, even if Shem didn't. I could give him enough money for each girl to have a fine dowry and be able to marry her suitor. That would make the daughters happy. Since Shem wouldn't have to support them anymore, it might mean he wouldn't have to work as hard mending nets. Then everyone would be pleased, most of all me, because I would have done something generous and shared my wealth.

I went back up to my room and pulled out the small sack of silver coins I kept under my bedding. If necessary, I could have gone to any one of several people in town who were keeping some of the money my parents had left for me, but when I spilled the coins out on my bed I saw I really had plenty for the dowries—twelve coins in all. Four silver coins per daughter would be just right.

But how could I give the girls the money without shaming their father? If I walked up to Shem's door and told him what I was doing, he would surely feel humiliated. And if I just left the sack of coins on his doorstep, some passerby might steal it.

The next day I went back to talk a little more to Phillip, the priest. This time he was gathering eggs and asked me to help him. We went from hen to hen, chatting all the while. As we walked, I performed some handstands, and then balanced myself on the log fence surrounding the chicken coops. As a boy, I wasn't as heavy as I am now.

"I see you're athletic besides being so clever, Nicholas," Phillip said. "You say you don't want to embarrass Shem. Well, do you think you can climb a ladder? His house has lots of windows, and everyone opens all their shutters at night so cool breezes can blow through them."

Phillip never actually told me I should sneak into Shem's house and leave the money, but his meaning was clear. It sounded like an adventure, and I set out to give my secret gifts that very night.

I waited until well after dark, when everyone in the village was asleep. We all got up very early, often before dawn, so we never stayed up too late at night. I wore my darkest robes and carried a small ladder borrowed from the workers' shed down the street, and moments after leaving the inn I was standing outside Shem's house.

Although he was poor, Shem and his daughters still lived in the house he had built when he was rich. It was just one story tall, but the walls were higher than those of most houses, rising almost twice as high as my head. The windows were up high, too, closer to the roof than to the floor. This was because heat and light were provided by fires, and as the smoke rose toward the ceiling it was supposed to waft out the open windows. Often, though, the winds blew in off the desert and the smoke just came back into the houses, making people's eyes water. Chimneys weren't invented yet.

I listened outside the house for a few moments. No one inside was making a sound. I guessed the house would have three rooms, one a big family room where meals were prepared and eaten, a bedroom for the three girls, and a bedroom for their father. I intended to leave the silver coins in Shem's room, but as I stood outside his house I began to wonder whether—when he woke in the morning and found the coins—he'd know they were for his daughters' dowries. A better plan would be to leave the coins in the room where the daughters slept. If they really had suitors who wanted to marry them, they'd know how the money should be spent.

My next problem was finding out which room belonged to the girls. The only way to find out was to look. I leaned my ladder against a wall close to the nearest window and climbed up. The shutters were half open. I peeked inside. It was very dark in there. There wasn't any fire lit, at least in that room, although I could hear the sound of someone snoring. Was it Shem or one of his daughters? I poked my head farther inside the room. Just then the desert wind gusted and the heavy wooden shutter was blown hard against my head. There was a loud thud as shutter and skull came together. I yelped with pain, waking up the snorer, who turned out to be Shem.

"Who's there?" he barked. "If you're a thief, I have a stick!"

I had no desire to meet Shem's stick. My head hurt enough already. Forgetting I was on a ladder, I pulled back from the window, toppled over into the street, and landed on a pile of straw. Pigs had spent time in that straw, and had deposited fragrant souvenirs. Dizzy from the knock on the head and smelly from pig droppings, I staggered to my feet, grabbed my ladder, and hurried back toward the inn. Shem was making a fearful uproar inside his house, screaming to his daughters to wake up and help him catch the thief. Startled, they began screaming, too.

As I ran, I heard behind me the sound of doors being thrown open and the voices of Shem's neighbors calling to ask him what had happened. Luckily, I was able to put the ladder away, creep back to my room, and slip into my night robes without anyone seeing me. I lay awake until almost dawn, my head throbbing and my nose offended by the way I smelled.

As soon as I could, without attracting notice, I went out into the early morning to fetch a bucket of water so I could wash off most of the odor. Over breakfast at the inn I heard people talking about how brave Shem had been to fight off six thieves who'd tried to break into his home. It put me in a poor mood.

When I'd finished eating, I went back to talk to Phillip. I didn't have to tell him what had happened. With no television or other way to hear world news, local tales were our main entertainment. Gossip spread fast.

"I hear a dozen burglars tried to break into old Shem's house last night," Phillip laughed. "He had a stick handy, I'm told, and beat some of them badly, although none so severely that they couldn't run away afterward. Did the noise wake you, by any chance?"

"I hit my head on a shutter and fell off the ladder into a pile of pig-fouled hay," I replied sourly. "I think this marks the end of my gift-giving."

To my surprise, Phillip's face reddened with anger. He started to say something, caught himself, turned redder, and finally said quietly, "You've suffered enough, have you? The pain of a fall into some dirty hay was so awful, you've forgotten the pain of Shem and his daughters? These feelings you've described to me, your pity for those with less than you and how you'd like to do good things for others, were lost at the same time you lost your balance on that ladder?"

"Not really," I protested. "I still feel sad for Shem's family, and for anyone else in need. It's just that I'm apparently not very good at giving presents. Look what a mess I made of it last night."

Phillip looked at me for a long moment, then said thoughtfully, "Do you recall the story of the three kings who traveled far to give gifts to the baby Jesus?"

I did; it was a favorite tale of mine. Apparently, three royal persons—or magicians, or astronomers, depending on who told the story—saw a bright star in the sky and knew they should follow it to where a special baby would be. They brought presents for this unknown infant—precious things such as gold and spices. They had to go a long way, riding camels for the most part. Eventually, they found Jesus, presented their gifts, and then went back to wherever it was that they came from.

"Of course I remember the three kings," I said to Phillip. "Why do you ask?"

"Did the kings have an easy time finding the Christ-child?" he replied. "Did they give up when they weren't successful in giving him their gifts on the first night of their journey?"

"Shem's daughters aren't the baby Jesus," I said sulkily.

"And you're not a king, either," Phillip responded, his words trapping me neatly.

"Your point is made," I conceded. "I'll try again tonight."

Actually, it was four nights before I could try again. It took that long before Shem and some of the other men of the village stopped lying in wait in the night shadows, watching to see if the band of thieves would again try to rob Shem's house, or perhaps another house in Patara. Every time I sneaked out of the inn, I quickly caught glimpses of people hiding behind donkey stalls and low fences. And each night I went back to my bed thinking, "That's enough. I won't try again tomorrow night." But I did, and finally on the fourth night no one was lying in wait for the thieves' return.

I got my ladder and quietly walked to Shem's house. I leaned the ladder by another high window and climbed up. I peeked through the open shutter and knew instantly that I had picked the right room this time. There was a low fire burning in the grate, and in its dim light I could see the shadows of three figures sleeping on rumpled bedding.

A new problem presented itself. It was a short drop down to the floor, perhaps six feet. I could do it easily, but once inside, how would I get back out again? The door to the street would undoubtedly be latched, and, anyway, it was in old Shem's room. I had no intention of waking him up and giving him a real chance to beat a presumed burglar with his stick.

The only thing to do was balance on the windowsill, draw up the ladder and place it inside the room. Then I could climb down, leave the coins, climb to the windowsill, pull up the ladder, lean it back out into the street, and climb down.

The first part of this plan worked admirably. My ladder was made of lashed-together wood, and I made little noise pulling it up from the street, easing it over the windowsill and then down into the girls' room. As soon as it touched the floor, I swung myself about and climbed down inside the house.

But just as I stepped away from the ladder, one of the sleeping girls began to moan from a bad dream. It was Sara, Shem's youngest daughter. As Sara whimpered, both her older sisters, Celina and Ruth, began to toss about, too. I worried either might awaken, get up to comfort Sara, and see me standing there. I froze where I stood, scarcely daring to breathe. After a few moments Sara seemed to settle back into a deeper sleep. I counted to fifty, then cautiously reached inside my robe for the pouch of coins. It was my intention to leave four coins under each girl's pillow; after all, my parents had often left little presents under my pillow when I was asleep.

I tiptoed toward Sara and was just reaching toward her pillow with four coins in my hand, when she again began to twitch and whimper. I jumped back and tripped over my own feet. I fought to recover my balance and nearly fell into the fire. Fortunately, I missed the flames and instead fell on the hard dirt floor. There was a soft thump as my head bounced off the floor. I expected the thump to wake the girls and their father, too, and briefly thought my head hadn't yet received all the punishment it was going to get. Fortunately for me, Shem didn't come rushing from his room. None of the girls woke up, either.

Still, it had been too close a call. I wanted to leave the coins behind and make my escape.

I was afraid to come near the girls again. My luck couldn't hold up much longer. Looking around the room, I noticed each had left her daytime clothes hanging on a line strung from one wall peg to a peg on an opposite wall. This was a custom in my country; quite often robes—made dusty during the day—were rinsed out, then hung up to dry during the night.

The idea came to me that I might leave coins in each girl's daytime robe, provided I could find pockets in them. But the room was too poorly lit to see the robes clearly. If I had to fumble around with them looking for pockets, I might knock down the whole clothesline and wake everybody up for certain. I had no sister or other female relative; I wasn't quite sure where pockets were on girls' robes.

But alongside the robes on the clothesline were three pairs of rough wool stockings. Everyone wore these during certain times of the year, sometimes to keep out the cold and other times to avoid burns on our bare legs when the desert winds blew sand about in hard, scratchy clouds. The stockings were obviously sturdy. Within seconds, I'd put four silver coins in each pair—two coins in each stocking. The girls couldn't help but discover the money when they woke in the morning and started to dress.

Thrilled to have given my gifts, I inched back across the room, grabbed my ladder, and leaned it back up toward the window. I clambered up, balanced on the sill, and pulled up the ladder. As I leaned it back from the windowsill to the street, Sara again began gasping. This time she woke herself up, and her sisters, too. All three sat up, and as they did I hurried a bit too much and the ladder clacked against the windowsill. I just caught a quick glimpse of their pale, startled faces looking up at me before I scurried over the sill and down the ladder, and began hurrying back toward the inn. I expected to hear screams behind me, but it remained quiet. I returned the ladder to the shed, sneaked back to my room, and then lay in my bed awake until dawn, feeling happier than I could ever remember. There's nothing better than giving gifts, I thought over and over.

In the morning the village was full of the news that old Shem's daughters had miraculously received dowries from an unknown stranger who'd somehow gotten into their house during the night to leave his wonderful gifts in their stockings. Almost immediately, it was announced there would be three weddings within the week. Everyone in Patara attended. Phillip wasn't the priest who married the three girls and their suitors, but I noticed during the service that he was looking at me and smiling with pride.

All three of Shem's daughters had long, happy marriages. I swore then and there I would find more opportunities to leave presents and make others happy, always coming in secret during the night.

And that's how my career as a gift-giver began.

TWO

Nicholas, Bishop

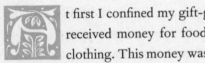t first I confined my gift-giving to Patara. Every hungry family received money for food, every ragged family got money for clothing. This money was always left with children, so their parents would not feel ashamed. Mostly, I visited houses, although sometimes I sneaked into tents if that was where need existed. I always gave my gifts in secret and at night. Not every night, of course, but once or twice every month.

However, I soon found that my simple plan had to be changed. By the time I'd been making my after-dark excursions for six months, everyone in the village knew some mysterious benefactor was entering homes at night and leaving money as a sign of his visit. Some greedy people who hoped to be next began sitting up nights, and sleeping during the day. A few went so far as to spend dusk until dawn in front of their houses hoping to spot the unknown gift-giver passing by, and to convince him to leave his coins for them, whether they really needed the money or not. Too many eyes were watching; I could no longer leave the inn and do my good deeds in secret.

I was frustrated. I consulted Phillip, who said I should simply think about it until a solution presented itself. Soon enough, it did. One evening at the inn I overheard a merchant who was staying overnight talk about a poor teenager in nearby Myra. This girl's legs had been weak from birth. She lived with her mother, who considered her to be a useless burden. A dressmaker in the young girl's town wanted to hire her to keep customer accounts, but, despite her spirit and intelligence, she could not walk from her home to the dressmaker's shop. If she had a stout pair of crutches, however, the girl could manage the short journey. But charity was scarce in Myra, and no one would buy the crutches for her.

"It's time to take my presents to other places," I told Phillip. "I'll go the twenty miles to Myra and leave money in the girl's stocking. Then she can buy her crutches, go to work for the dressmaker, and have a chance for a better life."

Phillip said it was a noble plan, and so that day I borrowed a mule from the inn's stable, telling the man who worked there that I wanted to visit a friend in Myra. I departed early in the morning and arrived just at dusk.

Discreet inquiries helped me learn where the girl lived—in a dirty, one-room house that looked to me like it was infested with spiders and mice. Still, it was easy enough to enter unnoticed after she and her mother were asleep. I left the money in the girl's stocking, took a room at the nearby inn, and allowed myself the pleasure the next morning of waiting to see the girl buy her crutches and begin her new life. But the girl's mother took the money from her, and spent it on herself while her daughter remained helpless at home.

"That mother needs to be punished," I complained to Phillip after returning home to Patara. "She's evil to deprive her daughter that way."

As always, my friend the priest was wiser than I. "It's not your place to assign blame, Nicholas," he said sternly. "Perhaps the greatest fault was with your plan, rather than with the mother. Did you leave a note with the coins, saying the money was to be used for crutches? No? I thought not."

"I know that woman would have ignored such a note," I said peevishly. "Writing it would have been a waste of my time. If you know a way I could have done better, why don't you tell me? I'm tired from the trip and I don't feel like guessing."

Phillip shrugged, "The answer seems simple enough to me. The girl can't walk from her home to the dressmaker's shop leaning on coins. If she needs crutches, give her crutches. Her mother can't spend those."

He was right, of course. I went to the market in Patara to buy crutches, only to learn none were available. Well, I had some basic skill at carving wood. I simply found a tree with proper-sized branches, cut two down, and trimmed them to the right shape. To make the gift more special, I removed the bark from the branches and spent the better part of a week carving intricate designs into the wood—birds and flowers and people with happy, smiling faces to remind the girl there was goodness in the world.

When the crutches were ready, I rode the mule back to Myra, waited until dark, entered the girl's house, and silently laid the crutches by her sleeping mat. I wasn't able to stay the next morning to see what happened next, but a few weeks later the merchant from whom I had first heard the girl's story returned to our inn and told how she had begun working for the dressmaker. Two months later the story took an even happier turn; feeling proud that her crippled daughter had done so well, the mother also took proper work. Together, mother and daughter earned enough money to move to a better, cleaner house.

I took heart from the experience. At night at the inn I made it my business to listen to the guests as they gossiped over dinner, telling stories about nearby villages and residents there in need. As often as possible, when I heard that someone needed help, I tried to provide it. Occasionally, I'd still leave money with children, but more often now I'd leave warm cloaks for a family in rags, or sandals for parents and children so poor they had to go around barefoot.

As my adventures spread farther and farther from my home village, so did the tale of the mysterious benefactor who left nighttime gifts. As usual, the stories far surpassed fact. I never was able to get much more than fifty miles from home, but myth had it that I'd made visits as far away as the far northern coast. There was immediate benefit; the greedy citizens of Patara stopped watching out for me every night, and I was once again able to make occasional stops in my own hometown.

Yet I still wasn't satisfied. Rumor had me traveling most of the known world, from Rome to Jerusalem and back again. Rumor or not, the thought intrigued me. My desire to give was unrestricted by borders between countries. I had the money to book passage by ship or wagon train to almost anywhere, and that is how I thought I'd spend my adult life. But, as usual, Phillip found a flaw in my plan.

"You're nearing sixteen," he told me one day, when I'd come to report another successful gift-giving trip, this one to the children of some nomads in a desert camp to the northwest. "You're now a man, and a man has to make some decisions. You need a profession. Otherwise, you'll gain a reputation as a wealthy, lazy fool. Besides, no matter what good deeds you do at night, you need an honest job for the daytime hours, if only so you'll better appreciate what other men and women do to earn their daily bread."

I hadn't thought about much of anything beyond giving gifts at night. Truly, I didn't mind the idea of finding a profession. The few people who'd inherited enough wealth to sit home all day were mocked by everybody else, and rightly so. There's nothing wrong with hard, honest work.

"What should I do?" I asked Phillip.

He replied that I ought to consider my interests and find a job where the work would be both enjoyable to me and helpful to the community.

"I'd like to travel more," I said. "Maybe I could invest some of my money in merchandise and open shops in all the civilized cities."

"Suppose your investments were bad and you lost all your money?" he replied. "How would you give your gifts then?"

Phillip smiled when he said this, so I knew he believed he had a solution. I must have spent ten minutes guessing before he finally said what was on his mind. "Why not become a priest? We're supposed to be poor, it's true, but the money you inherited would still be yours outside of the church. You could do good deeds by day as a priest and by night you could continue your other adventures. Besides, nobody finds out more about those in need than a priest."

I agreed immediately, although I knew the life I was choosing would be difficult. It was a harsh world then, as I suppose it still is today, but Christians might have been among the people who suffered most. Rome still ruled most of the known world (there were, of course, other countries and cultures, such as China, that dominated other parts of the Earth; those people knew as little of us then as we knew of them). There seemed to be a new Roman emperor every few years, and each had his own opinion about Christians. Some let us live in peace; others ordered terrible persecutions, starting with a man named Nero, who blamed us for burning down part of Rome, although no Christians were involved. Other religions were much more established than the Christian Church, which was still very, very new. Not long before my birth in 280 A.D., for instance, a Roman emperor named Aurelian worshipped Sol Invictus, a sun god, and that became the official religion of Rome.

The Christian Church itself had problems. Some of its leaders lived in Rome and had one idea of what the church should be like; there was another powerful group of leaders in Antioch who thought they were right about everything. Stuck in the middle were the bishops in charge of different regions and the priests who served in villages. Between Roman emperors and their own church leaders, Christians had to endure confusing times.

I always believed the whole purpose of being a Christian was to do good things for those in need, and so I chose to think about that and not about the negative aspects of becoming a priest. Phillip thought I should begin my career by going to Alexandria, in Egypt, where there was a school for priests. One of the school's first teachers had been a man named Origen, whom I admired for translating parts of the Old Testament into different languages so that more people could read them. Origen died thirty years before I was born, but his school was still open.

I said good-bye to my friends in Patara and sailed to Alexandria, excited about my new adventure. Very few people in my hometown could read, so it was especially enjoyable to be with other students who loved books.

Alexandria was the biggest city I'd ever seen. It had libraries and wonderful statues and marketplaces offering for sale everything I could imagine and many things I couldn't. The teachers at the school warned us not to wander around the street too much. They insisted we should concentrate on our studies. But I found I could study hard and still explore the city by night. I enjoyed meeting people from other cultures and listening to them talk about their customs. They, in turn, were curious about Christianity. I had many interesting discussions.

I also learned that the bigger the city, the greater the number of people in need. In Alexandria, I saw slums for the first time. Entire neighborhoods of poor people were always hungry, sick, and dirty. When my schedule permitted, I made some gift-giving trips, although when I did I was always saddened to think that for every child I helped, hundreds of others were still doing without.

It also was at school in Alexandria that I first gave much thought to something very important—how to celebrate the birth of Jesus. The teachers told us it shouldn't be celebrated at all, that we would insult Jesus if we celebrated his birthday as though he were just another human being. Origen in particular had believed that. It was one of the arguments dividing the church. Despite what Origen believed and preached, many Christians celebrated Jesus' birth anyway, usually on January 6. They'd have a feast and sing songs in his honor. I'd never seen anything wrong with this. In fact, on that day I usually brought cheese, bread, and wine to share with Phillip and the other priests of Patara.

After listening to my teachers in Alexandria, I still believed Origen was wrong. I was young enough to be very stubborn. I decided that I would find ways to celebrate Jesus' birthday with as many others as possible. There's nothing wrong with happiness.

I studied in Alexandria for almost two years. Despite our differences of beliefs regarding Jesus' birthday, the teachers decided I had learned enough to go out into the world as a priest. I wanted to travel to as many faraway places as possible, but felt I should start my new life back in my home country. I wanted to see Phillip again, and was anxious to get back to my old routine of giving gifts.

The place in Patara where Phillip and the other priests lived was called a monastery. I lived with them there for a year, and when I was nineteen they honored me by electing me abbot, or leader, after the old abbot passed away. Three years later the area's bishop also died, and I was elected to replace him. At age twenty-two, I was the church leader for all Christians in Lycia.

"I don't want to be bishop," I told Phillip one day. I'd had to move out of the monastery in Patara and into a fancy house in Myra, where the bishop was expected to make his home. "I have to spend too much time meeting with other bishops, arguing about church laws. I just want to give presents to children. That's my real interest."

Phillip coughed before answering. Lately, he'd begun looking frail, and that worried me.

"Nicholas, I respect you as my bishop. But I'm tired of constantly hearing you say you want to give up every time things get hard," he said. "Life will always be hard. You chose to become a priest, and you accepted when you were elected bishop. No one made you do these things. Well, I'm a tired old man. Give up, if you must. Otherwise, promise me that from now on you'll complete everything you start, and that no matter how hard something is, you'll have the courage to do whatever is necessary. I'm going to die soon, Nicholas, and you won't have me here anymore to talk you out of giving up."

I cried out of shame for my weakness and at the thought Phillip wouldn't live forever.

"I need you, Phillip," I sobbed. "I can't manage without you."

He smiled. "Everyone has his place in this world, Nicholas, and work to do before leaving it. Somehow, I think you were my work. Keep me in your heart and in your memory. And keep doing the work you were meant to do."

"Do you mean my work with the church, or my work with giving gifts?" I asked.

Phillip just smiled. He never did answer me, but that was his way. He always believed people were better off figuring things out for themselves. When he died a few weeks later, I swore I'd honor him by being the best bishop, and the best gift-giver, who ever lived.

THREE

Leaving Home

hat last chapter was rather sad, wasn't it? Well, please don't be unhappy. In that chapter and in this one, I'm telling about the days when I was still a very young man, growing in mind as well as in body. Growing up is never really easy, and we often learn our best lessons from the mistakes we make when we are young. The trick is to learn from those mistakes and go on; this is what I did.

After Phillip was buried, I went back to my house in Myra and did my best to fulfill my promises to him. I worked very hard, during the day as bishop and at night as the mysterious gift-giver. In some ways I was able to keep the two jobs separate. Bishops always had to settle disputes, some having nothing at all to do with the church. If two neighboring farmers couldn't decide the right dividing line between their properties, for instance, they might come and ask me to pray about it until God told me the answer. I always believed God had more important things to attend to, so usually I'd go out and see the situation for myself, then suggest a compromise. Most often they'd accept whatever I suggested, and afterward there might be a feast to celebrate their agreement. Bishops attended lots of feasts. I began to gain some weight.

Nights usually found me giving my gifts. As bishop, I had to travel, and if, for instance, I visited the small village of Niobrara and heard of a boy there who needed sandals, after my next overnight visit to that town he'd wake in the morning to find the sandals beside his sleeping mat. I was almost always able to get in and out without being seen; the few times I was glimpsed at all, it was by children or parents so foggy with sleep that they couldn't be sure they weren't dreaming.

It was inevitable, though, that descriptions of the mysterious nighttime gift-giver would emerge. I was variously described as short and tall, stout and thin, old and young, bearded and clean-shaven. I was said to be able to turn myself into mist and float into houses through cracks in doorways, or else able to fly from one place to another. The few hints I might be a demon were quickly hooted down. After all, it was immediately pointed out, I only gave good gifts, while a demon would prefer causing pain to bringing joy.

One portion of my description was usually the same, and properly so. The gift-giver was almost always described as wearing red robes with white trimming on the collar and sleeves. Well, as bishop I was usually required to wear the red robes with white trim that signified my office. More often than not, I was unable to pack other clothing for my trips, so I wore what I already had on when I sneaked off at night to give gifts.

You might wonder why, if the gift-giver and the bishop wore the same clothing, someone didn't use this obvious clue to solve the mystery and announce we were one and the same. Also, no one ever wondered aloud why the gift-giver always left his presents in the same villages where the bishop had just visited. Well, here's my conclusion, based on nearly two thousand years of observing human nature: People look, but they don't always know what they're seeing.

I must admit that sometimes my responsibilities as bishop interfered with my gift-giving. There were endless conferences to attend, where bishops from all over argued about points I personally found insignificant. When my turn came to speak, I'd always say I thought we could better spend our time helping the poor instead of debating issues that couldn't really be resolved anyway. As a result, I was not especially popular among my fellow bishops.

Please don't get the idea that I had no respect for the church, or that I always put gift-giving ahead of Christianity. Once I was even put in prison for more than a year; the Roman Emperor Diocletian had ordered all Christians to worship gods other than their own. I chose to go to prison rather than obey. I sat in a cell until that emperor died. Another took his place and allowed Christians to again worship as they pleased.

When I got out of prison, I was amazed to hear that, according to gossip, the gift-giver hadn't interrupted his services while Bishop Nicholas of Myra was otherwise detained. At first I thought these stories were all made up. In fact, many were. But upon further investigation I was pleased to find that, in a few cases, others had decided to imitate me and give presents to children in need. Instead of taking credit, they let everyone think it was the work of the original gift-giver. Being kind is its own reward.

The new century, called the fourth but including all the years numbered in the three hundreds, began badly for Christians in 303 A.D., when the emperor made new, harsh rules for us. But the Roman Empire was dividing under its own sheer size and population. For a while it was split into two empires, West and East, with each half ruled by a co-emperor. Eventually Constantine I, often called Constantine the Great in history books, took complete control. Constantine became a Christian himself, and gradually our church became the recognized religion of the empire, although this took some time. At first it was sufficient to know we could openly practice Christianity without fear of being thrown in jail or even put to death.

I took advantage of this new freedom to travel even more widely. Wherever I went, I tried to present religion as a cause for joy and not a source of fear. "Help each other the way you would want God to help you," I said over and over. To borrow a phrase, I practiced what I preached. The church had wealth, if not in coins then in rich farmlands, and I ordered the food grown on these lands to be given to the poor. Sick people were often shunned by those who were healthy. To set a good example, I would go to the sick in each town I visited, bringing them nourishing soup and bathing their heads with cool water. Many times, in those days, sick people simply died because they were ignored. After a few I visited regained their health, they began to tell others that I saved them through miracles, though I'd really done nothing of the sort. Others, fed when I ordered church farmland used for their benefit, began claiming I had called the food up out of thin air. Most people then weren't well educated, of course, and it was a time when most reported miracles were accepted as fact. That was certainly true of the stories involving me.

My new fame became a terrible burden. Wherever I went, people came up to me asking to be healed or fed. I did what I could, but there were limits to my abilities. Yet more and more often, people seemed to believe I could do anything if I really wanted. They began camping outside my door at night, ready to beg me to do impossible things the moment I stepped outside. Of course, this prevented me from doing any nighttime gift-giving. I hoped the myths about me would go away after a while, but they didn't. Instead, they spread farther and attracted more hopeful sufferers to my door. I had never felt so frustrated, by both the expectations of others and my own inability to do what they wanted.

For months, I tried to think of what I should do. The more people expected of me, the less I could actually do to help them. It was terribly frustrating. Then one night I had a dream. Phillip was in it, seeming as real as though he were right there with me. He said, "Nicholas, be brave just a little while longer. Get your church in order and wait for another dream, because there's a solution to your problems."

So I kept trying to do the best I could to cope with the demands on me. Every day started with requests for help and ended the same way. Days turned into weeks, weeks into years. I noticed everyone else around me growing old; I was doing the same. My hair began to turn white, and so did my beard. I neared my sixty-third birthday and assumed most of my life was over. Then the second dream came.

Phillip was in it again, of course. He told me to get up and look in the mirror. Whether I really did this or only dreamed I did, I can't say. But there was the mirror, and there was my reflection in it, and Phillip said, "Remember every line and wrinkle, because you will not grow any older."

"Then I'm going to die now," I answered, not really afraid of the idea at all.

Phillip laughed, the same dry chuckle I'd heard so often when I was a child and had just asked him a foolish question. "No, Nicholas. Your life so far is just a single grain of sand in an hourglass. It is only beginning."

"That can't be," I protested. "I'm nearly sixty-three years old. No one lives much longer than that."

"Remember this, Nicholas," Phillip said. "Time is different for each of us; a year to one man is one hundred years to another. Stop worrying about the end of life. Now it's time for you to start your gift-giving again."

"The people won't let me," I argued. "They stay outside my door. They follow me wherever I go."

"You haven't changed since you were a boy," Phillip said, not sounding especially pleased at the thought. "The simple solutions are always best. Just go."

Then the dream was over, if it really was a dream. I was sitting up in bed, with the words "Just go" echoing in my mind. I didn't go that night, though. I spent the next few days visiting with various bankers in Myra and Patara, bringing my financial affairs up to date and gathering the remaining money from my parents' estate. This was not an unusual thing for an old man to do. Word spread that Bishop Nicholas was settling accounts; obviously he felt he was about to die. Some of the supplicants surrounding my house respected this and went away, often calling back over their shoulders that they'd pray for my soul if I'd only work a few last miracles for them.

Beyond getting my finances together, I made no real plans. On the night of December 6, 343 A.D.—in my sixty-third year, if you're counting—I gathered a few things together in a pack, including my red bishop's robe, picked up a staff, saddled a mule, and rode quietly off to the north. I chose to go north because it seemed the right direction at the time. I had no idea what would happen to me next, but I believed I was part of some higher power's plan. This belief seemed to light my way as I ventured into the darkness and whatever future it might hold for me.

FOUR

Why the Calendar Changed

et's leave me heading north into the night for a bit. Even as I started my journey into the unknown, there were other things happening in the world, things that greatly affected my future.

The most important were changes involving the way Christians celebrated Jesus' birthday. Despite Origen doing his best to prevent it, many people chose to honor Jesus' birth with special meals, songs, or other ways to show how happy they were that he had been born on this Earth. But not everyone celebrated on the same date. Many chose January 6, but others preferred December 25. No one knew the exact date Jesus was born, so one guess was as good as another.

The first recorded December 25 celebration was in Antioch, in the middle of the second century. Some priests and members of the church there had a feast in honor of the occasion. They tried not to be too noticeable when they did it—Christians were being persecuted at the time. There were few of these celebrations for another hundred years or so. It was a real risk to have one. After Roman Emperor Constantine became a Christian, though, a lot of people in the church could openly express their joy by making their celebrations of Jesus' birth into elaborate festivities. Some of these celebrations lasted several days; all included lots of good food and drink.

(By the way, have you noticed I'm using phrases such as "celebration of Jesus' birth," but never "Christmas," the name you probably expect? That's because the word "Christmas" wasn't being used yet. It wouldn't be for quite some time. The same thing is true for "Santa Claus." For many centuries to come, I would still be known as Nicholas.)

Although Constantine had embraced Christianity, there wasn't an official holiday honoring Jesus' birthday at the time of my departure from Myra. That official recognition came seven years later, in 350 A.D., when Pope Julius I—who was head of the church in Rome—formally declared that December 25 would be celebrated each year as Jesus' birthday. Julius was late in making this announcement. Roman records already had noted a "nativity feast" on December 25 as an annual event going back as far as 336 A.D. It's interesting how the Romans chose December 25 as the correct date. For hundreds of years, Rome was the greatest military power on Earth, and its armies were constantly fighting to extend the boundaries of the Roman Empire farther in every direction, especially into what would become northern and western Europe and the islands beyond (which were eventually named Britain).

Rome almost always imposed its own laws on nations it conquered, but sometimes Romans also absorbed some of the customs of the countries they defeated, especially in matters of religion. Religion was important to the Romans, but they changed faiths like modern-day people change clothes. When Rome conquered Greece, for instance, they adopted the Greek gods, giving them new names, but essentially keeping the same ideas about them. Like lots of other pre-Christians, the Greeks celebrated something we now call winter solstice, or the time of year when the daylight hours are shortest and the weather turns cold. In ancient times, winter meant crops couldn't be grown and people had to live on whatever food they'd stored up during the harvest. To please the gods, and to convince them to bring back warmer weather, people in many different civilizations, both before and after the Roman Empire existed, would have feasts during the solstice, offering gifts to the gods as bribes to make the crop-growing seasons return.

One of the Greek gods was renamed "Saturn" by the Romans, who called their new solstice celebration "Saturnalia" in his honor. It was a long celebration, lasting from December 17 to December 23. The Romans were people who enjoyed parties. During Saturnalia all stores were closed down, except the ones selling food and wine. It became the Roman custom to give gifts to family members and friends at this time, not big things, but items such as candy, cake, and fruit.

Then along came Emperor Aurelian, whom we've talked about before. Aurelian wanted to worship Persian sun gods, and made his people do the same. They didn't really argue much; it certainly wasn't the first time Rome's official religion was changed, though it would only happen once more with Constantine. Aurelian proclaimed *"Dies Invicta Solis,"* or "Day of the Invincible Sun," on December 25. He did this because Mithra, the Persian god of light, was supposed to have been born on that day. His religion was known as Mithraism. Constantine believed in that faith until he became a Christian. When he did, he changed December 25 from a day of celebrating Mithra's birth to a day of celebrating Jesus' birth instead. As long as the Roman people got their day of feasting, I don't suppose most of them really cared whose birthday they celebrated.

In the centuries since, some people who don't like Christmas have criticized the holiday for its date, saying quite truthfully that it's almost certain Jesus wasn't born on December 25, during the winter. Scholars studying the Bible think it's likely he was born sometime during the spring, instead. To me, the specific date of Jesus' birth is less important than the fact that he was born at all, and that lots of people want to celebrate his birth. As you'll learn later on, December 25 is just one of the days on which I do my yearly gift-giving. Children in some countries expect me on December 6, my name day, and others on January 6, which is officially called Epiphany. In some countries, January 6 is thought to be the date that the Wise Men finally arrived in Bethlehem and gave their gifts to the baby Jesus.

All this is fine with me. It's the spirit of the season, being generous to others who don't have much and being grateful for the things we have, that really matters. Dates are, after all, just names and numbers made up by people long, long ago.

The first Roman calendar is supposed to have been introduced in 738 B.C. It had ten months and lasted 304 days. The names of some of its months ought to sound familiar to you: Martius, Aprilis, Maius, Junius, Quintilis, Sextilis, September, October, November, and December. The last six names are taken from the Roman words for five, six, seven, eight, nine, and ten.

That calendar was invented by Romulus, the first ruler of Rome. One of his descendants, Numa Pompilius, added the months of January and February, which made the Roman year 355 days long. If Pompilius had stopped there it would have been best, but then he got the idea of adding an extra month every other year. Within a few years, winter was arriving in September instead of November and December.

Which day was what got so mixed up that 46 B.C. was known as the Year of Confusion. Julius Caesar was emperor then, and he commanded that the calendar somehow be fixed. The solution was to make 46 B.C. 445 days long to get the seasons back to the right months. In his honor, the month of Quintilis was renamed July. Later on, Sextilis became August in honor of Caesar Augustus.

This new order, called the Julian calendar, was used for the next fifteen hundred years. But it still wasn't quite accurate. By 1580, the calendar and the people who used it were ten days off.

In 1582, Pope Gregory decided it was time for another calendar change. For that year, he ordered the ten extra days taken out of October, and then worked out what eventually became a complicated plan to add one extra day in February every fourth year, just to keep everything exactly in line. Some countries took a long time to agree to these changes. Russia didn't start using the Gregorian calendar until 1918, and it was 1927 before Turkey did.

I tell this to point out why it's obvious we can't ever be certain what date things happened around the time of Jesus' birth. Picking one day is as good as picking any other. I have enough trouble remembering the names of my friends at the North Pole, or Layla's and my wedding anniversary. As far as I'm concerned, people who argue that Christmas is all wrong because it's celebrated on December 25 should use their energy to help needy people instead. That's the best way to celebrate anything.

Anyway, making December 25 an official feast day was just one important step for the Christian church following Constantine's conversion. For the first time, it also was possible for many priests to travel about telling the story of Jesus without fear of being thrown in prison, tortured, or even killed. One of the big advantages Rome brought to nations it conquered was the constant building of roads, very good ones, some of which have lasted to this day. You can go to certain places in Europe and Britain and actually walk or drive on roads originally built by the Romans. Although they were fierce fighters, you see, Romans really wanted to control the world through trading. Roman merchants needed roads to move their goods from one market to another. These roads also came in handy for priests and other Christians who wanted to walk or ride long distances. All along the way, the mighty soldiers of Rome would now protect them from harm instead of hurting them. It made a big difference!

Of course, Christianity has lasted much longer than the Roman Empire, which began to crumble in the fifth century. Much to my amazement, I lasted longer than the Romans, too.

FIVE

The Beginning of Magic

his is the part of my story where the magic begins. There will be more magic times to come, but I'm going to tell you now about the first. Remember what we discussed earlier: Illusion can be explained, magic can't. So far, my adventures in gift-giving had been colored with illusion. I quietly entered people's homes and left gifts for their children. Because of this, they created myths about me being able to fly or to turn myself into the wind and blow inside. Yet I got in by using ladders or opening doors, nothing more special than that.

But I expect you're eager to hear about the magic now, so let's resume my tale.

After leaving my home behind, I kept traveling north and west from Myra. Sometimes I rode the mule, but not very often. I would have soon become tired of carrying him on my back, and I assumed he felt the same about me. I had left no family behind and had none ahead, so the mule was the closest thing I had to a relative. I named him "Uncle" and amused myself by talking to him along lonely stretches of road.

Since the Romans had built good roads, there were many other travelers along my route. I was going in the general direction of Constantinople, with the idea of getting ship passage from there to Rome. This wasn't unusual. Lots of tourists wanted to see the sights there—the Coliseum, the Appian Way, the Senate where the government conducted business, and so forth. I knew I wouldn't mind looking at these places and things if I happened to find myself standing in front of them, but I was going to Rome for a different purpose—because I had a feeling it was the next place I should be.

It was going to be a long walk before I reached Constantinople, hundreds of miles, and as a sixty-three-year-old man I expected I would tire easily. This didn't happen. I would walk all day and then walk through the night hours, and when the sun came up again I'd find I had walked thirty miles, or even forty or fifty. This was impossible; in one day at normal speed I might have been able to travel twenty miles if I rode the mule part of the way. My steps weren't longer than any other man's. I'd always needed as much sleep as anyone else. Yet somehow I was walking farther in one day than any man ever had, and still I wasn't feeling tired, although I rarely slept at all. In five days I was in Constantinople. The journey should have taken two weeks. This was the first magic. It wasn't anything spectacular like being able to fly, but there was no way to logically explain it. Somehow, as I walked, time and distance became different for me than for everybody else.

It was easy to get a berth on a ship to Rome. Merchant vessels let travelers pay for the privilege of sleeping in their holds along with whatever goods were being shipped. Some people would only sail on ships carrying cargos of aromatic spices or fresh-smelling linens. Although I wasn't sure why, I wanted to get to Rome as quickly as possible, so I paid to board the first ship sailing there from Constantinople. It was a cattle ship. The animals bellowed constantly. I didn't mind. I'd grown fond of Uncle the mule and was pleased to be able to take him to Rome with me. He was tethered down in the hold with hay to eat. I spent the twelve-day voyage on deck, enjoying the sea air and idly wondering what I was going to do when we arrived.

The other passengers were all seasick for the first few days. As for me, I never felt a twinge of discomfort. Indeed, I heartily ate all the food the crew offered me, and they offered a lot in hopes I'd get an upset stomach and turn green like the rest of the passengers. It was a game the sailors liked to play. When I consumed cheese and bread and jelly and fruit and candy and fish, and didn't lose my meal overboard right afterward, the sailors clapped me on the back and invited me to their cabin area to sing songs with them. When they asked my name, I said it was Nicholas. They were all strangers and I didn't think they'd know about a humble bishop from Myra.

"Say, you're named the same as that bishop who works miracles down in Lycia!" one of the crewmen boomed out.

Well, so much for that. Before I could say a word, the other sailors chimed in with stories they'd heard about the wonderful Bishop Nicholas, how he'd touched one finger to a blind man's eyes and made him see again, and how he'd planted a single grain of wheat in the ground and stalks sprouted for acres in every direction. They were very entertaining stories. I could even enjoy them, if I forgot they were supposed to be about me.

"On my next shore leave I intend to go to that bishop's town, Myra, I think it's called, and see him work some of these miracles for myself," a sailor said.

"Would you be very disappointed if this bishop turned out to be an ordinary man who worked no miracles at all?" I asked.

"Don't be so sour," he urged me. "Don't you think that, in this hard world, we all need some magic to believe in?"

He was right, of course. That night, for the first time since I'd left Myra, I curled up in a blanket and tried to sleep until dawn. I hoped I'd dream again about Phillip, and that he'd tell me something more about time standing still. Instead, I dreamed about snow, something I'd not seen in Lycia but had heard about—frozen rain coming down from the sky and turning into a soft white blanket over the Earth. When I awoke the next morning, I thought it was odd to have dreamed of such a thing.

When we docked in Rome, I found it to be the biggest, loudest, dirtiest place that ever could have existed. Most streets were paved and had gutters, but people washed many disgusting things down those gutters. The city seemed to stretch on forever. It was built on hills, and every hill was covered with buildings.

The winter cold was fierce. I used a little of my money to buy warmer clothes. Now that I'd arrived, I wondered what I should do next. On an impulse, I took a room at a small inn. At dinnertime, I went downstairs, ordered a simple meal of bread and cheese, and sat at a table to eat it. When I was done, I put on my new heavy cloak and walked outside.

"You! Yes, you!" hissed a voice from the shadows. "Come over here. I've got an important message for you!"

I looked, and there in an alley beside the inn was a scared-looking stout man. His round face was dirty and, though it was so cold, his forehead was shining with sweat.

"What do you mean, a message?" I asked. "No one in this city knows who I am, or even that I'm here."

"I was told to give you a message," the man insisted. "Won't you come and get it from me?"

"Certainly not," I said. "It's obvious you're a thief who wants to knock me over the head and steal my money, if I have any money. You're not even a good thief, either. Look—I can see that stick you're hiding behind your back. You hope to hit me with it."

The fellow looked behind himself and said, "A stick? What stick? Oh, that one? I've never seen it before. Someone must have put it in my hand. Please come and get your message. I'm very hungry."

"Why should my getting a message have anything to do with your hunger?" I asked. "This is a silly conversation. You want to rob me and I don't want to be robbed. I believe you must be the worst thief in the world, to be so obvious about it. You should be ashamed of planning to hit an innocent stranger over the head with your stick."

The man dropped the stick and took a few steps forward. I could see his clothes were torn and not heavy enough to keep out the cold.

"I'm sorry," he muttered. "I wasn't really going to hit you, anyway. I just wanted you to think I'd hit you if you didn't give me your money. I could never hurt anyone. That's why I'm so hungry now."

He didn't seem very dangerous, just sad.

"Why is that?" I asked. "Tell me your story. But first, why don't we go back inside the inn, where it's warm? I'll gladly buy you dinner. There's no need to rob me if you need money for a meal."

The would-be thief looked so grateful that I knew I'd said the right thing.

We went back inside the inn, and I told him to order all the food he wanted. At first I think he didn't believe I would pay for his meal, and asked for water and bread, the very cheapest things. So I pulled out a coin, big enough to pay for all the food in the kitchen, and soon my new companion was gobbling away from a mountain of meat, cheese, and pastry.

"You're a fat fellow to be starving," I noted. "I mean no offense, but how come you're so hungry? When did you eat last?"

"At midday," he said between huge bites on a leg of lamb. He held the meat in his hands; no one used knives and forks back then. "I can't help it. I just need more food than most. I've been stealing my meals for a week, ever since I ran away from my master."

He lowered his voice when he said this. Slavery was part of Roman society, and runaway slaves were severely punished whenever they were caught.

"Did your master beat you?" I asked. "Were you in fear for your safety?"

"I was in fear for my own life and the lives of others," he said. "My master said I ate too much, and ordered me to train as a wrestler. He meant to make me fight other wrestlers, and charge admission to watch. Well, I don't like other people hurting me, and I don't like hurting other people. So I ran away."

"Don't you miss your family?" I wondered. "Don't you miss your friends?"

"I have no family or friends," he replied, and his answer touched my heart. I quickly sensed he was a good person, and I admired him for running away from a master who wanted him to fight.

"Well, now you have a friend," I said. "My name is Nicholas. I'm alone, as well. I'm not sure where I'm going or what I'm doing next, but I have one plan you might like. I have some money. Why don't I go see your master and ask if I can buy you? Since I hate slavery, I'll set you free right away, and you can go wherever you like and not have to fight anyone."

Tears of joy filled the man's eyes. "Would you really do that?" he asked. "Are you sure this isn't a trick to learn my master's name and then take me back to him? I suppose he's offering some kind of reward for me."

"You have my word on it," I promised. "Let's get some sleep tonight, and in the morning we'll find your master and make everything right."

I paid the innkeeper a little extra to let the man sleep in my room with me. I would have gotten him his own room, but I thought he still might worry during the night that I really meant to trick him and force him back into slavery, and that might make him decide to run away before dawn. It wasn't until he was rolling himself up in the clean linen bedding that I remembered to ask him, "What's your name?"

"I'm Felix," he said. Then, before he could finish a huge yawn, he fell fast asleep.

Felix must have been very tired from running away and hiding. He snored loudly most of the night, but I was used to the cattle mooing on the boat and the noise didn't disturb me.

In the morning we went to see Felix's master, a mean old man who wanted to beat Felix for running away as an example to his other slaves. But I offered a great deal of money if he would sell me Felix instead, and unbeaten.

"Give me the money and make the sale official before I tell you this," the nasty old slaveowner growled. I gave him the coins and he snatched them from my hand, carefully tucking them into his purse before saying, "You've bought a useless slave. He eats too much and has too kind a heart."

"As of this moment, he's not a slave at all," I answered. Under Roman law, it was possible for owners to declare their slaves free at any time. "He's now as free as you or me." Felix, standing beside me, yelped with happiness.

His former owner cringed. "Don't let him near me! He'll attack me because of the way I treated him!"

Before I could reply, Felix said, "Slave or free man, I would never hurt anyone, even you. I do beg you to be nicer to the rest of your slaves, and to consider setting them all free. It's wrong for one human being to own another."

The slaveowner was too greedy to set any of his other slaves free, but at least Felix had asked. Afterward, we walked back to the inn, discussing where we might want to go next since neither of us really liked the crowded streets of Rome. It just seemed completely natural for us to assume we'd stay together. That's how Felix joined me and my next adventures began.

SIX

Felix and Me

suspect you didn't think there was enough magic in that last chapter—just being able to walk fast and sometimes not needing to sleep. Well, not all magic is fireworks and fanfare. Sometimes magic is quiet and sneaks up on you. An illusion is what needs all the bells and whistles to make itself appear grander than it really is, which is just a trick that can be explained.

It took Felix and me a while to realize magic was happening to us. We left Rome on foot, leading Uncle the mule. Before leaving the city we bought some provisions, and for the first few weeks of our travels we had a pleasant time exchanging our life stories. Felix was the son of slaves, and his parents were the children of slaves, and beyond that he had no idea of his family roots.

I told Felix all about my gift-giving and being the Bishop of Myra. I wanted to keep on giving my gifts to children, and Felix said right away he hoped to spend the rest of his life helping me do this. So we began to travel about rather aimlessly, finding towns and staying a few weeks while we discovered needy families, then delivering our presents—sandals, perhaps, or cloaks, or, less often, a few coins—during the dark of night and slipping away on the road to the next town before dawn. Mostly we stayed within a hundred miles or so of Rome, although sometimes we ventured into the countries that would later be known as Germany, France, and Spain. There was fighting going on everywhere—Huns and Vandals and Goths and Visigoths and Ostrogoths. Some of those names might sound silly, but the battles were always bitter. The Romans had tried to push the boundaries of their empire too far, and even their mighty legions couldn't fight successfully in so many places at the same time. Meanwhile, ordinary people tried to live their lives as peacefully as possible, keeping their children safe and fed and warm. It was pleasant to think Felix and I helped some of them do this.

We passed many nights gossiping with other travelers around fires at inns where we stopped for the night. It was on one such evening, perhaps a year after Felix and I had begun our travels, that I was stunned to hear a merchant returning home to northern Italy from Lycia tell me the people there had built a wonderful church above the tomb of Nicholas, who'd been Bishop of Myra.

"Tomb?" I asked doubtfully. "What did they put in that tomb?"

The merchant looked at me in wonder. "Why, the bishop's body, of course! What else would be put in a tomb? The man worked wondrous miracles during his life. One night he went into his house to sleep and the next morning they found him lying dead in his bed. So they buried him, and a fine ceremony they apparently made of it."

"Buried him?" I asked, too stunned to say anything more clever. "People went into the house of Bishop Nicholas and found him there?"

Now the merchant believed he was talking to a very stupid person. "I just said that. They took the body and put it in a great tomb, and then built a great church over that."

"But I—" I began, and Felix poked me in the ribs with his elbow. "I walked away in the middle of the night," I hissed in Felix's ear. "How could they find my body if I was gone?"

Felix and I hurried back to Rome and took passage on a ship to Constantinople. We couldn't find a ship with room for Uncle the mule, so we had to sell him. It was hard to part with such a faithful friend, but I felt his new owner would take good care of him.

We landed safely in Constantinople and walked from there back to Myra. Because I didn't want to be recognized, I camped outside of town and sent Felix ahead. He came back a few hours later shaking his head. "I don't know how to tell you this," he muttered. "You won't believe me."

"I promise I will," I said.

"Well, there is a magnificent church, and inside it is an equally magnificent tomb. This tomb has your name on it, and the date of your death—December sixth, 343 A.D. It even has your likeness carved on marble, although I think you're heavier now than the way they made you look. An old man who was standing beside the tomb said he'd been sleeping outside Bishop Nicholas's door—sorry, outside *your* door—on the fatal night, hoping when you came out the next morning you would heal his leg, which had been crippled from birth. The sun came up, but you didn't come out. By midday people were worried, and it was decided someone should go inside and see if you were all right."

"A crippled man, you say?" I asked. "I really didn't look too closely when I left that night. I tried to step over people quietly so they wouldn't wake up and prevent me from leaving."

Felix's eyebrows knitted together: I was to learn he often had this expression when he was trying especially hard to figure something out. "Well, maybe you didn't get away as completely as you thought. This crippled man was chosen to go inside, and he swears that when he did he found you on your bed, and that you must have died overnight in your sleep. People who had known you for years all agreed the body was yours. It must have resembled you exactly."

"How strange," I said rather faintly. It was odd to hear about someone finding me dead.

"Oh, don't worry, he said everyone mourned you greatly," Felix said quickly, mistaking my bewilderment for disappointment in public reaction.

"There were tears all around, and loud wailing, and the decision was made to build you the greatest tomb any bishop ever had."

"How flattering," I muttered.

"Oh, but you haven't heard the best of it," Felix warned. "The tomb was built and the body they found put inside it. Almost at once, this old man told me, a kind of wonderful oil began to drip from the tomb. He got some on his fingers and rubbed it into his crippled leg, which was immediately healed. He pulled up his robes just now to show me how both his legs were strong and healthy."

"This is too strange, Felix," I argued. "I'm sure he never was crippled at all. To find a body when the person hadn't died, and then to say some sort of holy oil seeped from the tomb, well, it's just impossible."

"Perhaps," said Felix, "but you've told me about being able to travel great distances without rest, and that you think time somehow doesn't affect you as it does ordinary men. Where these miracles exist, can't there be others?"

I insisted we go back to town so I could see this tomb for myself. Since I was supposed to be dead, there seemed no danger I'd be recognized, and I wasn't. I passed a few men and women who'd once been my friends, and they never gave me a second glance.

I felt embarrassed as we came to the tomb. It was a grand monument and I couldn't help thinking how many poor people could have been helped with the money it took to build it. No oil was oozing from it, but there were several people kneeling in prayer.

"What are you doing?" I asked one woman.

"Praying to the good Bishop, of course," she replied. "He does miracles for those in need. My daughter is blind. I'm asking the Bishop to restore her sight."

"What if he can't?" I asked.

"Then I'll keep on asking," the woman said. "I know Bishop Nicholas can't do everything for everyone at once. I'll just keep praying until I get my turn."

I couldn't think of anything else to say. Felix led me away. I was too confused to know where I was going. Eventually, I found myself in an inn that had been built after I'd left Myra. I told Felix I wasn't hungry, and went to our rooms. I immediately fell asleep, and dreamed of a young girl I'd never met who had been blind but suddenly could see. The next day I went back to Nicholas's tomb—my tomb, I suppose—and the woman was gone. Another woman praying nearby said, "Didn't you hear the glad tidings? Someone came running up to her yesterday to say her daughter had regained her sight!"

So I was dead and working miracles. Yet I also was alive and giving my gifts. That, my friends, is magic.

The magic continued. Felix and I left Myra, continuing our journeys and our gift-giving. Days became weeks, weeks became years. One day as we were walking along, Felix stopped short in the middle of the road and said, "Isn't this the year 410?"

"Of course," I said impatiently, for the question seemed foolish. Everyone knew it was 410, a year destined to be remembered as the time Rome was captured and partially destroyed by the Visigoths. The invaders had help; simple peasants and desperate slaves, disgusted with Roman taxes and cruelty, had opened the city gates of Rome from the inside to let the Visigoths enter.

"Well, weren't you sixty-three when we met, and didn't you, uh, change, in the year 343?" Felix wondered.

"You know this as well as I do," I grumbled.

"Well, then, friend Nicholas, doesn't that mean you're now one hundred and thirty?"

I thought about it and added up the years, though addition was never something I did well. "So I am," I finally agreed. "One hundred thirty years old! Tell me, Felix, do I look any different than when we first met?"

He peered at me. "Well, you weigh more."

"Don't be rude."

"Otherwise, you look exactly the same," Felix concluded. "You don't look young, of course. Your hair and beard are white. There are lines in your face and wrinkles around your eyes. But you certainly don't look like someone one hundred and thirty years old, not that anyone could even know what someone that age would look like."

I had attached to my belt a small pouch of personal items, among which was a small circle of polished metal to be used as a mirror. I used it when I trimmed my beard or hair with a small knife. Now, for the first time in a long while, I simply gazed at my reflection.

"See how your face is a bit more puffy from the extra weight," commented Felix, who was watching over my shoulder.

"Worry about your own weight," I snapped, although I knew what Felix said was true. Of course, he himself was shaped like a ball, so I felt he had no right to criticize my few extra pounds. All right, more than a few. But not many more. Ten at the most. With the dignity of my newly discovered years, I decided a man of one hundred thirty was entitled to a wider waistline.

"How wonderful for you," Felix continued, a note of awe in his voice as he considered our discovery. "You're never going to die, ever. You'll be here to watch the world change. Seas will dry up and mountains will crumble, and still you'll be alive to see what happens next. Lucky Nicholas, for some reason you are blessed above all other people!"

It was a sobering thought, and I felt uncomfortable with it. "I really don't think I'll live forever, Felix," I said slowly. "Time might be different for me than others, but it passes all the same. Perhaps a year for me is ten years for someone else, or even a hundred years. Who's to say what this means?"

"I know it means some higher power has special work for you to do on this earth," Felix said firmly. "It must be your gift-giving, for that's the way in which you're most different from ordinary people."

"Yet even when I give gifts I'm left with the feeling I'm not doing all I can and should," I reminded him. "We've talked of this often on our travels. For every child we help, so many more still have to do without. It's a terrible problem."

"Well, it seems you have plenty of time to come up with a solution," Felix replied. "If it's not too much trouble, could you please do this before I, myself, pass on?"

Another thought struck me. "Felix, how old were you when we met back in 343?"

He pondered, "I can't say for certain, Nicholas. The birth dates of slaves weren't always recorded. I suppose I was no longer a very young man, though certainly not much older than—wait! Are you saying what I think you are?"

He rather rudely rummaged in the pouch on my belt, frantic to grab hold of the metal disk and inspect his own reflection.

"Mind your manners!" I protested, slapping his hand away and pulling out the disk myself. "Here! Take a good look, but what you'll see is the same fat face I first encountered in that dark alley outside the Roman inn. You're a bit cleaner now, though still as stout." I couldn't resist this reference to his own poundage. "Let's say you were thirty. No? Is that too old or too young?"

"Too young, I think," Felix said distractedly, twisting the metal mirror this way and that as he peered hard at himself. "I was probably five years older, at least."

"Thirty-five years old, then," I suggested. "Well, add sixty-seven years to it. That would mean you're one hundred and two right now, my fine friend, and though you're not a handsome fellow, you're certainly not wrinkled with such age, either. It would appear that whatever power paused my aging has also chosen to interrupt yours."

"Amazing," Felix said. He sounded stunned, but then he had a right to be. "There was nothing very special about me before I met you—I was just another Roman slave. Do you think this means—?"

"I know," I interrupted. "It means my special mission of gift-giving can't be accomplished alone. I wonder if it's to be just the two of us, Felix, or if we'll be joined by others? Well, I suppose we have plenty of time to find out."

We continued on our way, walking thoughtfully. The packs on our shoulders were heavy. We'd never gotten around to buying a new mule to replace Uncle. Felix lagged a step behind me. After we'd gone perhaps another mile, I heard him say softly, "Nicholas, I'm afraid."

"I'm afraid, too, but I'm also curious," I answered. "Let's give it another century or two, and then maybe things will become more clear."

SEVEN

Carving Out Our Fortunes

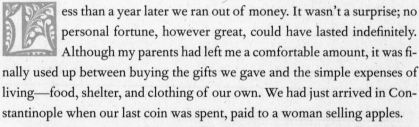ess than a year later we ran out of money. It wasn't a surprise; no personal fortune, however great, could have lasted indefinitely. Although my parents had left me a comfortable amount, it was finally used up between buying the gifts we gave and the simple expenses of living—food, shelter, and clothing of our own. We had just arrived in Constantinople when our last coin was spent, paid to a woman selling apples.

"What do we do now?" asked Felix, crunching his apple loudly. A little juice ran down his chin; my friend never could eat neatly. "What plan do you have to get more money?"

"I have no plan at all," I admitted. "Perhaps you should eat that apple more slowly. It might be your last meal for a while."

It was too late. Felix was already nibbling on the apple core. Carefully tossing it within reach of a camel tethered nearby, he remarked thoughtfully, "So no money means no meals. Well, that's serious. We'd better think of something." And we walked and we pondered, waiting for inspiration.

The plan we needed presented itself in a street market. As we wandered around stalls where all sorts of goods were being sold, we found one merchant surrounded by curious onlookers.

"They're genuine!" he was shouting. "Real copies of the new gospels, copied by the monks of Saint Benedict! If you can read, you'll find the story of Jesus here, and if you can't read, pay someone to read it to you!"

For the last hundred years, copies of so-called "new testaments" had been circulating. It was said that these were written by followers of Jesus to describe Christ's last days on Earth. Most people had heard of these gospels, but few had actually read them. Since each had to be carefully copied by hand, usually by priests, they were quite rare and in great demand among rich people. I had heard stories of churches selling a single copy of one gospel for enough money to support itself for six months.

Curious, Felix and I worked our way through the throng until we stood directly in front of the merchant. He had some parchment papers in his hand, each page covered with elegant handwriting. But the pages themselves weren't as elegant. They were torn in some places and creased along the edges.

"How much for one?" a tall, slender man inquired. He was dressed in wonderful woolen robes dyed bright blue, a tint so expensive only the very rich could afford it.

The merchant, quick to notice those blue robes, named an outrageous price. The rich man laughed and said mockingly, "Look at how your pages are falling apart! Look at the fingerprints made by sweat mixed with ink! And you have the nerve to ask such a high price?"

"What would you pay?" asked the humbled merchant. The rich man named a much lower price, and the sale was concluded. The rest of the crowd still found the new price beyond their means, and so they drifted away.

The merchant unhappily gathered up his remaining copies, preparing to put them in a canvas sack. As he did, and without a word to me, Felix walked up and said cheerfully, "You didn't make much profit on that sale, did you?"

"There was hardly any," the merchant agreed sadly. "The monks drive hard bargains, too. I'm supposed to pick up six more copies of this Gospel of Mark from them next week. I've already paid for those copies, and if I have to sell them at such low prices I won't make enough profit to buy myself a single decent meal."

He and Felix both winced at the thought of missed dinners.

"Well, just protect the pages better," Felix suggested. "If you can keep people from smearing the pages with their fingers and protect the pages from being torn and creased, you should be able to ask a much higher price. Put the pages between covers of wood, like some people in the Roman Empire have done. The wood protects the parchment. The pages remain clean and attractive."

"I like the idea, but I don't know where wood covers could be found on such short notice," the merchant replied. "The monks only make parchment copies. Even if they had the right sort of wood, I don't think any of them have the woodcarving skills to cut and decorate the covers properly."

I listened in amazement as Felix, sounding much like a modern-day salesman, smoothly suggested, "My friend and I can help you. Give us money to purchase the wood—treated oak is best, I believe, and I know we can find some in this great city—plus a few extra coins as an advance payment for our work. We're woodcarving craftsmen. Then next week we'll present you with six sets of fine wood covers. Take them with you when you get your new parchments from the monks; bind them about the pages and you'll sell every copy as quickly as rich men can pull out their purses and fill your hands with money!"

Felix must have sounded persuasive, because the merchant, whose name was Timothy, agreed almost immediately. He asked only that we first show him the inn where we were staying so he could be certain we wouldn't take his advance payment and run away. We took him there, and the innkeeper confirmed we had already paid for ten days' lodging. I stood watching in amazement as Felix then argued with Timothy over how much more we'd be paid when we brought him his book covers. They finally agreed on a price that, if we really got the money, would pay a month's worth of our traveling expenses and gift-giving costs.

After Timothy left, I asked Felix sharply, "What fix have you gotten us into? If we don't have those covers ready next week, that merchant might have us thrown in prison! Six sets of wooden book covers. Why, it would take both of us a week to carve decorations on one set!"

But Felix didn't seem worried. "Let's go find someone selling the wood

we need for the covers," he suggested. "Then I think we need to give ourselves a fine dinner so we'll have the energy to go back to our room and start
working."

We found the wood easily enough. We bought twelve small planks of it,
two for each set of covers. The planks were heavy, but Felix only carried
four of them back to the inn. I had to carry eight. When I grumbled about
having the heavier load, Felix casually told me he needed to save his
strength for the job ahead.

After using more of Timothy's money to buy dinner—some roast lamb
as well as the usual cheese and bread—we went to our room, pulled out our
carving knives, and got to work. The carving was a delicate process. Even a
single slip of the knife would mean a whole plank was ruined. As was the
custom, we planned to carve stars and angels and elegant patterns on each
cover. Some very rich people also decorated their covers with jewels, but we
had no jewels. Timothy's customers would have to settle for simple wood.

"I don't think we can do this," I told Felix. "Two men can't carve so
much in so little time."

"You've carved a lot of things," he answered. "You're good at it, too.
Remember the story you're always telling about the time you gave a little
girl a set of crutches? You carved them, didn't you?"

"That was just one set of crutches," I said, but Felix was already bent
over a plank. Sighing, I picked up another plank and began pushing the
point of my knife blade into the grain of the wood.

We worked for hours. My hands became very tired, and because it was a
hot night, sweat began to drip into my eyes. I felt discouraged, but whenever I looked over at Felix he was always carving away, looking very
pleased with himself.

Far into the night, I had only carved a small part of one plank. My design was clean and attractive, but there wasn't much of it to admire.

"This is going to be hopeless," I informed Felix. "Tomorrow we'd better seek out Timothy and admit we can't do the job he's paid us to perform.
Perhaps he'll give us an extra month or two. After all, the money he gave us
is mostly spent, and if he has us thrown in prison he won't ever be able to
get it back."

"Oh, are you tired already?" Felix asked cheerfully. "Well, why don't you go to sleep? I know you can walk all night while we're on the road, but it's still good to sleep when you can enjoy an inn's nice clean bedding. Go ahead, get some rest."

"What about you?" I responded. "You always need to sleep more than I do. Admit you had a bad idea. At least you tried. There's no disgrace in that. Get some sleep, too, and in the morning we'll face Timothy together."

But Felix just insisted I go to sleep while he kept working, so I did, and despite my sincere concern about what would happen to us when Timothy found out we hadn't kept our bargain, I soon nodded off.

I woke in the morning to find Felix carving away, and sitting amid a huge pile of wood shavings. Nine completed planks were stacked beside him, and he was almost finished with the tenth. Each was beautifully decorated with carved images that looked real enough to jump off the surface of the wood.

"What kind of miracle is this?" I gasped, jumping up, tangling my feet in the bedding and falling flat on my face into the pile of wood shavings. I got some of the shavings in my mouth and had a coughing fit. Even as I coughed, I could hear Felix laughing.

"It's not a miracle, it's just some of our magic," he chuckled. "Maybe I should say it's my magic, something special to me. I just kept on carving, intending to stop when daylight came, and the more I carved, the longer it stayed nighttime. I'm not tired at all. I feel as if I could keep right on carving all day, but I won't because we have six days left and just one more plank to complete, not counting the one you've been working on. Do you think you'll be able to finish it in time for Timothy, or should I just include it with the other I'll carve tonight?"

Of course, we had all the covers ready for Timothy by the date upon which we'd agreed. He was excited to have them, and offered many loud compliments on the quality of the craftsmanship. Timothy had gotten his new six sets of gospels from the monks, and Felix and I helped him bind these to the covers we'd carved. Then all three of us carried the books to the marketplace and offered them for sale. The rich man in the blue robe was back, and he bought four gospels, paying an amazing amount of money for the privilege of owning them. The other two were quickly sold as well. Even after Timothy paid us, he still made a handsome profit. Everyone was happy.

Felix didn't stop there. He immediately agreed to carve Timothy a dozen more covers during the next week. Timothy had a friend who owned a ship; this friend took six finished sets of covers with him on his next voyage to Rome, and sold them in one of the marketplaces there. We soon fell into a pattern. Felix and I would travel around, giving our gifts in secret. Every few months when our money ran low, we'd buy wood planks and Felix would spend a few nights practicing his woodcarving magic. Then we'd contact Timothy, who would take the covers, sell them, and divide the profits with us. In this way Felix and I were able to make a comfortable living and keep on with our mission and travels. Timothy became our good friend. Eventually we revealed some of our secrets to him, and he worked even more closely with us.

Meanwhile, being the one to solve our money problem did Felix a great deal of good. He gained self-confidence from it and felt more assured that he would play an important part in whatever the future might hold for us. That certainly proved to be true.

We spent a few months in and around Constantinople, building up our new business with Timothy and planning further travels. In particular, the islands of Britain sounded interesting and we decided to see them for ourselves. Then, just a week before we planned to leave, Felix and I went out one night to give gifts to several needy children we'd seen. They were living in tents on the outskirts of the city. It turned out to be perhaps the most important night of my life.

EIGHT

Layla

he first time I saw Layla, we were sneaking into the same tent.
Earlier that day, Felix and I had noticed some ragged travelers in
the Constantinople marketplace. They were trying to trade dirty
blankets for food, but none of the merchants were interested.

When the travelers gave up and walked away, Felix and I followed them
to the outskirts of the city, where they were camped in tents. Several hungry-
looking children ran up to them as they approached, obviously hoping
they'd returned with something to eat, but they hadn't. Felix and I nodded
to each other. We returned to the marketplace and bought loaves of bread,
large blocks of cheese, and lots of dried fruit. That night we loaded the food
in our sacks and went back to the travelers' tents. No one sat around the
smoking coals of the small campfire; everyone was obviously asleep.

We'd learned from long experience that Felix tended to trip and bump
into things whenever he tried to be stealthy, so I took the sacks and cautiously approached the first tent. Although it was old and patched, it was
still big, with several inside poles propping up the canvas and two entry
flaps, one at each end. The tent had room for six or seven people. I peeked
inside the nearest entry flap and saw the sleeping forms of two adults—

mother and father, probably—and two children. Motioning for Felix to stay outside and keep watch, I quietly eased myself inside. Being careful not to disturb anyone, I moved to the side of the nearest sleeping child, a little boy who looked much too thin. Reaching into my sack, I took out a loaf of bread, a block of cheese, and some sun-dried dates. I put these by the foot of his sleeping mat. When he woke in the morning there'd be enough food for him and his whole family to enjoy a good breakfast. Then I moved to where the next child slept. I reached into my sack for another loaf, and as I did someone else came through the other tent flap and nearly bumped into me.

I'd come close to being caught before, many times. Some people had caught glimpses of me, but never had I come face-to-face with someone whose house or tent I'd entered uninvited, although I'd done so for a good purpose. Remember, these were lawless times. Intruders were assumed to have come to steal or murder. You attacked burglars before they could attack you. So, expecting to be assaulted, I waved my loaf of bread like a weapon, hoping to frighten the other person enough so an alarm wouldn't be raised before I could get out of the tent, find Felix, and run.

The other person didn't cry out, but reached into another bag and withdrew what appeared to be a thick club, waving it at me. We made silent, threatening gestures: a pantomime of violence. For moments it was frightening, then quickly turned absurd. Obviously the other person didn't want to be discovered, either. Well, if it was a thief, Felix and I could at least see nothing was stolen. I stopped waving the bread and gestured instead for the other person to follow me out of the tent.

Felix looked startled when he saw two people coming. I raised my index finger to my lips; everyone in the tents was still asleep. The three of us quietly moved to a few hundred yards away. Even when we stopped and began to whisper, I still didn't get a good look at the intruder, who wore a dark cloak with a heavy hood.

"Who are you, and what are you trying to do?" I whispered. "If you're a thief, leave these poor people alone. They don't have anything to steal."

"Speak for yourself!" came the whispered reply. "Did I interrupt your robbery? Well, if the two of you want to kill me, I'll give you a hard fight first!"

"Give us the weapon you have in your pack, and then we'll talk," I suggested, still whispering. Felix moved quietly beside the stranger and put his hand into the pack. He looked puzzled as he pulled out a loaf of bread just like the one I'd been waving.

"Wait a moment," he said, and reached in again. "There's only food in here. Bread, olives, and fruit."

"Go ahead and steal it," sneered the stranger, hissing and sounding disgusted. "Fill your own fat stomachs while those poor people starve, and I hope you get the bellyaches you deserve afterward."

"We're not stealing anything, and don't call me fat," I hissed back. "Do you mean to tell me you were going into the tent to leave food, not to rob that family?"

The stranger snatched the loaf back out of Felix's hand and put it back into the pouch. "I've never robbed anybody, which is more than I can say for you. Where's that club you threatened me with?"

"I don't have a club," I replied. "Here's what I was waving." I pulled out my loaf of bread. "It seems neither one of us is a robber. Well, I'd like to know you better, friend. My companion and I have a clean, warm room back in the city. Would you care to accompany us there? We could find something to drink and be comfortable."

"Perhaps, but first let's finish our errand," the stranger whispered, and I remembered why Felix and I had come to the camp in the first place. Happy to share an adventure with someone who obviously was kind, I agreed. The stranger left gifts in some tents, I did the same in others. When all our food had been quietly distributed, we rejoined Felix and returned to the city.

As we moved farther away from the tent camp, Felix and I began to talk in our normal voices. But the stranger never did, speaking seldom and then only in a whisper. When we arrived at the inn where Felix and I had our room, our invitation to come in for something to drink was refused with a simple shake of our new friend's head.

"What's wrong with you?" Felix asked. "You know we're not thieves. We're just two gift-givers who are pleased to meet another. Come on up; if you don't have a place to stay, you can even sleep here."

I thought this offer was generous, but the stranger didn't, whispering, "I have to leave. Good night." But I reached out, grabbed an arm, and said, "At least let me see who you are." I pulled back the stranger's hood and found myself looking into the face of a woman who was perhaps thirty-five years old.

"Let me go," she said firmly, no longer whispering but sounding very definite. "I can fight if I have to."

"Well, you don't have to," I said quickly. "Please, my good woman, don't be afraid we'd harm you. Really, we honor you. Our offer of something to drink is made in friendship."

The woman had huge dark eyes, the kind that look into other people's hearts and instantly know all their secrets. She studied Felix and me carefully before saying, "Then in friendship I accept."

We sat in the room for hours drinking watered fruit juice—wine was too expensive; we preferred spending our money on things needed by others— and talking about ourselves. We learned her name was Layla, and that she came from a small village not too far from Patara, where I was born. Like me, Layla had been orphaned early in life. An aunt and uncle raised her. They were farmers who were lucky enough to have good harvests every year, and it was their pleasure to give all the extra food they had to those in need.

"As I grew up I began hearing stories about some mysterious man who, many years earlier, came secretly by night and left gifts by the sleeping mats of the poor," Layla explained. Felix looked amazed and poked me. I poked him back and muttered, "Be quiet."

"I always thought that was something I'd like to do, too," Layla continued. "When my aunt and uncle died, they left me their farm and a nice inheritance. Some of the men in my village thought they would marry me, but I knew it was because they wanted the farm and money and not because they loved me." She gestured at herself. "I'm not beautiful, after all."

"You seem beautiful to me," I said before I could stop myself, and, once the words were spoken, they seemed to hang in the air. Felix grinned like a fool. Layla blushed, and I swallowed hard. Soon afterward I asked where she was staying, and she named a place nearby that offered secure shelter to women traveling alone. "We'll escort you back," I suggested. "But will you please see us again tomorrow? I think we have a story to tell that might interest you."

She agreed. Felix and I walked back to her inn with her and waited while she knocked on the door. After she was safely inside, we turned to walk back to our own room.

"You like her, don't you?" Felix asked impudently.

"Of course I do," I replied carefully. "She gives gifts, just as we do."

"You like her for more than that," Felix teased. "She likes you, too. I think there's going to be a romance."

"There's going to be nothing of the kind!" I snapped. "Really, Felix, I'm more than one hundred thirty years old! That's too old to think about marriage."

"Well, you're the one speaking of marriage, or didn't you notice?" Felix pointed out.

"Don't talk to me," I mumbled, but when we were back in our room I dreamed the rest of the night about her beautiful eyes.

The next evening Layla joined us for supper. Later we distributed gifts to another poor family that had taken shelter in a rich man's barn. Layla insisted she buy her fair share of the cloaks and sandals we left behind as gifts. I could tell she was a woman of strong spirit and great self-confidence.

"If you like, we could go back to the inn and I could tell you a story you might enjoy," I suggested.

Layla agreed, and when we were seated and had fruit juice to drink, I began to tell her something of myself. It was strange to describe my early life again. Before, I'd only spoken of it to Felix. Layla listened carefully, her eyes peering into mine and apparently satisfying herself that I was telling the truth. I wasn't sure how much she should hear, but I ended up telling everything—about the first gifts to the daughters of Shem in Patara; my decision to become a priest; how people began to surround me all the time, and how I left Myra in the middle of the night to regain the privacy I needed for gift-giving; the way in which I first learned time and distance were different for me, and my meeting Felix in Rome. Finally, hesitantly, I told her how

Felix and I had stopped aging. This last information was so outrageous, I worried Layla might laugh at me or call me a liar, but she didn't. My story took until dawn to tell, and when I finally finished, she sat quietly and looked at me with those wonderful eyes.

"So it was you all along," she said. "You did the deeds that inspired me. Well, how splendid."

"You believe me?" I asked hopefully.

She seemed surprised by the question. "Of course I do! No one could invent such an incredible tale. So now you and Felix will spend eternity doing good things for others—how blessed you are, how lucky!"

I couldn't help myself. "But it's lonely sometimes," I blurted. Felix, seated near me, looked rather insulted. I ignored him. "The task is so great. So many people need so much. And I need your help. Will you join me, I mean, join us?"

"He's asking you to marry him, so I'm going to leave for a while," Felix interrupted, and bolted out the door before I could stop him.

"Are you?" Layla asked. "I'm not sure if you have or haven't."

I wanted to be angry with Felix, but I realized he'd only spoken the words I'd meant to say. "I suppose I am asking you to marry me," I admitted. "I've had no practice asking this before, so maybe I didn't do it properly. And it's all right if you say no."

"Of course I'll marry you, as long as you promise we can be equal partners in gift-giving," Layla said. "I can't imagine a happier life."

I wasn't certain what to do next. I thought about going to her and kissing her, but as I got to my feet another thought came to me.

"Layla," I asked. "What about how long you'll live? I mean, it seems Felix and I have stopped growing older, but what about you? I couldn't stand it if we married and I lived on and on, only to lose you along the way."

"Perhaps I'll be like Felix and stop aging, too," she suggested. "If I don't, well, who can tell the future, anyway?"

"I can't help but wonder——" I began, but she held up her hand for me to be quiet. What a strong-minded woman!

"Stop talking, Nicholas," she said firmly. "I think, since we're to be married, that you ought to come over here and kiss me instead."

So I kissed her, and a few days later we were married by the priest of a small church. He performed the wedding service in exchange for a set of Felix's finest carved-wood book covers. Then we moved on, Felix and Layla and me——three gift-givers ready for further adventures.

NINE

Travels with Attila

Because there were always so many wars going on, it was hard to travel from one part of the world to another. Although the three of us somehow could travel faster than other humans, that advantage was only possible in countries at peace. Where there was danger from marauding armies, we had to make our way carefully, like everyone else.

Layla, Felix, and I had decided we should concentrate on exploring those countries where Christianity had spread, often by priests who'd ventured into the wilderness. These priests were usually allowed to travel unmolested. Christian armies gave them free passage and other armies knew priests had taken vows of poverty and didn't have anything worth stealing.

So the three of us did our best to move about quietly, avoiding battlefields and spending as much time as possible in villages. Whenever we were stopped and questioned, we said Felix and I were priests and Layla was a nun. We certainly looked poor, and took pains to hide the money we had with us. Most of our funds were left with Timothy, who would send messengers to us with more as we needed it.

Nighttime gift-giving continued; we all enjoyed it, especially Layla. Felix and I soon found how helpful it was to have a woman working with us. When we'd reach a village, Layla would mingle with other women in the marketplace or at the river washing clothes, and later she'd return knowing exactly what each child in the village needed.

But we also tried to learn as much as we could about each country we visited. We didn't know why this might someday be important. We only knew it was something we should do. All three of us were especially interested in the islands of Britain, which had long since become legendary in other parts of the world. Tales had it that the original Britons painted themselves blue and lived in trees. Later, the myths said, they were led by great wizards known as Druids. The Romans eventually made Britain part of their empire, but it was easier to claim the islands than to keep them. The Britons were wild warriors and resisted the Romans as well as any Roman foe had. Finally, the Romans decided to concentrate their forces closer to their homeland.

As soon as the Roman forces left, the Saxons saw their chance. These fierce fighters crossed the narrow channel between Europe and England in warships, always eager to give battle and never in the habit of being merciful to anyone weaker than they were. The Britons soon found themselves in desperate trouble.

Still, the first Christian priests had made their way to the islands, so Layla, Felix, and I decided to follow them there if we could. The year was 453 A.D., and by my best estimate I was one hundred seventy-three years old.

"I don't see how we're going to get across the water to those islands," Felix grumbled as we slowly made our way northwest. "And if we do get to Britain, what if we're the only ones there who haven't painted ourselves blue?"

"Then we'll paint ourselves blue, too," said Layla, who hadn't seemed to age a day since she'd married me forty-three years earlier. "Remember, we don't want to draw attention to ourselves."

"Too late for that," I interrupted. "We have unwanted company, and they've certainly noticed us."

We were in a forest near the Rhine River, and had heard from other travelers that the army of the great Hun chief Attila might be nearby. The Huns were a warlike people whose tribes originated in what is now called Germany. They'd been a constant problem for the Romans, and Attila had long been one of the most feared warriors in Europe. But in 451 A.D., the Romans had formed a temporary alliance with the Visigoths and together they'd defeated Attila in a daylong battle. He and his army fled, although everyone knew they'd be back again in force. As Felix, Layla, and I neared the Rhine, local rumor had it that Attila had returned, this time determined to invade Italy and conquer Rome itself.

The rumor was right. While Felix and Layla had been talking, I saw six Huns dressed in wolfskins and armed with bows and short spears emerge from behind nearby trees. They quickly surrounded us.

We'd spent much of our time learning different languages, so we were able to talk with them.

"Whose army do you fight with?" one of the Huns asked, pulling an arrow back on his bowstring and looking quite eager to shoot it at us.

"No one's army," I answered as calmly as I could. "We're Christians trying to reach the islands of Britain. As you can see, we're very poor. But if you're hungry, we have bread and dried fruit in our packs. Would you like some?"

One of the warriors was very young, perhaps twelve. All six Huns were skinny, and this boy smiled when he heard me offer food. He started to move forward, but the first warrior, who seemed to be the leader, gestured for him to wait.

"You could be spies for the Romans," he said. "You look too fat to be a priest," he added, pointing at me. Layla giggled. "We'll take you to the leader and let him decide what to do with you."

The Hun camp was close by. We hadn't noticed it because Attila had ordered his men not to light many fires, thinking the smoke might give their presence away to the enemies. Our captors marched us up to the largest tent in the camp; it was made from stitched-together animal skins. When the leader came out, I knew he must be Attila. Though he was very short, his eyes were ice blue, and when he spoke it was obvious he was used to being obeyed.

"You say you're Christians on the way to Britain?" he asked harshly. "I don't believe it. The Romans sent you to spy on me."

"I don't think there are any Romans within a hundred miles," I said truthfully. "If there are, we haven't seen them, although you shouldn't take our word for it since we didn't see your army either. Look at how easily your men captured us. Could they have done this if we were really spies?"

Attila stuck a dirty finger in his mouth and began to pick his teeth with a long, cracked fingernail. Flies buzzed around him. I'm sorry to say he had a rather foul body odor.

"Well," he finally said, "I guess I have to either kill you or let you go. We've been marching fast and don't have any food to spare, so we can't keep you as prisoners."

"You really don't want to kill us," I said, trying to sound more confident than I felt. "We've done you no harm, and besides, aren't you tired of killing? Don't you often look at your sword and wish you never had to use it again?" I didn't know why I said this. The words just came hurrying out of my mouth.

Felix groaned, thinking I'd just said too much, and even Layla looked pale. Attila thought about killing us. I know I saw his fingers twitch near the hilt of his sword. But that tense moment passed. He looked at me thoughtfully and said, "Come into my tent. I guess I can feed one of you. The other two will stay out here. I won't waste guards on them. If they try to run, they'll regret it."

"Oh, we'll stay right here," Felix promised. Layla looked both relieved we hadn't been killed and angry that I was the only one invited into Attila's tent. She and Felix really didn't miss anything. It was dark in there, and smoke from the small fire hung in stinging clouds around our heads even after we seated ourselves on mats.

"How did you know I was tired of the killing?" Attila asked.

"Who wouldn't be tired of it?" I replied. "Hating wears a person down to nothing. Kindness is what brings true pleasure in life."

Attila leaned forward. "Tell me more," he begged, and I did. My whole story flowed out of me. My tale went back to the beginning at Patara, and all the way up to our capture by his scouts. Attila interrupted me once to call in one of his men and order food prepared for Felix and Layla, and that they be given a warm place to sleep. Then he and I talked until dawn, and when the sun rose there were four in our party, because Attila had decided to give up his life of war and join us.

"There's no sense in fighting, anyway," he admitted. "No matter how many battles we win, there is always another army ready to fight me. Oh, the Romans are weakening, but the Gauls are gaining strength, and the Franks and the Vandals prefer war to peace. I think I'll come with you to Britain and help you give your gifts there."

It didn't occur to Attila to ask if that was all right with me, and, anyway, it was. He was a scarred old warrior, but he had plenty of common sense. I knew he'd be especially useful in helping us locate and avoid other armies.

We left the next night. Attila picked a trusted captain to tell the rest of the Huns that their leader had died and would be buried in a secret place. They were to return to their homes and not fight any more if they could help it.

As a special favor, Attila asked if his wife could come, too. Dorothea turned out to be a very gentle woman who could sew beautifully, She soon patched all our ragged robes so well that they looked like new. Layla was worried Attila would get in fights with strangers we met—he never did, having fought as much as anyone could ever want already—but she was very pleased to have another woman to talk to. As for Felix, he developed a bad habit of teasing Attila, who would get angry and threaten him with terrible things, but never laid a hand on him.

So we were five when we finally reached the banks of the wide channel that separated our side of civilization from Britain. It was exciting to get that far, but we had no idea how to proceed.

"Maybe we could ask some Saxons for a ride on one of their warships," Felix suggested.

Attila fixed him with a fierce glare. "Saxons are terrible people," he snorted. "They'd rather kill someone like you, Felix, than give you a ride.

Why don't you just throw yourself into this water and drown? If nothing else, that would give all our ears a rest."

Dorothea frowned at her husband. "Leave Felix alone. At least he's trying to think of something. Can we perhaps rent a small boat and sail across?"

"I considered that," I said, "but I don't think any of us are good enough sailors to handle a small boat. We'd be as likely to get swept away as we would be to land on the British shore."

As usual, Layla had the best suggestion. "Everything always happens to us for a reason," she said. "We're here because we're meant to be. So let's simply wait until someone comes to help us. There's time for a meal, and to rest our feet after this long journey. We have bread and cheese and a few olives. Who's hungry?" Of course, we all were, though Felix later accused me of eating more than my share.

After eating, we spread out our blankets and slept. I stayed awake longer than the others, although Layla kept me company for several hours before she finally fell asleep. I lay there in the darkness looking up at the stars, wondering how far away they were and what was going to happen to get all five of us across the water to Britain. My answer arrived with the first pink streaks of sunrise against the black night sky. There was the sound of water slapping against the prow of a boat, and sure enough a small vessel came into view, hugging the shoreline near us and piloted by a tall, slender man of middle age dressed in the rough brown robes of a priest.

"Come ashore and join us for breakfast," I called out to him, the sound of my voice waking the others. The priest in the boat waved and steered his craft to the shore in front of us.

"Christians?" he asked carefully, eyeing Attila with particular suspicion. Though we'd convinced Attila to exchange his animal furs for more common robes, and although he washed more regularly than he once had, the Hun chief still looked too fierce to be an ordinary missionary.

"We are," I said hurriedly. "This is my wife, Layla, and this is Felix, and these two fine people are Attila and his wife, Dorothea. They're from the Hun tribe."

The priest raised one eyebrow. "Attila" was hardly a common name. "Not too many Christians yet among the Huns," he said carefully.

"Let's eat," grunted Attila, who was never much for polite conversation. We got out more bread and some dried figs. The priest ate heartily, with the appetite of a man who'd missed many meals. I waited until he had satisfied his hunger before asking who he was and where he was going.

"My name is Patrick," he replied. "I spent much of my boyhood as a slave on an island far to the west of Britain. Ireland, it's called. I escaped from my captors and made my way to Rome, where I became a Christian priest. Since then I've often returned to Britain and Ireland. There aren't many priests there. Sometimes I'm given credit for doing miracles when I've really done nothing at all."

"Tell me about it," I urged, remembering all the miracles I was supposed to have worked in Myra, but hadn't.

"The story of the snakes is the most common," Patrick said. "A few years ago in Ireland, a village was infested with snakes, or so it was said. I'd never seen any there myself. But the people in the village told me that if I was really a priest I could make the snakes go away. Well, I raised my hands to the sky and cried, 'Snakes, be gone!' And none of the people in the village ever saw any snakes again, not that I believe they were around to be seen in the first place. Those people probably had looked in the grass and seen some crooked sticks. Still, it's rather handy to have a reputation for working miracles. I go around the country, identify myself, and people are usually willing to do whatever I ask, including not fighting with each other."

"We have hopes of seeing Britain, and from your story, I think we'd like to see Ireland, too," I suggested. "Perhaps you'd give us a ride across this wide channel of water in your boat. Do you have enough room?"

"I'm sure I do," Patrick said agreeably, "although I could only take such a large load for a short voyage to the other side. I mean no insult about your weight, friend," he hastily added, though not before Felix started guffawing. "Let me take you and your companions across to Britain, and if you ever get far enough west I'll try to find you on that coast and bring you the rest of the way to Ireland."

So we gathered our things, got in the boat, and were whisked across the channel to Britain. It wasn't an entirely calm passage. Poor Attila got seasick and made quite a mess at Felix's feet. He apologized to Patrick, who told the Hun chief not to worry about it. I noticed Attila didn't apologize to Felix, who made a point of washing his feet over and over when we'd safely disembarked on the British shore.

TEN

Arthur of Britain

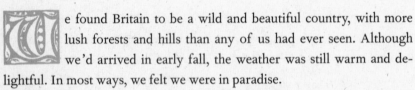e found Britain to be a wild and beautiful country, with more lush forests and hills than any of us had ever seen. Although we'd arrived in early fall, the weather was still warm and delightful. In most ways, we felt we were in paradise.

But war was as much a part of Britain as the land's lovely green fields. Its native people were a primitive, proud race ready to fight foreign invaders for every inch of earth. When we got there, the Britons were involved in a long battle with Saxon war parties for control of the island's south and east regions. For forty years, the Saxons had been winning, never decisively but always ending each year by extending their control a few miles nearer to the fertile British midlands.

As usual, we spent our first few months in a new place exploring the countryside, visiting villages, and learning as much as possible about the new place and its customs. Above all, we soon learned that, along the southeast coast, life for ordinary British peasants was hard. Villages often were raided by the Saxons, who stole what they wanted, killed any men they could catch, and took away women and children as slaves. Villages spared from the Saxons fell prey to Britain's own war parties—which also needed food, at the expense of the countrymen they were trying to save from the invading enemy.

So there were plenty of families in need, and plenty of children who could use a nighttime gift of food or clothing. But for the first time we were in a place where such goods were hard to buy. We had a fair amount of money with us, coins small enough not to attract too much attention, but easily worth the purchase price of such things as we needed. We did the best we could. It was so rare for any charity to be shown on this island that right after our first few gift-givings, the story of the gifts began to circulate quickly from village to village.

Attila was quickest to fall in love with Britain. Although he'd wearied of participating in battles, he still was a student of warfare.

"The Saxons will eventually crush the Britons completely," he predicted, "but they'll pay for every inch of land with blood. These Britons are good fighters, ones who know when to stand and do battle and when to retreat."

Attila was especially impressed with a tribal war chief named Arthur. This fellow was a special torment to the Saxons, moving his small band of fighters quickly from one place to another and attacking where and when he was least expected.

"I think this Arthur must be interesting," Attila said. "Could we try to find him, Nicholas? I'd like to talk battle strategy with him. Perhaps I could give him some useful advice. I once outfought the Romans, you know."

"We'd best stay away from Arthur, because where he is, the fighting is likely to be the bloodiest," I replied. "Put warfare behind you, Attila. Our business is giving gifts, not giving battle."

Layla noticed the strained tone of my voice. That night when the others slept she quietly said to me, "Being near battles weakens your special powers, doesn't it? That's why we can move so quickly when no armies are nearby, and why we creep along close to battlefields. Attila's scouts would never have captured us if we'd been going at our usual speed, and now here in the south of Britain we don't seem able to get ourselves from village to village as quickly."

"In a way, I'm glad you noticed," I told her. "I'd hoped it was my imagination, but now I'm convinced of it. Where war is, we can't be, or at least we can't be as effective as we are in other places. What a waste war is! Look at this beautiful country, with plenty of room for everyone. But the Britons want to rule themselves or die, and these Saxons are driven to conquer rather than come in friendship. Will the world always be like this? Surely someday people will know better."

"Perhaps," Layla said doubtfully. "Why not get some rest if you can? Tomorrow we'll find a village, and in that village will be children in need, and tomorrow night we'll visit them with presents. Think about that, instead."

We spent the next year going from village to village, giving our gifts and trying our best not to be discouraged by the fighting all around us. Twice we were taken captive by Briton war parties, who'd mistaken us for Saxons, and once by Saxons who'd mistaken us for Britons. On all three occasions we were able to convince them otherwise. Luckily the Christian religion had, to an extent, reached both sides, for when we identified ourselves as missionaries we were quickly set free.

"Thank goodness these people have been converted," Felix said with relief after the Saxons let us go. "They're devout enough to send missionaries safely on their way."

"It's too bad they're not devout enough to remember the phrase 'Thou shalt not kill,'" I said sadly. "Yes, they let us live, but how many innocent people will die at their hands tomorrow?"

Twice during the year we sent messages to Timothy, who now was a very old man. His children ran his businesses for him. Along with our requests for money, we shipped him more wonderfully carved book covers and, for the first time, intricate wood figures shaped like soldiers. Attila had a knack for carving these, and Timothy was able to sell them in faraway marketplaces for almost as much as the book covers. We'd more or less told him our secrets as the years passed and we learned he could be trusted. He always gave us fair prices, and once we saw the lack of goods in England he began to pay us in shipments of wool cloaks and stout shoes. We stored these in barns of Briton farmers we befriended. A few times we lost barnfuls of goods to Saxon raiders, but for the most part we were lucky.

Food for gift-giving was much harder to come by. There was very little for sale, and what there was to buy was frankly horrible stuff—wormy meat and old, tough vegetables. Anything worth eating was gobbled up by whichever Britons were fortunate enough to get their mouths to it first. So there were no marketplaces full of food for sale like we'd been accustomed to frequenting in Constantinople, Rome, and other major cities during our travels.

Sometimes a few of us—Felix or me, most often—would complain out loud that we did little good in leaving shoes for a child who was in danger of starving. But Layla, sensible as always, offered a constant reminder: "What we're really giving these children is hope, and the knowledge that there are people in this world who care about them. That's a gift even greater than food, so stop complaining." And we'd stop.

Although we were across the channel from Europe, word of events there would often reach us. The most important news was that the Romans had been driven from Gaul, the country that later would be called France. Clovis, the war chief of the Franks, not only defeated the Romans but the Visigoths, too. It seemed he might be the powerful leader who could eventually bring peace to the land, even if he had to accomplish this by killing off everyone else. I felt somewhat better when I learned that he chose Christmas Day 496 A.D. to be baptized, along with thousands of his followers. The Christian Church was delighted, of course, and Clovis proved himself to be more than a mere warrior by spending much of the rest of his life inventing laws to govern daily conduct.

There was no such clear-cut leader on the island of Britain. The Saxons continued their bloody invasion and the Britons persisted in defending themselves. Arthur became the unofficial leader of the Britons, who were divided into too many squabbling tribes to put up a united defense against the Saxons. Arthur tried to talk other tribal chieftains into joining together, and for a while it appeared he might be successful. In the year 500 A.D., Arthur even led a number of tribes against the Saxons in Dorset, a region of southeast Britain, and beat the invaders back toward the sea. Bards or storytellers of the Celtic tribes began traveling around singing songs and telling stories about the great and bold Arthur, the war chief who'd saved the

Britons, but they sang too soon. The Saxons returned more determined than ever to conquer the island, and Arthur's tribal alliance was smashed apart by the invaders' new attacks.

It became clear with Arthur's defeat that the Saxons would now rule Britain. Thousands of Britons sneaked to the coast and sailed across the channel, hoping life in Europe would be kinder than Saxon law. Most natives of the island, though, simply withdrew farther inland, up north to the wilderness they called Scotland, or into the rocky western plains of Wales.

Our group chose to stay close to the southeast coast. Most of the fighting was over. There were rumors that Arthur had been killed, perhaps stabbed in the back by one of his own captains who'd betrayed him to the Saxons. More hopeful Britons whispered that perhaps Arthur had only been badly wounded, and would come back in all his warrior glory someday to free their island of foreign rule.

The truth was, Arthur had been wounded, though not fatally. We knew this because a few days after he lost a final battle to the Saxons, an old woman cautiously approached us as we were walking by a small farm in the countryside a few miles from the battle site.

"Pardon, strangers, but are you some of those Christians?" she asked. I noticed the poor woman was wearing rags, and most of her teeth were missing. She went on, "If you are, and if you give help to others like they say Christians do, could you come see a wounded man? He's badly hurt, and I don't know what to do for him."

Dorothea had a great deal of experience assisting wounded men, having spent most of her marriage following Attila from battle to battle. She and Layla hurried ahead to the barn where the old woman said the wounded man lay unconscious. Felix, Attila, and I followed.

As soon as we saw the man, we knew he must be Arthur. There was a grandness about him, even as he lay in a bloody heap on the barn's dirt floor. With Attila's help, Dorothea raised him to a sitting position, and Layla got water from the old woman's tiny well. Dorothea bathed the wounded man's face. He had two deep cuts across his midsection and a nasty gash across his forehead. As Dorothea cleaned his face, his eyes fluttered open.

"Who are you?" he whispered, his legs jerking convulsively as he tried to get to his feet.

"Sit back, Arthur," Attila ordered in the softest tones I'd ever heard him speak. "Rest, brave chief. Your battle is done for a while, and the time to heal has begun."

"How do you know who I am?" Arthur wanted to know.

"One warrior knows another," Attila said briefly, and then told Felix, Layla, and me to wait outside while he and Dorothea inspected Arthur's wounds. The three of us left the barn and joined the old woman, who was fearful any Saxons hunting for Arthur would burn her farm if they found him there.

"It's him; it's the great Arthur, isn't it?" she asked, and we told her it was. "Well, he's got to leave right away. I came out to get eggs from my chickens and there he was in the barn, looking like he must have crawled in there during the night. I feel sorry for him, but I can't hide him here, don't you see? My husband's away hunting, and we're too old to start over if the Saxons find that man here and burn us out because of it."

Layla looked at me, the question reflected in our eyes. When I nodded, she said, "Don't worry. Let our friends tend to the man's wounds, and then we'll take him with us."

And that is what happened. Arthur was very weak, so for the first two days Attila fashioned a sort of stretcher with strong cloaks tied between a pair of long, trimmed tree branches. He, Felix, and I took turns two at a time carrying the stretcher with Arthur on it. His wounds healed quicker than his mind, which retained memories of what had to have been a terrible battle. At night Arthur would toss and moan, no doubt dreaming of Saxon warships and cruel invaders arriving on them.

On the third day he was able to walk part of the time. We were moving west. Attila thought the Saxons would be so proud of their victory that they'd stay near the coast to celebrate for a while. As we got farther from the battlefields, we were able to travel faster. I thought we might as well go all the way to Ireland and visit Patrick.

That night Attila drew Arthur aside and spent hours talking with him quietly. I could only guess, but I thought he might be telling Arthur about his own victories and defeats and how he'd eventually decided even the bravest warrior could only fight for so long. Apparently his words touched Arthur. The next day our newest companion walked along with the rest of us, despite having little to offer in the way of conversation. That took longer, but in another week when we'd reached the far west coast and gotten passage on a small ship to Ireland, Arthur had started entertaining us with stories of British history. He was a very good storyteller, far better than the rest of us, and a talented hand with a carving knife. Between Felix, Attila, and Arthur, we had three men who could turn bits of wood into almost anything imaginable.

It wasn't hard to find Patrick, who had become the most famous man in Ireland. His followers had built him a fine stone church, with a sturdy log hut covered with a thatched roof beside it so the good missionary would have a dry place to sleep. We sent word ahead to Patrick of our impending arrival, and when we arrived he welcomed us with a meal. He might have driven snakes out of Ireland, but he'd kept the rabbits. Two fine fat ones were roasting over Patrick's fire.

"I knew you and Felix would be hungry." He grinned. "After our meal, I'll want to hear about everything that's happened to you, and how you gained another companion. But take your time as you talk. All there ever seems to be in this world anymore is war and killing, so let's enjoy fellowship and peace here for a little while before we go out into the confusion again."

ELEVEN

The Dark Ages

Not much really worth telling about happened during the next six centuries. When scholars are feeling generous, they refer to this period as "The Middle Ages," but its most common—and correct—nickname is "The Dark Ages." Almost everyone living in Europe and Britain spent these hundreds of years in misery. Wars were fought everywhere. Different tribes battled each other for control of bits and pieces of land. Warriors did what they wanted and common people suffered for it. No one was safe from the sword.

The six of us—Attila, Dorothea, Arthur, Felix, Layla, and I—spent these centuries doing what good we could. Often, we couldn't do much. Our travel was slow; as I'd learned previously, being anywhere near fighting reduced our ability to travel at wondrous speeds, and there always seemed to be fighting wherever we went. Timothy's heirs continued to accept our carved book covers and whittled figures, and sell them for us, but their ships were frequently attacked by pirates. We had less money to spend and often there was nothing worthwhile to buy with the money we had. What a sad, terrible time!

Yet, while Europe wallowed in despair, other parts of the world flourished. In 570 A.D., a man named Muhammad was born in the Arab city of Mecca.

By the time of his death in 632 A.D., he'd sown the seeds of a new religion, Islam. In 589 A.D., China, a nation we'd heard of only in the vaguest terms, was united under one ruler for the first time in four centuries. Four years later, an island nation eventually known as Japan developed its first central government and laws.

Europe remained, for the most part, primitive. Brave missionaries gradually won most of the tribes over to Christianity, but this new religion seemed to have little effect on all the fighting. Stories about Jesus and his life were often intermingled with more superstitious tales. Legends sprouted everywhere. In some places, it was still believed dragons might be lurking.

People whose everyday lives are desperate often look to myths for comfort. In these years, the people of Europe wanted miracles to happen to them, so they easily accepted outrageous tales of miracles involving others. Our small, six-member band knew all about this, and we should have, because many of the made-up stories involved Attila or Arthur or me.

Attila, who'd simply left his army to join us, now was widely reported to have died in a fit of bad temper, then buried in a secret place made even more secret by his captains deliberately killing everyone associated with the burial. The rest of us knew from his own stories that Attila had been, in his time, a rather cruel fighter, but even he was amazed to hear stories of how he had preferred drinking his wine from human skulls.

"I suppose I might have done that if I'd thought of it," Attila said with a wry grin. "I must have shrunk, too. I heard recently that I was seven feet tall."

Still, tales of Attila were nothing compared to legends involving Arthur. As the years passed into decades, then centuries, it became widely believed in Britain that this simple war chief had actually been a king with a crown, one who lived with hundreds of fine knights and ladies in a magical castle called Camelot. Poems were written about Arthur; songs were composed and sung about him. At first, native Britons told these stories to give themselves hope that the hated Saxons would someday be driven back to Europe; but when the Normans crossed the channel in their turn and conquered the Saxons, the Arthur stories continued. Now, the stories went, he was being kept in some wonderful cave, asleep in the company of a magician named Merlin. Both would reappear soon, whenever "soon" might be.

And I, too, became the subject of more myths. Many of these stemmed from a new church policy of recognizing a select few men and women after their deaths as saints—people who were especially touched by God and who performed miracles during their lives. After saints had passed away, they were still supposed to be able to help those who prayed to them for assistance.

I was named a saint. Now memories of Nicholas, Bishop of Myra, became memories of Saint Nicholas, the man who in life was able to do wondrous things such as guide sinking ships safely into harbor and rescue children from all kinds of harm. In return for these acts, I was now considered patron saint of sailors and children, an embarrassing honor since I hadn't done any of it.

"If it's any comfort, I don't think I ever lived in the fabulous castle called Camelot," Arthur said jokingly. Often at night we'd entertain ourselves by reciting the latest myths we'd heard that involved each of us. "Nicholas, I once thought it was magic enough that I've joined you and lived to be—what?—three hundred years old already. But that's a little thing compared to living in enchanted castles and being named king of a whole country. I don't think the real magic would be splendid enough for the people who make up stories about us."

"Don't make fun of those who tell or believe the stories," Layla cautioned. "Many people have no joy in their own lives, so they let their imaginations work freely. Let's talk about other things, like the coronation of Charlemagne. Could he be the leader who will finally make things better?"

She said this just after December 25 in 800 A.D. Charlemagne, king of the Franks, had chosen that Christmas Day in Rome to be crowned emperor of the West by Pope Leo III. He picked the date because it was already a time of special celebration for Christians.

All over Europe and Britain, new ceremonies had gradually been added to the traditional Christian festivities on Christmas. In 529 A.D., Roman Emperor Justinian had declared December 25 a civic holiday on which none of his subjects could work. This news pleased me greatly. Most people had to labor too hard for their meager wages.

As Christian missionaries traveled throughout the world, they began to take winter customs of various nations and combine them with Christmas worship. In northern Europe and Britain, for instance, native peoples had long since had their own celebrations in December, mostly for the winter solstice. To symbolize their faith during snowy winter months that warm planting weather would eventually come again, they hung out evergreen branches in front of their homes. "Julmond," as these people called it, also required feasting afterward as another mark of confidence that times of plenty would return.

The Christian missionaries, seeing all this, carried tales back to central Europe of "Jul," pronouncing the "J" like a "Y." Soon enough, proper Christians began hanging out evergreen branches as part of their celebration of Christ's birth. A similarly named custom came to central Europe from Persia, where end-of-the-year customs included burning part of a log in the season called "Yole," the fire being an offering along with prayers for good weather during the next planting season. "Jul" and "Yole" eventually became "Yule," another name for the Christmas season that continues to be used to this day.

Amid all the other bad times, people began to consider the Christmas holiday a very special, happy occasion. For one day, at least, fighting was usually forgotten. Charlemagne's choice of Christmas for his coronation was the clearest sign yet that even the greatest war leaders recognized the significance ordinary people placed on December 25.

By this time, we were in the western Frankish region of Burgundy, now part of France, at the time of Charlemagne's crowning, news of which had been carried across the continent by messengers. After so many centuries of discouragement, we wanted to meet this new emperor whose rule promised to be special. Charlemagne was supposed to be spending the rest of the winter camped outside Rome—he had little use for the fancy palaces in the city—so we set off, traveling east and south until we crossed into Italy.

Ever practical, Layla wanted to know what I'd say to Charlemagne. "Will you tell him everything about us, and ask him to leave his army and come with us like Attila and Arthur?" she wondered.

"Charlemagne has his own important mission, so I'd be wrong to ask him to abandon it to join in ours," I replied. "I just want to meet the man so I can see with my own eyes that there's reason to hope for better times."

"It's probably going to be hard to see him," Felix predicted. "They say he's trying to do everything at once: build a government, start schools, and encourage artists to paint and write. Hundreds of important people every day are surely begging for an hour of his time. He'll hardly be interested in talking to strangers."

Felix was right; when we arrived in Charlemagne's camp and asked to see him, we were told the new emperor was much too busy. We left, spent a week giving gifts at night to poor children in the many villages surrounding Rome, then went back and asked again. The answer was the same.

"That's enough," said Attila, who was never especially patient. "This emperor has no time for us, so let's go back to the countryside somewhere and do our gift-giving as best we can."

"Let's go back to Britain," Arthur said hopefully. "We haven't been there in a hundred years. I'd like to see the green hills again, and give gifts to all the needy children who live in them."

"We will, we will," I said, being careful not to promise anything specific. "Tonight, when the rest of you are out leaving gifts, I'll stay at our campsite and think about this." But as soon as they were gone I put on my red bishop's robes—not the original ones, which long since had been worn out, but newer ones sewn by Dorothea—and crept into Charlemagne's camp. The emperor was living in a big tent. I hid myself in some bushes until Charlemagne sent away all of his staff for the night. Then I quickly, quietly ducked inside.

Charlemagne was a tall man with a long gray beard. He had something of the look of a warrior, standing straight and staring at me with an expression of curiosity, not fear. But there was great wisdom in his face, too.

He greeted me by saying, "I don't think you've come to try and kill me. I see both your hands, and neither is holding a weapon. Your robes are those of a priest, and I'm a good friend of the church, so you can't be angry about that. Why are you here?"

"I just wanted to talk to you, Emperor," I answered. "For a week, one of your staff has said you were too busy. So I thought I'd wait until you were alone and might have time for a conversation with a stranger."

Charlemagne raised his eyebrows a little; he wasn't used to being spoken to so plainly. Then he nodded, smiled, and said, "Well, then, here you are. Would you like something to drink or to eat? No? Well, here's a bench. Sit down and we'll talk."

And we did. I asked Charlemagne how he planned to use his new powers as emperor, and he told me of his plans for a united Europe that offered protection to people who needed it, with free trade between countries and free education so children could learn enough to earn good livings when they grew to be adults.

"I never learned to read very well, and I can't write at all," he admitted. "I was lucky enough to be born in a royal family, but if I'd been born to a poor man and woman I'd only have been considered fit for herding sheep. The more education people have, the less they'll fight, because they'll be smart enough to find other ways to solve their problems. Now, what about you? There's something about you that makes me think you're a fellow with many secrets, and that you're someone who's seen a lot of this world."

I didn't tell him everything. I just said some companions and I traveled about finding children in need and helping them with gifts. Charlemagne asked where we got money to buy these gifts and I told him how we carved book covers and figures.

"Don't you have any rich friends who will give money to buy the gifts that you leave?" he asked, and when I said we didn't, he got out parchment and a goose-quill pen. "Can you write? Well, then, write down what I'm about to tell you, which is an order to all my captains and officers to bring you into my presence whenever you like, and to give you food and other supplies for your party whenever you need them. I can't give you money. What I have comes from taxes and every coin is needed for the programs I'm starting. But at least getting more traveling supplies for free will let you use all the money you make to buy those gifts you give to poor children."

Charlemagne dictated a lengthy order. When I'd written everything down he heated wax and put a blob of it on the parchment. Then he took a heavy metal disk, his official seal, and stamped it on the wax. This seal meant that the emperor himself had given the written order to assist "Nicholas and any of his trusted friends, these being named Layla, Arthur, Felix, Dorothea, and Attila."

"Attila," Charlemagne muttered. "An unusual name, isn't it? The only person I've heard of called Attila was a fierce old Hun chief who—well, I suppose it doesn't matter. That other Attila was eight feet tall and drank wine from a human skull, you know."

"Really?" I said politely. "No, that's not my Attila at all. The Attila who travels with me is of normal height, and he uses a simple cup."

Charlemagne laughed. "Well, the man I'm thinking of had to have died a long time ago, anyway. If he were living today, he'd have to be three hundred or three hundred fifty years old. Impossible!"

"Right," I agreed, thinking to myself that Attila was really closer to four hundred. "Well, thank you for your time and your gift, great Emperor. We'll remember you in our prayers, and many more children will have warm clothing or food to eat because of your kindness."

"Do me one favor, Nicholas," Charlemagne said as I pulled up a flap and prepared to leave his tent. "Always keep December twenty-fifth special. It works wonders on human hearts, and I think more good is accomplished on that day than is done all the rest of the year. I don't know why I wanted so badly to tell you that, but now I have, and I feel very peaceful. Visit me again whenever you like. Just show that order to my guards."

I visited Charlemagne on several occasions before he died fourteen years later. He continued to be a good and just ruler. Not all of Charlemagne's fine plans worked. His son Louis succeeded him as emperor of the West; he died in 840. After Louis, Charlemagne's successors weren't quite as powerful. But they did rule what became known as the Holy Roman Empire, which existed from 962 until 1806.

And when people told stories of Charlemagne, they often mentioned his determination that children should grow up in peace, and be well educated. So that idea survived, and remained a beacon of hope as Europe stumbled through several more unenlightened centuries.

TWELVE

"Let's Give Gifts of Toys!"

ne night about three hundred fifty years after Charlemagne died, Felix, Attila, Dorothea, Arthur, Layla, and I were sitting around the campfire in the hills of southeast Britain. It was a large fire, because autumn had arrived and the night air was cool. We'd eaten dinner—bread, fruit, cheese; nothing fancy, but still good, filling food—and now we were all lounging on our blankets.

Our conversation stuck to ordinary subjects, such as how much money we had left with which to buy gifts, and when we ought to take a long trip southeast to Rome (where officials of the Holy Roman Empire still honored Charlemagne's order to give us all the traveling supplies we required). The parchment on which that original order was written had long since crumbled with age. We'd requested a replacement copy, and gotten it, then needed a replacement for the replacement, and a replacement for that replacement, and so on. None of the officials we spoke to seemed to notice we didn't age along with the parchment. They just gave us what we wanted without paying much attention.

"I think we should spend the whole next century in Rome," Felix said thoughtfully. "In this last century, Britain's been more of a battlefield than ever. You had the Saxons being conquered by the Normans, and the Danish wanting to invade, and the wild tribes up in Scotland threatening to come south. Anywhere else would have been more peaceful."

"Think again," Arthur said, sounding irritated. He always took it personally whenever Britain was criticized for anything. "Italy's just a stopping-over place for all those knights going on the Crusades. We'd see more swords and armor there than we would if we stayed here."

I sighed unhappily, because it was true. The worst of the latest wars found Christian soldiers from Britain and Europe uniting in armies to attack the Muslims, who'd taken control of the ancient lands of the Jews, including the holy city of Jerusalem. Instead of asking for permission to share the city, the Christians decided to fight for it. Sometimes they fought better than others; in the so-called First Crusade of 1095 they'd actually recaptured Jerusalem, but the Muslim leader Saladin soon won it back.

A recent crusade, led by kings Philip II of France and Richard I of England, had been a miserable failure. Richard, who was called the Lion-Hearted by his subjects, had been captured by the Duke of Austria on his way back home. The duke was asking for a large ransom. Richard's brother John, who'd been left in charge of Britain while the king was away fighting, didn't seem in any hurry to raise the money. No one in England knew what might happen next. Civil war, matching those lords and knights loyal to John against those remaining loyal to Richard, seemed to be coming.

"Well, what will we do then, Nicholas?" Attila asked. "When I was a younger man, say, perhaps two hundred years old, I might have thought people would sooner or later get tired of fighting. But with the wisdom of very advanced years, I have to say I'm not certain they ever will. We've been hoping for centuries that better times might be coming. Maybe they're not."

Layla, who'd been breaking up small branches and adding them to the fire, poked a stick into the flames so sharply that sparks crackled and jumped. We all had to slap our blankets to make sure they wouldn't start smoldering.

"You have no right to be discouraged, Attila," she said sternly. "Our long lives are all the proof we need that things will get better someday, and I think they'll get better a lot faster if we don't spend so much time moping."

Attila looked hurt. Tough old warrior that he was, he still had very delicate feelings. Dorothea reached over and patted him gently on the leg, saying quietly but firmly, "Attila wasn't moping. He was just saying what's been on all our minds, Layla. How many thousands of nights have we gone out and left food and clothing for poor children, and what difference has it really made? The wars continue; poverty is everywhere. There's no way to be sure we're really making a difference. Nicholas, you're our leader. Do you know something the rest of us don't, some secret you could share so we'd feel more hopeful?"

I shrugged. "Things keep changing for the worse. Sooner or later they'll have to change for the better. There are so many new nations now: Denmark, Norway, Germany, Iceland, Poland—maybe their armies will be satisfied with what they have and stop fighting."

"Don't forget rumors of a New World," suggested Arthur. In recent decades he'd become fascinated with tales about boats sailing west and not falling off the edge of the world, but instead discovering new lands, countries rich beyond belief with forests full of wild game. As early as 875, Irish sailors were said to have done this, although the Irish kept few accurate records. But it was almost certain that in 982 Eric the Red, son of a Norwegian chieftain, sailed to some far-off country after being banished from Iceland for murder; he called this new place Greenland for its color. In 1001, Eric's son—appropriately named Lief Eric's Son, or Ericson—followed his father's example by sailing west as well and discovering a place he named "Vinland" because he found grape vines growing there.

Sometimes Arthur suggested we take passage on one of these expeditions and see these wonderful places for ourselves. But the rest of us remembered how Attila often got seasick and wouldn't agree to such a long, turbulent voyage.

"Rather than speculate about a New World, I think we should talk about what we're doing in this old one," I suggested. "Does anyone else share this feeling I've had for quite some time that there must be a better way to do what we do? I mean, we all work hard to see poor children get food and clothing, but the comfort these bring is only temporary. Food gets eaten, and children soon outgrow clothing. Since we move about so much and try to give to as many different children as we can, the ones we feed and clothe one night will be hungry again the next night, and ragged again the next month. What real good are we accomplishing?"

I half hoped my longtime companions would all rise up and begin shouting that I was wrong, that my words mocked the great things we'd done. Instead, they responded with nods and murmurs of agreement.

It was no surprise that Layla, always outspoken, was first to reply at length.

"I've been wondering when you'd come to this conclusion, Nicholas," she said. "As much as I've loved the idea of helping you help others, for decades, maybe even centuries, I've had the same doubts. There's nothing wrong with our intentions, but perhaps we haven't thought enough about the way in which we carry them out. Food nourishes the body, and clothes keep the body warm and dry. But it's the spirit inside the body that's most important. I think we've neglected the spirit."

Felix spoke next. Though he'd never said so, I often guessed he felt he should be second-in-command because he'd been with me longest, longer even than Layla. "I want to say we've postponed this discussion too long, but it wastes time to think of what we might have done differently in the past," Felix commented, looking first at the fire, then at each of us in turn. "The right question is, what should we do in the future? It's not just the gifts we've been giving, either, but the way in which we acquire them. The carved wooden book covers are bringing less and less income. Books aren't that rare anymore, and more craftsmen are turning out covers the way trees turn out leaves. We need to find a different way of making money."

Attila said impatiently, "Let's think about money after we've decided how we want to spend it. Nicholas, if we're not going to give food or clothing, what should we give?"

"Toys." Dorothea, usually the quietest among us, spoke this one word and the rest of us fell silent. We were all thinking.

"Toys," Layla repeated. "There may be something to that."

We hadn't discussed this subject much before. In that year of 1194, toys weren't something every child owned. They weren't even common. Babies sometimes were given rattles—hollow gourds with pebbles inside. Marbles were made of river clay. There were occasional balls of cloth that could be thrown back and forth. Hoops and tops were rare, prized possessions. And at county fairs and bazaars, puppet shows had become instantly popular with adults and children alike. But the fact of the matter was that simply surviving occupied everyone's attention most of the time. Anything beyond the most necessary elements of life—food, shelter, clothing—had to be an afterthought. The money to buy toys, or the time to make them, were luxuries far beyond the means of most families. So children usually had no toys at all.

Adults had a few games. Chess was first played in India in about 500 A.D. The Persians learned the game there, and a few centuries later introduced it to Europeans. And it was about 500 A.D. that dolls made of cloth were found in Egypt. The Egyptians were clever craftsmen; they also gave their children carved wooden crocodiles with jaws that opened and closed.

There were no wooden crocodiles, though, in the European countries where we spent most of our time. Until Dorothea's comment, I think it's fair to say none of us had ever really thought much about toys at all. But now that she had mentioned them, it was easy to remember the way children's faces lit up on those rare occasions when they had wooden tops to spin or cloth dolls to play with.

"As you said, food gets eaten immediately and clothes wear out quickly," Felix mused. "But if we could give children toys so they could play—"

"Then the joy from the toys might last much, much longer!" Arthur interrupted excitedly. "Nicholas! Let's give gifts of toys!"

Sometimes new ideas, ones never considered before, are obviously perfect. This one was. We spent the rest of that night and the next several weeks camped there in England, not arguing about *whether* we should give toys, but rather deciding *how* we should give them.

The first and most obvious problem was how to get enough toys to give. No big companies were manufacturing toys, and there weren't any toy stores where we could buy them. To make them ourselves, we'd have to purchase large amounts of raw materials—wood, cloth, and so forth. The magic would probably allow the six of us to carve, sew, and otherwise build toys faster than any hundred other craftsmen could, but we still couldn't make enough each day to deliver them every night as gifts to all the children whose hard lives would be made happier by receiving them.

"Well, then, why don't we spend three weeks of every month making toys, and one week of the month delivering them?" Attila asked. All of us found this suggestion agreeable.

Felix added, "And, little by little, why don't we change the goods we make and sell from wooden book covers to toys? Rich parents would buy them for their children, and the money they give us for them will pay for the toys we give poor children. Doesn't that seem appropriate?"

"It does," I said enthusiastically. "Dorothea, we have you to thank for this." Dorothea, a modest woman, blushed. Attila gave her an enthusiastic hug.

"That's my wife," he boasted. "She should have been the war chief. Then we Huns would have won every battle!"

We spent the next few dozen years making a modest beginning. Our first toys were complete failures. We didn't make marbles from the right clay, so our first ones simply broke in pieces when they smacked into each other. None of us knew how to cure wood strips with water to make perfectly circular hoops. The egg-shaped ones Attila and Arthur made rolled in crazy directions. Even Dorothea's and Layla's puppets and dolls looked more like mittens, until they learned how to sew them better.

But we experimented until we got everything right, and when we did we took several sacks of samples to a fair in Rome, where every toy we had was sold within an hour. We used the profits to buy materials for more toys. These we distributed by night as gifts to poor children. How heartwarming it was to return the next morning and find them shrieking with delight as they rolled hoops, shot marbles, or played at make-believe puppet shows.

"I know they're still dressed in rags, and that most of them will be hungry when they go to sleep tonight," Layla said. "But at least they're happy today, and tomorrow they'll have their toys to play with again."

THIRTEEN

The Man Who
Changed Christmas

he man who changed Christmas forever wasn't always known as Saint Francis of Assisi. In 1182, a wealthy Italian merchant and his wife named their newborn son Giovanni Bernardone. Young Giovanni was twelve in the year Dorothea suggested we give toys for presents instead of food and clothing.

Unfortunately, Giovanni was quite spoiled as a youth. His family was rich; their home was one of the grandest anywhere in Italy. Giovanni had more clothes than he could wear, more food than he could eat, and, I'm sure, every kind of toy that had so far been invented. Giovanni's father expected his oldest son to gradually take over the family business, and this is exactly what Giovanni did.

But in those days, no city completely escaped war, and it was common for powerful Italian "city-states" to battle each other. When Giovanni was nineteen, Assisi got into a squabble with Perugia. As a member of one of Assisi's most prominent families, Giovanni was expected to help lead the fighting. Well, he ended up being captured instead. The Perugians tossed him into prison, and he had been in there for over a year by the time the war ended in 1203.

Giovanni was different when he got out of prison. He had spent most of his time in a cell thinking about the world and his responsibilities in it. He changed his name to Francis in 1205, the same year he told his father he no longer wanted to be a rich merchant. The name change was important—people who wanted to give up worldly things for a life of religion often did this. A different name showed that they were different, too.

The newly named Francis began living a life that was exactly the opposite of his pampered childhood. He gave up everything he owned and walked around in ragged robes. Any money given to him was immediately used to buy food for the poor. It seemed to Francis that many Christian leaders only told people about how they'd be punished if they didn't do what God wanted, instead of concentrating on how all Christians should be friends and help each other. Four years after he'd left his father's house, Francis started a new program for others—priests, monks, and laypeople—who felt the same way. In Francis's honor, they called themselves "Franciscans," and dedicated themselves to doing good things for people. This group is still around today, so obviously Francis had the right idea.

Francis wasn't afraid of traveling long distances to spread his message. In 1212 he tried to go to Syria with the plan of converting Muslims to Christianity, or, failing that, to at least convince them that Muslims and Christians shouldn't fight anymore. Francis never got there. His ship was wrecked on the coast of Croatia, and he had to return to Europe. Another attempted trip to Morocco didn't work out, either. Poor Francis got sick in Spain and once again had to turn back. He was very discouraged.

But no hero gives up, and Francis of Assisi was a real hero. In 1219 he finally managed to get to an intended destination—Egypt, where he spent a month with that country's leaders talking about Christianity and how we should all be kind to each other. The Egyptian leaders didn't become Christian, but they began treating their people better.

When Francis got back to Italy after that trip, he decided to concentrate on problems in his native country. Too many uneducated people didn't really understand what they heard about the church, he concluded, and so he left his small group to travel around by himself. Francis would go to tiny villages where most people couldn't read or write, and he'd sing the gospel passages, which is how priests usually conducted a part of their church services. But instead of singing in Latin, the official language of the church, he'd sing in Italian so everyone could understand the words. This thoughtfulness made ordinary people love Francis very much. Since he insisted on remaining poor himself, the villagers would often invite him to live in their small homes for a while, and to join them when they celebrated different holidays, including Christ's birthday.

And it was in a small Italian village on December 24, 1223, that the rest of us met Francis. Layla, Felix, Arthur, Attila, Dorothea, and I had been traveling nearby, visiting small farming communities for a few nights to learn which children lived there, and then using one last night to enter their homes and leave them toys. We didn't have to wonder which children might be poor; all of them in that area were. We did some night gift-giving on December 23, then found ourselves the next morning in a village where Francis also happened to be. It was a tiny place; Francis was standing in its square singing some gospels in Italian to about twenty people, and when we heard his high, melodic voice we stopped to listen, too.

After Francis was finished singing, he thanked everyone for listening. He said a short prayer, then prepared to walk to the next village and do the same thing again. Francis was a short, thin man dressed in very shabby robes. He looked tired and thirsty, so we offered him a drink from the water gourds we carried.

"Thank you," he said gratefully, and drank carefully so the water wouldn't run out of the corners of his mouth and be wasted. "God always blesses those who are generous to a stranger."

"You must be Francis of Assisi," Layla said. "As we've traveled, we've heard people talking about you. It's wonderful that you sing the gospels in a language people can understand. We're all honored to meet you."

Francis looked embarrassed. He wasn't a man comfortable with praise. "I'm no one special, unless you believe that in God's eyes we're all special. Thank you again for the water. I hope to get to the village of Lauria before nightfall, and it's a long walk. I've been asked to help the people there celebrate Jesus' birthday. When I was in Lauria earlier in the year, I made a suggestion about celebrating the holiday that they said they might try, and I'm anxious to see if they've done it."

"What suggestion was that?" asked Attila, who was usually the last among us to warm to anyone he didn't know. Apparently, he approved of Francis and the way he cared for ordinary people.

"Will you walk with me a while as we talk?" Francis asked. "I'd welcome the company, and the story takes some time to tell. I have to be on my way, so if you want to hear it I'm afraid you'll have to come along."

We had no reason not to; our current plans were only to do more gift-giving in the same general area, and the village of Lauria would be as good a place as any other. So the six of us joined Francis on the road there. We had two donkeys laden with packs. One of these packs held our supplies; the rest were crammed with toys. Francis had the good manners not to ask what the donkeys carried. He himself had no pack animal, and in fact didn't even have a small bag to carry on his own shoulder. Francis trusted so much in the kindness of others that he never traveled with provisions. Instead, he counted on meeting people who would share their food with him.

It was a cool day, but sunny. As we walked, Francis told about what he hoped would happen that night in Lauria.

"I have thought for some time that the real circumstances of Jesus' birth are being forgotten," Francis explained. "In our churches now we see great paintings of Jesus rising to Heaven, and so we forget that he came into this world as the child of poor parents, and even was born, it's told, in a Bethlehem stable. I think it would comfort poor people today if they remembered that the baby Jesus was really one of them. Religion should be a source of comfort, don't you agree?

"Anyway, I suggested to the people of Lauria that they remember Jesus and his humble beginnings by building another stable and acting out the night of his birth, complete with cattle lowing and the donkey Mary rode tethered near the baby's bed, which would be blankets placed on straw just as it must have been in Bethlehem."

This nativity scene sounded like a sight well worth seeing. It was late afternoon before we got to Lauria. As we reached the village square, Francis gasped with surprise and delight. A life-size stable, or manger, as it was called in those days, had been built. A small water trough was inside, and cattle were drinking from it. Several villagers were bustling about, placing piles of straw and pounding on the manger's dirt floor with heavy sticks to flatten out lumps of clay.

"Brother Francis!" one of them called. "See, we've done what you asked. Tonight, we'll act out everything, with someone as Joseph, someone as Mary . . . all of it! Then tomorrow on the holy day you can lead us in prayer, and afterward we'll feast. This will be the best Christ's Day ever!" (The word "Christmas" still wasn't in wide use, except in England. Since 1038, people there had referred to their annual December 25 church service as "Cristes Maesse" or "Christ's Mass." This special name for a special day would gradually spread from England to the rest of the world with English explorers and traders.)

And, afterward, we all agreed it just might have been the best Christ's Day, or Christmas, that anyone anywhere ever enjoyed. The whole reenactment of the nativity, or birth scene, added a special meaning to Christmas Eve. The humble villagers of Lauria were reminded that Jesus came into this world poor, and that he lived as a simple man, not as some sort of royalty. Francis sang appropriate gospel verses in Italian. The six of us traveling with him were invited to stay with some of the villagers. Their cottages were small, but very clean.

The next morning all the people of Lauria gathered for a breakfast that would not have been anything special for rich people, but was undoubtedly splendid for them—hot fresh bread, assorted fruit, bits of cold meat, and especially delicious pastries. The gingerbread was the best I'd ever tasted, and since everyone was so generous in urging me to have more I kept gobbling it until Layla pointedly told everyone that her husband Nicholas was getting much too fat.

After the meal came the presents. These, of course had been customary ever since the first Saturnalia celebrations in Rome. Everyone had a little something for each member of his or her family, and neighbors exchanged gifts as well. The gifts were really tokens, like cut straw for brooms or small squares of leather for patching sandals. Still, everyone made a fuss over what he or she had received, and there were hugs and loud expressions of thanks.

"Each person is so grateful for the gifts, yet they're just small items anyone could acquire at any time of the year," Felix said quietly to Francis, who hadn't eaten much of the wonderful food, preferring to sit and happily watch the villagers rejoice over their presents.

"It's not the value of the gift, but the philosophy of the giving and receiving," Francis replied. "It's a hard world, all in all, and to receive a present means someone else cares for you, that you're not alone."

"I already know that," Felix said a little huffily, and I knew he was thinking he'd been secretly giving gifts eight hundred years before Francis had even been born. But Francis's words were further proof, if we needed it, that he was someone who would perfectly understand our mission. I'd been thinking since soon after we'd first met Francis that it might be a good idea to invite him to join us. But just as Charlemagne had his own job to do that was separate from ours, so, I decided, did Francis. We ended up saying goodbye to him that afternoon. He walked off toward another small village, while we stayed one more night in Lauria, leaving before dawn. When the children of Lauria awoke that morning, they all found toys beside their bedding.

Two years passed; Francis's idea of a nativity scene to help celebrate December 25 spread quickly. A few villages had great debates about whether it was really proper to act out the night of Jesus' birth since the actors would be mere humans, while Jesus, Mary, and Joseph were holy. Other communities were so small and poor that sufficient wood and other building materials for a life-size manger couldn't be spared. So, many families made miniature mangers instead, and filled them with little clay or stick figures representing the baby, his parents, the animals, shepherds, even the three Magi, or Wise Men. The nativity scene custom then spread throughout the rest of Christian Europe; within two centuries, few households celebrated December 25 without one.

Then, in 1225, we happened upon Francis again, once more in a small Italian village, and once more just a few days prior to December 25. This time we met at a crossroads. He looked exactly the same as when we'd last seen him in Lauria, except perhaps a little more tired.

After hearty greetings, we suggested he join us along the roadside for a meal. Francis accepted, saying he hadn't eaten for almost two days.

"Sometimes the villages I come to are so poor I don't accept offers of food because I know none can really be spared," he explained. "Obviously, your group is especially blessed and always has enough to eat, if the waistlines of Felix and Nicholas are any proof."

We took out cheese, fruit, and bread. I was careful not to eat too much, feeling somewhat embarrassed by Francis's comment. Felix, I noticed, felt no similar shame. He ate his share and most of mine, too.

"What have you been doing lately, Francis?" Layla asked. "Your idea of the manger scenes was certainly successful. We feel so lucky to have been part of the first one in Lauria."

"Would you like to be part of another first effort?" Francis asked. "I've been thinking more about December twenty-fifth celebrations, and it seems to me that music should be included, too. I've heard some church officials grumbling lately that there's too much drinking and other inappropriate behavior used to celebrate Christ's birthday. Well, ordinary people love to sing and dance, and their everyday lives are so busy that they can't indulge in these pleasures too often. Of course, they want to sing and dance whenever they have one of their rare chances to stop working and enjoy themselves! So I've been thinking it might be best for everyone if we found some way to connect celebrating Jesus' birth with songs as well as feasting and presents."

Francis paused to sip some water and swallow a few bites of cheese.

"Tell us more," urged Felix, who always liked to sing and dance. "I like this idea even more than the mangers."

"It involves carols," Francis explained. Now, in 1225 the word "carols" didn't mean what it does today. Medieval carols were dances in village streets. Flutes would be played to provide the proper music. The people who danced would join hands in a circle and move to the rhythm. Sometimes words would be sung, too.

"So there should be carols written that celebrate Jesus' birth," Francis said. "I have a few already prepared, just the parts of the new gospels dealing with Bethlehem, really. I've spent some time lately at the village of

Banyoli. There are some brothers there who play flutes as well as the angels must in Heaven. We're going to attempt some carols at Banyoli's December twenty-fifth celebration. Would you like to come along and see what happens?"

Of course we wanted to come, and it was just as splendid a success as the nativity scenes had been. People laughed and danced and sang, all in celebration of Jesus being born, and somehow it seemed right that such joy should be part of their thanks for his birth.

"Feasts, presents, mangers, carols—what a very special occasion December twenty-fifth has become!" Arthur chuckled. "I believe I'll find myself looking forward to this day all during the rest of the year!"

"The most important thing is that people are being happy together," Francis emphasized. "For at least one day of the year, past quarrels are forgotten and strangers are greeted as friends."

The next morning we ate breakfast with Francis. He had plans to be in another village that night, singing the gospels in Italian. In the early light, I noticed how the lines around his eyes were much deeper, how his hands trembled just a little when he raised a crust of bread to his mouth.

"What's troubling you, Francis?" I asked. "For all the happiness you're bringing others, I sense you're not very happy yourself."

Francis shrugged. "It's just that often, now, people expect me to be able to do things I can't. I'm a man, a human being, no more than that, but I'll come to a village and find they've heard stories of how I've magically made the real manger fly to Italy from Bethlehem, or how I call down choirs of angels to sing the gospels with me. When they find I can't do those things, that all I have to offer is my own poor voice, well, sometimes I know they're disappointed. I gladly give all I can, but for many that isn't enough. I wanted to help bring about a world that treated every day as specially as December twenty-fifth, but I wonder if instead I'm not somehow ruining all the other days of the year."

Sitting beside me, Layla gave me a powerful poke in the ribs with her elbow. I grunted in surprise. Francis, lost in his sad thoughts, didn't seem to notice.

I leaned toward my wife and whispered, "What did you do that for?"

Layla whispered back, "Tell him everything, Nicholas! This is the right time."

"What about leaving him alone to accomplish his own mission?" I muttered.

"Maybe it's been accomplished; perhaps it's time to help him find another one," she replied.

I trusted Layla's instincts above those of all others. I asked Francis to postpone his travels for a day, and to walk out into the fields with me and my companions for a talk. We spent that day telling our story, which, since it involved ten centuries, took its usual long time to explain. Francis listened intently, looking especially amazed when we explained who Attila and Arthur really were. I spoke, Felix spoke, Layla added several comments; it was a lot for poor Francis to take in.

But he did, and he believed us, too. "In this great world, all things must be possible," he said. "Somehow I know I'm really talking to Saint Nicholas of Myra, and Attila the Hun, and Arthur, legendary High King of Britain. King Arthur, I've read of you just lately in Geoffrey Monmouth's *History of the Kings of Britain!*"

"I was only a tribal chief," Arthur said gently. "Don't believe everything you read. But in that sense, several of us here know what you mean when you say stories of what you've done are so exaggerated that no reality can measure up. Who wants to believe I was a war chief who lived in a straw and mud hut, when they can picture me sitting on a golden throne in imaginary Camelot?"

"We should get to the point," Layla interrupted. "Francis, you've done as much in a normal life as anyone could. Join us, and you'll have limitless time to do good deeds, but without the pressure of being recognized and expected to work miracles every day."

"I'm not sure I can," Francis said humbly. "I'm a simple priest; I don't think I will be able to live forever, or at least hundreds of more years."

"Well, why not try?" boomed Attila. "Nicholas's magic has somehow attached itself to us, too. If for some reason you join us and aren't as lucky, well, you haven't really lost anything, have you?"

And so Francis of Assisi was persuaded to join our band, and a wonderful addition he was, too. Above all we treasured his marvelous mind and his knack for understanding the simple needs of ordinary people. Determined to properly close out what he called his "mortal" life, Francis first returned to Assisi, where he arranged for trusted friends to announce he died unexpectedly while praying in the Portiuncula Chapel, his favorite church and the first headquarters of the Franciscan movement he founded.

After staying out of sight for a few months, during which he rested and regained much of the strength he'd lost earlier, Francis met us outside Rome. No one else paid any attention to the slight, smiling man in ragged robes and patched sandals. They would have been very surprised to learn he was the same Francis of Assisi who, just a year later, was named a saint by the church.

"Saint Francis and Saint Nicholas," Arthur laughed when the news of Francis's new title reached us. "I feel second-class because I was only supposed to be a king!"

FOURTEEN

Gunpowder, Chimneys, and Stockings

oon after Francis joined us, many other things happened, and quickly, too. The world went through one of its periods of great change. Of course, some changes were more welcome than others.

In 1270, Europeans first heard about gunpowder. The Chinese had invented this explosive material much, much earlier, but since Europeans really didn't travel into China until the late 1200s, it took that long for the information to spread west. An Italian writer published a report on gunpowder he called "Book of Fires for Burning Enemies." While the rest of us thought this new thing called gunpowder sounded extremely dangerous, Arthur and Attila were curious to see how it really worked.

They got their chance twenty-five years later. While traveling in Venice, our party met a merchant-explorer who had just returned from a long series of adventures in China. The man's name was Marco Polo. Although he was constantly surrounded by people who wanted to hear more about the mysterious place where he'd been, we were lucky enough to catch up with him near a big house where he was staying. A friendly fellow, Marco Polo invited us all inside. When Arthur and Attila asked him about gunpowder, he took a small container from a wooden chest. Opening the container, he spilled some black smelly particles into their palms.

"That's gunpowder," Marco Polo said. "What do you think of it?"

"It looks like dirt," Attila said bluntly. "How can something like this burn with enough force to injure an enemy? What are you supposed to do, throw the powder on them, and then ask them to hold still while you build a fire to light it?"

Marco Polo grinned; obviously, he was used to doubters. "The powder is collected in containers," he explained. "The powder is packed in tightly and a twist of cloth or paper is forced into it, like a wick is used for a candle. This wick into the gunpowder is lit, and when the flame reaches the powder there is a loud explosion. The force of the explosion can be used to launch weapons at great speed and height."

"I can hardly believe it," Attila said, so to prove his point Marco Polo fashioned a small paper tube, stuffed gunpowder and a wick into it, led us back into the street, motioned for passersby to move away, and lit the wick. The subsequent loud crack hurt my ears; there was quite a lot of smoke, too, which stung my eyes.

"Are you now convinced?" Marco Polo asked, looking over his shoulder to the spot where Attila had been standing. But Attila wasn't there any longer. Panicked by the exploding gunpowder, he'd dived under a nearby cart.

"I hate to think what terrible injuries that gunpowder will inflict on brave soldiers and innocent people," Attila said sadly, after we'd helped him to his feet and brushed off the street dirt and straw that had stuck to his clothes.

We spent several more days in Marco Polo's company. He was an interesting person and told us many stories about China and the people who lived there. Felix thought we should ask Marco Polo to join us, and I almost did. But before I could make the suggestion, he told us he intended to stay in Venice and possibly fight for the city in a war he expected to occur between Venice and the neighboring city of Genoa.

"I wouldn't do that if I were you," cautioned Francis, who remembered his own experiences in a war between Italian cities, but Marco Polo was determined to stay and fight. He ended up being captured and spent three years in a Genoa prison, where he wrote a book about his Chinese travels. The book was widely read. For the next five hundred years, it provided most of the information Europeans had about China, a country that rarely encouraged outsiders to come and visit.

We never had a chance to speak with Marco Polo again, but we'd have many more experiences with gunpowder. Attila's prediction was unfortunately correct. Almost immediately, nations outside of China began to use the new material in their wars. The earliest recorded instance was in 1304, when Arabs used gunpowder rammed into bamboo tubes to shoot arrows at enemies.

Other inventions were more welcome. Eyeglasses first appeared in Italy in 1286. By 1300 they were being manufactured in Marco Polo's home city of Venice. These eyeglasses used specially shaped lenses of glass, which were placed in frames and worn so that the lenses rested in front of each eye. If the shape of the lenses matched the weaknesses of the eye, the person wearing the eyeglasses could see much more clearly. Felix, Arthur, Francis, Attila, Dorothea, Layla, and I all tried on eyeglasses, and Felix and I were astonished to each find a pair that helped us see better. We purchased several pairs and carried them with us on our travels. The lenses of these glasses were convex, thicker in the middle than at the top and bottom. They helped us see things that were close up, such as writing on pages. Concave lenses, thinner in the middle than at top and bottom, were only invented a century later. These helped people see things better that were far away. And it was only in the late 1700s that a future friend of ours in America, a fellow named Ben Franklin, invented bifocal lenses, ones that were half for farsightedness and half for nearsightedness.

It was about 1300 that a long period of about four hundred years called the Renaissance began. This was a very welcome time when people became more interested in art and music—things that enriched lives instead of threatening them. Painters and composers got some of the glory that previously belonged only to generals. To put it simply, the world started to become more civilized.

This didn't mean that things were perfect. Wars continued, and there still wasn't much knowledge about medicine, which meant diseases could and did spread widely. How many people were fed still depended mostly on the weather—when seasons were moderate, farmers could grow plenty of crops. But let one winter be especially severe or a spring go by without enough rain, and starvation was always possible. From 1314 through 1317, there was a great famine. England, Ireland, and Poland were especially hard hit. Then in 1347, a terrible disease killed almost one-third of all the people in Europe; later on, in history books, this plague was called "The Black Death."

But, as with time itself, disease didn't seem to touch us. We all remained healthy, and did everything we could to ease suffering when we found it— and we still found it everywhere.

"The good that is happening will last longer than the bad things," Layla said firmly. "At last, people are using some of their energy in positive ways. What's the game that was just invented in Germany, and that we all played there? The one that was so enjoyable?"

"Bowling," Felix said. Bowling did seem like lots of fun. To play, ten wooden bottle-shaped pins were set up in a sort of triangle, and people would roll wooden balls and try to knock down as many of the pins as they could. It took a long time to play, however, mostly because setting the pins back up was a lot harder than knocking them down.

"The greatest invention in history will be the one that picks up the bowling pins for the players," Attila grumbled. "And I'm not saying that just because all of you beat me, either."

"You tried to roll the ball too hard," Arthur said helpfully. "Bowling is a game of skill, not strength. You didn't bowl well for the same reason your Huns never could defeat the Romans. You just went into battle without any real plan, and they thought things through before they fought."

"I didn't notice your British tribes doing any better against the Saxons," Attila shot back. "Don't tell me about fighting, and don't tell me about bowling, either." He and Arthur glared at each other.

"It's ridiculous for you two to argue about a friendly game of bowling, let alone battles that occurred almost a thousand years ago," I said. "Instead, why don't we think about making miniature bowling games to give to children? Arthur, you figure out a way to make the small wooden balls, and, Attila, you decide how we should carve the pins." It was always a simple thing to make them stop arguing. Like the rest of us, they enjoyed making and giving gifts more than anything else.

The 1350s saw widespread use of another relatively new invention, and one that would become part of our legend. One night in France, Felix and I crept into a small country village with several sacks of toys we meant to distribute to the children who lived there—maybe fifty children in all, living in two dozen cottages. We'd never been to this village, but Layla and Dorothea had visited the day before. They'd told us how many children lived there and how many presents we should pack for our gift-giving.

Felix and I quietly approached the village, taking care not to wake up the many dogs sleeping nearby. Interestingly, dogs rarely bothered us, anyway. They always seemed to sense we came for a good purpose, not to rob or otherwise hurt anyone they loved. We neared the first cottage; I was reaching into my sack for two wooden tops. Layla had said two young brothers lived there. As I took out the tops, Felix suddenly hissed, "What's that?"

"Where?" I asked, worried someone had seen us.

"That, that—well, that thing on the side of the cottage!" Felix spluttered. I looked where he was pointing, and there attached to one outer wall was a squarish-looking stone structure tall enough to stick above the roof. Little swirls of woodsmoke were coming out of the top of it.

After a few moments of thought, I whispered, "That must be one of those newfangled chimneys we've been hearing about. You know, with fires built in the bottom of them to provide homes with light and warmth. That part is known as the fireplace. Then the smoke from the fire comes out the top of the chimney and doesn't settle back inside the house."

"Amazing," Felix answered. We both stood looking in wonder at this chimney. Then he added, "Well, let's go inside."

We rarely had any trouble getting into a house or cottage. Fancy locks for doors hadn't been invented yet. Later on, when they were, Attila proved masterful at teaching the rest of us how to open them. So Felix and I easily opened the wooden door of the cottage and slipped inside.

As with most cottages in small European villages of this time, there was only one large room. Seven people were sleeping in it, apparently the two parents, the two children, a grandmother and a grandfather and an aunt. Often lots of relatives lived together, for shelter was scarce. We quickly identified the straw bedding where the two boys slept, but before we left our gifts beside them we found ourselves drawn back to the marvelous fireplace. A tiny blaze burned at the bottom of it.

"Look at how the smoke is drawn straight up," Felix muttered. "If you weren't so wide in the middle, you could get into houses just by getting on the roof and jumping down the chimneys."

It was rare that we ever talked while inside a house, for fear of waking someone up, but I couldn't let this insult pass.

"You're quite wide yourself, my friend, so don't mock my waistline," I said. "Besides, if I jumped down the chimney I'd burn my feet on the fire when I landed! Still, you've given me an idea. Look, for instance, at how the whole family's stockings have been hung up by the front of the fireplace to dry in front of the flames while everyone sleeps. Remember my story of leaving my first gifts ever in the stockings of Shem's daughters? Let's leave these toys in the stockings of the boys. They won't burn—the fire isn't that large or hot—and in the morning maybe the family will think the mysterious gift-giver came down the chimney, just as you suggested!"

So we put toys in the stockings and hurried on to the next cottage, and the next, and the next, and the next. In each one with a chimney we found stockings drying in front of the fire, and we always left our gifts in the smaller stockings worn by the children.

After sunup, Felix and I made a point of going back to the village and listening to the excited gossip there. Everyone was talking about how all the children had found toys in their stockings that morning, and how whoever had left the toys must have come down the chimneys without being burned by the flames in the fireplaces.

"Surely whoever gave these gifts must have great magical powers!" declared one elderly woman, and everyone around her nodded in agreement. Felix and I grinned and hurried back to our camp to tell the tale to the others. Forever afterward, in houses with chimneys, we always left our gifts in stockings by fireplaces, if the children in those families had left their stockings hanging there.

FIFTEEN

At Court with Columbus

ntil about 1400, our group of seven traveled everywhere together. Felix, Arthur, Attila, Dorothea, Francis, Layla, and I were
good, close friends. But as the world changed, the way we did
things had to change, too. We began to feel the frustration of not being able
to be in enough places at once. Since we were always going someplace or
another, there was never any opportunity to settle in one spot for a while
and concentrate only on making toys of the highest quality. This especially
frustrated Arthur and Attila, who were by far the finest craftsmen among us,
better even than Felix, who himself was much better than me. At the same
time, Layla and Dorothea constantly suggested we try to make some specific
toys for girls, as well. They felt tops and the like were mostly favorites of boys.

Finally, Arthur and Attila came to me with a suggestion: For the first
time, they said, the group should divide, with some of us traveling and gift-
giving, and the others remaining in one place to concentrate on crafting as
many fine toys as possible.

"And the ones who travel can be constantly on the lookout for new
places where gifts should be given," Arthur said. "That's obviously the role
for you, Nicholas, and for Francis and Felix and Layla. You're the ones who

really enjoy the traveling. As for me, I'm never entirely happy unless I'm in England, and Attila longs to remain in Germany, and Dorothea wants to be there with him. So let us go to the places where we love to be the most, and once there we'll do what we love doing the most, which is making toys."

It was soon agreed. Arthur would set up toy-making operations in London, and Attila and Dorothea in the German city of Nuremberg. Quietly, they'd acquire property and build workshops, then recruit the finest craftsmen they could find. Half the toys manufactured in the workshops would be sold in city markets to raise the money necessary to pay the workers' salaries and buy materials. The other half would be turned over to those of us continuing the gift-giving.

Felix and Francis went to Germany with Attila and Dorothea to help get everything started in Nuremberg. Layla and I accompanied Arthur to London, and a very unhappy place we found it. The London streets were filthy; people threw garbage everywhere. England was involved in ongoing wars with France and also in its own civil wars, with rival families taking turns claiming the English throne.

"How can you be happy here, with so much fighting going on?" Layla asked Arthur.

He shrugged. "It's my home," he said simply. Almost one thousand years after he'd given up fighting the Saxons to join us, Arthur still had the force of character necessary to be a good leader. He quickly found a dozen fine craftsmen to come to work in the new toy factory, men and women skilled in carving and sewing and painting. They were delighted to have a chance to earn their livings in such a happy way.

Arthur's toy factory was operating within six months, and Attila's in Nuremberg opened a few weeks after that. Felix, Francis, Layla, and I—who were left to do the traveling and gift-giving—missed being with our good friends very much. But there was comfort in knowing they were happy to be in permanent homes, and a few times every year we'd go to one toy factory or the other to replenish our supply of gifts, and then we'd have happy reunions with them.

Layla took special pride in Dorothea's role at the Nuremberg toy factory. Dorothea insisted on hiring several special German craftsmen herself
and having them do nothing but create wonderful wooden dolls. Nobody
knew for certain where the word "doll" came from, although Dorothea always believed it was based on the German word "tocke," which literally
means a small block of wood. This is what dolls were carved from in those
days.

To everyone's joy, Attila and Dorothea met and hired perhaps the finest
craftsman who ever lived—Willie Skokan, a short wiry fellow who could
take a sharp knife, a bit of wood, some string and paint, and literally create
any toy imaginable. It became Willie's job not only to make toys, but to invent them. Some of his first inventions in Nuremberg were small wooden
models of Noah's Ark, complete with tiny animal figures to move in and out
of the boat; toy musical instruments, flutes and recorders that children
could blow into and compose tunes; wooden puppets, marvelously jointed
and able to do all sorts of tricks for those who pulled their strings; dollhouses for dolls to live in; and, finally, toy weapons, blunt-edged wooden
swords and bow and arrows.

These last toys worried the rest of us. We wanted children to play with
the gifts we gave so they'd forget the bad things in life, not pretend to be
doing the bad things themselves. But Willie, in his unique, halting way,
explained why he thought someday children would no longer find toy
weapons interesting.

"Children follow the examples of their parents," he told Layla and me
one night at his cottage in Nuremberg as we ate a plain dinner of toasted
bread and cheese. Willie could build elaborate toys, but his personal tastes
were always quite simple. Once, when asked his philosophy of life, he
replied, "Moderation in all things." At dinner we debated whether war toys
were appropriate for gift-giving. "There's a lot of fighting in this world,
and when children play they often reflect real life," Willie said.

"But if they didn't have toys that reminded them of violence, maybe
they wouldn't grow up to be violent themselves," Layla argued.

Willie looked thoughtful and took a moment before replying. "What we
should do is hope that grown-ups learn to set better examples. When they

give up their instruments of war, children will no longer want toy weapons." And from that time we kept making and giving pretend swords and bows, and later toy guns and rifles, to the children who wanted them.

The 1400s had other moments of special significance, and as usual some were better than others. Besides the wars, the saddest time for me was in 1444, which was when the ship fleet of Henry the Navigator began to bring captured African natives to Portugal, where these innocent African men and women were sold as slaves in the marketplace. In previous history, and in the centuries yet to come, there had been and would be nothing more disgusting than some human beings believing they had the right to own others. We made special efforts to bring gifts to slave children, but this was often quite difficult. Slaveowners guarded their so-called "human property" all through the night hours to be sure none of them escaped. Only rarely could we elude detection by these guards and get into slave quarters to leave our presents.

In the later 1400s, Francis had the urge to spend time in the Western European kingdoms of Aragon and Castile, which eventually would be combined into the nation of Spain. These lands were, in many ways, the cultural and political centers of Europe. It was important that we knew everything happening there. So, while Felix, Layla, and I concentrated on central Europe and England, Francis spent several years getting to know Ferdinand and Isabella, the king and queen of Aragon and Castile. Eventually in the spring of 1492, Francis wrote to me in care of Attila's Nuremberg toy factory, asking my permission to tell the king and queen about us and our mission. Isabella in particular, Francis said, might be persuaded to give us financial help in much the same way that Charlemagne had nearly seven hundred years earlier.

I wrote back telling Francis that I trusted his judgment. He was right; Isabella was thrilled to learn about us and our mission. Ferdinand was less enthusiastic. He wanted to use his government's money for wars. Francis wrote me again, asking me to come to their court and meet Isabella for myself.

"Though she respects her husband the king, she also will do things she believes to be right whether he approves of them or not," Francis wrote.

Able to travel at ten times the speed of normal mortals, Layla, Felix, and I were Isabella's guests less than a week after we received Francis's letter.

The three of us were introduced to Isabella by Francis in the privacy of the queen's chambers. I wanted to like Isabella, but I found it difficult. She had decorated her rooms with the most expensive furnishings available. We could have made toys for every child in her kingdom for much less than she'd spent on curtains and chandeliers. Also, Isabella had a rather forceful way of speaking, usually interrupting whoever was talking to her and immediately forming rigid opinions about everything.

"So you're Saint Nicholas himself," she said immediately, her voice so loud I feared everyone in the castle might have heard her. "Did you really work all those miracles, the saving of sinking ships and so forth?"

"I've only heard the same stories that you have, Your Majesty," I said politely. "As I'm sure Francis has told you, my time is spent giving gifts to children, and nothing more heroic than that."

"Exactly why I like you!" the queen announced. "I, too, am very fond of children. Perhaps you would like to give a gift to my daughter Catherine."

"I doubt your daughter needs our modest gifts," I replied, thinking to myself that this woman didn't really understand what we did at all. I caught a glimpse of Francis standing just behind Isabella; when his eyes met mine, he grimaced and shrugged. I must admit, though, that later in our visit to Isabella when we met Princess Catherine, I felt so sorry for the child that I wished we had brought something to give her.

Catherine was a very solemn girl who looked much more like her father than her mother, and King Ferdinand was big-nosed and jut-chinned, rather than handsome. It was quite clear Catherine was going to be one of those unfortunate princesses who someday would be married off by her parents to create some sort of political alliance with another country and its ruler. As it turned out, in 1501, when she was sixteen, Catherine's parents ordered her to marry Prince Arthur of England, who was the oldest son of King Henry VII. This marriage had a great impact on our mission, although the proper time to tell more about it comes later in this story.

In any event, Queen Isabella pronounced herself truly committed to helping us. King Ferdinand would not allow her to give us money from the national treasury, she said, so instead she would simply give us all her jewelry, which we could sell for a great deal of money.

"It was rather a hard choice about who should get this jewelry, you or that Italian captain who also has been asking us for financial help," Isabella added. "What was his name, again, Francis? You met him a few weeks ago."

"Christopher Columbus," Francis added helpfully. "He said he thinks, or rather he knows, a quick trade route to the Indies and Japan could be found simply by sailing directly west instead of circling east around the Cape as the trading ships do now. An interesting fellow, really. I'm sorry your decision to help us comes at his expense."

Isabella told us we would have to remain at the castle for a few weeks while she collected all her necklaces, earrings, rings, and other jeweled finery. She kept some items at other castles and had loaned others to family and friends. When I told her it probably wouldn't be necessary for us to be given every item she owned, Isabella just laughed and said it was always easy for queens to get all the jewelry they wanted. After she gave us what she had, she'd just tell rich noblemen who wanted the king's favor to give her more.

So we waited, and on the third day after we'd met Isabella, we were walking in the courtyard when Francis said, "Look, over there. That fellow is Columbus, the Italian captain I told you about."

Columbus was older than I'd expected, certainly more than forty. His hair had turned gray and, like many people of that time, his teeth were yellow and nasty-looking. But he had a nice smile, though a sad one.

"I'm told by the queen that there's no longer a chance she can help me because she's going to give her jewelry to you," Columbus said, sounding depressed but not angry at us. "She won't say why you need the jewels, but I suppose it's for some fine purpose. I have a final appointment with King Ferdinand this afternoon, and I'll ask him one last time for money for my voyages. If he refuses, as I'm certain he will, I suppose I'll have to go back home. I've already been turned down by the King of Portugal, and by every nobleman in Italy."

"Perhaps King Ferdinand will decide to help you after all," I said cheerfully. "Francis has told us about your idea of a new way to sail to Japan or the Indies."

"It's not just an idea to make me rich, you know," Columbus said. "Everyone would benefit, even the Japanese and Indians. We have goods they want, and we want theirs. Craftsmen in every country in Europe would be able to sell more, and thus make more profits. People could live better. Fewer children would go hungry."

After we left Columbus, the four of us talked about what he had said. "Do you really think he can reach Japan or the Indies just by sailing west?" I asked Francis. "There are still many people who think ships going west will just fall off the edge of the world."

"The oceans have been sailed enough for anyone intelligent to know there are no edges to fall off," Francis replied. "I do wish Columbus would get his chance. If he did, I'd like to go with him. We need to know more about Japan and the Indies, Nicholas. No doubt there are many children there who need gifts, too."

The more we discussed it, the more it became clear that Christopher Columbus was just as deserving of Isabella's help as we were. This wasn't convenient for us, of course. We needed all the money we could get. Every day, each of us felt frustrated because we never had enough gifts for all the deserving children we wanted to please. Anyone trying to do good things has to believe in the cause being served, and that can make it easy to forget that others are trying to do good things, too—different things, perhaps, but still important.

So, that evening we went back to Isabella to ask if she might spare a few items of jewelry for Columbus after all. At first she was surprised we didn't want it all for ourselves, but eventually agreed to spare him enough to buy and outfit no more than three small ships. Francis ran to find Columbus and tell him the good news, only to be informed the captain had left court an hour earlier, headed home to Italy after King Ferdinand had refused his final request for money. Undaunted, Francis borrowed a mule and tracked Columbus down, bringing him back to court for a private meeting with the rest of us and Queen Isabella. When she told him she would finance his trip, he began to offer his thanks. Isabella interrupted him.

"There are conditions, of course, Captain Columbus," she said firmly. "Most important, whatever new lands you might find must be claimed in the name of King Ferdinand and myself. Second, we must receive nine-tenths of all the wealth you find. And third, my friend Francis must sail with you on this adventure."

Except for Francis, we all looked surprised. Columbus was so pleased to get his money that he was glad to have Francis come along, especially when Isabella explained he was an Italian priest. Columbus was very religious and told Francis it would be an honor to have him aboard.

Isabella collected her jewelry and divided it between us and Columbus. The captain then bought three ships, which he named the *Niña*, the *Pinta*, and the *Santa María*. On August 3, 1492, he sailed from the harbor of Palos; Felix, Layla, and I stood on the dock waving good-bye to Francis.

Later, Francis told us colorful tales of the trip. Columbus did not turn out to be an especially good leader of men. Several times, his crews were ready to mutiny. But more than two months after leaving Palos, they sighted land on the western horizon. Poor Columbus thought this land might be Japan, but it turned out to be one of a series of sandy islands inhabited by native tribes who certainly weren't Japanese. Always ready to fool himself and others with grand exaggeration, Columbus instantly decided he must have reached the Indies. As he had promised, he claimed the first island, which he called San Salvador, in the names of Ferdinand and Isabella.

He also called the natives "Indians." Columbus then ordered his ships to sail a bit farther, and they discovered and claimed several other islands in the next few days. One of these islands, which Columbus named "Juana," would eventually be known as Cuba. Columbus and his crew were shocked to see natives on this island smoking a dried plant. This was the first time Europeans had seen tobacco.

Columbus didn't turn out to be a very good sailor, either. On the night of December 24, he wrecked the *Santa María* on another new island, one he named Hispaniola. Today it is home to Haiti and the Dominican Republic.

"On the night of that shipwreck, after all the sailors were safe and as many goods as possible salvaged from the wreckage, I reminded Captain Columbus that it was Christmas Eve," Francis said. "I asked his permission to lead the sailors in a mass honoring Christ's birth. Although he was already losing himself in dreams of gold and glory, the captain said I could. I felt special sensations during the mass, Nicholas. It's not quite time yet, but you should mark my words. Much of our future and this mission of gift-giving lies in the New World. You'll have to go there and see for yourself."

"Perhaps so," I answered. "But before I set foot on a ship, I'll want to see what happens to Columbus and the rest of the explorers who'll undoubtedly follow him there. For now, we have enough work to do in the countries we already know about."

The New World did, in fact, turn out to be a glorious place, but Columbus himself didn't come to a glorious end. In March 1493, he returned from his first voyage to promise Ferdinand and Isabella that the lands he had claimed for them were full of gold and other valuable things. They sent him back three more times, but he didn't find any gold to bring them. Columbus was disgraced, and he died a very poor, unhappy man.

Francis didn't return to the New World on any of Columbus's last three voyages. Instead, he rejoined Felix, Layla, and me. The jewelry we'd received from Isabella was used by Arthur and Attila to expand their toy factories. Soon we had toys for almost every child in Europe and England, with some left over. We decided we should have a regular schedule to distribute them, and this decision led us into the next phase of our mission.

SIXTEEN

The Christmas Legend
of Saint Nicholas

ver since I started giving gifts back in Patara and Myra, people told stories about the mysterious person who came at night to leave presents for children. Over the centuries, as the territory where I gave gifts and the number of those gifts grew, so did the myths. It wasn't until about 1500, though, that the gift-giver was identified as me, or rather as Saint Nicholas.

Although we hadn't realized this at the time, it was inevitable at least some of the truth would become widely known after Arthur and Attila opened their toy factories and hired staff to work in them. Back then, simply the presence of factories that only made toys was unusual enough to arouse local interest, and, try as Arthur and Attila might, there were workers who learned something of what we did and couldn't resist telling family and friends. In centuries to come, some companies would require employees to sign "secrecy agreements," where they promised not to tell anyone else about the work they did. But in 1500, that hadn't been thought of yet.

A few very trusted workers knew everything: Willie Skokan, for instance, occasionally would come with Felix, Francis, Layla, and me when we delivered toys he had made. Willie wanted to watch children at play with their gifts. He would take notes on any problems they had with the toys, and then try to fix these design flaws when he got back to the Nuremberg factory.

At any rate, once the first Saint Nicholas tale was told there was no stopping the story from spreading. People seemed relieved to have a name by which to identify the mysterious gift-giver they'd been wondering about for so long. From Rome to London, and in every city and village in between, children began to hope they'd get a nighttime visit from Saint Nicholas.

"This is going to be very awkward," I told Layla one night as we sat by a tiny campfire in the hill country of France. Felix and Francis were asleep, rolled up in their blankets as close to the warmth of the fire as they could get without setting their bedding ablaze. "I understand many children now pray at bedtime that Saint Nicholas will visit while they sleep and bring them something. I certainly don't want to disappoint anyone. What are we going to do?"

As always, Layla's commonsense approach to problems was helpful.

"You know that for some time we've been thinking about picking just a few very special nights each year for the gift-giving," she reminded me. "That way we can spend most of our time preparing the toys and choosing which children should receive them. We'll recruit more people to help deliver the gifts on these nights. That way, we'll be better organized and more children can wake up to delightful surprises."

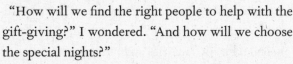

"How will we find the right people to help with the gift-giving?" I wondered. "And how will we choose the special nights?"

Layla favored me with the sort of lovingly impatient look wives use when their husbands ask especially silly questions.

"Somehow, Nicholas, when you are concerned, things simply happen because they need to," she said. "When you needed Felix, you found him. When you needed me, you found me. The same is true of Attila and Dorothea and Arthur and Francis and Willie Skokan. The right people will find us. As for the nights to choose, well, I think we already know the most important one."

And, of course, we did. Christmas had become an almost universal day for exchanging gifts. What better time for children to receive our gifts, too?

"For reasons of time and convenience, in some countries we could choose other dates associated with Christ's birth and presents," I mused, suddenly inspired. "For instance, in some places gifts are given on January sixth, the day the three Wise Men are supposed to have arrived in Bethlehem and offered their presents to the baby Jesus. So there are two dates. Don't you think we need at least one more?"

We did, and, as Layla had guessed, that day was chosen for us. December 6, the anniversary of my supposed death, had been declared "Saint Nicholas Day" by the church. As soon as my name was connected with the mysterious gift-giving, families in some countries assumed I would come visit their children on that day instead of Christmas.

It took a few dozen years for us to arrange this new schedule. Eventually a plan evolved where Arthur and helpers would distribute gifts in England and the British Isles; Attila and Dorothea and assistants in Germany, France, and the European "middle countries"; Willie Skokan and helpers in Eastern Europe; Francis and associates in Spain, Portugal, and Western Europe; Felix and helpers in Scandinavia; Layla and helpers in Italy; and me assisting wherever I liked, working with one group one year and with another the next. Everyone went in Saint Nicholas costume, the traditional red robes trimmed with white that I had worn in my days as a bishop. They also glued on white beards to match mine, and Felix began the rude custom of stuffing a pillow under the belt of his robes—to imitate, he said, my "considerable" waistline.

Traveling faster than normal mortals could imagine, the various groups moved from city to village, from house to cottage, leaving gifts inside for the children who lived there. Whenever possible, presents were placed in stockings hung to dry by fireplaces. This quickly caused a new flurry of myths about how Saint Nicholas must prefer coming down chimneys to any other way of entering a home, and how children wanting to be certain of gifts should hang up their stockings there on the appropriate night.

It came as a welcome surprise that some parents, who hadn't before now, began using these special nights of December 25 and January 6 to give their children gifts, too. We might leave a doll for a little girl, and on that same night her mother and father might add a new dress, pieces of fruit, and perhaps even some candy.

The helpers we recruited came from all sorts of places, and from all kinds of professions. They were good-hearted men and women, sworn to secrecy, and people we somehow knew we could trust not to talk out of turn. Many helped us for a few years; some assisted us for decades, and a special few became part of our core group and stopped aging altogether, just as we had.

Even as our ranks grew and we were able to distribute more toys to more children, the quality of the toys we gave improved as well. One of our finest new companions came to us from Italy in 1519. Leonardo da Vinci was the greatest painter of the time, and his *Mona Lisa* might be the most famous painting ever. It is still on display to the public in Paris's Louvre museum.

Francis had first met Leonardo in Milan, Italy, in the late 1400s, and kept in touch with him after that. Leonardo's style of painting was quite unique; he liked to use dark colors as backgrounds, believing this made light colors stand out better. Leonardo also was a great scientist. He filled whole notebooks with ideas for flying machines and boats that moved underwater. But in 1519, he told Francis he was tired of being such a public figure, saying, "The greatest artists work in private." Very soon Francis helped spirit Leonardo away from France, where he had been living, to Arthur's toy factory in London. Almost immediately, Leonardo came up with wonderful new ways to paint faces on dolls. He and Willie Skokan would meet once or twice a year to invent new toys. It was a happy time for Leonardo—indeed, it was a happy time for all of us.

"I believe we have finally done everything necessary," I told Felix one afternoon after we'd spent most of the day visiting Arthur in London. For a change the city seemed almost clean, and it was a fine, sunny spring day. "The factories here and in Germany are producing all the toys we need, we have special days to distribute our gifts, and since it's spring, with winter so far away, we can even relax a little and simply enjoy ourselves."

I should have known better. Life is never as uncomplicated as we'd prefer. Even as Felix and I chatted, a German priest named Martin Luther was breaking away from the Catholic church because he didn't agree with some church teachings. Because Luther's followers were said to be protesting, they eventually became known as "Protestants." European Christians no longer all belonged to the Catholic church.

There were religious changes in England, too. Little Princess Catherine of Aragon had, of course, grown up to marry Prince Arthur of England in 1501. Prince Arthur was expected to become England's king, but the poor fellow died unexpectedly before he ever had a chance to inherit the throne of his father, King Henry VII. Arthur's younger brother Henry became the new heir, and in 1509 Catherine had to marry Henry when he became king.

It wasn't a very happy marriage; Catherine was much older than Henry VIII, and by 1527 he wanted to divorce her. The Catholic church wouldn't allow the divorce; while Henry was arguing with church officials in Rome, he met a woman named Anne Boleyn and decided to marry her. Kings usually do what they want, and Henry ordered the English church to break away from the Catholic church. His new Church of England allowed Henry to divorce Catherine and marry Anne. This second marriage wasn't happy, either; Henry ended up getting married six different times. But the result for Christians in England was that, while Henry was king, they weren't encouraged to worship as Catholics anymore.

After Henry VIII died in 1547, his daughter Mary became queen and ruled England. She wanted everyone to become Catholics again. Eleven years later Mary died and her sister Elizabeth became queen. She was a Protestant. The whole issue of religion, in England and in Europe, became quite confused.

This confusion affected our mission very much. I always loved children of all religious faiths and backgrounds, but the mythical Saint Nicholas who was supposed to give toys was traditionally a part of the Catholic church. People thought Saint Nicholas might only give toys to Catholic families. When our gift-giving continued as usual in every country regardless of whether children receiving them were Protestants or Catholics, the stories about who was giving the presents began to change.

For instance, Catholic saints weren't welcome in the England of Queen Elizabeth I, so parents began telling their children about "Father Christmas," who came down chimneys on Christmas Eve after everyone was asleep and filled the stockings of children who'd been good throughout the year. In France, the same mission was carried out by "Père Noel," and so on until each country seemed to have a different idea about who gave children presents and the nights on which he or she did it. You notice I say "he or she." In Italy, children began to believe that Befana, a very old woman, brought them their presents. Some Italian parents even told their children that Befana was a friendly witch.

Truthfully, it didn't matter to us what name this mysterious gift-giver was given, or what he or she was supposed to look like. We wanted to help children be happy. If that meant being Saint Nicholas in Belgium, and leaving gifts there on December 6, then being Father Christmas in England on December 25 and Befana in Italy on January 6, well, that was all right. Layla was especially pleased about the Befana tale, and insisted on dressing up in old robes and distributing the presents in Italy herself.

Sometimes it took a while for countries to separate our gift-giving from the religious purpose of Christmas, which of course was and is to celebrate the birth of Jesus. We never intended to interfere with that much more important part of the Christmas season. Rather, we wanted to add to it.

In Germany, for instance, parents told children that Saint Nicholas came on December 6, and that the Christ Child brought more gifts on December 25. "Christkind" was the German name for him. As years passed, that name began to be pronounced "Kris Kringle," by German settlers in other parts of the world, especially in America. German children today still expect their Christmas presents from the Christkind, who is usually accompanied by little gnomish helpers.

We heard all of these tales and considered them carefully before deciding on one simple rule. In each country, we would gladly take on whatever identity its children preferred. We would leave presents for children in every home where we were welcome. In a few cases, we learned that parents did not want us to come, and we regretfully avoided those houses.

Wars continued to trouble us. Our powers were always weakened whenever there was fighting nearby. Children whose countries were at war often had to do without gifts from us. It seemed like an unfair penalty for them, and our greatest pleasure was being able to return to these countries and give gifts there when the fighting was over.

As the 1500s passed and the 1600s began, we continued our mission in Europe and England. But reports continued to arrive from what everyone thought of as the New World. Columbus had been the first captain to sail across the Atlantic Ocean and claim land for Spain. England and France were among the other countries to hire explorers whose job was to establish settlements in the New World and bring back any treasure they might find.

"The biggest treasure in the New World is going to be the land itself," Francis kept insisting. "It's a special place, Nicholas, and one day it's going to be full of special people. When will you go there to see for yourself? We'll take care of things in the Old World for you while you're away."

I resisted the trip for quite a while. There was still so much work to do in England and Europe. It was especially enjoyable now to see new Christmas customs being developed—people in Germany decorating Christmas trees, for instance. Keeping green boughs during winter had long been traditional in many parts of the world—the idea was that these cheerful decorations promised spring would come again. But the Germans were the ones who connected this longtime belief to Christmas around the year 1500. Legend, which is almost always interesting but not always accurate, indicates the great German Martin Luther took some fresh evergreens into his home on Christmas, and after that, his friends and followers began to do the same.

But in the early 1600s, such lovely new Christmas traditions hadn't yet made their way across the Atlantic Ocean. It was reported that settlers in the New World were having hard times of it. They suffered from bad weather, strange diseases, and simple loneliness for the families and friends they had to leave behind. One complete English settlement called Roanoke simply disappeared.

"You know you want to go across the ocean and bring Christmas comfort to those suffering people," Layla scolded me one morning. "Arthur writes from London that some people calling themselves the Saints are going to sail to the New World in a ship called the *Mayflower*. Why not sail with them?"

"Will you come, too?" I asked.

"I think I'd better stay behind and make sure things run smoothly here," Layla replied. "Don't look so sad at the thought! It won't hurt us to be apart for a little while—after all, we've been married for over a thousand years!"

"I'll need someone to help me," I pleaded.

"Well, then, take Felix," Layla suggested. "It's been centuries since the two of you were out on your own together. It will almost be like a vacation for you."

So Felix and I went to London, where we met William Brewster, the leader of the Saints. He told us his group was leaving England because they weren't allowed to worship as they pleased, and that they called themselves Saints because they were willing to suffer to enjoy freedom of religion.

"We have exactly one hundred passengers, and one-third are part of our group," Brewster explained. "The others are craftsmen and physicians and such, who will be needed to help us establish our new colony. How could the two of you help out if we let you join us?"

"Well, I'm very good at carving wood and fixing things," Felix said quickly. "As for my friend Nicholas, well, he's a hard worker, if not a good one."

I was offended by Felix's remark and became even more offended when Brewster added, "Well, I can tell by his weight that he's at least good at eating. You might find yourself losing a few pounds in the New World, my friend!"

"I'll take my chances," I replied, feeling insulted.

Brewster agreed to let us come, so 102 passengers left England on the *Mayflower* in September 1620. All during the long, hard years ahead of them, these people called themselves Saints. It was only two hundred years later that historians renamed them "the Pilgrims."

SEVENTEEN

Hard Times in the New World

he Saints and the rest of the 102 people bound for the New World were supposed to sail in two ships, the *Mayflower* and the *Speedwell*. But at the last minute, someone decided the *Speedwell* wasn't safe enough to cross the ocean. Felix and I thought this meant the trip would be delayed until another ship could be found, but instead all 102 of us were crowded into the ninety-foot-long *Mayflower*.

If everyone had acted pleasant it would have been hard enough to get along when we were packed so tightly together, but the thirty or so Saints weren't a very friendly group. They tried to keep separate from everyone else, which was practically impossible, and spent a lot of time criticizing the rest of us for not acting properly. What they meant by that was not doing everything exactly the way the Saints wanted. Several times there almost were fights. At one point during the voyage everyone was asked to sign an agreement to create a fair government when we landed, so that there would be reasonable laws for all of us to follow, Saints and non-Saints alike. Everyone couldn't wait for the day that we arrived at our destination, which was supposed to be near the area in Virginia where, in 1607, Captain John

Smith of Britain had founded Jamestown, the first permanent British colony in the land most Europeans were already calling "America."

Well, we only missed landing in Virginia by hundreds of miles. Instead of sailing into a friendly harbor, the *Mayflower* ended up on the coastal rocks of Plymouth, Massachusetts, well to the north. Most passengers had already been in very bad moods, and this made them feel even worse. Everyone started accusing everyone else of all sorts of things.

"The so-called Saints certainly aren't living up to their name," Felix whispered to me, ducking a heavy plate some Saint had thrown at a non-Saint. "Nobody's gotten off this ship yet and already the trip seems to be a complete disaster."

William Brewster and another Saint leader, William Bradford, tried to get people calmed down. They reminded everyone about the agreement they'd signed to set up a good government, and it was only after the passengers stopped arguing that we were allowed to get off the ship—which by then, we all hated—and take our first steps on American soil.

Felix and I joined in as everyone concentrated on building a strong fort. Some natives—whom we called "Indians" just as Columbus had, although we, of course, knew we weren't in India—wandered out of their own villages to stare at us. It was December 21, and already very cold.

It came as no surprise to Felix and me that little notice was taken of Christmas Day. There were some prayers said, but that was the extent of it. Felix and I wished we could give toys to the few children in the group, but we hadn't been able to bring any with us on the voyage and there wasn't time after we landed to make gifts before December 25.

"Next year, though, we'll help these children have a wonderful Christmas," I assured Felix.

The winter was a harsh one. The Saints insisted on wearing rather odd clothing, mostly black with white collars and wide belts. They believed wearing bright colors was a sin. Their cloaks were ragged and did little to keep out the cold. The non-Saints had it a little better, dressing for warmth rather than in the plain styles favored by the Saints. The food brought over on the *Mayflower* soon ran out, and we couldn't expect any other ships arriving from England for quite some time, especially since we'd ended up landing so far from where we'd been expected to settle.

In the spring, the Indians saved the people of Plymouth. They showed their new neighbors how to plant crops, and how to use fish as fertilizer. Eventually, there was enough to eat, and in November 1621 William Bradford, who'd been elected governor, announced there would be a special feast called Thanksgiving to celebrate the group's survival. Quite properly, the Indians were invited to join in. Everyone ate a lot; afterward, in the crude shelter we'd built inside the fort, I told Felix, "This wonderful Thanksgiving is a sure sign that Christmas here in Plymouth will be celebrated joyfully!" Felix and I had spent several months secretly making toys out of wooden sticks, bits of cloth, and lumps of clay. Felix still carved beautifully. We eventually made a doll for every little 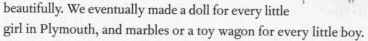 girl in Plymouth, and marbles or a toy wagon for every little boy.

But we weren't allowed to give these gifts. Right after that first Thanksgiving, Governor Bradford announced Christmas would not be celebrated in Plymouth—ever. Astonished, Felix and I rushed to his tent and demanded to know why.

"To set aside December twenty-fifth would be to admit another day is as important as Sunday, the Sabbath," Bradford droned. He was a boring man both in appearance and speech. "If you two have studied your Scripture, you would realize no one truly knows the date of our Lord's birth. So there must be no celebration on the twenty-fifth, none at all."

"You mean, there can be no presents given?" I asked. "Presents are a happy Christmas tradition, and have been for centuries."

"We have come to America to begin new, more proper traditions," Bradford lectured.

Felix shot me a warning look, but I was angry and said to Bradford, "Saint Nicholas won't like this!"

Bradford looked irritated. "There is no place in Plymouth for that ridiculous myth, either. I think I know my history as well as any man, and I'm sure if the real Saint Nicholas were standing here, he'd completely agree with me."

"I wouldn't be so certain," I growled, and Felix grabbed me and hurried me away before I could say more.

Despite our protests, Bradford banned Christmas. All the Saints accepted his decision. Some of the other settlers didn't. Although they weren't allowed to have a Christmas service, they simply took the day off from work and ran around the fort playing games with their children. Bradford wouldn't permit even this. He told them it wasn't right for them to play while the Saints worked. He took away their hoops and sticks and balls and told them that if they had to celebrate at all, they should do it quietly in their tents and log shelters.

Oh, I was furious. I told Felix we should leave Plymouth at once and never, ever come back. "How dare that man Bradford refuse to let people enjoy Christmas?" I fumed. "I've had enough of these Saints, and of this New World called America. As soon as the first ship finds us, you and I are going back to Europe, where Christmas is properly celebrated!"

"Don't be too impatient," Felix suggested. "Surely someone like you, who's almost fifteen hundred years old, must realize some things take time. This place known as America isn't always going to be ruled by such stiff-necked people."

"They don't want Saint Nicholas and his gifts here," I complained.

Felix smiled. "Why don't we spend a year looking around?" he asked. "You just might find that Saint Nicholas is here already." When I said I didn't understand, he added, "These Saints from England aren't the only European settlers, you know."

I'd quite forgotten.

A few hundred miles to the south of Plymouth, Dutch explorers and traders had begun establishing towns. The Dutch had reputations as hard-headed businesspeople, but they also loved celebrations, especially those involving Christmas. Felix's plan was for us to pack up our few belongings and visit some of these Dutch settlements. I agreed, and when Governor

Bradford said he wouldn't give us permission to go, we simply left quietly in the middle of the night. The winter weather was harsh, but as usual Felix and I could travel faster than normal humans. We reached the Dutch trading village of Fort Orange in two days.

These villages didn't have as many rules as Plymouth, and the people were friendlier. A British explorer named Henry Hudson had been hired by the Dutch a few years earlier to sail to America and find good land there for them to colonize. When he reported finding a huge harbor, with a wide river connecting it to wonderful green valleys, the Dutch were quick to send over their first ships full of colonists. Unlike the Saints, they weren't looking for religious freedom, but for trading opportunities.

In 1621, the main Dutch settlement was Fort Orange in the northern part of what eventually became the state of New York. The people there welcomed Felix and me. Right away they told us they were sorry we'd just missed their celebration of Christmas, when they'd had great feasts and exchanged presents. A little boy named Hans added that on December 6, Saint Nicholas had brought marbles for him and a hoop for his sister.

"The good Saint Nicholas doesn't forget the little children in America," laughed Hans's father. I smiled; obviously, parents in Fort Orange had brought Saint Nicholas's spirit with them to America, and provided little gifts to their children when I hadn't been around to do so. Well, come next Saint Nicholas Day, I promised myself the pleasure of giving these children their presents.

Felix was quite proud of himself for bringing us to Fort Orange. We decided to stay for a while. We didn't trap animals for their fur, which was what most of the other men in the settlement did. Instead, Felix made some money with his carving, and I spent my days exploring the hills all around the settlement. The Indians were friendly to me once they understood I didn't mean them any harm. It was a pleasurable, peaceful time. I missed Layla terribly, of course, as well as the rest of my longtime friends, but as soon as they learned Felix and I were in Fort Orange they sent letters on every ship that sailed there from European ports, and Felix and I wrote letters back.

Our letters to Europe were filled with happy news, all about how Saint

Nicholas and America—at least the Dutch parts of America—were a perfect match. But the letters Layla, Francis, Arthur, and Attila sent us weren't as pleasant.

Europe was still torn by war. When people weren't fighting armies from other countries, they were fighting among themselves. Arthur in particular warned that England was bound to be split apart by civil war. King Charles was unhappy with his Parliament—the elected leaders who helped him govern the country—so he'd simply told the members of Parliament to go home while he ruled all by himself. The Puritans in England opposed Charles. "Sounds like Plymouth all over again to me," Felix commented.

Layla's advice was that Felix and I should stay in America and continue establishing our mission there. The rest of our group would continue on as best they could in Europe. I was pleased to have more time in America, and reluctant to be away from Layla for so long. But my wife and I apparently had thousands of more years to spend together, so Felix and I remained among the Dutch colonists.

These people were, mostly, a very friendly, happy group, and we enjoyed their company. But they weren't perfect, either. As early as 1619, some Dutch colonists earned their livings by importing African slaves to the colonies, where they were often sold to British settlers.

It was about this same time that Dutch leaders met with some trusting chiefs of Indian tribes and bought from them the island called "Manhattan." It was hardly a fair exchange. The colonists got a large island guarding a wide natural port, and the Indians got a few bags of cheap beads. But they'd never seen anything like these beads and considered them to be treasures. The Dutch were careful to have the Indians mark all sorts of legal documents. By European law, the sale was legal.

As soon as the island was theirs, the Dutch sent word back to Holland that more colonists should sail for America. In 1626 a whole fleet arrived, dozens of ships bringing people of every age and profession. These newcomers made up most of the population of a new village on the southern tip of Manhattan Island. The village was named "New Amsterdam" after the most important city in Holland.

Felix and I were watching on the shore as the ships arrived. The leading vessel was called *Goede Vrowe*, Dutch for "Good Housewife." Like all ships of this time, *Good Housewife* had a carved wooden figurehead nailed to its front, since sailors believed these figureheads would protect them from storms. Usually they were the figures of mermaids or other sailors. But as Felix peered at *Good Housewife*, he suddenly blurted, "Nicholas! Look at that figurehead!"

"It looks rather familiar," I replied. "The face, and the robes that are painted such a bright shade of red. I wonder who it's supposed to be?"

"It's you!" Felix shouted. "These settlers carved a figurehead of Saint Nicholas to safely lead them to the New World! It's a sign, Nicholas, don't you see? Christmas has arrived in America, and it's never, ever going to leave!"

But Christmas had to leave England for a while. Even as the Dutch settlers built a statue of Saint Nicholas in their village of New Amsterdam, the Puritans in Britain began an armed uprising against King Charles I. Led by Oliver Cromwell, they eventually captured Charles and executed him. Just like Saints in Plymouth, those Puritans didn't approve of celebrating Christmas with feasts and gifts. In 1645 they ordered everyone in England to treat Christmas like an ordinary day, and said anyone who tried to celebrate the holiday would be punished.

"People all over England are very unhappy with this law," Arthur wrote. "There have been riots in some cities. Canterbury was the worst. Quite a few people were hurt in the protest there. About ten thousand protestors signed a proclamation that they'd have their holiday back even if it meant they had to have a king again, too. I've decided to close down the London toy factory for a while, since these Puritans don't like toys, either. But don't worry; we're just biding our time. Christmas will return to England."

And it did. In 1660, after more civil war, England had a new king, Charles II. Soon afterward, Christmas was restored.

But as Arthur and Layla both wrote, the holiday there wasn't quite the same. Afraid that the Puritans might come back to power, lots of English families stopped openly celebrating December 25, preferring quiet family dinners to singing carols in the streets. Owners of many British companies had taken advantage of the Puritan law to require their employees to work on Christmas Day. Even after King Charles II took the throne, these owners continued to insist that Christmas be an ordinary working day.

"I think we should go back to England for a while," I told Felix. "Something has to be done to make Christmas there what it used to be. Let's find a few special people among these Dutch settlers in New Amsterdam and teach them the ways of gift-making and gift-giving. Then we can return to Europe and rejoin our friends."

But this plan had to be postponed. England and Holland got into a war, one that raged in Europe and affected their colonies in America. England got the better of it. In 1664, the Dutch colonies of Fort Orange and New Amsterdam had to be surrendered to England. The English renamed both villages. Fort Orange was called Albany and New Amsterdam became New York. Fortunately, the English settlers who arrived along with these new names weren't stern Puritans. They not only allowed the Dutch colonists to continue celebrating Christmas with gifts and feasts, they enjoyed joining in the fun. Holland and England continued their war in Europe, which meant Felix and I couldn't safely take a ship back to London, and fighting still occasionally broke out in America between colonists from those two countries. In 1673, the Dutch even retook New York for a little while, but in 1674 the English won it back for good.

New York grew from a village into a city, one of the three largest in America. The other two were Boston to the north and Philadelphia to the south. Colonists flocked to the New World. The hope of religious freedom and lots of green, fertile land was irresistible to people tired of crowded, war-torn Europe.

Late in the 1600s, two new, wonderful names became part of the New World's vocabulary. In 1697, a minister in Boston named Cotton Mather described all New World settlers as "Americans." And, about the same time, English settlers arriving in New York and Albany and other villages established earlier by Dutch colonists found themselves gladly swept up in the Christmas celebrations that had become traditions there. Because most of these settlers had been born after the Puritans banned Christmas in England, they didn't know any legends about a Christmas gift-giver. Their children were thrilled to learn they might have surprise gifts when they woke up on Christmas morning, and begged the Dutch children to tell them all about it.

Since the British now ruled what had been Dutch colonies, English became the official language there and the Dutch had to learn to speak it. This wasn't easy. They had trouble pronouncing certain words in the new language. So when they earnestly began to tell the Christmas stories to their newly arrived English neighbors, they couldn't quite say "Saint Nicholas" clearly. What the English listeners heard was "Sintnicklus" and walked away thinking the gift-giver was "Sinta Klass," which they soon pronounced in a more traditional English way.

For the first time in America, some children began believing that their Christmas presents were delivered by "Santa Claus."

EIGHTEEN

Reunion in America

 knock on the door of our log cabin woke Felix and me up from a sound sleep. It was a cool spring night in the thriving village of New York. We'd spent most of the day making toys and had gone to bed feeling very tired.

"I hope it's not another fire," Felix muttered. There had been several blazes in the past months. As New York grew, so did the number of careless people living in it who didn't put out their fires properly before turning in for the night.

Still half-asleep, I stumbled to the door and opened it. Layla rushed in and was hugging me before I realized it. Thrilled to be with my wife again, I hugged Layla back enthusiastically while Felix jumped up to welcome Willie Skokan and Leonardo da Vinci, who came into the cabin behind her.

"Whatever are you doing here?" I asked. "We're happy to see you, of course, but I thought the plan was for Felix and me to train some new helpers here in America and then rejoin you in Europe."

"You weren't the only one eager to see America," Layla replied briskly, taking off her scarf and not looking a bit older, even though I hadn't seen her for eighty years. "Francis, Attila, and Dorothea have everything in Europe under control, and I'm sad to say that Arthur needs very little help right now in England, since they're still not openly celebrating Christmas there. We decided that it's time to spend the holiday in this country, and we didn't want you and Felix to have all the fun of doing it."

"A new land means a need for new toys," Leonardo added. "Willie Skokan and I want new challenges."

"It would be challenging to fix up these walls a little bit," Willie muttered, feeling along the edges of the logs with his callused fingertips. "Who built this cabin, anyway? There are gaps between the logs."

"Thank you for the compliment, Willie," Felix laughed as he bustled about getting drinks and food for everyone. "Santa and I have been busy learning about this country and making gifts for the many children who are growing up here. We haven't had time for little things like making our own home very comfortable."

"What did you call my husband?" Layla asked, tilting her head to the side as she sometimes did when she heard something that surprised her.

"Santa," Felix answered. "We've told you in our letters about the *Sinta Klass* mispronunciation, and how some children around New York expect Santa Claus to bring their presents. It's a good nickname for Nicholas, don't you think?"

"Santa," Layla repeated thoughtfully. "Yes, it really suits him. I suppose we all ought to call him that from now on."

The five of us spent the rest of the hours before dawn chatting excitedly, catching up on each other's news and making plans for further adventures in America. Felix and I astonished Layla, Leonardo, and Willie Skokan by serving them hot cocoa, a new drink that had become very popular in America but wasn't yet common in Europe. They smacked their lips, enjoying the chocolate taste. When we also served fresh bread with homemade blackberry jam, Leonardo sighed with pleasure.

"Does everyone in America eat so well?" he asked. "When Nicholas— excuse me, when Santa—gives his gifts all over the colonies, do children leave him delicious snacks as they've started to do in Europe?"

"Actually, we haven't had much chance to find out," I admitted. "Because the English now control the colonies along the coast, those unhappy

Puritan traditions still are common almost everywhere. Except for New York and Albany and other areas where Dutch Christmas celebrations took hold, December twenty-fifth is almost as poorly celebrated in America as it is in England."

"We think that's just because most of the American colonists haven't heard about Santa Claus yet," Felix chimed in. "Give us a century or two to recruit the right helpers, and every American will look forward to December twenty-fifth. And with three of you here to help us now, it can happen that much sooner!"

The five of us had good intentions, but other events prevented us from accomplishing much in the next few decades.

The American colonies had grown, both in territory and population. By 1700 there were 275,000 settlers. New York had five thousand residents; six thousand people lived in Philadelphia, and seven thousand in Boston. In the next few years, the first American newspapers were published. Farther to the west and south, French-Canadian trappers founded New Orleans and Spanish missionaries built San Antonio. All over the American continent, men and women with ambition and energy wanted to create their own great nations.

But the nations where they had come from weren't eager for these new Americans to become too independent. England, in particular, which had by far the most colonists, also had the strongest interest in keeping them under control. In the 1740s the first great cotton mills were built in England, but American colonists were forbidden to build their own mills. This meant they would have to buy their cotton cloth from England. Next, the English government told its American colonists that they couldn't settle anywhere west of the Allegheny Mountains, because if settlements were too far inland it would be hard for British soldiers to be stationed there.

Naturally, the colonists felt resentful. They became even angrier when, in 1754, England and France became embroiled in a war over boundaries between each other's American colonies. While the French government cleverly recruited Indians to fight on their side, the English ordered their colonists to enlist and go to war. A lot of them didn't want to fight and were forced into battle. During this nine-year war, a young Virginian named

George Washington was made an officer for the English. In fact, he fought in the very first battle of what became known as the French and Indian War.

As usual, we found our powers weakened by being near the fighting. Leonardo and Willie Skokan spent most of their time making gifts, while Felix, Layla, and I began to travel around in hopes of meeting people who could become new helpers. And, of course, all five of us enjoyed those special nights when we delivered our gifts; December 6 in a few communities, December 25 in others, and, for a few years, New Year's Eve and New Year's Day in some Dutch settlements. It so happened that, for whatever reasons, their children hoped for gifts on those two new dates, and, since it made them happy, we were pleased to oblige. After only a hundred years or so, though, almost all children in America wanted their stockings filled when they woke up on Christmas morning.

We recruited our first American helper in 1727. Sarah Kemble Knight was a schoolteacher who wrote the first book about traveling around the country. It was called *A Private Journal of a Journey from Boston to New York in the Year 1704.* That doesn't sound like much of a trip now, but in those days it was a journey that took the better part of two weeks, and required stagecoaches and canoes. Sarah filled her book with comments about the towns she passed through, and the customs of the people who lived in them. Layla happened to meet Sarah in New York in 1726. Over several weeks she explained our mission, and a year later Sarah left her old life behind and joined us. She was wonderfully helpful. It was a great advantage to have someone with us who knew so much about the country and its people.

In 1768 we added another member to our group, though not as a full member who knew all our secrets. Daniel Boone was the first great explorer who had been born to settlers in the colonies. Daniel—he and everyone else really pronounced his name "Dan'l," so that's what I'll call him for the rest of this story—had a restless spirit that reminded me very much of Francis, although Francis was well educated and Dan'l could just read and write simple sentences.

Felix ended up traveling with Dan'l for several years. In 1769 they began to explore the mountain country west of what would be known as North Carolina, and in March 1775, Dan'l led the first settlers along the instantly famous "Wilderness Road" that curved through mountain passes to the rich grasslands of Kentucky. Felix left him there to return to us in New York. When Felix came back, he reported that there seemed no end to how far the American continent stretched toward the western horizon. Someday, Felix predicted, we would need many more helpers to deliver hundreds of thousands of gifts to American children.

"I've asked Dan'l to keep in touch with us so we'll know where new settlements are when we've got enough helpers to deliver presents there," Felix said excitedly. "As soon as this current war business is over with, we can help all Americans learn how to celebrate Christmas properly!"

But what Felix called "this current business" wasn't going to be over as soon as we wished.

For several years, it had been obvious that the American colonists wanted to break away from English rule. In 1774, the group calling itself the First Continental Congress met in Philadelphia. This group, made up of elected representatives from each colony, voted for Americans to stop buying all goods shipped to their country from England. The English weren't pleased. They sent more soldiers to America and, in April 1775, tried to seize a warehouse full of ammunition in Concord, a village in Massachusetts. A silversmith named Paul Revere and several others made frantic, nighttime horseback rides to warn people living in and around Concord that the British were coming. On April 19, 1775, the first shots of the American Revolution were fired.

It turned out to be a very long war, with fighting continuing until 1781. Things were not really over until a peace treaty was signed by the Americans, English, French, and Spanish in 1783. The English armies had better weapons and usually beat the colonists when both armies stopped and faced each other, but the Americans were smart enough not to get into too many battles. Instead, George Washington, picked by the Continental Congress to lead the colonists, kept his soldiers moving continually and attacked the English when they weren't expecting it.

I always hated wars, and I didn't care much for this one. It seemed to me that negotiation would have been better than shooting. But the Revolution was under way, and we in America were in the thick of it. When New York came under attack from the English army, we decided to move south to Philadelphia for a while.

As soon as we arrived in Philadelphia, Leonardo and Willie Skokan told me they wanted to meet a man they'd heard about who was a great inventor.

"This fellow once flew a kite in a thunderstorm to find out more about electricity," Leonardo explained.

"That sounds less like an inventor than an imbecile to me," I replied. "What does a thunderstorm have to do with electricity?"

Willie and Leonardo launched into a long, complicated explanation that just confused me more. People had known about electricity for centuries. It had been William Gilbert, the physician of Henry VIII's daughter Queen Elizabeth, who gave electricity its name. Leonardo even suggested that someday normal people would be able to use electricity in their homes, but for purposes he couldn't yet predict.

Leonardo and Willie Skokan told me that this Benjamin Franklin of Philadelphia thought there might be electricity in lightning, so he went out in a thunderstorm with a metal key attached to the tail of a kite to see if lightning would strike the key and produce electricity. They also talked about Franklin's printing company, and how every year he'd publish a book called *Poor Richard's Almanack*, which was full of useful information about weather and other things.

Meeting Benjamin Franklin sounded like a more productive way to spend time than worrying about the war. After learning his address, we all went to his home and introduced ourselves. Franklin invited us in, offered us food, and almost immediately fell into deep conversation with Leonardo and Willie Skokan about, of all things, eyeglasses.

"Some people need one type of lens for help with seeing things that are far away, and others need help to see objects that are near," Franklin said. "But often when people get older, they need both kinds of eyeglasses and can only wear one at a time. But I have an idea . . ." The three of them disappeared into some side room Franklin used as his laboratory, leaving Felix, Layla, and me behind.

Within two weeks, they'd invented a type of eyeglasses they called "bifocals," with each lens half convex and half concave. And within two months, Benjamin Franklin was a full member of our group.

"I'll have to postpone most of my involvement with you until this war is concluded," he told us. "I'm spending much of my time in France, trying to gain our new nation more support there. Christmas is wonderful, but independence is necessary."

Ben—this is what he told us to call him—understood our dislike of war, and never asked us to help with the Revolution. That December we did help the colonists, however, quite by accident.

General George Washington came to Philadelphia during the third week of that month in 1776 to report to the Continental Congress and to visit his good friend Ben, who was back home briefly from France and invited us one night to have dinner with his famous guest. George Washington was very tall. Later on I read somewhere that he had wooden teeth, but they certainly looked real to me. Ben naturally didn't tell the general who we really were, simply saying that we were visiting from Europe and knew everything there was to know about Europeans and their customs at Christmas.

"Is that so?" General Washington asked. "I wish I knew more about Europeans and their countries. The English have just brought some German soldiers to help against us. We call these troops 'Hessians,' and by reputation they're very good fighters. They've set up a strong camp at Trenton, which isn't too far from here. My soldiers don't believe they can beat the English troops, let alone these Germans. Most of my army is in the countryside around New York, and I'm afraid the Hessians will attack us there."

"Oh, I don't think they'll do that, at least not until after Christmas," Felix observed.

"Why do you think so?" General Washington asked quickly, leaning forward and looking very interested.

"Why, among all people on Earth, Germans may very well like to celebrate Christmas most!" Felix laughed. "I expect the forest around Trenton to be quickly stripped of its evergreen trees, for instance. Your Hessian foes will want to take those trees indoors and decorate them with ribbons and fruit and even candles. Then, on Christmas, I have no doubt they'll gather around those trees all day to sing Christmas carols and drink hot rum."

"Oh, really?" General Washington asked again, now leaning so far forward it appeared he might fall out of the chair onto his face. "They'll spend all Christmas night singing, and drinking, too?"

I suddenly felt uncomfortable with the way the conversation was going. "Perhaps we should change the subject, Felix," I said quickly, but my old friend was already saying more.

"You can count on it, General," Felix babbled cheerfully. "Go back to your troops in New York and tell them they can spend a peaceful Christmas, too."

One week later, on the night of December 25, the Hessian troops in Trenton gathered in their barracks. They stood around Christmas trees and sang carols and drank rum, just as Felix had predicted. And while they did, George Washington and his troops stealthily crossed the Delaware River and surrounded the Hessian camp. On the morning of December 26, while the Hessians were just waking up after their night of celebrating and drinking, Washington's army attacked and overwhelmed them. It was the first major military victory for the colonists, and because of that battle the colonial troops began to believe they could defeat their powerful opponents after all.

Nearly five years later at Yorktown, General Cornwallis of England surrendered to George Washington. Cornwallis said, both then and later, that Washington's Christmas victory over the Hessians was the most important battle in the Revolutionary War, and the moment when the Colonists began to win.

"Well, Felix, it seems you gave George Washington the best Christmas present possible," Ben laughed soon after Cornwallis had surrendered and the war was over. "What a helpful fellow you are."

"Too helpful," I grumbled. We were all crammed into the laboratory at Ben's house. He, Leonardo, and Willie Skokan were hard at work trying to copy a new toy called "roller skates" that had been invented by a helper of Arthur's in London. Apparently, this toy involved putting wheels on the soles of shoes.

"Well," Felix said, "at least the war is over. Now everyone in America can finally learn about Christmas."

NINETEEN

Diedrich Knickerbocker
and "Silent Night"

Newly independent America was, in most ways, an exciting place to be. We certainly enjoyed being able to travel up and down its Atlantic coast without worrying about the British army. Sarah Kemble Knight and Ben Franklin were wonderful guides. Layla, Felix, Leonardo, Willie Skokan, and I learned a great deal from them.

The problem we now faced was simple. Except for areas of New York and Pennsylvania where Dutch colonists had settled, Christmas celebrations in America were still inhibited by old-fashioned Puritan influence. In Boston, for instance, people still had to work on December 25, unless that date happened to fall on a Sunday. Each year after the Revolutionary War ended, we could and did choose areas where, on Christmas Eve, we'd quietly enter homes and leave gifts for children to find on Christmas morning. The children would wake up and be delighted with their presents, but they had no idea who had left them. Often their parents were more concerned that someone had come into their homes uninvited, and the next Christmas Eve might even sit up on guard to keep anyone from getting in again. And, as always, if parents didn't want us to come, we felt we shouldn't.

"What we need is some good publicity," Ben Franklin suggested one day in 1808. "You know—stories about Santa Claus and his helpers, and how their gifts can be such a pleasant part of celebrating Christmas."

"Do you mean stories in the newspapers?" Layla asked nervously. There were now quite a few newspapers in America, but none were especially known for telling the truth. "Do you mean we should go to reporters and tell them who we are? I don't think that's a good idea at all."

"She's right, Ben," Leonardo agreed. "If too many people knew our secrets, we'd lose the sense of wonder and magic that makes Santa Claus so special."

It took Sarah, herself an author, to come up with the best solution. "There are several writers in America whose articles and stories are especially well written," she said. "Perhaps we could choose just one writer, someone who could capture Santa's legend on the printed page so that it would inspire everyone's imagination. This way we'd only be sharing our secrets with one person, but that writer could tell our story to parents and children all over America!"

We all thought Sarah's idea was wonderful, and began talking about various American authors whose works we had read and enjoyed. It was Ben, who perhaps read the most of any of us, who insisted he had just the right author in mind.

"There's a fellow in New York named Washington Irving," Ben suggested. "He's an odd sort, by all accounts, someone who hated school, but then studied law for six whole years because he found the subject interesting. Irving has written several excellent short stories in newspapers about New York and the colonists who came to live there. Let's go meet him and see if he might be interested in helping us."

We found Washington Irving to be a fascinating man. He was short, slender, and balding prematurely at age twenty-six. To arrange our first meeting, we left a note for Irving at his home saying two men who knew all about the early Dutch colonies in Fort Orange and New Amsterdam wanted to talk with him. And this, of course, was true—although it had been almost two hundred years since Felix and I had first lived in them. Still, we both remembered those villages well.

Irving invited us for tea, and didn't seem surprised when seven strangers showed up instead of the two he was expecting. Ben made a good first impression by praising some of Irving's stories that he'd read.

"Right now, most of my new stories are appearing in a newspaper called *Salmagundi*," Irving explained. "I'm not paid very much for writing them. I make most of my money working as a lawyer. I'd rather write. It's my hope one day to spend all my time writing books."

"Why not write a book about the early Dutch colonists?" Ben suggested cheerfully. "I imagine lots of Americans would want to buy such a book to learn more about their customs."

"And their Christmas traditions," Felix added helpfully.

"Do you mean that Saint Nicholas nonsense?" Irving laughed. "I don't think there's anyone left alive who's really certain where that tall tale came from."

"Think again," I replied, and for the next few hours Irving's eyes grew ever wider as he heard the true story of Santa Claus all the way back to when plain old Nicholas first became bishop of Myra. It was especially hard for Irving to believe he was sitting in the same room with Leonardo da Vinci and Benjamin Franklin, but when he was finally convinced he began to chatter frantically.

"I must write this story," he chattered. "I must, I must. What a wonderful tale, Saint Nicholas living forever and coming to America!"

We agreed with him that the story was wonderful, but explained what we really wanted him to write was only the part about how Dutch colonists had welcomed Saint Nicholas to help them celebrate Christmas.

"Why not do what Ben suggested and write a book all about the Dutch colonists," I said. "Let Saint Nicholas be a part of the book. Use that name instead of Santa Claus, the way the Dutch did. This way, everyone who reads it can ease into the whole idea of Santa Claus."

Irving agreed, and for the next six months we stayed with him at his house while he wrote steadily. Irving worried he'd have to work as a lawyer during the day and only write at night, but we arranged for Francis to send us money from Europe, which made up for the salary Irving lost because he wasn't practicing law.

Washington Irving was a great writer, and eventually he would achieve his dream of writing books that were both famous and best sellers. The book he wrote with us, which was called *Diedrich Knickerbocker's 'A History of New York from the Beginning of the World to the End of the Dutch Dynasty,'* sold quite well by the standards of that time—several thousand copies. You must remember that many Americans still couldn't read in the early 1800s. Irving wouldn't let us read the book while he was writing it. He'd sit in his study, scratching words on paper with his goose-quill pen, and we'd amuse ourselves playing croquet in his yard. Sometimes he'd call us in to give him extra information on one subject or another. Eventually, Irving pronounced the book completed, and he took his hundreds of pages to a printer. Only after the book was bound between covers and displayed for sale in shops would Irving let us read it.

Mostly, we were pleased. Irving wrote of Christmastime in the old Dutch colonies and how "the good Saint Nicholas came riding," with the purpose of bringing "his yearly presents to children." This was good. What wasn't as pleasant was Irving's made-up description of how Saint Nicholas did this by "riding over the tops of trees" in a wagon.

"I can't fly," I spluttered to Irving the first time I read that description. "Why did you say that I could?"

"It seemed to make the story better," Irving replied. "You told me you wanted readers to be thrilled by your Christmas magic."

"Well, my magic doesn't include flying," I grumbled. "I hope everyone who reads your book skips over that part and concentrates on my gift-giving instead."

But when *Diedrich Knickerbocker* was published in 1809, at first it didn't seem as though I'd have much to worry about. As I said, a few thousand copies were sold, and we were able to go into that many more homes on Christmas Eve and leave presents for American children to find on Christmas morning. It was a good start. Then someone who read it was inspired to write a children's book entitled *A New Year's Present to the Little Ones from Five to Twelve*, and in this book I was supposed to ride in a sleigh pulled by a reindeer.

We thanked Irving for his trouble and wished him future success.

Though we invited him, he didn't want to leave his home and travel with us. "Writing is my life's purpose, the same way giving gifts to children is yours," Irving explained.

"We'll see you again, I know," Ben told him as we departed. "Meanwhile, happy times are coming for you. With your talent, you're certain to be a world-famous author, and soon."

"I wish you could stay longer," Irving said. "Maybe I could write another book about Saint Nicholas that might sell even better, if you'd stay and give me more good ideas."

"Don't feel badly," Layla suggested. "I have a feeling that *Diedrich Knickerbocker* is going to give us exactly the help we need, although it might take longer than we expected. Write other books. We all agree with Ben that when we see you again, you'll be famous."

We were sorry to say good-bye to Washington Irving, but excited to be on our way because, after so many years, we had decided to take a ship back to Europe. We wouldn't stay there forever—it was understood among us that America would probably be our permanent home—but we wanted to see Arthur and Francis and Attila and Dorothea again. Sarah, Felix, and Ben Franklin stayed behind to open up a toy factory in Philadelphia and keep building the American Christmas tradition until the rest of us returned.

In the spring of 1810 we sailed back to London. Arthur met us at the dock. Francis was with him, and so were Attila and Dorothea, who'd come all the way from Nuremberg to greet us. That night we had a wonderful reunion dinner at Arthur's home, and heard about the latest news in Britain.

"You might have left America just in time," Arthur suggested. "Everyone here in England believes we'll soon be at war with the colonists again."

"They're not 'colonists' anymore, Arthur," Layla said gently. "They want to be called Americans now."

"Whatever they call themselves, I think they were lucky to defeat the British," Arthur snorted. "If I didn't know better, I'd think that General Washington had some sort of special help. None of you would know anything about that, would you?" We all shook our heads and did our very best to look innocent.

But Arthur was right about another war between America and Britain. The two countries got in a fierce argument over shipping rights—whose ships could go where, carrying what—and finally war was declared in 1812. Again, it was fought in America, and mostly the British got the best of it. In May 1814, their army actually burned some of Washington; President James Madison had to run away as part of the White House went up in flames. But four months later an American named Thomas Macdonough won a terrible naval battle on Lake Champlain in New York state, and soon afterward leaders from both sides met in Belgium and signed a peace treaty. They did this on Christmas Eve, saying it was appropriate to stop fighting on Christ's birthday. There was one more battle in this war to be fought, though. News of the peace treaty didn't reach New Orleans before January 8, 1815. Thinking America was still at war, General Andrew Jackson routed his British foes. Thank goodness, this was the last battle ever between America and Britain.

We were still determined to help make Christmas a happier holiday in America, but we also wanted to enjoy a few European Christmases in countries that celebrated the season properly with traditional visits from Saint Nicholas, by whatever name and on whatever date. Leonardo and Willie Skokan happily went right back to work at the Nuremberg toy factory. Layla and I joined Arthur, Attila, and Dorothea on some of their gift-giving adventures, and went out on our own several times, particularly in Italy. How wonderful it was to be among people who held Christmas in their hearts, with carols and Christmas trees and nativity scenes and presents and, most of all, honest, grateful joy for the birth of Jesus that didn't have to be concealed for fear of someone else thinking such happiness was inappropriate.

In 1818, a few years after we'd come back to Europe, Layla asked me if the two of us might spend a special Christmas together. "I love our friends and our gift-giving, Santa," she said, using the American name for me that all of us liked best. "But just once, after all these years, I wonder if we couldn't spend one Christmas Eve quietly, just the two of us, going somewhere special and celebrating at a midnight church service just as normal people do?"

In all our years together, this was the first favor Layla had asked of me. I was more than happy to agree. When we told our friends, they all had suggestions about where we should go for our holiday.

"A second honeymoon for you!" Dorothea laughed. "How wonderful! What fun!"

"We never had a first honeymoon," Layla replied. "We were married in the afternoon, and we helped Felix give gifts that night. It's taken me thirteen centuries to get this husband of mine alone for a while!"

Attila had heard of an Austrian village named Oberndorf, just eleven miles north of the city of Salzburg.

"It's lovely country; the Salzach River runs right beside the town," he said. "Best of all, the villagers there have their midnight worship service in Saint Nicholas's Church! It's named for you!"

Obviously, Layla and I chose to spend our holiday in Oberndorf. We arrived there a few days before Christmas and arranged to stay at a comfortable inn. I hadn't ever had a vacation, and was surprised how pleasant one could be. Layla and I slept late, ate what we pleased, and took long walks along the banks of the river. It was on the last of those walks, during the morning of December 24, that we passed Saint Nicholas's Church and saw a tall man wearing a priest's robes standing outside talking with a stocky fellow. They were obviously upset, although not with each other.

"Pardon us, gentlemen," I said as Layla and I approached them. "We don't wish to interrupt, but tonight we plan to attend Christmas mass and wonder when the service will begin."

"There might not be a midnight service, or, at least, there might not be a very special one," the heavyset man mumbled. "Christmas mass without music won't seem like Christmas at all."

"We can't give up so easily, Franz," the priest said. He smiled at Layla and me and added, "I'm Father Josef Mohr, assistant priest of this church, and this is Franz Gruber, our church organist. We pride ourselves on our Christmas midnight mass, especially since our church is named for the saint who many believe is the example of true holiday spirit. People come from all over to celebrate Christmas with us, but we've just discovered our church organ is somehow not working. Franz thinks mice have been nibbling too much at the pedals, and I believe mist from the river must have damaged the pipes."

"It doesn't matter what's wrong with the organ, Father," Franz said unhappily. "It won't play and there's no time to have it repaired before tonight's service. Christmas without music just isn't Christmas, as I said before."

"Can't everyone just sing without music?" Layla asked.

"The organ music is necessary for all the traditional carols," Franz brooded. "Tonight's mass will be a disappointment to everyone. Well, I'll go back inside and work on the organ some more. Maybe Saint Nicholas himself will arrive tonight with a new organ so we can have music after all."

"Don't think badly of Franz," Father Mohr cautioned after the organist disappeared into the church. "It's just that he loves music so much, and loves Christmas so much, too. We can still have a happy service without music. We'll celebrate the birth of Jesus with songs in our hearts and not on our lips, I suppose."

Father Mohr seemed very agreeable. Layla and I invited him to eat lunch with us. Afterward, he invited us back to the church and showed us all around. There was a beautiful stained-glass window of Saint Nicholas in his old-fashioned red bishop's robes trimmed with white.

"Quite a handsome fellow," I said.

"A thin fellow, too," Layla whispered rudely. I chose dignified silence as my best response.

Because it was winter, darkness came early to Oberndorf. Although it was cold, the air felt crisp and the sky was clear. Layla, Father Mohr, and I stood outside the church looking up at the stars. In the village, families were inside their homes getting ready for dinner. Afterward, they'd walk to the church for midnight mass. Then there would be much bustling in the streets, and loudly shouted wishes to each other of "Merry Christmas." But for now, everything was blissfully silent.

"This is such a silent night," Layla mused. "And somehow it feels like a holy night, as well."

Father Mohr's brow furrowed. He pulled a stick of charcoal and a scrap of paper from his pocket and began scribbling. "Did you say this is a silent night, a holy night?" he asked Layla.

"Yes," she replied, looking puzzled.

"Come with me—hurry!" Father Mohr blurted, turning and running into the church. "Franz Gruber! Franz Gruber! Come here quickly, and bring your guitar!"

Three hours later, and just minutes before the first worshipers arrived at Saint Nicholas's Church, Father Josef Mohr and Franz Gruber had written a new Christmas carol. It began with Layla's words: "Silent night, holy night." Using simple, heartfelt rhyme, Father Mohr had continued, "All is calm. All is bright." From there, he let his song with its lovely melody and plain words tell the story of the night of Jesus' birth.

Just after midnight on December 25, 1818, the climax of mass at Saint Nicholas's Church in Oberndorf came when Father Mohr and Franz Gruber stood before the congregation. Father Mohr held a sheet of paper in his hands, with words and musical notes written on it. He held the paper in front of Franz Gruber, who strummed his guitar. Father Mohr sang tenor. Franz Gruber sang bass. As their listeners sat transfixed, they sang:

Silent night, holy night.
All is calm. All is bright.
'Round yon virgin mother and child.

As they continued to sing, many men and women in the church began to weep with joy. Tears running down their faces, they begged to hear the song again, and again. By the fourth time Father Mohr and Franz Gruber sang, the entire congregation was standing and singing with them. Standing with my wife, Layla, singing and crying at the same time like everyone else, I somehow knew, *knew,* that our voices were carrying up through the roof of the church, through the cold Christmas night air, all the way up to Heaven, where the one whose birth we were singing about was listening and smiling, pleased with the love and joy reflected in this new, incredible carol.

After the service, the villagers of Oberndorf walked quietly home, as though speaking might somehow break a special spell. There was no need for Layla and me to hurry away from the church. We knew Attila and Dorothea and their helpers had delivered presents to the children of Oberndorf and all of Austria on December 6, Saint Nicholas Day.

"Thank you," Layla said softly to Father Mohr.

"Thank you," he replied. We took turns hugging him, and then Layla and I, too, returned to the village. I looked back once and saw Father Mohr staring up at the dark Christmas sky. Abruptly, he raised his hand toward the stars, waving to the Savior he'd just celebrated in a song that would be part of Christmas forever.

We left Oberndorf the next day, feeling especially joyful, and returned to Nuremberg, where we happily rejoined our friends and continued our gift-giving work. Then one morning, five years later, Attila told me he'd received a message from Arthur, who wanted Layla and me to return to London as soon as possible.

"Has someone been hurt?" I asked worriedly. "Has there been an accident at Arthur's toy factory?"

"The message said it was nothing bad, but still a matter that required you to come right away," Attila said. Layla, Leonardo, Willie Skokan, and I left immediately, traveling as quickly as we could, which was ten times faster than ordinary mortals.

When we reached London, we hurried to the toy factory and burst into Arthur's office. "What's happened?" I asked.

Arthur raised an eyebrow; in reply, he handed me a letter in Felix's handwriting.

It said simply, "Come back to America at once. Everyone knows about you now. You're famous."

There was also a mysterious postscript: "Please bring flying reindeer. Eight, if possible."

TWENTY

Reindeer Fly, and So Do I

mong those who had read *Diedrich Knickerbocker,* Washington Irving's book that included the Dutch colonists' belief in Saint Nicholas, was Clement Moore, well known in New York as a great scholar and historian. Moore loved Irving's book, and his favorite passages were about the long-lived saint who gave Christmas presents to children.

In 1822, Moore invited several relatives to join him and his family for Christmas. Moore's favorite daughter, Charity, begged him to write a poem for the occasion, because her father often wrote verses for special family gatherings.

Now, Clement Moore was a busy man. For a while he forgot about his promise to Charity. On December 23, relatives began arriving for the Christmas celebration, and that afternoon Mrs. Moore asked her husband to go to the market and buy some food they needed for that evening's meal. It was a snowy day, and Moore made the trip in a horse-drawn sleigh. He had allowed his daughter Charity to come with him, and on their ride home she asked if he'd written his special Christmas poem yet.

"I didn't want to disappoint my little girl," Moore told us nearly ten years later, when we'd become his friends and often joined him for long evening talks. "When we got home, I went upstairs to my study and closed the door. I remembered reading *Diedrich Knickerbocker,* and took the book down from a shelf. Washington Irving is such a wonderful writer! I loved his descriptions of Saint Nicholas, especially when the saint would place his finger beside his nose and fly away."

Moore also referred to another small book, titled *The Children's Friend.* That one included a sketch of Saint Nicholas driving a sleigh pulled by reindeer.

"An idea for a poem began to form in my mind," Moore said. "All my children loved the Christmas holiday, after all, and we'd always kept the tradition of having presents for the children to open on Christmas morning. From the history I'd studied, I'd long suspected Saint Nicholas really did exist, and that he somehow was able to bring gifts to children during the holidays. So I was determined to write my poem about him, and include all the wonderful stories from the Dutch colonists. My remaining problem was describing what he looked like, for I wanted my children and family to be able to perfectly picture him in their minds as they listened to my poem."

As it happened, the Moore family employed a gardener named Jan Duyckinck. He was of Dutch descent, white-bearded and somewhat overweight. Also, Jan was a jolly fellow who always did his work cheerfully, and with a small pipe clenched between his teeth.

"When I thought of Jan, the whole poem seemed to come into my head at once," Moore concluded. "I wrote for several hours. Then, after dinner on that night of December twenty-third, 1822, I called everyone into the parlor and began to read to them."

Every line, every word, was to become famous. Moore titled his poem "A Visit from Saint Nicholas." It began:

'Twas the night before Christmas, and all through the house
Not a creature was stirring, not even a mouse.

It was a short poem, fifty-six lines in all. When Moore completed his recitation, everyone clapped and cheered. He was pleased by his family's response and thought that one reading was the last anyone would ever hear of "A Visit from Saint Nicholas."

But someone among Moore's listeners that night—he never found out who—considered the poem too good to be forgotten. This person secretly copied the poem and gave it to the editor of the *Troy Sentinel,* a newspaper in a nearby town. The editor obviously loved the poem, too, because exactly one year later, on December 23, 1823, "A Visit from Saint Nicholas" was published in the *Sentinel* and became an immediate sensation. Every copy of that day's newspaper was sold. Newspapers and magazines all over the rest of America reprinted the poem in its entirety. It seemed every American parent who read the poem immediately decided to make Saint Nicholas welcome, and all the children who heard the now-famous lines went to bed on Christmas Eve with visions of sugarplums dancing in their heads, and in hopes that Saint Nicholas soon would arrive to leave them presents.

There were two other important, immediate reactions. Felix, Sarah, and Ben Franklin, my poor helpers who had stayed behind in America, were suddenly overwhelmed by the number of homes in which they were welcome, and in which they were now expected to leave gifts on Christmas Eve. They worked frantically to satisfy as many eager children as possible. And Clement Moore, who considered himself a serious scholar, felt embarrassed by the attention being given to something he thought of as an enjoyable but still silly little poem. The *Troy Sentinel* hadn't printed the name of the poet, and for many years Moore tried to keep his identity a secret.

Felix and the others thought the sensation caused by the poem might die down after a year or so, but instead the popularity of "A Visit from Saint Nicholas" spread. Children now believed they knew all about me from that poem. By 1825, Felix felt he had no choice but to summon me back to America from Europe, and sent his urgent message to Arthur.

Layla, Leonardo, Willie Skokan, and I were able to get back quickly. The first steamship had crossed the Atlantic Ocean in 1819, and this new method of sea transportation cut sailing time between England and America in half. Felix, Sarah, and Ben met us at the dock.

"Whatever did you mean, 'Bring flying reindeer. Eight, if possible'?" I asked Felix as soon as my feet touched land.

"You'll understand soon," he assured me, and within hours we new arrivals were sitting comfortably in the house Felix and the others had built in New York, reading "A Visit from Saint Nicholas" for ourselves.

I very much enjoyed the first dozen lines or so. "This is simply wonderful!" I chortled, but Layla, who read faster, suggested I save my rapturous comments until I'd read further. And when I got to the lines describing what the father saw as he "tore open the shutters and drew up the sash," I began to choke. Everyone jumped up to pound me on the back.

"I can't believe this," I bellowed. "Reindeer pulling my sleigh through the sky? Eight reindeer? Reindeer with names, for goodness sakes! Why, this fellow has me landing on a roof!"

Most of the rest of the poem was acceptable, even pleasing—the part about filling the stockings was my favorite—but I didn't feel I could overlook Moore's rude comments about my weight.

"He says I've got a little round belly," I complained.

"Well, actually, you've got rather a big round belly," Willie Skokan observed, meaning, I suppose, to be helpful. Everyone enjoyed a good laugh at my expense before Felix added carefully, "You might also note the forty-sixth line."

I reread it and gasped with horror. "Why, I'm not an elf! I'm a full-grown man, and don't you say what I know you're thinking, Layla!" My wife had opened her mouth to make a sarcastic remark, but now she closed it again. "This poem is going to cause us problems, my friends. Now, I'm glad it was written, and gladder still it's become beloved and made Americans want us to be part of their Christmas holiday. But it's always been our rule to become whatever children of each country expect us to be, and in this case it may be impossible. I'm not an elf, for one thing, and can't become one to satisfy the expectations created by this poem."

"I really don't think the children will care if you're an elf or not," Layla commented. "That can be like the myth of you coming down chimneys, part of the illusion but not really vital to the real mission, which is delivering the toys. It's the flying-reindeer issue that we have to deal with."

"We actually have gone down a few chimneys if the chimneys were wide enough and if there was no other easy way to get into a house," Felix noted. "The problem here in America, as I see it, is that countless children will be peering out windows every Christmas Eve, hoping for a glimpse of Saint Nicholas and his sleigh flying through the night sky."

"Let me just correct you by noting many American children, perhaps the majority of them, use the name 'Santa Claus' instead of 'Saint Nicholas,'" Sarah interrupted. "On my last trip along the coast I learned this. I wish Clement Moore had chosen to write 'A Visit from Santa Claus' to avoid future confusion, but I assume he was trying to remain faithful to the Dutch traditions, and—"

"I don't mean to be rude, but can we please concentrate on the flying reindeer?" I asked impatiently. "Everything else can be worked out, but we have a simple problem that can't be ignored. Reindeer cannot fly."

"I think they can," Leonardo said in a soft but assured voice. "That is, I think they can under the correct circumstances and with the proper equipment."

Leonardo, Ben, and Willie Skokan were sitting together by the front of the fireplace, and I saw that they had one of Leonardo's notebooks in front of them. As usual, its pages were full of diagrams and mathematical formulas.

"I don't think reindeer can sprout wings, Leonardo," I said as patiently as possible. "Do you know of a herd that has?"

Leonardo was a very serious person. I don't think he realized I was being sarcastic. "No, Santa, but wings on the reindeer themselves might not be necessary for flight. I've been pondering the possibility of flight for the better part of three centuries now, and I'm convinced that flying is a matter of speed and air mass. Look at these sketches in my notebook." He handed me the notebook, but I hadn't the slightest idea of what the diagrams I was looking at might mean.

Before I could say anything more that might have hurt Leonardo's feelings, Ben interjected, "Willie Skokan and I are convinced there must be a way reindeer can fly, too. Of course, it's not really a matter of the reindeer flying so much as it's a question of how to put them in a position where they can be attached to the right device that would allow flight."

"Can you say it more simply?" I asked wearily.

"Let us get some reindeer and start working," Ben said. "Leonardo and Willie Skokan and I will find a way reindeer can fly, if only you'll be patient."

"Santa will be patient, Ben, but I wouldn't count on American children doing the same," Layla advised. "Please find some brilliant solution as quickly as you can."

And so Leonardo, Ben, and Willie Skokan set to work. They sailed back across the Atlantic Ocean to Europe, then went north to the remote Scandinavian snows of Lapland. This was where reindeer roamed, handsome animals standing three and one half feet high and weighing about three hundred pounds. Both male and female reindeer have wide, heavy antlers, and heavy hoofs. Fortunately, they can be tamed, though not easily. Some Laplanders used them to pull sleds. My three helpers could have purchased reindeer from Lapland farmers, but they preferred venturing out onto the frozen tundra and capturing their own.

"We wanted only the very best," Ben explained when they finally returned to America after a hard trip home. It had taken them nearly ten months to round up eight reindeer Leonardo considered suitable: great, powerful animals whose eyes shone with intelligence. In anticipation of their arrival, we had purchased property in the far hill country of New York state, near a village called Cooperstown. This property was far enough removed from public gaze that we felt it might be possible for Leonardo to conduct his flying-reindeer experiments in relative privacy.

The reindeer were installed inside a snug barn. The rest of us were given boring daily chores to perform—buying grain for their feed bags, raking out stalls—while Leonardo, Ben, and Willie Skokan would put halters on the reindeer and lead them off into the hills for training they wouldn't describe to the rest of us. Helpers and reindeer never got back until well after dark each night. Sometimes Ben and Willie would be smiling. More often, they'd look tired and frustrated. Leonardo's expression never changed. He always looked thoughtful.

Christmas of 1826 passed, then Christmas of 1827. We gave gifts as best we could, and children all over America peeked out their windows on Christmas Eve, watching in vain for Santa flying by with his reindeer.

"I don't think Leonardo can do it," Felix said sadly as Christmas 1828 approached. "We have to face it: As great as our magic has been, some miracles are beyond us, and flying reindeer happen to be one of them."

"I still have faith in Leonardo," Layla replied.

It was just the next night when the three would-be reindeer trainers came trooping into the house with huge grins on their faces. Even Leonardo looked pleased.

"We need Felix to come with us tomorrow," Ben announced. "He's not as good a carpenter as Willie Skokan, but we'll need his help, if only to carry wood and tools."

"I can come help, too," I said quickly, but Ben shook his head.

"Just Felix, I think," he commanded. "We want you to be surprised."

Felix left with the other three in the morning, and looked tired when he returned with them after dark. His hands were scratched from hard labor. When I asked what kind of work he'd been doing, he shook his head and wouldn't tell me.

"I promised I'd keep the secret," he muttered, and fell asleep in front of the fire soon after supper.

Felix began working with Leonardo, Ben, and Willie Skokan in early October. By mid-November, my curiosity was too great to control.

"Tell me what's going on!" I demanded one night as we all sat around the dinner table. "I can tell by your smiles that even Layla and Sarah are in on the secret. I'm the only one who doesn't know. Tell me now, quickly—will there be flying reindeer this Christmas?"

"Wait and see, Santa," Ben advised.

"I've waited long enough," I grumbled, and everyone else laughed.

One morning three weeks later, I was awakened at dawn by Layla. "Put on your warmest clothing," she ordered. "We're all going out with the reindeer." I quickly dressed and waited impatiently while the others ate breakfast. When they finally finished, we put halters on the reindeer and hiked some two miles to the top of the highest hill on the property, where a large, mysterious object was concealed under an equally huge sheet of canvas.

"Are you ready?" Ben asked me, grinning fiendishly as Willie Skokan and Leonardo took hold of the canvas. "Are you prepared to discover whether reindeer really know how to fly?"

"Enough of this foolishness," I snapped. "I see the reindeer standing right here, and they're no different than they were when you first brought them to America. They surely can't fly, Ben. They have no wings!"

"But they will, and besides, this does, too!" Ben announced, and with a theatrical flourish of his hand gestured for Leonardo and Willie Skokan to reveal what was under the canvas.

I saw a sleigh, but a sleigh unlike any that could ever have existed before. It had the usual wide bed, and a long front pole to which harness could be attached. And extending from the sides of the sleigh, not very far but still sticking out, were what appeared to be curved, shaped wings.

"What does all this mean?" I asked.

Leonardo hurried to my side, brandishing one of his notebooks and pointing to a sketch on one page. "You see, Santa, it's not really the reindeer themselves who fly," he explained. "The reindeer provide the thrust, the power, if you will, to make the wind flow under the wings of the sleigh and also under the smaller wings we've attached to each reindeer's harness. This wind mass under the wings lifts up the reindeer and the sleigh."

"I have no idea what you're talking about," I replied honestly. "Can you or someone else please use words I can understand?"

Ben said, "In the simplest terms, Santa, if the reindeer can pull the sleigh fast enough, it will fly. And these reindeer can do just that. Back in Lapland, we selected the eight fastest reindeer. When they're hitched to the sleigh and begin to run, the wings on the sleigh and the harness cut through the air. Enough air gets under the wings to lift the sleigh and the reindeer, too."

Eager to tell me more, Leonardo added, "We've factored in the weight of a load of toys, and also the weight of a driver, who is meant to be you, Santa. I didn't know how much you weighed, but Layla said she could guess, so I took her word for it."

I swung my gaze over to my wife. "And how much did you say I weighed?"

Layla smiled. "Don't ask. Why not just thank Leonardo for his brilliance, and everyone else for their hard work?"

So I offered my thanks, and suggested we might as well take the sleigh and the reindeer back to the house.

"Wait, Santa," Felix said. "Don't you want to see the reindeer pull the sleigh and fly through the sky?"

"I'm sure you've tested the whole process thoroughly," I answered. "Good for you. Well, let's go home."

"Wait, Santa," Layla said in a tone that made it clear she expected me to do as I was told. "All this work has been done so you can fly this sleigh on Christmas Eve, just a month from now. You must climb aboard the sleigh. Look, Willie Skokan is loading toys on it so the weight will be exactly right. Try it for yourself."

Before I could protest, Ben took one of my arms, Felix took the other, and they propelled me toward the sleigh and onto its seat. There was a belt attached to the seat, and this was secured around my midsection—"So you won't fall off," Felix said alarmingly. Leonardo hitched up the reindeer and handed me the reins.

"They've been very well trained," he assured me. "We have a signal that tells them to start running. It involves their names."

"What names?" I spluttered.

"Why, the names given to them in Clement Moore's poem," Leonardo said innocently. "I assumed you wanted to keep everything as close to that story as possible, so American children won't be disappointed. I'll whisper the command now, so they won't hear me and start too soon. Simply shout out, 'Now, Dasher, now, Dancer, now, Prancer and Vixen; on, Comet, on Cupid, on, Donder and Blitzen!' Then they'll run and the sleigh will take off."

Everyone but Felix backed away, waiting for me to give the reindeer their signal. Even the reindeer themselves seemed pleased at the prospect, as all eight looked back at me with expectant eyes. The small wings on each reindeer's harness seemed to flutter with anticipation. I sat still and didn't make a sound.

Felix leaned over and whispered to me. "What's wrong?"

I whispered back, "I can't remember the whole signal."

"That's all right. Just in case, we've also trained them to run when the driver shouts, 'Go!'" Felix assured me.

I still didn't move.

"What's the matter now?"

Felix inquired softly.

I told him the truth: "I'm afraid of heights."

"Well, time to get over it," Felix muttered unsympathetically. He stepped back and, to my absolute horror, shouted, "Go!"

The reindeer responded instantly. My arms were nearly tugged from their sockets as the reins tightened and the eight-animal team surged forward. They ran madly over the snow, the sleigh bumping along the ground behind them. For twenty yards, I bumped along, then fifty, and I started thinking Leonardo had been wrong, and then the wind began to whistle and the sleigh took a sudden lurch. I looked in front of the sleigh at the reindeer, and then down, and the ground was well below me. Layla, looking no larger than an ant, was waving. I suspected she was also laughing.

TWENTY-ONE

A Christmas Carol

fter I learned to drive a team of flying reindeer properly—and it took me a few years, too, with some very embarrassing accidents I choose not to describe here—I made it a point every Christmas Eve to make my last American stop for the night at Clement Moore's house. The first time I landed on his lawn—not on the roof, because roofs as a rule are too steep to make good landing areas for reindeer—I saw him peeking through his bedroom window curtain. Smiling in spite of myself, I motioned for him to meet me inside.

We ended up chatting for almost an hour, sitting comfortably in his parlor beside a huge Christmas tree, and had such a pleasant time we decided to make a tradition of it. Poor Clement apologized profusely when I told him what great trouble his description of flying reindeer had caused me, but I assured him things had turned out well. In fact, I had even overcome my fear of heights and quite enjoyed soaring through the skies with Dasher and Dancer and the rest of my four-legged friends.

On Christmas Eve 1842, Clement had a surprise for me. I landed on his lawn as usual, tired from my long night's work and looking forward to the delicious chocolate chip cookies Mrs. Moore always baked fresh that afternoon for me. Clement welcomed me inside and, before I could ask for my cookies, said he wanted me to shake hands with someone.

"Don't worry, Santa, I haven't given away your secrets to a stranger," he laughed. "I think you already know this gentleman." We went into the parlor and there, sitting beside the warm fire, was none other than Washington Irving.

"It's wonderful to see you again," I told him by way of greeting. "Your *Diedrich Knickerbocker* made me welcome in America after all, with its influence on Clement's 'A Visit from Saint Nicholas.'"

"Actually, most people have begun to call that poem 'Twas the Night Before Christmas' after its first line," Irving corrected. "The original title is well on its way to being forgotten. Still, I'm proud that my book was Clement's inspiration."

Clement bustled about getting us all hot cocoa to drink. As he did, I told Irving, "Congratulations, of course, on all your success as an author. You certainly accomplished your goal of becoming world famous and widely read. What was the name of that one book, the collection of short stories, and the title of that popular story in particular?"

"I think you mean *The Sketch Book of Geoffrey Crayon*," Irving laughed. "You might remember I was living in England when I wrote that one. And the story in it to which I'm sure you refer is 'The Legend of Sleepy Hollow.' I have to admit I'm surprised it was so popular, what with its references to a headless horseman and so forth. Perhaps it will become closely associated with that so-called holiday of Halloween, the way Clement's poem is eternally linked with Christmas."

The three of us chatted until almost dawn, when I rose to take my leave before Clement's countless children and grandchildren spilled down the stairs to see what presents Santa might have left for them. As I gathered up the handful of sugar lumps Clement always gave me as a parting present for the reindeer, Irving asked me, "Now that you've conquered America, so to speak, what do you want to do next?"

"It continues to trouble me that Christmas is still so poorly celebrated in England," I replied. "My friends, I tell you that once upon a time there was no country that enjoyed happier Christmas holidays. Oliver Cromwell and his henchmen ruined that, and I won't be completely at peace with myself until British Christmases return to their old, joyous heights."

Irving looked thoughtful for a moment, then said, "I received a letter not long ago from an English writer whose work I admire. In it, he said how much he'd enjoyed a short story of mine about a mythical Christmas celebration at the home of a fictional English squire, and how he was determined to restore the tradition of wonderful Christmas holidays in his country. His name is Charles Dickens. He might be of help to you, and you could be of help to him."

Within a month, I'd written to Dickens asking to visit him in London, identifying myself only as someone who shared both his enthusiasm for the Christmas holiday and his desire to again make it a special part of British life. In October, having received a warm and enthusiastic invitation to Dickens's home, Layla and I sailed back to England. We had a happy reunion with Arthur when we docked, and the next morning I strolled across London to meet with Charles Dickens.

Please understand that, except on my holiday gift-giving excursion, whenever I was out in public I wore ordinary clothing so as not to draw attention to myself. My full white beard and somewhat stout stature never seemed to remind anyone I passed of Santa Claus. But the moment Dickens opened his front door and saw me standing on the step, he immediately said, "You're Father Christmas!" Remember, this was the name by which I'd once been widely known in England, and what I was still called by the remaining English children who were allowed to believe in me and expect my Christmas visits.

"Not so loud!" I cautioned. "May I please come in?"

"Of course!" Dickens boomed, and ushered me into a very nice home. "My study is just to the left. Please make yourself comfortable sitting on this chair, not that other, which has seat-spring cushions which sometimes cause discomfort.

"Well, Father Christmas is here in my own home! I knew you really existed, I just knew it! There's been too much joy surrounding the holidays, too much happiness for there not to have been someone special involved for countless centuries! You really must tell me all about it!"

I did, and Dickens sat listening for hours. Sometimes he'd interrupt with questions, but mostly he nodded. The poor man actually had tears in his eyes as I described the wonders of English Christmases past. When I finally finished with the tale of how Washington Irving had suggested I come to London, Dickens pulled his handkerchief out of his pocket and blew his nose in a series of loud honks.

"Father Christmas, please help me find a way to restore proper Christmases to England," he pleaded. "Although I've tried, I'm afraid my own poor talents aren't equal to the task."

"How have you tried?" I wondered.

Dickens frowned, an expression I later learned was usual for him. The man truly had an odd face, pinched around the eyes and dominated by one of the largest noses I'd ever seen. Even Dickens's hair was strange, very thin on top and thick and curly around his ears.

"As you know, I'm a writer," he explained. "By most standards, I'm a rather successful one, too. Some of my novels have sold very well, particularly *Oliver Twist*, *Nicholas Nickleby*, and *The Pickwick Papers*. But the public likes my books better than it does the other causes I promote, namely better working conditions in the factories and better treatment of the poor. These are hard times for the less fortunate, Father Christmas, and that's a fact. This is why I think it's so important for Christmas to become glorious again, so everyone, young and old, rich and poor alike, can have at least one day of the year where problems and differences are put aside and everyone can celebrate together."

It was an impressive speech; Dickens was out of breath at the end of it. I sat thinking for a few moments, then said, "Have you tried writing stories about Christmas? The right book or poem can work Christmas wonders; in America, Washington Irving's novel and Clement Moore's poem have done that."

Dickens ducked his head, looking ashamed. "I've tried, Father Christmas. Some years ago I published 'A Christmas Dinner,' a short story about how a family sitting down for their holiday meal is able to forgive past arguments and insults."

"A lovely theme," I commented.

"Perhaps, but the story was ignored," Dickens said ruefully. "I then attempted to stir up interest in Christmas by including a holiday tale in *The Pickwick Papers*. I called this story 'The Goblins Who Stole a Sexton,' and in it a cold, unfriendly man who hates the Christmas happiness of others is taken one night by ghostly beings on adventures which teach him how wonderful Christmas is, after all. Well, *The Pickwick Papers* was widely commented upon, but no one reading it seemed to understand the special Christmas message I meant to convey."

"That certainly is too bad," I said with great sympathy. "You are obviously someone who truly holds Christmas in his heart, and long ago I learned to put my trust in fate. Since we've been brought together, I believe it's meant for us to work on behalf of the holiday. However, I notice it's getting late, and by the toys scattered about your home I perceive you must be a married man with children."

Dickens nodded. "My children are truly the joy of my life, Father Christmas. My wife has taken them today to visit with her parents, and I expect them home momentarily."

"It's best I leave, then," I said, standing up and stretching. "Be careful not to tell your family about my visit or the things I've told you. I always prefer as few people as possible knowing such secrets. Could you, perhaps, lend me copies of your Christmas stories? I'll read them tonight and tomorrow you might call on me, my wife, and our friend Arthur at his toy factory. We can talk more there."

Walking back to Arthur's in the early evening darkness, enjoying the coolness of the crisp late autumn air, I felt pleased to have met Dickens and wondered how to help him. Arthur, Layla, and I sat up most of the night reading his stories, which were truly excellent. We exclaimed over especially well-written scenes and agreed that such a talented writer as Charles Dickens surely could create a story so wonderful, so moving, that everyone reading it would pledge to celebrate Christmas properly forever afterward.

"Do you suppose we should pay to have these stories printed again and distributed all over England?" Arthur asked.

Layla shook her head. "For whatever reason, they have not accomplished their purpose despite being written so well," she reminded him. "My suggestion would be for Mr. Dickens to try again with a new story."

The next morning, Dickens arrived at Arthur's toy factory promptly at nine. We offered him tea and pastries, then took him on a brief tour of the premises. He was thrilled with the craftsmanship, but positively overwhelmed to find himself in the presence of the man he kept referring to as "King Arthur."

"Just yesterday, you didn't seem surprised to meet Father Christmas," I said jokingly. "Now, you're almost hopping up and down in your excitement at meeting my old friend and helper. Why, my feelings might be hurt!"

"It's just that I always thought you existed, but never suspected King Arthur did," Dickens babbled.

Arthur was red-faced with embarrassment. "Please calm yourself, Mr. Dickens," he suggested. "When time permits, I'll be glad to tell you about my real experiences, if you like, not those grand, made-up adventures you've apparently heard and believed. For now, I think we all should listen to Santa—Father Christmas—because he has an idea for you."

"I enjoyed reading your Christmas stories last night, and truly believe you are one of the finest writers ever to live on this Earth," I began, and it was Dickens's turn to blush. "I found 'The Goblins Who Stole a Sexton' to be especially good, but I think most readers would find it less a tale about Christmas than a ghost story that accidentally took place on December twenty-fifth. Why not take the best parts of that story—the mean-tempered man who hated the Christmas joy of others, and his nighttime visitors who changed his ways—and build a whole new book around them, making certain this time that every reader would realize the author is delivering a message about Christmas, and how everyone should celebrate it!"

Dickens smiled and replied, "Why, that's exactly what I'll do! It will be a few months before I begin, of course. Right now, I'm writing a novel called *Martin Chuzzlewit* and I must finish that book first."

Arthur said quickly, "Mr. Dickens, in ten weeks it will be December twenty-fifth. You'll find that, when working with Father Christmas, people can accomplish things in a tenth of the time normal jobs take to be done. If you mean what you say about loving Christmas and wanting to restore it again in England, I suggest you drop everything else and begin writing the story Father Christmas has suggested."

Arthur's voice had a tone of great authority; Dickens was visibly impressed. "I'll do exactly as you say, King Arthur."

I added, "Mr. Dickens, I don't know your normal method of writing. I believe, though, if you close yourself in your study with a good supply of paper, ink, and quill pens, you'll find you have all the inspiration, energy, and time you need."

Dickens hurried away. We waited, not wanting to contact him for fear of disturbing his writing. Then, late one night during the second week of November, there was a knock on Arthur's door. Charles Dickens came in clutching a cloth sack.

"I've brought you the manuscript of my new book," he said nervously. "I have no idea whether it's good or not. Every day as I sat at my desk it seemed as though an invisible hand gripped mine and made my pen write unexpected words at terrifying speed. If you would, please read this book, and when you've finished come call on me at my home and tell me what you think. Its title is *A Christmas Carol*."

So that night Arthur, Layla, and I read all about Ebenezer Scrooge and the ghosts who came to visit him. We spent hours laughing and crying and finally rejoicing when the old man repented his meanness and promised to forever "keep Christmas in his heart."

The next morning we hurried to Dickens's house. Although it was early, his wife and children were already gone. Dickens asked us to come inside, offered us refreshments, then blurted, "Is my story all right?"

"Is it all right?" Arthur asked incredulously. "Mr. Dickens, you have written the finest story of Christmas that will ever be printed on a page! Bless you, sir, and may you feel great satisfaction for a job well done!"

I echoed Arthur's sentiments, but Layla hesitated.

"I agree *A Christmas Carol* is wonderful, Mr. Dickens," she observed, "and I hope I might mention one small concern without seeming unappreciative of your effort."

"Newspaper critics have said many harsh things about my work," Dickens chuckled. "Please, say whatever you like."

"This concerns the crippled son of Scrooge's employee Bob Cratchit," my wife explained. "He's a wonderful boy as you describe him, and I'm so glad he doesn't die as Scrooge once foresaw, but I just don't think you've given him an appropriate name."

"You mean Little Fred?" Dickens asked. "I chose that name because it's so common. Everyone who reads *A Christmas Carol* will know someone named Fred."

"That's just the problem," Layla said. "Your story is wonderfully uncommon, and so are the names of the rest of your characters—'Ebenezer Scrooge,' 'Jacob Marley.' The very names of the ghosts of Christmas Past, Present, and Future will help readers picture them in their minds. But 'Little Fred' lacks any flair, and I'm afraid his character will be overlooked as a result."

"My wife never offers criticism without a solution, as well," I told Dickens. "Layla, do you perhaps have another name to suggest?"

"The child should have a name that springs from the tongue," she replied. "I've always loved the sound of the letter 'T,' and I wonder if you might consider renaming your character 'Tiny Tim'?"

"It's perfect!" Dickens barked, and snatching his manuscript from Arthur's hand, he took a quill pen and made the necessary corrections immediately.

Everything went rapidly after that. To help keep down the price of the book and make it affordable to even the poorest readers, we provided Charles Dickens with money to pay some of the cost of having *A Christmas Carol* printed. It was published shortly before Christmas in that year of 1843 and was an instant sensation. Christmas 1844 found all of England ready to celebrate the holiday again with open joy and merry festivities. Father Christmas was once again welcome in almost every English home, and it was a special thrill for me to deliver those presents.

We'd hoped Charles Dickens would eventually join us forever, but this was not to be. He had other books to write and, only a year after *A Christmas Carol* was published, tried his luck with another holiday tale, *The Chimes*. Dickens told friends that this new work "knocked the *Carol* out of the field," but of course this didn't happen. Charles Dickens went on to write several great books, *David Copperfield* being perhaps the best, but he had already outdone any writers of the past or future in creating the finest Christmas fiction possible. Certainly for the rest of his life Charles Dickens was identified with Christmas, and this was only right.

Layla and I stayed with Arthur for several more years, enjoying the pleasant task of gift-giving in a country where we'd too long been unwelcome. Just as I was beginning to think of myself as Father Christmas instead of Santa, the urge came upon us to return to America. Felix, Leonardo, Sarah, Willie Skokan, and Ben Franklin undoubtedly had things under control there, but that exciting new nation was certain to suffer the inevitable pains of political and social growth. We wanted to be there, and took a steamship back across the Atlantic.

TWENTY-TWO

"Yes, Virginia,
There Is a Santa Claus"

elcome back!" Felix called out as Layla and I stepped off the ramp of the steamship and onto the dock in New York harbor in the spring of 1860. "The reindeer missed you. The rest of us did, too, of course."

We had to take a series of trains from New York to Cooperstown. Willie Skokan was waiting there at the station with a horse-drawn carriage. After we'd loaded our luggage and climbed aboard, it was still another hour-long drive to our farmhouse. Ben Franklin, Leonardo, and Sarah greeted us there, along with someone we'd never met. Layla and I were struck by his dark, intelligent eyes and the bright cloth turban wound around his head.

"This is Sequoyah, a Cherokee who invented an alphabet so his people could have a written language as well as a spoken one," Ben explained.

Sequoyah smiled and shook our hands. "I see you're staring at my scarf," he said politely to Layla. "Not all Indians wear feathers and head-dresses, you know. This cloth keeps my head protected from the sun when it's hot, and from the dampness when it's raining."

"It's a very attractive scarf," Layla said politely. "I didn't mean to stare; I haven't met many Indians before."

"Except for the color of our skin, we're the same as you," Sequoyah replied. "Sadly, many people don't understand that."

"Sequoyah can't even go to town since many people there insult him because he's an Indian," Sarah said sharply. "It's disgraceful. Felix and I first met him in Washington, D.C., where he was representing his tribe in 1829, when the government decided to force the Cherokee to move from their homes in North Carolina to Oklahoma."

"I didn't do a very good job of representing," Sequoyah admitted. "We were forced to move anyway. Many of us died on the way. The Cherokee now call that journey 'The Trail of Tears.'"

"We've always made a point of giving gifts to the Cherokee children on that Oklahoma reservation ever since," Sarah continued. "After you left for England, we were able to convince Sequoyah to come and join us, so his talents can be useful forever."

"Soon I hope to translate Mr. Dickens's wonderful story *A Christmas Carol* into the Cherokee alphabet," Sequoyah said. "The children in our tribe will love it."

"Isn't it a terrible thing that this intelligent, gifted man can't even walk into a store in our village and be treated like everyone else?" Sarah asked indignantly.

"There's more trouble coming about skin color, and soon," Willie Skokan said solemnly, and we all were surprised because Willie seldom said much, preferring to listen to the rest of us. "The coming war's all about the slaves. It will be terrible."

Willie wouldn't say any more, so Felix offered details. "Santa, Layla, so much has happened since you've been gone. Abraham Lincoln's just been elected president. All of the Southern states are going to try and leave the Union because their citizens believe slavery won't be allowed anymore. President Lincoln won't let the states leave—*secede* is the word being used—so everyone expects there will be a civil war, with the Northern states fighting the Southern ones. Slavery is the worst thing in the history of the world," he concluded, sounding bitter.

I wondered for a moment at the anger and pain in his voice, then remembered Felix had once been a slave himself.

The United States had been steadily expanding to the west, Felix explained. Where the original thirteen colonies had mostly hugged the Atlantic coast and extended partially inland, now American explorers and settlers were swarming all the way to the far Pacific Ocean.

"In 1847, only twenty thousand people lived in the region called California," Felix said. "In 1848, gold was discovered there. By 1852, two hundred fifty-five thousand people had settled in California."

"Our gift-giving will have to cover a lot more territory," I said thoughtfully.

"We'll have plenty of time to plan," Felix predicted glumly. "This so-called civil war has got to come soon, and I expect it to last for a long while. Since war reduces our special powers, many American children will wait in vain for Santa until the fighting is finally over."

Felix was right. The Civil War broke out in April 1861 and lasted until 1865. All wars are terrible, but this one was worse than most. Families argued over the issue of slavery, and sometimes brothers fought on opposing sides. Battles raged across the country. As far as gift-giving was concerned, we had to content ourselves with delivering presents to those areas where armies weren't lurking.

But even while my friends and I were so limited, the story of Santa Claus became more widespread. Soldiers in both armies dressed up like me on Christmas Day to hand out presents to their comrades. Books, magazines, and newspapers contained stories about me, made-up stories where I did amazing things. Often these stories were accompanied by pictures, and no two pictures were alike. Some artists drew me rail-thin, others roly-poly. Sometimes I had a long white beard and other times just a mustache and goatee. The reindeer and sleigh made popular by Clement Moore's poem were always shown, though.

And the renewed holiday spirit in England caused by *A Christmas Carol* continued to flourish. In 1862, a British company even printed and sold something called "Christmas cards," cards wishing people "A Happy Christmas" or "A blessed New Year."

It took another dozen years for the idea to catch on in America, but once it did every family seemed to send Christmas cards to friends and loved ones. It was a fine new tradition.

Arthur, Francis, Attila, and Dorothea pleaded with the rest of us to leave America and return to Europe, but there were always wars there, too. The eight of us in the United States were determined to bide our time until the Civil War was finally over. But when it was, in 1865, bad feelings remained between the North and South. President Lincoln, who might have been able to help both sides work out their problems, was assassinated less than a week after Confederate General Robert E. Lee surrendered to Union General Ulysses S. Grant. The next few years were difficult for everyone.

We did our best to help heal the country, hoping to remind everyone that Christmas is the season of forgiveness and love by bringing our gifts to as many children as possible every Christmas Eve. My team of reindeer whirled me all over the night skies, and the rest of the group fanned out across the country to deliver their loads of toys by less spectacular means. Still, we found we couldn't cover all the necessary territory if we kept our only base in upstate New York. Fortunately, in 1869 the first railroad tracks were completed that linked the American East and West. In 1872, Yellowstone became the first American national park, a lovely area of wild, natural beauty. Its trees, lakes, mountains, and wild animals were protected by the government. Quietly, Sarah, Sequoyah, and Willie Skokan established another base for us there.

Great strides were made in science. Alexander Graham Bell invented the telephone in 1876. Three years later, Thomas Edison perfected the first electric lamp. Seventeen years after that, Henry Ford built his first automobile.

America was becoming a modern country. But as people learned more about science, they somehow began to doubt things that couldn't be explained with formulas and blueprints. They lost the ability to know the difference between illusion and magic.

"This is getting ridiculous," Ben Franklin announced one day in the autumn of 1896. "Adults all over this country are deciding there can't really be a Santa Claus because he wasn't created by a scientist. Why, Leonardo da

Vinci, the greatest scientist of all time, is the one who made it possible for reindeer to fly! For two cents I'd grab all the grown-ups in America and make them take a long ride in your sleigh!"

"They wouldn't all fit," Leonardo said helpfully. He didn't understand sarcasm; many scientists don't. "If you really want to have all of them flying with the reindeer at once, I'll have to build a much larger sleigh, and carve bigger wings for the sleigh and the reindeer."

Layla looked up from a book she was reading and said, "At least most newspapers and magazines aren't against us, Ben. Why, many of them publish lovely stories about Santa, and Thomas Nast at the *Harper's Weekly* draws those wonderful Santa cartoons."

"I don't think they're wonderful," I grumbled. "He makes me look too fat, and he draws me the size of an elf instead of a man."

"Blame Clement Moore for that," Layla reminded me. "He called you an elf in his poem."

"That's no excuse," I replied, irritated at the thought. Not only were Nast's cartoons unflattering about my height and weight, they had proven so popular with readers that, all across America, anyone familiar with them assumed this was exactly the way I looked. Worse, except for the height, Layla and the others kept insisting that was the way I *did* look.

"Let's get back to the adults who no longer believe," Felix urged. "Many of these adults are fathers and mothers. When they have doubts about Santa, those doubts are often shared with their children. And that, my friends, is a disgrace! To think that some children no longer believe in Santa Claus! Something has to be done!"

We tried to calm Ben and Felix down, reminding them that many grown-ups, far from disbelieving, were doing their best to contribute to universal holiday good spirits.

"Remember Ralph E. Morris of the New England Telephone Company?" Layla asked. "He's the one who looked at those strings of electric lights on telephone switchboards and suggested they be hung on Christmas trees. Those make such a nice display! And there's that police commissioner in New York City—what was his name?"

"Theodore Roosevelt," Leonardo said, looking up for a moment from a diagram he was drawing in a notebook. I glanced at the diagram, which was of a giant sleigh. Apparently Leonardo was getting ready just in case we did decide to take all the adults in America on a ride through the sky with our reindeer.

"Yes, Commissioner Roosevelt," Layla continued. "During the Christmas season he likes to go out in the city streets and lead carolers in singing that new song, 'One Horse Open Sleigh,' that many prefer to call 'Jingle Bells.' And, of course, there's Thomas Nast."

"Nast's cartoons are ridiculous," Felix snapped.

"Because they make me look short and fat?" I asked hopefully.

"No, because the man draws us living at the North Pole!" Felix replied. "Isn't that the most foolish thing? Nobody's even been able to reach the North Pole. Robert Peary's tried and failed. I think Nast and all the doubting adults ought to be sent there. A little snow and ice might do them good. No one could live at the North Pole!"

"Oh, I think I could," Leonardo said quickly. "In fact, I have a diagram here that shows how—"

"Later, please, Leonardo," Felix interrupted. "Santa, what can we do to make everyone believe in you again?"

"I don't think we can do anything, Felix," I answered softly. "I can't go out and fly my sleigh in front of every doubting grown-up and child in America. Even with our powers, there's just not enough time. If it's meant for these disbelievers to start believing again, someone else will have to make them do it for us."

Just a year later, someone did. Two someones, really.

The first someone was an eight-year-old girl named Virginia O'Hanlon, who lived in New York with her parents. Virginia's father considered himself a man of science. He was a doctor who sometimes advised Commissioner Theodore Roosevelt and the rest of the New York City Police Department. Dr. O'Hanlon decided there wasn't any Santa Claus, although I had personally come to his house on several Christmas Eves to leave presents in Virginia's stocking. Perhaps Dr. O'Hanlon didn't talk much to Mrs. O'Hanlon, and thought she left the gifts for their daughter. In any event, some of Virginia's friends at school wondered out loud if there really was a

Santa Claus, and when she got home that afternoon she asked her father whether or not I was real.

Dr. O'Hanlon wasn't an evil man, just a skeptical one. Although he no longer believed in me, he didn't want to make Virginia sad. So he suggested she write a letter to the "Question and Answer" section editor of the *New York Sun* newspaper asking him if I existed. I don't think he ever expected Virginia to write that letter, but she did.

Virginia's letter read:

> *Dear Editor:*
>
> *I am eight years old, and some of my little friends say there is no Santa Claus. Papa says, "If you see it in the Sun, it's so." Please tell me the truth, is there a Santa Claus?"*
>
> *Virginia O'Hanlon*

Now, the "Question and Answer" editor of the *New York Sun* was a man named Francis Church. Mr. Church had once been a famous reporter, but now he had what the newspaper considered an unimportant job. Sometimes Mr. Church answered questions in ways that made readers of the *Sun* very angry. It's possible he didn't like his job very much at all.

But Francis Church did love Christmas, and he did believe in me. Maybe it was the marbles I'd left for him one Christmas Eve when he was a boy. In any event, on September 21, 1897, Mr. Church printed Virginia's letter and his answer to it right on the editorial page of his newspaper, where untold thousands of people read them.

Mr. Church's reply was so perfect I found myself wondering if Felix and Ben Franklin might have written it for him. It began:

> *Virginia, your little friends are wrong. They have been affected by the skepticism of a skeptical age. They do not believe, except they see . . .*
>
> *Yes, Virginia, there is a Santa Claus. He exists as certainly as love and generosity and devotion exist, and you know how they abound and give to your life its highest beauty and joy. Alas! How dreary would the world be if there were no Santa Claus. . . . You might get your papa to*

hire men to watch all the chimneys on Christmas Eve to catch Santa Claus, but even if you did not see Santa Claus coming down, what would that prove? Nobody sees Santa Claus, but that is no sign that there is no Santa Claus. The most real things in the world are those that neither children nor men can see . . .

No Santa Claus? Thank God, he lives and lives forever. A thousand years from now, Virginia, nay, ten times ten thousand years from now, he will continue to make glad the heart of childhood.

I don't know if Virginia cried when she read Mr. Church's answer to her letter, but I certainly did. I cried with joy, because I knew anyone reading those beautiful words would believe in me again and never stop believing in me anymore. The editors at the *Sun* must have thought so, too, because they reprinted Virginia's letter and Mr. Church's reply every Christmas season for the next fifty-two years, until the paper was finally closed down.

Virginia herself became a teacher, and a very good one, who always told her students they should believe in me. After teaching in public schools for a while, she taught in a school for children who were very, very sick. Virginia's special pupils there were always visited by me or my helpers on Christmas Eve.

Of course, I'd long had a rule about giving my gifts only to children, not grown-ups, but I decided to make one exception. On Christmas morning 1897, Mr. Church awoke to find the finest set of marbles ever made had been left in a new stocking tacked up by his fireplace. There was also a note that said simply, "Thank you. Love, Santa."

That same Christmas morning found Layla, Ben Franklin, Leonardo, Felix, and me back at the Cooperstown farmhouse, worn out from our gift-giving activities of the night before. As we sipped cocoa before enjoying some well-earned sleep, Ben commented, "I truly believe that letter from Virginia and Mr. Church's answer may have done the trick! More children than ever believe in you, Santa."

"And though that's a problem we're glad to have, it's still a problem," Felix noted. "It soon will be impossible to keep track of all the children who believe in you, and all those children must get presents. It's awkward being so far away from our friends in Yellowstone National Park, from Arthur and Francis in London, and from Attila and Dorothea in Nuremberg. It would be so much more efficient if we could all work together in one place. But I wonder, where could that place be?"

"Thomas Nast has shown us," Leonardo blurted. "Do you have time to listen to me now? In Nast's cartoons, Santa lives at the North Pole, and for the reasons I'm about to share with you, I think the North Pole would be perfect. . . ."

TWENTY-THREE

Theodore Roosevelt
and Our North Pole Home

In the late 1800s, the North Pole seemed like a very mysterious place. Everyone knew it existed, but no one had ever been there. It was the absolute top of the Earth, a region of snow and wind and bitter cold, scientists said, destined by its unique location to have months where the sun would not shine at all, followed by six months of constant sunlight. When he drew his cartoons of Santa living there, Thomas Nast thought it was a joke. But Leonardo da Vinci didn't.

"Consider the location, Santa Claus," Leonardo pleaded with me during early 1898, just a few months after Virginia O'Hanlon's letter to the *New York Sun* inspired new widespread belief in me. "The number of children we must serve grows every year. We can't continue to have some of our helpers in one place and some in another. Besides, it's becoming harder to keep the locations of our toy factories and reindeer barn secret. With so many people around, there's less privacy. At the North Pole we could all work together again as one team, and few, if any, visitors would disturb us."

"What about all the snow, Leonardo, and what about the ice?" I protested. "I have wonderful friends, gifted individuals like you—but no one among us is a penguin."

"Penguins only inhabit cold areas in the Southern Hemisphere," Leonardo said helpfully.

"Oh, you know very well what I mean," I huffed, but in the end I gave Leonardo permission to study how a permanent Santa headquarters might be established at the North Pole. He quickly traveled to New York City to meet with Robert Peary, a civil engineer who was determined to become the first person ever to reach the North Pole. Such visits to people involved in projects he found interesting were common for Leonardo. About this same time, he frequently made his way to Dayton, Ohio, where, in his words, he "helped out" brothers Orville and Wilbur Wright. Leonardo said he liked visiting the brothers because they were experts at building and repairing bicycles, a new form of two-wheeled, self-pedaled transportation that had become very popular with children. But the rest of us suspected our old friend was curious about how long it might take the Wrights to invent an airplane using the same principles of flight Leonardo had applied to my sleigh and reindeer so many years earlier.

While he traveled and studied, the rest of us went on about our increasingly complicated business. Earning the money to pay for our mission became harder every year. We certainly weren't the only toy manufacturers in the world anymore. It also was necessary to constantly monitor countries where we wanted to give gifts, but were kept from doing so by revolutions and other political problems. Russia, for instance, had a great religious tradition that included extended celebrations of Christ's birth, but more and more it seemed a possible new government there might discourage these celebrations, and, indeed, religious freedom altogether.

And in 1898, America got itself into another war, this time with Spain, though the conflict's few battles between April, when war was declared, and August, when a treaty was signed, were all fought on islands adjacent to the United States—Puerto Rico and Cuba. Theodore Roosevelt, the former New York City police commissioner whom Layla had so much admired, turned out to be the dominant figure in the Spanish-American War, leading a troop of soldiers he called the "Rough Riders" on a charge up San Juan Hill in Puerto Rico that thrilled his fellow Americans. Soon afterward,

Roosevelt was elected governor of New York, then vice president of the United States. He became president in 1901 after the assassination of William McKinley. When Roosevelt assumed the office of president, I decided to carry out a plan I'd long been considering.

"I'm off to Washington, D.C.," I told the others in the spring of 1902. "It's been obvious to me for some time that, in order to properly carry out our mission around the world, we'll need to make ourselves known to leaders of governments. That way, we'll be welcome wherever we go and not suspected of being invaders or spies. President Theodore Roosevelt seems to be a person of intelligence and imagination. I want to tell him about us first, and then get his help in introducing us to the other world leaders."

It was a simple matter to take the train to Washington and arrange an appointment with the president. Government wasn't so complicated then. In fact, it was a tradition that once a year the White House was opened to the public, and thousands of men and women lined up to walk through it and shake the president's hand.

When I was ushered into President Roosevelt's office, he got up from behind his desk and, like Charles Dickens sixty years earlier, recognized me right away.

"Santa Claus! Bully!" the president blurted, peering at me from behind tiny, round-lensed eyeglasses. At first I was offended, thinking he was accusing me of picking on someone, but then I remembered that "bully" was his favorite expression of excitement and pleasure.

"Thank you for seeing me, Mr. President," I began. "I've come to ask for your help—"

"Not at all, Santa, not at all!" He grinned. "Do call me Theodore, won't you? Say, let me send for some cocoa and cookies. You do like cocoa and cookies, don't you? I used to leave them out for you every Christmas when I was a boy. Oh, this is bully! You say you want my help? Anything, my friend, anything! Let's get our refreshments and talk all about it!"

I ended up spending several days with Theodore. He insisted that I be his guest at the White House and introduced me to his wife and children, all of whom were as energetic and outgoing as their father. Theodore didn't tell his family who I really was, of course, simply saying I was Mr. Nicholas from upper New York State who'd come to work out some land problems. Mrs. Roosevelt and most of the children seemed to accept this, but I caught one of the Roosevelt daughters, Alice, watching me closely and taking special note of my white beard and somewhat generous waistline. I think she knew.

Theodore himself I found delightful, despite his outspoken love for war and fighting. Though tremendously intelligent, the president had somehow retained the enthusiasm of a young boy. He immediately announced he would give up politics so he and his entire family could join us in our mission. It took me some time to convince him that the country needed him as president more.

"Well, could you at least name a toy after me?" Theodore pleaded, and I was happy to oblige. The most popular toy of 1903 became the teddy bear, which was named after Theodore in honor of his great interest in animals. Theodore even looked a little like a bear, with his bristling brown mustache and somewhat prominent teeth.

Theodore was happy to help me make contact with other world leaders, and in several cases used a combination of personal charm and polite threats to make them agree to assist me and my helpers whenever we required it.

That dilemma solved, I told Theodore a little about our problems in establishing a central headquarters and toy factory. He suggested we simply move into the White House—"Plenty of room here, just plenty, and wouldn't it be bully to have you and Ben Franklin and Leonardo da Vinci and the others under the same roof with me?"

"Thank you for the offer, Theodore, but it wouldn't be right for us to seem to belong more to one country than any other," I explained. "As it is, we will never be able to deliver gifts to every deserving child everywhere, since our powers are limited by wars and because some parents prefer we don't visit their homes. If we lived in the White House with you, children in other countries might think we favored American children above any others, and, as you know, we love all children equally."

"Well, the North Pole certainly isn't the property of any single nation, but it's a very cold place, and unfit for humans," Theodore replied. "I don't care how intelligent your Leonardo da Vinci is, he'll be hard-pressed to invent some way for you and your helpers to live up there, let alone reach it in the first place. Tell you what: We'll get you together with Robert Peary and perhaps you can find some way to reach the North Pole successfully. That would be a good start, wouldn't it?"

It didn't seem polite to tell the president that Leonardo already had been talking to Robert Peary. Theodore wrote me a letter of introduction, which I didn't have to use; Leonardo invited Peary to visit us at the Cooperstown farmhouse. He seemed very discouraged when he arrived.

"I've made several unsuccessful expeditions," Peary complained. "Something always goes wrong. We head north from Canada or Alaska, and then we run out of food, or important equipment breaks down. It's depressing."

"Why go to so much trouble just to get to a place that really isn't that important?" Layla asked. "I realize the North Pole is the top of the world, but, after all, once you did get there all you could do is plant a flag or something."

Peary's eyes gleamed. "It's a matter of being first, Mrs. Claus, of doing something no one else in the whole history of the world has ever done before."

"We know all about that," Felix commented dryly.

In any event, Peary agreed Leonardo could come with him on his next attempt to reach the North Pole. That one didn't succeed, either, but Leonardo came back convinced that the North Pole would make the perfect home base for us.

"Once we were settled there, no one would bother us except occasional passing polar bears," he insisted. "There would be so much space. We could make our toy factories as large as we wanted."

"It would be impossible for our craftsmen to build toys if they were exposed to freezing winds and blizzards," commented Arthur, who was visiting us from England. "The strongest-walled houses would blow down in some of those Arctic storms. Besides, none of us knows how to make an igloo."

"We'd use the principle of igloos, not igloos themselves," Leonardo urged. "We'll create a man-made, self-contained environment. See, the snow and ice can be used as insulation. You must factor in density; let me write out the formula." He did, and it was the strangest set of unreadable chicken scratchings I'd ever seen.

"You've lost me," I admitted.

Ben Franklin took the notebook from Leonardo, glanced at the scribbled formula, and said, "Basically, Santa, Leonardo wants to use the snow and ice as outer walls to protect us from the bad weather. As an outer shell, so to speak. Inside that shell, we can build roofs and walls, toy factories and apartments."

"We can use generators to supply power," Leonardo added. "There aren't any portable generators yet, but I'll invent them immediately. I have some ideas, too, for other inventions that will eventually allow us to get energy from the sun itself, or, rather, from the light it radiates. Just let us locate the right spot at the North Pole, Santa, and I'll teach the craftsmen from our toy factories to build the finest snow- and ice-covered facility possible.

"By the way, there's one more advantage," he continued. "If our outer shell is made up of snow, ice, and earth, then, in the near future when airplanes fly all over the skies, pilots looking down at the North Pole won't be able to tell anyone is living there at all. They'll just think we're an especially big hill or bit of glacier."

"What do you mean, airplanes flying all over the skies?" I asked peevishly, since I didn't really understand anything else Ben or Leonardo had said.

"Oh, it will happen, Santa," Leonardo assured me. "In fact, just before Christmas this year I'm going to go to Kitty Hawk, North Carolina, with my friends the Wright brothers. They think they might be able to make their airplane fly there. I could, of course, tell them exactly what to do, but I think it's better for them to figure things out for themselves with just a few hints from me."

I snorted, less from disbelief than from a growing sense that someday soon I'd be living at the North Pole. Leonardo had proven through the centuries that he was capable of solving any scientific problem.

The Wright brothers became famous at Kitty Hawk on December 17, 1903, when their primitive engine-powered airplane first flew 120 feet in twelve seconds, then 852 feet in fifty-nine seconds. It was hard for me to feel too impressed; every Christmas season, I flew thousands of miles in my sleigh. Later on, in history books for schoolchildren, there were photographs of that airplane and the Wright brothers standing beside it. If you study some of those photographs carefully, you'll see a tall, slender man in the background. It's Leonardo, of course.

Leonardo came back to the Cooperstown farm from Kitty Hawk and set to work inventing plans for our new North Pole home. It took him more than five years. In the meantime, Theodore was elected president for a full four-year term, and he kept pestering me to give up the idea of the North Pole and move into the White House instead.

"What I'll do is make the Congress vote that you and your helpers can live there no matter who is president," he promised.

"But, Theodore, you can't tell Congress all about us," I reminded him. "Some of those elected officials wouldn't be able to keep our secrets."

Theodore frowned. "I would threaten to shoot anyone who told on you. They know I'd do it, too."

"Please don't," I asked. "Besides, Leonardo's determined that we're going to go and live with the polar bears."

"Well, let me finish this term as president and I'll move up there with you," Theodore suggested. "Things around here are getting too civilized. You might need someone to protect you from the polar bears. I'd like to shoot a polar bear or two."

"We can talk more about that when the time comes," I suggested. "Right now, the country and the world need you more." Theodore seemed pleased when I said that; he always enjoyed praise.

Finally, in early 1909, after several months of building odd-looking igloos in the fields of our farm, Leonardo announced he had perfected what he called his "self-contained environment" plans and was ready to proceed.

We knew from the newspapers that Robert Peary planned to make his next attempt to reach the North Pole in March. We contacted him, and he invited Leonardo to go along, as well as anyone else from our group who wanted to come. Willie Skokan did, of course, and so did Arthur and Attila, who always craved new adventures. Disgustingly, Layla wanted to go, too, which meant I was expected to go with her.

"I hope you're satisfied," I grumbled four weeks later, as all of us in Peary's group huddled in drafty igloos. We were swaddled in fur cloaks provided by Eskimos; I later found they treated the fur with fish oil, which made the cloaks waterproof and very, very smelly. After spending three weeks in the cold and snow, Peary still thought we were another two weeks away from the North Pole.

"Oh, stop complaining," Layla said sharply. "Leonardo thinks he found an error in Peary's map. We'll be at the North Pole in just a few days, he says. So eat a little smoked caribou meat and get some sleep."

"I'd rather have cocoa and cookies," I mumbled.

Six days later, on April 6, 1909, Peary and Leonardo, who were walking a few hundred yards ahead of the rest of us, suddenly stopped in their tracks. Peary jumped up and down for joy. "It's the North Pole! We're here!" he shouted. Personally, I didn't see any real cause for excitement. Where we were looked no different than anywhere else as far as the eye could see—just more snow and ice. But apparently it was the North Pole, and we were there. Peary planted an American flag, which the wind promptly knocked down and blew away. Then we turned around and headed back.

When we returned to civilization, Peary went to New York City and reported his achievement. A few months later another explorer named Frederick Cook, a doctor who had previously traveled with Peary, claimed he had reached the North Pole first. If he had, we hadn't seen him, and he hadn't left behind any markers to prove he'd been there. A fierce debate followed, with some people believing Peary and some believing Cook. We stayed out of it.

For the next four years, Leonardo, Willie Skokan, Arthur, Attila, and dozens of our best craftsmen would head for the North Pole right after we'd completed our holiday season gift-giving. Eventually, Leonardo and some of the craftsmen stayed there year-round. Whenever I asked if I could come and see what they were doing, I was informed they were working hard, didn't need to be interrupted, and would invite me when they were ready. I waited impatiently. So did Theodore, who desperately wanted to be part of what he called "the bully Santa Claus adventure." He left the presidency in 1909 and traveled around the world. Bored, he returned to run for president in 1913, but lost. Theodore then resumed his requests to join us.

"Wait a while longer," I urged. "When the time is right, I'll tell you."

Finally, in May 1913, Leonardo returned to the Cooperstown farm. He told everyone else to pack their belongings and come with him, then instructed me to wait three weeks and fly to the North Pole with the reindeer.

"How will I find you?" I asked. "From the air, I won't be able to tell one snowdrift from another."

"Trust the reindeer and the stars," Leonardo said mysteriously. "When you've acted on faith before, you've always succeeded, haven't you?"

So I spent three weeks all alone, the first time I'd been by myself for so long in centuries. It was quite peaceful; I fed the reindeer and ignored cablegrams from Theodore begging me to let him stow away on the sleigh.

On the appointed day I got up well before dawn, so the reindeer and I could fly away under cover of darkness. Not a stick of furniture or scrap of food was left in the farmhouse. I put my red Santa outfit on over my regular clothes. Somehow when I was up in the sleigh, the red suit seemed to protect me from the weather.

The reindeer and I flew north, and gradually the land beneath us changed from green grass to brown hills and, finally, to rocky ground with patches of snow and ice. I had learned from Leonardo that even the North Pole wasn't always cold and freezing. Sometimes the temperature reached forty degrees, and bits of stringy grass popped up and waved in the wind.

And that was how it looked below as the reindeer and I moved into what was called the Arctic Circle, flying farther north as the sky around us darkened and stars began to twinkle. I watched the stars, and it gradually occurred to me that several of them seemed to shine all in a row, a neat row pointing down. Then I looked at where those stars seemed to be pointing, and there was the tiny figure of Leonardo da Vinci waving at me.

I tugged the reins gently; the reindeer turned downward in a graceful arc. As we drew close, I saw Leonardo was pointing to his left. Doors suddenly swung out of what seemed to be a lumpy hill covered with a layer of snow. Without further direction from me, the reindeer gracefully swooped through the doors and landed on a long, carpeted runway.

I looked around. I was in some sort of enclosed area that seemed to go on forever. It was well lit and warm; as the sleigh came to a stop, Layla and all my old, dear friends—Felix, Attila, Dorothea, Arthur, Francis, Willie Skokan, Ben Franklin, Sarah, Sequoyah, and, of course, Leonardo—crowded around with cries of welcome.

"Come see, Santa, come see!" they chanted like excited children. For the next two hours I was escorted through a wonderland of toy assembly areas, storerooms for tools and raw materials, laboratories, kitchens, dining rooms, bathrooms, guest rooms for visitors, and, finally, private quarters for each of my special friends. It was astonishing, all built under a protective cover of snow and ice and earth, and everything snug and comfortable and somehow welcoming.

"Come over here, Santa, and see your new office," Felix urged, and I found myself in a lovely room with a large desk, couches and overstuffed chairs, bookshelves groaning with volumes of every shape and on every subject, a fireplace with a crackling fire, maps of the world on the walls, an attractive oil painting of Layla—"I do like to keep up my portrait painting," Leonardo confided. "I think this one of Layla is much better than the *Mona Lisa*"—and a wide window offering a panoramic view of the horizon and sky.

"Don't worry about anyone in airplanes being able to look down and see you," Leonardo assured me. "I've invented a type of tinted glass which lets people inside look out, but doesn't let anyone outside look in."

Layla nudged me with her elbow. Actually, she poked me rather sharply. "Thank Leonardo," she commanded in a whisper.

I tried to find the right words and couldn't. Tears came to my eyes, and I reached out and hugged Leonardo da Vinci, the greatest genius who ever lived.

"Is this place all right, Santa?" Leonardo asked anxiously.

"It's better than all right, Leonardo," I answered. "It's home. After all these centuries, after all our wandering, we finally have a home of our own."

TWENTY-FOUR

Happy Christmas to All

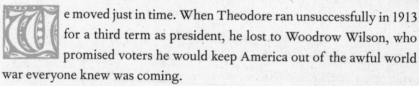e moved just in time. When Theodore ran unsuccessfully in 1913 for a third term as president, he lost to Woodrow Wilson, who promised voters he would keep America out of the awful world war everyone knew was coming.

It came in 1914. The country of Austria-Hungary declared war on Serbia; one after another, more countries became involved, including the United States in 1917. That same year, there was a revolution in Russia. Leaders of the new government soon made it clear they wanted no part of us or our gift-giving.

This sad situation was made a little easier for us by the fact that we were finally away from fighting. No country was especially interested in conquering the North Pole. If, during this war, there were few countries where we could go and give gifts as we pleased, at least we could make toys and wait for peace, which was finally declared in November 1918 after terrible destruction. The war became officially known as World War I, and unofficially nicknamed "the war to end all wars." You know, of course, that it wasn't. Wars still go on today, often in the same countries where World War I was fought. I think we've talked about war long enough. There's not much time left to tell the rest of my story, and there were wonderful things happening, too.

A special moment came in 1919, when we finally allowed Theodore to pack his things and join us. I made the decision a few days after World War I ended. I was visiting Theodore and he talked for a long time about how he'd learned to hate war, too.

"You've never really given me credit for what I did in 1906," Theodore complained. "As president, I helped Russia and Japan work out an agreement that settled their war. I was awarded the Nobel Peace Prize for that effort, I might add."

"Quite true," I agreed. The Nobel Peace Prize was named for Alfred Nobel, a Swedish engineer who'd invented, among other things, dynamite and better gunpowder. He'd come to regret those inventions because of the new violence they made possible, and as a result gave all his money when he died to establish prizes for those who, each year, did the most to bring world peace. Nobel also provided yearly prizes for exceptional achievement in economics, medicine, literature, chemistry, and physics, but the annual Nobel Peace Prize was considered the greatest honor anyone could win.

"Let me come help you, Santa," Theodore continued. "My own son died in this latest war. Let me dedicate myself now to making other people's sons and daughters happy."

I couldn't refuse; when I told Theodore to pack, he whooped like a cowboy. And before daylight on January 6, 1919, I added a final stop on my yearly visit to children in countries where gifts were expected on that date. My sleigh landed right beside Theodore's home. He leaped aboard and positively shouted with glee as I prepared to order the reindeer to fly us away to the North Pole.

"May I, Santa, oh, may I?" Theodore pleaded, and, since I knew what he meant, I nodded.

"Now, Dasher, now, Dancer," hollered President Theodore Roosevelt, naming all eight just the way Clement Moore had first described in his poem. "This is so bully!" Theodore added as we swooped into the night sky.

Sky-swooping soon became more complicated. The first flight credited to the Wright brothers was followed by many more. In 1927, Charles Lindbergh stunned the world by flying his airplane nonstop between New York and Paris. The trip took Lindbergh a little more than thirty-three hours. Up at the North Pole, we were all happy for him, though for us, thanks to Leonardo and his sleigh, flying from New York to Paris took thirty-two hours less.

Lindbergh made the first official long-distance flight, but far from the last. About one year later, a woman named Amelia Earhart joined two men in flying across the Atlantic Ocean in twenty-two hours. I noticed they named their airplane "Friendship." And, as airplanes quickly improved in both power and air speed, people flew farther and faster. In 1932, Amelia Earhart became the first woman to fly alone across the Atlantic, and it took her only thirteen hours and thirty minutes—still not close to our North Pole speed, but respectable enough.

"It seems quite probable that every child in the world will want toy airplanes for Christmas," I predicted over supper in April 1932, about a month before Amelia Earhart made her solo flight. It had been a fine supper; Theodore, who always loved everything to do with the Wild West, had taken a trip to Oklahoma and Texas earlier that year and, in a small Texas town, discovered a cook named Worth, who, Theodore insisted, made the best fried chicken in the world. The rest of us were all especially fond of fried chicken; we visited Worth, sampled his cooking, and immediately talked him into moving to the North Pole with us. Our meals improved considerably, but, after nightly second and third helpings, my waistline didn't.

"Those airplanes are all well and good, but to my mind most boys and girls are soon going to want cowboy toys, too," Theodore argued. "You know, little guns, toy horses, cowboy hats and boots, those sorts of things."

"Perhaps you're right," I admitted. Already, new entertainments called "movies" were very popular, and many of the most popular movies were westerns. Books about cowboys could be found in many homes, too. "Well, Theodore, I suppose you and Sequoyah can advise Willie Skokan and Leonardo and the rest of our craftsmen about how cowboy toys should work and look."

Sequoyah grinned and replied, "I know about alphabets and books, not about cowboys."

To my surprise, Theodore shook his head, too. "Santa, I love cowboys too much to claim to be an expert. We need someone else, a real cowboy, here to help us out, and I have just the cowboy to suggest."

A warm fire was crackling nearby, and we all gathered around Theodore as he told us about the adventures of a man named Bill Pickett, the son of a former slave. Bill Pickett grew up to star in something called *The 101 Ranch Wild West Show* and, Theodore claimed, won wrestling matches with wild steers by biting the animals on the lip or nose.

"Oh, be serious, Theodore!" Felix complained. "No self-respecting wild steer could be beaten that way! I always enjoy your tall tales, but this one is just too much. Try telling us another."

"I promise you, it's the truth!" Theodore growled; he hated anyone making fun of him. "What Bill Pickett does is called 'bulldogging,' and besides wild steers, some say he's even wrestled down a buffalo and a bull elk! I understand he's retired from the rodeo now and living on a ranch in Oklahoma. Do let's go find him, Santa. You'll see, Bill Pickett would be a great addition here. I was right about Worth and his fried chicken, wasn't I?"

It was hard to argue with Theodore on that point, especially since I'd just been wondering if I might be able to enjoy one more piece of fried chicken before dessert; the next day Theodore and I left for Chandler, Oklahoma, where Bill Pickett had his ranch. As always on non-holiday trips, we took more common transportation—dogsleds south until civilization, where we switched to trains.

Bill Pickett turned out to be a wonderful man, quite small and wiry, built much like Willie Skokan. And, as Theodore Roosevelt had done a few decades earlier, Bill recognized me right away.

"Why, it's Santa Claus," he chuckled, shaking my hand. "Good to see you down here in Oklahoma!" Actually, it was somewhat surprising no one else had given me a second glance on my trip south to meet Bill. A year earlier, an artist had finally painted me the way I really looked. The Coca-Cola Company had hired a Swedish-American artist, Hans Sundblom, to do a

"Santa" painting for a series of holiday advertisements on behalf of their popular American soft drink. Without telling anyone else at the North Pole, I discreetly visited Hans, introduced myself, explained my frustration at constantly being drawn elf-size, and ended up posing for his portraits myself. Hans drew "Santa" ads for Coca-Cola for thirty-five years, and I was his model in every one. We kept my real identity a secret. Whenever Hans had to have other people in his studio at the same time I was there, he introduced me to them as "Les Prentice," a retired salesman. At any rate, I was finally pleased with the way I looked in print.

Bill Pickett's rugged ranch in Oklahoma was a long way from Hans Sundblom's comfortable studio. After telling me, "You sure look like those Coca-Cola pictures," a comment I supposed was meant as a compliment, Bill cheerfully took us out to his corral, where he pointed to a huge, snorting bull.

"Think that one would be hard to wrestle down?" he asked.

"Please don't try, Bill," I said anxiously. "That animal must weigh a thousand pounds. Don't hurt yourself trying to impress us."

Before I could say more, Bill vaulted over the fence. The bull charged. Almost faster than eyes could see, Bill grabbed the bull's head, bit its lip, and twisted with his arms, and the bull flopped over on the ground. Then both the bull and Bill got up, neither worse for the experience, although the bull obviously had learned who was boss.

"So, how was that?" Bill asked, laughing at the expression on my face.

"Bill, we have something important to talk with you about," I replied, and just eleven days later, on April 13, Bill left Chandler to move to the North Pole.

Bill and Ben Franklin almost instantly became best friends. Both were curious about absolutely everything. Whenever Bill took breaks from working in the toy factory with Leonardo, Willie Skokan, and Ben, he got in the habit of visiting me in my study to ask questions.

"You've told me how you can't give holiday presents every year to every child in the world, sometimes because of war or sometimes because parents simply prefer that you don't," he began one day.

I was busy reading letters from children. Thanks to our continued communications with friendly governments around the world, we received regular deliveries of mail at the North Pole, first by dogsled and later by airplane. Bill's question interrupted my reading, but it was a pleasant interruption. "True," I replied.

"Well," Bill continued, "you don't give gifts to grown-ups or even teenagers, usually, so how do you decide when each child should stop getting presents from Santa?"

"I don't decide that," I answered. "It's really decided by the children themselves. You see, there comes a time in the life of each child who truly loves Christmas when that boy or girl realizes even Santa Claus can't give presents to every young person who hopes for one from me. That's when these children gladly give up what I would have brought them in order for boys and girls somewhere else to receive those gifts. It's called generosity of spirit, Bill."

Bill looked a little unhappy. "It surely seems sad, Santa Claus, for those generous young people to end up not getting any gifts themselves, after being so understanding and all."

"That's the wonderful thing about Christmas, Bill!" I exclaimed. "Besides you good friends who live with me here at the North Pole, parents and other adults all over the world are truly Santa's helpers, too! They're proud of their children for making the right, unselfish decision, and they make sure these youngsters continue to get gifts, too. True, the children know their Christmas gifts aren't presents from Santa anymore, but those gifts are just as special as mine because they're given with love, as all gifts should be."

"One question more, Santa," Bill continued. "What if someday, every child in the world made that decision, so that Christmas came and no boys or girls expected you to bring them presents?"

"I don't think that will happen, Bill, and frankly I hope it doesn't," I replied. "First, every child who loves the holiday season ought to get some presents from Santa. It's a wonderful, natural thing. Second, not all children make their generous decision at the same age. That's fine, too. It's good we're all a little different. And, finally, you know how I always say my motto is 'It's better to give than to receive.' Well, it's more fun, too. When they believe in me and my presents, it makes me happy. So I don't plan to ever stop giving children gifts!"

"Unless we get this flying problem fixed, you might have to," Felix interrupted. Apparently, he'd been standing in the doorway listening to Bill and me. "Santa, most countries, including some very friendly ones, have rules now about who they allow to fly overhead. 'Restricted air space,' they call it, as though people on the ground also should be able to rule the sky over their heads! Well, they're afraid of bombs, I suppose, and some of them probably wouldn't believe you had a sleigh full of toys instead."

I nodded; it was a very serious problem. "Felix, do you have any suggestions?"

"Well, Layla and I have been talking," he admitted. "You know how she's always admired that woman aviator, the one named Amelia Earhart?"

"And rightly so," I agreed. "Amelia Earhart is clearly the greatest pilot in the world."

"The best pilot in an airplane, but not the best in a sleigh," Bill interrupted quickly, trying to make sure my feelings weren't hurt.

"Probably the best pilot, period," I said firmly. "Don't worry, Bill, I'm not ashamed to admit someone else may be better at something than me. But, Felix, what does Amelia Earhart have to do with our problem?"

"Layla found out Amelia Earhart plans to try to fly all the way around the world," Felix said. "Apparently, Amelia's spent years studying maps of every country. She must know better than anyone else every flight pattern and plane route from one place on Earth to another."

"I'm sure Layla has a reason for thinking this is so important," I commented. "Why hasn't she told me about it herself?"

"Oh, I will, right now," my wife announced, joining Felix, Bill, and me in my study. "And please, Santa, stop asking Worth to fix you extra bedtime snacks. Soon there won't be room in the sleigh for the toys and you at the same time!"

"About Amelia Earhart," I suggested, taking a deep breath and trying, without much success, to suck in my stomach.

"It's very simple," Layla said in the patient tones of a wife who thinks her husband hasn't understood something obvious. "Let's see if Amelia

Earhart will become one of our North Pole helpers. Then she can plan all your sleigh routes, working with governments that are friendly and finding ways for you to fly undetected by the unfriendly ones. Don't you remember how Sarah helped us so much when she wrote that first book about traveling around America?"

Stated that way, the solution to our flight problems was very simple. With a little help from the current president—as it happened, he was a distant cousin of Theodore's, named Franklin Roosevelt—we met with Amelia Earhart. She said she'd be honored to join us, and offered to cancel her upcoming round-the-world flight in order to do so.

"That's quite generous, but do you think you might make at least part of that flight?" I asked. "Up at the North Pole we don't have as much information as we should about the islands of the Pacific Ocean. Perhaps if you could explore them before you come to join us, you could help us get gifts delivered to more children in that part of the world."

Amelia said she'd be delighted, if, in turn, we'd allow her to bring her trusty navigator, Frederick Noonan, on the flight with her and later to the North Pole as well. Everything worked out as planned. On July 2, 1937, everyone else in the world except President Roosevelt and those of us at the North Pole thought Amelia Earhart and Frederick Noonan somehow became lost forever on their flight. Actually, they turned north from the Pacific Ocean and flew to join us. We threw a grand party to welcome them, featuring Worth's fried chicken and plenty of homemade chocolate chip cookies for dessert. Layla wanted me to have just one helping of each, but I thought it was only right to have seconds—well, thirds, too—in the proper spirit of celebration.

With the help of Amelia and Frederick, I was able to fly my sleigh more efficiently, meaning more children got gifts. This is always our annual goal at the North Pole, to deliver presents to more children than the year before.

Modern technology and better management plans have helped us do this. It finally became necessary to put all our records on computer. Arthur and Francis spent a few decades dividing the countries of the Earth into what they called "regions." Senior staff were each put in charge of a specific region, with the responsibility of recruiting helpers from each country as needed and keeping track of which children wanted what. Arthur naturally oversaw our operations in England, Ireland, Scotland, and Wales. Francis took Spain and Portugal. Attila and Dorothea directed Germany and Austria, and so on.

We ended up having to divide types of gifts into separate divisions, too, with new helpers to keep track of all the latest developments in their areas of specialization. Zonk and Andy handled drums; Mary Elizabeth and Alison were our doll specialists; Scoop recommended the right books—his favorite was *Beautiful Joe,* the story of a wonderful dog. Bill and Theodore turned down jobs as regional directors to continue being in charge of all cowboy toys. Sequoyah, too, preferred the toy factory to other areas of management; he made it his special concern that our toys reflected the interests of children of all races.

There were other helpers with other jobs; gift-giving started to become complicated with the invention of chimneys so many centuries ago, and never got any simpler. We ended up needing a North Pole library, since we subscribed to many magazines; Marsha was our librarian, and Marilyn our chief researcher. Ira was the North Pole doctor, because even Santa's helpers don't feel well sometimes. Amelia Earhart and Frederick Noonan handled our air travel, and Sarah Kemble Knight decided on all land routes. We even had a public relations department to meet privately with people who didn't understand why Santa Claus should be part of Christmas. This was delicate work sometimes. Leonardo and Willie Skokan ended up having to expand our North Pole home to three times its original size to make room for all the new helpers, but they didn't mind. They were always happiest when there were new chores to be done.

So we became computerized and compartmentalized, but never subsidized. We continued to pay for all our own expenses by inventing ideas for toys and selling some of these ideas to companies in the outside world. For instance, we were delighted when video games became popular. Leonardo and Ben invented literally hundreds of games they sold to outside video-game companies at great profits to us. They thought their best game ever was about a plumber, his brother, and a princess; I always liked the one they invented that involved a hedgehog.

We did most of our toy business with companies in the United States, but had a longtime understanding with the American government that we wouldn't have to pay taxes. Instead, the Internal Revenue Service declared us a "nonprofit" company. From Theodore Roosevelt to the present, every American president has agreed and not bothered us about taxes.

Lately there has been especially good news. Felix and Sarah Kemble Knight came into my study last week and asked if they could speak to me. Both of them were grinning, and Felix announced, "We're going to be married."

"Really?" I asked, delighted at the thought. "When did you decide to get engaged?"

"We've been talking about getting married since the 1800s, but we didn't want to rush into anything," Sarah answered. "Couples really need to take the time to get to know one another before they go racing to the altar. No offense to you and Layla, of course. Sometimes short engagements work out, too."

Later that night I told Layla the happy news, only to be informed she'd known about Felix and Sarah for more than a century.

"Anyone with common sense could tell just by looking at them," Layla said smugly.

"I couldn't tell," I replied, slightly offended.

Layla gave me a warm hug and a kiss. "That's what I love about you, Santa. No one with common sense would have walked out into the night nearly two thousand years ago not knowing what would happen to him, but trusting some higher power would show him how to spend the rest of his life giving gifts and making other people happy. You've got a loving heart, and that's more important than common sense any day."

"I think I have a lot of common sense," I grumbled, but Layla gave me another quick kiss and hurried off to find Sarah and begin planning the wedding.

The marriage took place yesterday. I performed the ceremony. After all, I never really stopped being a bishop. The bride looked beautiful; the groom looked nervous. Afterward, Worth served a huge wedding dinner. Layla thought I ate too much. Everyone at the North Pole went outside into the sparkling snow to wave good-bye to Felix and Sarah as they flew off; I'd lent them my sleigh for their honeymoon. Just before they departed, Amelia consulted her state-of-the-art radar and assured them the weather was perfect all the way from the North Pole to Rome. The pope had invited the newlyweds to stay at one of his mansions there, and Felix wanted to show Sarah where he'd once lived as a slave.

"At least there are no more slaves," I commented to Arthur as we waved good-bye to the rapidly disappearing sleigh. "And maybe one day there'll be no more wars, either."

Then we all went back inside and ate some more. Fried chicken, cocoa, and homemade chocolate chip cookies make the best meal in the world.

Well, that's about all of my story, at least so far. I'm certain there will be more adventures, just as I'm certain there will always be people who truly love Christmas and who, understanding that the main purpose of the holiday is to celebrate the birth of a child and the love he brought with him, have a special place in their hearts for Santa Claus, too.

It's been my pleasure—even more, it's been my honor—to share the holiday spirit with so many of you. Don't ever apologize for loving me as much as I love you. After all, for those who don't want to believe in me, no amount of proof would ever be enough. But for friends like you, who believe what they know to be true in their hearts, no further proof is necessary.

Well, it's getting late. I have many things to do before morning, and you need to be off to bed.

My old friend Clement Moore was the first to write these words as a message from me, and they can't be improved upon, so I'll conclude with them here:

"Happy Christmas to all, and to all a good night."

Santa's Favorite Recipe

WORTH'S NORTH POLE DELIGHT TENDER FRIED CHICKEN

INGREDIENTS AND SUPPLIES

fresh chicken parts (two to six pieces per diner—
    Santa likes six for his dinner)
4 medium- or large-size mixing bowls
ice and water
lemon or lime juice
honey (optional)
salt and fresh ground pepper to taste
    (Santa likes a light seasoning touch)
4 fresh eggs or egg whites
½ cup milk or skim milk
lots of bleached or whole wheat flour
canola, olive, and corn oils

2 large but fairly shallow frying pans,
  preferably with nonstick surface
large platter with plenty of paper towels

PRE-FRYING PREPARATION

1. Buy the freshest whole or cut-up chicken available. Cut into your favorite chicken parts. (Preferred but optional to taste: remove skin and extra fat.) Wash thoroughly in running cold water.

2. Fill one bowl with ice water. Fill second bowl with ice water and lemon or lime juice.

3. In third bowl, gently beat four whole eggs or egg whites with ½ a cup of milk or skim milk.

4. In fourth bowl, fill with layer of flour.

5. Mix four parts canola oil with one part olive oil and a splash of corn oil in each of the large frying pans. Be sure the pans are only about half full of oil. Preheat oil mixture in one frying pan. Keep other pan of oil ready for backup.

    Note: You want your chicken pieces to be half under and half out of the oil mixture while frying.

    Caution: Test oil for proper temperature with pinch of flour. If the oil sizzles instantly, it's ready for the chicken.

6. Double-dip chicken in flour: Move chicken from cold-water bath into ice water.

7. From there, remove and dip thoroughly into the egg and milk mixture.

8. Remove and dip it in the flour.

9. Sprinkle lightly with salt and fresh-ground pepper or other spices, as desired. Return seasoned, floured chicken to lemon or lime ice water.

10. Remove quickly and re-dip it in the flour.

    Note: Be ready to pour more flour over chicken for the second dip to get even coating. But even single-dip chicken will be crunchy and tasty.

FRYING

1. Slip floured chicken immediately into the hot oil.
2. If oil gets too hot, it will pop or splatter out of the pan. If so, slightly turn down heat.
3. Keep constant watch on frying chicken. As it begins to brown on one side, turn it over. As it browns on other side, turn again. Turn at least two more times for even frying on both sides.
4. Chicken is ready when it's rich, golden brown, and crisp on both sides, and the sizzle begins to wane. Remove chicken and place on paper towel–covered platter. Turn over once to let oil drain off both sides. Dab with towels as necessary.
5. If frying a lot of chicken, put second pan of oil on another burner and preheat the oil. As the first oil's frying capacity breaks down, switch frying to the pan of fresh, hot oil. Then empty, clean, and refill the first pan, and preheat another batch of oil for more frying.

     Note: Don't let oil get old and weak while frying.

     Caution: Don't cover chicken while it's frying. Don't put finished chicken in warm oven or under heat lamp. Don't cover finished chicken.
6. Serve immediately, fresh fried and hot from the platter.

     Note: This is also good as a cold snack later from the fridge. Ask Santa.

Resources

Ball, Ann. *A Litany of Saints*. Huntington, Ind.: Our Sunday Visitor, Inc., 1993.

Barraclough, Geoffrey, ed. *The Times Atlas of World History*. Maplewood, N.J.: Hammond, Inc., 1989.

Crichton, Robin. *Who Is Santa Claus? The True Story Behind a Living Legend*. Edinburgh, Scotland: Canongate Publishing Ltd., 1987.

Cross, F. L. *The Oxford Dictionary of the Christian Church*. New York: Oxford University Press, 1957.

Del Re, Gerard, and Patricia Del Re. *The Christmas Almanack*. New York: Doubleday and Company, 1979.

Ebon, Martin. *Saint Nicholas: Life and Legend*. New York: Harper and Row, 1975.

Encyclopedia Americana. Danbury, Conn.: Americana Corp., 1980.

Garraty, John A., ed. *Encyclopedia of American Biography*. New York: Harper and Row, 1974.

Goldsmith, Terence. *Saints*. New York: Blandford Press Ltd., 1978.

Humble, Richard. *The Travels of Marco Polo*. New York: Franklin Watts, 1990.

Ickis, Marguerite. *The Book of Religious Holidays and Celebrations*. New York: Dodd, Mead, and Company, 1966.

Imbert, Bertrand. *North Pole, South Pole: Journeys to the Ends of the Earth*. New York: Harry N. Abrams, Inc., 1992.

Jackson, Kenneth T., ed. *Atlas of American History*. New York: Charles Scribner's Sons, 1978.

Jones, Charles Williams. *Saint Nicholas of Myra, Bari, and Manhattan*. Chicago, Ill.: University of Chicago Press, 1978.

Jones, E. Willis. *The Santa Claus Book*. New York: Walker and Company, 1976.

Metford, J. C. J. *Dictionary of Christian Lore and Legend*. New York: Thames and Hudson, Inc., 1983.

The National Christmas Tree Association, Milwaukee, Wisconsin.

Professional Rodeo Cowboys Association, Colorado Springs, Colorado.

Sanders, Dennis. *The First of Everything*. New York: Delacorte Press, 1981.

Snyder, Phillip V. *December 25th*. New York: Dodd, Mead, and Company, 1985.

Taylor, Michael J. H., and David Mondey. *Milestones of Flight*. Alexandria, Va.: Jane's Information Group, Inc., 1983.

Weis, Frank W. *Lifelines*. New York: Facts on File, Inc., 1982.

Whyte, Malcolm. *The Meanings of Christmas*. San Francisco, Calif.: Troubador Press, 1973.

The World Book Encyclopedia. Chicago, Ill.: World Book, Inc., 1993.

Acknowledgments

TWO PEOPLE above all others deserve special recognition for helping Santa and me write this book. Besides Layla, it was Mark Hulme who originally urged that it be written. Back in 1994, Susan Besze Wallace was absolutely invaluable, doing an amazing amount of research and making sure all our dates and facts were accurate.

Other special Santa's helpers include Sara Carder, my editor, and Ken Siman, my publicist, at Tarcher/Penguin; Robert Fernandez; Felix Higgins; Del Hillen; Mary Arendes; Art Cory; Don Jesse; Dot and Frank Lauden; Zonk Lanzillo; Rich Billings; Wilson McMillion; Scott Nishimura; Doug Perry; Julie Heaberlin; Rick Press; Charles Caple; Marsha Melton; Mary and Charles Rogers; Ira Hollander; Kelly Goss; Dorit Rabinovitch; Michael and Barbara Rosenberg; Jerry Flemmons; Mike Cochran; Ralph Lauer; Cecil Johnson; Karen Potter; Anita Quinones; John Ryan; Bob and Betty Burns; Jim and Barbara Firth; Buck, Debbie, Jeanne, and Jonathan Firth; Speaker Jim Wright; Sandy Smith; the Reverend Linda McDermott; Max and Cissy Lale; and Larry Wilson.

Santa dedicates this new edition of his book to everyone who keeps Christmas in his or her heart. I agree, and also dedicate it to Louis and Marie Renz.

Everything I write is always for Nora, Adam, and Grant.

HOW
MRS. CLAUS
SAVED
CHRISTMAS

FOR SARA CARDER

Thanks

Foreword

WE NEVER STOP WORKING at the North Pole. Though children all over the world only expect to find presents from us on one of three mornings— December 6, December 25, or January 6—we need the rest of the year to design and build their toys. In fact, we work just as hard during the spring, summer, and fall as we do around those wonderful winter holidays of St. Nicholas Day, Christmas, and the Epiphany. Most people, I find, don't realize this. Over the years, I've seen thousands of cartoons about where Santa likes to take his vacations. These are often funny drawings of me on the beach sipping a drink through a straw, or at a baseball game enjoying a hot dog. And it's true I enjoy baseball and hot dogs, but I mostly do so in my den at the North Pole, watching the game on television and eating the hot dog from a tray on my lap. Beaches are less enticing. As someone who is well over seventeen hundred years old and, I admit, perhaps a few pounds overweight, wearing a bathing suit in public is not something I'm eager to do.

Besides, there simply isn't leisure time to spend at the beach. There are no magic North Pole buttons we can push to make toys instantly appear for every deserving girl and boy. I explained in a book I wrote about my life that there is a fair share of magic in what we do, but there's plenty of hard work, too. Everyone living here at the North Pole—and there are hundreds of us—is kept very busy from the time we gather for breakfast each morning, at eight o'clock sharp, until about six or so in the evening, when there's dinner and, afterward, well-deserved relaxation and fellowship until it's time to go to bed.

Designed by the great inventor Leonardo da Vinci, our North Pole home is a complex series of buildings and tunnels mostly underneath the snow, so that no one in planes flying overhead will notice us. The long, well-lighted workshops and assembly lines are separated from everyone's private living quarters by a large dining hall and several other rooms where comfortable chairs and sofas and widescreen televisions and well-stocked bookshelves make it pleasant for friends to gather and chat, read, or watch movies. No one is required to be anywhere doing anything. It's all very informal. Those who want quiet to enjoy their books can have complete peace in one place, while in another, dozens may be happily gathered to watch a hilarious film. Leonardo was careful to make each room soundproof, so that hearty laughter from one room does not disturb companionable silence in another.

Though everyone is free to choose what to do and whom to spend their evenings with, it often happens that one group is comprised of what we call "the old companions"—those of us who have been together longest in this eternal mission of helping everyone celebrate the joy and wonder of the holiday season. I'm never happier than when these very special people are gathered with me—Felix, the Roman slave who became my first companion; Attila, known through the ages as The Hun, and his wife, Dorothea; Arthur, the British war chief who, in legend, became celebrated as a king; St. Francis of Assisi, who wrote some of the first Christmas carols; Willie Skokan, the incomparable craftsman; Leonardo da Vinci and Benjamin Franklin, two great inventors and significant figures in world history; Sarah Kemble Knight, Felix's wife, who wrote the very first book about traveling in America; Teddy Roosevelt, the former president of the United States; Amelia Earhart, the wonderful aviator; and Bill Pickett, the great cowboy who could wrestle any steer to the ground in a matter of seconds. And, of course, there's the person I love and admire most of all, my wife, Layla, whose common sense and courage have inspired us during many challenging times.

Although we've known one another for a very long time, being together remains quite agreeable. Sometimes we don't even get around to watching a movie or reading books at all, because someone tells a favorite story and then everyone else begins reminiscing about wonderful times or places or people. Even though we've heard these same stories hundreds or even thousands of time before, they're still enjoyable. Felix, for instance, loves to tell about how he met George Washington and informed him that the German troops opposing him in the Revolutionary War would be spending Christmas night celebrating rather than guarding their camp. Based on this information, General Washington crossed the Delaware after dark on December 25, 1776, and took the Germans by surprise. Teddy Roosevelt is always ready to jump in and talk about his great adventures, including how he helped create eighteen national monuments. Leonardo might recall painting his masterpiece, the *Mona Lisa*. Every so often, I'm coaxed into recounting my first days of gift-giving, when I was a bishop in the early Christian church and even before that, as a small boy whose dream it was to bring comfort to those in need. Actually, I need very little coaxing.

Everyone always seems to have a story to share, and occasionally that includes Layla. But on most evenings, she prefers sitting quietly and listening to others. It isn't that she's too shy to speak. As Layla has demonstrated throughout the sixteen centuries we've been married, if she feels there is something that ought to be said, she will say it, and always in her pleasant, practical way. Layla is so intelligent, and so perceptive—she was the one back in the 1100s who helped us decide we must give toys to children instead of food, because the food would soon be gone but the toys would be lasting reminders that someone cared enough about them to bring gifts. It was also my wife who suggested that we deliver these gifts on three special nights rather than randomly throughout the year, so that we would have time to properly prepare, but more important, to help keep holiday traditions alive. And it was Layla, in the middle 1640s, who saved Christmas.

That's a story no one but Layla, Arthur, and I really knew until recently, when it came up by accident. We had not deliberately kept it a secret. For more than three and a half centuries, Layla simply didn't feel like talking about these particular Christmas-related events, which have been mostly overlooked by historians. Oh, they get some of the basic facts right—for a while in England, celebrating Christmas was against the law, until finally the people protested and got their beloved holiday back again—but they have no idea of the important part Layla played in it.

None of our other North Pole companions did, either, until the night we sat down to watch a movie about one of history's more controversial figures. I should perhaps explain how we came to watch this particular film. It is our custom to take turns selecting what movie will be watched. If, for instance, Ben Franklin chooses on one night, it will not be his turn again until each of the other "old companions" has had the chance to make a selection. Everyone's choice is always honored, and it's interesting to see who likes to watch what. You would think, for instance, that Bill Pickett would want movies about cowboys, but he loves those colorful films about a boy wizard named Harry Potter. St. Francis likes the Disney cartoon *Peter Pan*; we've worn out several cassette copies, though the DVD version has lasted longer. Attila would watch *Some Like It Hot* every night, if he could. Christmas-themed movies like *It's a Wonderful Life* and *A Christmas Story* are always popular. None of us like films that contain a great deal of violence. We are people who love peace, not war. But movies based on history are always interesting. After all, some of us might have been there.

We all find it amusing that Arthur enjoys movies about himself. There are so many, most based on the colorful but inaccurate myth that Arthur was a British king who lived in a magical place called Camelot and fought evil-doers with the help of a great wizard named Merlin. Arthur always claims to be embarrassed by such embellishment. In fact, he'd been a war chief in the 500s who, for a while, helped hold off Saxon invaders before they finally overran Britain. Layla, Felix, Attila, Dorothea, and I had found him lying wounded in a barn. We nursed him back to health, and he joined us in our gift-giving mission.

But books were written about mythical King Arthur, and poems and songs, too. When movies were invented (by Leonardo, Willie Skokan, and Ben Franklin, though they let others take the credit) there were soon films that also emphasized the Arthur legend rather than real history. We some-times watch these at the North Pole, always at Arthur's suggestion. He tries to make it seem that he isn't secretly flattered; "Let's watch this new exag-geration," Arthur might say. "How silly it is." But his eyes stay glued to the huge widescreen television on which our movies are played.

One of the better versions, perhaps because of its wonderful songs, is a musical called *Camelot*, based on a fine book, *The Once and Future King*, by T. H. White. The theme of the movie, and the book, is that more is always accomplished by kindness than by violence. An actor named Richard Harris plays King Arthur in the movie. He does it quite well, though he doesn't look exactly like Arthur. He wears a beard in the movie, and Arthur never had a beard.

But a few weeks after we saw *Camelot* for perhaps the twentieth time, when Arthur's turn came around again he suggested we watch Richard Har-ris in another movie. We had just settled into our seats that evening, each of us enjoying a thick wedge of Candy Cane Pie, a special recipe by a wonder-ful Norwegian pastry chef named Lars. He makes the most fabulous desserts you can imagine, and many more you can't. We were thrilled when he agreed to join us at the North Pole. And, afterward, some of us began to put on a bit of additional weight, me perhaps most of all.

"This movie has more real history than *Camelot*," Arthur explained, set-ting down his plate of pie. "It's called *Cromwell*, and it's about the British Civil War in the 1640s."

"You were in England during that time, weren't you?" asked Sarah Kemble Knight. Sarah hadn't joined us until 1727, so she often requested such clarification.

"I was, along with Layla and Leonardo," Arthur replied. "That was the same time that Santa and Felix were trying to introduce Christmas to the colonies in America." Before he started the movie, he talked a little about Oliver Cromwell, a leader of the revolution against the British king. Leonardo added a few comments. Layla didn't. I thought she looked rather sad.

Then we lowered the lights and the film began. Richard Harris, playing Cromwell, stormed across the screen, pounding his fist and shouting. He did this in scene after scene, until after one particularly loud episode Layla spoke for the first time.

"He wasn't like that at all," she said. Though her voice was low, everyone instantly paid attention, because it was unusual for Layla to comment during a movie.

"You knew Oliver Cromwell?" Teddy Roosevelt piped up. "I had no idea, Layla. Did you actually speak to him?"

Arthur paused the DVD and reached over to turn on the lights.

"Did Layla ever speak to Cromwell?" he replied. "Why, several times! If you knew the entire story—"

"There's no need to tell it," Layla interrupted. "I'm sorry I said anything. Please, Arthur, start the movie again."

But now everyone was curious. "It surely seems like there's something interesting here," Bill Pickett remarked in his slow drawl. "I'd rather hear about it than watch the movie." Several of our other companions loudly agreed.

Dorothea, who has been one of Layla's closest friends for over fifteen hundred years, quickly said, "If Layla doesn't want to talk about it, she shouldn't have to. Though, of course, I'd be very happy to listen if she does."

Layla frowned. I could tell that there were things she was tempted to say, but for more than three hundred years she had never talked about her time with Cromwell, except to me in 1700 when we reunited back in America. Some memories can be painful as well as happy at the same time, and this, I knew, was one of those instances.

"You hardly ever tell stories, Layla," Amelia Earhart pointed out. "It's usually Felix, or Teddy Roosevelt, or Santa. Please, take a turn now. You say that Cromwell wasn't loud, that he didn't shout like the actor in the movie?"

"No, I never heard him shout," Layla said, choosing her words carefully. "He was a determined man, someone who I completely disagreed with about Christmas. Oliver Cromwell thought Christmas was sinful, and tried to end it forever. But he wasn't *evil*, you see. That was what made it harder when—"

"When what?" Amelia urged.

Layla looked at me, a question in her eyes. I knew she was silently asking whether I thought she should continue. It wasn't a matter of me granting permission. Layla never asks, or needs, my permission to do anything. But she values my opinion, as I always do hers.

"I think this might be a story that should finally be told, Layla," I said, looking around the room. Most of our good, dear friends were perched on the edges of their seats, watching Layla and obviously hoping she would tell whatever the story was about Oliver Cromwell and his attempt to end Christmas. "I've often said that it's wrong for me always to get credit for almost every good thing in Christmas history. Perhaps everyone here should know about your incredible accomplishment, too."

"I really did very little," Layla replied. "It was the others—Elizabeth and Alan Hayes, for instance, and all those brave apprentices in London, and Avery Sabine, though he surely didn't mean to help us. And. . . and—"

"And Sara," Arthur added, his voice very soft.

"And Sara most of all," Layla agreed. She sat quietly for a moment, thinking hard. "All right. I'll tell the story, if everyone wants to hear it."

"Please do," begged Teddy Roosevelt, who usually preferred telling stories to listening. "Who were Elizabeth and Alan Hayes, Layla, and what about apprentices and this Avery fellow? Who was Sara, who seems so special to you? And why haven't you mentioned any of this before?"

"Some things are almost too important, and perhaps too painful, to mention," Layla said quietly before drawing a deep breath. "All right, then. In 1645 and again in 1647, the British Parliament voted that celebrating Christmas was against the law. I had spent quite a bit of time with Arthur and Leonardo at our secret toy factory in London, and—"

"Please, Layla, share more than that," Amelia pleaded. "Why were you in England in the 1640s, when Santa was in America?"

"Well, remember, he wasn't called Santa then," Layla reminded. "That name only came fifty or sixty years later. Before that we all called him by his given name, Nicholas. He was in America because we wanted to encourage Christmas celebrations there. I stayed behind since there were still things to do in Europe and England, especially in England. Now, Oliver Cromwell wasn't the only Englishman to oppose Christmas. The story goes back a very long way. There are lots of details. One is even related, in a manner of speaking, to the Candy Cane Pie that Lars baked for us tonight. Are you sure you want to hear it all?"

This time, I answered. "Yes, Layla, tell everything. And start, please, at the very beginning, because I doubt some people here even know very much about your childhood. Don't imagine that we'll be bored. It will be our pleasure to listen."

And so, Layla told her story. It was such a magical evening that the next day I called a writer from Texas who helped me with my autobiography. I asked him to capture Layla's words on paper so that you, too, could enjoy the story of how Mrs. Claus saved Christmas.

—*Santa Claus*
The North Pole

One

If I start at the very beginning, we must go back to the year 377 A.D., when I was born in the small farming town of Niobrara in the country then known as Lycia. Its modern-day name is Turkey. With a population of two hundred, Niobrara was, in those days, a medium-sized community. Almost everyone living in my hometown at that time had something to do with growing, grinding, or selling grain, though a few families had groves of dates instead. I know many people today believe most of Turkey is just sand and wind, but there are some very green, fertile places, and Niobrara was in one of them. Most visitors to Niobrara were travelers briefly passing through on their way to bigger, more important cities and ports. And, always, bands of poor nomads would briefly camp on the outskirts of town, hoping to earn a few days' wages by helping harvest crops.

I lived on one of the wheat farms with my Uncle Silas and Aunt Lodi. They took me in while I was still a baby. My mother was Aunt Lodi's only sister, so when she and my father died unexpectedly of some unnamed disease, it was natural for my aunt and uncle to bring me into their home and raise me as though I were their daughter. There was nothing unusual about this. There were many orphans in those days. People didn't live very long.

Even if they were healthy, fifty or sixty was considered great old age. No one knew much about medicine, so if you did get sick the chances were good you would die rather than get better. When I was a child, Aunt Lodi sometimes called me "Layla the Miracle Girl," because I didn't catch whatever disease it was that took my parents. "God must have special plans for you," she would tell me, keeping her voice low so Uncle Silas wouldn't hear.

Like most men of his time, Uncle Silas wouldn't have accepted the possibility that any girl could be special. He loved me, I knew. Childless themselves, he and Aunt Lodi never acted like I was a burden passed on to them because of my parents' bad luck. Uncle Silas often carried me on his shoulders as we passed through town. He told me funny folktales and bought fine soft blankets for my bed and even let me have real leather sandals, a rare treat for a child. But, when I asked, he never let me come into the fields with him to work. Nor was I allowed to go to school to learn to read or write. By tradition, only boys were allowed to do these things, and Uncle Silas was a very traditional man.

"Honor God by knowing your place, little Layla," he would tell me over and over. "Let your Aunt Lodi teach you all the womanly tasks, and learn to be satisfied by them."

Well, I wasn't. By "womanly tasks," Uncle Silas meant I should become expert at cooking gruel and wheat cakes and lamb stew, and at washing clothes in the nearby river and fashioning brooms from river reeds and stout limbs of wood. My aunt did these things with a smile on her face, for she loved Uncle Silas dearly, but sometimes in the evening when he was out talking with his friends she would quietly tell me to not only keep my dreams, but to make them come true if I could.

What were those dreams? Not to settle for a woman's secondary place in a small farming village, for one thing. I had no quarrel with others who wanted nothing more out of life. Each of us should have the right to decide who and what we want to be. But when travelers passed through Niobrara on their way to somewhere else more exciting, I heard them mention Constantinople and Athens and Rome and I yearned to see these places for myself.

I also badly wanted to learn to read and write. We were a Christian community, and there were priests who would gather the boys several days each week for informal lessons. No one had paper and ink to spare back then. The priests would take sharp sticks and scratch letters and numbers into the dusty ground, while their pupils gathered around. When I tried to quietly join them, hanging back at the edge of the group, the priests would eventually notice me and shout that I had to go away immediately. But I kept trying, and each time I might learn a new letter or a new combination of letters that spelled a word before I was ordered to leave. By the time I was ten I was able to read and write quite adequately, though Aunt Lodi and I kept this a secret from Uncle Silas.

It was no secret from him, though, that I could do what in those days we called "sums," adding and subtracting numbers. At night in our hut, Uncle Silas would sit by the fire and try to do the accounts for the farm, adding up the money from the bushels of wheat he'd sold that day, and subtracting the wages he'd paid his nomad helpers to harvest it, then factoring in the cost of new seed. He was a kind man, but not good at math. He would say all the numbers out loud, hoping that would help him get the totals right: "Sixty-four coins for three bushels, plus seventy coins for four more, less sixty-nine coins for the help and forty-four for the seed, and that leaves . . . twenty-two? That doesn't sound right. Sixty-four and seventy, less sixty-nine and forty-four. Twenty-three? Twenty?"

"It leaves twenty-one, Uncle Silas," I said from across the room, where I was already wrapped up in my blankets for the night. Children went to bed quite early then, usually as soon as it was dark.

"What? Are you certain?" Uncle Silas blurted, and he spent the next several minutes muttering various sums until, finally, he saw that I was right. "Layla, how did you know that? Have you sneaked over to the boys' school again while they were studying mathematics?"

"No, Uncle Silas," I said, and it was the truth. That morning, I hadn't sneaked over during their math lessons. They'd been working on reading and spelling instead.

"Then how in the name of heaven are you able to calculate sums so quickly?" my uncle demanded. "It's quite unwomanly, I fear."

"Layla has a natural gift for sums," Aunt Lodi said, looking up from the shirt she was mending. "God-given ability is not unwomanly, I'm sure."

Uncle Silas was less certain, but he still found it convenient to have me help him keep his daily accounts—so long as I did this in the privacy of our home, where no neighbors could observe it. It was pleasing to me to have this special privilege, but I still wanted something more out of life. And, as I grew up, I became more aware of what that was, because of certain stories I kept hearing.

Throughout Lycia, there were tales of a mysterious gift-giver who came to poor people in the night and left them things they needed—cloaks or blankets or sandals. Those who were hungry sometimes awoke to find bread or cheese or dried fruits beside their beds. This was a wonderful, even miraculous thing, because times were hard and most people had all they could do to provide sufficiently for themselves and their own families. Charity was rare.

But this unknown gift-giver, who apparently was ageless since he'd been carrying out his wonderful mission for over ninety years, took charity to previously unthought-of heights. He bestowed his presents in big cities like Myra and smaller towns like Lycia—and Niobrara! Several times during my childhood, some of the nomads camping outside the village came whooping into town, crying out with joy that someone had left new cloaks for their children, or enough bread and cheese to feed their families for a week! Though none of the gifts was ever enough to supply anyone's needs for years or even months, it was the gesture itself that brought such happiness. Someone cared enough about poor people to seek them out and quietly minister to their specific needs.

I don't mean to imply that no one else cared for the poor. At the end of each harvest, after all our bills were paid and enough money set aside for the rest of the year, Uncle Silas was pleased to distribute the remaining grain to the men he'd hired. They, in turn, could sell the grain in other markets and use the money to feed and clothe their wives and children for a little while. This was one public task Uncle Silas gladly shared with me. I loved going with him to the nomad camps and handing the small sacks of grain to the hungry, ragged people there, though afterward I remembered their thin cloaks and thinner bodies and wished I could do even more. Twice, Uncle Silas punished me for giving my nice sandals to nomad girls who were barefoot. My punishment was only being sent to bed without supper. Even when he ordered me to go to my blankets, Uncle Silas added that he understood why I had done it.

"It's a sad thing, Layla, to see the poverty in this world," he said, gently patting my shoulder. "But you must learn, girl, that there's only so much any of us can do to help other people. If they're meant to be hungry or barefoot, that can't be any of our concern."

"Who means them to be hungry or barefoot?" I asked. "If I could, I would spend my whole life bringing gifts to people."

Uncle Silas sighed the way grown-ups often do when children ask difficult questions.

"I suppose God decides who is rich and who is poor," he said. "We must leave these things to him. As for you, girl, no life of gift-giving is possible. Get that thought out of your mind. You're almost twelve now, and in another year or two it will be time for you to take a husband and have a family of your own. Think of that instead."

I *was* thinking of that, when I wasn't dreaming of traveling the world and going out anonymously in the night to give gifts to the poor. All the other girls my age in Niobrara acted obsessed with the idea of marriage. They seemed to believe they would be asked to marry a young man, move into a home with him, have and raise children, and live happily ever after. When they talked about it, they never mentioned the endless chores that made up most of a married woman's life. I didn't mind chores, ever, if I thought they were accomplishing something worthwhile. Planting wheat would have been exciting, had Uncle Silas allowed me to do it, because stalks would grow and grain would be harvested and people would eat. But sweeping a floor just moved dust from one place to another. It seemed to me there was no real accomplishment in that. I had nothing against marriage, either, if I could be an equal partner rather than my husband's servant.

Because Niobrara was a small town, everyone knew everyone else and families often planned from the time of their children's birth who might grow up to marry whom. Though Aunt Lodi understood my dreams of travel and independence, Uncle Silas made a point on too many nights of mentioning various village boys to me, always adding what there might be about them that would make them desirable husbands.

"Have you noticed Hiram's son Matthew lately?" he might ask Aunt Lodi over dinner, pretending to be talking to her but really intending to be heard by me. "He's just turned sixteen, and he's a strapping young fellow, a very good worker. Of course, he's got three older brothers and Hiram's farm isn't big enough to support all the extra families when the four boys marry, but if Matthew married the right girl who inherited her own place, I think he'd be a fine provider."

At twelve, I was not pretty and seemed unlikely ever to become so. My jaw was long, and everyone said my eyes had the unwomanly quality of looking right through people, instead of my gaze being modestly cast down at the ground, which was more proper for a nice girl. No prospective husband was likely to want me for my looks, or for my attitude.

But I was going to inherit Uncle Silas's farm when he and Aunt Lodi passed away, and a very good farm it was. Enough wheat could be grown there to support a family in comfort, if not luxury, and all but the very richest young men in our area were very aware of this possibility. And so, as I became thirteen and then fourteen, boys and even older widowed men began dropping by our home, supposedly to visit my uncle and aunt but really looking over our barn and fields and the niece who would someday own them. When they greeted me, often praising my beauty and charm, I knew they were lying. They thought the farm was beautiful and charming, not me. After each one left, Uncle Silas would ask what I thought of him. My response was never satisfactory.

"Blast it, girl, there must be some man you would like to marry!" Uncle Silas shouted in the spring of 395, raising his voice because he was so frustrated. "I'm not like other men who order girls to marry someone specific. I'm letting you make your own choice. But you must make it soon, Layla! Your aunt and I are getting older, into our fifties, and we could die at any time. You are eighteen, already almost past the prime age for marriage. You must have a husband to take over the farm and care for you!"

"Why must I have a husband at all?" I asked for the hundredth, or perhaps the thousandth, time. "I could run the farm. I can certainly take care of myself, too."

Uncle Silas shook his head. "Young women must have husbands, Layla. That's all there is to it. Talk to the girl, Lodi! See if you can get her to see the sense of what I'm saying."

Aunt Lodi was gentler than Uncle Silas, but she was concerned about me, too.

"I want you to be happy, Layla," she said as we carried a basket of clothes down to the river to wash them. "You are intelligent, and warm-hearted, and I understand all your dreams to travel and help the poor. But you must be practical, too. It is hard, even impossible, for a woman to make her way alone in the world. Perhaps you could find a husband who wanted to do the same things."

"There's no one like that in Niobrara," I said gloomily. "When any man here looks at me, he sees the farm instead of Layla. And if I can't travel away from here, how can I meet a man who would love me for who I am, rather than what I'm going to inherit?"

"We'll pray about this, you and I," Aunt Lodi replied. "You are too special for your dreams not to somehow come true."

A few days later, Aunt Lodi suggested to Uncle Silas that the three of us make the forty-mile trip to Myra.

"We all need new clothes, and I've heard so much about the wonderful tomb there that I'm eager to see it," she said. Of course, my uncle and I both knew about the tomb to which she referred. For many years, Myra and its surrounding towns had been blessed by the presence of Bishop Nicholas, by all accounts a wonderful man who loved everyone and who encouraged generosity of spirit. It had been during his lifetime that the mysterious gift-giver began leaving his presents, and there had been some rumors that Nicholas was the one doing it. But in 343 he died quietly in the night. The community responded by building a splendid new church in his honor, and his body was placed in an elaborate tomb. Almost immediately, sick people began coming to the tomb to pray for cures, and some of them claimed they had miraculously been healed. And when the gift-giver continued coming quietly by night and leaving food or clothing to those in need, everyone knew it couldn't have been Bishop Nicholas after all—which is when the stories really took on new, fantastic tones. Now people whispered that the mysterious person had magical powers—he could turn himself into the wind, perhaps, and whistle into houses through cracks under doors.

So, a trip to Myra was exciting in several ways. The possibility of new clothes meant little to me. I never really cared what I wore. But I did want to see the wonderful tomb, and any time I could be somewhere different than my old familiar hometown, I was ready to go. Though I had been taken by my uncle and aunt to small communities near Niobrara, I had never traveled so far before, or to such a big city. If going to Myra wasn't quite the adventure of which I'd been dreaming, it was still closer to that dream than anything I'd previously experienced.

It took several days to prepare for the journey. Uncle Silas had to rent a cart, and a mule to pull it. Aunt Lodi and I baked extra loaves of bread and bought some dried fruit in the town market. Going forty miles would take at least two days. We needed food to eat on the way. There were no paved roads between Niobrara and Myra, just well-worn paths where dust swirled a little less because the dirt was so hard-packed by generations of feet, hooves, and wheels.

I loved the trip to Myra, though it also frustrated me. It was wonderful to watch other travelers, many of them wearing exotic-looking robes. We passed caravans of heavily-laden camels and could smell the aroma of the rare spices they were transporting. But the trip took so long! When the wheel of our cart caught in a rut, it took an hour for my uncle, sweating, to wrench it out. I wanted to help, but as a woman I was required to stand quietly to the side, the hood of my robe pulled modestly around my face. How boring!

But there was nothing boring about Myra, which had so many buildings you could actually see them hundreds of yards ahead before you even entered the city! People milled about, and animals added moos and bleats to the general cacophony, and the market in the center of the city must have had a hundred different stalls. Uncle Silas left Aunt Lodi and me at the market, telling us to look around for good bargains on new cloaks while he found a stable for the mule and an inn for us to sleep in that night—we would be staying for several days. Aunt Lodi was eager to begin shopping, but I wanted to do something else.

"Please, let's go right away to see the tomb of Bishop Nicholas," I pleaded. "The cloaks will still be for sale in the morning."

"The tomb will be there in the morning, too," Aunt Lodi replied. "Why are you so anxious to see it?"

I didn't know. I just felt I had to go there. It took several minutes, but I convinced my aunt that it would be all right for me to find the tomb by myself while she shopped. Aunt Lodi made me promise that I would take only a brief look at the tomb, then rejoin her at the market.

"You and Silas and I can go take a long look at it tomorrow," she said. "Be certain you meet me right back here by sunset. I don't want you walking the streets of a strange city all alone after dark."

I promised I would, and hurried off. It wasn't hard to find the tomb. The first woman I asked knew exactly where it was, though she warned me I might not be able to get a very good look at it.

"The cripples, you know, gather around it before dawn and spend all day praying to be healed," she said. "Bishop Nicholas, of course, is given credit for granting such miracles, and perhaps he does. My hands get very swollen and sore sometimes; I'm thinking of going to the tomb and praying to him myself."

And she was right. The tomb was actually inside the church, and a magnificent thing it was, higher all by itself than any structure I had ever seen before, with the date of Bishop Nicholas's death carved into the stone—December 6, 343, it was—as well as his likeness. He had been, apparently, a striking-looking man, with long hair and a beard. He appeared a bit stouter than most, but then bishops also ate better (and, apparently, more) than the rest of us. I wanted to look closer at the carving of the bishop, but dozens of cripples surrounded the tomb and I didn't want to push them aside. Some were blind, others couldn't walk, and their crutches lay beside them as they prayed, silently or out loud, to be healed. As I stood behind them, I also noticed in the shadows to the side of the tomb a number of other people, all ragged and hungry looking, quietly waiting, though I had no idea for what.

"Who are they?" I asked a reasonably well-dressed man who was standing beside me.

"It's an odd thing," he said. "Ever since this tomb was built, poor people passing through Myra seem to get comfort from just being near it."

As I stood as close to the tomb as I could, a strange feeling came over me. It wasn't sadness, though I felt very badly for the crippled and poor people, and wanted with all my heart to do something to help them. And it wasn't exactly excitement, either, though I was thrilled to be in a large city for the first time in my life. If I had to describe it, I would say I felt inspired. My eyes moved from the poor people to the carving of Bishop Nicholas's kind face, back and forth between them while time passed and I didn't notice the afternoon shadows growing long and deep. Finally, as night fell, everyone began to leave. I felt as though I was being jostled awake from a wonderful dream. Then I realized it was nighttime, and I remembered Aunt Lodi waiting back at the market.

She was very angry with me when I finally returned, a bit out of breath because I'd run all the way from the tomb.

"If Silas knew you'd been out gallivanting until after dark, he'd pack up the cart and have us back on the road to Niobrara at dawn. What was there about the bishop's tomb that made you forget your promise to come right back?"

I don't recall my answer, though I do remember she didn't tell Uncle Silas about how I had disobeyed. The three of us stayed in Myra for four days. We bought clothes and ate wonderful food and wandered around the city marveling at its size and all the people who lived there. Twice, we went to see the bishop's tomb. Both times, I was overcome by the same sense of inspiration. I did not tell my uncle and aunt about it, but afterward when we were back home in Niobrara I found myself having the same dream almost every night. I would be in a different place in each dream, but in the company of the same man. He was older than me and somewhat overweight. His hair and beard were white. No one who looked like him lived in Niobrara, yet his face was very familiar.

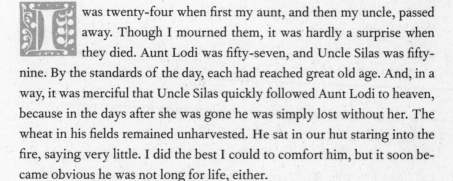I was twenty-four when first my aunt, and then my uncle, passed away. Though I mourned them, it was hardly a surprise when they died. Aunt Lodi was fifty-seven, and Uncle Silas was fifty-nine. By the standards of the day, each had reached great old age. And, in a way, it was merciful that Uncle Silas quickly followed Aunt Lodi to heaven, because in the days after she was gone he was simply lost without her. The wheat in his fields remained unharvested. He sat in our hut staring into the fire, saying very little. I did the best I could to comfort him, but it soon became obvious he was not long for life, either.

"Marry, Layla," he said during our last conversation. His voice was quite weak. "Find a good husband."

"I promise," I replied, and felt somehow I was telling the truth, even though I was no more willing than ever to marry a man from Niobrara and become a farmer's wife.

Uncle Silas's death created a very difficult situation for me. As his only heir, his farm became mine. But no woman in Niobrara, or anywhere else that anyone in Niobrara knew of, lived alone and managed a farm by herself.

This was supposed to be done on her behalf by a husband or son or uncle or cousin, or at least a close male friend. I had none of these.

"Choose a man and get on with your life," people told me over and over. When I tried to hire workers to harvest the grain, they all refused to work for a woman. A year after my uncle had passed I was still unmarried, and even the other women in the village began to act uncomfortable around me. Once, several of them pulled me aside and told me I was acting "unnatural."

I knew better. I had spent the year making plans. Never forgetting Aunt Lodi's words, I was not only keeping my dreams, I was going to try to make them come true.

Besides the farm, which was worth something itself, Uncle Silas had bequeathed me some money. It wasn't a fortune by any means, but the small pile of coins he'd accumulated over the years amounted to enough for what I needed—a sum sufficient to keep me in simple food and clothing for a long time, with quite a bit left over. And I knew what I wanted to do with the money that was left.

The mysterious gift-giver of local legend might be magical, or might not. I could not be that person—I certainly had no special powers—but I could do some of the same things. I would take my money and use it to buy blankets and cloaks and food for people in need. During the year between my uncle's death and the time I left Niobrara, I thought long and hard about how best to do this. Gradually, I realized several things.

First, as a giver I, too, must remain anonymous. Even the very poorest people still had pride and might be insulted by a strange woman simply handing them gifts. The legendary gift-giver, whoever that was or might have been, was right to leave presents at night and in secret.

Second, I must distribute my gifts as widely as possible. There were poor, deserving people everywhere. To stay in one place for too long would also cause another problem. After a while, people in the area would begin to stay awake at night in the hope that they could find out who the gift-giver might be. Besides, I wanted badly to travel.

Third, it would be impossible to give anyone in need all that he or she might require. If I helped a few in a substantial way, all my money would soon be gone and I would have nothing left for anyone else. But if I did something small but important for each one, then hundreds, perhaps even thousands, of good if impoverished men, women, and children would at least know that, in a hard world, someone had cared enough about them to leave tokens of respect and assistance. In a very real sense, my gift to them would be hope.

There was, of course, another inevitable dilemma. Even if I was very frugal regarding my own needs, and kept the gifts I gave small and inexpensive, the money I had would only last for so long. In seven or eight years, ten at the most, it would all be gone. I had only one farm to sell, only one accumulation of coins to spend. When they were used up, I would have no way to get any more. It was possible, even probable, that when my final gifts were given I would then become exactly the same as those I'd done my best to help—an impoverished person who would have to depend on the charity of others. Starvation might be my eventual fate.

I accepted this. It didn't frighten me, perhaps because I did not expect something like that to happen. I believed—somehow, actually, I *knew*—my future held something different, something wonderful. At night I still dreamed of being in many places with the white-bearded man, and the inspiration I felt that first afternoon at the tomb of St. Nicholas had remained with me ever since.

So it was just after my twenty-fifth birthday that I walked into Niobrara and announced to the men gathered near the well there that I was selling my uncle's farm. Did anyone want to buy it at a fair price?

Oh, the men made a fuss, and told me I shouldn't sell, that I should marry and let my husband run the farm instead, but I knew that they were already making calculations in their heads. What was the lowest price they could offer to a woman who, by reason of her gender, certainly wouldn't have the intelligence to recognize the amount wasn't nearly enough? So over the next few days, one by one they came to my hut and made their bids, and every time went home shaking their heads and muttering about this extremely unfeminine woman who drove such a hard bargain. But it was a good farm, certainly a profitable one, and after a week or so I made a very fine sale indeed. I collected the money, got together the few belongings I wanted to take with me, and prepared to leave Niobrara and embark on my great adventure.

This was when I began to understand the extent of my challenge.

I had a good-sized pouch of coins strapped inside my cloak, with cotton mixed in with the coins to keep them from jingling. I hadn't yet been out much in the world, but I knew well enough that thieves lurked everywhere, and any of them would be eager to rob a female traveler with money. Still, I could afford to rent a cart and mule—my plan was to return to Myra, pray at Bishop Nicholas's tomb myself, and then begin my own gift-giving mission wherever whim and fate might take me.

But no one in Niobrara would rent me a mule and cart. Everyone said it was simply too dangerous for a woman to travel to Myra all by herself. I was certain I would be safe, so long as I was careful, but no one would hear of it. When I said I would walk to Myra instead, they said they could not allow it and would restrain me if necessary. I had to wait impatiently for almost three days before a farm family from town set off to Myra, and allowed me to ride along with them in their wagon. It was a very frustrating trip. The whole way, the husband and wife kept telling me how foolish I was to be leaving such a nice, safe place—surely I would rather marry and settle down instead of risking my life on some dangerous, lonely trip.

They dropped me off in the market at Myra with many final recommendations that I should come to my senses. I managed not to reply that I was being quite sensible, thank you very much. Then I found that things would be just as difficult for me in Myra as they were in Niobrara, if not more so.

Since I planned to stay for several days, buying and then distributing gifts to the very poorest people in Myra I could find, I first needed to take a room at an inn. I wanted the inn to be clean but inexpensive. Every coin I spent on my own comfort would be one less I had for gifts. But I must have gone to a dozen inns where I was turned away. In the big cities, it seemed, unmarried adult women traveling by themselves were assumed to be of very bad character. How could they be otherwise, if no men were willing to marry them? It was almost dark when I finally found a place to stay. The innkeeper grudgingly took my money and warned me to behave myself.

"I run a nice place here," he said, waving a hand at a very dirty collection of bug-ridden rooms.

"And a very expensive place, too," I replied, handing over more coins than I'd intended to pay for a few nights' shelter.

"If you don't like the price, feel free to go elsewhere," he said, his tone quite insulting. "My guess is, no one would have you, and you'd have to sleep in the street."

"Is this the same price you would charge a single man for a room?"

"It's what I'm charging *you*."

I hoped that he would be unique in my travels, but, sadly, he wasn't. No matter where I went, people always seemed to look with disdain on me for being a woman who traveled alone, and I knew I was often charged more than what was fair for rooms. And, as I would soon discover, unfair costs of lodging were to be among the very least of my problems.

Still, that night in Myra I could hardly sleep, as much for being excited as for the nasty bedbugs that crawled everywhere along the floor and walls. In the morning I would visit Bishop Nicholas's tomb, pray, and then make my way to the market. There I would buy bread and dried fruit and some blankets, and spend much of the next few nights quietly distributing them by the sleeping mats of the poor.

Only the first part of my plan went as expected. I was up with the sun and hurried to the tomb, which was already surrounded by cripples and other pilgrims. That was all right. I simply bowed my head and asked God to bless me as I tried to do good works. I raised my head and found myself looking again at the carving of Bishop Nicholas, focusing on his strong, kind face. Though I knew it was impossible, it seemed as though his eyes, carved in stone to look straight ahead, somehow briefly turned to gaze at me—and did that stone mouth momentarily widen into a *smile*? How odd!

But I had no time to spare on further speculation. Before leaving the inn, I had carefully removed several coins from the pouch sewed into the lining of my cloak—enough money to buy a dozen loaves of bread, some containers of dried dates, and several blankets. At the market, I lined up and bought these things, only to find that I had too much to comfortably carry. I had to leave some of my purchases in the stalls where I bought them, promising to retrieve them the next day. Even so, it was an awkward walk back to the inn with bread loaves tucked under my arms, and the blankets I was balancing on one shoulder spilling over in front of my face. Several people I passed pointed at me and laughed.

After making a simple supper from a bit of the bread and two of the dates, I waited impatiently in my nasty little room for night to come. During the day, I had seen several ragged nomads in the city. I knew some of them were camped just outside Myra; I'd noticed their patched tents set up by the side of the road when I arrived with the farm family in their wagon. These wanderers, surely, were just like the ones I'd known back in Niobrara—poor, honest families who had no permanent homes because they could not afford them. Instead, they moved from place to place, finding temporary work and never certain which nights there would be food for themselves and their children.

Finally it got dark. I put on my cloak and gathered up some bread, fruit, and two blankets. I was just able to carry everything. My heart pounded as I slipped out into the street, where I immediately realized I had no idea how to find the nomad tents outside town. There were no streetlights. There were many more buildings than I was used to. Clouds kept me from seeing the stars, which would at least have let me figure out north and south. It took several hours of wrong turns and unexpected dead ends before I finally stumbled out of the city and into the countryside, where I found myself on a road that might or might not have been the one to Niobrara.

No matter; the clouds shifted and there was enough moonlight for me to see tents, tattered ones, and I knew the people sleeping in them must be desperately poor. Stealthily, I approached the nomad camp. My gift-giving was about to begin!

Then a dog started barking. I'd forgotten that many of these wanderers kept canine pets, as much for protection as for companionship. This dog had caught my scent, and, of course, did not understand I was coming to give his owners presents rather than rob them. People who'd been sleeping in the tents jumped up, many of them shouting. The first dog kept barking, and several more joined in the thunderous chorus. There was nothing for me to do but turn and run. As I did, I dropped the loaves of bread, which were long and thin, and then I lost my grip on the blankets as I dashed madly through the darkness back toward the city. I arrived at the inn without the gifts I had meant to deliver, and without the satisfaction of actually giving them. My sleep during the few hours left before dawn, though, was curiously refreshing. The bearded man I had been dreaming about—how familiar his features seemed; *where* had I seen him before?—appeared to me again, and this time he winked and said, "You'll learn, and it will get better."

Well, my dream-friend was right about that. I had learned how important it was to scout out during the day those places where I planned to leave my gifts at night. It was, for instance, important to know where watchdogs might prowl. So on my second day in Myra I spent the morning locating another nomad camp just outside the city, making certain no one in that group had a dog, and carefully studying the best route between the camp and the inn, so I would know my way even in the pitch dark.

My reconnaissance yielded other useful information. I counted five children in the group. All were barefoot, a painful state in a time when roads were strewn with rocks. I returned to the market to claim the bread, dried fruit, and blankets I hadn't been able to carry the day before—they still comprised quite an armful—but I also added five child-sized pairs of sandals to the load.

That night, I went out again, and this time things went smoothly. I found the camp, quietly made my way to the tents, and left bread and fruit by the sleeping mats of the snoring adults. Two of the older ones shivered in the cool night air, because they had nothing to cover themselves with. I left a blanket for each. Finally, I left a pair of sandals by the side of each sleeping child. I took a moment to study their faces, which were streaked with dirt. How hard their lives must be, I thought, constantly moving from place to place, often required to do the same hard fieldwork as grown-ups, always worried about whether, at night, there would be any supper at all. Well, they would have one very special morning, at least.

I made my empty-handed way back to the inn and lay down, but I simply couldn't sleep. I was too excited. As soon as it was dawn, I hurried back toward the nomad camp, and there by the light of the still-rising sun I saw five little figures dancing with glee, twirling in the dust on their new, treasured sandals even as their parents called for them to come to the fire and enjoy a tasty, nourishing breakfast of bread and fruit.

It was a wonderful moment for me, too, and in the next years I was blessed to have many, many more of them. We learn in the Bible that it is better to give than to receive, and I was reminded of the truth in this every time I did my gift-giving. The satisfaction I felt, and the joy that washed over me, when I left food or clothing or blankets for those in need more than made up for the frustrations that continued to plague me.

The main problem was that each wonderful moment of gift-giving required whole days and weeks of preparation. I had known from the start that I would have to keep moving about, traveling as far as I could between the places where I left the gifts. To stay in one place too long would be to invite discovery of who I was and what I was doing. My intention had been to divide my time between big cities and small villages, enjoying diversity in my happy task. There were plenty of poor folk everywhere. But I discovered it was difficult to make my way to country villages and impossible to properly carry out my mission once I was in them. In small towns, strange single women were objects of scorn, pity, or a combination of both. There was no way for me to quietly blend into the population, watching to learn where the poorest people lived, what food or clothing they needed most, and then purchasing these things before quietly leaving them beside the right sleeping mats during the night. Just the act of a lone woman buying many loaves of bread or pairs of sandals would set all the residents of small towns to gossiping, and when these very same things were left in the night for the poorest people in the village to enjoy, well, it would be no mystery who had done the gift-giving. A few times I tried buying these things in big cities, then transporting them with me to the country communities, but that proved much too difficult. If anything drew more attention than a lone woman arriving in a hamlet, it was a lone woman arriving with great packs of provisions and clothing.

That was one reason I mostly had to keep to the cities. The other involved transportation. It might take me several weeks just to find some way to get from one place to another, let alone make the journey. I didn't mind walking, but, as my former Niobrara neighbors had told me, that was too dangerous. Bandits lurked along every road, waiting to prey on travelers foolish enough to be on their own. I thought about buying a mule and wagon, but their price would have substantially reduced the money I had to purchase gifts. The only economical, and safe, way for me to get from one place to the next was to find caravans heading to the same places I wished to go. Usually, it would not cost much for me to rent a place on one of the wagons or carts in the caravan. Then, along with dozens or even hundreds of others I would make my slow, bumpy way to another major city. At the very least, every trip would take days, and some took weeks. If roads were bad or wagons broke down, the caravan might make only a few miles' progress between dawn and dark.

Upon arriving in the new city, I would then have to find a place to stay for a few days, and that was never easy. As was the case in Myra, most innkeepers did not want to rent rooms to a single woman. Those who would always wanted more money than the rooms were worth, but most of the time I had no choice but to pay whatever was being asked. After that, it took more time to scout out everything, to find where the poorest people lived or camped, and which camps had dogs or were too well-guarded. I would estimate that I spent two weeks traveling and planning for each night that I was actually able to leave gifts.

I don't mean to make it seem as though I was generally unhappy. During those moments that I crept up to campfires, laid down bread or fruit or blankets or clothing, and then stealthily disappeared back into the night, I felt a joy that warmed me even during the most frustrating times in between. No life is perfect, and no dream is realized exactly as it was imagined. Unless we accept the unwelcome parts of our lives instead of resenting them, we can't completely enjoy all the good things that come to us. I grumbled sometimes, but I would not allow myself to brood. As the years passed, I was able to look on my problems as challenges, situations to be overcome if only I had enough common sense and determination. If I let certain things discourage rather than inspire me, it would be more my own fault than anyone else's. Realizing this, I was able to maintain a positive attitude.

Even so, the time came in the year 412 when the coins I carried were so few that I no longer needed to keep them in a pouch hidden under my cloak. I could drop them in a pocket of my robe instead. The fact I had managed to stretch my inheritance for ten years of gift-giving gave me great satisfaction. The additional fact that I'd be penniless within days was also something I had to consider.

I was staying at an inn in Constantinople, by far the largest city I'd visited during my decade of journeys. I found myself there quite often during the years. The larger the place, the more poor people in and around it, of course; because the population of Constantinople was so immense, more than three hundred thousand by some counts, no one took much notice of a woman on her own. There were even a few inns that specifically offered shelter to those like me, and for a reasonable cost. It was a relief not to be stared at, and to be treated with respect instead of insolence.

In my room, which was, for a change, clean and bug-free, I sat on the sleeping mat provided and took out the few coins that remained to me. I had paid in advance for one week's lodging, because that left me just enough to buy supplies for about that many nights of gift-giving. When the week was up, so, apparently, would be my wonderful mission. I had just passed my thirty-fifth birthday. By the standards of the day, I was in my late middle age. I still felt healthy and strong. Somehow I'd avoided the common diseases that claimed lives so regularly. By God's grace I had all my teeth, and my hair remained brown instead of gray. But old age had to be well on its way. I'd been lucky my money and health had lasted so long.

After I spent these last coins and passed my last night at this Constantinople inn, I wondered what would become of me. In such large cities, there were usually places where unmarried women could live and work in the Christian church. That was a possibility; I certainly believed in and loved the Lord. Otherwise, I could become a nomad, perhaps joining with some band or another that would take me in and give me a place in a torn tent at night. While I had any strength left, I had no intention of becoming a street beggar. Well, for these last few days I would simply go on as I had been, and let fate or divine grace determine what happened next.

Reminding myself that self-pity is the worst disease of all, I stood up, put the coins I had left in the pocket of my robe, and made my way to one of Constantinople's many marketplaces. The day before, I had spied a nomad camp on the outskirts of the city, one with many ragged children and hungry-looking old people huddled around tiny fires. They were wrapped in thin, dirty blankets, which was sad, but they seemed to have nothing at all to eat, which was worse. I counted almost twenty people.

Now, in the market, I took out my few coins and estimated how much would buy just enough food to fill all twenty of their stomachs for a few days. While that wouldn't permanently improve their lives, at least it would give them a chance to gain some strength and, perhaps, some hope, because they would know someone cared about them. So I bought bread, and dried fruit, and some blocks of cheese. It was certainly plain fare, but it was nourishing and cheap enough for me to buy quite a lot. Over my ten years of gift-giving I had learned better how to carry large loads. My robes and cloak had many deep pockets.

As I stood in front of one vendor's stall, shoving cheese and fruit into those pockets, I happened to glance at another stall nearby. Bread was being sold there to a pair of customers who were putting the loaves into large pockets in their robes, too. The first thing I noticed about these men was that they were, to say it kindly, both somewhat stout. Because their robes were so wrinkled and stained with dust, I suspected they, too, must be travelers. Their backs were turned to me as they tried to pack away all the bread they had purchased—why would two men need so many loaves? Then, chatting away to each other like old, beloved friends, they walked past me and I was able to see their faces. The fellow on the left looked to be about forty. His hair was mostly brown but streaked with gray. He had no beard, unusual for the time, and he squinted his eyes a little. As was true of many people before glasses were invented, this was an obvious sign he was nearsighted. He seemed in every way to be a pleasant, even kindly person, but it was his companion who drew my attention.

I could have sworn I recognized that long white hair and beard, and that smile, which was at once warm and welcoming. Other people automatically smiled back as they stepped aside to let him pass. There was about him a unique sense of *goodness*, if that isn't too strange a description. Very briefly, our eyes met, and when they did I nearly gasped, because I realized this was the man from my dreams. As a sensible person I knew this had to be impossible, yet here he was! I wanted to say something, I meant to reach out and pull at his arm and speak to him, but the shock I was feeling left me too confused to move, and by the time I recovered myself he and his companion had been swallowed up in the marketplace crowd.

Still stunned, I slowly made my way back to the inn, trying to make sense of what had happened. Surely I'd just been granted a sign—but of what? Should I now do nothing else but search every street in Constantinople until I found this man again? And, if I did, what should I say to him? He might be repulsed by a strange woman saying to him that she knew him from many years of dreams. But beyond the dreams, I had the sense that I had seen him somewhere else, too.

As night fell, my only instinct was to go ahead and bring my gifts out to the nomad camp. After all, because I had spent the last of my money, this would be one of my last moments of gift-giving, too. I would take most of the provisions I had just purchased. The few things remaining I would bring to others in need, and when the final loaf and dried fig and bit of cheese were distributed, the next part of my life would begin. I wondered, perhaps even allowed myself to hope, that the man with the white beard and wonderful smile might be involved.

Three

here were four tents in the nomad camp, with two small fires burning nearby. I always found it easier to leave gifts when tents were involved rather than proper huts or houses, which usually had doors. Though door locks weren't yet in use, sometimes families would block their doors from the inside by placing heavy objects against them, since, particularly in cities, there were thieves who might try to sneak in. I, of course, was also sneaking in, but to leave things rather than take them. Tents only had entryway flaps, and these were easily pushed aside.

I approached the camp carefully, as I always did, trying to be certain no one else was around. On this night, I couldn't escape the feeling that someone was lurking nearby, but after an extra half hour of waiting and watching I decided to get on with my task. The camp was about a half mile outside Constantinople, but it was beside a good-sized road, and someone might ride or walk by at any time. At least there were hills all around. Even if that made it easier for others to hide from my sight, this meant in case of emergency I, too, would have a good chance of getting away.

I quietly walked toward the nearest tent. I knew from my scouting earlier in the day that a mother and father and their two children would be sleeping there. Just before I eased aside the flap to go inside, I reached into the deep pocket of my cloak and put my hand on a long, thick loaf of bread. In those days, a loaf might be the entire dinner for a family of four or six or even ten, so they were quite substantial. Think of how long a modern-day baseball bat usually is, and that was about the length of a loaf in 412, only the loaf was easily twice as thick as the bat. Years of practice made what I would do next completely automatic. The pockets inside my cloak were quite long, from my waist all the way down to the hem around my ankles. I could put several loaves into them at once, along with other smaller items of food or clothing. On this particular night, I would begin by entering this first tent, pulling out one loaf, and placing it gently by the side of one of the sleeping mats. Then I would take out smaller things, in this case some dried fruit and cheese, and put these items by the other mats, so that each sleeper would find something when he or she woke up. I didn't want anyone to feel ignored. After that, I'd leave gifts in each of the other tents, in turn. So my hand was on the bread as I slipped into the closest tent, but almost instantly I recoiled in near panic, because someone very large was standing inside, and he was holding a heavy-looking club.

Now, I had nearly been caught many times over the years by someone who hadn't been able to get to sleep, or else I bumped into something and made a noise, but I had always been able to make a quick escape. I'd never come into a tent to find someone not only wide awake, but on his feet and armed. At least he seemed as astonished to see me as I was to see him; we both peered at each other in the darkness for several seconds, and then, since he didn't call out a warning to anyone else, I realized he must be a thief who was cruel enough to want to rob these poor people of the very few things they had. Anger boiled up in me, and before he could swat me with his nasty club I yanked the long loaf of bread from my cloak and waved it in front of his face, though I couldn't clearly make out his features. In the dark, I hoped he would think I had a club, too, and apparently he did, because after shaking his own club at me for a few moments he gestured for me to follow him and exited the tent through a flap on the other side.

Here was a real dilemma. If I went with him, this hulking fellow might just hit me over the head with his club and rob me, too. But if I didn't go, he might shout out an alarm and send all the nomads running after me, while he made his own escape in the opposite direction. Well, I was a woman, perhaps, but I still could fight if it came to that. More than once in my ten years of traveling, I'd had to defend myself with a punch or a kick. I could do it again.

So I followed the man out of the tent and a few dozen yards beyond the nomad camp. There, in the first swell of hills, another man was waiting. That was when I knew I should turn and run, since I was outnumbered, but the second man, who was large, too, stepped forward quickly and I couldn't get away. Showing signs of fear would only make me a more inviting victim, so I tugged the hood of my cloak tightly around my face, hoping they would not realize I was a woman.

The man I'd followed out of the tent hissed, "You thief, why can't you leave those poor people alone? They don't have anything for you to steal!"

That made me furious rather than frightened. I still couldn't see his face clearly, but his mean words were certainly uncalled for.

"Don't accuse me," I whispered back. "You're the robber. Well, if the two of you want to fight, I'm ready!" I'd put my long loaf back in my robe pocket as I'd left the tent, but now I reached to pull it out again. But the second man, moving quickly for someone so large, was faster. He reached into my pocket first and pulled out bread instead of a cudgel. Then he reached back in and rummaged about a little before whispering, "There's only food here, bread and fruit."

"Well, go ahead and steal it," I whispered, still keeping my tone harsh and, I hoped, masculine-sounding. "Eat it while those poor people starve, and may you get bellyaches afterward, you fat fiends."

"We're not going to steal this food, and don't call me fat," whispered the first man. My eyes were adjusting to the darkness, and I could see him better. But, like me, he and the other man had the hoods of their cloaks pulled around their faces, too, so I still had no idea what they might look like. "Were you going into that tent to *leave* food rather than commit robbery?"

"I've never robbed anyone," I replied, snatching back my bread loaf and returning it to my pocket with as much dignity as I could muster given the strange circumstances. I didn't want to lose the bread. After all, I had so very few things left to give before my mission was over. "Where have you put your club? Are you going to hit me with it?"

He chuckled, and pushed into my hand another long loaf, which I had obviously mistaken for a weapon. "Neither of us seems to be a robber, my friend. I think I want to know you better. My companion and I have a warm, clean room back in the city. Join us there; we'll eat and drink and talk."

Well, I certainly couldn't accept this invitation. I still wasn't sure I could trust these men, and if they were somehow bad and they discovered I was a woman, my situation would only become worse. So I suggested we first distribute food to the poor nomads in their tents instead, hoping that in the process I would have a chance to run away. But while the second man waited outside the camp, the first one I'd stumbled into stayed right by my side as we left bread and fruit and cheese. When the last item was placed by the final sleeping mat, the man gently took my arm and led me back to where his friend was waiting. I was caught.

As we walked back into the city, the first man let go of me, but I noticed he and his companion walked on either side of me, perhaps so I couldn't get away. They began to talk in their normal voices. I kept whispering. My cloak was baggy, its long empty pockets flapping since the food I'd stored in them was gone. Apparently, these two still thought I was a man.

We arrived at the inn where they were staying, and they invited me to come up for something to eat and drink. Sensing my chance, I simply shook my head and turned to walk away, but the man who'd waited outside the nomad camp caught me and said somewhat impatiently, "What's the matter with you? You know now we're not thieves. If you don't have a place to stay, you can even sleep with us."

"I have to leave," I whispered. "Good night." I meant to go. I would have, but then the first man reached out toward me. I could have avoided his touch. But somehow I was frozen in place.

"At least let me see who you are," he said, gently tugging my hood away from my face. My long hair tumbled out, and as the light coming through the windows of the inn fell upon my face, I knew it was clear I was certainly not a man.

"Let me go. I can fight if I have to," I said with as much force as I could summon.

"You don't have to," he said reassuringly. "Please, my good woman, don't be afraid we'd harm you."

I couldn't be sure of that. The two men were standing close together, staring at my newly revealed face. Impulsively, I reached out and, one after the other, pulled their hoods away from their faces. At least if I was attacked by them and survived, I might be able to identify them afterward to the city authorities. When I saw the first face I gasped. I recognized this man. He was one of the two men from the market, the beardless one with the nearsighted squint. That must mean the other was— Yes! The man with the long white hair and beard and warm smile, the man I'd dreamed about for so long. I couldn't help staring into his eyes. We must have looked at each other for a full minute or more before he said, "Our offer of something to drink and eat is made in friendship."

I knew I could trust him—why else had he been so long in my dreams?—so I replied, "Then in friendship, I accept."

Up in the room, they produced jars of fruit juice—I very much preferred drinking such healthy stuff rather than wine—and some bread and cheese. Our conversation instantly bubbled over. I had never been someone who liked to talk about herself, but as soon as we sat down on the floor mats I found myself almost babbling as I recounted my childhood in Niobrara with Uncle Silas and Aunt Lodi, and how I decided while still very young that I wanted to be, *would* become, a gift-giver.

"The inspiration came from the old stories, you see," I explained. "In Lycia, people had spoken for a hundred years about a mysterious gift-giver who came silently in the night to give gifts to the very poorest people." The nearsighted man whispered something to the wonderful man with the white hair and beard, who sharply whispered to him to keep quiet. "Well," I continued, "ten years ago when my uncle and aunt died, they left me the farm and some money as my inheritance. Men in my village offered to marry me, but I realized it was the farm they really wanted, not me. I mean, it's obvious I'm not beautiful."

Now the white-bearded man couldn't keep himself from speaking. "You seem beautiful to me," he blurted, and his nearsighted friend laughed and slapped him on the shoulder. For a moment, everything felt quite awkward. I felt myself blushing, and the white-bearded man's cheeks turned bright red, too. I thought I should perhaps feel offended—the remark had been quite forward, as we used to term such a personal comment. But instead I was pleased. Never before had I really cared what any man thought of my appearance. But now I did.

After several silent moments, the white-bearded man composed himself, poured all three of us more fruit juice, and remarked, "Do you know, we've been talking for some time and we haven't even properly introduced ourselves. May I ask your name?"

"Layla," I said.

"Well, Layla, we are honored to meet you. This fat grinning fellow here is Felix. He has been my friend and traveling companion ever since we met in Rome many, many years ago. And my name is—"

Before the word was out of his mouth, I knew. A carved image on a tomb in Myra flashed into my mind.

"Your name is Nicholas," I told him. "I should have known. I recognized you right away, from the likeness on your tomb and from—" I was about to add, "my dreams," but thought better of it.

Nicholas and Felix exchanged a long look. Then Nicholas said carefully, "Well, it's getting quite late. I suggest Felix and I escort you back to your own lodgings. Will you meet us again tomorrow night? We have gifts to give; a very needy family is spending hungry, cold nights hiding in a rich man's barn. You could join us as we help them. Afterward, there are certain things I would like to tell you about."

"It would be my pleasure," I replied. There was a great deal I wanted to ask them, most importantly how a man who had died of old age in 343 still appeared very much alive sixty-nine years later. The odd thing was, though I wondered how it was possible, I never doubted it was true.

Felix lagged a little behind Nicholas and me as we walked back to the inn where I was staying. It wasn't a long walk and only took about ten minutes, but it seemed like much less even than that. Nicholas and I didn't say much to each other, just casual comments about the coolness of the night air and how much more bread and cheese cost in the Constantinople markets than in Myra. When we reached the inn I found myself wondering, unexpectedly, whether Nicholas was going to kiss me good night, which certainly would have been forward and definitely unacceptable upon such short acquaintance. It was only after he formally shook my hand and turned and walked away with Felix that I realized I'd hoped he would kiss me. I'd sometimes kissed my Uncle Silas on the cheek, but I'd never kissed any man in a romantic way and had never really wanted to before.

Needless to say, that night I slept very little. Perhaps I should have been awake because I was worrying. My money was all gone, I had only a bit of bread and cheese left to distribute, and after that, what would become of me? Instead, I couldn't close my eyes out of sheer pleasure. Nicholas wanted to see me again! Something special was happening.

I was right about that. The next evening, just as the sky turned dark, Nicholas and Felix came to fetch me at the inn. I met them outside the front entrance, my pockets filled with the very last bread and cheese I had. Before I had met them, my intention was to make these things last for several more days of gift-giving. Now, I brought everything that was left. Just to make certain I had been invited as a full contributing partner rather than a welcome but essentially useless companion, I informed them right away that I expected to contribute my share to the night's gifts. Both Nicholas and Felix seemed quite pleased to hear this. They led the way to an extensive property just north of the city. It was a large farm, much bigger than my uncle's. Livestock nestled in wide corrals. The bright moon silhouetted an impressive house fifty yards from a fine barn. Nicholas whispered that sleeping in this barn were a mother and father and their three young children. He and Felix had met the father two days earlier in the Constantinople market when he was begging everyone he passed to hire him for any sort of work so he could buy food for his family.

"His name is Tobias, and he seems to be a very fine fellow," Nicholas said. "There are so many men like him—poor due to bad luck, not laziness. He is very talented at threshing wheat and shoeing horses. He learned these trades on a small farm perhaps a hundred miles from here, but when the owner of the farm died a year ago, Tobias and his family were ordered off the property without any sort of explanation. He hasn't been able to find steady work since, and some nights his children cry because they're so hungry."

"Well, they won't be hungry tomorrow morning," Felix added, brandishing a handful of dried fruit and handing it over to Nicholas. "You two go on inside the barn and leave your gifts."

"Aren't you coming, too?" I asked.

Nicholas chuckled. "Felix, here, is a fine fellow with many admirable talents, but stealth isn't one of them. Our custom is for him to stand guard outside while I am inside."

But Nicholas seemed quite glad to have me inside the barn with him. Without any prior plan, we instinctively shared the gift-giving tasks there. He left bread and cheese where the two parents slept on piles of hay. I placed dried fruit by the sides of the sleeping children. Because all five lay in a dark corner of the barn, we knew instinctively the owners of the farm had no idea their barn housed uninvited guests. Probably, the family had been subsisting on a few eggs stolen out from underneath the chickens who perched on the barn's many rafters. Well, for one morning, at least, they'd have a breakfast equal to the one undoubtedly being enjoyed by those living in the fine house a few dozen yards away.

I should have felt sad as Felix, Nicholas, and I walked back into the city. For ten years, I had loved the experience of anonymously leaving gifts, and it was over. If my two new friends now told me it had been wonderful meeting me and good luck in the future, I would be left alone with no real prospects. But I didn't think about this. Instead, I wondered what Nicholas and Felix—all right, mostly Nicholas—wanted to talk about next. It had to be something wonderful.

It certainly was. Back in their room, jars of fruit juice close to hand, Nicholas began by confirming who he was.

"By normal measure, I'm one hundred and thirty-two years old," he said. "I'll certainly understand if you don't believe me."

"Tell me more," I urged, and for several hours he did. I heard about his childhood in Patara, how his parents had died when he was young and he ended up being raised by village priests. How, while still very young, he had felt inspired to use the money he had inherited to help those in need. How his first gift-giving attempts were clumsy and almost ended in disaster. All these things sounded familiar to me, because they were so similar to my own life, ambition, and experiences.

Then came memories of great wonders—how, in the year 343 at age sixty-three, he rode off from Myra in the middle of the night because too many people expected him to work wonders for them, and how, in the years following, he realized two things. First, that he could travel hundreds of miles in the time ordinary people might manage one or two. Second, that he had somehow stopped aging. He had no explanation for how these things had happened, he added. They simply did.

"And when I met and joined Nicholas a year later, I stopped aging, too!" Felix interrupted. "The magic that graces him is also extended to anyone who joins him, we believe."

I couldn't help shaking my head at the wonder of it all. Nicholas, though, interpreted the head-shaking as a sign I didn't believe what I'd just heard.

"It seems impossible, I know," he said. "Perhaps if you consider it a bit longer before you decide it's not true—"

"Oh, no," I replied. "I believe every word. I mean, I see you here in front of me, and I saw your likeness carved on your tomb, and, of course, I've seen you so long in, well . . ." I was still too embarrassed to admit I'd been dreaming about him for years. I sat up a little straighter on my mat, composed myself, and said briskly, "So it was you all along who did the gift-giving that inspired me to do the same, and now I've met you. How splendid!"

Nicholas seemed both pleased and anxious. "Then you do believe everything I've told you?" he asked.

"Of course I do," I said. "No one could invent a story like that. So now you and your friend Felix, here, will spend eternity doing good, generous things. You're more than lucky—you're blessed!"

"But I'm lonely, sometimes, too," Nicholas said, and I thought Felix, sitting on a mat beside his longtime companion, looked rather offended. "The challenge is so great, and so never-ending," Nicholas continued, his eyes locked on mine. "So many people need so much, and I need your help. Will you join me?" He suddenly remembered Felix. "I mean, will you join us?"

"What exactly do you mean?" I asked. I hoped I knew what he meant, but I wanted to hear him say it.

Nicholas blushed and stammered, so Felix said it for him: "He's asking you to marry him, so I'm going to leave you two alone for a while." He got up and left the room. In the silence that followed, I could hear his heavy feet thumping as he made his way down the hall.

Nicholas remained tongue-tied. It was almost comical to see him try to say something, consider his words, begin to make the first sounds, panic, and have to start all over again. He sputtered for some time, and I finally lost patience.

"Look, are you asking me to marry you or not?" I asked. "It would be nice to know."

He took a deep breath. "Yes, I'm asking you to marry me. I'm sorry to make such a bad job of it. Even though I'm a hundred and thirty-two years old, I've never done this before."

"Are you certain?" I couldn't help asking.

"Oh, yes," Nicholas said. "I've never had such feelings for anyone. So, will you? Marry me, I mean. I know it's a complicated life I'm offering, and that there's a great difference in our ages. If you're thirty-five, why, I'm ninety-seven years older than you. Someone so youthful might not want to burden herself with someone so, well, senior."

"I don't care how old you are," I replied, feeling rather pleased that someone actually considered me to still be young. "I'll gladly marry you, but there's a condition. You must promise we'll be equal partners, in gift-giving and in marriage. I will always love and respect you. Will you feel the same toward me?"

"I already love and respect you," Nicholas said, and my heart pounded and I found myself smiling so widely that the corners of my mouth hurt. I thought he would now come over and kiss me, but instead he suddenly looked uncertain again.

"What's the matter?" I asked, afraid that he was having second thoughts and might take back his proposal.

"It's just that I'm still learning about special powers and this gift-giving mission," Nicholas said. "I mean, how long will you live, Layla? Felix and I have stopped growing older, but what about you? I couldn't stand it if we married and I lived on forever, only to lose you along the way."

I hadn't considered this. The possibility of living forever, or at least for a much longer time than the average person, seemed almost unimportant compared to marrying Nicholas.

"Maybe, like Felix, I'll stop aging, too," I said. "Maybe I won't. No one can know the future. We'll have enough to do giving gifts. Let's not waste time worrying about something we can't control." Nicholas started to reply. Apparently, he wanted to keep talking. But I was a newly engaged woman and the time for talking was over. "Hush up and come kiss me," I told him—and he did.

Nicholas knew a priest in Constantinople. He married us the next day. Felix was best man. After the short ceremony, the three of us immediately departed for Rome in Italy, a city Nicholas and Felix already knew well and one I had always longed to see. As a wedding present, Nicholas had told me we could go give gifts anywhere in the known world. He and Felix seemed delighted when I asked to go to Rome.

"There are plenty of needy people there," Nicholas told me as we walked arm-in-arm to the dock where we would board a boat and begin the trip. "We're going to be busy. You may regret very soon that you ever married me."

But I never did.

CHAPTER

Four

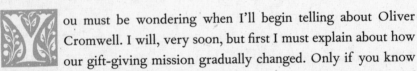ou must be wondering when I'll begin telling about Oliver Cromwell. I will, very soon, but first I must explain about how our gift-giving mission gradually changed. Only if you know about how toys and Christmas and America came to be part of what we did can you understand why I happened to be in England without my husband in the 1640s when Oliver Cromwell tried to do away with the holiday, and why I was so determined that he wouldn't succeed. Things that happened as much as twelve centuries earlier had their effect—on me, on Cromwell, and on Christmas itself.

My early days with Nicholas were fascinating. I found it quite different to be traveling and gift-giving in the company of my husband and his friend. As a married woman, I was welcome in any clean, reasonably priced inn; a wife arriving with her husband was not looked on with suspicion in any community. We gave our gifts in small villages as well as large cities. And, of course, I loved traveling formerly impossible distances at equally impossible speeds.

Oh, sometimes we had to make voyages on boats or travel in carts as part of caravans, but most often we simply walked, moving at night, and though there was no sense of hurry we would still find, by sunup, that we had gone eighty or one hundred miles. I was also amazed not to feel at all tired at the end of such lengthy treks. It seemed as though the act of walking refreshed rather than tired us.

I learned that Nicholas and Felix paid for the gifts they gave by carving elaborate wooden covers for books, which were relatively new in the early 400s. Most people still didn't read much, if at all, but those who did now wanted to protect their manuscripts from dust and decay. Every so often, Felix would announce our money was about to run out, and we would purchase a dozen small planks of treated wood. Then he and my husband would spend a few days carving designs on the planks, which were then sold to a friendly merchant they knew named Timothy. He, in turn, would bind the planks around sets of manuscripts, sell the finished books with covers to wealthy customers, and everyone was pleased.

"Though I started my gift-giving with the help of a good inheritance, even that large amount of money had to run out sometime," Nicholas explained. "There was a time I feared my mission would have to end because I had no funds left."

"I know the feeling," I replied, and told him how we had met at the very moment my own money for gifts was completely spent.

"God's grace is a wonderful thing," he replied before giving me a big hug. As a former priest and bishop in the Christian church, Nicholas never, ever doubted that his special powers came to him directly from the Lord. "Layla, there is truly no coincidence where this mission is concerned. When my money ran out, for instance, was the same moment Felix and I learned that we could carve book covers with the same speed that we could walk great distances. It was true—*is* true—of Felix in particular. You will have noticed how I might carve one cover in a night, and, in the same few hours, Felix can carve five or six."

"Felix is amazing," I said, making sure my voice was loud enough for Felix to overhear where he stood a few yards away. My sudden presence was not always easy for him. He'd been used to being Nicholas's only companion for almost seventy years, and now he had to share his friend with someone else. Though Felix and I were very cordial to each other, I sensed sometimes that he felt uncomfortable, if not resentful, now that Nicholas had a wife who received so much of his attention. So I went out of my way to make sure Felix understood how special he was to my husband, and how I very much wanted us to become good friends, too. I think, over the centuries, we eventually did.

There was another benefit to traveling and working with Nicholas. I stopped aging, too. I know that in the thousand and more years since, many of our later companions took this for granted from the start, but they had the benefit of our experience. Then, we had no idea whether the magic would touch me as well, and so for months and even a few years—all right, decades—a day didn't pass without me taking out a disk of polished metal—because we had no glass mirrors then—and peering anxiously at my reflection, looking for lines around my eyes or my first gray hair. They never appeared. By the time I had been with Nicholas for about forty years, making me seventy-five and extremely elderly by the standard of the day, I still looked exactly the same and knew I had stopped aging, too.

Those forty years were full of love and excitement and, I admit, some sadness and frustration. We gloried in our mission, and our ability to range so far across Asia Minor and Europe to give our gifts. We gave thanks for the special powers God had granted to us. But we were always aware that even these powers had their limits. Any time we came near wars, our speed was reduced to that of normal humans. It seemed, in those years, that all the world we knew of was torn by war. The Roman Empire was gradually crumbling. Tribes with names like Vandals and Visigoths made bloody bids for supremacy. We were able to avoid capture, perhaps even execution, because in those days Christian priests were known to be noncombatants, and so were allowed to wander where they would. Nicholas and Felix were assumed to be priests, and, in the case of my husband, that was close to the truth. Any time we were stopped and questioned, we simply said we were on our way somewhere to minister to the poor—and that, too, was certainly true.

As he had promised, my wonderful husband treated me as an equal partner, both in our marriage and in gift-giving. No decisions were made by Nicholas alone. He always consulted me, and Felix, too. Sometimes Felix or I might suggest where to go next. Of course, in some ways having a woman along was very helpful. In a small village, I could casually join other wives washing clothes in a stream or gossiping by a well. I would hear about local families who were hungry or wearing ragged clothes. More and more, we concentrated on gifts for children. This was not because we didn't care about grown-ups. It was just that there was so much need that we had to set priorities, and, more than anything, we wanted all children to grow up feeling loved and hopeful about their lives. A constant source of frustration was that, no matter how hard we tried, we could never bring gifts to every deserving, needy child. There were so many children, and in so many places!

I had the great pleasure of seeing Rome, and Alexandria, and other famous cities. Gradually I became familiar with hundreds of towns and villages in what we called "the known world." But all three of us never stopped feeling curious about those countries we had yet to visit, and finally in the year 453 we decided it was time to travel to the legendary, mysterious land of Britain. What we knew of the island nation was fascinating. The Romans had conquered some of it for a time, but according to most stories it was still inhabited by wild people who painted themselves blue and lived in trees. It sounded too interesting to resist, so we began making our way there. Under peaceful circumstances we could have made our way from Rome to Britain with three or four nights of magically fast walking, but there were battles all around us and we could only manage about ten miles a day. In particular, a famous Hun war chief named Attila was known to be marching toward Rome. As it happened, we met him, or, I should say, were taken prisoner by him. But after some conversation with Nicholas, Attila admitted he was tired of war. When Nicholas impulsively told him about our special mission, Attila asked to join us, along with Dorothea, his wife.

This was a turning point. Until that moment, we had never even discussed adding to our number. "Do we really *want* a warrior coming along?" Felix asked me, and I believe it was then that he finally accepted me as an equal rather than just as his best friend's wife.

"I think we have to trust Nicholas's instincts, and he wants Attila and Dorothea to join us," I replied. "We'll watch Attila carefully, because he's used to fighting with anyone he meets. And it will be nice for me to have another woman to talk to."

In fact, our two new friends fit in right away. Because he'd had to study so many maps while planning battles, Attila knew his way around better than the rest of us. Dorothea was very kind and, though soft-spoken, quite intelligent. By the time we crossed the channel to England—a monk named Patrick happened to be floating by in a small boat on his way to Ireland and offered us a ride—we were all enjoying one another's company very much, except for Attila and Felix, who constantly argued with each other. But these arguments were entertaining, and kept the rest of us amused as we traveled.

We loved England immediately, for it had the greenest hills and clearest streams any of us had ever seen. Sadly, the lives of the people there did not match the beauty of their land. There was fighting everywhere, with fierce tribes in the north and west constantly assaulting the people of the central and southern regions. At the same time, Saxons from across the sea often sailed over to conduct raids. Why, we kept asking each other, couldn't everyone stop fighting and begin enjoying the wonderful world given to them by God? Then Attila would remind us that too many people measured themselves by how much they could take from others.

"I was like that," he would always point out. "Though I'm pleased to have learned giving gifts is more satisfying than owning things myself, it was a hard-earned lesson. But if I can learn it from you, then others can, too."

Almost everyone in Britain was desperately poor. Though we'd arrived with plenty of money, very little food or clothing was for sale. What we did find in sad marketplaces were old, stringy vegetables, and sandals and blankets so filthy and tattered that beggars in other parts of the world would have disdained them. So we had to arrange to buy proper gifts like cheeses and dried fruits and well-made blankets from markets in Europe, and have these shipped by boat over to Britain. Then we paid English farmers to let us store these things in their barns. So long as we paid in advance, no one ever asked us why we were doing this. They were just grateful for the few extra coins.

And yet, with the awful fighting and nearly universal poverty, there was still something special about this country. If the people were poor, they were also hopeful, certain that somehow, some way, they would eventually live in peace. Instead of moping in times of trouble, they made up songs and stories about wonderful heroes who would one day come to their rescue. For fifty years we wandered among them, leaving our gifts when we could, trying to avoid battlefields and hoping along with all the ordinary folk that better times for them would soon be coming.

Around the year 500, a British war chief named Arthur won several spectacular victories against Saxon invaders. Many people in Britain believed he must be the longed-for hero who would save the land, but Attila told us that there was no chance Arthur could hold off the Saxons for very long.

"There are too many of them," he said, looking rather sad. "This Arthur is a brave man and a great leader, but anyone who fights constantly must eventually lose to someone stronger. This is true now, and will be throughout history. I only hope he escapes with his life."

With our help, Arthur did. One day we found him lying badly wounded in a barn, with his Saxon enemies all around. Obviously, we couldn't leave him there, and he became our sixth member. After he recovered, Arthur proved to be a very good addition to the group. He was brave, as Attila had guessed, and quite resourceful, too. He could carve wood book covers even better than Felix, and his love for his country despite its terrible wars was sincere.

I believe it was because of Arthur that Britain remained so important to us all. For the next six hundred years we divided our time between that island nation, Europe, and Asia Minor, meeting people and giving gifts and trying always to bring a little joy and comfort to children who most desperately needed reminding that the world was not entirely a cruel, dangerous place. All of us were happy anywhere we went, but it was during our visits to Britain that Arthur seemed the most content.

"Though battles and invasions continue—the Saxons who conquered my people are now being challenged in their turn by the Normans sailing in from France—I know that the English people themselves are especially noble in spirit," Arthur said one night as we gathered around a campfire in the hills outside the town of London, which had originally been built by the Romans a thousand years earlier. "If peace ever comes to this land, the rest of the world will look to Britain for inspiration and leadership."

Britain itself often looked to Arthur for inspiration, though the man of its legends had little in common with the war chief who'd joined us. Ordinary people comforted themselves in times of trouble—and, in Britain, it seemed always to be a time of trouble—with tales of Arthur the mythical king, who defeated enemies with the help of a magic sword and the advice of a wizard. There were tall tales about Nicholas and Attila, too, but the stories about Arthur were, at this time, the most widespread. We would tease him about them, always understanding that if they brought some comfort to frightened people, then they were good rather than harmful.

We had great adventures in Britain and everywhere else we went. My husband, Nicholas, wrote about many of these in his own book, so in most cases I won't repeat them here. It was our great good fortune to be befriended by Charlemagne, the king of the Franks who became the leader of the Holy Roman Empire. Thanks to his generosity, we were less dependent on carving and selling wooden book covers to pay for our gifts and travel costs. We studied with great interest events in far-off lands—how a man named Muhammad, for instance, founded the religion of Islam, and how there were rumors that Viking sailors had crossed a great ocean and discovered some vast, fertile new land. Though we could not travel to these places yet—our gift-giving services were so badly needed where we were—Nicholas, Felix, and I declared that someday we would explore them for ourselves. Arthur's main interest was Britain; Attila and Dorothea remained especially devoted to Europe and Asia Minor.

Sometime in the middle of the twelfth century, the nature of our mission changed. We still gave gifts, but of a different sort. As Britain, Europe, and Asia continued to be torn by war—the latest flare-ups were called "the Crusades," with Christian rulers raising armies to march to Jerusalem and try to take back that holy city from the Muslims—our efforts to bring comfort and happiness to children began to seem almost foolish. If we left food, it was eaten and gone in a day or two. Cloaks and sandals wore out, if the children didn't outgrow them first. The times people of all ages had to live in seemed to be getting worse rather than better. What difference did our gifts of a little food or new clothing make, really?

One night in 1194, Nicholas called us together for a full, honest discussion. We all agreed something had to be done differently. We couldn't do much to lessen the violence of the world, but at least we could find a way to carry out our own mission more effectively. I spoke for a while about the difference between the body and the spirit. Food and clothing were temporarily good for the body, but we needed to give gifts that gave more lasting comfort to the spirit. It was Dorothea, the quietest among us, who eventually made the best suggestion—she thought we should give gifts of toys instead. Now, at this time toys were not something every child, or, indeed, many children, actually owned. Those that existed were very primitive—marbles made of clay, hoops fashioned from bits of wood, dolls carved from wood or sewn together from rags. But the more we thought about it, the more sense the idea of giving toys made. Bread or fruit would be gone after one meal; children could play with toys for years, and in the process forget, at least for a while, about the dangerous world all around them.

We couldn't purchase toys as we could buy cloaks or loaves of bread. There were no companies that made them, no stalls full of toys in city marketplaces. So we learned to make them ourselves, and it took some time. The first dolls Dorothea and I sewed looked more like socks or mittens than pretend people. Our earliest attempt to make marbles found us using the wrong sort of clay, so they didn't roll straight and then broke on the rare occasions that they actually hit the other marbles at which they were aimed. Still, with some practice we were able to craft toys at the same incredible speed with which we'd been able to carve book covers. We took this as a sign that we should keep trying, and finally we made some that we considered good enough to take to Rome, where we offered them for sale at a market. We sold everything, dolls and marbles and hoops, within minutes, and at a good enough profit to buy materials to make hundreds more. We left those as gifts for poor children in Naples to the south of Rome. The next morning we returned to their neighborhood, and how wonderful it was to see boys and girls shouting with sheer joy as they shot their marbles or played with their dolls or rolled hoops across the meadow.

"Perhaps they're still wearing rags, and too many of them will go to bed hungry tonight," I said. "But for now, they're happy, and tomorrow they'll still have their toys to play with. We must keep on giving gifts of toys."

"Then we have to keep making them," Felix observed. "That's going to be the hardest part. Food and clothing we can buy anywhere and give away the same day. Crafting toys is far more complicated. It will be impossible for us to have some to give away every night, no matter how fast we work."

Though we wouldn't realize it for another three hundred years, the solution to that problem was already in progress. Gradually, people in Britain and Europe were defining specific dates when special gift-giving was most appropriate. Today, many people think that Santa Claus or St. Nicholas or Pere Noel or Father Frost—the name is different in almost every country— simply selected December 6 or 25 or January 6 as the day he brings gifts to children. In fact, those dates were picked for us.

Forget the word *Christmas* for just a moment. Though not known by that name, the date of December 25 became especially holy in the Christian church in the early 300s, when it was arbitrarily selected as the day to celebrate the birth of Jesus. That date was borrowed from other, earlier religions. Mithra, the Persian god of light, supposedly had been born on December 25. The Romans traditionally enjoyed a weeklong celebration called Saturnalia from December 17 through 24. They had parties and ate special food and gave each other little gifts. When Christianity became the official religion of Rome in the 300s, people still wanted their holiday. In 350, just seven years after my husband supposedly died in Myra, Pope Julius I used December 25 as Jesus' birthday on the new Roman calendar. Of course, the holiday was intended from the start as a special time to give thanks to God for sending Jesus, and not everyone carried over the old Saturnalia tradition of giving gifts on that date. But many people did. In some places, grown-ups began giving small presents to children on January 6, called Epiphany, and supposedly the day that the three Wise Men arrived in Bethlehem to give their gifts to Baby Jesus.

Going to church on December 25 was something most Christians wanted to do; the service held then was known as a mass. Because this particular mass was devoted to Jesus, it was called Christ's mass. In the year 1038, people in Britain started using the term *Christmas,* combining the two words. Christians in other countries began doing the same, altering the wonderful new word to fit their own languages. In Holland, for instance, people now looked forward to Kersmis, since the old Dutch word for Christ was *Kerstes.*

We were thrilled with the celebrations of Christmas and Epiphany; not only did they celebrate the birth of Jesus, they also gave common people a better chance to forget their troubles for a little while. Their holiday feasts might be the only time all year that there would be a little meat with their vegetables, or sweet candy for the children afterward. Many villages would hold dances or put on holiday plays. This may not seem very exciting today, when almost every family has a big meal every night and then settles down to watch television or listen to music or play videogames. But in those times, life for adults and children alike mostly consisted of hard work all day, little to eat, and bedtime when the sun went down, since there were no electric lights and candles cost too much to use very often. Perhaps the date of Christmas was based on old pagan beliefs, but why did that have to matter? What counted was that December 25 had become a time to give joyful thanks for Jesus' birth, and the opportunity for everyone, rich or poor, to put aside worries and be happy, even for only a day.

In 1224, one of the people who made these early Christmases so special became the seventh member of our group, and the first new one since Arthur joined us seven centuries earlier. St. Francis of Assisi encouraged poor villagers to create nativity scenes with a manger and animals to remind themselves that Jesus came into the world humble and poor, just as they were. Francis wrote some of the first popular Christmas carols, so common people had special songs to sing and dance to during their holiday celebrations. Francis's contributions to Christmas traditions made people love December 25 more than ever—and only about two hundred years after he joined us, St. Nicholas finally became part of those traditions, too!

Again, this happened *to* us rather than because of anything deliberate we did. By the late 1300s, it again became obvious that the way we did things had to change. It was getting too hard to craft all the toys we needed by campfire light in locations that changed every few days. In order to have the most toys possible, and the ones that were made best, we needed some permanent place to make them—a factory, perhaps, or even two. While Nicholas, Felix, Francis, and I loved traveling most, searching out children who needed gifts and then delivering them in the middle of the night, Arthur much preferred staying in his beloved Britain, while Attila and Dorothea were happiest in their native country of Germany. So it was decided that Arthur would establish a toy factory in London, while Attila and Dorothea did the same in Nuremberg. Meanwhile, the rest of us would continue traveling and distributing half of the toys made in these factories. The other half would be sold in city markets; Arthur in London and Attila and Dorothea in Nuremberg would use the money to buy materials and pay their employees.

It all worked very well, though we missed our three longtime friends. But every few months we had to replenish our supplies of toys, and so we would go to London or Nuremberg—both large cities for their time, though dirty and small by today's standards—and enjoy reunions there.

I really think it was because of these two toy factories that St. Nicholas and Christmas became linked in the minds of so many people. Arthur, Attila, and Dorothea tried very hard to hire good craftsmen and craftswomen who just wanted to make toys and not gossip about their employers, and mostly they succeeded. One fellow in particular was a very welcome worker who soon was accepted as a full member of our special companions. Willie Skokan was a Bohemian who could take a bit of string, a splinter of wood, and a few drops of paint and combine them into literally any toy he wanted to make. Willie was absolutely marvelous, and we soon couldn't imagine how we'd ever been able to get along without him. He seldom spoke, and when he did he was careful never to reveal our secrets.

But that wasn't true of some others, though I don't believe anyone deliberately tried to expose us. Some of our workers in Britain or Germany just couldn't resist whispering things to their families and friends. By the middle 1400s, stories had spread through Europe and Britain about Nicholas, the ancient Catholic saint who somehow was still around and brought gifts for children at holiday time. In some countries, Germany especially, people began to think that perhaps his special gift-giving time was December 6, the date of Nicholas's "death" in 343.

So now, in addition to our year-round tasks, we were faced with not one but three special days when children particularly hoped to receive our gifts. I finally suggested that we gratefully accept these new obligations as opportunities rather than problems.

"In this way, we can make our night visits three times each year and spend the rest of the time planning our gift-giving and helping Arthur and Attila and Dorothea at the factories," I said. "Why, we can each choose one or two countries for our special individual attention. It will be more efficient, and great fun besides."

So it happened that, each year at holiday time, while Nicholas might roam anywhere, Arthur and his helpers brought gifts in England and all other parts of Britain. Attila and Dorothea took much of Western Europe, while Willie Skokan concentrated on Eastern European countries. Francis led the holiday gift-giving in Spain and Portugal, Felix found Scandinavia to his liking, and no one was surprised when I asked for Italy. The reason, of course, was Befana.

Everywhere else, legend now had it that holiday gifts were brought by a man—St. Nicholas or a similar male gift-giver with another name. But in Italy, children woke up on January 6 hoping for toys or treats from Befana, an old woman. As Italian tradition had it, when the three wise men began their search for the Baby Jesus, they came to Befana's house, asking directions to Bethlehem and inviting her to come with them. She wouldn't give the directions, because she didn't understand who Jesus was. Afterward, when Befana learned Jesus was the savior, she wished she had gone to give presents to him, too, and so ever since she went out before dawn on Epiphany to leave gifts for any child she could find. What fun it was for me to spend that special time leaving dolls and tops and marbles for children all over Italy! Of course, every few years we would switch countries so we could share in all the different traditions. But it's also true Befana and Italy remained especially dear to my heart.

The excitement for us only increased in 1492, when Francis met Queen Isabella of Aragon in Spain and was able to make a place for himself on the first voyage to the fabled New World by Italian sea captain Christopher Columbus. Francis returned with tales of this wonderful new land, and his enthusiasm was contagious. Everyone, especially Nicholas and Felix, couldn't wait to visit the New World. None of us, though, felt we could leave immediately, for we were still helping build holiday gift-giving traditions in Britain and Europe. Still, I didn't miss the longing in my husband's voice as he talked about crossing the Atlantic Ocean someday. I decided then that it might take fifty years, or a hundred, but as soon as it was practical I would insist that Nicholas get on a boat and travel to that new place he so clearly yearned to see for himself.

About this same time, in 1501 Princess Catherine of Aragon was given in marriage to Prince Arthur of England. Though we didn't know it at the time, this began a series of events that would result in Oliver Cromwell and his Puritans banning Christmas 144 years later.

Five

ou know you want to visit what they're calling the New World,"
I said to Nicholas one fine early fall evening in 1620. We were
spending a few weeks in Nuremberg with Attila and Dorothea,
helping the confectioners at our factory there. When we left our gifts of
toys for children, we often added a few pieces of candy, leaving these, when
we could, in the stockings that their mothers washed and left hanging by
fireplaces to dry overnight. Because the candy was always some kind of
hard-boiled sweet, it wouldn't melt from the warmth of the fire. Candy was
almost as rare a treat for boys and girls as new toys. We had recently tried
something called peppermint candy, which had become available in a few
places, and it was very, very good. Attila and Dorothea wanted to be able to
make a lot of it at the Nuremberg factory, and quickly—the holidays were
only a few months away. But it took time to get the taste just right—too
much peppermint flavor made your tongue feel like it was burning instead
of pleasantly tingling—and so Attila and Dorothea and Nicholas and I,
along with Willie Skokan, who lived in Nuremberg, and Felix, who was also
visiting there, were volunteer tasters. The first few attempts were not too

agreeable, but as the day passed the peppermint candy tasted better and better, until by late afternoon we thought the confectioners had got it just right.

Afterward, Nicholas and I returned to the nearby inn where we were staying. Attila, Dorothea, and Willie, who worked in Nuremberg full time, lived in a small house. Felix was staying in their extra bedroom. Since that used up all the available space for guests, my husband and I took a room at a clean, modestly priced inn, and very much enjoyed some rare private time together. We loved all our old companions, but it was also pleasant to have an opportunity to concentrate on each other. In particular, I wanted to talk to Nicholas about the New World of English, Dutch, Spanish, and French colonies across the Atlantic Ocean in a vast land unofficially named America on many maps. Ever since Francis had returned from his voyage with Columbus over a century earlier, my husband had clearly longed to see America himself. But there was always a reason he just couldn't go quite yet—new toys to test in London, additional Christmas customs in Germany that we had to learn and adopt, or something else of that nature. So, alone together at the Nuremberg inn, with an hour or so to spare before we joined Attila and Dorothea and the others at their house for supper, I decided Nicholas and I would settle the issue for good. I intended for him to go to America, and soon.

"It would be selfish for me to leave my friends behind," Nicholas said, pacing about our little room while I sat comfortably in a chair before a small, glowing fire. "Everyone here in Nuremberg works so hard, and Arthur has more than he can handle at the factory in London."

"Arthur has Leonardo now," I reminded him. "That's lightened Arthur's load considerably." It was true.

In 1519, we'd added another full-time companion. Leonardo da Vinci was a brilliant painter and equally imaginative inventor. He colored canvases with extraordinary scenes and filled notebooks with diagrams of machines that could soar through the air like birds or move underwater like fish. Having joined us, he eventually based himself in London with Arthur. There, he did what Willie Skokan did in Nuremberg—inventing new toys was a constant, though delightful, challenge for them both.

"Leonardo is amazing," Nicholas agreed. "But that doesn't change the fact all of us are kept busy every waking minute. Yes, I'd love to visit America, but it wouldn't be fair for me to have a vacation while everyone else had to remain on the job."

"It would hardly be a vacation," I pointed out. "From all the reports, colonists in America are having a terribly hard time. Most of them have little to eat, some of them fight with the natives, and I believe that one British settlement called Roanoke simply disappeared. We've been married for twelve hundred years, Nicholas. I know perfectly well you want to go to America to bring Christmas to the desperate people there whose daily lives consist mostly of hardship. And you should—they deserve Christmas joy, too, and what better way to experience it than to have St. Nicholas among them for the first time?"

"That's true," Nicholas admitted, sitting down in a chair opposite mine. "But we must always be practical, Layla, and though we haven't spoken of it much, these are dangerous times for Christmas in places other than America. That's true in England, especially. My place—our place, I mean—may be with Arthur just now, instead of across the Atlantic Ocean. So many things in England have been confused since 1527, when King Henry VIII decided to divorce Princess Catherine of Aragon."

From the time we first crossed the channel to England in St. Patrick's boat, the country had constantly been ravaged by some sort of upheaval, usually war. When there weren't invaders storming ashore, the English seemed to turn on themselves, fighting each other when there wasn't some enemy from the outside. When the conflict known in history as "the Wars of the Roses" ended in 1485, it seemed for a while as though there might be peace on the beautiful island nation, particularly when King Henry VII married his son Prince Arthur to Princess Catherine of Aragon. But Arthur, who was going to be the next English king, soon died, and his widow Catherine was then married to Arthur's younger brother, Henry. When Henry became king, he and Catherine did not get along very well. Henry met another woman named Anne Boleyn who he wanted for his wife instead, but the Catholic Church would not let him divorce Catherine. Furious, Henry simply left the church, taking his country with him, and established a new Church of England. Catherine, who believed very deeply in the Catholic Church, considered herself still married to Henry and raised their daughter, Mary, as a Catholic. Henry ended up marrying four more times after Anne Boleyn and had two more children, Edward and Elizabeth, who were raised as non-Catholics, or Protestants. And this is where problems for Christmas in England began.

Henry didn't want anything to do with Catholicism left in England. He gave most of the property owned by the Catholic Church to his friends. New, non-Catholic religious leaders weren't comfortable with a Catholic saint named Nicholas bringing presents to English children. The name Father Christmas was substituted, which was fine with us. But even the word *Christmas* became unpopular with the king and his clergy. Some Protestant leaders insisted *Christmas* was just another way of saying "Christ's mass"—which was a fact—and mass was Catholic. To them, anything Catholic was bad. They ordered everyone to say *Christ-tide,* instead. Most people kept saying *Christmas* anyway.

"I have the feeling that the attacks on Christmas in England are just beginning," Nicholas said sadly, staring into the fireplace in our room at the inn. "It might even become dangerous there for Arthur, Leonardo, and our employees at the London toy factory. True, we've mostly been able to keep the existence of the factory there a secret, as we have in Nuremberg, but the wrong people might find out. I simply wouldn't feel right going to America while Arthur was left to deal with such problems."

"Leonardo is there to help Arthur," I said.

Nicholas smiled. "I love and honor Leonardo, but his talent is for art and invention. He's not an especially practical man. We need someone in England who has a lot of common sense, who can study complicated matters and suggest solutions. Someone like, well, *you,* and you can't help Arthur if we're off in America."

"No one said *we* had to be off in America," I replied. "Nicholas, you and I haven't been apart for twelve centuries. Though we'd certainly miss each other, this may be a time when we each have something important to do in different places. It won't last forever—ten years, maybe twenty. Colonists in America need Christmas desperately. Bring it to them. I'll go to London and work with Arthur to help Christmas through difficult times there."

"I think I'd be very lonely in America without you," Nicholas said, sounding mournful and excited at the same time. I knew he would genuinely miss me—just as I knew he was thrilled at the thought of bringing joyful Christmas traditions to a whole new continent.

"Well, take Felix with you," I suggested. "You two haven't had any adventures on your own since our marriage in Constantinople. Arthur wrote in his last letter that some group is organizing a boatload of colonists to sail to America. They're going to settle near a previous colony called Jamestown. Let's get Felix and go to London; surely the two of you can join that brave band or another one, and soon be on your way. Who knows? America may prove to be so wonderful that in a decade or two you'll send for me, and we can establish a new toy factory there!"

Nicholas grinned, the same warm smile I'd seen in my dreams so many centuries earlier. "But if I go to America, who will help you taste the peppermint candy?" he asked.

I glanced pointedly at his waistline. "It's obvious you've sampled more than enough candy for too many years. I expect that in America you'll lose a few pounds. From all reports, you'll be lucky to have even a little bread to eat. A diet will do you good."

Over supper, we told the others about our plans. Dorothea said she thought Nicholas would miss me even more than he realized. Attila was a little jealous that he wasn't the one going off to a new land for adventures. Felix whooped with joy when Nicholas asked him to come along to America. Willie Skokan didn't say very much. He'd brought more samples of peppermint candy from the factory and sat off in a corner tasting them. Willie took such things very seriously. He wanted our peppermint candy to be the best anywhere.

"I think you should take some of this along with you to London," he said. "Arthur and Leonardo will enjoy it, and I don't think there is a lot of peppermint candy in England yet."

Nicholas, Felix, and I set off for England the next day. We'd hardly arrived in London before my husband and his friend disappeared, hurrying to the docks where Arthur told them the group of colonists was signing on for the voyage to America.

"But there's something you should know about——" Arthur shouted toward their backs as they disappeared down the street.

"What would that be?" I asked, as Arthur helped me carry my bags to the guest room in the cottage he and Leonardo lived in not far from their toy factory. Arthur looked and sounded a bit concerned, and this worried me.

"It's just that the people organizing this colony are, well, rather different," Arthur explained. "Have you heard about the group of Protestants here in England who call themselves the Puritans? No? Well, surely you're aware of how Catholics are quite unpopular with the government and the Church of England. It's all been very confusing for everyone. First King Henry VIII broke the country away from the Catholic Church, then his daughter Queen Mary made Catholicism the religion of the land again, then her sister, Queen Elizabeth, ordered the country to return to Protestantism, and now King James says Catholics may worship as they please, but clearly favors Protestants."

"I've heard of all this," I replied. "As much as possible, we cannot allow it to affect our gift-giving. You know our rule is to always respect the faith of others, even when it is different from our own."

"Of course I know our rule," Arthur said, sounding exasperated. "The problem is not with people like us, but with those who insist the only correct faith is identical to what they themselves believe, and that anyone with any different opinion is automatically evil. Which brings us to the Puritans. They are Protestants who disagree with all but the very simplest forms of worship. They're the ones who are complaining about *Christmas* and insist everyone calls December 25 *Christ-tide* instead. This group Nicholas and Felix want to join is led by Puritans, who say they're going to America so they may worship as they please. I very much fear that in America they will establish a colony where only their religious beliefs are tolerated. By 'religious freedom,' they mean the right to force everyone else to believe as they do."

But Nicholas and Felix returned from the London docks so excited that Arthur and I couldn't bring ourselves to warn them about the people they'd just met. They told us all about it when we sat down for supper. Leonardo joined us. William Brewster, Nicholas said, was the organizer who met with them. Brewster explained he and his friends called themselves the Saints. Within a month, they hoped to have one hundred volunteer colonists, who would sail to America aboard two ships. Upon arrival, they'd start a new community near Jamestown, where everyone would farm and hunt and be happy.

"Only about one-third are actually members of the Saints," Felix said happily. "Everyone else brings some sort of necessary talent—a black-smith, a doctor, some toolmakers, and so on. I told Mr. Brewster that I was a good craftsman and wood-carver, while my friend Nicholas was a willing worker, if not an especially good one. Do you know what Mr. Brewster replied?"

"We hardly need to mention this, Felix," Nicholas interrupted.

"No, it's funny. Mr. Brewster said he could tell that Nicholas was at least good at eating, and that he'd certainly lose weight in America."

It was obvious Felix and Nicholas had their hearts set on joining the Saints on their voyage, so Arthur and I decided we wouldn't caution them about their new companions. After all, we thought, Nicholas in particular had been successfully bringing Christmas to people around the world for centuries. Even if William Brewster and the Saints didn't cooperate, he was bound to succeed eventually.

In the three weeks between the time we arrived in London and the day the Saints set sail for America, Arthur and I did not bring up our concerns about Christmas in England. Nicholas and Felix were so excited about America that we didn't want to spoil the moment for them. Instead, we talked about what the new colony might be like, and whether it would be cold enough around Jamestown to require them to wear warmer cloaks, and how they would spend their time secretly crafting toys for the children in the new colony to wake up and discover by their beds on Christmas Day.

The Saints sailed aboard the *Mayflower* in September 1620. The 102 colonists were supposed to be divided between two ships, but the second had problems with leaking and William Brewster didn't want to delay the voyage for repairs. So everyone was crammed aboard a single vessel. We learned from Nicholas's letters that things turned sour immediately, with the thirty or so Saints trying to impose their ways on everyone else. In history books, the Saints would be called the Pilgrims, and most of their early squabbles would eventually be forgotten. But when they finally landed on the coast of Plymouth, Massachusetts—hundreds of miles north of Jamestown—Brewster and the other Puritan leaders instantly imposed their religious will on everyone else. Nicholas and Felix weren't surprised in December 1620 when Christmas was hardly mentioned. The new colonists were spending every waking minute trying to build shelters and find food in the harsh winter. But in 1621 the Puritan leaders decreed that Christmas would not be celebrated at all in Plymouth.

"This has made Nicholas and Felix so furious that they've left Plymouth and joined Dutch settlers in their colony of Fort Orange," I told Arthur and Leonardo as I read a letter from my husband that had arrived by ship. "They say that, as awful as it sounds, Christmas has been made completely against the law in Plymouth, and celebrating it will result in severe punishment."

"I'm sorry, but not surprised," Arthur observed. "I suppose, in all their excitement of going to the New World, Nicholas and Felix forgot this has already happened in an entire country. Christmas has been against the law in Scotland since 1583."

This was very sad, but still a fact. In Scotland, a nation separate from England to the north, Puritans were especially anxious to rid themselves of anything to do with the Catholic Church. Christmas, their leaders insisted, was more than just a bad Catholic name for a holiday. In fact, when people celebrated Christmas with singing and dancing and feasting, they violated the way Puritans thought Jesus should be worshipped. They felt people should sit quietly and think about all God's blessings, especially sending his son among us. And choosing December 25 as Jesus' birthday was, to their minds, an insult—Jesus was better than any ordinary person, and only ordinary people had birthdays. They were certainly entitled to these opinions, but they wanted everyone to share them. So the Scottish Puritans and elected leaders made celebrating Christmas a crime. And, as Arthur pointed out, if it happened in Scotland, it could certainly happen in England.

"Our current King James ruled in Scotland before Queen Elizabeth of

England died without children in 1603," he reminded me. "So James has allowed Christmas to be banned in one country already. Puritans don't yet control government in England, but they are louder than anyone else, and if they ever are in charge I suspect Christmas will be the first target of their wrath."

"Christmas means too much to too many people in this country," I said firmly. "For poor families in particular, December 25 is the only day of the year when they can feast and dance and sing and forget, for just a little while, how hard they have to work, and how little they have to call their own. It's just a different way of thanking God for Jesus than sitting quietly in a room, thinking. I can't believe the Puritans want to prevent others from having a little holiday happiness."

Arthur's eyes narrowed, and he looked quite grim.

"Layla, we've both lived long enough to realize something," he said. "There are always those who want to control the way everyone else lives, including how, when, and why they are happy."

"Well, the Puritans have picked the wrong place for a fight over Christmas," I replied. "No country celebrates Christmas better than England. Of course, no country needs Christmas more, either." Then, upset at the possibility of the holiday being taken away, I donned my cloak and hurried outside. I walked for hours through the London streets, and everywhere I looked I was reminded why the ordinary people of Britain should not be deprived of their beloved holiday.

Six

ondon in the 1600s was nothing like the sprawling city we know today. Because some of its very oldest buildings and monuments— Parliament, the Tower of London, some castles and mansions— still stand, many people think the city hasn't changed very much. But it has. The London where Arthur and I fretted about the Puritans and Christmas almost four hundred years ago was a much dirtier, desperate place, where most citizens lived in poverty and seldom survived past the age of fifty. A few rich people enjoyed lives of luxury, living in fine homes and riding everywhere in gilded, horse-drawn carriages. Almost everyone else, including many children, labored for little pay at difficult, physically demanding jobs and went home to dark, damp huts at night with nothing to look forward to but a supper of scraps and then a few hours of sleep before they had to get up and do the same discouraging things all over again.

Four million people lived in England then, and about two hundred and fifty thousand of them were in London, making it by far the largest city in the country. It was one of the oldest, too, originally built as a fort and supply depot by the Romans in 43 A.D. on the south bank of the River Thames, a mighty waterway. When the Romans left four hundred years later, the

Saxons gradually took it over, and then the Normans. It became clear that whoever ruled England would do so from London.

That meant the city attracted lots of people, starting with the lords and ladies who made up the royal court. They wanted great houses of stone and later brick to live in, and servants to tend to their needs. Building materials and food and clothing had to be supplied by merchants, who made up a sort of in-between social class. They, in turn, needed people to build their shops and the much more modest homes middle-class families lived in—houses cobbled together from wood and plaster, not more expensive stone. Still others were needed to prepare the food and sew the clothing the merchants sold to the rich, and these workers were paid very small salaries—pennies every week, not every day—and their homes were really tiny huts, often with thatch roofs that would burn far too easily. And so the population of London always grew, with dozens of very poor people added for each rich one.

I walked through London after my conversation with Arthur. It was late November in 1622. Nicholas and Felix had been in America for almost two years. I missed my husband terribly, and, of course, I missed Felix, too. But as I walked, my thoughts were about the people and places I was seeing. What a difference there was between the lives of the rich and poor! Most of London's streets were narrow and dirty. A few avenues were paved with cobblestones, but these were the ones that led directly to the fine mansions. Everyone else walked to and from their homes and jobs on paths of dirt. When it rained, the mud was ankle-deep. During dry weather, dust blew up into everyone's eyes, noses, and mouths. Garbage was everywhere. There were no organized pickups of trash. If you were lucky enough to have an apple to eat and not so hungry that you'd gulp down every bit of it, including the stem and seeds, then you'd toss the core into the street. It would lie there, swarming with flies, until it rotted away, or until it was gobbled by one of the hundreds of pigs that waddled around loose. Stray dogs and cats roamed everywhere, too, fighting beggars and cripples for bits of bread or cheese tossed from passing carriages—not in charity, usually, but by someone riding along in comfort who'd eaten his or her fill and was discarding the leftovers. And rats ate whatever the humans and other animals somehow missed.

As I approached the Thames, I saw that, as usual, its banks were lined with fishermen. The wide river teemed with salmon, trout, perch, and eels. Those who traded in seafood had boats and nets; they could go out in the deepest parts of the river and often haul up a bountiful catch. Common folk who would either catch a fish or go hungry that night often had one poor line to toss in the water, its hook baited with a bit of animal fat. There were at least enough fish in the Thames that they had a good chance of landing their supper. Several times, in fact, whales were spotted, though the last of these was reported in the 1400s.

Food was of constant concern to all but the very rich. Meat came with most meals only in the mansions, where five or six courses might be served as dinner, accompanied by expensive wine. In the small cottages and fragile huts, porridge or bread smeared with lard frequently made up the entire menu. Vegetables grown in tiny garden plots were considered treats. When potatoes were introduced to England and Ireland from Peru in the late 1500s, these became another diet staple. If there was anything besides water to drink, it might be cheap, weak beer, which was shared by children as well as adults. Poor people seldom left their tables feeling comfortably full, only less hungry.

The rich and poor dressed quite differently, too. Wealthy people wore clothing made from cotton and silk, with lots of lace sewn on. They had plenty of shirts and dresses. These well-to-do men and women often wore elaborate wigs, and their shoes were shiny because they seldom had to step in the dirty streets. Their carriages whisked them wherever they wanted to go. Poor people wore mostly woolen clothes, and didn't change them often because they had no other clothes to put on. And, while the clothing of the rich came in all colors of the rainbow, the poor would try to brighten their drab garments with bright vegetable dyes, and, when it rained, these often ran and stained their arms and legs.

The London I wandered was, quite frankly, a smelly place. This wasn't just caused by the garbage and the animals on its streets. Rich or poor, few people bathed very often. Water was difficult to come by. You could haul buckets of it from the river, but even in the 1600s people realized much of the water there was fouled with garbage. There were places in the city where you could buy barrels of clean water, but this kind of purchase was well beyond the means of most. Water bearers sometimes passed along the streets, selling smaller quantities for a few farthings, but with money needed for food and clothing, buying water for washing was too much of an extravagance. And, though it's not pleasant to think about, there was no indoor plumbing either. Rich people had chamber pots, poor people just plain pots. After they were used, they had to be emptied—often in the same streets where everyone walked.

For entertainment, rich people in London could have parties and dances whenever they liked. They often had country estates where they could ride horses or stroll through flowery meadows if they grew tired of the city crowds and smells. Everyone else had more limited choices. Many poor people couldn't read, and for those who could, books were both rare and expensive. Under the best of circumstances, they might make an occasional visit to a theater. There were plays to see. King James, among others, had encouraged a playwright named William Shakespeare. You could enjoy dramas and comedies for a penny, though at that price you had to stand up the whole time in a crowded area in front of the stage, while those who could afford more expensive tickets sat in nice chairs on elevated platforms. And the working class enjoyed sports, too. Some, like cock-fighting, where roosters were encouraged to attack each other, or bear-baiting, which is exactly what its name describes, were cruel beyond modern belief. But others would be familiar to almost anyone today—football, for instance, which in America is better known as soccer. Football was by far the most popular sport because you didn't need much to play it, just a ball (perhaps a blown-up pig's bladder, or something of that sort), two areas designated as goals, and players with enough energy to run around for a while.

Mostly, though, nine out of every ten people in 1600s London worked hard every day with very little to show for it. Religion, which should have been a comfort, hadn't been much of one since King Henry VIII abruptly left the Catholic Church a century earlier. Ever since, there were confusing, constantly changing rules about how everyone could worship. During the reign of Queen Mary, some Protestants had even been burned at the stake. Now King James supposedly would allow anyone to worship as he or she pleased, but everyone remained afraid that the rules would change again without notice, and they might be in danger because of how they chose to practice their faith. Always, too, there was the threat of war to further complicate things. When England wasn't enduring civil war, its leaders were generally embroiled in battle against foreign foes, most often the French. In matters of daily life, in religion, in national issues, all the poor people of England felt little but stress or even fear. Their opinions didn't count. Nobody powerful really cared what they thought or what they wanted. Their monarch James firmly believed in the divine right of kings— if God allowed someone to be a king, then whatever the king wanted must be God's will, and no one was allowed to disagree. Perhaps the hardest thing for poor people was knowing there was nothing most of them could do to improve their lives. If you weren't born rich, there was little chance you could become wealthy. Property and titles were handed down from one generation to the next. Working-class people had no chance to acquire such things.

But they also had one time each year when all this could be put aside, a time when the most poverty-stricken families could expect that their rich employers would be generous, even thoughtful, to them. That time, of course, was Christmas, and as I walked through London on this early winter evening I smiled as I spied several people already festooning the doors of their humble cottages with holly and green boughs, two popular decorations at holiday time. Of course, the source of this pleasant tradition originally came from earlier, non-Christian faiths—in the winter, primitive people would set out greenery as a sign they believed spring would come again—but now they were just tokens that almost everyone was preparing to celebrate the birth of Jesus.

Certainly they were eager to celebrate by having fun instead of worrying about their next meal! December 25 was a holiday; shops would be closed, so nobody had to go to work. Even well before that special, happy day, common people in England were preparing themselves for a few fine hours when good things would momentarily be part of their lives.

I passed a doorway where two elderly women chattered happily as they tacked a sparse sprig of holly to their front door. I could tell they were desperately poor. Their clothes were ragged and they were painfully thin. And yet, preparing for Christmas, their smiles were very wide.

"A lovely bit of holly, this," one remarked. "Look at the green of the leaves, and the red rosy berry!" There was only one berry on that tiny sprig, but it was enough to bring them holiday joy.

"Nothing like Christmas, I vow," replied her companion. "I can taste the pudding already! Oh, I wish it was the wonderful day right this minute!" When the sprig was properly in place, they stepped back to admire it, their arms around each other's waist.

No one celebrates Christmas better or with more enthusiasm than the English poor, I reminded myself again, tucking my hands under my cloak, since the November winds were already quite cold. Even though Christmas was still a month away, I knew, somewhere groups of singers were rehearsing traditional carols, since music was such an important part of the national festivities. Soon the streets would be filled with *waits,* carolers who would please everyone with their renditions of holiday songs. Originally, waits were night watchmen who would call out the hours, but they gradually evolved into this more festive role. And, as the waits sang, hardworking men and women and children would begin to smile, because Christmas was finally drawing near. They would spend precious pennies for boughs and holly, so their homes would briefly be filled with color and fresh scent. Many saved all year to buy a single scrawny goose; after its bones were picked clean at Christmas dinner, they would be boiled for soup. And goose wouldn't be the only thing served at this special, once-a-year meal. There would be dessert, too, usually a mince pie or plum pudding. Ingredients for these fabulous concoctions were expensive, but on this holiday occasion everyone who could possibly afford to shop for them gladly did so.

Even though St. Nicholas was not welcomed by British rulers and clergy anymore, Father Christmas tried hard to bring little gifts to poor British children while they slept on Christmas Eve. Before he left for America with Felix, my husband very much enjoyed doing this. In his absence, Arthur and Leonardo and I took up the task. Because there were so many deserving boys and girls who had so very little, anything we left was precious to them—a rag doll, perhaps, or a wooden top. One reason we wanted to perfect our peppermint candy was that these children seldom tasted sweets during all the rest of the year. How fine it would be to add to the joy of their Christmas by leaving them such a special treat!

And yet even a visit from Father Christmas was not the highlight of the holiday. That came when everyone was up and dressed.

After church on Christmas Day, working-class people were allowed to call on the very richest people in their neighborhoods. Out in the English countryside, village peasants would gather and happily walk to the manor of whichever lord they served. In city or country, the poor would then serenade their social superiors with loud, happy songs. One that is still sung today captures the spirit of the tradition. Surely you've sung "We Wish You a Merry Christmas," though you may not have sung or even know all the original verses.

Huddled together in the December cold, dressed in their best clothes and with smiles on their faces, the common people would sing:

We wish you a Merry Christmas,
We wish you a Merry Christmas,
We wish you a Merry Christmas
And a happy New Year.

Good tidings we bring,
To you and your king.
Good tidings of Christmas,
And a happy New Year.

You know that part, don't you? But then the singers would continue,

Oh, bring us a figgy pudding,
Oh, bring us a figgy pudding,
Oh, bring us a figgy pudding,
And a cup of good cheer.

We won't go until we get some,
We won't go until we get some,
We won't go until we get some,
So bring some out here.

This, you see, was the custom. On just one annual occasion, rich people would allow poor people into their homes, and they would give them good food, offer something to drink, and, for a little while, treat them as welcome guests, or even equals. Perhaps some of the wealthy class would have preferred not to, but they wouldn't—couldn't—ignore tradition. Of course, afterward they remained in their warm, fine homes, while their visitors had to resume their normal, difficult lives. For rich people, holiday festivities were only beginning on December 25. They would continue enjoying feasts and gifts through Epiphany on January 6—these were the twelve days of Christmas. Poor people went back to work on December 26. But, as Nicholas and the rest of us concluded centuries earlier, at least Christmas Day had brought momentary joy to those who needed it most.

So Christmas on December 25 was, in some ways, all most people in England had to be happy about, and now these Puritans argued that it should be taken away from them. I simply could not imagine why anyone would be so cruel. Though there still weren't that many Puritans in London, there seemed to be a few more every day. As I walked, it was easy to pick them out.

While everyone else, rich or poor, enjoyed wearing clothes of pleasing colors, Puritan men and women generally preferred black, white, or gray. They thought wearing any other colors might encourage pride, and pride was, in their opinion, sinful. Most Puritan men kept their hair clipped short—one nickname for them was Roundheads—and they would stop and glare at anyone acting in ways they considered inappropriate. They considered almost anything inappropriate— dancing, singing anything other than hymns, even laughing out loud. Above all, they hated any form of religion that worshipped God except in the most basic of ways, sitting in an unadorned church listening to a long sermon. They didn't even want music played in church—that, too, was supposedly insulting to God. The only respectful music, to their minds, came solely from the human voice.

Christmas became the focus of their unhappiness because, they said, it reduced gratitude for Jesus being born to an occasion where people got drunk and acted badly. They weren't completely wrong—sometimes that would happen. Though hundreds of thousands of people behaved properly, inevitably a few others would take the opportunity to misbehave. Every Christmas, there would be isolated incidents of someone drinking too much beer and shouting out insults to his upper-class host or of children getting so excited that they became unruly. But the Puritans chose to present these unfortunate moments as typical rather than exceptional—proof, they insisted, that Christmas had become nothing more than an excuse for rowdy, sinful behavior.

Further, they claimed, God was not pleased by so-called Christian celebrations that were simply extensions of pagan ceremonies. Christmas was on December 25 because, prior to Rome embracing Christianity, one of that nation's emperors worshipped the Persian sun gods. Mithra, the Persian god of light, supposedly was born on that date. In 350, it was just changed to be Jesus' birthday, instead. Nobody, the anti-Christmas Puritans argued, really knew the date when Jesus was born, so how could anyone be so presumptuous as to simply pick a day instead?

They hated everything about Christmas, including the custom of exchanging gifts. That, they complained, harkened back to Saturnalia, the weeklong celebration in old Rome that lasted through December 23, when people would give each other little trinkets as part of the celebration. Imitating the way the Wise Men brought gifts to the Baby Jesus had nothing to do with this terrible modern tradition of awful Catholic St. Nicholas bringing gifts to British children, the Puritans insisted. It didn't matter if he was now officially known as Father Christmas. By any name, he was a Catholic saint, and anything remotely connected with Catholicism must be eradicated. Over the years, all of us who traveled and worked with Nicholas had learned everyone has the right to his or her religious beliefs. But we also felt, very passionately, that it is wrong to force your opinions on others who believe differently. I did not dislike the Puritans for what they chose to believe, but I was very offended by their inability to tolerate, let alone respect, the beliefs of others.

"No matter how they try, the Puritans will never be able to take Christmas away from the British people," I insisted to Arthur and Leonardo when I had finally finished my long walk and returned to their house in London for dinner. We were eating a meal that was very middle class, since there was fruit juice to drink and a little meat to go along with cheese and some asparagus that Leonardo had grown in a small garden. Unlike the wealthy, we had only that one course, with no wine or dessert, but unlike the poor, at least we had more than bread, potatoes, and water. "Celebrating the holiday is ingrained in the national spirit. If the Puritans try to take it away, all they'll do is make the common people hate them."

"I wish I felt as certain, Layla," Arthur replied, wiping his mouth with a napkin before he took up his knife and spoon again. We didn't have forks. In 1622, few people did. You picked up your meat on the point of your knife, or else you cut off a tiny slice and used your fingers to transfer the morsel from plate to mouth. "But in our history, too often a few give the orders that must be obeyed by everyone else. King James may protect Christmas for now, but he could change his mind about it tomorrow. Or our next king or queen could agree with the Puritans."

"They might take everything else, but nobody could ever take Christmas," I said suddenly, finishing my last bite of cheese and pushing my plate away. "The Puritans can try, but there aren't enough of them."

Arthur looked thoughtful. "Actually, their numbers are growing. People still remember their terror when Queen Mary sent Protestants to the stake. So many in England are frustrated with their lives, which are controlled by the beliefs or even whims of those in power. Ordinary folk want power over someone or something, too. The Puritans tell them they can raise their voices against anything that remotely seems Catholic, and for the first time many of these people feel their opinions might make a difference. They're told by the Puritans that if they join the cause, they'll instantly be better than anyone who believes differently, even if it's a king or queen. How tempting that must be to anyone who has never before been shown respect! But I'll agree with you that the Puritans can't touch Christmas so long as two things don't happen. There cannot be a weak English king, someone who says and does foolish things that give the Puritans excuses to encourage outright rebellion. And the Puritans can't have a charismatic leader, someone intelligent enough to harness their energy, to organize and lead them. If ever we have that terrible combination in England, watch out!"

Less than three years later, Charles I succeeded his father, James, as king of England. Three years after that, an obscure country squire named Oliver Cromwell became a member of Parliament, the elected body that was supposed to advise the king. As Arthur predicted, catastrophe resulted.

Seven

I met England's new king in a London marketplace soon after his coronation. I was there at Leonardo's request, shopping for beets, a reddish-colored vegetable that was quite popular with poor people in 1625 Britain. Leonardo didn't want beets to eat, however. He planned to extract the juice of the vegetable and see if it could be used to dye peppermint candy.

"The appearance of a sweet is almost as important as its taste," he explained to me in his laboratory at the toy factory. "The peppermint treats we make here are pleasing to the tongue, but insulting to the eye." He brandished a handful. "Here, look! Round and white—how boring! But if we could only add some color, some flair, how delightful it would be. Bright red, I think, would be the most attractive. But this candy should not be completely red, either. I am picturing it as white with red stripes. Don't you think this would be just right?"

I agreed that combination would be attractive. In those days, no one yet decorated hard-boiled candy with vivid colors. Remember, there were no modern machines to shape and color products. Everything had to be done by hand, and, besides, people were still in the primitive stages of learning how to dye clothes, let alone confectionary. But Leonardo da Vinci never had the same limits of imagination as anyone else. He asked if I would go to the market for him and buy beets, since he had noticed recently at dinner that when beet juice was accidentally splashed on clothing, the resulting stain was hard to get out.

"Perhaps this juice can be altered in a way that would allow it to retain the red color without the nasty beet taste," Leonardo said. "Then I can discover a way to make the color stick to the candy, but not to fingers or clothing. Please, Layla, go to the market and buy some beets for me. I'm anxious to begin my experiments."

Leonardo did not want to go to the market himself because he didn't want to attract attention. Arthur rarely ventured out in daylight hours for the same reason. They had lived in London now for more than two hundred years, and didn't look a day older than when they had arrived. If too many people saw them often enough to remember them, at some point there would be gossip about why these two fellows apparently never aged. That attention, in turn, might lead to discovery of the toy factory. So it couldn't be risked. Having no real friends besides the other longtime companions was a sacrifice we all had to make. In London, Arthur and Leonardo mostly stayed inside.

I had no such restriction because I didn't always live there. Even after Nicholas and Felix left for the New World, I never moved permanently into the cottage near the London toy factory. I spent much of my time there, to be sure, but I also traveled back to Nuremberg to help out Attila and Dorothea, and, as always, I visited countries in Europe to study their changing Christmas customs and to seek out all the deserving children we would want to reward with gifts. And, unlike Arthur with his forceful personality and Leonardo with his distracted, scholarly airs, I looked and acted perfectly normal. There was nothing remarkable about me. So long as I was careful to keep conversations short and avoid meeting the same people too often, there was little chance they'd even remember me, let alone notice that I never seemed to get older.

It was a sunny summer day, and despite the dusty streets I quite enjoyed my walk from the cottage to the market. Today when people shop in air-conditioned, well-lighted, sterile grocery stores, I think they are missing something. The old outdoor marketplaces of Europe exploded in colors and smells, as people milled about bargaining for squawking chickens and dangling bunches of onions and flapping sets of pantaloons. Vendors set their prices as starting-points for friendly negotiation. If you wanted, let's say, a bushel of apples, you never bought the first ones you saw. Instead, you visited several stands selling the crunchy fruit, and made your final purchase based on which merchant combined the lowest prices with the freshest produce.

I spent many enjoyable minutes shopping for Leonardo's beets, which I placed in a wide basket I held by the handle, and then decided I might buy some fish for our supper, since this marketplace was close by the Thames. It was usually easy to get good prices on freshly caught fish, because they would have just been pulled out of the river and needed to be sold before they spoiled in the heat. In a pleasant sort of way I was telling a vendor he was asking far too much for a few pieces of cod when someone bumped violently against my arm. The basket I was holding overturned, and beets rolled everywhere. I turned and found myself staring into the thin, mournful face of Charles I, recently crowned king of England, Scotland, Wales, and Ireland after the death of his father, James.

"I do beg your pardon, madam," Charles said, stammering a little over the *b* and the *p*. He had a slight speech impediment, though it wasn't severe enough to make understanding him difficult. "Here, let my guards pick up those vegetables for you." He had trouble with the *v*, too.

"Please don't bother, Your Majesty," I replied, bowing as protocol required but not feeling in any way intimidated by the presence of royalty. After all, in my more than twelve hundred years of life I had met many legendary figures. Charles I might currently rule England, but in a few hours I would be sharing supper with "King" Arthur, not to mention Leonardo da Vinci.

Besides, seeing the king and even speaking to him was not unimaginable in that time and place. Though Charles had several country estates, he often had to be in his capital city to meet with counselors and converse with members of Parliament gain the required permission of their elected body to raise money through taxation. It was a testy relationship. Parliament wanted the king to consult them about all important policy decisions, including if and when to fight wars and how religion should be regulated. Like his father, James, Charles very much believed in the divine right of kings. Parliament, he insisted, should be told what their ruler wanted and then always support his decisions. As we stood face-to-face while some of his soldiers scrambled about retrieving beets, I guessed Charles must be in London because Parliament was in the process of considering his request for money to attack the Spanish port of Cadiz. Of course, he had no reason to come to the marketplace to buy his own food; the king had plenty of servants to do that. But since he was in London anyway, a royal visit to one of its busiest marketplaces made political sense. Common people would have a chance to see their new ruler, and be both pleased by the opportunity and awed by his appearance. Charles was dressed in the finest coat and trousers, and his long brown hair—what you could see of it under a wide, broad-brimmed hat—glowed in the sunshine. His mustache and beard were freshly barbered. The colors the king wore—gold and green and spotless white—were in absolute contrast to the grim blacks and grays of the Puritans. I noticed that even his hands were spotlessly clean, with the nails of his fingers neatly trimmed. A half dozen guards stood around in close proximity, and I expected Charles, now that he had acknowledged me and seen to it that my vegetables were picked up and put back in my basket, to move on and greet some of his other subjects. Instead, he smiled and continued speaking to me.

"I see you have purchased beets, and now perhaps some fish," Charles remarked. Having heard his mild stutter, it no longer really distracted me. "Will these be the things you prepare for your family's delicious supper?"

"Yes, Your Majesty," I said, pleased by his courtesy and not wanting to explain the beets were for one of Leonardo's experiments, not dinner. "That is, we'll eat fish if I can convince this merchant to sell me some for a fair price."

Charles laughed. "I, too, have problems receiving fair prices, and even in getting money to make purchases at all. Parliament is very miserly—often,

I fear, to the detriment of our nation. But they will see reason, as this fish-monger will. Now, madam, what is your name?"

"Layla, Your Highness."

"Layla," Charles said. "An odd name, certainly. French, perhaps? Italian? Well, no matter. Tell me, what profession does your husband pursue?"

It was not an unusual question. Women of middle age, as I appeared to be, were simply assumed to be married. If I answered the king's inquiry honestly, though, he would believe I was insane, so I simply responded, "Nicholas is across the ocean in the New World colonies, Your Majesty." I didn't add he'd moved to a Dutch settlement because of his disgust with anti-Christmas rules in the British settlement of Plymouth.

"Well, how wonderful!" Charles said. "My father, of course, was responsible for our first New World colony. They called it Jamestown in his honor. I assume your good spouse will soon send for you. And how do you earn your living while he is so far away?"

I thought of the beets, and Leonardo. "I make candy, Your Majesty," I told the king. "It's of the new variety flavored with peppermint."

Charles beamed. "Your new queen is very fond of sweets, and of peppermint candy in particular. It is much more common in her native France than it is here in England. She will be pleased to learn supplies of it may be more convenient than she believed."

As the king and I talked, a crowd had naturally gathered around us listening to all that was said. When Charles mentioned the queen, there was some angry muttering. Just months after her marriage to Charles, Henrietta Maria was already a very controversial figure. In those times, marriages in royal families were arranged more for political advantage than love. In this case, Charles married Henrietta because she was a princess of France. For the moment, England's chief foreign enemy was Spain, so the British king took a woman of French royal blood as his wife in hopes her country might become an ally against the Spanish if England needed military help. There were two immediate problems with this marriage. One involved the royal couple themselves. Charles was twenty-four, in those times considered a very mature age, since few people lived past fifty. (King James died when he was fifty-nine.) But Henrietta was only fifteen, a grown woman by some standards but still, really, a young girl who did not fall in love with her stuttering, shy husband right away.

Meanwhile, many of the British people, especially the working class, did not like what they knew of Queen Henrietta. Mostly this involved her religion. She was a very devout Catholic. King Henry VIII had rejected the Catholic Church a century earlier, so most current English subjects thought of themselves as Protestants. Part of the formal contract of marriage between Charles and Henrietta stipulated that the new queen must be allowed to continue practicing her Catholic faith. Charles went to a Protestant church, but that wasn't enough to silence the queen's many critics. Puritans especially argued that husbands could be influenced by their wives, and because all Catholics were treacherous, Queen Henrietta must privately be trying to convince the king to return England to the Catholic faith. This was highly unlikely since, in these early days of their marriage, they hardly spoke to each other at all. Yet, as is often the way with hateful, unfair gossip, some people kept repeating that Henrietta was treacherous, and almost everyone else eventually assumed that she was.

"Do you have any of your peppermint treats with you, madam?" Charles inquired. "The queen is in our coach just over there"—he gestured to the edge of the market, where a magnificent carriage drawn by four coal-black horses was guarded by a dozen soldiers—"and she would surely enjoy a tasty surprise."

I couldn't see the queen inside the carriage. The window curtains were drawn tight, which wasn't surprising, since if the crowd had seen her they might very well have called out insults. I wondered why the king would have brought her along, and decided he was trying, honestly though probably uselessly, to show his subjects that their queen was a normal woman rather than the scheming monster her critics proclaimed her to be.

"I have none with me, Your Majesty," I answered.

Charles looked disappointed. "Well, then, perhaps you will at some future date. Please, madam, prepare some of your finest confectionary and bring it to the palace some time when Her Majesty and I are in residence. Identify yourself as Layla the Peppermint Woman, and if it is a convenient time you will be admitted. And don't fear—I will pay a fair price for your product."

"It would be my pleasure to offer the candy as a gift, Your Highness," I replied, and bowed again. I could see that the king's guards clearly wanted him to move on, and Charles, too, looked ready to leave. Just as he turned away, though, I thought of something else.

"May I ask a question, Your Majesty?" I called out.

Now, this bordered on rudeness, and even on being dangerous. It was one thing for me to speak after the king had spoken first, but quite another to address him when the conversation he had begun was concluded. Several of the guards glared, and one stepped toward me, but Charles gestured for him to stop.

"Your king is always pleased to respond to his subjects, madam," Charles said. "The queen waits in the carriage, and I have business with Parliament, but as all here can see, I pause to take this question from you. What might it be?"

"It concerns Christmas, Your Majesty," I said boldly. "There are some now in positions of influence and power who say it is sinful and should be abolished. Though their voices are loud, many, many more of us love this special day. I wonder, will you protect it for us, so that we may keep Christmas as a time of joyful celebration?"

The king smiled. "I too love Christmas," he said. "It is the day to give thanks to God for sending his most holy son, and I realize the feasting and singing brings great happiness to my people. Do not fear, Madam Layla. While I rule this land, your beloved holiday is safe. I only hope Father Christmas will leave some peppermint candy for the queen this year."

"He very well might, Your Majesty," I replied. "Thank you for your courtesy, and for your protection of Christmas."

That night, after we'd finished our dinner of fish and Leonardo had retired to his laboratory with the beets, I told Arthur about my meeting with Charles.

"He loves Christmas too," I said. "If only he can be strong enough to withstand the Puritans' demands to ban the holiday."

"I'm afraid the Puritans squabbling about Christmas may prove the least of his worries," Arthur replied. "The king is truly at odds with Parliament. He believes they must obey all his commands, and they believe he must be guided by their collective wisdom. At some point they will either compromise or fight. Another civil war in England is a very real possibility, Layla."

Charles's disagreements with his Parliament continued. Parliament met at the king's command, and three times in the next three years Charles summoned it to meet, then angrily dismissed it when its members refused to give him the tax money he wanted and tried to keep him from appointing the royal ministers he preferred. There was much grumbling about this, not only in the London streets but throughout England. Though its members were all country lords, prominent ministers, or well-off merchants rather than real representatives of the poor working class, Parliament was still considered the one opportunity for the king's subjects to have some influence on his decisions.

Meanwhile, in my own small way, I tried to encourage Charles's support of Christmas. Occasionally, I took some ordinary white peppermints to the palace. I never actually asked to see the king or queen, but just left the package with a servant there. And, though it was not easy making my stealthy way into the royal palace on the night of every December 24 for almost the next two decades, each year England's Queen Henrietta awoke on Christmas Day to find a small package of special peppermints beside her pillow. It was especially lovely candy, from the batches Leonardo was able to successfully decorate with bright red stripes. I was careful, in delivering my occasional packages during non-holiday times, to leave only plain white treats so no one would guess the identity of the Christmas gift-giver. As it turned out, the queen, who had little belief in the Pere Noel of her native France or England's Father Christmas, decided the striped candy was a thoughtful present from her husband. She began to feel happier with Charles, and soon their marriage blossomed into a real love affair.

But the king's relationship with Parliament remained anything but loving, and several events during the next few years moved England ever closer to civil war. In the process, Christmas was in even greater danger.

CHAPTER

Eight

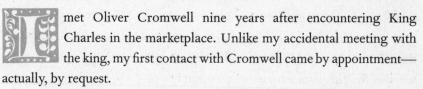met Oliver Cromwell nine years after encountering King Charles in the marketplace. Unlike my accidental meeting with the king, my first contact with Cromwell came by appointment—actually, by request.

In 1634, religious and political problems in England remained unresolved. The Puritans were more outspoken than ever against all forms of worship other than their own. Charles infuriated them in 1633 by appointing William Laud to be archbishop of Canterbury. Laud supported what Puritans considered "liberal" church services with music and altar decorations. One of the Puritans, William Prynne, responded by writing a book titled *Histromastrix, or the Player's Scourge,* which attacked as sinful all forms of public entertainment from plays to sports, and particularly argued that Christmas encouraged bad behavior, not worship of Jesus. Few people could read at the time, and if the king had been sensible he would simply have ignored the book. But instead Prynne was arrested, and as a punishment for writing what he truly believed, he had part of his ears cut off. This unfortunately proved that Charles could be as harsh as his critics. "Half-Eared" Prynne became a symbol to the Puritans that they were in terrible danger for openly advocating their religious beliefs, and, frankly, it was hard to blame them, even though I disagreed with them completely about Christmas.

Puritans comprised only part of the king's political opposition. Almost everyone in Parliament was against him. Three times in three years Charles called Parliament to meet, and each time demanded money to fight wars. All three times, Parliament refused to immediately do what he wanted, and all three times Charles told its members to go home, instead of thoughtfully discussing with them how both sides could work together instead of remaining angry and adversarial. Then the king got his money by forcing rich people to make loans to him and by imposing new taxes on some businesses. This was clearly against English law; Parliament had to agree with any form of taxation. Charles said the law was wrong; kings had the God-given right to do as they pleased. Parliament was supposed to help him, not tell him what he could or couldn't do.

The members of Parliament responded by writing what became known as the Petition of Right, which stated that whoever held the English throne could not tax anyone or anything without Parliament's approval—and, further, that no one could be arrested and punished without proof of a crime and that the king could not impose martial law on the country in peacetime, something Charles was always threatening to do. The Petition of Right was delivered to Charles in June 1628, when he either had to get the money to keep fighting his wars in Spain and France or else bring all his troops back to England. So Charles signed it, and in return Parliament gave him some of the money he wanted, but neither side was really happy. Charles believed Parliament had assumed too much power. After signing the petition the king just ignored it, levying taxes and arresting people as he pleased. Then, in March 1629, Charles went further. He announced that, for the time being, Parliament would no longer exist. He would govern without it. And, for the next eleven years, he did, despite continued criticism. If members of Parliament hoped English working people would rise up and demand that their representatives again be involved in government, they were disappointed. People in the so-called "lower classes" had enough to do keeping their families clothed and fed.

So in 1634, the king's political and religious opponents were feeling especially frustrated. There was no swelling of popular support for their causes. This is why some of them, including a rather obscure man named Oliver Cromwell, were ready to give up. Now, in a few more years everyone in England would know Cromwell's name, but at that time he was just another outspoken Puritan.

I certainly had never heard of him until one afternoon in the spring of 1634, when one of the women who worked in Arthur's toy factory hesitantly approached me. Arthur employed several dozen people, who would come to the factory in the morning, work during the day, and then go home to their families. He paid a wage that was more generous than most salaries of the day, but not so high as to attract undue attention. None of these people acquired our special powers of not aging and the ability to work and travel much faster than normal folk. We were careful that they wouldn't work at our toy factories for so long that it would become obvious we weren't growing older. Anyone employed for ten years or so was given a generous pension and, if he or she still wanted to work, help finding a new job. Of course, Leonardo's inventions included some remarkable machines that helped us make toys at a more rapid rate than was possible anywhere else, but this was the result of science, not magic. We asked our employees not to talk much about the toys they helped craft and, mostly, everyone obeyed this rule, especially since their pay was so good and they were treated with such respect by Arthur.

Whenever I was in London, I enjoyed visiting with these employees, chatting with them about their families. So in 1634 when Pamela Forrest asked if I could spare a moment, I was glad to do so. Pamela was in her late twenties and we often spoke about her two sons and her husband, Clive, a London barber. Poor people trimmed their own hair with knives, but wealthier men and women enjoyed having this task done for them. Pamela, who had then worked at the toy factory for about three years, often shared funny little stories about her husband's customers, but I noticed on this occasion that she seemed very concerned about something.

"You appear upset, Pamela," I said. "I hope nothing is wrong. Are your husband and children all right?"

"They're fine, Layla, praise God, but I hope I haven't done something wrong," she replied. "Now, I know none of us are to discuss what we do here, and I promise you I haven't. I'm very grateful to Mr. Arthur for the kindness and generosity he shows to all of us who work for him. But I did have a word with someone about you and your husband, Nicholas, who I've heard of but never met because he's over in the New World colonies."

I was immediately concerned. "Who did you talk to, Pamela, and what did you tell them?"

"Only about your husband in America, ma'am, and precious little about that, because, if for no other reason, I don't know much," Pamela answered, wringing her hands nervously. "It was all quite innocent, and quite natural. My husband, Clive, the barber, was trimming a gentleman's hair the other day, and the man told him he was thinking of going to America as a colonist because he found living here so distasteful."

"I know some people do, Pamela," I said. "Please continue."

"Well, this gentleman is a good customer of Clive's, and as it happens I also know his wife, who I meet now and then in the market. Her name is Elizabeth and she's a lovely lady. Well, her man told mine about maybe going to the colonies, and then I met Elizabeth yesterday and she said she was frightened by the thought, that to her mind all there was across the ocean was starvation and attacks by the natives. Well, you get letters from your husband who's there, and I thought perhaps you could talk to Elizabeth and her husband about what it's really like. I hope I haven't made you angry. I'm just trying to help my friend."

I felt quite relieved. After fourteen years in the New World, Nicholas's letters were increasingly positive. He still disdained the Puritan settlers and their refusal to celebrate Christmas, but both he and Felix felt quite at home with the Dutch and their continued enjoyment of visits from St. Nicholas. In fact, Nicholas had begun urging me to cross the Atlantic and join him, but I was worried about Christmas in England and didn't want to leave Arthur alone to face an uncertain future.

"So long as you didn't mention our toy factory, Pamela, there's no problem at all," I told her. "Am I to call on your friend Elizabeth and her husband? I can only tell them what Nicholas has told me, of course, but I'd be glad to be helpful if I can."

Pamela smiled, happy that I wasn't displeased with her. "That would be ever so nice," she exclaimed. "Though they live most of the time on a farm in St. Ives about seventy miles north of here, they're often in London and have a small cottage near the Thames. Elizabeth suggested, if you were agreeable, that you meet them there for conversation and refreshments this Saturday about four o'clock. I'll see her in the market tomorrow. May I tell her you'll come?"

I had no particular plans for Saturday afternoon. "Please do, Pamela. Now, your friend's name is Elizabeth. Who is her husband?"

"His name is Oliver Cromwell," Pamela told me, and went on to explain that he had been a member of Parliament, who, having suffered some business misfortunes, was currently farming in St. Ives. "He and Elizabeth are Puritans, by the way," she added. "Will that bother you?"

"No, it will only make our conversation more interesting," I replied, and on Saturday afternoon I walked to the Cromwell's London cottage, which was quite small and undistinguished. When I knocked on the door, it was opened by a fresh-faced woman in her early thirties dressed in the usual Puritan colors of black and gray.

"You must be Pamela's friend Layla," she said cheerfully. "It's so good of you to come. My husband is in the kitchen. We're just enjoying some fruit—apples and pears, nothing fancy. But I hope you'll have a bite or two."

The afternoon sun cast shadows through the kitchen windows. Seated there at a table was an average-sized man with close-cut hair and a small mustache. When he stood to greet me, he smiled pleasantly and said, "I'm Oliver Cromwell, missus." This was a common way for Puritans to address adult married women; they preferred the simpler term to the more formal *madam*, which they believed copied the social style of the French, who, in turn, they found to be influenced by Catholicism. "Please remind me of your given name."

"I'm Layla, Mr. Cromwell," I replied, being friendly but formal in my turn. "Thank you for inviting me to your home."

"Layla?" he answered, gesturing for me to sit down at the table with him and Elizabeth. "An unusual name, which I hope isn't French. And what is your last name?"

Now, here was a problem. In my youth, people just went by their first names. Further identification involved where you were from, like "Layla of Niobrara" or "Bishop Nicholas of Myra." By the time cultural custom got around to requiring last names, too, people like me and my husband and Arthur and Felix simply kept the shorter names we were used to. No one, over the centuries, had ever asked me my last name before. I would learn, though, this sort of question was typical of Oliver Cromwell. He was always every bit as interested in other people as he was in himself, a rare quality in someone with the ambition to become a national leader.

"Your last name, again?" Cromwell repeated, sounding pleasant but determined to keep asking the same thing until he got an answer. This, too, I would learn was typical of him. Once he started something, he never stopped until it was accomplished.

"Nicholas, Mr. Cromwell," I finally replied. It was, after all, my husband's name, and could be a last name as well as a first one.

"Layla Nicholas," he said, cutting a bit of pear and using the tip of his knife to raise it to his mouth. "And your husband's name?"

"Nicholas," I answered.

"You've said that already. I mean, what's his first name?"

"Nicholas."

"That's his last name. What's his first?"

There was something about Oliver Cromwell that made me feel not nervous, but perhaps unsettled. Over the centuries I had met many famous people, and a few who were great, which is an altogether different thing than being famous. Cromwell had an air about him that was only common to great men and women, individuals who had rare qualities of leadership. My husband had this quality, too. Something about them made everyone else feel compelled to be honest. In times of crisis, you would look to them for guidance. Now, in his kitchen, I could have made up some name or other for my husband, but I simply could not lie to Oliver Cromwell.

"Nicholas is his first name, too," I answered, because this was, after all, the truth.

Cromwell looked amused. "Nicholas Nicholas, is it?" he asked. "Well, that's quite a name. How long has Nicholas Nicholas been in the New World, and what took him there?"

This was not much safer a topic. As a Puritan, Cromwell would not be pleased by the prospect of the real St. Nicholas bringing Christmas to the New World. What I told him, though, was accurate enough in itself—that my husband and his friend Felix (I was glad Cromwell didn't ask what *his* last name was) had longed to see this place known as America, and they'd now been there for several years. They wrote that they were happy enough, and at some point I expected to sail across the ocean myself and rejoin my husband. The Cromwells didn't seem surprised when I mentioned they were living in a Dutch settlement rather than an English one. Traders and craftsmen went wherever they could make their fortunes, and most New World colonies founded by one country would soon include settlers and merchants from other lands.

"I am considering taking my family to this place called America," Cromwell told me. "Though Elizabeth here fears that those natives they call Indians will slay us as we step off the boat onto the shore, I've heard America is a place where a man can make his living based on his own ability. Here in England I'm only a person of very modest means—I have a small farm, and must make my living from my own sweat. Though I've been elected to Parliament, the king won't allow Parliament to meet. And you know, of course, how we who call ourselves Puritans are persecuted. In America, at least, you can worship as you like without fear of reprisal."

I thought about Plymouth, and how the Puritan leaders there refused to allow anyone to worship differently than they did. "This seems to be a time when few people are willing to tolerate different faith in others," I said carefully. "That may be the case in the New World as well as in England. I, myself, find it sad when anyone attacks the religious beliefs and activities of anyone else. Take, for example, the matter of Christmas."

"Ah, Christmas!" Cromwell exclaimed, putting down his knife and pear.

If he had been Richard Harris in the *Cromwell* film he would have stamped his feet and pounded the table, but he was Oliver Cromwell in real life, and not so theatrical. "A day that has become an occasion for bad behavior rather than worship. Do you celebrate Christmas, Missus Nicholas?"

Elizabeth Cromwell gently laid her hand on her husband's arm. "Our guest is here to talk about America, not to debate the merits of Christmas with you."

"No, she is the one who raised the subject," Cromwell replied. "I can guess the holiday is dear to you, Missus Nicholas, but do you deny that it encourages drunkenness and other sinful activities?"

"Nothing in this world is perfect, and certainly there are isolated instances of bad judgment," I said. "But will you, Mr. Cromwell, deny that the poor working people of England look forward all year to Christmas, and that it is the one time they can set aside their problems and give thanks for Jesus in the happiest of ways?"

Cromwell shook his head. "If the purpose of the holiday is to give thanks, why must anything else be involved, like singing loudly in the streets or marching as a mob to rich men's houses and demanding strong drink from them? Giving thanks to God ought to be a constant thing, and something done solemnly. December 25 is nothing more than a date based on old pagan beliefs, which in themselves are insulting to God."

"You would ban Christmas, then?" I asked carefully, trying to keep the anger out of my voice. "You would take that joy away from the English people?"

Cromwell looked thoughtful. "I have nothing against joy, so long as it is tempered with respect for God. Given the opportunity, I would try to persuade people that there are better ways than Christmas to express pleasure in all God has given us, including his son. Unless the situation was dire, though, I do not believe anything involving religion should be forced on anyone, or taken away, for that matter. Surely you do not deny me my right to believe Christmas is wrong?"

I was always ready to defend Christmas with all my heart and spirit, but I saw Elizabeth Cromwell looked very uncomfortable. I was a guest in her home, I reminded myself, invited to discuss America rather than the holiday, so I tried to bring my debate with her husband to quick conclusion.

"Certainly, so long as you do not deny me my right to believe Christmas is precious and must be preserved," I replied.

"So be it," Cromwell said, smiling, and then he cut me some pieces of pear. The Cromwells and I sat at their table for another hour, talking about the New World and the possibilities in it. A few weeks later Pamela Forrest met Elizabeth Cromwell in the marketplace, and learned that the Cromwells had decided to stay in England because they could not find a buyer for their farm. Two years after that, Oliver Cromwell inherited a considerable fortune from an uncle and didn't have to plow his own fields anymore. This enabled him to focus more on politics, so in 1640 when King Charles finally recalled Parliament after eleven years, Cromwell was among its many members who were determined that this time, the king was going to learn that "divine right" was a thing of the past. As Parliament reconvened, Oliver Cromwell was still not considered one of its leaders. But that would come, and soon.

Nine

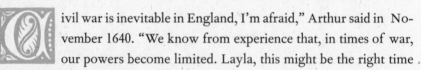ivil war is inevitable in England, I'm afraid," Arthur said in November 1640. "We know from experience that, in times of war, our powers become limited. Layla, this might be the right time for you to go join Nicholas and Felix in the New World. Leonardo and I must stay here, to keep the toy factory operating if we can. But there's no reason for you to take the risk of remaining, too."

"Perhaps there won't be war," I said hopefully. "The king has just recalled Parliament again. This time things may go better than in the spring." In April, Charles had summoned Parliament for the first time since 1629, mostly because he needed money to put down an uprising in Scotland. Instead, members of the House of Commons—the largest branch of Parliament, designed to be the voice of ordinary people—wanted to talk about unfair taxes, and about Charles's continuing habit of doing whatever he wanted without consulting Parliament first. So, once again, the king told Parliament to go home, but later in the year there was a rebellion in Scotland, and he needed money to raise an army to put down that threat. So now in November, he had asked Parliament to re-form, but its members, including Oliver Cromwell, were in no mood to cooperate.

"There are more Puritans than ever in Parliament," Arthur noted. "They have no intention of compromising with the king about anything, particularly since they learned the two oldest princes have gone to Catholic church services with their mother. They're now convinced the king might return England to the Catholics at any time. Wait and see—something is going to happen that will make war inevitable." Sadly, he was right.

Instead of giving the king the money he wanted, Parliament voted that William Laud, Charles's archbishop of Canterbury, and the Earl of Stafford, the king's military advisor, were guilty of treason and had to be removed from office. Stafford was executed. Then, before finally giving Charles some of the money he requested, certain new laws were made, taking away many of the king's powers and requiring him to allow Parliament to meet at least once every three years. Charles hated these laws. As he had in the past, he agreed to them and then ignored them. He still believed in divine right—God had made him king, and so anything he wanted to do was what God wanted, too.

While Charles was away fighting the Scottish rebels in 1641, Parliament went even further. It wrote prospective laws that required the king to get Parliament's approval for any ministers he wanted to appoint, and created the Assembly of Divines, a committee that would make new rules for religion in England—rules that would reflect the beliefs of the Puritans.

"They're going to ban Christmas right away," Arthur predicted when the news reached us at the toy factory.

I thought of Oliver Cromwell, and how he had told me he would try to persuade people to give up Christmas rather than order them to do it. Though he was still not the most prominent member of Parliament, people were starting to mention Cromwell's name more often. Many poor people in particular admired him. Whenever he made speeches, he always emphasized that the best government was one that let ordinary people have some influence—"democracy" was what he called it.

"If the Puritans truly want to respect the wishes of the working class, they'll soon learn that Christmas is too important to too many people for it to be outlawed in England," I said. "I've told you about Oliver Cromwell. Surely if reasonable people like him are involved, Christmas can still be preserved, and peace in England, too."

"Don't be too certain that this Cromwell is going to be around much longer," Arthur said. "There are rumors that the king intends to charge his main opponents in Parliament with treason, and have them arrested and perhaps even executed. Cromwell could be one of them."

On December 25, 1641, Christmas in England was celebrated as usual. Waits strolled through cities and villages singing their joyful holiday songs. Poor people scraped together their few pennies to buy a goose, and on the wonderful day itself groups of working-class people marched to the homes of their wealthy neighbors and shared fine food and drink with them there. Some churches held special holiday services, though Puritan congregations ignored the holiday completely. Arthur, Leonardo, and I had a wonderful time making our quiet way into many, many English homes to leave small gifts of toys and peppermint candy for the children living there. We regretted very much that we could not leave something for Puritan children, but our tradition had always been to avoid homes where, for one reason or another, parents did not want us to go. Still, the overwhelming number of families in England very much wanted visits from Father Christmas, and it was our pleasure to oblige.

As soon as our special night of gift-giving in England was over, I left for Italy, since the children there hoped to discover gifts from Befana when they woke up on Epiphany, or January 6. There were no Puritans in Italy complaining about this wonderful way of helping celebrate the birth of Jesus. I dressed up as the old woman who had given directions to the Wise Men and loved every moment of it.

From Italy, I returned to Nuremberg, intending to spend some time there with Attila, Dorothea, and Willie Skokan. In Germany, as in Italy, holiday celebrations were universally enjoyed. For the past hundred years, Germans had started the fine new custom of bringing small evergreen trees into their homes around Christmas, and decorating these trees with candles and bits of bright paper. These Christmas trees were lovely to look at, and their clean scent would perfume the room. Willie Skokan had an idea about these trees, and shared it with me when I briefly stopped in Nuremberg before Epiphany to collect the toys and candy Befana would leave in Italy a few days later.

"Candles are dangerous, and these trees, once they dry out, might easily catch on fire," Willie told me. "I'm certain there are already many people who would like decorations that involve less risk. Someday, Leonardo and I will invent some safer kind of lights, but this will take awhile. Meanwhile, I think we ought to find other colorful things to hang from these trees— peppermint candy, for instance."

"You're experimenting with peppermint candy, too, Willie?" I asked. "You know that back in London, Leonardo has found a way to decorate peppermints with bright red stripes."

Willie looked reproachful. "Of course I do. Leonardo and I write to each other constantly. He was interested in improving the appearance of the candy. I propose to change its shape. If, instead of round little lumps, we could stretch them longer and thinner, then perhaps we could wedge these bright red-and-white sticks between the fir tree boughs. Even better, what if this candy took on some sort of curved shape, so it could then dangle from the Christmas tree branches?"

"You mean, something like the kind of cane old people sometimes lean on, Willie?" I replied.

His eyes lit up with excitement. "Perfect, Layla!

Peppermint candy *canes*! I'll get to work right away!" I knew Willie would soon have samples to show me, but I wasn't able to remain in Nuremberg long enough to see them. A letter arrived from Arthur telling us that a final, terrible mistake had been made by the king and that war would erupt in England at any moment.

"Under no circumstances should you return to England, Layla," Arthur wrote at the end of his letter. "Any war is bad enough, and this one may cost everyone here their beloved Christmas holiday. Leonardo and I will do our best to carry on, but things in this country are so dangerous that you must go over to the New World and help your husband spread Christmas joy there."

Three days later I walked back into the London toy factory and informed Arthur in friendly but firm fashion that I would decide when and where I went, not him. "I married Nicholas to be a full partner in his mission," I told my old friend. "You wouldn't tell my husband it wasn't safe enough to stay and help you. I know you're trying to protect me, Arthur, but I really don't need protection. Now, tell me what has happened."

The king, Arthur said, had finally had enough of Parliament telling him what he could and could not do. Acting on their own authority, its members had already tried and convicted his archbishop and his most trusted general, and right after Christmas rumors began to circulate that Parliament next intended to accuse the queen of treason, too, because the Puritans believed she was telling the king to make the country Catholic again. Now, Charles dearly loved Queen Henrietta, and he immediately decided he would eliminate her enemies. He had his staff draw up warrants for five members of Parliament, all of them outspoken critics of the king. Then, leading one hundred musket-bearing soldiers, Charles actually marched to Parliament, interrupted its meeting, and announced he was there to arrest the men.

"But they had learned he was coming and left the building before he arrived," Arthur told me. "The king demanded to know where they had gone, and no one would answer. He then dismissed Parliament and told everyone to go back home, but no one left. He stormed out and Parliament carried on with its daily business." Now, Arthur added, the king had left London for the north of England, where he was beginning to gather an army. Not enough Englishmen were willing to fight for him, so he was trying to hire what were called "mercenary" troops from Europe. Some of the European royal families had also promised to send soldiers to Charles—the last thing they wanted was for their own subjects to see a king deposed in favor of democracy. Queen Henrietta supposedly was ready to cross the English Channel and meet with foreign rulers to make sure they supported her husband.

In London, Parliament recruited its own army, one consisting mostly of landowners and their workers. Leaders of this rebel army were working very hard to convince working-class people that their lives would be better without a king. For once, the Puritans among them were careful not to threaten Christmas. Instead, they talked about taxes based on what was best for the majority instead of what a single ruler wanted, and how law should be based on the common good rather than a king's whim. What reasonable poor person could disagree? Other than Charles and Parliament, though, it soon became clear that nobody else wanted this inevitable war. In the end, Charles and the rebels would collectively have about fifteen thousand troops, even though almost a million British men could have enlisted to fight.

When I heard that Oliver Cromwell was going to make a speech in a public park about the war, I decided to go. He stood on a tree stump so everyone in the crowd of about two hundred could hear him, and he spoke very well.

"We did not choose to quarrel with the king, and still don't wish him any harm," Cromwell insisted. "If he will simply abide by the law and honestly consult Parliament before he imposes taxes or makes new laws, then Charles may come back to London and we will welcome him."

"You Puritans just want to take over so you can force your religion on us," someone called from the back of the crowd.

"Not at all!" Cromwell replied. "This war, sir, is not about religion. It is about whether the king will listen to the voices of the people. I hope that someday all of you might understand God's will as we Puritans do. I pray for this constantly. But all we would impose on anyone is a nation where every voice has importance."

"So you would not take away Christmas?" I called out.

Cromwell's eyes locked on mine, and I knew he recognized me, though it had been eight years since we met in his kitchen.

"No one is mentioning Christmas just now, missus," he replied. "The fate of our nation is at stake. Let us discuss Christmas after the larger matters are settled."

Cromwell talked a little longer, about how he was raising a company of soldiers in Cambridge and why the able-bodied men listening to him should sign up to fight against the king. One or two asked directions to his estate and set off to enlist. Everyone else drifted away, but not before several muttered to me that they were also worried that the Puritans would ban Christmas if they won the war against Charles.

I was leaving, too, when Cromwell came up behind me and tapped my shoulder.

"So, Missus Layla Nicholas, wife of Nicholas Nicholas the colonist, I perceive you still love your sinful holiday right well," he said, a slight smile on his face. "I had hoped, because you seem to be an intelligent woman, that you might have changed your mind by now."

"I'll never change my mind about Christmas," I replied.

"Then you entirely support the king and his Catholic ways," Cromwell said. "I would not have suspected you for a royalist sympathizer."

"My sympathy is for the poor people of England, and I understand, as you apparently still do not, how much Christmas means to them," I said. "Can you not look all around you, Mr. Cromwell? Most of the people you see are wearing rags. They work hard all day and have very little to eat at night. But they still love God and their special day on December 25 to give thanks for his son while having some brief joy for themselves. Why would an apparently decent man like you want to take this away from them?"

Cromwell sighed. "Why cannot *you* understand? I see the same poverty you do. I see the backbreaking labor, the empty stomachs, the desperation. But I also see the everlasting glory ahead for all who renounce this pagan celebration. God will give eternal reward to those who worship respectfully, not obscenely. Christmas represents all the sin in our modern age. It is no surprise that the king and his evil queen love the holiday. One day soon we will remove its temptations from this land, and when we do God will be pleased and bless Britain accordingly."

It would have been easier for me to think Cromwell was just using Christmas as one more excuse to go to war with the king, but that wasn't true. He hated Christmas just as passionately as I loved it, and we both felt we knew what was best for the people of England.

"You told me you would never simply take Christmas away," I reminded him. "You said you would try to persuade the people to give it up instead."

"And so I will, missus, once the king is brought to his senses," Cromwell replied. "With God's grace we will avoid war, the king will listen to Parliament instead of his Catholic queen, and once political peace is restored we Puritans will convince everyone about Christmas and its evils. Perhaps you and I can debate the issue here in the park. But that must come later. As you can see, my friends are ready to leave." He gestured toward a half-dozen men gathered nearby. Their hair was cut short in the Roundhead style. All but one wore somber black garments. The other man wore black trousers, too, but his cloak was blue.

"I thought Puritans found bright colors to be sinful," I said to Cromwell.

He grinned. "Ah, missus, Richard Culmer wears blue as a sign to the common people that he holds their interests close to his heart. A godly man, Richard, but beware. He is less inclined than I to respect the opinions of others. If he believes you are set on preserving Christmas, he is likely to mark you down for future reference."

"Is that some sort of threat, Mr. Cromwell?" I asked.

"I hope you know that I personally wish you no harm," Cromwell said, looking directly into my eyes. "But understand there are those who feel the best way to ensure God-fearing, Christian democracy is to eliminate all dissenting voices. It was not wise, Missus Nicholas, for you to raise your question about Christmas in such a public place with men like Mr. Culmer present. If you make that mistake again, it may have painful, even fatal consequences."

I looked at the man in the blue cloak. Richard Culmer was tall and thin, and his smile bothered me. It was an odd smile because his lips were stretched in a wide grin, but there was no matching pleasure in his eyes. These remained dark, hard, and cold. I was reminded less of another human being than a shark baring its teeth just before biting.

"How can you associate with such people?" I demanded.

Cromwell shrugged. "We must use the tools God sends, missus, and in Mr. Culmer he has given us a hammer. Don't let yourself become a nail."

All during the spring and early summer, both sides prepared for war. It was a leisurely process. This was the way, in those days, that war was often conducted. The two armies gave each other time to get ready, and when they finally did fight it was often in an agreed-upon place at an agreed-upon hour. The king had the support of most of the wealthiest lords, many of whom lived in northern England. The parliamentary, or Roundhead, troops came primarily from the small landowners and other members of the middle class. London was solidly Roundhead, probably because Parliament continued to meet there.

As the summer days of 1642 grew long and warm, a preacher in London calling himself Praise-God Barebone began delivering fiery street sermons about the sinfulness of non-Puritan worship in general and Christmas in particular. To my dismay, large crowds began to gather and, often, cheer his words. Many of them were the same people who, I was sure, still intended to go out on Christmas day to sing and feast. But to hear Praise-God Barebone tell it, Christmas was a trick devised by Catholics and pagans to lure innocent Protestants into terrible sin.

"They're cheering the entertainment as much or more than the message," Arthur reassured me. "If you listen carefully, his real theme for the common folk is that rich people have too long taken advantage of them and that support for the Puritans is the best way to become powerful and important themselves."

"He shouldn't tell such terrible lies about Christmas without someone standing up and disputing him," I said. "Perhaps, whenever he is speaking, I should be there, too, and present the other, truthful side."

"You can't do that, Layla, and for two very good reasons," Arthur cautioned. "First, you know it is our rule to never personally interfere in major historical events. Yes, Nicholas spoke with Charlemagne, and several of you supported Columbus with Isabella the Queen, but never did you tell anyone what to do in matters of public policy. We are gift-givers, not history-changers. Second, Oliver Cromwell warned you about coming to the attention of Puritan thugs like Mr. Culmer, who is becoming known as 'Blue Richard' because of his oddly colorful cloak. If you attract Culmer's wrathful attention, you do more than place yourself in danger. He might then discover the toy factory, and, from there, begin to guess all our gift-giving secrets. I realize it is hard, but you must remain quiet."

I knew Arthur was right, and because of his advice I refrained from engaging Praise-God Barebone in any sort of public debate. But I couldn't resist joining the crowds listening to Barebone and other fanatics like him. This was a mistake. Over the many centuries of my life, I have made my share, but this was one of the most foolish. True, I never raised my voice to disagree with Barebone, but his Puritan allies, keeping careful watch on those who came to listen, must have noted my obvious disgust. I discovered this in October 1642, when Pamela Forrest again said she had to speak with me, this time because she had dreadful news.

Ten

y old friend Missus Cromwell searched until she found me in the market yesterday," Pamela began after pulling me into a small storage room inside the toy factory. Its shelves creaked pleasantly under the weight of blocks of wood and containers of paint. "She didn't come out and say that her husband wanted to pass a message to you, but her meaning was clear."

"What would Oliver Cromwell want to tell me?" I asked. "Perhaps once again that he's right and I'm wrong about Christmas?"

Pamela looked stricken. "No, Layla, it's more serious than that. It seems that Blue Richard Culmer has your name on a list of possible spies for the king. All the people on this list are to be arrested on sight tomorrow, because the Roundheads are about to go into battle against His Majesty, and they fear a few royalist sympathizers might pass him information about their troops and war plans."

"That's ridiculous," I replied. "I know absolutely nothing about any war plans, and, if I did, I would not take sides in this war by telling the king about them."

"I know that, Layla, but Richard Culmer doesn't," Pamela said. "Missus Cromwell says he has your name right at the top of the list."

"How can he do that?" I replied. "To my knowledge, I've only seen Culmer once, and that was when I spoke to Oliver Cromwell after a speech he made. I asked a question there about Christmas, but how, based on that, am I considered a king's spy?"

"It's far worse, I'm afraid," Pamela said. "According to what Mr. Culmer has told Mr. Cromwell and other Roundhead leaders, you have taken to stalking Praise-God Barebone. Mr. Culmer, it seems, has his people watching everywhere for such acts of dissent. And then there's what seems to be the worst evidence of all, though I'm sure it can't be true."

Everything I'd heard so far seemed nothing less than ridiculous. "What could that possibly be?" I asked.

"According to what Mr. Culmer told Mr. Cromwell, for several years you have been seen making visits to the royal residence in London, obviously to inform on Puritan activities to the king and queen."

I couldn't help laughing. "Pamela, that is so silly. I would go there occasionally to leave peppermint candy for the queen, since she is so fond of it. I never even see her or her husband. If Blue Richard Culmer bothers to get the full story from his own spies, surely he'll learn that I was never in the palace for more than a few moments, certainly not long enough to pass any sort of information to his royal enemies."

Pamela Forrest shook her head. "All Mr. Culmer needs is the *appearance* of guilt to accuse you, Layla. He has decided he dislikes you, and that's all the reason he needs to have you arrested."

The foolishness of the whole situation astonished me. "But Pamela," I protested, "one of the reasons Parliament is going to war against the king is because they didn't want Charles arresting his opponents without solid evidence of wrongdoing. If Blue Richard arrests me on such flimsy charges, the Puritans are doing exactly the same thing!"

"But the Puritans are in control now, at least here in London, and so they no longer have to justify their actions," Pamela said gently. "That is the way of power, I suppose, to feel no real need to explain yourself beyond the general principle of, 'I am completely right, so anyone who disagrees must be wrong.'"

Well, there was no doubt I was in danger, and I honestly didn't know what I should do. In all our centuries of gift-giving, none of the companions had ever before found himself or herself being hunted by the authorities. I had to discuss this with Arthur, of course, and asked Pamela if she would go into the factory to get him. I sat down at the small table in the storeroom and rested my chin on my hand, thinking hard.

When Pamela brought Arthur, we told him about Blue Richard and his warrant for my arrest. For a few moments Arthur was furious on my behalf, and then, with great effort, he tried to calm down.

"No problem is ever solved with impulsive decisions based on anger," he said, more to remind himself as anyone else. "Certain facts are obvious. First, we can't reason with Blue Richard Culmer because he doesn't care about the basic truth, which is that you never collaborated with the king and queen. Second, you cannot allow yourself to be arrested. Torture and even execution is not uncommon for political prisoners. Third, whatever we do now must not in any way reveal the existence of this toy factory. Pamela Forrest, I hope you understand this. And now, so that you are not placed in further danger yourself, please return to work, with our thanks for this warning."

"I'd prefer to stay, Mr. Arthur," Pamela said firmly. "My loyalty is to you and Layla, not Blue Richard Culmer and his nasty accomplices. Let me help you, if I can."

Arthur was about to refuse, but I caught his eye and nodded. Pamela Forrest was placing herself at considerable risk by passing on the message from Oliver Cromwell. Though she shouldn't—couldn't—be made aware of all our secrets, she had at least earned the right to involve herself in my escape, if we could think of a way to accomplish that.

"All right," Arthur said. "Culmer and his henchmen are to arrest you on sight tomorrow, which must mean they do not know where you live. Maybe you can just stay inside the toy factory for however long it takes them to forget about you."

"We can't take the chance that they will, at some point, begin a door-to-door search," I replied. "If they found me here at the factory, and if they saw the toys, they might make the connection to Christmas and gift-giving and then you and Leonardo and everyone working here might be arrested, too. No, I can't stay here."

"But you can't go out on the London streets, either," Pamela noted. "They'll have posters of you up on every wall. Mr. Culmer and his helpers are fearfully efficient, Layla."

"Then I have to leave London," I said. "I'll pack a few things and leave as soon as it's dark tonight. I'll quickly make my way to the channel and take the short voyage across to France, and from there I'll go on to our friends in—" I remembered Pamela must not know much about our other operations. "Well, I'll go to our other friends and their factory. Blue Richard's reach doesn't extend outside of England, surely."

Now it was Arthur's turn to point out something obvious. "If the war is about to finally begin, and if Culmer is preparing to make his first arrests, then Parliament has set guards on all the ports. They expect Queen Henrietta to try and flee across the channel to France, you know, and it's very likely Culmer has warned the soldiers placed at the ports to watch out for you and the other so-called spies he intends to arrest. As Pamela has pointed out, Culmer is fearfully efficient. I'm afraid, Layla, that you're stranded here in England."

"But if I can't stay here in London, then where in England can I go?" I asked. "Truly, we don't know anyone who might offer shelter." This was no exaggeration. To protect our privacy, to keep our secrets of being ageless and able to travel much faster than ordinary people, we had not made friends outside our small circle of longtime companions. This now caused a terrible problem. I was going to be a fugitive on the run, but I had no particular place where I *could* run, no trusted friends somewhere in England away from London who would hide me without asking too many questions. For the first time since Pamela had told me the news, I felt some fear. Perhaps I *would* be arrested and thrown into prison. I hope my confessing this doesn't disappoint you too much. But anyone in that dangerous situation would have been afraid.

"If only Nicholas were here," Arthur mused. "He might see a way out of this."

"I wish he were, too, but there's no sense wasting time on forlorn hopes," I said. "There seems to be no other choice than for me to pack a little food, wait for nightfall, and be on my way. I'll have to trust to God to somehow protect me until this terrible time is over. I'll try to get word to you, Arthur, when I find a place to take shelter. Meanwhile, don't write to my husband about this and alarm him. He has plenty to do in America, and in the time it would take him to return here, who knows what the situation might be. In your letters, tell him I'm just too busy to write."

"Think this through carefully," Arthur warned. "You'll be a wanted criminal on the run. You won't know who to trust, who might betray you to the Puritans. And, if there's truly war, you know how that will affect your ability to travel fast." He suddenly remembered Pamela, and added, "I mean, with battles all around you, you won't be able to make your way directly to many places."

"I'll just have to do my best," I said. "Well, Pamela, I really think you should go back to work now. I'm grateful to you for helping me avoid immediate arrest, and I pray you won't find yourself in trouble for doing it. I'll go pack now and be gone as soon as it's dark."

"Wait, Layla," Pamela said haltingly. "I think I may know somewhere you can go, someone who would take you in. Do you know about the town of Canterbury?"

Of course, I did.

Canterbury, about sixty miles southeast of London, grew from a camp scratched out of swamps by primitive tribesmen. The Romans established a town there, and later St. Augustine arrived, sent about the same time we met Arthur, to strengthen Christianity in what was a pagan land. In 597, construction began on a great cathedral, which, almost five hundred years later, had expanded into one of the most towering, impressive places of worship in all the world. In 1170, King Henry II had his archbishop Thomas à Becket murdered in the cathedral, which brought Canterbury a great deal of national attention and shame. Pilgrims began to come to Canterbury for special worship after the Catholic church declared Becket to be a saint. As in

Myra at the supposed tomb of my husband Nicholas, many people thought if they came to Canterbury and prayed to St. Thomas à Becket they would be cured of all sorts of diseases.

In the late 1300s, an official of the English government wrote a book called *The Canterbury Tales,* all about some very odd pilgrims who were on their way there to worship. This book, which poked fun at its characters, became one of the most popular ever written. You can still find copies quite easily today. It only added to the town's reputation. Except for the income generated by visiting pilgrims, who would buy food and rent places to stay, Canterbury was mostly a farming community. When King Henry VIII broke away from the Catholic church, Canterbury particularly felt his wrath. He ordered the shrine of St. Thomas à Becket completely destroyed— Henry did not want any of his subjects worshipping at the grave of a Catholic saint. As soon as the shrine was gone, so were most of the pilgrims, so with their tourist trade evaporating it was lucky people in Canterbury had farming to fall back on. In particular, they raised sheep. Wool from Canterbury was prized in foreign markets.

But Canterbury's religious reputation continued to work against the town. In the 1550s, when Henry VIII's Catholic daughter, Mary, was queen, she ordered some Protestants burned at the stake in Canterbury. All the English monarchs since—Elizabeth I, James I, and Charles I—had supported Protestants over Catholics, and Canterbury became a haven for Protestants fleeing persecution by Catholics in Europe. Now the town was considered by the Puritans to be one of their strongholds, and I wondered why Pamela Forrest would mention Canterbury to me as I tried to pick a place to hide.

"Who would shelter me in Canterbury, Pamela?" I asked. "I don't know anyone there, and, to hear the Puritans tell it, no one there would want to know me."

"That isn't so, Layla," she replied. "Most of the people in and around Canterbury are just good, hardworking folk who want all war to go away and with it any people who try to tell others how to worship and what to believe. It's true that Avery Sabine, the town's mayor, happily serves the Puritans in any way he can, but the vast majority of Canterbury citizens still love Christmas. I know all this because I have a younger sister who lives there. Elizabeth is a wonderful, warm person who I know would become your good friend. She and her husband, Alan Hayes, live in a pretty little cottage about a mile outside the town walls. Alan is often away, because he is a fine sailor and much in demand on voyages to and from the New World, so Elizabeth and her eight-year-old daughter, Sara, are left to carry on as best they can. Elizabeth, in fact, works in the manor of Mayor Sabine and his wife, Margaret. I know she and Alan would give you shelter if I asked."

"I couldn't impose on strangers like that," I said. "Your sister hardly needs to be placed in danger by hiding a fugitive."

"She would want to help, I promise," Pamela said firmly. "Elizabeth has a warm heart and a keen sense of justice. Let me write a note for you to take to her. I'll tell her something about your circumstances, asking that she let you stay with her, at least for a little while so you have time to make further plans. Canterbury is far enough from London for you to be safe there, I'm sure."

"I can't do it," I repeated, but Arthur agreed with Pamela.

"It's already getting dark, and you're to be arrested in the morning, Layla," he pointed out. "There is very little time left. And I like the idea of Canterbury, since the Puritans believe they are so popular there. They would never expect you to hide in *their* city. Also, to be honest, it doesn't seem that you have any better option."

"Let me write the note to Elizabeth," Pamela urged.

It seemed I had no real choice. I privately decided that if this Elizabeth Hayes in any way seemed reluctant to take me in, I would not stay at her home at all. Even if she was willing, I would still leave as soon as I came up with another idea. The thought of running, of hiding, was so disturbing to me. I was branded a spy because I loved Christmas. How foolish! How very, very sad!

While Pamela wrote her note I packed a few items of clothing, along with some bread, fruit, and cheese.

"I really don't need to take along food," I reminded Arthur. "Sixty miles is nothing to you or me. Even walking, I'll probably be in Canterbury in less than a day."

"It never hurts to be prepared," Arthur said. "You might have to leave the road to avoid patrols and hide along the way for a while. If you do, the food will come in handy. And if you don't need to eat it, you can contribute it to the larder of your hosts."

He hesitated a moment, then said, "There is one other thing I must ask you, and I didn't want to while Pamela was here. Layla, why on earth would Oliver Cromwell want to warn you about Blue Richard? Could this be some sort of trick on his part?"

I shook my head. "Although we disagree about Christmas, I think Oliver Cromwell is an honorable man who acts on his beliefs, just as you and I do. He realizes I'm no spy for the king. Cromwell will always be faithful to those causes he believes are just, but never at the expense of truth."

Then I took a few moments to write a hasty letter to my husband, telling him I was off for a while to scout the English countryside for children deserving of gifts from Father Christmas. I hoped he and Felix were well and happy. Then, after a long pause, I added: *"Remember always how much I love you, and how glad I'll be when we're together again. I especially thank you for letting me be your equal partner in this grand gift-giving mission. You are the finest man in the world, and I'm so honored to be your wife."*

After twelve hundred years of marriage, Nicholas and I seldom put into spoken or printed words our feelings for each other. We usually felt we didn't have to. Our mutual devotion was obvious. But this one time I wanted him to have those words to remember me by if my flight from Blue Richard Culmer did not prove successful.

In a while, Pamela finished her note to Elizabeth. She pressed the note into my hand and whispered, "God be with you, Layla."

"And with you," I replied. Farewells should be kept brief under the best of circumstances, and this particular moment was dreadful. I hugged Arthur, patted Leonardo on the arm—he was absentmindedly gazing at a circling moth, wondering, perhaps, how its wings carried it through the air—and then I swung my small pack onto my shoulder, pulled the hood of my cloak tight around my face, and went out into the London night.

Streetlamps were lit at varying intervals, but mostly I walked through the city in shadow. For the first time ever, I felt the need to occasionally look behind me to be certain I wasn't being followed. I didn't see anyone, but the very thought of being pursued made me nervous. Still, I encountered few people, and no one challenged me when I walked through a city gate and out into the country on the road to Canterbury. If Blue Richard was going to put up posters with my likeness on them, he hadn't gotten around to it yet.

At that same moment forty miles to the north, the armies of the king and Parliament were preparing to clash. The Battle of Edge Hill wouldn't officially begin until the next day, but cavalry scouts from both sides were picking their way through the dark to determine the best routes of attack. A few of these scouts accidentally encountered one another and fired some futile shots. Though I had no way of knowing the exact particulars, I had immediate evidence that there was fighting. With my usual powers to travel at great speed, I could have covered the sixty miles between London and Canterbury in a few hours. I had expected to greet Elizabeth Hayes as the morning sun rose. Instead, it took me that night plus three full days to make the trip, walking at the usual human pace. Any sort of fighting had that effect on our special powers. So, to my great dismay, I realized that somewhere in England a dreadful civil war had begun, and Christmas hung in the balance.

CHAPTER

Eleven

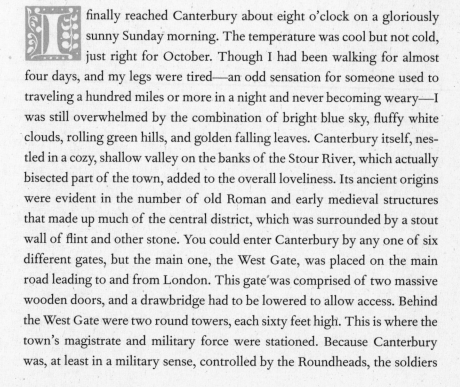 finally reached Canterbury about eight o'clock on a gloriously sunny Sunday morning. The temperature was cool but not cold, just right for October. Though I had been walking for almost four days, and my legs were tired—an odd sensation for someone used to traveling a hundred miles or more in a night and never becoming weary—I was still overwhelmed by the combination of bright blue sky, fluffy white clouds, rolling green hills, and golden falling leaves. Canterbury itself, nestled in a cozy, shallow valley on the banks of the Stour River, which actually bisected part of the town, added to the overall loveliness. Its ancient origins were evident in the number of old Roman and early medieval structures that made up much of the central district, which was surrounded by a stout wall of flint and other stone. You could enter Canterbury by any one of six different gates, but the main one, the West Gate, was placed on the main road leading to and from London. This gate was comprised of two massive wooden doors, and a drawbridge had to be lowered to allow access. Behind the West Gate were two round towers, each sixty feet high. This is where the town's magistrate and military force were stationed. Because Canterbury was, at least in a military sense, controlled by the Roundheads, the soldiers

there had close-cropped hair and dressed in much simpler, drab uniforms than the colorful costumes of the king's forces. The left-hand tower also housed the town jail, which seemed to be a rather fearsome place. Its few windows were crisscrossed by massive bars.

But the forbidding wall and gates and towers and jail still didn't spoil Canterbury's overall impression of country welcome. On this Sunday morning, all the gates stood open and the drawbridge was down. Few people were stirring yet. The calls of the birds and the gentle rushing of the river were easy to hear. Soon, though, everyone would be up, and most, after breakfasting, would make their way to church. There were several churches in the town, but all of them paled in comparison to the limestone Canterbury Cathedral in the eastern corner. This glorious cathedral towered high, dwarfing everything else in both height and breathtaking majesty. Seeing it in daylight for the first time—my few previous visits to Canterbury had been by night to deliver Christmas gifts—I was especially struck by the gorgeous stained-glass windows that adorned all the cathedral's long walls. Even from the outside, they reflected the sun in great rainbows of colors. How wonderful, I thought, that human beings had mastered the skills necessary to craft such beautiful things.

Before Henry VIII's edict changing England from a Catholic to a Protestant country, long lines of pilgrims would have circled the cathedral, each waiting for a turn to pray at the shrine to St. Thomas à Becket in a small side chapel. So many pilgrims went there for so long that grooves were worn into the hard stone chapel floor—often they would fall on their knees when they entered and actually *crawl* to the altar to pray. Now such behavior was frowned upon, especially with Puritans running the town, and so no pilgrims came and crawled and prayed.

About eight thousand people lived in Canterbury, quite a respectable number for that time, and their homes were much the same as those in London. The few wealthiest residents resided in fine stone structures. From my vantage point of a roadside hilltop a quarter-mile from the West Gate, I could look down over the town wall and see clearly where these well-to-do folk lived. I suspected that one particularly large home must belong to the city's mayor. Then there were the middling homes of merchants, their plaster walls supported by wooden beams. The vast majority of the houses were modest, squarish cottages with thatched roofs. The portion of the town streets I could see looked much cleaner than those in London. At least, there were fewer pigs on the loose, rooting through trash.

I was tempted to go into the town and find some small, quiet church at which to do Sunday worship, but there was another matter that needed immediate attention. I had Pamela Forrest's letter to her sister Elizabeth, and no real idea of whether or not this Elizabeth Hayes would even consider taking in a stranger, and a fugitive from the Roundheads at that. If she turned me away, I wasn't really sure what I could do next, besides try to hide myself away in the country until I could think of a different plan. Pamela had assured me Elizabeth would make me welcome, but I couldn't be certain this would be the case.

The same number of people lived outside the town walls as inside them. These "outer" families usually owned or worked on farms, and their cottages were within easy walking distance of Canterbury's shops and churches. Elizabeth Hayes, I'd been told, lived a mile to the east of the city with her husband, Alan, and daughter, Sara. Anne's directions to me were to go to the river just past town and follow the path beside it past a grove of poplars. I would soon see a cottage surrounded by flower bushes, with a mighty oak tree towering over it. That, Pamela said, was her sister's home. Of course, Pamela couldn't provide me with a specific address, because these things were not yet in use. People lived where they lived, and you found them by looking around and asking.

Church bells had begun to peal back in the town by the time I saw the Hayes cottage. The cheerful ringing echoed down the road as I walked, and I thought again how foolish it was for a country to go to war, even in part, because people could not agree to let each other worship as they pleased. Then I paused, because the door of the Hayes home was opening, and I got my first look at my prospective hostess.

Elizabeth Hayes was slender and dark, a lovely looking woman of perhaps thirty. Her brown hair cascaded past her shoulders, and her smile was warm and unforced. I liked her on sight, but didn't have the chance to speak, for she was dressed in a long, clean frock and clearly on her way to church. She paused just outside the door, gesturing for someone to follow, and a moment later was joined by a sturdy-looking child I knew must be her eight-year-old daughter, Sara. If I liked Elizabeth Hayes the first time I saw her, I loved her daughter. Unlike her dark-complexioned mother, Sara was light, almost pale, with white-blonde hair and sparkling blue eyes. It seemed to me that there was something very special about this child, a sort of inner glow. Was it obvious to everyone else, or only to me? Sara had a serious expression as she tugged a kerchief in place over her hair, and took her mother's hand as they walked toward the town. They nodded to me as they passed where I stood perhaps twenty yards from their cottage. Elizabeth said, "Happy Sabbath," in a bright, friendly voice, while Sara quietly murmured, "Good day," and looked quickly away. It was obvious she was a very shy child. It would be a bad thing, I decided, to interrupt their stroll to church by presenting Pamela's letter, and so I decided to sit for a while in the shade of the towering oak and eat the last of my fruit and cheese. Time enough when Elizabeth returned from worship to introduce myself. I did wonder where her husband might be, since only mother and daughter had left the cottage. Either he was sleeping in—not likely in those days and that place—or else he was away on one of his voyages.

I rested my back against the tree and munched an apple. Families made their way down the path, heading into town and church. Many people called out greetings to me. It seemed almost impossible that the same England that was home to such warm, friendly folk was at the same time split by civil war. During the time it had taken me to walk from London to Canterbury, I had heard bits of gossip about the first clash between royalists and Roundheads at Edge Hill. The king's forces, apparently, had barely gotten the better of the fight, and the Roundheads had retreated back toward their strongholds near London. Oliver Cromwell, I guessed, would have taken part in the fighting, and I hoped he had survived.

The breeze was cool, but the sun was warm, and after I'd eaten I suppose I must have dozed, for suddenly I snapped awake with the feeling of being watched. My pleasure in the fine morning had made me forget, for a while, that I was on the run, but now my fear of capture overwhelmed me. I gasped, opened my eyes, and there, perhaps five feet away, was little Sara, who must have been as frightened as I was, for she whirled and scampered back to her mother, Elizabeth, who stood at the cottage door.

"Sara, remember your manners," Elizabeth cried. "Ma'am, I apologize for my daughter. She should not have approached you as you slept. Are you hungry, perhaps? I'm about to prepare our Sabbath meal, and you're most welcome to join us."

For English country folk of the time, inviting a stranger in to eat was not an uncommon thing. Hospitality was cherished, even among the poorest people. Whatever God gave you was to be shared with open arms and a generous heart. Elizabeth's invitation provided me with a perfect opportunity to introduce myself, and I took advantage of it.

"Missus Hayes?" I asked politely. "Please don't be surprised I know your name. Mine is Layla, and I'm a friend of your sister Pamela Forrest in London. We work in the same place."

"Well, now!" Elizabeth exclaimed, her smile growing even wider. "Pamela has told me often about how much she enjoys where she works and the kind people there. Though, you know, I can't ever get her to provide many details, like what, for instance, you *make*."

It was gratifying to know that Pamela was keeping our secrets, even from her beloved sister. "Oh, we make many things," I said vaguely. "I don't know from one day to the next what we'll be putting together." That, certainly, was true.

"Well," Elizabeth said, "by the sun I can see it's getting past noon, and some food will make a pleasant day seem even better. Sara, get out an extra plate, and please see the table is free of dust." The child hurried inside. Elizabeth took my arm and led me through the door.

The cottage was unremarkable. It was, in the 1640s tradition of rural England, one large room with a narrow ladder leading up to a small loft. In one corner of the downstairs room was a fireplace, which provided both warmth and a means to cook. Pots dangled over the fire on hooks, while pans might be placed directly in its embers. A pallet covered by a quilt in another corner was where Elizabeth and her husband slept. I knew little Sara would have her own place up the ladder in the loft. There were a few simple chairs with high, straight backs in front of the fire, and there was a small table where Sara was busily setting out three sets of plates, cups, and knives. She had taken these from a cupboard standing against the plaster wall. I could see these things clearly because the sun was shining through several open windows. The windows had no glass—only the very richest people could afford such luxury—but were protected by heavy wooden shutters that could be closed and latched in case of bad weather or when the people inside wanted privacy. Somewhere behind the house, I knew, would be the "privy," and some yards away from that, a well.

"I'm sorry my husband, Alan, isn't here to greet you, too," Elizabeth said as she poured some water from a bucket into a bowl. "Here, please soak this cloth and wipe the dirt from your face and hands. I can tell you've been traveling for some time. Anyway, Alan has just left as part of a crew sailing over to the Americas and will be gone at least a year, since they are delivering goods in several places and then picking up other goods to bring back to English markets—mostly tobacco, I believe."

"You and Sara must be lonely with him gone," I said.

Elizabeth reached out and affectionately ruffled her daughter's fine blonde hair. "Well, of course we miss Alan, but we're a sailor's family and have learned to accept his lengthy absences. Are you hungry, Layla? What we have to offer isn't fancy, but it's healthy and filling. Bread to start, from local wheat. Fine cabbage and carrots from Sara's garden in the back. I'm sorry we can't offer you beer, but the water from our well is so fresh and clear that it's what we prefer to drink. The cheese is good; all our local dairy is excellent. And, for an after-sweet, we'll have pears from our very own tree. Will that do?"

"It all sounds delicious," I replied, and helped Elizabeth get out the food and set it on the table. Sara helped, too, but I noticed she still avoided looking directly at me, and she didn't say anything at all. When everything was ready, we pulled chairs to the table. Elizabeth offered a short but eloquent blessing, thanking God for both food and a new friend to share it with. As we ate, Elizabeth and I enjoyed pleasant conversation. Sara didn't talk, but I could sense she was listening and remembering every word I said about my husband, Nicholas, being a colonist in the New World, and how someday soon

I planned to join him. Elizabeth told some amusing stories about Pamela and their happy childhood together. She'd always thought her older sister would live right beside her in Canterbury, Elizabeth said, but then Pamela met Clive, whose ambitions took him to London—"We country folk don't need barbers, really"—and so now the sisters seldom saw each other.

"We send letters back and forth though, whenever someone we know comes to Canterbury from London or vice versa," Elizabeth said as we finished the last of our cheese and prepared to wipe the plates with cloths to clean them.

"That reminds me of something," I said, though I really hadn't needed reminding. I'd just been waiting for the right moment. "Your sister sent you a letter that I hope you'll read." I took it from my pocket and handed it to her.

"Lovely!" said Elizabeth, and she walked over to a window where she would have more light. I watched anxiously as she bent over the note. A moment later, she began to frown.

"Sara," she called out to the little girl, who was putting the cleaned plates back into the cupboard. "Go out, please, and pick us some pears from the tree. Take them over to the river and wash them before you bring them in."

"The well is closer," Sara replied. It was the first time I'd clearly heard her voice, which was soft and sweet.

"I prefer you rinse them in the river," her mother said firmly. "Now, get to it." Sara disappeared out the door. Elizabeth looked at me thoughtfully, then returned to her sister's letter. After several long, silent minutes, she folded the note, placed it in the pocket of her dress, and said to me, "This message is quite interesting."

"I can leave at once," I said carefully, not certain of her mood.

"No," Elizabeth said. "Pamela tells me you are her good, honest friend, but that you've somehow come to the attention of bad people and must stay away from London for a while. I already know Richard Culmer's name. He was minister for a brief time at a church here, but he spent his pulpit hours informing everyone they were doomed unless they embraced God exactly as he did, with no music or altar decorations or even, it seemed, happiness. Archbishop Laud removed him from office. Of course, now the archbishop is in a Roundhead prison, and Blue Richard is free to arrest whoever he will. And that number includes you. Why?"

"He claims I must be a spy for the king," I answered. "It isn't true. I believe my real crime has been to believe in the celebration of Christmas, which, as you know, the Puritans would take away if they could."

Elizabeth nodded. She wasn't smiling now. "Christmas is important in this house, always a welcome time to celebrate Jesus with songs and treats. I too would hate to lose it. But I also realize it can be dangerous to flaunt opposing beliefs around those with the power to arrest anyone who disagrees with them."

"Unfortunately, you're right," I said. "In any event, I certainly don't wish to put you or your child in any danger. Pamela said I might be able to stay with you for a time, but if you feel that isn't possible, don't be embarrassed to say so. I know there's no real reason for you to risk what you have to help a stranger."

Elizabeth smiled again. "There's a very good reason. The Bible tells us that the blessing works both ways when strangers are treated as welcome guests. My husband is away for a long while. I'd be glad to have another grown-up for company. I will ask you not to tell Sara about this arrest warrant. There's no reason for a child to be implicated if, for some reason, they find you here. But otherwise, please be a welcome guest in our home. Though the Puritans rule in Canterbury—our mayor is outspoken in his support of their cause—the rest of us just want to live in peace and have goodwill toward people of all beliefs. So long as you don't draw too much attention to yourself, you should be safe here."

Relief washed over me. I hadn't realized, until that moment, how nervous I had felt as a fugitive on the run with no specific place to find shelter.

"If, at any time, you feel I'm imposing, don't hesitate to tell me," I said. "And, of course, I'll want to do my share of chores and help out in any other way I can. I have a blanket in my pack, so just show me where you'll want me to sleep, and I thank you for your generosity."

"If you don't mind, I'll have you sleep up in the loft with Sara," Elizabeth said. "She has a wide pallet, and you'll find it more comfortable than just a blanket on the floor. And it will do her good to have company, even if she doesn't want any. You may have noticed she's very shy and doesn't talk much. She's always been that way, hesitant to make her opinions heard. But she is a very intelligent child, and I love her dearly."

"Will your neighbors wonder why you suddenly have a guest?" I asked. "I know, in the country, such events can cause gossip."

"We'll just say you're a cousin who's come to stay a while," Elizabeth said. "It makes perfect sense, with my husband away on a voyage and your husband being a colonist across the ocean. Sara," she called out to the child, who was just coming back in with an armful of pears that dripped river water on her arms and dress, "it turns out that Layla is a distant cousin. She's part of our family, and will be staying with us for a bit. Isn't that splendid?"

Sara nodded.

"Can't you welcome our cousin?" Elizabeth urged.

The little girl looked up at me, and I again was struck by her lovely blue eyes and sweet face.

"Welcome," she muttered, and blushed as she spoke that single word.

"Do better than that," her mother suggested. "Say, 'Welcome, Cousin Layla.'"

Now Sara spoke up, though to her mother and not to me. "It's rude to call a grown-up 'cousin,'" she said.

"All right," Elizabeth said, "then call her Missus—" She looked at me, a question unspoken but obvious. I didn't want to repeat my mistake with Cromwell, when he had ended up thinking my husband's name was Nicholas Nicholas. I thought furiously for a moment.

"Please call me Aunt Layla, Sara," I said.

The girl looked at me, and this time she smiled just a little.

"Welcome, Aunt Layla," she said softly, and put the pears down on the table. For a moment I hoped she might hug me, but she didn't. I still felt pleased. This was the first time in my life, I realized, that a child had ever addressed me as anything other than an adult stranger. I liked it very much.

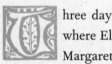hree days later, Elizabeth and Sara took me into Canterbury, where Elizabeth worked at the house of the mayor. "Avery and Margaret Sabine do a great deal of entertaining, both for business and political reasons," Elizabeth explained. "Mr. Sabine has made his fortune as a trader in cloth goods, and also in farm tools like plows and lathes, buying them from factories in big cities and selling them to local people. He and Mrs. Sabine have some hopes of him getting an important place in national government, at least if the Roundheads prevail in this current struggle. So, quite often, they have prominent dignitaries in to dine. Mostly my job is to help keep their home clean, but sometimes at these dinners I also help serve food. It's not a bad job, and we need the money I earn. Sara keeps outgrowing her dresses."

Walking along between her mother and me, Sara made a face, but didn't say anything.

"Oh, my sweetheart, I'm just glad you're a healthy girl," her mother said gently. "And a smart one, too. She can already read, Cousin Layla, and write almost any word in the English language."

"How wonderful, Sara," I exclaimed. "Do you go to school in town?"

Again, Sara grimaced, and let her mother answer for her.

"Canterbury has no school for girls, I'm afraid," Elizabeth said. "There's some basic grammar instruction for the boys when it's not harvest time. But the Sabines have a daughter named Sophia who is the same age as Sara, and the girls are good friends. Sophia has begun private instruction in reading and spelling and sums, and Sara has been allowed to share these classes with her. It's a rare opportunity, and one we appreciate very much."

"Sophia says she will marry a great lord some day, and when she does I will become her lady-in-waiting," Sara said. I waited, hoping she would say more, but she didn't.

"Do you want to be a lady-in-waiting, Sara?" I finally asked.

After a few moments of silence, Sara said, "I want to *see something*," and skipped on ahead. Her mother shook her head and smiled fondly.

"Sara is a quiet little girl with big dreams," Elizabeth confided. "She has heard of wonderful cities around the world, and longs to visit them."

"Do you want her to do this?" I asked.

"I want my daughter to be happy, and it's a hard world we live in," she replied. "If Sophia does marry well and travel with her husband, and if she does make Sara her lady-in-waiting, well, perhaps some of Sara's dreams will come true. But you and I are old enough to know about the danger of dreams, aren't we? If a poor girl wishes for too much, she's likely to be bitterly disappointed. I hope Sara will be realistic as she grows up."

"I believe in dreams," I said. "Well, back to present problems. Do you think Mrs. Sabine will hire me?"

After just three days as Elizabeth and Sara's guest, I was entirely bored with staying inside the cottage all day. I didn't know whether keeping out of sight was really necessary. The civil war had erupted, and surely Blue Richard Culmer's attention was directed at something other than a woman who loved Christmas. Today with modern technology, perhaps my picture would have been circulated everywhere, but this was 1642 England and the sixty miles between Canterbury and London were, probably, as good as six thousand. As long as I didn't call too much attention to myself, I decided, I would probably be safe.

This was another reason why I thought I'd better find employment. In country towns, people took notice of everyone else's business, and while a distant relative staying for a time with her cousin wouldn't be considered worthy of gossip, an able-bodied woman remaining home while her hostess worked certainly would. Elizabeth said Mrs. Sabine often hired women to do menial, time-consuming chores like laundry and cooking. The work certainly wouldn't be very interesting for me—I was used to traveling the world and giving gifts, after all—but it would fill the hours and help me blend into the community.

We came into Canterbury through Riding Gate, one of the town's easternmost entrances. There were two guards at the gate, and Elizabeth had to stop and let them look through the basket she was carrying.

"Sorry to trouble you, missus," one of the guards said. "But we've got orders to be extra careful, what with the battle and all." He was referring to the fight at Edge Hill, where the king's army had gotten the better of the Roundheads. Everyone in Canterbury, and, I assumed, England, was talking about it. Parliament's army had marched in shouting that God was on their side, but their soldiers were mostly untrained farm hands and the king had somehow found enough money to hire a few experienced foreign militia. The result wasn't what the rebels had thought God had guaranteed them. According to the rumors, Oliver Cromwell—who was an officer in the Roundhead army, but not its commander—was angry because his troops hadn't received the training they'd needed before being sent in to fight. Cromwell had retreated with his soldiers—who were mostly the men who normally worked for him in his fields—to his estate near London, promising that he would only return when his troops were properly prepared. The king's victorious army stayed farther north. His commanders wanted to get better organized, too, and finish off the rebels for good when next they fought.

Since Canterbury was a Roundhead town, everyone was afraid of what would happen if the king triumphed. Certainly, those who had sided with the rebels might be punished. And, truthfully, most of the people living in and around Canterbury really didn't care about the war, except for wanting it to be over. They had farms to tend or shops to manage. They wanted, on Sundays, to go to the churches of their choice and worship as they pleased. But their city government, led by Avery Sabine, was firmly Roundhead. He controlled the local militia, which meant his word was law. Even if there was popular demand for a new election, Sabine's people would be the ones counting the ballots.

"If the king's forces win, won't that mean the end for Avery Sabine?" I asked Elizabeth as we made our way through the town's streets toward the house of the mayor. "If he and his family have to flee, I supposed that's the end of your job, and Sara's chance to be a lady-in-waiting."

"Somehow, I believe Mr. Sabine will do quite well no matter what," Elizabeth said, looking to be certain Sara was too far away to overhear. "When you meet him, you'll understand. He's one of those people who know how to be a good friend to whoever is in power. He's with the Puritans now because he thinks they'll eventually win, but if it turns out that the king retains control, then Mr. Sabine will be His Majesty's most loyal, and most visible, supporter. Meanwhile, here we are at the house. Let's go through the kitchen in back, and I'll see if Mrs. Sabine is available." She called sharply, "Sara, wait with Cousin Layla."

The mayor's home was a sprawling brick structure, obviously very expensive to build. I stood in the kitchen watching people bustling around, carrying loads of food or clothes and talking to one another about the big dinner party the next day, and *would* the venison haunches arrive in time to be properly grilled before serving? But there was order to the bustle; someone ran this great household with efficiency, and soon enough Elizabeth returned with her. Margaret Sabine was a towering woman, almost six feet tall in an era when men seldom surpassed five and a half feet, and she was wide to match. Mrs. Sabine's dress was silk, rare for everyday wear, and her auburn wig was spectacular in both size and color.

"Elizabeth tells me you are her cousin who wants work," she said briskly, her tone matter-of-fact without quite becoming rude. "We may have some for you. Sara, Sophia is upstairs and her lessons are about to begin. Hurry if you want to join her." Sara hurried, and Mrs. Sabine returned her attention to me. "Please look directly at me, missus. Well, you've got an honest face. We have an organized household here. Phyllis, do *not* fold the towels that way. Here. Watch. See? Isn't that better? Well, Missus—Layla, is it? Odd name. I've had one of the washing women leave me at a *very* inconvenient time, since some of Mr. Sabine's suppliers from Portsmouth—very wealthy, influential people, all of them—are coming to dine tomorrow, then staying for another day, and we must impress them and everything from sheets to shirts needs cleaning. I'll take you on to help with the washing for a while. Two pennies a day is the wage. If you please me, we'll talk about a permanent position. Oh, and you get your dinners here in the kitchen. Elizabeth, take your cousin back into the washing shed and get her started, then come back and help me arrange things in the parlor."

We watched as Mrs. Sabine marched from the room, barking out suggestions on how best the kitchen floor might be swept and *don't* let that pitcher of milk spill; Sophia wants two cups of it sent up to her room immediately.

"One cup of milk will be for Sophia and the other for Sara," Elizabeth explained. "I know Mrs. Sabine seems gruff, but in her way she's very kind. Most rich employers wouldn't allow their children to mingle with the children of servants. Sophia treats Sara almost like a sister. Well, you're hired, so let's take you over to where you'll work. Washing is hard business, I know, but with luck you'll please Mrs. Sabine and she'll soon set you to more pleasant tasks."

Like the kitchen, the washing shed was a bustling place. There were two huge wooden tubs, one for soaking and the other for rinsing. My job was the most demanding. There were dozens of sheets and lots of outer garments and underclothes and towels and pillowcases and every other imaginable item to be washed, and to accomplish this water had to be hauled in from huge vats in the backyard. I would lug wooden buckets to the vats, fill them with water, then bring the heavy, swinging buckets into the washing shed, where I would empty their contents into the tubs. A fire burned under the soaking tub, so the water could be heated, and all the clothes in there had to be scrubbed by hand with soap. It was hard work, but not as hard as hauling the water, which I was doing. Then, when the things in the soaking tub were considered finished, they were transferred to the rinsing tub and wrung out by hand again. Finally, they were hung on long lines in the backyard to dry in the sun.

I had wondered, before I began, if I would be able to work at much greater speed than everyone else. But I quickly learned I had no special powers as a washerwoman. Soon enough my arms and back began to ache from hauling the heavy buckets, and the heat from under the soaking tub made me feel sweaty and uncomfortable. By the time someone came in to tell us it was time to break for dinner—that was what the midday meal was called—I was having some difficulty standing up straight. I could not remember ever having worked so hard.

"Tie a little cloth around each palm, dearie, so you won't get no blisters from carrying the buckets," an old woman who worked at the rinsing tub suggested. Her face, though deeply wrinkled, was very kind, and I asked what her name was. "I'm Janie," she said, and remarked that she'd been working for the Sabines, mostly in the washing shed, for twenty years.

"What did you do before that?" I asked, mostly to be polite. My back throbbed horribly.

"Why, I helped my mother in the fields," Janie replied. "Now that I'm thirty-five, I hope I'll stay healthy enough to keep working here a while longer. But it wears you out, it does."

I was thirty-five when I met Nicholas and stopped aging. Janie looked haggard and ancient, old enough to be my mother or perhaps even my grandmother. I'd never really understood before how constant hard, physical work could age people. Though I was an enthusiastic gift-giver, I realized that, in my more than twelve hundred years, I'd never really had to do anything so exhausting before.

Elizabeth joined me at the long kitchen table as we ate the bread and cheese provided for our meal. It was good bread and cheese, and there was plenty of it. I asked why Sara wasn't eating with us, and Elizabeth said she usually ate with Sophia in her room. I valued the break from hauling water even more than I did the meal, which seemed to be over in minutes. Then Elizabeth went off to another part of the house and I trudged back to the washing shed. For the next five hours, I took water from the vats to the tubs, slowing considerably as the day wore on, but never completely stopping. Janie's advice about wrapping cloth around my hands helped, but I still wore blisters on my palms. Finally, though, the last sheet and shirt were hung up on the line, and everyone got ready to go home.

"You've tried hard," said a voice behind me, and I turned to see Mrs. Sabine. "You've not done this kind of work before, have you?"

"It was quite tiring," I admitted.

"But you kept at it, and that's commendable," she said. "Because of your attitude, I have something better for you. So you're staying with Elizabeth and Sara? Elizabeth is a good worker, and little Sara gets along so well with my daughter. I like them both. Well, I'll need you here by sunup tomorrow, since the guests will arrive around noon. Lots to do, lots to do. Have you polished much silver before? No? By this time tomorrow you'll be expert at it. Now go home and rest."

The walk back to the Hayes cottage seemed endless. Elizabeth had to slow down so I could keep up. Sara scampered ahead, not tired at all.

"They worked on sums today," Elizabeth told me. "Sara likes to practice them, but I'm hopeless with numbers and can't help her much. Say, should I carry your pack for you? I'm sorry you're so tired."

I could barely keep my eyes open. "Elizabeth, I can't understand how people can work so hard every day of their lives," I moaned. "If I'm suffering so much after just one day, imagine how weary Janie must feel after twenty years! No wonder working folk are desperate to keep the few pleasures they have, like Christmas."

"Eating is a pleasure, too, and we have to work to earn money for food," Elizabeth replied. "People find the strength to do what they must, Layla. I saw you talking to Mrs. Sabine just before we left. She must have been impressed with you to take time for conversation. I'm to be at the house by sunup tomorrow. What about you?"

"She asked me to come then, too," I said. "Something was mentioned about polishing silver before the guests arrive at noon. That sounds easier than hauling water."

"Ah, the silver," Elizabeth said thoughtfully. "Well, I'm sure you'll at least find it different from water hauling."

Working-class people didn't have forks. No one in England did until the early 1630s. But the Sabines had hundreds of them—no exaggeration!—and hundreds of knives and spoons and fine plates and goblets, all of them tarnished and desperate for cleaning. I sat down in the kitchen a good hour before dawn, and didn't stop polishing until, finally, the last silver was shining brightly just as a carriage pulled up outside with the Sabines' guests. My fingers ached, and my eyes stung—the polish had a harsh aroma that burned as well as smelled bad. But the silver did look lovely, and Mrs. Sabine even complimented me on it as she bustled past to greet the men and women who suddenly filled her parlor. They were all Puritans, as evidenced by their sober dress. Mrs. Sabine wore plain black instead of the brighter silks I'd seen her in the day before. Her husband stood by her side, looking stout and prosperous in his formal black coat and trousers. The greetings were long and loud, with God repeatedly thanked for welcome guests and gracious hosts, and Mrs. Sabine said how everyone must be tired and hungry after their journey, and please come into the main dining room, where a little light refreshment had been prepared. The light refreshment would have fed a dozen families for a week. There were all sorts of rare, wonderful treats—things like tomatoes and grapes, and perfectly roasted venison, which had arrived in plenty of time. We servants were kept busy picking up this and moving that. The women guests praised the furnishings and the shining quality of the silverware—I felt proud—while the men huddled over glasses of wine and talked about the war.

"I hear Cromwell swears he won't fight again until his troops are ready," one said. "Imagine that, a glorified farmer telling lords and real gentlemen how they're supposed to fight!"

"Don't underestimate Oliver Cromwell," another responded. "There's a sense of destiny about the man. Say, Sabine, are your people here getting nervous about the royals' battlefield success? Can you keep your pro-Catholics in line?"

"My people will always obey me," Sabine said confidently. "They're really good and God-fearing, I promise. We'll find a way to get the king whipped, and then we can really get this country straightened out."

"Cromwell's been saying he doesn't want the king deprived of the throne at all," the first man said. "He just wants him to learn a lesson about sharing power with Parliament. Be a shame to win the war and still have Charles and his Catholic queen."

"Mr. Cromwell hasn't thought this through," Sabine said. "It may be he isn't tough enough for leadership. But we have others who are sufficiently stern, and useful for keeping doubters in their places."

"Blue Richard Culmer, perhaps? Is that who you mean, Sabine?"

"Certainly, I mean Mr. Culmer."

The man sipped some wine. "Now, Culmer's one fellow I wouldn't want after *me*!" and the others laughed and agreed. I winced; with all my exhaustion from hauling water and polishing silver, I'd almost forgotten that I was one of the unfortunate ones Richard Culmer was pursuing.

After the guests had eaten and we'd cleared the dishes away, the Sabines brought down their daughter to present to the company. Sophia came dashing down the stairs, with Sara trailing quietly behind. The two girls were complete physical opposites. Where Sara was sturdy and blonde, Sophia was tall and slender and her hair was almost black. There was also another obvious difference—while Sara hardly ever talked, Sophia never seemed to stop. She ran from one guest to the next, chattering constantly, asking where they were from and what they'd seen on their journey and telling about her latest lessons—"Sara thought eight and three made eleven, but I told her they made twelve."

"Well, eight and three *do* make eleven, dear," one of the women told her, and instead of becoming angry Sophia threw back her head and laughed.

"Sara, you were right after all," she called to the back of the room, where Sara perched quietly on the staircase. "Let's go back up and practice numbers some more." In the manner of well-raised children in company, Sophia curtsied to the grown-ups before she turned to leave the room.

"Is Sara your sister, dear?" the woman asked. Before Sophia could answer, her mother said sharply, "Oh, no, not at all. She's the daughter of one of the servants. We sometimes allow her to play with Sophia, however."

"How *democratic* of you, Margaret," the woman said, and back on the staircase I saw Sara's cheeks flush bright red before she turned and followed her friend Sophia. So, along with intelligence and ambition she also had pride.

Thirteen

hat night, Elizabeth asked if I would take Sara home. She explained she'd just heard a friend was about to give birth, and needed to go to her and help with the delivery of the baby. While rich women brought their babies into the world surrounded by physicians and midwives, poor women usually had to rely on their friends. I told Elizabeth I'd be glad to, and went upstairs to fetch Sara from Sophia's bedroom. I found the girls sprawled on a wide bed with silk covers and a canopy. Sophia was talking about a dress her father had promised to buy her, and Sara was bent over a slate, studying arithmetic.

"Time to go home, Sara," I interrupted. "Your mother has to go help a friend, so it will be just you and me."

"You're Sara's Aunt Layla, aren't you?" Sophia inquired. "The one who's come to stay at her house while your husband's in the colonies? Do you like living with Sara and her mother? How long do you expect to stay with them?"

"I really don't know," I replied, trying to sound respectful as befitted a servant speaking to an employer's child. "I'm just glad Sara and her mother have offered me their hospitality."

"Sara says she likes you," Sophia observed, and I felt immensely pleased to hear it, though Sara had never said anything to me that indicated like or dislike, for that matter. "She's glad you're her aunt."

"I'm glad, too," I said, and Sara and I set out for the cottage. Since it was just the two of us, I thought the girl might chat with me along the way, but she didn't. We walked in companionable silence though. I found pleasure simply in her presence. It occurred to me that, although Nicholas and I and the rest of the companions had devoted our lives to children, we never actually spent time with them besides briefly coming into their homes at night to leave holiday gifts.

When we reached the cottage we went inside and lit some candles. Today, with electric lights that shine brightly at the touch of a switch, that Canterbury cottage in 1642 would probably seem like a dark, depressing place. But back then, a few candles and their meager light were what we were used to, and so Sara and I found their glow cheerful. Neither of us had eaten, so she fetched water and I sliced bread and washed a few carrots and pears. As we ate our simple meal I asked, "What cities do you want to visit someday?"

"Paris," Sara said promptly. "Athens, in Greece. Rome, of course, and Alexandria. I suppose I'll start with London, since it's the nearest great capital and I haven't even been there, yet. What is it like?"

I told her about the high towers and palaces, the great hall of Parliament, and the other impressive buildings. Then I described London Bridge over the wide Thames, and the marketplaces where so many things were for sale, and the theaters and gardens and the streets with cobblestones. I did leave out details about trash and smells, because this little girl had plenty of time to temper her dreams with reality, as we all must eventually do. Sara smiled hugely as she listened, and after I'd talked about London I couldn't resist beginning to describe Paris.

"You've been to *Paris?*" she exclaimed. "However did you get there?" I explained that my husband Nicholas was a craftsman and trader, and that his work had brought us all over the world. When Elizabeth finally came home around midnight, reporting that her friend had given birth to a healthy baby boy, Sara and I were still at the table, and I was describing the unique scent of tabouli that permeated the streets of Constantinople.

"Cousin Layla, I'm glad you and Sara have had such fine conversation, but eight-year-olds need their sleep!" Elizabeth said. "Young lady, off to bed with you! We all have to get up early."

Sara obediently rose and walked over to the short ladder that led to her pallet in the loft. "I'm glad the baby is fine, Mother. Good night. And good night, Auntie Layla." Now I was *Auntie* rather than the more formal *Aunt*. That thought warmed me as Elizabeth chatted for a bit about her friend and the baby, and when we blew out the candles and went to bed ourselves I almost hoped Sara was still awake in the loft pallet we shared so I could tell her more about the places she wanted to go, but the child was fast asleep. And soon, so was I.

For a few more weeks, life remained simple and mostly good. All day from Monday through Friday, and then half-days on Saturdays, I worked in the Sabine house, doing all sorts of chores. Saturday afternoons were spent with Elizabeth and Sara shopping in town or enjoying walks through the green hills around Canterbury. On Sunday mornings there was church—I was pleased Elizabeth attended one where the minister did not adhere to the stern tenets of the Puritans—and then, afterward, perhaps a picnic.

After so many centuries of magical gift-giving, it was in some ways pleasing to live what would be considered a "normal" life. I was often reminded, though, that I was still a fugitive. Reports of the war reached us regularly, often in my letters from Arthur and Elizabeth's from Pamela, which they sent whenever they knew someone who was going between London and Canterbury. In those letters, we learned the king was winning most of the battles against the Roundheads, but he was never quite able to end the war by marching all the way into London.

"Even without Cromwell, who is still supposedly training his troops, the rebels fight just well enough to keep the king from complete triumph," Arthur wrote. "The Puritans still go around saying God will not let them lose. They're trying to convince the working people that few, if any, real Englishmen are fighting for Charles at all. Their new rude nickname for the king's troops is *Cavaliers*, which, I think, is based on the French *chevalier* or 'cavalry.' If the rebels don't win a major battle soon, I don't think they can hold out much longer."

But besides the English rebels, Charles had other troubles. The Scots kept raiding up along the northern border, and there was outright rebellion in Ireland, where most people were Catholics who wanted English Protestantism completely gone from their country. It was rumored that the Roundheads were holding talks with the Scots, Arthur said, hoping to form an alliance with them against Charles—who, other rumors had it, was trying to get the Irish Catholics to join him!

It was all very confusing, and ordinary people had trouble keeping track of who was doing exactly what. So long as Avery Sabine was in charge, Canterbury would officially belong to the Roundheads, but as fall 1642 turned into winter, it seemed quite likely Charles was going to beat the rebels of Parliament. In Canterbury's markets and streets, working people began to grumble about Sabine, and how the king might just wreak some awful vengeance on the town in retaliation for its mayor supporting his enemies.

Almost everyone, I think, began looking forward to Christmas that year as an especially welcome time to forget the war. I personally found it quite odd, when October gave way to November, not to be part of annual holiday preparations at either the London or the Nuremberg toy factory. There, I knew, Arthur and Leonardo and Attila and Dorothea and St. Francis and Willie Skokan would be overseeing toy production and planning who would deliver what and where, while, over in America, Nicholas and Felix were doing much the same. I hadn't heard directly from my husband while I was in Canterbury. Arthur mentioned he'd had one letter from Felix saying everything there was fine, and that he'd replied all was generally well in England, though I was away from London for a while.

I missed Nicholas terribly, and planned to join him in America just as soon as the war in England was over, which promised to be soon. The king would win, the Puritans would be commanded to give up trying to force their beliefs on everyone else, and Christmas would once again be safe. At that time, I would no longer be a fugitive, and it would be possible for me to move on and resume my life as an ageless gift-giver. I longed for that moment and, yet, I knew I would be sorry to leave Elizabeth, who I'd grown to love as a sister, and Sara, who I certainly loved like a daughter. She talked to me all the time now, about her dreams and also her disappointments, such as often being reminded in little ways that although she could be friends with Sophia, she could never be considered her equal.

"I'm actually better than Sophia at spelling and sums, but the teacher only praises her and not me, Auntie Layla," Sara said. "Sophia talks all the time about *her* education and the important man *she* will marry and how I'll be *her* lady-in-waiting. It doesn't matter how smart I am; I'll always be the servant, and, if I marry at all, it will probably have to be to some farmer in Canterbury. I don't think it's fair."

"Much in life isn't fair, Sara," I replied. "It's for us to find and take advantage of its possibilities, though, instead of being controlled by gloomy thoughts. I had a dear aunt who told me often to keep my dreams and make as many of them come true as I could. That's my advice to you, my love."

"Your aunt sounds very special," Sara said. "What was her name?"

"Lodi," I answered.

"That's a pretty name. Is she still living?"

"In my heart, at least, and now in yours," I said, and gave Sara a huge hug.

In early December, a package arrived from Arthur along with the usual letter. Anticipating Christmas morning, I had asked that Leonardo personally craft a fine doll for Sara, one with blonde hair and painted blue eyes. He'd outdone himself, fashioning a marvelous wooden toy with real working joints, and I felt some satisfaction that Sophia Sabine, for all her father's wealth, would never own a finer one. There was something in the package that I hadn't expected, too, wrapped carefully in paper. I had never seen the likes of the candy that spilled into my hands.

"Leonardo and Willie Skokan have been collaborating," Arthur wrote. "These things they call 'candy canes' are the result. Willie says you were the one who suggested them."

The peppermint sweets had been stretched into sticks about four inches long, and then one end had been curved around in the shape of an upside-down *u*, mimicking exactly the sort of canes older people used to walk, and also resulting in a shape that could, as Willie hoped, dangle as a decoration from the branches of Christmas trees in those countries like Germany that had developed this new holiday tradition.

Leonardo's striking red stripes remained on the canes, and they were lovely in their color and simplicity. Since neither Elizabeth or Sara was around—I wanted to keep the confectionary as a surprise holiday treat—I sampled a cane, and the sharp peppermint taste was astonishing.

I knew it would be all right for Sara to wake up on Christmas day to discover Father Christmas had left her a doll and some candy, because Elizabeth had assured me he was a welcome visitor in their home.

"Of course, Father Christmas can't be everywhere, so my husband, Alan, and I are careful to help him with Sara's presents," she said. "It's been a hard year with Alan away at sea, but still there will be a new dress for her on Christmas morning." When I told her I would like to give a doll, she hugged me in thanks for adding to her child's holiday joy.

"It's really a gift straight from Father Christmas and his companions," I said truthfully, and Elizabeth stared at me in surprise.

"Father Christmas has companions?" she asked.

"Of course," I replied, smiling.

In my months at Canterbury, I had been accepted into the community, with my plain looks and unremarkable job. Though I'd been careful to make no close friends other than Elizabeth and Sara—I didn't want questions about where I'd come from, because in Avery Sabine's town I assumed there would be Puritan informers—I did have passing acquaintance with a number of people, including the other women who worked for Margaret Sabine. They began talking, during the second week in December, about what the Canterbury mayor might do to discourage the celebration of Christmas.

"I hear he thinks his Puritan masters in London will be angry if people here do the usual things on the holiday," Janie confided one weary day as I lugged water buckets into the washing shed. Occasionally I still had to perform this backbreaking chore. "You know, Layla—the feasting, and the singing in the streets, and all that. He'd like to impress them with his control of the city by making sure that doesn't happen."

"I don't really see how he can prevent it," I replied. "There are no laws against celebrating Christmas—at least, not yet."

"He'll try to find a way," Janie predicted, and she was right. Only a few days later, town criers began walking around Canterbury's streets urging people "at the suggestion of our beloved mayor" to treat Christmas like an ordinary day. Shops should remain open. Everyone should go to work. If the savior's birth must be celebrated at all, it should be with a moment's silent meditation. No gifts, either, because that was only continuing a pagan tradition.

"Are Christmas gifts really bad, Auntie Layla?" Sara wanted to know after listening to the criers.

"Not at all, my darling," I said. "Gifts anytime are simply a token of love and caring, and gifts at Christmas are meant to add joy to a wonderful celebration. Please remember that the kind thoughts of the giver are even more important than the gift, and then you'll have the perfect spirit of Christmas."

Christmas fell on a weekday that year, and on the Saturday before Margaret Sabine called her servants together to tell us we would be expected to report to work as usual on December 25.

"I know some of you may disagree with my husband's—that is to say, my *family's*—position on Christmas, which is more properly called Christtide, but that is just too bad," she said. "Those who do not report for work will have to find employment somewhere else, and there are few other jobs to be had in Canterbury right now. And if any of you have any thoughts of the usual caroling at our home with drinks and food provided for all, forget them. We are a godly Puritan household and will no longer honor drunken, pagan traditions."

No one dared argue, most because they knew Margaret Sabine would certainly fire them for disobeying, and me because my husband and his companions had long ago decided to always respect the beliefs of others. If the Sabines did not want Christmas celebrated in their home, it should not be. But the rest of us could certainly do as we wished in *our* homes.

So eight-year-old Sara woke up on the morning of December 25, 1642, to discover a dress and a doll by her pallet, as well as several candy canes on her pillow. She shrieked with delight, trying to pull the dress on over her nightgown while cuddling the doll at the same time. As soon as those contradictory tasks were accomplished, she jammed a candy cane in her mouth, mumbling in wonder over the shape, color, and taste.

"And just last night she was privately asking me to tell her the truth about Father Christmas," Elizabeth confided. "Sophia told her they were too old to believe in some made-up Catholic saint."

"Sophia was wrong," I said, and handed a candy cane to Elizabeth, who liked it very much. Leonardo had sent along dozens, so I had plenty. When Sara was sufficiently calm, we fed her breakfast and walked to town and our jobs at the Sabines. Sara reported later that, despite Sophia's parents telling everyone else not to celebrate the holiday, they had given Sophia dozens of Christmas gifts, though Sara much preferred her own doll and dress and candy to anything her friend had received. When the day's work was over, Sara and Elizabeth and I walked hand-in-hand back to the cottage, softly singing Christmas carols. Later, we ate goose and mince pie, both special, once-a-year treats, and only after I climbed into the loft bed I shared with Sara did I realize with a start that not once during the whole day had I even thought about my usual magical gift-giving.

Though the working people in town reluctantly obeyed the Sabines' edict not to come to their fine home for caroling and treats, most of them openly defied their mayor's wishes and celebrated Christmas as best they could. The shops in town that Sabine didn't own were shuttered in honor of the holiday. His remained open, but had few customers. The town's non-Puritan churches held worship services, and the grandest of these was in the fine Canterbury Cathedral. Because we had to work, Elizabeth and I were unable to attend, though we badly wanted to. Well, we told ourselves, we had kept Christmas as best we could, with joy and gifts to celebrate the birth of Jesus.

"Sophia says her father is afraid his reputation has suffered because so many people here kept to their Christmas traditions when he asked them not to," Sara told us a few days later. "She says he wrote to someone in London asking for help."

"What sort of help?" Elizabeth asked absently. Sophia talked about so many things it was impossible to know what was important and what wasn't.

"Just help, Sophia said."

At dawn on the second Sunday in January 1643, there were loud shouts outside the cottage. "Someone's destroying the cathedral," a man bellowed, and Elizabeth, Sara, and I quickly pulled on our clothes and ran with the rest into town. What we saw there was horrifying. A number of men with heavy clubs, some high on ladders, were smashing the cathedral's lovely stained-glass windows, howling, "Death to Christmas!" Dozens of others, dressed in full Roundhead armor, stood pointing muskets at the dismayed crowd.

"The mayor called in troops!" someone said, and it was true. Avery Sabine stood safely inside the line of soldiers holding everyone at gunpoint, his arms folded as he watched the destruction of the church windows with every appearance of satisfaction.

"It's horrible, Auntie Layla," Sara whispered to me. Elizabeth and I held her tight between us. Then my own blood ran even colder, because one of the stick-wielding men broke away from his terrible work and walked to Avery Sabine's side. In the early morning light, I could see that his cloak was a color other than traditional Puritan black.

Blue Richard Culmer turned to the crowd and shouted, "Your mayor told you not to celebrate Christmas. You should have listened!" As in London, his lips split wide in a happy leer while his eyes remained dark and joyless. "If you do it again next year, we'll break you like we broke these sinful windows!" Then, with an animal-like howl of triumph, he signaled for the club-wielders and musketmen to march back toward London through the West Gate while Avery Sabine preened solemnly and almost everyone else stood numb with despair.

"Don't test me on Christmas again," Sabine said to the stunned crowd, and walked back to his fine house.

Fourteen

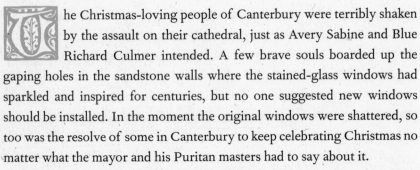he Christmas-loving people of Canterbury were terribly shaken by the assault on their cathedral, just as Avery Sabine and Blue Richard Culmer intended. A few brave souls boarded up the gaping holes in the sandstone walls where the stained-glass windows had sparkled and inspired for centuries, but no one suggested new windows should be installed. In the moment the original windows were shattered, so too was the resolve of some in Canterbury to keep celebrating Christmas no matter what the mayor and his Puritan masters had to say about it.

"I doubt there'll be many around here welcoming Father Christmas from now on," Janie suggested as we wrung out tablecloths in the washing shed. It was the spring of 1643, and I had been employed by the Sabines long enough that I was no longer the newest servant. Much of my time was spent indoors, where the work was easier. Melinda, hired soon after the assault on the cathedral, now had the dubious honor of always being assigned the hardest chores, which included water hauling. But there was a lot of washing to be done on this particular day, and I had been instructed to go out and help.

"No act, no matter how terrible, can destroy Christmas," I replied. "Somehow, the holiday will prevail."

Sometimes, though, I wondered, especially when, over the next months, the Roundheads won a series of victories over King Charles and his army. Oliver Cromwell had returned with properly trained cavalry, and his troops were instrumental in winning several battles. There were rumors the king might now be willing to negotiate a settlement that would allow him to remain on the throne in return for certain concessions, which would give more power to Parliament. In general, I simply hated the whole idea of civil war, and hoped it would end as quickly as possible. But I also knew men like Blue Richard Culmer would never really compromise about anything, although they might pretend to for a time. If Parliament defeated the king, the Puritans would find ways to dominate Parliament, and, eventually, force their beliefs on everyone else in England.

By late summer, the Scots had allied themselves with the Roundheads, and the king's forces gradually lost control of their few ports. Avery Sabine strutted down the streets of Canterbury, and was often called away to London on mysterious business, which Sophia told Sara her father would not even discuss with his family, though he promised his wife and daughter that great things were in store.

"He sometimes mentions Christmas, and laughs when he does," Sara reported. "Sophia says I should throw away that doll Father Christmas left me, but I won't."

In September 1643, just after the king's forces suffered a terrible defeat at Newbury, Alan Hayes came home from his long voyage. Elizabeth, Sara, and I returned one night from work to find there were candles already lit in the cottage. Both mother and daughter knew what this must mean and ran shouting through the door. I followed, and found them wrapped in the arms of a tall, wide-shouldered man who nodded briefly in my direction before burying himself back in this joyful three-person embrace. I went outside for a little while, to give the reunited family some privacy, and wondered what I would do if Alan Hayes did not want a houseguest who had already been living in his home for more than a year.

It turned out I had no cause for concern. After about ten minutes, Sara came to fetch me, saying her father very much wanted to meet his wife's cousin.

"If Elizabeth and Sara love you, then so do I," Alan proclaimed, and by the time we had finished dinner—eggs from a neighbor's chicken made up the main course—Alan was insisting I stay as long as I liked, "up to and including forever." Actually, I had no idea of how long I wanted to remain in Canterbury, or even in England. If the Roundheads won—it now seemed possible they might— then Christmas would soon be abolished. Avery Sabine and Blue Richard Culmer had demonstrated the lengths to which the Puritans would go to frighten people into giving up the holiday. If England had no Christmas, there was no longer any reason for Arthur and Leonardo to operate the toy factory in London, and certainly no reason for me to delay any longer my reunion with my husband, whom I now had not seen in twenty-three years. True, for ageless gift-givers like Nicholas and me, twenty-three years was the merest hiccup of time, but I still missed him so very much, and knew he missed me equally.

But somehow I believed I must stay where I was. Arthur, certainly, thought I should get out of England immediately. He said as much when, in November 1643, he came to Canterbury to see me.

"I decided this couldn't be communicated as effectively in a letter, Layla," Arthur said. We were off in the hills outside Canterbury on a late Saturday afternoon, out of sight in a grove of trees so no passing neighbors might start wondering aloud to their friends about the stranger visiting Alan and Elizabeth's longtime guest. "We hear constantly at the toy factory in London that Parliament is determined to eradicate Christmas and everything about it. Blue Richard Culmer grows more powerful each day. I doubt he's forgotten you—such men remember everyone they consider to be their enemies. The Roundheads now control almost every port city, but we can find some way to get you through. Go back to Nuremberg, or, better, across the ocean to join Nicholas and Felix. But leave England—*now*."

"What about you and Leonardo?" I asked. "You're in danger, too. If

Culmer ever discovers the factory, and why we make toys there, you'll end up in the Tower of London."

Arthur sighed. "I've come to the conclusion that, at some point, it will be better to close the toy factory down. I won't until I absolutely have to, and for now there still is no specific law against Christmas, just strong suggestions by the Puritans that it's no longer wise to celebrate it. Everyone in England has heard about what happened here in Canterbury."

"Do you think Parliament will legally outlaw Christmas, Arthur?"

"It's only a matter of time," he said. "If, in another year or two, enough people in England don't voluntarily accept the Puritan view of the holiday as sinful, then the Puritans will stop trying to persuade and start commanding instead."

I reminded Arthur of how Oliver Cromwell once told me no one should force religious beliefs on anyone else. "Cromwell is growing in influence among the Roundheads," I said. "Maybe he will prevent them from passing anti-Christmas laws."

"Cromwell is a devout Puritan who hates Christmas as much as any of them," Arthur replied. "Besides, power changes the way people do things. When he told you he believed in persuasion rather than force, he was an unimportant member of Parliament who had very little power. Of course he believed in persuasion. That was the only way he could get things done. But now he's one of the most important men in England, and as people grow in power they usually grow less concerned about the opinions of others. Don't fool yourself that Oliver Cromwell will protect Christmas if he sees the chance to destroy it." He shrugged. "But we really can't do anything about Cromwell. Let's talk about you."

I wasn't accomplishing anything for our overall gift-giving mission by staying in England, Arthur pointed out. I couldn't be in London, helping at the toy factory, because of the warrant for my arrest issued there by Blue Richard Culmer. In Canterbury, all I did was wash clothes and sweep floors for the wife of a Christmas-hating Puritan. In Europe, children in Italy still waited for Befana on January 6 and French children loved Pere Noel, who'd leave gifts in their shoes while they slept on Christmas Eve. A holiday custom unique to France was that children could open their presents on Christmas morning, but adults had to wait until New Year's. So many countries had their own special traditions, meaning Attila and Dorothea and St. Francis and Willie Skokan had all they could do preparing for the holidays and delivering all the right toys to all the right places. They badly needed my help. And what about the New World, where Nicholas and Felix were working so hard to spread the wonder of Christmas? Didn't I think they needed me, too?

"Isn't it possible, Layla, that you're being selfish by insisting on staying here?" Arthur concluded.

That stung me, because, in a way, he was right. *Selfish* is such an awful word, implying a person cares much more for himself or herself than about others, and for twelve centuries I had devoted my life to gift-giving. I had been granted very special gifts, and while I remained in Canterbury I was not using them.

I was quiet for a few moments, thinking—about my husband, so far away in America; about Oliver Cromwell, and whether he was as special a leader as I had once believed; about all the children in the world who depended on holiday gift-givers for moments of joy; and, yes, about the person in the world who, next to Nicholas, had become dearest to me. Every moment I spent with Sara was a delight. I had to admit that part of the reason I refused to flee England was that I couldn't bear to leave her. She was so hopeful, so anxious to see the world and do special things and not become just one more country farmer's wife. So much, I realized, like I had been back in Niobrara.

But there was something more at work here, and finally I tried to explain it to Arthur and, perhaps, to myself.

"Not long after we married, Nicholas told me he felt there was no coincidence where our gift-giving mission was involved," I said. "He believes, and helped me to believe, that we find ourselves in certain places at certain times because there is some great purpose to our being there. You've heard the story more times than you wanted, I'm sure, of how Nicholas and Felix and I just happened to bring gifts to the same nomad camp outside Constantinople one night in 412, or 1,231 years ago. Constantinople is a sprawling city in a huge world—what brought us together there in that one modest spot? I'm here in Canterbury now as a result of many apparently coincidental things—Nicholas wanting to see the New World, the Puritan 'Saints' making a voyage just as we came to London, Pamela Forrest working at your factory and having a kind, generous sister here when I needed some place of refuge . . . Arthur, I believe if I leave now, I ignore a message from God, who has so generously given us the special gifts to carry out our mission."

"A message to do what, Layla?"

"It's hard to say," I admitted. "Surely it has to do with Christmas, and the danger to the holiday. Canterbury is where Blue Richard Culmer made clear the Puritan determination to eliminate Christmas forever. Canterbury, then, may be the place where it is saved."

Arthur looked doubtful. "Who will save it, Layla?" he asked gently. "You? Remember, you're running from Blue Richard because you're not strong enough to fight him. I understand why you say God is with you, but don't forget the Puritans believe just as strongly that God is with them. Please, be practical."

I took a deep breath. "I'm staying, Arthur," I said. "We have been friends now for more than a thousand years. Support me in this, as we have all supported one another for so many centuries. There is no coincidence in our lives, and somehow Christmas will be saved."

Arthur embraced me and returned to London. I went back to the Hayes cottage and resumed my life there. Parliament continued to combat both king and Christmas. December 25, 1643, was one of the saddest holidays in memory. Parliament still did not demand that Christmas no longer be celebrated, but it deliberately met on Christmas Day as a sign business should be carried on as usual. Across England, a few brave church leaders put holly on their doors and invited working people in to celebrate. Many of those who conducted services soon afterward received visits from vandals sent by Blue Richard Culmer.

The vast majority of the English people still loved Christmas and kept the holiday quietly in their homes, sharing special dinner treats and summoning up their courage to sing some carols, though not too loudly. Those with Puritan employers reported for work. Arthur wrote me that so many families feared reprisals that they made it clear Father Christmas should not enter their homes and leave gifts for hopeful little ones. Reluctantly, he complied, since we never left gifts where we were not welcome. "For the first time, we had a surplus of toys left over after Christmas," Arthur wrote. "We sent them immediately to Attila, so they could be distributed on Epiphany." He added that he didn't think he could keep the factory open much longer, especially since there was so much less gift-giving to do now in England.

On December 25, 1644, Parliament took another step toward eliminating Christmas completely. Just before King Charles had fled two years earlier, in a last-minute effort to appease his rivals he had agreed that the last Wednesday of each month should be set aside for fasting, since Puritans believed the act of going hungry would remind everyone of how grateful we should be to God for providing us with food. Now, in this year, the twenty-fifth happened to be the last Wednesday of December. In towns like Canterbury where the Puritans had control, town criers offered reminders that, by law, December 25 was a day to fast, not feast. Singing Christmas carols in your home might not be illegal, but eating a Christmas goose or holiday pudding certainly was.

Though there still was not one final, heavy-handed decree that Christmas was unlawful, these acts and edicts gradually wore down the Christmas spirit all across the land. Fewer people grumbled about having to work on December 25 because it seemed like one more permanently sad fact in life, rather than something temporary. Poor villagers were much less likely to band together and march singing to the homes of their richest neighbors because, in too many cases, they would be met with curt reminders that Christmas was a pagan holiday, and then have heavy doors slammed in their faces.

Not everyone rejected Christmas out of either conviction or, more likely, fear. Some wealthy families encouraged their poorer neighbors to make the traditional holiday visit and gave them wonderful things to eat and drink when they arrived. Brave working-class families declared what happened in their homes was their business, not Parliament's, and feasted on

Christmas and exchanged small gifts. The very bravest even ventured out to church, knowing spies among their neighbors might report them for doing it. In Canterbury, the Hayes family tried to balance Christmas spirit with common sense. Elizabeth and I were employed by Margaret Sabine, so we had to work. But Alan Hayes was home between voyages, so he had the whole holiday free to celebrate if he wanted—and he did.

"When I was a boy, my family was probably the poorest one in Canterbury," Alan explained. "We counted ourselves lucky, during the year, if we had vegetables more than once a week to go with our bread at mealtimes. Then my father got work with a farmer who loved Christmas. One of the ways he celebrated it was to give a goose to each of his employees to enjoy for their holiday supper. I cried on that first Christmas when we had goose, Layla, because it was the most wonderful thing I'd ever tasted. When my parents brought me to church that day, I thanked God for sending us his son *and* the tasty goose. When my mother served it to us, that was the one time that year I can remember her smiling. I promise you, while I live we *will* celebrate Christmas in my home, and I feel sorry for all those who deny themselves and their families the joy of the holiday."

So while I went to work with Elizabeth, Sara stayed home with her father, and Elizabeth and I returned home at the end of the day to find the cottage decorated with holly and a fine goose sizzling on a platter.

Sara received another dress that Christmas morning, and Leonardo had sent me more candy canes from London, which I left on her pillow. But she announced as Alan carved the Christmas goose that Father Christmas probably shouldn't bring her gifts in the future.

"I'm ten now, and will be eleven next month," Sara said. "I know this is a hard time for Father Christmas, and so I'm ready to do without presents."

"Is this because of something Sophia has said to you?" her father asked sharply. "I know her father is a powerful Puritan and won't allow Christmas in their home, but in this house your mother and I make the decisions—and Auntie Layla, too. If you want Father Christmas to keep coming, I promise you he will."

"I do want him to, but I know there's danger in it," Sara replied. "I would not want Father Christmas or anyone helping him to get in trouble.

Sophia does say her father expects new, stern laws about Christmas to be passed very soon, since the king's troops are losing nearly every battle and the war will be over before next year's holidays."

I was proud of Sara for putting concern for her parents ahead of any desire for Christmas gifts. It was another sign that my beloved girl was indeed growing up fast, in mind as well as body. She was almost as tall as me, and the instruction she still shared with Sophia Sabine now included drawing and dancing in addition to reading, writing, and sums, since privileged young ladies were expected to master such social graces. Of course, the purpose of the instruction was to prepare Sophia, not Sara, for society life, but Sara admitted to me she enjoyed dancing very much, though, being so shy, she would never dance anywhere but in a small room with only her best friend and the dancing instructor there to see. Then she wanted to know if I had ever done much dancing. I replied that I hadn't—but didn't add that twelve centuries of making and giving gifts all over the world had left little time for such things.

The year 1645 in England started with very bad news. Meeting on January 4 in London, Parliament began considering a rule that would allow only Sundays to be considered holy days. Confident now of complete victory, not long afterward its members put former Archbishop Laud, who'd been appointed by King Charles and then appalled the Puritans by not restricting religious worship, on trial. He'd been held for a long time in the Tower of London, but now he was brought out, sentenced to die, and promptly executed.

Oliver Cromwell caused a stir by temporarily leaving the battlefield to make a speech. In it, he accused Parliament of still promoting rich men to be military leaders rather than more talented working-class men. Hearing this, I felt hopeful about him. Clearly, power had not altered Cromwell's commitment to the common people.

Then members of Parliament turned their attention back to King Charles, and soon they convincingly defeated him at Naseby, with Cromwell leading what was known as his New Model Army to victory there. Now the king's soldiers were in full retreat, and the holiday haters were about to have the power they had craved for so long.

But they hadn't destroyed Christmas quite yet. As December 25 drew near, I found myself wondering if it was right for me to remain safe in hiding in Canterbury, while Arthur and Leonardo and their employees risked so much operating the toy factory back in London. Dusting in the parlor while some visitors from London chatted over tea there with the Sabines about the war and its most prominent figures, I overheard that, on Christmas Day, Blue Richard Culmer intended to prowl some northern English cities, punishing those who celebrated the holiday there. Meanwhile, Oliver Cromwell was going to be visiting his wife back in London.

I told Alan, Elizabeth, and Sara that I would be spending Christmas 1645 in London. They were dismayed, Sara in particular.

"But if you're on a trip, how will Father Christmas find you, Auntie Layla?" she asked.

"Oh, I never have to worry about that, my love!" I said, and I knew Sara wondered why her innocent question had caused me to laugh. Her parents, of course, had another concern, and asked me quietly if I really wanted to risk being seen by Blue Richard Culmer. I replied that, to the best of my knowledge, he would be away to the north, and I should be safe if I only stayed in London for a day or two.

Just before I left, I informed Margaret Sabine that I would not be able to come to work on December 25. "There are some people in London who might only be there on that day, and I must see them," I told her.

"You've worked for me for three years, honestly and well," she replied. "With someone else, I might suspect this was an act of defiance over that pagan Christmas holiday. But if you say you must see someone in London, I believe you. I would not want you to have to walk all the way there. My husband is sending some goods to London by wagon on the twenty-third. You may ride along, though you must find your own way back."

So the Christmas-hating Sabines helpfully gave a ride to someone who intended to save Christmas from people like them.

Fifteen

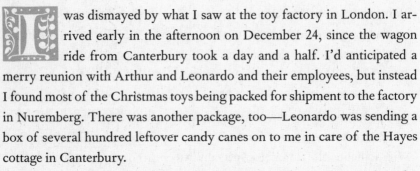 was dismayed by what I saw at the toy factory in London. I arrived early in the afternoon on December 24, since the wagon ride from Canterbury took a day and a half. I'd anticipated a merry reunion with Arthur and Leonardo and their employees, but instead I found most of the Christmas toys being packed for shipment to the factory in Nuremberg. There was another package, too—Leonardo was sending a box of several hundred leftover candy canes on to me in care of the Hayes cottage in Canterbury.

"This is the last Christmas we'll have this London operation, at least for a while," Arthur informed me. "Blue Richard Culmer has his spies everywhere in London, so it is only a matter of time before we are discovered. Tonight we're going to distribute gifts to those few remaining children in England whose parents defy the Puritans by allowing Christmas presents. With the very limited number of boys and girls who are still allowed to accept our gifts, it won't take very long. Then Leonardo and I will be off to Germany. The fine people who work for us will have to find other jobs, I'm afraid. Within a year or two, I'm sadly certain, Christmas will no longer be celebrated in England. For a while, at least, its enemies have won, Layla."

"Perhaps they haven't, Arthur," I argued. "I suppose you're right to close the factory for a while, though it breaks my heart to see you do it. But this new government may very well find it is harder than they imagine to make the holiday simply go away. It won't. Those who cherish it so much won't allow that to happen."

That night, I helped Arthur and Leonardo distribute gifts—dolls and puppets and hoops for spinning and balls for bouncing, tokens to remind children throughout the coming year that they were loved. Even in such a sad time for Christmas itself, there was still so much joy in giving presents as one way to celebrate the wonderful gift God gave the world so many, many centuries before. Then, on Christmas morning, I hugged my dear friends good-bye as they prepared to leave for the toy factory in Germany. By government order, all the British ports were open despite the holiday, and so Arthur and Leonardo could leave immediately.

"Give my love to Attila and Dorothea and St. Francis and Willie Skokan," I reminded them. "Arthur, when you write my husband to inform him you've closed the London factory, please tell him as well that I send my love and hope to see him very, very soon."

"You really should come with us," Arthur said. "I'm worried that you have some dangerous plan in mind. If you like, I can send Leonardo on ahead and stay to help you."

I smiled and said gently, "I really don't have a specific plan, Arthur. But I'm not going to give up on England and Christmas quite yet."

I had two visits to make on that holiday morning. Many of the shops in London were open, signifying December 25 was just another ordinary working day. Most of the people who were at work wore sad expressions, for they truly believed it was wrong not to celebrate Jesus' birth with songs and small gifts and feasting. When I arrived at my first destination, Pamela Forrest told me her husband, Clive, had been summoned to cut the hair of some Roundhead generals and asked if I had brought any messages from her beloved sister Elizabeth. I had, of course, and spent some happy minutes sitting with her in her small, pleasant home while describing to Pamela how much her niece Sara had grown. Pamela had a few small tokens she wanted me to take to Elizabeth, Alan, and Sara, and they, of course, had sent some modest gifts for Pamela, Clive, and their two sons.

"With the factory closed, Pamela, how will you make your living?" I asked.

"I'm not certain," she replied. "There are some businesses that hire seamstresses, and I'm very talented with needle and thread. But no matter where I go to work, I'll keep hoping that Mr. Arthur and Mr. Leonardo return someday, so I can go back to helping them make toys. I'm not going to ask you any awkward questions, Layla, but I think I have a rather good idea of what the three of you really do. I'll just say that Father Christmas is *very* real to me, and we'll leave it at that."

When I stood up to go, Pamela hugged me. I thanked her again for sending me to her sister Elizabeth in Canterbury and promised I would keep in touch. Then I went on to my second stop, a fine brick house near Parliament. Oliver Cromwell's dwelling reflected his rise in rank; though he was not officially the commanding general of the Roundhead army, everyone knew he made all the important decisions. Years ago, I had just knocked on the front door of his middle-class cottage, then joined him in the kitchen. Now he had guards outside his home, and it took several minutes before they would even agree to tell their commander that a Mrs. Nicholas wanted to see him.

After another quarter-hour, a young Roundhead soldier came out to fetch me.

"Colonel Cromwell is fearsomely busy, missus," he said. "I'm surprised he'll see you at all. Please state your business and then be on your way."

Cromwell received me in a large, well-lit room. He stood by a table that was strewn with maps. Looking up as I entered, he said, "So it's Layla Nicholas, wife of colonist Nicholas Nicholas. Missus, I would have hoped by now you'd be safely across the ocean with your husband, and instead you come knocking on my door in London. Aren't you afraid Blue Richard Culmer may run in and catch you?"

"I'm sure Mr. Culmer has more important things to do," I replied.

"Don't be so certain," Cromwell said. "Blue Richard is never pleased when someone escapes his clutches, and he surely hasn't forgotten how you avoided arrest—what, three years ago?"

"Three years," I agreed. "I assume you know I was never a spy for the king, and thank you for your warning so that I could escape. I don't deny I am a great friend of Christmas, but I don't believe that is, at least as yet, a crime. Will you make it one, now that you've beaten the king and England is yours to do with as you wish?"

Cromwell rubbed his face. He looked very tired. "We began to debate this Christmas issue once before in my home and again in a public park. We obviously will never agree. But I wish you would at least try to understand what I am really attempting to do, what we true Puritans have intended from the moment this terrible civil war began. Yes, the king is defeated, and I believe that, within a few months, he will finally negotiate the peace that we have sought for so long. Charles will be welcome to return to London and reclaim his throne—don't look so amazed! We never said we didn't want a king at all. We just want one who will consult with Parliament, which is elected to give voice to the people, before the king makes his decisions. When Charles agrees to this, why, I'll dust off his crown for him myself."

"And if the king refuses?"

Cromwell rubbed his face again. "He won't. He doesn't have much of an army left. So Charles will come back to London, Parliament will have its rightful influence, England will be at peace, and I can return to my farm. See if it doesn't happen just that way."

"It won't be as simple as you make it sound," I argued. "People like Blue Richard Culmer will shut down any churches that don't worship God the way they want. Christmas, the happiest, most joyful day in the lives of almost every working family in England, will be banned. You say you want a government that listens to its people. But you don't seem eager to hear what they say, only to impose your will on them. How is that an improvement?"

Cromwell walked over to me and looked hard into my eyes. "Yes, there will be some new rules. Only godly men, those who truly understand the will of the Lord, shall control this government. We will allow worship for any faith—Catholics or Jews or whoever. But non-Puritans will never hold any positions of power, as, indeed, they should not. Though we will protect them, we will not allow them to taint our laws or godly nation with their false beliefs. As for Christmas, all right. I will state it for you one more time. Christmas is not a true Christian holiday. December 25 is not the actual birthday of Christ, but instead a pagan date appropriated by sinful people who want to practice bad behavior. Singing and gift-giving and feasting are not proper ways to give thanks to God. In short, missus, Christmas is not holy."

I stared right back at him. Years before, I had held my tongue in deference to Elizabeth Cromwell, but now there was no reason not to reply in detail. I had come to London hoping to meet with this man and offer a complete defense for the celebration of Christmas. I would take advantage of the opportunity.

"Very well, Mr. Cromwell," I began. "You have told me what Christmas is not. Now allow me, sir, to tell you what Christmas *is*.

"Christmas *is* a day when we can reflect in our words and deeds the same generosity of spirit that moved our Lord to send us his son. It *is* a day when, for a few fleeting hours, every man, woman, and child can remember all the joyful things in their lives instead of being worn down by problems and hardship. It *is* a day when, for a little while, there are no masters and servants, no rich and poor, just human beings equal in their love of Jesus and in their respect for one another. In short, Mr. Cromwell, Christmas *is* holy."

Cromwell looked frustrated. "Surely, missus, you cannot see these Christmas drunks and troublemakers and tell me their actions are appropriate in the eyes of God?"

"I suggest, Mr. Cromwell, that you consider the actions of Blue Richard Culmer smashing windows in churches and arresting people on trumped-up charges. Are these things holy? Just as you, I know, would tell me Mr. Culmer does not really represent the Puritans, so I promise you that those who abuse the holiday for their own purposes do not represent Christmas. Let us be honest with each other, Mr. Cromwell. We both know very well that even if King Charles regains his throne, you personally will be the real power in England. When you have that power, will you use it to represent the people or to force your own beliefs upon them?"

Oliver Cromwell started to say something, stopped, thought a while, and then sighed. "I will always do what I know is best for England. I've learned a hard lesson during this war, that sometimes right-thinking leaders must impose their will if the common people prove incapable of understanding. At first, some new rules may seem harsh, but everyone will accept them after they see how much more improved their lives are, living as God wants. When Christmas is gone, it will only be missed until a pleased Lord bestows new blessings on England, a country that turned away from pagan celebration. I am acting as I think right for the land I love, Layla Nicholas, and I hope you accept that."

I did. It is very hard, when you believe in something as completely as I believed in Christmas, not to decide anyone who disagrees must be evil. Oliver Cromwell and many, perhaps most, of his Puritans thought they were doing the right things for England, including making everyone give up Christmas. I wanted everyone to celebrate it. The difference between us was that I would never force my beliefs on others, and Cromwell and his supporters would. This did not make them evil, but it did make them wrong.

I held out my hand, and Cromwell shook it. "We understand each other, even if we cannot agree," I said. "You can defeat a king, Mr. Cromwell, but Christmas will prove too powerful."

"Please leave London immediately, missus," he replied. "This is not a safe place for you. Neither is England, for that matter. Go to your husband in the New World, and I will pray that God helps you understand the sinfulness of this holiday you mistakenly love so much."

"Good-bye, Oliver Cromwell," I said.

"I sense that you might be very dangerous, Missus Nicholas," he replied, and turned his attention back to the maps on the table.

I had wanted to make a final appeal to Cromwell, and I had done it. The London factory was shut up tight. I had visited with Pamela Forrest. I had no other friends in the whole city. There was nothing to prevent me from beginning the long walk back to Canterbury, where I would do—what? The Roundheads controlled England. I had no doubt, now, that Parliament would order Christmas ended forever. It seemed there was nothing I could do to stop them. I walked along the London streets, avoiding pigs and piles of garbage and thinking my gloomy thoughts until, quite suddenly, I became aware of a great commotion.

Even though it was officially a workday, many people were bustling about in the central marketplace on the banks of the Thames. They were mostly young men of what was called the apprentice class, hired out to work for pennies for carpenters and cobblers and other tradesmen, serving until they had learned the craft for themselves. Christmas was a special holiday for apprentices, who were otherwise required to work from dawn until dark every day but Sunday. Christmas was their one day a year to sing and feast and do silly, enjoyable things like playing football in the streets. But Parliament's order to keep December 25 as an ordinary working day took that single holiday away from the apprentices, whose masters were glad to have them putting in extra work. Now, in the marketplace, some of these young men were congregating, defying the law that required them to work on Christmas Day. Many of them were quite young—a boy could be apprenticed out at eleven or twelve—and none seemed much over twenty. Quite a few looked fearful as they defiantly walked away from the shops where they worked. They were taking a considerable risk. Their masters, of course, could tell them never to come back and the years they'd served to begin learning a useful trade would be wasted. They could also be arrested by the Roundheads, if not officially for celebrating Christmas then for some made-up charge like disturbing the peace.

And yet hundreds of them were gathered together in the marketplace, apparently without any prior planning, and they were running about chanting in unison, "God bless Christmas! God bless Christmas!" until even more others like them heard the shouting and couldn't resist leaving their jobs to join in. Later, there would be reports that a thousand apprentices joined in courageous protest that day, and it might be true. I was there to see it, and though I didn't count the participants, I know there were many of them.

Despite what the Puritans subsequently claimed, the Christmas protestors did not overturn marketplace displays and threaten shop owners who refused to close in honor of the holiday. No one was beaten, or even spoken to harshly. Instead, these brave young men were making it clear that no law could prevent them from thanking God for his son as they saw fit. They kicked footballs around the streets and market stalls, cheering and laughing and enjoying the lives that God had given them. By high noon, they were singing "We Wish You a Merry Christmas" over and over, somehow louder every time, and Roundhead soldiers stood by watching helplessly, not certain what they should do. There were too many of the apprentices to arrest, and even the Roundheads didn't want to fire their muskets into the crowd. Then, older men began to join in the singing, and women and children, too. I really believe almost everyone in London would have been swept up in the excitement, had not, at that moment, several carriages rolled up in the marketplace. The Lord Mayor of London got out of one, and Oliver Cromwell was at his side, whispering in his ear.

The Lord Mayor waved his arms for silence; the singing stopped. "What is this gathering?" he cried. "Everyone, back to work at once, do you hear me? In this godly nation, December 25 is a working day!"

"We want Christmas!" several apprentices shouted back.

Cromwell whispered again in the Lord Mayor's ear. Nodding at Cromwell, he shouted, "If you disperse at once, there will be no arrests. I will forgive this terrible behavior. Tell your masters I said you were not to be punished. All will be as it was."

There was a great deal of murmuring. Cromwell nodded to the Roundhead soldiers, who brandished their muskets. The apprentices had no leader to rally them, to assure them that the soldiers most certainly would *not* fire in fear that the peaceful protest would then become a riot. So, first one by one and then in pairs and finally in dozens, the apprentices dispersed, walking unhappily back to their jobs, but warmed, I hoped, by the knowledge they had made their love for Christmas known.

Cromwell and the Lord Mayor remained in the marketplace. Cromwell talked; the Lord Mayor listened and nodded. Finally, the apprentices were all gone, and the marketplace activity went back to normal. The Lord Mayor got back into his gilded carriage. Just as he, too, was about to climb inside, Oliver Cromwell took one last long look around and saw me standing there. He thought about ordering some of the soldiers to arrest me, I'm sure, but didn't. Instead, he gazed at me thoughtfully before getting into the carriage and closing the door behind him. The horses pulled the carriage down the street and past me; Cromwell watched me from the window, his face wrinkled with concern. I knew he was wondering how it happened I was in the very place where the apprentices' Christmas protest took place. I did not believe in coincidence, and neither, I guessed, did Oliver Cromwell. He would think I had somehow organized that protest, even though I had not.

On the long walk back to Canterbury I had much to consider. One surprise was that the walk took a single day rather than three or four. I was regaining some of my power to travel faster than normal men and women; that was because the English civil war was finally winding down. Soon, once a peace treaty was signed, I would be able to go from one border of England to another in hours rather than weeks.

But there was something else to occupy my thoughts. The apprentice protest in London had been a spontaneous event, yet one that made a powerfully effective statement. The Lord Mayor and the Roundhead soldiers had been confounded by the sight of so many citizens insisting boldly, yet peacefully, that Christmas not be taken from them. Had Cromwell not been on hand to offer guidance, I believed, the Lord Mayor would not have acted decisively, and all of London might eventually have joined in sending the holiday message. What if there was another such protest, one that was better organized, one that had strong leadership? I had seen Oliver Cromwell in the marketplace afterward; I had looked into his face. He had been worried. If the people spoke in defense of Christmas again—even more of them, and louder—then perhaps Cromwell would not be able to ignore what they were telling him.

Sixteen

he power of the protest came from so many voices uniting in their demand to be heard," I told Elizabeth and Alan Hayes as we sat at the table in their cottage. "One person shouting out support for Christmas would certainly have been arrested. The same is true for five or ten or two dozen. But hundreds of men, women, and children standing shoulder to shoulder, peacefully but forcefully demanding the right to enjoy their beloved holiday, was too much for the Puritans. If the crowd had been better organized, I think they might be singing 'We Wish You a Merry Christmas' yet!"

It was mid-January in 1646. Sara, who had just celebrated her twelfth birthday a few days before, was up in her loft bed. Almost everyone in and around Canterbury was surely asleep at this late hour of perhaps ten o'clock, but my two friends and I had much to discuss. Ever since I had returned from London, I'd burned with excitement whenever I thought of the apprentices' Christmas protest. Rumors about it had swept through England, gladdening the hearts of everyone who still loved their special holiday and wanted to keep it as an important, joyous part of their lives. Elizabeth and Alan sat transfixed as I offered them my eyewitness account.

"It must have been amazing, Layla," Alan said, lighting his pipe and puffing happily. In those times, of course, no one realized how bad smoking was for your health. "I wish I could have seen it. Very soon I'll need to go to London myself and sign on with some company for a new voyage. But I doubt there will be more Christmas protests there until the holiday draws close again."

Elizabeth looked sad, and I certainly couldn't blame her. Families of sailors had to accept long, frequent absences of their loved ones, but that didn't make the separation any easier. I knew how it felt to miss your husband. I hadn't seen Nicholas now for more than twenty-five years. When I wasn't thinking about how to save Christmas in England, I often found myself remembering his warm smile or the softness of his wide white beard.

"Perhaps the next protests won't happen in London," Elizabeth mused. "Country folk don't want Christmas taken from them, either. Sometimes I believe the members of Parliament only think about what happens in London, because that is where they spend most of their time. If they really want to know what people want in England, they ought to get out into the rural villages for a change."

"Some sort of big demonstration out in the country supporting Christmas could be very effective," I agreed. "Why couldn't it happen, for instance, here in Canterbury?" I began imagining some grand gathering on High Street near the cathedral, with hundreds of participants, even a thousand, so many people singing songs and shouting out their love for the holiday that their example would inspire similar pro-Christmas demonstrations in every corner of England.

Alan, though, said he doubted it could happen.

"The livelihoods of so many people here depend on the goodwill of Mayor Avery Sabine," he reminded me. "Sabine, for instance, owns all the mills that grind local farmers' corn. They can't sell the crop as it comes directly from their fields. If the farmers join a pro-Christmas protest and Sabine sees them, he can simply refuse to grind their corn, they'll have nothing to sell, and their families might starve."

"Think about those of us who work for Mrs. Sabine, Layla," Elizabeth added. "If she saw any of us, or any members of our families, involved in some Christmas protest that might embarrass her husband and hurt his prospects in politics, she would certainly dismiss us immediately."

"I think the Sabines couldn't retaliate if there were enough protestors," I argued. "The mayor's mills, for instance, can't make profits for him if they have no grain to grind up. If enough of the farmers were part of the protest, Sabine couldn't deny them the use of his mill because, at the same time, he'd be shutting down his own business. And Mrs. Sabine has no intention of ever doing her own laundry or sweeping her own floors."

Alan shook his head. "You make it sound easier than it would really be, I'm afraid. Just persuading enough people to participate in that sort of demonstration would take months, perhaps even years. As much as all of us love Christmas, we have to consider our responsibilities to our families, too. The risks for anyone involved would be great."

That night, up in the loft bed beside the sleeping Sara, I thought about what Alan had said. He was right, of course. I reminded myself that the risk for any of the working-class folk in and around Canterbury would be much greater than the danger to me. They would have to stay and face the conse-quences of their actions. I, on the other hand, would be leaving soon to rejoin my husband in America. I had to, and not only because I missed Nicholas so much.

All of us involved in the gift-giving mission had to be careful not to stay in one place for too long or if we did, like Arthur and Leonardo in London, to keep out of sight. Normal people aged quite rapidly. In Europe and in England, living to sixty was rare. The passage of three or four years re-sulted in obvious signs of aging. Peoples' faces creased with wrinkles. Their hair rapidly turned gray. I had been in Canterbury since 1642, arriving as a thirty-five-year-old woman, about the same age then as Elizabeth Hayes was now. She was still lovely, but there were new lines around her eyes and streaks of white in her lustrous brown hair. Sometimes, now, she teased me a little, saying things like I must have a guardian angel who kept my hair from turning gray, and wasn't it wonderful how a few lucky women like me never seemed to get wrinkles around their eyes and mouths? In another year, perhaps, certainly in two or three, it would be obvious that I was not growing any older. Though I knew there was nothing sinister in this or my other special powers, that view would not be shared by the Puritan clergy or a superstitious public. Arrest and burning at the stake for being a witch would not be out of the question. So I would have to leave soon, whether Christmas in England was saved or not.

In the spring of 1646, Alan Hayes made several short trips to London, talking to various captains about their upcoming voyages and trying to choose which ship's crew to join. He didn't want to be away from his family for two or three years on some around-the-world adventure; instead, Alan hoped to find a berth on a ship making a direct voyage from some British port across the ocean to America, taking on tobacco or some other cargo, and then coming straight back to England.

"Six months is as long as I want to be gone from now on," he told us. "My little girl is growing up, and I've missed too much of her life already. You're going to be thirteen, Sara, and for all I know I'll come back from my next voyage to find you've married a young man and started a family of your own."

Sara squirmed and made an awful face. "I don't want to marry anyone," she insisted. "All Sophia ever talks about now is what rich man might become her husband. It's boring!" I sympathized with Sara, but I also knew what Alan meant. Being with Sara had helped me understand how precious every parent should find each day of a child's life. Already, my darling girl no longer played with dolls. She was becoming a beauty. At church on Sunday, some of the boys couldn't stop staring at her. As yet, she didn't notice, but someday soon she might. At least up in the loft at night she still whispered to me about her wish to travel and see all the great cities in the world. I would tell her to keep her dreams and make them come true, just as my Aunt Lodi had once encouraged me.

When he returned from London, Alan also brought us up to date on the latest news. For anyone who loved Christmas, it wasn't good. By June, the civil war was officially over. Commanders of the royal army had signed peace treaties, and King Charles had surrendered—to the Scots, not the Roundheads. While in their custody, he was rumored to spend his days secretly communicating with leaders in Ireland and France, trying to convince them to send armies and restore him to his throne. Queen Henrietta was in Europe trying to do the same thing; the two oldest princes, Charles and James, were with their mother.

In London, Alan reported, Parliament seemed divided on what to do next. Some wanted to settle with the king on almost any terms, as soon as the Scots could be persuaded to hand him over. These members were mostly businessmen who had made great profits during the war and now hoped to have a royal blessing to do the same in times of peace. Oliver Cromwell led a faction that wanted the king to remain on his throne, but only if he would agree to accept Parliament as a full partner. Then there was another group called the levelers—they wanted to abolish the crown and, indeed, every form of social class. All who lived in England must be equals, they insisted.

Many leaders in Parliament wanted the Roundhead army to be disbanded. Now that the king was defeated and the English government no longer planned to meddle in Europe, there was no need for a standing army, they argued. Cromwell loudly disagreed; the army, he insisted, was necessary because the king's supporters might, at any time, attack with new troops. It was also true, although Cromwell didn't say it, that so long as the Roundhead army remained intact, he, as its chosen leader, was the most powerful man in England. Though he never threatened it, no one could doubt that if Parliament didn't do what Cromwell wanted, he could muster the army and take over the country. Some people even believed Cromwell eventually intended to make himself the new king.

So the last months of 1646 were nervous times, because no one could be quite sure what was going to happen next. Would Charles again be England's king? Would Queen Henrietta be successful recruiting invaders from Europe to sweep Parliament out of power? And, of course, everyone wondered about Christmas. Charles had always supported the holiday—I knew this from our single conversation—but the Puritans would never let him remain on the throne without extracting certain concessions, one of which would surely be his support in abolishing Christmas celebrations. It may seem to some of you now that one holiday would count very little in the minds of working people, compared to who would rule their country.

But you must remember how hard these times were for the poor, and how December 25 was really the only day when they could forget their troubles and deprivations by celebrating the birth of Jesus. The more it seemed obvious they would lose their single real holiday, the more precious it became to them.

Alan Hayes left on a voyage to America in September 1646, promising his wife and daughter he would return to them no later than spring. At the same time, I began mentioning to Elizabeth and Sara that I might soon be leaving, too, and my departure would be permanent. I couldn't tell them I had to go before they discovered I wasn't aging, of course. I told them that it was soon going to be time for me to join my own husband, though I loved my Canterbury "family" dearly.

"We can't be selfish about Auntie Layla," Elizabeth reminded her daughter; Sara had burst into tears at the thought of my going away. "She wants to be with her husband just as you and I want to be with your father. Do you know for certain when you will leave, Layla?"

"Probably within another year," I replied. "It will take some time to book passage on a ship, and, of course, I don't want to cross the ocean during the cold storms of winter."

"You are welcome in our home for as long as you want to stay," Elizabeth reminded me. "At least we'll have you with us for one more Christmas."

That was another reason I didn't plan to leave right away. With the Puritans and Roundheads in full control, Blue Richard Culmer wasn't constantly on the track of those he accused of being royalist spies. He spent most of his time now in London, waiting, perhaps, for orders to persuade reluctant members of Parliament to do whatever it was Cromwell and the Puritans wanted. I wasn't in quite as much danger of discovery and arrest if I tried to organize one last, great Christmas protest in Canterbury. But I had to be certain that the time was just right.

In 1645, Parliament had essentially banned Christmas, but many celebrated it that year anyway, usually quietly in their homes, and they had not been arrested or otherwise persecuted. People had begun to hope that Parliament, having passed its Puritan-inspired law against the holiday, might now be content after making that gesture to let each English citizen decide whether or not to completely comply. As long as there wasn't any *public* celebration, some believed, perhaps the Puritans really didn't care who enjoyed a goose dinner or some family carol-singing on December 25. I knew that wasn't the case—the Puritans were just distracted with setting up a whole new system of English government. When they had completed that task, they'd turn their attention to Christmas again, because Oliver Cromwell was their leader, and Cromwell never left anything uncompleted. Because people were so uncertain how to celebrate it, and what might happen to them if they did, I realized it would do no good yet to organize a protest supporting the full enjoyment of the holiday. In a few more months, when the unsettled state of English government was resolved, then we would all know for certain what the fate of Christmas would be. Until then, no one would be willing to do too much.

So Christmas 1646 was a very curious day throughout England. Some churches, usually only one or two in each community, bravely sported holly and evergreen boughs on their doors, windowsills, and altars, and there were services in them giving thanks to God for sending his son. In almost every case, black-robed Puritans made a point of gathering outside the churches and staring hard at the worshippers as they left. This was rather unpleasant, but there were no physical attacks, just shouted threats of God's stern judgment if they didn't renounce the celebration of a "pagan" holiday. Most people couldn't go to church, anyway, because all the shops were open and lots of men and women had to work. A few shopkeepers did ostentatiously keep their doors bolted and their windows shuttered, and, afterward they received no further trade from Puritan customers. Because most of the major landowners now were either Puritans or defeated royalists who wanted to get back in the government's good graces, no wealthy families encouraged or accepted Christmas Day visits by groups of townspeople to their homes. No waits strolled singing through the streets, but there weren't any protest marches, either, even in London. Out in public, the day was subdued.

In private homes, of course, it was often different. With the toy factory in London shut down, I wondered if Arthur, Leonardo, or any of the other companions were making Christmas visits to children in England. I had not heard from them since they left for Germany the year before. This did not particularly worry me. There was no official mail service, so getting a letter to me in Canterbury from Nuremberg would have been difficult. If there was something they thought I needed to know, they would find a way to bring me word.

On the morning of December 25, Elizabeth and Sara found candy canes on their pillows. Leonardo had sent along a whole boxful, and it was only right to share the bright, tasty treats with my friends, though there were many dozens left over. We went to the Sabine house, Elizabeth and I to work, Sara to visit upstairs with Sophia. She told us later that Sophia's gossip once again concerned her father: Avery Sabine had hopes that if he could exhibit one last year of firm control over Canterbury he might be appointed to some important government office.

"Then, Sophia says, she and her parents will move to London," Sara reported as we walked slowly home afterward. "She told me not to worry, though, because she will surely marry some nobleman soon after that, and then I will be called to London as her lady-in-waiting." Elizabeth and I sighed. Sophia was a very pretty girl, and a rich one, too. If she did move to London, she wouldn't lack for suitors, and her ambitious parents would be eager to make a good social match as quickly as possible.

"And will you go to London if Sophia asks you?" Elizabeth asked carefully, trying and failing to keep concern out of her voice.

"I want to see London, but I don't want to be anyone's servant," Sara replied. "When I tell Sophia that, she just laughs."

That Christmas night, Elizabeth and Sara and I dined on vegetables and fruit, but not goose. Alan was still away on his voyage, and his wages for the trip would be paid after his ship returned to England. Elizabeth and I had our earnings from Margaret Sabine, but lately prices had increased on every kind of food, and we simply could not afford goose that year. It made little difference, though. The three of us heartily enjoyed the food we did have, and after dinner we sat in front of the fire and sang carols. If Oliver Cromwell doubted that the spirit of Christmas mattered less to those celebrating it than fine food and gifts, he could have learned better by watching us that night. After we had sung every carol we knew, some of them twice or three times, Sara asked me about the wonderful candy canes, and I explained to her that a special friend of mine had made them. When she tried to learn more about this mysterious friend, I changed the subject, telling her about the waits who used to walk the streets of London and about the great churches I had seen where thousands gathered to praise God and his son on Christmas Day.

I meant, very soon afterward, to make my plans to go, only waiting until Alan Hayes arrived home in the spring so Elizabeth and Sara would not be left on their own. I thought about how wonderful it would feel to be with Nicholas again and tried very hard not to imagine the empty place that would be left in my heart without Sara. So long as the Puritans allowed people to at least quietly celebrate Christmas in their own homes, I believed, I might as well leave. Even the smallest spark of Christmas spirit and joy was better than none. Somewhere, someday, enough people in England would demand their full, wonderful holiday again, and it would be restored. Until then, I reasoned, my place was with my husband, fulfilling our gift-giving mission in lands where Christmas was still completely welcome.

Alan's return home was delayed until late May, which still left me plenty of time to book passage to the New World and be with my husband before the onset of winter. But the news Alan brought with him from London convinced me I could not leave England after all.

Seventeen

he first months of 1647 were difficult for the Puritan-controlled Parliament. The war was over, and the king was defeated. But victory did not guarantee the love and loyalty of the common people. Many working-class English men and women, perhaps even a majority, had liked it better when the king was on his throne. They were very suspicious of the Puritans and of Parliament. Even though its members were supposedly voted into office at regular intervals by the taxpayers, this Parliament had been in session since 1640 without benefit of reelection. They kept extending their own current terms without requesting public approval. Many called it the Long Parliament, and they didn't intend the nickname as a compliment.

Parliament made an agreement with the Scots for the return of King Charles. In exchange for several large payments, the Scottish leaders handed the king over to England, where he remained a prisoner while rebel leaders negotiated with him. If Charles agreed to Parliament's terms, there was still the chance he would regain his throne. If not, he faced a life in prison and perhaps even execution. But as soon as Charles was in Parliament's custody, a stunning thing happened. As the defeated king's carriage proceeded south to the estate where he would be kept captive, the common folk of England lined the road and cheered him as he passed. This made the leaders of Parliament *very* nervous—what if there was a popular uprising to restore the king? Parliament had just voted to stop raising money to pay the army, so the Roundhead soldiers might very well refuse to fight anymore.

"Parliament feels it must do something to prove it is in complete control of England," Alan reported after his arrival home in Canterbury. "I believe one of its members, Lord Manchester, called it 'Bringing the rabble to heel.' Rumor has it there will be a new, harsher law against Christmas, because, so far, so many people have ignored the ruling of two years ago that it should no longer be celebrated."

"What can Parliament really do if people want to sing carols or feast in honor of Jesus' birth, so long as we do this in our own homes?" Elizabeth wanted to know. "They can't punish everyone who does. Under the laws of this country, no one is supposed to tell us what we may or may not do within the walls of our own homes, so long as we are not plotting treason."

"No," Alan said thoughtfully, "but they can try—and they might. I'm sorry to say, my love, that those presently in power seem to define 'treason' as any beliefs that do not exactly match their own. Those they cannot persuade, they are quite willing to intimidate. Blue Richard Culmer is stalking through the streets of London once more, followed by his gang of nasty-looking thugs. Parliament meets again during the first week in June. That, I expect, is when we'll have more laws about Christmas. It is on that issue—whether or not it is sinful to celebrate the birth of Christ on December 25—that the Puritans intend to make their stand and to prove once and for all that they can force their beliefs on the rest of us."

Sadly, Alan was right. In early June, Parliament announced again that celebrating Christmas—or Easter, for that matter—was against the law. Violators would be punished. There was no explanation of *how* they would be punished. That was left to the public's imagination. But there was no flexibility in this edict. Christmas could not be celebrated publicly *or* privately. No church services, no carol singing, no gifts, no feasts. Any of these activities would be cause for arrest. Though Parliament still couldn't find money to pay its army, it did set aside funds to pay for a militia, or Trained Band, in each county. These men would enforce the new no-Christmas law.

As a gesture to the poor working class who were losing their beloved holiday, Parliament added that, from now on, one Tuesday of each month would be made into a nonreligious holiday when no one would be required to go to their jobs. This only proved Parliament had no real understanding of what Christmas truly meant; the wonderful, traditional celebration of December 25 had nothing to do with not having to go to work, and everything to do with giving joyful thanks to God for the gift of his son.

After the new, stern law was announced, Parliament was concerned by the negative public reaction. I, on the other hand, was thrilled. The time had finally come. With the right planning, it might just be possible to rouse the public spirit and save Christmas in England after all.

I began cautiously in mid-June, right after news of Parliament's edict reached Canterbury. I asked Alan and Elizabeth to quietly talk with their friends and sound out whether any of them might be willing to risk reprisal by joining in a public protest on behalf of Christmas. I realized, of course, that for the greatest impact the demonstration should take place on December 25 itself, but six months would be barely enough time to recruit sufficient participants.

"You must be aware, Layla, that every town in England is riddled with spies for the Puritans," Alan warned. "Here in Canterbury, that is especially true. Mayor Sabine must have informers all over. If the wrong person learns that you are attempting to organize a Christmas protest, something terrible might happen to you."

I was willing to accept the risk. I had now been living in Canterbury for five years. I knew that most of its people were good-hearted, hardworking men and women who loved Christmas and resented being told they could no longer have it. Avery Sabine's spies might be numerous, but they were mostly obvious, too, in their Puritan black and with their disdainful, superior expressions.

It would be enough, at first, to suggest to people that there might be some way to make it clear to Mayor Sabine and to Parliament that Canterbury and its surrounding towns would have Christmas whether the law allowed it or not. There need be no immediate mention of a demonstration on Christmas Day. Otherwise, people might decide to march before we had recruited a large enough number to defy reprisals—a group of fifty might all be arrested, but there was no jail in Canterbury or anywhere else in England that could hold a thousand. Public indignation was already widespread, but it would grow even more intense when the holiday was imminent.

And so Alan and Elizabeth began making discreet inquiries, and I did the same. At work in the Sabine house, I was particularly careful since I knew at least some of the employees there had to be informers. Only to Janie and Melinda did I carefully mention the possibility of public action on behalf of Christmas, and they both told me they would be willing, even eager, to participate. Shopping for Sunday dinner in the Canterbury marketplace, I made the same suggestion to several people I saw there on a regular basis. A few replied that they had no desire to incur Puritan wrath, and I could not blame them for that. But most liked the idea, and one or two even mentioned the Apprentice Protest of 1645 in London, which pleased me. If that event was still in public memory, think how effective a larger, better organized demonstration might be!

Not surprisingly, I found strong, if secret, support among non-Puritan church leaders, who were being allowed to conduct services so long as they did not violate the new Parliamentary strictures. In particular there was Father Joel, a staunch Catholic who had been reduced to holding Sunday services in a barn. Because his responsibility was to protect his small congregation's beliefs in general, he told me, he would not personally be part of any Christmas protest I planned. But he could, at least, offer me the use of the barn. Large, clean, and well away from view several miles outside the walls of Canterbury, it stood atop a sprawling hill. No one could approach closer than two hundred yards in any direction, Father Joel said, without being visible, so if I held meetings there I could post lookouts and not have to worry about the area's Puritan-funded Trained Band sneaking up to arrest us.

By late September, I felt we had enough supporters to call a meeting at the barn, where we could discuss more specific plans for a demonstration. Parliament's attention, for the moment, was on issues other than Christmas—the king was being stubborn during negotiations, refusing to give up most of his divine right powers—but December 25 was now just three months away, and more people were beginning to realize that this year Christmas really *was* being taken away from them for good, unless they did something to prevent it. We now had to begin our work in earnest.

"How many people do you expect to come to this meeting?" Elizabeth asked, keeping her voice very soft. It was late at night and Sara had long been in bed, but we still didn't want her to overhear if she happened to be awake. "Six? A dozen? More?"

"I would think twenty or even thirty," I said. "All of them are known and trusted by you, Alan, or me. There won't be any strangers there."

"Well, there will be a few you haven't met, Layla," Alan corrected. "I've made the rounds of the surrounding farms and found a few good fellows who ought to be great additions to our group. We've done what we can to emphasize to everyone that we must keep our effort completely secret. I believe they understand. We all certainly remember Blue Richard Culmer's smashing of the stained-glass windows of the cathedral. No one doubts how severely we'll be treated by the Puritans if they find us out, but we all are willing to take that chance."

"You've made it clear to them that there will be no violence on our part?" I asked. "Everyone understands that whatever we do, it will be peaceful?"

"Christmas is dedicated to the glory of the Prince of Peace," Alan said solemnly. "It would dishonor him if we raised a hand against anyone, even those who might raise their hands against us."

The night of September 30 was unseasonably chilly. A brisk wind blew in from the north and recent rainstorms had left the ground damp. Leaving Elizabeth home with Sara—who indignantly demanded to know why her father and auntie were off somewhere after dark and was told that some friends needed help planning a party—Alan and I walked about two miles to the barn, which was to the north of Canterbury, past the river and across rolling fields of recently harvested wheat. The scent of freshly cut grain carried quite pleasantly on the cold air. We pulled our cloaks about us and didn't need to light our lantern for a while, since the moon was full and the road was wide. A few riders passed us, including members of the Trained Band, but no one stopped us to ask where we were going. The war was over, and, though Alan thought we were walking at a very good pace, I could have made it all the way from Canterbury to London in the thirty minutes it took us to get from the cottage to the barn. But I made certain to match his much slower, normal pace.

The barn was on the property of a farmer named Stone, a devout Catholic who'd had to stop practicing his faith openly, but who allowed Father Joel to hold Sunday services there for the Stone family and other Catholics. Accordingly, it was quite clean inside, with fresh straw strewn across the dirt floor and a thick bale of hay off to one side. I guessed that, on Sundays, Father Joel used that hay bale for an altar.

Alan and I were the first to arrive, but soon afterward we saw flickers of small lanterns being carried by people making their way up the hill toward the barn. Father Joel had been right—it was easy to see anyone coming from any direction. Many of the new arrivals were farmers, but to my surprise I also recognized some town craftsmen and a few shop owners. While I had expected twenty people, perhaps thirty at the most, almost sixty eventually arrived.

"I hope you don't mind, Layla," my friend Melinda from the Sabine house whispered to me. "It's just that my two chums Katie and Kenneth love Christmas so much, and I knew they would want to come."

"Do you trust them to keep our secret?" I asked, and when Melinda nodded, I greeted both her companions, who assured me they wanted to be part of any effort to save Christmas in England. And, like Melinda, it was obvious some of the other people Alan and Elizabeth and I invited had decided to recruit some of their Christmas-loving friends, too. Alan was worried because there were so many arrivals he didn't know personally, but I took it as a good sign. People cared enough about Christmas to come out to a secret meeting on a cold fall night!

Alan called the meeting to order, first suggesting that only a few lanterns remain lit: "We don't want the Trained Band to receive a report that a local barn is on fire!" he joked. "Let me welcome you all, and thank you for coming. I'll begin by emphasizing things I hope you already know. First, we must keep our activities secret. None of us want a visit from Blue Richard Culmer. Second, our purpose is to help save our beloved Christmas holiday by planning some activity, a protest, if you will, that will be so impressive in style and message that all the way back in London Parliament will realize it cannot take Christmas from us. Third, there is to be no violence of any sort. No matter what might be done to us, we will not raise our hands against anyone else. Are all here agreed?"

There were murmurs of assent. Then Alan introduced me as "Layla, aunt of my beloved daughter and someone who has lived here among us for five years now. Though we may not have any official leader, I would suggest that she is the beating heart of this body. No one I have ever met loves Christmas more than Layla or understands better how the holiday can reflect the best in human spirit."

Then I talked for a little while, mostly about the Apprentice Protest in London, how brave it was, and how effective. I was not used to speaking to an audience and found it somewhat uncomfortable. My voice shook a little as I told about the look on Oliver Cromwell's face as he realized there was stronger opposition to the abolition of Christmas than he and his Puritan supporters had ever imagined. I pointed out that the demonstrators had been easily dispersed because they had no real plan. If they had remained organized, no one could have made them stop protesting until they themselves decided they'd done enough.

"If we do something similar here, it will only be effective if we act as one," I pointed out. "Everyone must be agreed beforehand that we will stand together and not waver in any way. Mayor Sabine will certainly order us to go home, and he will threaten us with prison or even the possibility of direct musket-fire from the Trained Band. But if there are enough of us, nonviolent but defiant, all he can use against us are words. The mayor is not a stupid man. If a peaceful Christmas demonstration is marred by bloodshed caused by the Puritans, the whole country might well rise up against them, and Sabine can't risk that."

"You say we need a thousand people involved, maybe more," a gap-toothed farmer said. "How are we supposed to find them?"

"In the same quiet way the first few invited here tonight took it upon themselves to invite others," I replied. "All of you have friends you trust, and those friends will have friends, and so on. An abiding love of Christmas, and a determination not to lose that wonderful holiday, are the only qualifications necessary. Of course, the more people who know, the greater the danger that someone will be a spy for the mayor. Well, that's a risk we must take." As I spoke, I worried I wasn't effectively communicating the urgency of our task, and what I was asked next proved me right.

"Do we really need to do this?" an elderly woman wanted to know. "I miss singing carols in the streets, but last Christmas my family still enjoyed roast goose. We gave each other little gifts, and no one came to arrest us."

"The laws are stricter this year," Alan pointed out. "Blue Richard and his gang are promising that, on December 25, they'll break into homes where Christmas is being celebrated and drag everyone there off to jail. They might miss your home this time, but sooner or later it will be your turn. We're not trying to save Christmas just in 1647. We're trying to preserve it for the future. If we don't act now, people will gradually decide that the Puritans really can take Christmas away, and if enough of them eventually accept this awful new law, then Christmas *will* be gone forever."

"And there's even more danger to Christmas than that," said another man, and my eyes widened and my heart leaped, because his face and voice were so familiar. Arthur, my friend of more than one thousand years, had come back to England!

"Christmas has been gone from Scotland for sixty-four years, taken from the people by Scottish Parliament then and never restored since," Arthur said, grinning as he looked toward me and saw I'd recognized him. "At first, the people there thought it would only be a matter of a year or two before their Puritan leaders came to their senses and let everyone choose whether or not to celebrate the holiday, but it never happened. Across the ocean in their American colonies, the Puritans have banned Christmas for more than twenty-five years. Now, if they succeed in banning Christmas in England, why, they may try the same thing in other countries until, finally, a December 25 will come where no one in the world will dare sing a carol or give a small gift in honor of the birth of Jesus. But we're gathered here tonight. Let this be the moment when we decide this cannot, will not, happen. Let this be the moment when we agree that, no matter what the risk, we join together and take the first step to save Christmas forever."

I understood something then, listening to Arthur. Because we know them so well, we often take our family or friends for granted. We don't appreciate them as much as they deserve.

Now, after spending over a thousand years in Arthur's company, I finally realized the extent of his ability to persuade people to act. Perhaps he had only been a war chief and never a magical king, but he was a great leader. He could put words together in a speech to inspire followers in a way I never could. When I talked about the Apprentice Protest, I made the people in the barn think about the possibility of a single demonstration in local streets. Arthur talked about saving Christmas for the whole world, and suddenly everyone understood all that was really at stake. It wasn't just the holiday. It was the right of people to believe as they chose, rather than being told what they could and could not believe. By protecting Christmas, we would even be protecting the rights of those who *didn't* want to celebrate it.

Everyone cheered, and some began chanting, "This is the moment!" until Arthur finally raised his hands and asked them to stop "because we don't need the sound of our voices reaching the mayor's ears just yet!" But now there was a sense of excitement, of exhilaration, that hadn't been there before. Arthur suggested that everyone think about how to recruit more supporters and that we meet back at the barn in two weeks. There was a roar of approval, and people slapped one another on the back and chattered happily as they began making their way home through the chilly, dark night.

Arthur came over and hugged me. I introduced him to Alan as "a dear old friend of mine and my husband's. I thought, though, he was living in Germany."

The two men shook hands, and Arthur said, "I'd heard such fine things about the countryside around Canterbury that I just had to come see for myself. I'm staying with a farm family, helping out with the chores, and when one of them told me about this meeting tonight I just thought I'd come with him, since I love Christmas so much. Layla, perhaps we can meet tomorrow evening and catch up with each other. I just had a letter from your husband Nicholas in America, and I'm sure you'll want to read it."

Alan invited Arthur to join us tomorrow for dinner and gave him directions to the cottage. I hugged Arthur a second time, and then walked home with Alan feeling completely elated. *This is going to happen,* I thought to myself. *Christmas is really going to be saved.*

Eighteen

Sara didn't like strangers coming into her home. When Arthur arrived for dinner, she nodded stiffly in his direction, then resisted all his efforts to coax her into conversation. But Alan and Elizabeth warmed to my old friend quickly, so despite Sara's shyness—which, I informed her afterward, bordered on rudeness—we shared a happy meal and pleasant talk. Arthur told about himself—that he was a native of England who'd been living in London, then moved abroad for a bit "because of political and religious discomfort" before returning to his homeland, since he missed it so much. By apparently telling everything, he was able to conceal his deepest secrets, specifically how he was about eleven hundred years old and an important member of Father Christmas's gift-giving companions. Once again, I marveled at his amazing ability to draw people to him. After an hour of his company, I could tell Elizabeth and Alan would have followed Arthur anywhere. Only Sara didn't seem captivated by him. As soon as dinner was over, she excused herself and climbed up to the loft.

"I don't think your young friend likes me," Arthur commented when the dishes were cleared away and he and I had gone outside to walk a bit and talk. "Did I say or do something to offend her?"

"That's just Sara's way," I replied. "She is bashful around those she doesn't know very well, but she must learn to be friendly and gracious even when she feels uncomfortable. I'll speak to her about it. Now, last night you mentioned a letter from my husband. Did you bring it with you?"

"Of course," Arthur said, reaching into a pocket and handing me several pages of creased, well-worn paper. "After Leonardo and I arrived in Nuremberg I wrote to Nicholas right away, telling him we'd closed the London toy factory, at least for a while. I *didn't* tell him you'd remained behind in Canterbury. Perhaps you wrote him about that yourself? You didn't, did you? Well, that, of course, is your decision. Anyway, it must have taken him a long time to receive my letter, and it certainly took months for his reply to reach me. Here it is; I'll just wander around a bit while you read."

Arthur disappeared over a small knoll, and I settled down in the fading fall grass with Nicholas's letter. Even his handwriting, so grand and flowing, made me miss him. It had been so many years since we had been together! Well, we wouldn't be apart much longer.

The first part of the letter described his life with Felix in the New World. They were now living in the Dutch colony of New Amsterdam, and very much enjoying the holiday customs there. Dutch children expected visits from St. Nicholas on December 6, and there were enough of them to keep Nicholas and Felix quite busy making and delivering toys on time. But the British colonies were still Puritan-dominated, and Father Christmas was not welcome in them—an extension, Nicholas noted, of the Christmas troubles in England.

"Though I'm sorry you felt the London toy factory must be closed, I certainly understand and agree with that decision," he wrote. *"What a terrible thing it is when a few close-minded people force their own prejudices on everyone else. But I hope that, like me, all of you continue to believe in the overall goodness of human nature. Bad times do not last forever. Because the vast majority of the English people want Christmas, I know that they will, somehow, get it back again."*

Then, to my amazement, my husband addressed me directly. He had not done this in his previous letters. After more than twelve centuries of marriage, we did not need to constantly reassure each other of our love. But, separated from his wife by a vast ocean, Nicholas still instinctively understood that just now I did need some extra words from him.

"Layla, none of Arthur's recent letters have made much specific mention of you," Nicholas wrote. *"I don't know for certain, but I suspect that you are planning, in some way, to challenge the English Parliament's outlawing of Christmas. I won't insult you by pointing out the dangers of such action. You will have considered them for yourself. I will only remind you that whatever you do, you have my complete support. We are now, as we have always been, equal partners. Though I can't share these difficult times with you in person, I am always with you in your heart. Do whatever you believe is right, and then board a ship and come across the ocean to me, so I can put my arms around you again after so many years."*

I suppose I sat there for a half hour or more, tears dripping down my cheeks onto the grass, before Arthur returned. He sat down beside me and patted my shoulder.

"I miss my husband so much," I murmured. My throat felt thick, and my eyes burned from the salty tears.

"Of course you do," Arthur said. "You know, Layla, we have received these wonderful gifts—apparently endless life, the ability to travel at amazing speeds, the opportunity to spread joy and comfort to children through our holiday mission. But they come with a price, as all worthwhile things do. You can no more let the Puritans' banning of Christmas go unchallenged than you can resist breathing. That's why I came back to England. I knew you would be planning something, and now the moment draws close. I'll help in any way I can and, afterward, I'll take you to the dock and smile as you board a boat that will take you across the ocean to your husband."

"Thank you," I gulped. Then I resolutely wiped my eyes, cleared my throat, put Nicholas's letter in the pocket of my cloak, and got to my feet. "All right, Arthur," I said. "I've had my weepy moment, and that is the end of that. Now, we have a Christmas Day protest to plan."

And we did. Back in the Hayes cottage, gathered with Alan and Elizabeth around the table while Sara sulked up in her loft, Arthur and I discussed what might happen, and where. His experience as a war chief came in handy, because he could guess how the Canterbury authorities and Trained Band would react.

"If we have two thousand protestors, and I believe we will, we can't have them all trying to enter the city through the same gate," Arthur warned. "The guards will see them coming—the town is in a valley, after all—and simply shut the gate tight. The protest won't be as effective if Mayor Sabine and his holiday-hating cronies stroll the streets while the demonstrators are held outside the city walls. There are six gates in all. We'll need to have the protestors divided into six groups, each entering the city at the same time through a different gate. That way, even if one or two of the gates are closed to prevent some of us from entering, the others will still get inside the walls."

"What about once we all are inside?" Elizabeth wanted to know. "If we're in six different parts of the city, won't that lessen the impact of having thousands of people involved?"

"We should all meet in one central place," Alan said. "And, by the way, I still haven't said you can march, my darling. It will be quite dangerous. The Trained Band might attack. It would be better for you to stay home with Sara."

Elizabeth looked at her husband, and then said, in tones made all the more frigid by their apparent blandness, "I'm afraid I don't require your permission. Do you intend to insult me by implying I don't love Christmas as much as you do, or that only men have the right to take risks for the sake of a good cause?"

"You know it's not that," Alan sputtered. "But if things turn ugly, Sara must have a parent left to raise her."

"Then *you* stay home," Elizabeth said briskly. "Now, Layla, what time of day do you think would be right for the protestors to enter the city?"

For more than a month, we continued to plan. There were so many little things to consider, and a few big ones, too. As our numbers gradually swelled, it was no longer possible for everyone to gather at the barn for nighttime meetings. Arthur suggested that we appoint captains, who would come to the meetings and then, in their turn, inform everyone else of what had been discussed and decided.

"These captains should be the people we know best and trust most," he added. "They will understand the need for secrecy. We need to establish some sort of password for them, or some secret sign, so we can identify ourselves to one another without anyone else knowing."

I had an idea for that. The box of Leonardo's lovely striped candy canes was still beside the bed Sara and I shared in the loft. I brought it down. There were several dozen canes left.

"No one else would have these," I suggested. "They will provide perfect identification, and Mayor Sabine and his men surely won't consider candy to be something suspicious."

"They're festive, too," Elizabeth agreed. "I think they're just perfect."

That night, about thirty of us met back at the barn. It was much colder now, and everyone wore heavy cloaks. Arthur distributed the candy canes—no one had ever seen anything quite like them before—and explained how they were to be used. When one of us needed to meet with everyone else, he or she would leave a small drawing of a candy cane stuffed in a crevice of the big tree outside the Hayes cottage. Arthur or I would check for such messages every day, and, if we found one, we would come to the barn after dark.

"Don't ask for a meeting unless you really need one," Arthur added. "The more often we gather, no matter how careful we are, the greater the chance we'll be noticed by the Puritans. Also, whenever we meet, hold out your candy cane as a sign everything is safe. If, for some reason, you think you've been followed or there is some other sort of danger, hold out your empty hands, and that will be a sign to the rest of us."

Everyone remarked at the candy canes, about their color and unique shape. A few wanted to taste the candy, but I reminded them that if they ate their secret symbols, they would no longer have them to use.

"After we've marched on Christmas Day, we can have the pleasure of eating this candy," I said. "It will taste very good, I promise." Though Arthur still was much better than me when it came to addressing the group, I was gradually becoming more comfortable in speaking to them.

Arthur and I checked the tree for messages each day, and a few days later we did find a candy cane sketch. That night, up in the barn and after showing us his candy cane, as we showed him ours, a Canterbury bootmaker named Peter told us he thought he'd mentioned the protest to the wrong person.

"He's been coming to my shop for years and has always been very friendly, and sometime we talked a little about how sad it was that Christmas can no longer be celebrated," Peter said. "So this past week I told him there might be some sort of demonstration in favor of the holiday on Christmas Day and would he be interested in participating? He said he might, but then he asked so many other questions, like who exactly was *organizing* everything, that I suddenly had the feeling he was going to run to Mayor Sabine with whatever he could find out."

"You were right to tell us," Arthur said. "I know it is inevitable that some rumors about what we're doing will reach the wrong people. But we can't let any outsiders learn too much. Now, you didn't tell this man anything else? Very good. I expect he'll be back in your shop tomorrow asking more questions. Just tell him that you had misunderstood; there's no demonstration planned at all, and sorry for the confusion. Then be very careful that you're not followed by any of the mayor's spies. They ought to be easy to spot, with their black cloaks."

I still could not really understand why anyone would be against Christmas. This can happen sometimes, when we believe in something so completely that we lose the ability to appreciate someone else's right to a different opinion. Many Puritans sincerely believed God and Jesus were being dishonored by holiday celebrations. Their arguments—that the date of December 25 was based on pagan rituals, that too many people used Christmas as an excuse to get drunk or otherwise act badly—weren't entirely wrong. In choosing to fight for Christmas, I could not, or at least should not, disregard inconvenient facts. But to me and, I believed, to almost everyone else in England, the positive things about Christmas—thanksgiving for Jesus, gifts and food to remind men, women, and children that even hard lives could include moments of joy—far outweighed the problems. How could Puritan-controlled Parliament even consider taking the holiday away from people who drew from it almost the only joy they experienced throughout the whole year?

My own resolve to save Christmas was reinforced one day in early December, when several of Margaret Sabine's servants missed work because of illness and I had to help Janie back in the washing shed. The work there, filling and lugging buckets of water, or wringing heavy sheets and curtains by hand, was still hot and exhausting. I couldn't help but notice Janie's already-exhausted face had gained many more lines and creases in the five years since I'd met her. She was a tired, aging woman who told me repeatedly that she looked forward to Christmas all year long. How thrilled she had been when I invited her to the first barn meeting to discuss the Christmas Day protest, and then I had delighted her further by presenting her with a candy cane and making her one of our group's captains. I really didn't do this because I felt Janie had a shrewd mind and could help us plan. Rather, I just wanted to let her feel important for once in her life, which had mostly been spent doing menial work for Margaret Sabine. It was, in a sense, self-indulgence on my part, but I didn't regret it for a moment.

Now, as I carried buckets of water over to the rinsing tub where Janie was twisting pillowcases to wring water out of them, I saw she was smiling.

"Why, are you enjoying your work today, Janie?" I asked as I poured water into the tub.

"You know why I'm smiling, Layla," she replied, lowering her voice so no one could overhear. "Our big day is coming, and I'm quite looking forward to it!"

I dropped down beside her as she squatted by the side of the tub. "I'm glad you are, Janie, but please promise me that, on Christmas Day, you'll be very careful. Even though I doubt it will happen, Mayor Sabine or his wife might see you taking part in the demonstration, and then you could lose this job. There will be no disgrace if you decide to hang back behind most of the marchers, so there will be less chance you'll be identified."

"But I won't mind being seen!" Janie said proudly. "All my life, I've taken orders, and I've tried to do good work in return for my wages. But this will be a moment when I can speak up for something I believe in, and if it costs me my job I'll just have to find another one, won't I? Christmas is so wonderful, Layla, and don't make any mistake about it. I know that even though Mr. Arthur is getting most of the attention, you're the one who must have really thought of this, because you're so smart and so brave, like."

All of us enjoy compliments, and I am no exception. Janie's words warmed me more than a little. I was never jealous of Arthur being considered the leader. He had so much more of what would one day be called *charisma* than I did. But it was still nice to know that someone recognized and appreciated some of my qualities, too. I gave Janie a brief hug and told her not to work too hard, because she was going to need all her strength very soon. Janie hugged me back and furtively reached into an apron pocket.

"See, I've got my candy cane with me," she whispered. "Just in case I have to use it for a signal, you know."

"Well, be certain not to let it melt around all this steam and hot water," I laughed, and spent the rest of the day feeling happy despite the aching in my arms from hauling heavy water buckets. Janie had reminded me why saving Christmas in England was so important. I wanted to do it for people like her, who really had nothing else.

When there were only two weeks left before Christmas, Mayor Sabine instructed the town criers to begin announcing that any form of Christmas celebration was forbidden by law. Shopkeepers were required to tack up posters announcing all stores, including their own, would be open on Christmas Day. This was mostly a symbolic gesture, since so few people could read.

Arthur and I called another meeting of group captains. As each arrived at the barn, he or she brandished a candy cane. That meant no one was following them, but also represented a certain holiday spirit as well. We'd talked about the Christmas Day protest for so long, and in just fourteen more days it would happen!

"It will soon be time to decide which groups enter the city through which gates," Arthur said. "You all know that we have selected the noon hour to begin. Everyone else in the city, including the mayor, will be up by then."

More strategy was discussed, and all of it involved things Arthur and I had talked about earlier with Elizabeth and Alan at their kitchen table, while Sara, as usual, stayed out of sight up in the loft. We told everyone now that we would only meet once more, on the night of December 24. As always, messages for emergency meetings should be left in the crevice of the big tree.

"Be of good cheer," Arthur called out to everyone as the meeting concluded. "It won't be long now."

I walked back to the cottage with Elizabeth; it had been Alan's turn to stay behind with Sara. We talked about what might happen after the protest. Would Margaret Sabine dismiss all of us who had participated? Would the Trained Band have the nerve to arrest anyone at all? How would Parliament react when it learned two thousand men and women gathered to defy their laws against Christmas?

"I'm a little nervous, but even more excited," Elizabeth confessed. "This may be the only time in my life that I make my voice heard. That's a special thing, isn't it?"

"It certainly is," I agreed, and silently prayed that Elizabeth and all the others would not suffer too much for their moment of honest protest.

Nineteen

en days before Christmas, Sara and I took an evening stroll after dinner. It was a beautiful night. There had been some snow the day before, so the hills were covered with pure white. But the clouds had cleared, so the black night sky was decorated with hundreds of stars and a crisp quarter-moon. We pulled our cloaks tightly about us and wore mittens. It was chilly enough to make our cheeks and noses tingle, but not so cold that we were uncomfortable.

"Don't you cherish this time of year?" I asked cheerfully. "The snow is so beautiful, and in winter I think the stars seem to shine just a little bit brighter. From my husband's letters, I know there are stars and snow in America, but I can't imagine them being as lovely as they are in England."

"When you leave for America, Auntie Layla, will I ever see you again?" Sara suddenly asked. Now I knew why she had asked me to take a walk with her. I had made it clear in the past weeks that right after the winter snows melted I would be leaving Canterbury to join Nicholas in the New World. Of course, I'd already stayed much longer with the Hayes family than I'd ever expected, but five years was the absolute limit before it was obvious I was not aging as they were. Whether the Christmas protest was effective or not, I would still have to go almost immediately afterward. Following this final effort to save Christmas in England, I would help Nicholas and Felix spread holiday joy in America.

But Sara's question tore at my heart. "No one can know the future, my love," I answered gently. "The ocean is quite wide, but people can cross any distance if they want to badly enough. Who knows? Instead of me returning to Canterbury, you might come to the New World instead. Then we could have a wonderful reunion there!"

Sara sniffled, probably as much from holding in tears as from the winter wind. "I think that after you leave, we'll never see each other again. I hate it. Why can't you stay? If you and your husband miss each other so much, he can just come back to England."

I thought of my own frustration with Parliament's banning of Christmas, and how Nicholas would despise it, too. At least in the New World, he had Dutch and French colonists who welcomed his gift-giving. "Right now, England isn't a place where my husband would feel welcome," I replied. "Sara, you know I'm going to miss you, too. I love you as though you were my own daughter. It has been one of the great joys of my life to share these past five years with you."

And this was true. I realized Sara was not a perfect child. There has never been one. Sometimes she was a little too proud of her own intelligence, since her ability to read and write and do sums was so far superior to her friend Sophia's, and Sophia was herself a very clever girl. Often, Sara indulged her natural shyness, giving in to the urge to hide from almost everyone and refuse to talk when it would have shown great maturity on her part to overcome her bashfulness and behave more appropriately. And there had been, lately, some testy flare-ups between her and her parents. At thirteen, Sara was beginning to consider herself a full-fledged adult, and it was certainly true that some girls her age were already married, and a few had children of their own. Alan and Elizabeth, naturally, still thought of Sara as their little girl, and sometimes she responded too sharply when she felt they were treating her like a helpless child rather than a responsible grown-up.

But those bad habits paled beside all her good qualities, which included offering her unqualified love to those she knew best and trusted—her mother, her father, and me. Sara had a generous heart, too. It hurt her deeply to see people in need. If her parents had permitted it, she would have given away all her clothes and food to the beggars who lined Canterbury's streets (the poor, in fact, lined the streets of every English town). And Sara had great spirit. She refused to limit herself to those basic things society allowed young working-class women of her time. It had been her great good fortune to be allowed to study with Sophia, but Sara had also worked hard and taken full advantage of that opportunity. She did not intend to marry some local farmer and spend her days doing chores and raising children, the life working-class girls like her were supposed to accept, whether they wanted to or not. Nor did she intend to become her best friend's lady-in-waiting, accepting that servant's role because Sophia had been born rich and she had not. Instead, Sara planned to somehow find a way to travel the world and do good deeds. She believed in this fine future as deeply now at thirteen as she had when I first met her five years earlier. What a precious, special girl, and how hard it was going to be for me to go on without her.

So we walked in silence for a few minutes, each thinking our own thoughts, until Sara suddenly blurted, "But you can't go to America if Sophia's father puts you in jail."

I whirled toward her. "What are you talking about?"

Sara sighed, the sort of sigh traditionally heaved by teenagers when adults fail to understand the obvious. "I know all about your plans for Christmas Day, Auntie Layla. You and my parents and that man Arthur are going to lead a parade or something through the city streets to protest Christmas being taken away."

My heart was pounding. "Sara, where did you ever get that idea?"

"Oh, Auntie Layla," she said disdainfully. "All those nights when I've gone up to my bed and the four of you have sat downstairs talking around the table, don't you think I could hear every word being said? Just because you couldn't see me, that didn't mean I couldn't hear you."

"It isn't nice to eavesdrop on other people's conversations, young lady," I said sternly. "But why would you say that Sophia's father might arrest me?"

"Well, not *you* in particular," Sara replied. "But Sophia says her father has heard there will be some sort of demonstration, and he's getting ready to put it down and impress everyone in London with his firmness. She thinks he'll arrest some of the demonstrators and keep them locked up for a while, to teach everyone else that it's futile to try to save Christmas."

We had guessed all along that Avery Sabine would hear some rumors about the protest, of course, but now I wanted to be sure he didn't know everything about our plans.

"Has Sophia said how many protestors her father is expecting?" I asked. "I don't want you to betray your friend's confidence, of course, but anything you feel you could tell me would be helpful."

"Sophia never has secrets because she talks too much to keep any," Sara said. "I don't think her father is expecting much trouble. But that's one reason I asked you to come on this walk. I don't want you to go to jail, or my mother or father, either. I think the three of you should stay home on Christmas Day, and let whoever else wants to march get arrested instead."

"I thought you loved Christmas, Sara," I said.

In the silver light from the stars and moon, I saw her give me a sharp look. "Of course I love Christmas, Auntie Layla. I'm going to miss it very much now that it's against the law."

"And why will you miss Christmas, my love?" I asked. "Is it the presents you will no longer receive, or perhaps the goose we had for Christmas dinner on those years when we could afford it?"

Sara snorted. "I haven't expected presents from Father Christmas since I was eleven! Last year we didn't have goose, and it was still a wonderful holiday because we sang carols and thanked God for sending Jesus. I love Christmas because it's happy. You can forget all the sad things in life for a little while. I'm going to miss there being one special day when everyone is friends with everyone else, and we are reminded of all the good things we have."

"Then if Christmas is such a precious day, don't you think it is worth trying to keep?" I asked.

"Yes," Sara replied, "but I still don't want you being arrested. They'd put you in that big ugly jail by the West Gate. I don't want you or my parents there. It would be horrible for you."

I put my arm around her. "My darling, you're right that it would be horrible. I certainly don't want to go to jail, and I know your parents don't either. But we will, if it comes to that."

Sara jerked away from me, and, in the faint silvery light, I could see tears finally streaking her cheeks. *"Why?"* she whimpered. "Why would you take the chance of going to jail?"

I reached out for her hand. At first she tried to pull her hand loose from mine, but then she relented. "Sara, I'm going to tell you something very important, and I hope you'll remember it. In life, no great achievement is possible without equally great risk. Anything worth having comes with a price, my love. A few moments ago, you described perfectly why Christmas is so important, as a time to thank God for sending us his son and a time when even the poorest, saddest people can have moments of hope and joy. The men who control England now don't understand this, either because they are genuinely mistaken or because they simply don't want to. They say they have taken Christmas away because it is sinful, but there is more involved than that. Taking Christmas, even though most of the English people want to keep it, is a way of demonstrating that they have complete power over everyone else. And if we let them take Christmas, who knows what they might decide to take next?"

"I don't care about that," Sara said stubbornly. "I just care about my mother and my father and you."

I gently turned her face toward me. "You may not care now, Sara, but someday you will. No, don't argue. I know you as well as I know myself. Any time a great wrong is being done—and taking away Christmas is completely wrong—those who know better must not allow it to happen. If we do, then we are as much at fault as the people who are doing the bad thing. Here in Canterbury on Christmas Day, a thousand or more men and women are going to bravely stand in front of the mayor and tell him they will have their Christmas whether he agrees or not. There will be too many for him to arrest, I believe, and so he will have to stand and watch. Then the story of what happened will begin to spread—not just back to London and Parliament, but all over England. In other counties, other towns and cities, all the people who cherish the holiday will be inspired to do the same thing, until finally the men in power realize that, despite all the laws they might pass and the threats they might make, they cannot take Christmas away. It may take another year, or ten, or twenty, but there will be waits singing carols in our streets again and we will all enjoy the grateful fellowship that only Christmas can really bring."

"Do you really believe that's going to happen?" Sara said doubtfully.

"I have always believed in Christmas because I have always believed in the best of human spirit," I told her.

We walked a little more, both of us silent and thoughtful. Then, just as I was about to suggest that we'd been out in the winter cold long enough and should turn back toward the cottage, Sara said something that surprised me.

"Will you let me march with you on Christmas, Auntie Layla?" she wanted to know.

"I thought you found the possibility of prison quite horrifying," I said. "What if you marched, and the Trained Band was called out, and you were the one they arrested?"

Sara shrugged. "I would take that chance. You're right—we must all stand up for what we believe in, and I believe in Christmas."

I was proud of Sara, but wanted her to think it all through. "If you marched, my darling, you would have to be among strangers, and they would look at you and talk to you. You're the girl who runs to the loft whenever anyone but your parents or I are in the cottage. Are you certain you could overcome feeling so shy?"

"I'm not sure," Sara said honestly. "But at least I would try."

"That's all any of us can do," I said. "Well, angel, this isn't my decision to make. You must discuss it with your father and mother. If they agree, you may certainly come with us, provided that you understand the risks and are willing to accept them. If the mayor or Mrs. Sabine happen to see you, at the very least you would never again be allowed to play or study with Sophia, and she is your best friend. How would you feel about that?"

"Mrs. Sabine doesn't think I'm as good as her daughter," Sara replied, and she sounded resentful, which I could certainly understand. "She reminds me in many little ways that she could keep me away from Sophia any time she chooses. I wouldn't care if I never saw Mrs. Sabine again."

"But I asked you about Sophia," I reminded her.

Sara was silent for several moments. "Sophia and her parents will move to London soon," she finally said. "Since I don't want to be her lady-in-waiting after she gets married, I suppose I won't see her anymore. I'll be sad about that. She isn't like her mother. She mostly treats me like we're equal. Sometimes she even says we're like sisters. But deep down we both know we're not. We'd be separated soon anyway. But——" and here her voice broke a little—"I'm going to miss her."

I pulled Sara close, and we walked that way a while, moving back toward the cottage where a warm blaze roared in the fireplace. We had almost arrived when Sara tugged free, ran ahead a few paces, and called back to me, "I'm going to lose Sophia, and I'm going to lose you, but I'm not going to lose Christmas!" By the time I came through the door, she was already huddled with Alan and Elizabeth at the table, making a case for marching with us on Christmas Day. I could have joined them, but I decided this was something for parents and child to work out among themselves. I lay up in the loft bed for more than an hour, and Sara was correct—I could hear every word being said. She insisted she had the right to stand up for what she believed in, and they talked about the possibilities of the Trained Band using violence to disperse the marchers. Elizabeth flatly informed Sara that she would not be allowed to come, but Alan was wavering, and then they finally sent Sara up to bed so they could discuss it further themselves. An hour later, when Sara was finally asleep, her mother and father were still talking about it, but now I could tell Elizabeth was beginning to change her mind. In the morning, Sara was informed she could march, but only at the back of one of the groups, and that at the first sign of possible violence she was to turn and run back to the cottage.

"Will you promise you'll do this?" Elizabeth asked, looking her daughter straight in the eye.

"Will *you* run away, too, if it gets scary?" Sara shot back. "Will my father? Will Auntie Layla?"

"We'll certainly try not to be hurt," Elizabeth replied, which really didn't answer Sara's question. They both knew it. But Sara was pleased that she would at least be allowed to march, and so she didn't press her mother further.

When Arthur and I spoke later, he assured me there should be no real danger to Sara. "I know of several other parents who will be bringing their children on the march," he told me. "Their presence should make it even more certain that Mayor Sabine's constables and the Trained Band won't resort to violence. Think of the massive public reaction if children were injured as they demonstrated on behalf of Christmas Day! I think Sara will be fine, Layla."

In fact, Arthur's main concern was that the march wouldn't have its desired effect on Parliament no matter how many men, women, and children participated. Back in London, he said, it was possible government leaders were more concerned about the king than Christmas.

"You know Charles escaped Parliament's custody for several weeks in November," he reminded me. "Cromwell and his Puritans are starting to realize that the king won't do the convenient thing and cooperate completely with them. There is so much royalist support throughout England. A second civil war is certainly possible, and within months unless Parliament does something drastic. They could ignore our march altogether."

"They *are* doing something drastic, and it involves Christmas," I replied. "You wait and see. In ten days they're going to unleash Blue Richard Culmer and his minions on anyone who celebrates the holiday, and this will be meant to frighten everyone into complete submission, and not just about Christmas. That's why they won't ignore our march. They'll understand exactly what it means, that the people *will* have their voices heard whether Parliament permits it or not. I just hope nothing goes wrong. We're so close now."

"I think, if something was going to prevent us, it would have happened by now," Arthur said. "You've told me that Mayor Sabine has heard some rumors, which we expected. But the magnitude of our march will catch him by surprise."

For a few more days, I thought so, too.

Twenty

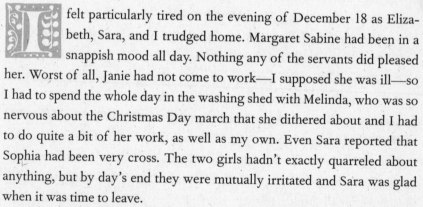 felt particularly tired on the evening of December 18 as Elizabeth, Sara, and I trudged home. Margaret Sabine had been in a snappish mood all day. Nothing any of the servants did pleased her. Worst of all, Janie had not come to work—I supposed she was ill—so I had to spend the whole day in the washing shed with Melinda, who was so nervous about the Christmas Day march that she dithered about and I had to do quite a bit of her work, as well as my own. Even Sara reported that Sophia had been very cross. The two girls hadn't exactly quarreled about anything, but by day's end they were mutually irritated and Sara was glad when it was time to leave.

So we walked slowly home, mostly in silence. I was thinking about the protest. We had told our team captains we would meet once more in the barn, on the night of December 24, and now I was wondering if we shouldn't meet on the twenty-third instead, since Avery Sabine's spies might be especially active on the day before Christmas. I asked Elizabeth what she thought, but she was worn out from her own long working day and made it clear she didn't want to talk.

It was already dark when we reached the cottage. I was surprised to see

Arthur there, sitting at the table with Alan. The glow from candles was sufficient for me to see that Arthur had a scrap of paper in his hand.

"There was a message in the tree," he told me. "I came by about an hour ago to check, and there it was." He handed me the bit of paper, which had the outline of a candy cane scrawled on it with charcoal—that is what many poor people of the time used to write or draw. "We'll have to walk over to the barn, Layla. Whoever left this might already be waiting, since night has fallen."

"What could someone need to tell us?" I asked. "Christmas Day and the protest are only a week away. Do you think there's a problem?"

"There could be," Arthur mused, "but it's more likely that one of our captains is feeling nervous and wants some reassurance. You must remember, Layla, that most of the people who joined with us have never done something so bold in their lives. As the moment approaches, they're bound to worry. So why don't you and I go to the barn and see if that isn't what's happening. Probably a few soothing words will do the trick."

"I'll go with you, too," Alan said. "It's a cold, clear night and I'll enjoy the walk. Besides, if there is some sort of problem, perhaps I'll be able to help."

Elizabeth then said that she would go, while Alan stayed with Sara. It had been a frustrating day at work, she said, what with Mrs. Sabine acting so angry, and so she wanted a chance to get out and clear her head and think of something else besides why there had been dust under one of the beds when Mrs. Sabine happened to look there. Several minutes went by while Alan and Elizabeth debated who should be able to go with Arthur and me, until finally Sara shouted crossly from her loft that they should both go, she was fine, and after all she was thirteen years old! Just *go*, for goodness' sake!

"I suppose she's right. She's old enough to be left by herself for a while," Alan muttered, and so all four of us adults took the two-mile walk across hills to the barn. We brought a single lantern, but didn't need to light it. The moon was half-full, the stars twinkled, and by now we knew the way very well, even in the dark. As we walked, we talked quietly about the protest, and how wonderful it would be to see thousands of people joining together on behalf of Christmas, and this discussion put us all in better moods.

"Exactly one week from now, we'll be back in the cottage celebrating Christmas with extra enthusiasm," Alan predicted. "The protest will go well, our message to Parliament will be clear, and the holiday in England will be saved. Just wait and see."

When we reached the bottom of the steep hill with the barn above us, we lit the lantern so that if someone was waiting for us there he or she would see us approaching and not be startled when we arrived. Halfway up the slope we could see the silhouette of the barn against the night sky, and in the doorway there was also a lantern casting a small glow.

"Whoever it is, is waiting," Elizabeth said. "Let's hurry and deal with this problem, whatever it might be. I really don't like Sara being alone back at the cottage. I don't care if she's thirteen."

"Remember to be cautious," Arthur warned. "Pull the hoods of your cloaks around your faces. Wait to see the candy cane before you go all the way into the barn and reveal yourselves." But as we reached the crest of the hill and a small, dark figure also wrapped in a cloak stood in the doorway, I knew who it was even before she pulled her beloved candy cane out of a pocket and waved it at us.

"Janie, you weren't at work today," I whispered. "Is something wrong?"

"Come inside, Layla, so we can talk, and bring your friends with you," she replied, and turned back into the barn, her small lantern barely radiating enough light to see where she was going.

"It's Janie," I said to my three companions. "It's all right." We pulled our cloaks away from our faces and filed inside. It was very dark in the barn. Beside me, I could sense rather than see Arthur taking flint and stone from his pocket to strike a spark and light our lantern, too.

Then there was rustling behind us and to either side, and Janie said, "I have some people here, too." The clicking of stone and flint echoed in several places, as did the louder *clack* of musket hammers being drawn back. Lanterns flared with sudden light, and Arthur, Elizabeth, Alan, and I saw we were surrounded by at least a dozen members of the Trained Band, each of them pointing his gun directly at us. The four of us were not armed. There were too many of them to fight, and they were all around us, so we couldn't run. Directly in front of us, Janie stood beside two cloaked figures, both very tall, one of them thick-bodied and the other thin as a wraith. The heavy one threw off his hood, and I saw it was Mayor Avery Sabine, whose expression was disapproving and solemn. Then the thin one pulled back his hood, and I looked into the leering face of Blue Richard Culmer.

"Ah, Missus Layla Nicholas," he hissed with sarcastic courtesy. "You avoided becoming my guest in London five years ago. I'm so pleased to greet you now, and also your friends. *No,* sir!" he barked as Arthur moved to step between us. "You will stay still, or these men will shoot you down where you stand. I don't know your name, or that of these others."

"The second woman is named Elizabeth Hayes," Avery Sabine told him. "She works for my wife as a maid. The fellow with his arm around her is her husband."

"I'm Alan Hayes," my friend said bravely, his voice trembling a little. It is very frightening to have guns pointed at you. "What is the meaning of this? Mayor Sabine, why do you threaten peaceable citizens?"

"You're hardly peaceable," Sabine replied. "You and your fellow conspirators, here, planned to incite a terrible riot in my city on Christmas Day. It was your intention to destroy property and set fires and encourage other citizens to join in the violence. Well, you're caught."

"Who told you such lies?" Arthur demanded, but, my heart sinking, I already knew.

"Why, Janie?" I asked.

She stood behind Sabine and Culmer and had a sad smile on her face.

"From now on, I'm to be the upstairs maid instead of toiling in the washing shed," Janie said. "That will make every working day like Christmas for me, Layla. And I never said nothing to this man about any violence. I told him the whole thing was to be peaceable, like." She turned to Sabine. "Your honor, may I go now? Your missus wants me at work quite early tomorrow."

"Yes, yes, go," Sabine muttered. "Wait, here's a coin for you. Now, begone while we finish our business here."

Those words chilled me. There were soldiers with guns, Blue Richard

Culmer with his evil smile, and no witnesses. Perhaps Alan, Elizabeth, Arthur, and I were all to be shot. Culmer, watching me intently, guessed what I was thinking.

"There will be no executions here tonight, missus," he said. "I have other plans for you and your friends. How foolish you were, what amateurs! Did you really believe you could confide your plans to so many people and not have one of them, at least, betray you? If you're the best defenders Christmas has, no wonder the holiday is going to be gone forever! You trust people, Missus Nicholas, and that's always a fatal flaw."

"I'm the one who planned this, Culmer," Arthur interjected. "These other three only did what I told them. They're frightened now by you and these guns. They've learned their lesson. Let them go."

Culmer laughed—at least, the cackling sound he made was probably intended as laughter. "Oh, no, Mister—what is your name?"

"Arthur."

"Well, Mr. Arthur, you and Missus Nicholas and these Hayes people are going to be helpful to me, which means helpful to England. Even traitors like you can be of use."

Arthur bristled. "I'm no traitor to England, Culmer, now or ever. You're the traitor, terrorizing anyone who doesn't act exactly as you demand. And I don't care what you might have been told about plans for Christmas Day. Violence was never part of them. That's your way, not ours."

"Oh, sometimes cracking heads or smashing windows is effective, but I have other ways, too," Culmer replied. "You're about to find that out. You meant your Christmas riot to symbolize resistance. Now I will use you to symbolize the futility of resisting. Men, get out rope and tie these people up. Then let them sit down on the floor. There's hay strewn all about, so it shouldn't be too uncomfortable. We need to settle in. The night is still long, and we must wait until daylight."

"I can't stay here all night," Avery Sabine protested. "I have many important things to do tomorrow, and I need my rest."

Culmer waved his hand. "Go back to your home and your bed, then. Mind you don't tell anyone about what happened here tonight. We want everyone to be surprised tomorrow."

"Surprised by what?" Arthur asked.

"You'll see," Culmer said. The mayor hurried out of the barn, and we could hear him stumbling down the steep hill. Avery Sabine was not a graceful man. Then Culmer watched as a few of the Trained Band set down their muskets and tied our hands behind us. We were forced to sit down. Elizabeth was crying a little. The sound of her sobs seemed to soothe Culmer, who lit a pipe and sat with his back to the bale of hay I presumed Father Joel used as an altar.

"I hope you're not uncomfortable," he said sarcastically. "We'll be here until dawn. You'll understand why after that. Meanwhile, you may talk quietly, but if I even suspect you are trying to loosen your bonds and escape, I'll have one of you shot in front of the others. Four would be better for what I have planned, but three will do. Perhaps you might sing some Christmas carols to pass the time."

Alan squirmed over to Elizabeth's side. Because his hands were tied he couldn't put his arm around her, but he leaned so that their shoulders touched.

"Don't be afraid, love," he said softly. "I don't think they'll do anything too terrible to us."

"You don't believe that for a moment, and I'm not crying about our predicament," Elizabeth replied. "I'm afraid for Sara. She's all alone at the cottage, and both her parents are prisoners."

Panic shot through me. I had forgotten about Sara. I wondered how long she would sit up waiting for us to return. Maybe, after hours and hours, she would come to the barn herself to see what was delaying us. Culmer might take her prisoner, too! "Don't mention Sara," I hissed to Elizabeth. "If Culmer overhears, he might send his men to arrest her, too, just to make you and Alan feel even worse. She's Sophia's best friend. I don't think Margaret Sabine will let anything bad happen to her. But don't talk about Sara now!"

The four of us talked quietly a little longer. We thought it odd that Culmer was not questioning us about others involved in the Christmas Day protest plan. It was as though he didn't care. Why? And why were we being kept in the barn until dawn? After a while, Elizabeth and Alan, exhausted by fear and stress, dozed. Arthur and I remained awake. Every so often I would glance over at Blue Richard Culmer, who leaned back against the hay bale smoking his pipe and never taking his eyes off of us. Finally, as the first faint streaks of dawn appeared on the eastern horizon, Culmer stood up, stretched, and nodded to one of the Trained Band. That fellow went to a far corner of the barn and, with some effort, picked up a heavy canvas bag that clanked as he carried it over to where we four prisoners sat. The clanking woke Alan and Elizabeth.

"Chains," Arthur said grimly, and he was correct. "Now, I understand. Culmer means to make examples of us."

"Exactly, Mr. Arthur," Culmer snarled. "Men, secure them properly, and take no chances. Keep those ropes tight around their arms until all the chains are in place."

It was horrible. The chains were very heavy. Manacles were snapped around our wrists, which were still kept behind our backs. Then lengths of chain were placed around all of our waists, with about two feet of additional chain linking us up one to another—me to Arthur, Arthur to Elizabeth, and Elizabeth to Alan. Finally, Culmer stepped up and personally secured a final shackle around my neck, much like a master will place a collar and leash on a dog. "Time to go to town," he crooned, and tugged the length of chain attached to my neck. I was jerked forward and forced to follow him, and my three friends staggered along behind me in a grotesque parade. The Trained Band soldiers took up their muskets and fell in on either side of us. "Slowly, now," Culmer cautioned as he led the way down the hill. "Don't stand too close to the prisoners, lads. We want all their friends and neighbors to get good looks at them!"

Country people around Canterbury rose with the sun, so as we reached the main path toward town there already were many people moving along it. As we made our ghastly walk, I recognized quite a few of them—they were all participants in the planned protest. Now their eyes widened and their mouths fell open in shock to see their leaders in Blue Richard Culmer's clutches.

"See what happens to Christmas plotters?" Culmer bellowed over and over as we made our slow, awful way into Canterbury. "All those who unlawfully celebrate Christmas face swift and certain punishment! Would you want this to be *you*?" People who had greeted me every day for five years turned away, trying not to look me in the eye. Culmer was using us to frighten the rest of the people into submission, just as he had used the smashing of cathedral stained-glass windows a few years earlier. And his plan was obviously working. No one called out comforting words to us; onlookers were too afraid for their own safety to offer any show of support.

Culmer led us into Canterbury through St. George's Gate on the eastern wall, and the guards there snapped to attention and saluted him as we passed. High Street, the main city thoroughfare that was lined with shops, ran straight through the center of Canterbury and ended at the West Gate, with its two hulking towers, one of which housed the city dungeon. Culmer obviously intended to take us there, but along the way he wanted as many people as possible to see us in our chains. We tried to walk with some dignity, but with our hands chained behind us it was hard to do. Every so often Culmer would deftly tug at the chain linked to my neck, and I would stumble a little, and in turn Arthur, Elizabeth, and Alan would be pulled off balance and stagger for a few steps. Right through the central marketplace he led us, calling out for the Trained Band soldiers to make the crowd stand clear. As word of our procession spread, black-cloaked Puritans began to appear all along High Street, calling out insults to the four of us and jeering that Christmas was gone forever, and look at the dreadful fate we'd brought on ourselves by not accepting that! I was terribly afraid, though not for myself. I was thinking about Sara. When she woke and discovered that her parents and auntie hadn't returned to the cottage, what would she do? The girl was so shy that she would probably not run to a neighbor and ask for help. Perhaps she'd make her way into Canterbury and her friend Sophia—what if my darling girl was seeing us in chains right now? I began desperately looking at the people lining both sides of the street, my head swiveling back and forth, and Blue Richard Culmer saw me and misunderstood.

"You're feeling panic, I can tell!" he crowed. "Well, missus, not one of those people is going to help you, so there's no sense searching for a friend. You have no friends left!"

We finally reached the West Gate, where the north tower served as the town prison. I thought Culmer would immediately throw us into cells, but he had other plans. Outside the tower were four sets of "stocks," wooden stands with openings that closed around prisoners' necks and wrists, forcing them into an awkward standing crouch until, finally, the stocks would be unlocked and they could move around again. Culmer ordered us locked into these stocks. Hundreds of people gathered about; criminals were usually put into the stocks for extra embarrassment after some particularly disgusting crime, like stealing from church coin boxes. Then Mayor Sabine appeared—I could only see him out of the corner of my eye, because the stocks were tight and I could not move my head.

"Behold the Christmas criminals!" Sabine roared to the crowd. "This is what happens to traitors who plan riots on behalf of sinful holidays! These evildoers hoped to lead many of you into crime, but your mayor and Mr. Culmer have saved you! Look on them, and learn your lesson! There is no longer any Christmas in England, or in Canterbury!" Then Culmer directed the Trained Band soldiers to festoon the stocks with green boughs and holly, in a mockery of traditional Christmas decorations. There was nothing for Arthur, Elizabeth, Alan, and me to do but stand where we were locked in place as the sun traveled across the winter sky. All day, we were offered no food or water, and all of us were feeling weak when, in early evening, Culmer finally ordered us taken out of the stocks. Our legs were so stiff that we staggered as, at gunpoint, we were marched into the jail. Down stone steps we went, until, finally, we came to a heavy, barred door, which creaked ominously as it was opened and we were forced inside. The stone walls of this dungeon were damp and reeked of rot.

"There are empty buckets for you when you need to do the obvious," Culmer said. "Bread and water will be brought in the morning. By then you'll be so hungry, you'll think you're dining on fine holiday goose. In the meantime, why don't you pray to Father Christmas? Perhaps he'll come to save you." Then Culmer stepped back and nodded to a jailer, who grunted as he swung the heavy cell door shut. The single lantern lighting the hallway was extinguished, and we were prisoners in the dark.

Twenty-one

We only knew it was morning when two jailers lumbered down the stone steps to our dungeon cell carrying a bucket of water and two loaves of stale bread. One stood outside with a musket and torch while the other unlocked the heavy door, growled "Breakfast," shoved the bucket and bread inside, then slammed the door shut and locked it again. The only light we had came from the torch, and it was a relief when the second jailer jammed it into a holder on the wall outside the cell and we could see a little by the flickers it cast through the barred window. As the jailers went back up the steps without another word, we took turns having long sips from the bucket—the water was sour tasting, and I tried not to think of where it might have come from—and then Arthur insisted we each eat some bread. None of us felt especially hungry, despite the fact we hadn't had a meal since noon the day before. Our troubles had overwhelmed our appetites. But Arthur pointed out we needed to keep up our strength, so we ate.

"I must know what's happened to Sara," Elizabeth moaned after she reluctantly gulped down a few mouthfuls of the awful loaf. "Surely someone has found her by now."

"I'm certain the Sabines have brought her to their home," Alan said reassuringly, though I could tell he was not as confident as he was trying to sound. "These people might have arrested us for trying to save Christmas, but they surely won't punish an innocent child." He chewed on his bread for a few moments and then asked, "What do you think they will do to us today?"

"Probably nothing," I said. "Culmer knows it is much more cruel to leave us here for a while wondering about his intentions before revealing them. Meanwhile, we'd better save what's left of the bread and water. It may be all we get for a while."

I was right. No one came down the stairs to our cell. Sometime during the day the torch went out, and we were plunged back into total darkness. The hours crawled by. I knew Alan and Elizabeth were tormented by their fear for Sara, and I felt the same. Arthur undoubtedly was devising escape plans, though nothing of the sort seemed possible. There was only the one door to our cell, and the narrow stone stairway leading up from it was undoubtedly guarded at the top. None of us speculated what Blue Richard Culmer and the Puritans might have in mind for our further punishment. Anything was possible. They could twist the laws in any way they pleased to suit themselves. We talked very little, because we were so discouraged and also because Arthur warned there might be some jailer perched on the stairs hoping to overhear information about the protest plan that he could report back to Culmer.

"We have to protect everyone else if we can," Arthur whispered. "I believe Janie only identified the four of us. With luck, all our captains and other supporters might be spared."

"Perhaps they'll march anyway, even though we've been taken prisoner," Alan said hopefully.

"That would surprise me," I replied. "You saw how everyone remained silent when we were pulled down High Street in chains. An effective protest needs leaders, so even if some of them do try to march without us on Christmas Day, they'll be confused and easily dispersed by Sabine and the Trained Band." As soon as I spoke these gloomy words, I regretted them. Our situation was bad enough without adding to it. So I didn't say anything more, and neither did the others. After a while I began thinking about my husband. I knew Nicholas was far across the ocean, preoccupied with bringing Christmas gifts to colonial children in the New World. How many more months would it take before he noticed there had been no letters from Arthur or me, and what would he do when he learned of our fate, whatever it might turn out to be?

I suppose all of us slept a little, though afterward it seemed to me I hadn't closed my eyes at all when the rattle of boots on stone steps indicated another day had passed. A new torch flared its light into our cell, and when the heavy door was unlocked and swung open, there stood Blue Richard Culmer.

"How are my guests this fine morning?" he jeered. "How wonderful you all look." This, of course, was sarcasm. All four of us were dirty from sprawling on the cell floor, and smelly from not bathing. After so many hours spent in darkness, even the feeble torchlight made us blink and rub our eyes.

"What do you mean to do with us, Culmer?" Arthur demanded. "You can't keep us prisoners without telling us what we're charged with and allowing us a fair trial on those charges."

Culmer emitted his usual odd cackle. "You don't understand our special new laws. In emergency situations dealing with obvious traitors, we can keep prisoners as long as we like without going through the usual motions of charges and trials. We decent English people are at war with sinners like you, and so you have no legal rights. But of this, you may be certain—for planning a violent riot in support of the illegal Christmas holiday, your punishment will be quite severe. Well, I'll leave you to wonder what will happen to you. Now that you're in custody, I'm off to London. We've heard rumors of Christmas plotters there. Please continue to make yourselves at home. Bread and water will be served soon."

As Culmer turned to go, Elizabeth cried, "What about my daughter? Where is Sara?"

He paused, then replied, "Someone mentioned that girl to me. You'll have to ask the Sabines about her."

"Then let me speak to the Sabines," Elizabeth pleaded. "She is only thirteen years old!"

"As far as I'm concerned, children of traitors should be treated like traitors as well," Culmer snarled. "I've got more important things to think about than your brat. Take it up with the Sabines, if they decide to waste time talking to you. And a Merry Christmas to all." He stalked out of the cell, the door was slammed shut and locked, and Elizabeth spent most of the next few hours sobbing uncontrollably.

Eventually there were more footsteps on the stone stairs. Unlike Culmer, Margaret Sabine did not come into our cell. Instead, she stayed outside the thick door, calling through the barred window for Elizabeth to stand up and speak to her.

"You, girl," she called. "Come over here at once! Are you ready to offer an apology?"

"What do you mean, an apology?" Elizabeth asked as she stumbled to her feet and over to our side of the door.

"You have betrayed my trust, and showed no gratitude for my years of kindness to you," Margaret Sabine declared. "I gave you work. My money, paid to you in salary, bought your family's food. In return, you planned to participate in, even help lead, a hateful, violent act that, had it been successful, would have destroyed my husband's career. Well, now you're caught, and I don't feel sorry for you. But I do expect you to at least ask my forgiveness."

"Mrs. Sabine, what about Sara?" Elizabeth pleaded. "Is she with you? Is she safe?"

"The apology first," Margaret Sabine demanded.

"I'll apologize for anything you like, but please tell me about my daughter!" Elizabeth cried.

"Well," the mayor's wife said, "I have very little to tell. When news reached me of your arrest, and that of your husband and this other woman, Layla, who also has repaid my kindness with betrayal, I sent some of my people to your cottage to fetch Sara. You are, of course, an unfit mother, since you recklessly threw in with these plotters without a care in the world about what might happen to your child. Angry as I am with you, I'm a Christian woman and would not let the girl suffer because of her parents' sinfulness. But they reported back to me that the cottage was empty. Sara was not there."

"Then, where is she?" Elizabeth asked in horror.

"I'm sure I don't know," Margaret Sabine replied. "It had been my intention all along to bring Sara with us when our family moved to London. You could not have objected. Being Sophia's lady-in-waiting would have been a far better life than you and your sailor husband could ever have given to her. But now that won't happen. Sara is gone, and I haven't time to spare seeking her further. After my husband makes clear on Christmas Day how he foiled your plot, Sophia and I are moving to our new London home, where Mr. Sabine will soon join us after a grateful Parliament names him to some very high government position."

"But Sara—" Elizabeth pleaded.

"Speak no more to me of her," Margaret Sabine said. "I was becoming somewhat annoyed with her, in fact. This is how people of my class are rewarded for trying to be generous to our inferiors. Your daughter, a peasant girl, too often seemed to think she was the equal of my little darling, a child of much higher breeding. Well, now I know where she got the idea. Her mother and father thought they could somehow challenge their social betters, and look where it got you!"

"Please find Sara," Elizabeth pleaded. "You're a mother, just like me."

"Oh, I'm nothing at all like you," the mayor's wife replied. She seemed about to say more when there was much thudding on the steps, and Mayor Avery Sabine stumbled outside the cell door.

"Come away, Margaret," he said impatiently. "Don't waste your time on these pathetic traitors."

"Mayor Sabine, please find my daughter!" Alan shouted from the back of the cell. "Sara can't be left out there all alone."

Sabine drew himself up and peered through the barred cell window. "You'd best worry about yourself, fellow. As for your daughter, well, there's always room on the streets for one more homeless girl."

Despite our rule against violence, Alan threw himself at the mayor. But his shoulder bounced off the locked, heavy door between them, and he sprawled on the cell floor. He lay there pounding his fist in frustration while Sabine, roaring with laughter, guided his stout wife back up the stairs and out into the sunlight it seemed that we four prisoners might never see again.

The last few days before Christmas passed in an agony of combined tedium and worry. Much of the time we had no light and had to sit in the dark. The hours crept by. Every so often, we'd be given bread and water. This poor diet sapped our strength. We worried about Sara, about the rest of the Christmas protestors, and, I admit, about what would finally happen to us. Culmer had made it clear we could be held without trial for as long as he wanted. We could be whipped, have our ears "notched," or even be executed. The longer we sat in the darkness, the more we couldn't help imagining various horrible fates. No one came to speak to us. Culmer had apparently gone back to London. Mayor Sabine had other things to do. By the third day, we'd mostly stopped talking among ourselves, because there was really nothing left to say. Sara might be anywhere. Every so often, I would think that it was my fault all this had happened to her, and to Elizabeth and Alan and Arthur. If I had just joined my husband in the New World, or if I had followed Arthur's advice and at least moved to the toy factory in Nuremberg instead of stubbornly insisting on staying in England and trying to save Christmas . . . had never felt so terrible, or so helpless. And yet, deep inside I still believed that there was no coincidence in our Christmas mission and that I had remained in Canterbury for some great purpose.

On what we reckoned must be December 24, the day before Christmas, there were more footsteps on the stone. Two guards unlocked the door, and one called, "Layla Nicholas, come forward." I stood up with some difficulty. My legs were stiff from sitting on the floor for so long.

"What do you want with me?" I asked, trying to sound brave.

"I don't want anything," the guard said. "There's someone to see you, so come on up. I've been told not to tie your hands, but don't get any ideas about trying to escape. There are men with guns upstairs, and they wouldn't mind shooting a violent traitor like you."

"I'm not violent, and I'm not a traitor," I said.

"That's not how Mr. Culmer and the mayor tell it," he replied, and gestured for me to come out of the cell.

I slowly made my way up the stairs. When I reached the main floor I had to shield my face with my hands to block out the sunlight coming through the windows, because the glare hurt my eyes. When I lowered my hands again I saw someone familiar. Oliver Cromwell, dressed in plain Puritan black, looked at me sorrowfully.

"You can leave us alone," he told the guards. "Missus Nicholas will not attack me or attempt to escape."

"Our orders from the mayor are not to leave her," one of the guards said. "She's a nasty one, she is."

"My orders outrank the mayor's," Cromwell said. "Go." The guards did. He turned back to me and said, "I thought you'd be hungry, missus. There is cheese here on the table, and clean water in a cup. Refresh yourself."

It was a kind gesture, and I grabbed a hunk of cheese and began eating it. I was sorry I had to touch the food with my filthy hands; in the light of day I could see the dirt caked under my fingernails. I was sure I smelled very bad, but Cromwell was enough of a gentleman not to mention it or to wrinkle his nose at my odor.

"Missus Nicholas, I regret very much to find you in this situation," Cromwell said. "I did my best to warn you. Now, you must have the sense to cooperate fully with the mayor tomorrow on the so-called Christmas Day, so that we can end your suffering and all get on with our lives."

"What do you mean?" I asked suspiciously.

"Christmas is gone from England, and your plot to save it has failed," Cromwell said. "You must surely realize that. We can't have any more Christmas riots like the one you helped organize for the apprentices in London two years ago. If the people think they can have their holiday just by demanding it, then they next might decide to demand the restoration of the king. He, of course, has greatly disappointed me. He never intended to bargain in good faith, and give Parliament its proper influence. Well, a bad end is coming for him. But it doesn't have to be that way for you. Tomorrow, Mayor Sabine expects you and your three friends to stand up in front of this prison and call out to everyone that you renounce Christmas Day and all of its sinfulness. Do it, and afterward you'll be set free."

"Does Blue Richard Culmer know about this?" I asked. I knew there was no use trying to convince Cromwell I had nothing to do with the Apprentice Protest.

Cromwell sighed. "He didn't like it, but it was not his decision. I have consulted with Mayor Sabine. If Culmer had his way, the four of you would already have been executed. But the vast majority of us now in power are not bloodthirsty, missus. Be reasonable. You cannot save Christmas, so save yourself."

"And if I don't do as you and the mayor want?"

"Then you and your friends will be placed in the Canterbury stocks for all of Christmas Day, and afterward you will be taken to London for trial before Parliament. The charge will be treason. After you're found guilty, and of course you will be, all four of you will be thrown into the Tower of London and kept there forever. Don't let that happen. Speak against Christmas tomorrow, and I myself will take you to the London docks and pay your passage on a ship to the New World and your husband."

"I can't renounce Christmas," I said. "I love all the good things it stands for. I disagree with some of your beliefs, Mr. Cromwell, but I would never tell you to renounce them or be judged a traitor. That, I suppose, is the difference between us. And I promise you this: You will never successfully ban Christmas. You can't imprison everyone who supports the holiday. There wouldn't be a thousand people left free in England if you did. It may happen gradually rather than immediately, but all you believe you have accomplished—removing the king, giving full power to Parliament, creating a country that abides by your beliefs and no others—will be undone because you tried to take away the most wonderful celebration of the year. I don't want my freedom lost, but I want people to have Christmas more."

"So you refuse."

"I do."

Cromwell reached for his wide-brimmed black hat. "Then, Missus Layla Nicholas, I will see you next in the halls of Parliament, perhaps in a week. And I will take no pleasure in what happens to you there."

I was returned to the cell, where Arthur, Alan, and Elizabeth asked me what had happened. I told them, and added I thought they could each save themselves if they would stand up the next day and renounce Christmas as Cromwell and Sabine wanted.

"But you won't do that?" Alan asked.

"No," I said. "Perhaps outrage over what Parliament does to me will rouse public spirit and help save Christmas after all. There will be no disgrace if any of you makes a different choice."

But they didn't. I spent the rest of the day thinking about what I had told Sara—that great achievement always requires great sacrifice and how we each must decide how much we are willing to risk for our beliefs.

It was just dawn on December 25, 1647, when a troop of armed guards came to the cell and roughly pulled us up the steps. We were brought outside into the cold morning light. Our appearances, I knew, were appalling. Our clothes were nasty and torn, our exposed skin was filthy, and our legs were so weak we could barely stand as we were locked into the stocks. The guards hung holly and green boughs and signs saying "Christmas Criminals" in front of us. Town criers began to stroll up and down High Street, calling out that Mayor Sabine expected all shops to be open and business conducted as usual. Then they shouted that anyone defying these orders would join the Christmas criminals in the stocks. A dozen black-cloaked Puritans gathered in front of us and called out insults. A few tossed handfuls of dirt and pebbles in our faces, but we were already so grimy the added filth made little difference. The rest of the townspeople tried to hurry by without staring. After an hour the criers changed messages. Now they informed everyone that at high noon, Mayor Sabine would come to the stocks to make a public address.

Alan, Elizabeth, Arthur, and I remained hunched over in the stocks. We didn't talk. It took all our strength to keep our legs from collapsing, which would have been even more painful since we would then have hung from the stocks by our necks and wrists. About noon, as the winter sun shone weakly overhead, we sensed movement behind us, and Mayor Sabine appeared, surrounded by members of the Trained Band. He had a long, written speech in his hand and maneuvered in front of the stocks as a crowd began to gather. I waited almost numbly for him to begin what I knew would be a tirade against Christmas and a reminder to look hard at the traitors, because their fate would be shared by anyone who continued to support the sinful holiday.

Sabine turned and gave the four of us in stocks a long, disgusted look, turned back toward the crowd, held his speech in front of him, cleared his throat loudly, and proclaimed, "Good people of Canterbury, it is pleasant to see you going about an ordinary day instead of indulging in unlawful Christmas activities. As a sign of its love for godly people, your Parliament has condemned Christmas as illegal, and all those who continue to celebrate it are criminals. You see before you four evildoers who intended to terrorize you today at the head of a mob, burning shops and beating people in an attempt to force you to engage in drunken, evil acts that insult Jesus rather than indicate thanks for his birth. But we have saved you from them! I find great pleasure in announcing that tomorrow they will be taken in chains to London, where they will be tried by Parliament and—"

My head was held in place by the stocks, so I couldn't be sure what Mayor Sabine saw, only that, whatever it was, it caused him to stop talking, drop the pages of his speech, and motion for the dozen soldiers from the Trained Band to raise their muskets. Elizabeth, in stocks to my left, had a better view toward the West Gate and the beginning of High Street, and suddenly she gasped, "Is it really possible?" Then there was the thudding of footsteps from every direction, and a great procession swept in front of me, and I saw that, yes, it *was*.

Twenty-two

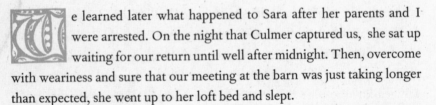e learned later what happened to Sara after her parents and I were arrested. On the night that Culmer captured us, she sat up waiting for our return until well after midnight. Then, overcome with weariness and sure that our meeting at the barn was just taking longer than expected, she went up to her loft bed and slept.

But when Sara woke at dawn, the cottage was still empty and she knew something must be wrong. She got up and dressed, quickly ate a little fruit for breakfast, put on her warmest cloak, and went outside into the cold winter morning. She intended to walk from the cottage to the meeting barn atop the high hill, but she had only gone a few hundred yards when she noticed a commotion along the road toward Canterbury. Peeking around the adults lining the thoroughfare, she saw a horrifying sight—her parents, auntie, and Arthur chained together and being led toward town by blue-cloaked, leering Richard Culmer. Sara's instinct was to scream and run to us, but my precious girl had enough sense to realize that would only make things worse. She might be arrested, too, and used as a bargaining chip to make her parents and me do whatever Culmer wanted. So she ran back to the cottage and raced up the ladder to her loft bed, where she lay shivering with fear—but only for a few moments.

As soon as Margaret Sabine heard of her parents' arrest, Sara guessed, she would send some of her servants to the cottage with instructions to bring her along to the mayor's house. That would still leave her at Culmer's mercy, so she had to run. The problem for the girl was that, because she had always been so shy, she had no friends other than Sophia whose family might take her in and hide her. So she had to make a decision, and quickly—would she stay cowering in bed until her parents' enemies came to get her or would she overcome her lifelong shyness and seek help from neighbors she'd never really gotten to know very well?

Sara chose not to wait for capture. She resolutely put some fruit and cheese and a small gourd of water in a pack and left the cottage, walking east away from Canterbury rather than west toward the city. She didn't know that she barely left in time—perhaps fifteen minutes after she shut the door behind her, Margaret Sabine's people arrived looking for her. But all they found was an empty cottage; Sara was out of sight in the nearby hills.

She knew that she should go to one of the other houses in the vicinity, identify herself to whoever lived there, and ask for shelter. Almost all the neighbors, she knew from overhearing conversations between her parents, Arthur, and me, opposed the banning of Christmas and were unlikely to turn a thirteen-year-old girl over to the nasty clutches of Blue Richard Culmer. But the thought of talking to someone she didn't know was almost as frightening as the sight of her loved ones as prisoners. Sara truly *was* shy, and the habits of a lifetime, even one that had so far lasted only thirteen years, were hard to overcome. So, that first awful day, she wandered and occasionally tried to find the nerve to ask for help, and always panicked at the last moment. Finally she found a small grove of trees in the space between two low hills. The spot was out of sight of the road, and Sara huddled there as the day dwindled into night, chilled by bitter December winds and petrified by the horrible turn her life had taken.

As she crouched for hours with her cloak pulled tight around her though, she began to think about overcoming fear, and about each person's responsibility, if something wrong is being done, to try to stop it. The three people she loved most in the world, the adults she looked to for guidance and protection, were undoubtedly in a Canterbury dungeon. There was nothing she could do about that. But she could, at least, do something about the Christmas protest they had so deeply believed in that they were willing to risk their freedom, even their lives, to help organize and lead it.

Just as the sun rose the next morning, December 20, a farmer named John Mason heard a knock on his cottage door. He opened it to find a young girl standing outside, shivering both with cold and nerves.

"My name is Sara, and I need to talk to you," she said, almost choking out the words because she so much wanted to turn and run instead. "You know my parents, Alan and Elizabeth Hayes, and my Auntie Layla. You've been meeting with them about the protest on Christmas."

"I'm afraid they've been arrested, child," Mason said, gesturing for his wife to come over and help him bring the shuddering girl inside. "It is a sad thing, indeed." The Masons fussed over Sara, putting extra wood on the fire to help her get warm, and insisting she eat some hot mush. Sara swallowed several spoonfuls before she felt strong enough to say anything more.

"They trusted you very much," she finally said. "At night, they would talk about how brave you are, how they expected you, Mr. Mason, to be one of the best captains on Christmas Day."

Mason shrugged sadly. "I would have been proud to take part in any way I was needed. Now, of course, there will be no protest, since our leaders are captured and our plans are ruined. It would have been a good thing to save Christmas, but now all we can do is hope your parents and auntie don't give the rest of us away to Blue Richard Culmer."

Sara took a deep breath. "You're wrong, Mr. Mason."

He looked worried and asked, "You mean, you think your family will identify the rest of us in hopes of saving themselves?"

"No, not at all. My parents and auntie are very brave people. But now we have to be brave, too, and hold the protest that all of you have planned for so long."

"Our leaders are gone, child," Mason protested.

"Then *we* have to be the leaders, sir," Sara replied. "Those who stand by watching something wrong being done are as guilty as the people who do the bad thing. My auntie taught me that. Help me talk to all the people who were helping to plan the protest. We have to march on Christmas day. We have to."

For the next few days, Sara and John Mason walked dozens of miles, quietly visiting all the captains who'd been named by Arthur and convincing them that they still must march. A few could not be persuaded. Because of the arrests at the barn, they were now too afraid of Blue Richard Culmer, Avery Sabine, and the rest of the Puritans. Many were shocked to see a teenaged girl assuming leadership of such a complicated, important effort. No one realized how hard it was for that thirteen-year-old to overcome her bashfulness and talk to so many people. But Sara did this, and very effectively. She remembered all she had overheard from her loft bed when the adults downstairs were talking—how, above all, they wanted thousands of marchers, so sheer numbers would prevent arrests or other reprisals by Culmer, Sabine, and the Trained Band. So, when she had convinced most of the captains to continue the protest, she emphasized to them that they, in turn, must recruit as many other people as possible.

Then, leaving the adults to that task, Sara herself spent hours talking to other children. It was hard, at first. Besides her natural shyness, Sara also had a bad reputation among her peers to overcome. Boys and girls in Canterbury were all aware of her special friendship with Sophia, the richest child in town. While the rest of the working-class children had to help their parents in the fields or in shops, Sara had been enjoying private lessons and fine meals with Sophia, and so she was often resented. Her bashfulness was mistaken for snobbiness. But now, for the first time, she sought out other young people and talked to them about Christmas, how special it was, how it must somehow be saved. She explained the purpose of the march and its intended message to Parliament. Even more than the adults, the children understood: No one should have the right to force beliefs on others. And so a whole new youthful battalion of protestors was added to the demonstrators' ranks.

By the time of the final planning meeting, on the night of December 24 in the barn high atop the hill, the protestors accepted Sara as a leader. A week earlier, everyone would have considered such a thing impossible, particularly those who realized just how bashful she was. But, in times of emergency, intelligence, imagination, and courage are the most important traits, and no one had more of these than Sara. Mayor Sabine and the Trained Band assumed the plans for protest were dead, so Sara and the five dozen adults with her were able to meet in the barn without too much concern that soldiers might come for them. If they were still understandably nervous, they were excited, too.

"We have to remember tomorrow to approach all six gates at once," Sara cautioned. "One big crowd at one gate will just alert the guards. So let's gather everyone here just after dawn, then divide into six groups."

"How do you think of such things, young lady?" someone asked.

Sara smiled. "I heard Mr. Arthur say it to my parents and auntie." Here, she was displaying another sign of true leadership by not taking credit for someone else's good idea, even though she could have. Then, Sara and John Mason, who had also stepped forward to lead, reminded everyone that there was not to be any violence on the part of the protestors.

"The moment even one of us strikes a blow or throws a stone or breaks a shop window, that will give the mayor and Trained Band an excuse to claim we were rioting rather than protesting," Mason explained. "They'll use it as further evidence that Christmas is sinful and that those who support it are criminals. So we will march—"

"And sing," Sara added.

"And sing," Mason agreed, smiling fondly at the girl who he had come to admire very much. "We will have ourselves a very special Christmas celebration right on High Street, and when Sara gives the signal, waving her hands over her head, then we will all march back out of town to our homes. If we begin at noon, the whole business should take no more than an hour. This will be sufficient to make our message clear. Anything longer, and one of our people or one of the Trained Band might do something unfortunate. We want a brisk, peaceful protest."

Mason paused a moment, then said, "There is one thing more. We know, of course, that Sara's parents and auntie, along with their friend Arthur, are being held in the town jail. Certain information has reached us. By Mayor Sabine's order, tomorrow on Christmas Day they are to be taken out and put in the stocks as examples of how anyone who celebrates Christmas will be punished from now on. Those entering town from the West Gate must immediately get to the stocks and free them. Place them in the middle of the marchers, so that Sabine and his Trained Band can't recapture them. Clark, you are a blacksmith by trade." A massive man nodded. "Well, then, bring along a hammer and chisel for breaking the locks on the stocks. But use them only to strike the locks, no matter how tempted you might become to tap Mayor Sabine once or twice, as well."

Afterward, Mason and Sara walked back to his home, where she was staying with him and his wife. "We're going to save your parents and auntie," he promised.

"We're going to save Christmas, too," Sara replied.

She did not sleep that night. During the hours before dawn, she thought about many things—what if, for instance, the protest failed? It was possible Avery Sabine might be smart enough to order the city gates locked all Christmas Day long, to keep potential protestors out. Or what if not enough people showed up to march? Originally, her parents, Auntie Layla, and Arthur had hoped for a thousand marchers, perhaps two thousand. But if only a hundred or so actually participated, then the march would have no effect other than reassuring Mayor Sabine that few people really cared about saving Christmas after all.

Then Sara shed many tears, not from fear of failure, but because she missed her parents and auntie so much. She was being very brave by overcoming her shyness and stepping in to lead the protest, but she was still a thirteen-year-old girl who loved her family and was afraid for them. What if the marchers frightened the mayor and Trained Band so much that they turned their guns on the four Christmas prisoners?

Gradually, though, Sara calmed herself by realizing she had done all she could to prepare. She could not control the future. It had to be enough, just then, to know that she had tried to do the things she should. After a while, Sara slept, and she dreamed about a stout man with a white beard and warm smile, who patted her arm and told her that her courage was going to help save Christmas. When she woke, she remembered the man in her dream, and somehow this comforted her very much.

Christmas Day of 1647 in England dawned clear and cold. Fluffy white clouds decorated bright blue sky. Sara and John Mason gulped down porridge and hurried to the high hill where the protestors were to gather. As they walked, they talked quietly, mostly wondering how many people would come to join the march.

"Five hundred, at least," Mason guessed. "All our captains report they have met with enthusiastic response. Five hundred people gathered together on High Street will make for a very impressive demonstration, Sara."

"Five hundred won't be enough," she told him. "We must have a thousand or more. Only that kind of multitude will convince Parliament that Christmas can't be taken from us or intimidate Mayor Sabine and the Trained Band so none of us are arrested."

"Perhaps you shouldn't get your hopes up," Mason cautioned, and just then they passed a bend in the road and the steep hill with the barn on top sloped up before them. Usually, the barn looked quite striking, standing alone, silhouetted against the sky. But on this Christmas morning, there was a far more remarkable sight.

All up and down the hillside, a massive crowd of men, women, and children were waiting. They were wrapped in cloaks against the cold, and the raggedness of many of those cloaks indicated that the very poorest people of Canterbury and the surrounding area had come to march on behalf of Christmas. Though the morning was frosty and the act they were about to carry out was so risky, there was still about them a sort of excitement, even joy. As Sara and Mason approached, they were greeted with hearty shouts of "Merry Christmas." For the first time in her life, children her own age swarmed to Sara, greeting her like the special friend she had become to all of them, and this pleased her so much that she smiled despite the nervousness she still felt. And, even as those already there milled about, many more people kept coming to the hill, arriving from every direction.

"How many—" Sara began, awed by the crowd.

"Five, six, even seven thousand," John Mason gasped. "Who ever would have believed it? The love of Christmas truly runs deep in many hearts."

He and Sara called over their captains, who in turn gathered about them the people they had recruited for the march, and as they did, even more men, women, and children continued arriving, until finally about an hour before noon Mason estimated ten thousand were ready to march. He told the captains to get everyone's attention. It took several minutes. Someone had written a proclamation stating that the people of England would have Christmas back, even if it meant having the king back, too. He was asking everyone to sign, and the Xs most of them made—few could actually write their names—took up many pages. Arthur would have forbidden the proclamation, because he wanted to keep the issue of celebrating the holiday separate from the fate of Charles I, but Mason and Sara didn't think of this and let the petition be passed around and signed. Finally, when the crowd was mostly silent, Mason and Sara stood before them. She was quaking inside. It had been one thing to talk in front of a few dozen people. Ten thousand seemed like too many, and for several panic-stricken moments she was sure she couldn't do it. But then she thought of Christmas, and her parents, and about what her Auntie Layla had taught her, and so she spoke. Her voice was still low rather than loud, but in a way that helped quiet the crowd, since they had to stop whispering among themselves to hear her.

"Merry Christmas to you all," she began, and ten thousand shouts of "Merry Christmas" came in response. "Today, we will march into Canterbury and save Christmas. There's really nothing left to say, except to remind you that we must enter all six gates at once, meet in the High Street market, and carry on from there."

"And no violence," John Mason added. "Any blow you strike will hurt Christmas more than it hurts the holiday-haters."

"Can we hit them back if they strike us first?" inquired a short, feisty man.

"As the Bible instructs us, turn the other cheek," Mason replied. "Remember this young lady's parents and aunt are Mayor Sabine's prisoners. We must not give him an excuse to do anything awful to them. All ready? Then let's march to Canterbury!"

The throng overflowed the road as they walked swiftly toward the town. Just before they came into sight of its walls, the march captains divided the marchers into six separate units. These half-dozen battalions of more than fifteen hundred each took different routes to Canterbury, arriving at the six town gates at approximately the same time. Sara, John Mason, and the blacksmith named Clark made certain they led the group at the West Gate, since it was their intention to rescue the four "Christmas criminals" from the stocks.

As the town bell tower tolled noon, the marchers surged forward from six different directions. The guards at the gates were simply overwhelmed. Even if they had thought of trying to slam the gates shut, all at once there were so many people surrounding them that they couldn't have done it anyway.

Down into the city swept the six groups of protestors, hustling past the few dozen armed Trained Band soldiers who, at any rate, had no idea of what to do. Coming through the West Gate, Sara and her group saw ahead of them the four sets of stocks, with Mayor Sabine standing in front preparing to address a crowd. They increased their pace, and the pounding of their feet on the street echoed off the buildings and alerted the mayor to their presence. He turned, saw them approaching, turned pale with fear, and dropped his written speech into the dirt. Then, in his heavy, graceless way, he ran for his home, more anxious to save himself from any possible danger than to confront the marchers.

It was only as the mayor turned to flee that first Elizabeth, then the other three of us in the stocks were able to see an apparent multitude of demonstrators spill into High Street, with a very familiar blonde-haired, blue-eyed thirteen-year-old girl in the lead. That sight caused her mother to gasp, "Is it really possible?" and then the burly blacksmith was smashing the locks that held us in the stocks, and we were free to throw our arms around Sara and gaze in wonder at all the people who had come to protest on behalf of Christmas.

"Sara is responsible for this," John Mason shouted to us.

"So many people, Sara," I cried as I took my turn hugging her.

"Oh, there are many more, Auntie Layla," she replied, and as we hugged I saw over her shoulder that thousands of men, women, and children were pouring into the High Street marketplace from every direction.

"I have to go do some things," Sara said, causing me to reluctantly let her out of my embrace. "We want our demonstration to be efficient as well as peaceful."

Her parents and I watched in wonder as this painfully shy child stood in front of ten thousand people and led them in singing "We Wish You a Merry Christmas" so loudly that the sound must have echoed inside the fine brick home where the mayor of Canterbury was cowering.

"It's a Christmas miracle!" Elizabeth Hayes exclaimed. "Everything is going to be perfect." But Arthur nudged me with his elbow and pointed. One of the Trained Band had mounted a horse and was galloping away through the West Gate.

"He's off for reinforcements, Layla," Arthur said. "The protest isn't successful yet." Everyone else, it seemed, was singing, and I wondered what would happen next.

Twenty-three

For about an hour, everything went according to plan. Arthur suggested that we set our own sentries at each of the six city gates, so that reinforcements from the Trained Band couldn't storm in and take us by surprise. This was done—those few dozen Trained Band members already inside the walls of Canterbury were so overwhelmed by the number of demonstrators that they simply leaned on their muskets and watched as we marched and sang. Mayor Sabine, apparently, had no intention of coming back outside his house. Our thousands of protestors were behaving admirably. They sang Christmas carols, marched along all the main streets chanting "God bless Christmas," and courteously requested those merchants who had their shops open for business to please close their doors in honor of the birth of Jesus.

Most of the shopkeepers were happy to comply. They, too, loved Christmas, and only were working that day because Mayor Sabine had ordered them to do so. Perhaps a dozen others, mostly Puritans whose stores were owned by the mayor, haughtily refused to close. Because the purpose of our march was to support the right of anyone to believe as he or she wished, we took no further action. If they wanted to remain open for business on

Christmas Day, this was their perogative—just as it was our perogative to celebrate the holiday we loved so much.

Initially, Arthur, Elizabeth, Alan, and I were kept in the middle of the protestors. Everyone was worried that the mayor and his soldiers would try to recapture us. But it soon became clear that we were in no immediate danger, and, besides, Arthur simply couldn't resist joining Sara and John Mason at the head of the marchers. I found myself there, too, with Alan and Elizabeth not far behind.

It was grand fun to go up and down Canterbury's streets, singing carols and seeing the smiling faces of city residents who suddenly realized that it might be possible to keep the holiday as an important part of their lives. The sun was shining, we were out of the dungeon, and it was Christmas! So an hour flew by, and Arthur whispered to me that it was now time to conclude.

"I'm rather surprised that more of the Trained Band hasn't arrived here already," he murmured in my ear. "I wonder what is keeping them." We didn't know until later that our Christmas protest wasn't the only one that day. In towns like Ipswich and Oxford, there were smaller but still effective demonstrations by working-class people who wanted their beloved holiday back. Some Trained Band troops were on their way to those places. In London, the Lord Mayor had another protest to quell. Canterbury's, though, dwarfed all the others, and it obviously was only a matter of time before more soldiers reached the city. Mayor Sabine had hopefully learned a permanent lesson, our protest had been potent but peaceful, and Arthur was right—we needed to go.

"I'm the one to give the signal, Auntie Layla," Sara called to me, and I was struck by how happy she looked, how excited. She raised her arms high in the air and waved. John Mason and our other captains all along the line of the march started shouting, "Disperse! Disperse!"

But then things began to go wrong. We'd set sentries at all six entrances to the city, and at this exact moment the ones at the North Gate shouted, "Soldiers coming! Maybe a thousand!" and that caused great concern among our number, though there was really no reason to panic. Even if a thousand Trained Band troops really were coming, we still outnumbered them ten to one. They could hardly arrest us all. But instead of filing quickly through the other five city gates and heading for their homes, almost everyone followed a natural instinct of gathering again as a large group in the town marketplace, while the North Gate sentries swung the heavy wooden doors closed and barred them from the inside. Arthur, Sara, Alan, Elizabeth, John Mason, and I tried to tell everyone to just remain calm and go home as we had planned, but instead thousands of voices suddenly raised again in "We Wish You a Merry Christmas," with the addition now of percussion—the soldiers were pounding on the North Gate and loudly demanding to be let in.

The man with the proclamation produced a hammer and nails. He ran to the mayor's house and tacked the thick packet of papers on its heavy wooden door. Then some of the teenaged marchers were overcome by youthful exuberance. Two footballs were produced, and a wild game broke out, with boys running and kicking the ball and shouting out friendly insults to one another. One of the footballs, kicked crookedly, bounced through the door of a dry goods shop that had remained open, and a dozen of the players charged in after it, accidentally knocking over some display shelves. Bolts of cloth rolled into the street, and the Puritan shopkeeper ran after them, shrieking that criminals were destroying his store. The crowd outside was between carols, and so his cries were clearly audible to the soldiers outside the North Gate, who understandably assumed that a mob was rioting inside the walls. They stopped banging on the gate, took up axes, and began knocking it down instead. Afterward, the Puritans would claim that pro-Christmas rioters not only broke down the gate, but burned it, too. Nothing was burned in Canterbury that day, but the rumor has persisted ever since.

The sounds of the wooden gate cracking apart frightened our demonstrators, who now expected to be attacked by the soldiers any minute. Despite instructions to remain calm from Arthur and me, some reached down for stones to throw or lengths of wood to use as clubs. Then the gate broke open and a long column of Trained Band forces marched in, all of them armed with muskets or heavy cudgels. The newly arrived soldiers seemed stunned at the vast number of demonstrators in the marketplace. Our ten thousand protestors were unnerved by the presence of the soldiers. An open space of about twenty yards separated the two groups, and, with tension mounting, Arthur and I knew something had to be done. We stepped in between. Sara tried to come with us, but her mother, reasserting parental authority, grasped her arm and firmly pulled her back.

The leader of the soldiers came forward to meet us, and identified himself as Colonel John Hewson. "What's the meaning of this unlawful gathering?" he demanded. "How dare you riot like this!" Our demonstrators had fallen silent. Everyone could hear what he said to us, and what we said to him.

"This is a demonstration, not a riot," Arthur corrected. "We have come to celebrate Christmas, which is our right."

"Parliament says different," Colonel Hewson replied. "We heard shouts from someone who'd been attacked. What's that all about?"

The owner of the dry goods shop scurried to the colonel's side. "These ruffians charged into my shop, breaking things and shouting they'd do the same to anyone who didn't join them in celebrating Christmas," he claimed. "I've been savagely beaten, and I demand that you arrest them all!"

"That's not true!" I shouted. "Some of the boys were playing football, and the ball was accidentally kicked through his open shop door, and there was some damage. But nobody did it on purpose, and certainly no one hit or threatened him. He's making that up."

"You'll have to tell it to the courts," Colonel Hewson said. "Quick, now, all those who broke things in this man's shop step forward and surrender." I had to admire the colonel. He was vastly outnumbered, and faced with a very difficult situation. But he was remaining calm, and that, at least, was reassuring.

"No one will come forward," Arthur said firmly. "Colonel, there are perhaps five hundred teenaged boys here today. I doubt this shopkeeper can specifically identify those who, for a few seconds, were inside his store. You know you can't arrest them all. Listen to me, please. I promise you that we will disperse now, and go back to our homes. A collection will be taken up to compensate this man for the goods that were lost, even though he lied about what happened. We'll also raise money to repair the gate your men broke down, if you like. So there will be no permanent loss or damage. You'll get credit for resolving such a potentially dangerous situation, which you would certainly deserve. We can all leave here in peace. What do you say?"

Colonel Hewson looked past us at the thousands of demonstrators milling nervously in the marketplace. He certainly noticed some had stones or sticks in their hands, obviously ready to fight if they thought it was necessary. The colonel was a soldier with enough experience to recognize a good offer when he heard one. He compressed his lips into a tight smile, and nodded.

"That seems like common sense," he said. "If you all go quickly; if, in twenty minutes' time, not one of you is still inside these city walls, then—"

Just as I allowed myself a sigh of relief, the front door to the mayor's fine brick home flew open, and clumsy, heavyset Avery Sabine once again lurched toward the marketplace. Colonel Hewson never finished agreeing to Arthur's proposal, because the mayor interrupted him.

"Colonel! Colonel, I say!" Sabine bellowed. "Shoot these Christmas rioters. Shoot every one!" He shoved his way through the line of Trained Band soldiers, and stood, snorting, by Hewson's shoulder, glaring at Arthur and me.

The colonel said reasonably, "Your honor, these people have just promised to disperse peacefully. They're going to pay for any damages. Let's leave it at that, and be glad we had no bloodshed."

"We *won't* leave it at that!" Sabine blustered. "I'm a man of great influence, and if you don't do your duty here, I'll see you reduced in rank and sent to serve in the loneliest outpost in England! Do what I say! Shoot them all, starting with these two! They were arrested by Blue Richard Culmer last week, along with another man and woman, for planning to incite this terrible riot!" He made a threatening gesture toward Arthur and me. Someone in the ranks of demonstrators behind us, panicking, launched a rock in the mayor's direction. It missed him, and bounced off the leg of a Trained Band soldier. He, in turn, raised his musket and pointed it at the crowd.

"Stop this at once," Arthur shouted. He turned toward our protestors and said, "There must be no violence. None!" Some of our people had their arms raised to throw rocks or swing sticks, but Arthur's air of command was sufficient to make them lower these weapons. Colonel Hewson did the same with his troops. "Muskets down!" he cried.

But Avery Sabine, his courage restored by the presence of armed soldiers, had no further interest in a peaceful conclusion. He snatched a stout club from one of the Trained Band troops, and, swinging it over his head, charged directly at me, probably because I, as a woman, seemed less formidable than Arthur. Alan jumped up in front of me and took Sabine's blow on his arm. The force of it knocked him down. Seeing Alan on the ground, the mayor turned from me, stood over the fallen sailor, and raised his club again, ready to finish him off. Colonel Hewson and Arthur desperately shouted for their respective followers to stand back, and as they did Alan ducked away from the mayor's second blow and regained his feet. Moving nimbly, he yanked the club from Sabine's grasp. Suddenly unarmed, Sabine reverted to his natural cowardice and turned to run. But his clumsiness betrayed him. He tripped over his own feet and sprawled in the street.

Alan Hayes was a kind, decent man. From the day when we first began planning the Christmas Day protest, he had not only understood but insisted on a strict philosophy of nonviolence. But in the last week he had been arrested, along with his wife. He'd been frantic with worry about his daughter. He'd been held prisoner in a dark, smelly dungeon with only stale bread and dirty water for nourishment, and twice he'd been locked into public stocks. Now his arm ached terribly from the mayor's unprovoked attack, and Sabine, the one who'd laughed at the possibility Sara would have to live in the streets, lay fallen before him. Gradually, almost mechanically, Alan raised the club while the mayor cringed at his feet.

It was one of those terrible moments when everything seems to happen in slow motion. Arthur and I both began to rush to Alan's side, desperately wanting to prevent him from clubbing the mayor, which would certainly force Colonel Hewson to order his troops to shoot, which in turn would result in panic and more death when the  demonstrators fought back against the soldiers. But Alan was too far away. I saw the club come up and knew we couldn't reach him in time.

But as the club rose, the door to the mayor's house swung open again. Thirteen-year-old Sophia Sabine raced out and threw herself over the prone form of her father. The sight of the child caused Alan to hesitate. As he stood there uncertainly, Sara pulled out of Elizabeth's grasp and ran to wrap her arms around him.

"No violence, Poppa," she reminded Alan.

Then everything was quiet for a long moment. I remember how, despite the throng all around me in the marketplace, I could hear birds chirping, and the rushing of the Stour River. The Trained Band soldiers shuffled in place, waiting for Colonel Hewson's instructions. Everyone stared at the four figures in front of them—Sophia shielding her father, Sara embracing hers.

Then, fearfully, Mayor Sabine stumbled to his feet. Alan lowered his club. They, too, seemed uncertain what to do next.

Sophia and Sara gazed at each other. Then they both took a step forward and hugged one another tight, tears streaming down their faces.

"Merry Christmas, Sophia," Sara said.

"Merry Christmas, Sara," Sophia replied. She reached out, took her father's arm, and gently led him back into their house. Sara stood looking after them as the door shut. Then she turned, took Alan's hand, and pulled him back toward the rest of the demonstrators. The club dropped at Alan's feet. There was no more anger left in him.

In moments, it seemed, the crowd began to melt away. The protestors quietly walked toward the various city gates that led to the right paths home. The Trained Band lowered their muskets. Colonel Hewson shook Arthur's hand and signaled for his soldiers to form a column.

"You'll see to raising the money for repairs?" he asked.

"I promise," Arthur said.

"That's enough for me," the colonel said. "I don't know what will happen next. You may be wanted in court. Do I have your word of honor you and the other three who were originally under arrest will stay in the area until everything is settled? Good. Then our work here is finished for today."

Arthur smiled and wished the colonel a Merry Christmas. The colonel wished him one back. "I hope your message gets to Parliament loud and clear," he said. "I love Christmas, too!"

Finally, only Arthur, Alan, Elizabeth, Sara, and I stood in the marketplace. All four of us adults looked like quite a sight, since we were all dirty and ragged from our week in prison.

"You need baths!" Sara suggested, reverting in that moment from a poised protest leader to a mischievous thirteen-year-old child. "The smell is making my eyes water!"

"I'll smell *you*, young lady!" her father joked, grabbing Sara and nuzzling her hair while she squealed with laughter. "Well, let's all go home. Arthur, I have no idea of what food we might still have left, but will you join us for Christmas dinner?"

"Please do, Mr. Arthur," Sara added. "It would be so nice if you did."

Arthur's eyes widened in surprise. "Are we friends, now, Sara?" he asked.

"I'm sorry if I seemed rude before, sir," she answered. "From now on, I'm going to try harder not to be so shy."

"Then you've just given us a fine Christmas present, my darling," I said to Sara, and held her hand as the five of us walked happily back to the cottage, singing Christmas carols and feeling thankful for our lives and all the blessings we enjoyed.

After scrubbing ourselves thoroughly with well water and changing into wonderfully clean clothes, we ransacked cupboards and finally assembled a Christmas dinner of dried fruit, potatoes, a few stringy winter vegetables, and fresh water. There was also bread, but Arthur, Alan, Elizabeth, and I had already consumed quite enough bread during our week in prison. We wouldn't want any more for quite a while. Afterward, I produced some candy canes for dessert, and we sang a few more carols. Almost as soon as it was dark, we all felt quite exhausted and were ready for bed. Arthur, who was staying with us for the night, paused as he prepared to go outside for a final washing-up at the well.

"Now, *that* was quite a Christmas!" he declared. By the time he came back inside, everyone else was already asleep.

Twenty-four

istory includes many great events, but very few neat, tidy endings. What happened in Canterbury on December 25, 1647, did save Christmas. It also contributed to the eventual fall of the Puritan government and the restoration of the monarchy in England. But all this took quite a long time. We didn't wake up on December 26 to find everything back the way it was before the king lost his throne and Christmas was abolished.

What we did find was that, sometime during the night, Margaret and Sophia Sabine were whisked off by carriage. Word reached Canterbury later that the mayor's wife and daughter had moved permanently into the family's house in London. Margaret Sabine informed all her new neighbors that Canterbury was no longer a fit place for godly people to live. Sophia Sabine, I suppose, soon did meet a suitable husband, and I hope she enjoyed a long, happy marriage. What a brave girl she was, rushing out to save her father from the clubbing he was about to receive! But I really don't know what happened to Sophia. I do know that she and Sara never saw each other again.

Mayor Sabine stayed behind in Canterbury. It quickly became clear that most of the people there now thought of him as a laughingstock. Whenever he would bellow out commands, nobody listened. His reputation among the Puritan leaders in London suffered, too—all of England heard about the Canterbury Christmas March, and how the city's mayor had acted like such a coward. Avery Sabine never did get the high position in government he had both coveted and expected. Instead, he had to keep operating his Canterbury businesses. Customers came into his mills and shops because it was convenient, not because they respected the owner.

In the spring of 1648, Sabine made one last attempt to regain his local influence. He formally charged Arthur, Alan, Elizabeth, and me with assault. Sabine also brought assault charges against a dozen or so other protestors who he had noticed during the demonstration, John Mason among them, and the man who had nailed the "Christmas and King" proclamation to the mayor's front door was accused by Sabine of treason. But this time, there was no Blue Richard Culmer swooping into Canterbury to arrest us. After our impressive Christmas march, Culmer never came to Canterbury again. He was a cruel man, but also a clever one. He realized his nasty tactics would not be effective anymore in a community where ten thousand people were ready to stand up against him. Instead, Colonel Hewson politely notified us all that we would be tried by a jury of our peers, as traditional English law required. He and his men escorted us—*not* in chains—to Leeds Castle, where we were kept in comfortable quarters rather than cells while the trial took place. Elizabeth arranged for Sara to stay with John Mason's wife. Mayor Sabine testified at the trial that he had been pulled down by Arthur, Elizabeth, Alan, and me and thoroughly beaten by our "hooligans" before he had been able to fight his way to freedom. His ability to make up stories was amazing, but in May the jury unanimously found us all not guilty, and we were free to get on with our lives.

And those lives were different. Elizabeth could no longer work for the Sabines. She had to take a job as a milkmaid on a local farm. She was paid much less, and the work was harder. But she gladly accepted this, saying it had been well worth the sacrifice to speak out on behalf of Christmas. Because his role in the protest had become well known and because Puritans still controlled most of England's shipping business, Alan could not find a place on any crews. So he had to start doing farmwork, too. At least he was no longer away from his wife and daughter on long voyages.

Sara, of course, had no more daily lessons with Sophia. But she did, finally, have lots of friends her own age and that helped ease her sense of losing someone who had been as close to her as a sister.

Just as soon as the jury set me free, I left Canterbury. I had to. I had been there almost six years and hadn't aged a bit. It was very hard to go. I told my friends there that I was going to briefly visit people I knew in Nuremberg, and then finally cross the Atlantic Ocean to reunite with my husband. Alan and Elizabeth told me I was always welcome in their home and that they would miss me very much. Sara cried, and begged me to never forget her. That was an easy promise to make. I had plans for my precious girl. As part of them, I did sail for Germany in the summer of 1648, but I had no intention of making the longer journey to America for some time yet.

Arthur guessed the reason. "You mean to ask Sara if she will become one of our gift-giving companions," he said one night in Nuremberg, where he and Leonardo were helping at the toy factory until they felt the time was right to reopen their factory in London. "That's why you've written to Nicholas that you can't come to the New World immediately."

"She is perfectly qualified to join our company," I replied. "You saw for yourself during the protest that she is brave and intelligent and completely dedicated to Christmas. I would reveal our mission to her now if she weren't still a child. I know if I did, she would come with me immediately, but it would break her parents' hearts to lose her. So I'm waiting until she is completely grown—twenty or twenty-five, let's say. Then she can come with me to America, and we'll join Nicholas and Felix in spreading Christmas joy there."

"What if she doesn't want to go?" Arthur asked. "I know she's told you she dreams of traveling to great cities, but young people do change their minds."

"Sara won't," I said confidently, and I waited. While I did, the events in Canterbury on Christmas Day 1647 had further effects on the future of England.

All over the country, people who were unhappy with heavy-handed Puritan rule took note of the march and how it intimidated their new, rigid rulers. They were also pleased when the grand jury refused to convict the march's leaders of any crimes. Support for King Charles spread to the point that, by the summer of 1648, there was civil war again. It was eventually put down by Oliver Cromwell, who led his army all the way into Scotland and Ireland, ruthlessly beating back opponents until, finally, England was really run by the military rather than Parliament—and Cromwell led the military. I hated the fighting, of course, and was especially grieved when King Charles I was executed in January 1649. It was Oliver Cromwell's idea, and I was so sorry that this essentially decent man had decided it was all right to use such awful tactics to achieve his purposes.

For Oliver Cromwell, afterward, things only got worse. Like King Charles before him, he became frustrated when Parliament wouldn't do exactly as he wanted. When its members voted to keep themselves in office rather than schedule elections, Cromwell dissolved Parliament and ended up creating a new one composed entirely of his own trusted supporters. These included the street preacher Praise-God Barebone, and the group became known as "Barebone's Parliament." They really had no power. Cromwell was named Lord Protector of England. He could have called himself the king, but that office had been legally abolished in 1649.

Oliver Cromwell tried hard to rule fairly, based on his religious and political beliefs. Non-Puritans like Catholics and Jews were allowed to quietly worship as they pleased, though they were given no power in Cromwell's government. Cromwell tried to establish schools for working-class children and to make laws based on the best interests of everyone instead of just the rich. He never wavered in his hatred of Christmas, and, while he reigned, celebrating it was still against the law. But, after what we did in Canterbury, there were no more threats of punishment for those who wanted to sing carols or feast on goose or exchange gifts in the privacy of their homes. Parliament couldn't risk more rebellion. The Puritans could, and did, pretend they had ended Christmas forever because there was no longer singing in the streets, and because many shops remained open on Christmas Day. But everyone knew better. Still, without public festivities there was a difference. We had managed to *save* Christmas, but it would be quite a long time before it was entirely restored as a wonderful holiday.

The anti-Christmas laws remained in partial effect until 1660. When Oliver Cromwell died in 1658, Puritan rule was highly unpopular with most of the English people. Cromwell was succeeded as Lord Protector by his son Richard, but Richard had little of his father's charisma and determination. Two years later, he stepped down and Parliament invited Prince Charles, the oldest son of the former king and queen, to come back to England and rule. King Charles II immediately announced "the Restoration," which effectively abolished all the laws passed by the Puritans.

So, celebrating Christmas, in private *and* in public, was once again perfectly legal. But, for more than another one hundred and fifty years the magic and wonder of the holiday didn't entirely return to England. Many business owners *liked* the idea of their employees having to come to work on December 25, instead of enjoying a paid holiday. Working-class people still felt intimidated by the long years of holiday oppression. Arthur returned to London and reopened the toy factory there, since enough families once again allowed their children to receive gifts from Father Christmas. But no more happy crowds marched through cities singing and playing games and calling on their richest neighbors to share holiday snacks. Most people only dared to celebrate the holiday in their homes. And not all of Britain enjoyed even that limited pleasure. Christmas was not officially restored as a full holiday in Scotland until 1958. So, while Christmas flourished across the English Channel in Europe, it remained almost a halfhearted holiday for many in England until two important events.

First, in 1840, England's young queen Victoria married a German prince named Albert. Albert loved all Germany's wonderful Christmas traditions, including caroling in the streets, church services thanking God for sending his son, and even Christmas trees. With their queen encouraging Christmas celebrations, people in England began to openly enjoy the holiday. Then, in 1843, a fine British author named Charles Dickens published a short novel called *A Christmas Carol*. (I'm glad to say my husband and the rest of our company played a part in this; that story is included in Nicholas's book.) Mr. Dickens's amazing tale of an old miser named Scrooge and a crippled boy named Tiny Tim was a sensation all over the country. Between Prince Albert and *A Christmas Carol,* by 1844 Christmas in England was once again a time of great happiness, even for the poorest people.

By then, of course, I had been reunited with my husband for almost one and a half centuries. But Sara was not with us.

After I left Canterbury, I stayed with Attila and the others in Nuremberg. Several times each year, I would go back to England, and, from a distance, feel my heart swell with pride as I watched my beloved girl continue to grow up. Sara was so intelligent, so *good*! Though, for the time being, I could not let her see me, I still could enjoy being near her. When she was sixteen, she started a free school for farm girls, teaching them to read and write and do sums. Only three or four came at first, for it was unusual for girls to learn these things. But they told their friends, and more girls came, until finally Sara was giving lessons to a hundred. This was, I knew, more proof that Sara not only deserved but needed to join our gift-giving mission. If she took so much pleasure in helping a hundred children, how much more delightful she would find bringing gifts and hope to hundreds of thousands! I decided I would reveal myself and our secrets to her when she was twenty. I was anxious to be with her again, and also anxious to join Nicholas in America. When I arrived with Sara, it would be like presenting my wonderful husband with a grown daughter! He would love her as much as I did, I knew.

But when Sara was nineteen, she met a farm boy named Robert. Suddenly, I could tell, she dreamed of something other than travel and adventure. A home and a family of her own became what Sara truly wanted. She married Robert, and they had five children, four daughters and a son. I knew then that I could never ask Sara to come join us. She would not want to be separated from her husband and children. I settled, over the next forty years, for watching her whenever I could. I personally delivered Christmas presents to her son, Michael, and to her daughters. The three youngest were Elizabeth, Gabriella, and Rose. The oldest girl, the first child born to Sara, was named Layla.

Sara lived a fine, full life, using her many talents to benefit others. She was a loving wife and mother, and a doting grandmother when her children married and had families of their own. As I watched her grow old, I couldn't help regretting what might have been. How I would have loved to have had my girl with me forever! But I had no right to force what I wanted on Sara, just as Oliver Cromwell and the Puritans had no right to force the abolition of Christmas on England. Instead, the most important thing was that Sara was happy. I reminded myself of this in late 1699, when she was buried in a Canterbury cemetery. More than a thousand people came to the service, many of them middle-aged women she had taught to read and write. After everyone else had left, I approached her grave and left on it a brightly colored candy cane. Then I booked passage on a ship to America, where I rejoined my husband, Nicholas, in 1700 after eighty years of separation. Until now, only he and Arthur knew about what really happened at the Canterbury March—and about Sara.

Now you have heard the story, too, and I want to ask you to do something. If you love Christmas, if you really cherish the hope and joy that the day can bring to everyone, spend just a moment each December 25 remembering those who made great sacrifices to preserve the holiday despite the efforts of its misguided enemies to destroy it. Instead of scorning someone who makes fun of Santa Claus and gifts and Christmas carols, invite him or her into your home to share genuine holiday happiness. Christmas will never be a perfect holiday, because people are not perfect. But, celebrated in the right spirit, it is as close to perfection as anything on this earth can ever be.

And, perhaps, when you see a candy cane, you will think of Sara and the Canterbury Christmas March. I always do.

Lars's Candy Cane Pie

This is a perfect holiday dessert, and everybody's favorite here at the North Pole. Besides being delicious, it's quick and very easy to fix.

1 8- or 9-inch pastry shell
12 candy canes
3 large eggs
1 14-ounce can sweetened condensed milk
¼ teaspoon cream of tartar
⅓ cup sugar
½ teaspoon vanilla extract

1. Bake a pastry shell in an 8- or 9-inch pie plate. We use a refrigerated pie crust we pick up at the North Pole Grocery, and bake according to directions on its package. If you like, feel free to use your own favorite pie crust recipe. Place the cooked and slightly browned pie shell on a cooling rack. Lower your oven temperature to 350° F.

2. While the pie crust is cooking, crush the candy canes into very, very small pieces and set aside for use later. We use a food processor so

there's less mess, but you might have more fun placing them inside a strong, sealed food storage bag and crushing them with a rolling pin or even a small hammer.

3. Separate the eggs, placing the yolks in a small saucepan and the whites in a medium mixing bowl. Set both aside.

4. Add the sweetened condensed milk to the egg yolks in the saucepan. Stir the mixture over medium heat until it begins to thicken—which should happen before it boils! The longer you heat this mixture, the firmer your pie filling will be. Remove the mixture from the heat.

5. For the pie meringue, beat the egg whites in a bowl until soft peaks form. With your mixer still running, add the cream of tartar, then slowly add the sugar (about one tablespoon at a time). Now beat until stiff peaks form. Finally, beat in the vanilla extract.

6. Fold about two-thirds of the candy cane pieces into the egg yolk mixture in the saucepan. Don't overstir. If you do, the candy pieces will dissolve, which is all right, but the pie looks niftier when it's speckled throughout with little bits of candy cane. Now, pour this mixture into the baked pie crust.

7. Pile the meringue on top of the pie, being careful to seal the edges by spreading the meringue to the edges of the crust. Sprinkle the remaining candy cane bits on top of the meringue.

8. Bake the pie for 12 to 15 minutes, or until the top of the meringue is lightly browned. Let the pie cool before eating.

If you have extra candy canes, you can always serve this pie with a candy cane garnish! And here at the North Pole, we all agree it tastes best with a cup of coffee or a glass of very cold milk.

Merry Christmas!

Acknowledgments

Thanks above all, as usual, to Sara Carder, my editor. I'm also grateful to Andrea Ahles Koos, researcher *extraordinaire*; Jim Donovan, a fine literary agent; Joel Fotinos; Ken Siman; Katie Grinch; Robert I. Fernandez; Larry "Lars" Wilson; Carlton Stowers; Doug Perry; Felix Higgins; Charles Caple and Marcia Melton; Mary and Charles Rogers; Marilyn Ducksworth; Steve Oppenheim; Michael Barson; Elizabeth Hayes; Brian McLendon; Frank and Dot Lauden; Jim Firth; Del Hillen; Mary Arendes; Molly Frisinger; Sophia Choi for special inspiration, unintentional though it might have been; and Iris Chang, a brave, brilliant woman whose memory will always inspire those who were lucky enough to know her.

Everything I write is always for Nora, Adam, and Grant.

Let me offer my sincere thanks to everyone who read *The Autobiography of Santa Claus* and enjoyed it enough to also read this sequel. I wish you all a very Merry Christmas, this year and forever.

Further Reading

YOU CAN READ MORE about Oliver Cromwell, King Charles I, the British Civil War, Blue Richard Culmer, Avery Sabine, the London Apprentice Protest, and the Canterbury Christmas March in lots of history books, many of which should be available in your local library. Layla's story includes all the basic facts. Dates and the events taking place on them are accurate. You can get a good start by finding and reading *The British Civil War* by Trevor Royle (Palgrave/Macmillan, 2004); *Elizabeth's London* by Liza Picard (St. Martin's Press, 2003); *The Struggle for Christmas* by Stephen Nissenbaum (Vintage Books, 1996), and that favorite tool of so many historical novelists, Gorton Carruth's *The Encyclopedia of World Facts and Dates* (HarperCollins, 1993). If you don't own a copy, treat yourself to one. Every page is fascinating.

The

GREAT SANTA

SEARCH

FOR FELIX HIGGINS

Lunch is on me.

Foreword

YOU DON'T LIVE as long as I have—more than seventeen hundred years so far, and counting—without becoming something of a philosopher. After all the things I've seen and the people I've met, I've concluded it's true that most problems are really opportunities. Everyone's life includes moments of crisis when everything seems to be going wrong, and we feel discouraged or even helpless. But if we are determined enough, we can find ways to make the best of these situations, and afterward find ourselves happier than we were before. The story I'm about to tell is proof.

Let me set the scene.

Sometimes, during the few quiet moments we have at the North Pole, I reflect on how lucky I've been. Of course, my greatest privilege has been to help so many children all around the world celebrate Christmas, and the other holidays of St. Nicholas Day and Epiphany. The presents that they've received from me and my wonderful friends have always been intended as symbols of caring, a sign that on the most special of holidays someone loved them enough to leave a gift, just as on that happiest of days some two thousand years ago God demonstrated his love for us all with the gift of his son Jesus. I have never meant for my mission to divert attention in any way from that. As Santa Claus, I want to contribute to the celebration without being mistaken for the cause of it.

This is what I have tried to do for many centuries, and I hope I've mostly been successful, though I'm aware that there have always been and will always be those who twist the traditions of Christmas to suit their own selfish purposes. Part of my good fortune is that I've encountered so few of them. Instead, I've known many fine people whose actions were sparked by generosity of spirit, and some of them live and work with me now at the North Pole. You've heard of several: Benjamin Franklin, Amelia Earhart, St. Francis of Assisi, Leonardo da Vinci, Attila the Hun, and Theodore Roosevelt. There are others who should be better known than they are: Sarah Kemble Knight, who wrote the first books about traveling in colonial America, and Bill Pickett, the great African-American cowboy. One has a colorful reputation that has very little to do with the actual facts—King Arthur, who was really a British war chief rather than a crowned head of state. Then there are three dear people whom popular history has never noted at all, because they have never sought the fame they so richly deserve—Willie Skokan, the fine Bohemian craftsman; Felix, the former Roman slave who became my first companion in this gift-giving mission; and Layla, my beloved wife, whose courage and common sense have meant so much to all of us for so very long.

You may be wondering what all this has to do with problems actually being opportunities. Well, in 1841 an acquaintance of mine had an idea that eventually threatened to ruin Santa Claus and the spirit of Christmas altogether. His name was J. W. Parkinson, and he owned a dry-goods store in Philadelphia. Though the story I want to tell is concerned with what happened more than 160 years later, we can trace everything back to J.W.'s plan to drum up a little extra holiday business at his shop. He had no inkling, and would never have believed, that because of his marketing brainstorm the entire nature of Christmas celebrations throughout America would eventually change forever, and that the generous spirit of the holiday and reputation of Santa Claus would one day hang in the balance. Everything I've tried to represent came very close to being destroyed forever.

But it wasn't. In the end, some wonderful people refused to let this happen. In the process, they taught me that "Santa's helpers" are even more numerous than I had realized, and reminded me that the only time it's certain there can't be a happy ending is if we give up trying to make one happen.

I hope you enjoy the story, and learn from it, too. No one, including me, is ever too old to learn.

—Santa Claus
The North Pole

One

don't see why you won't agree, Santa Claus," said J. W. Parkinson, pacing in front of the stone fireplace in the living room of his home. "It would be great fun for you, and extra holiday profit for me. We'd both be benefiting."

"That's just it, my friend," I replied, taking another sip of the delicious hot chocolate he'd just served. "I would enjoy myself, and your general store would sell extra toys. But what about the other merchants in Philadelphia who have toys for sale? Wouldn't they feel you had an unfair advantage because Santa Claus invited children to meet him at J. W. Parkinson's? I know you've promised to use some of the additional income to buy gifts for needy children, but I still can't do it. I love and treat everyone equally, you see. In anything regarding Christmas, I can't favor you over your competitors. I suppose the best way to put it is that Santa Claus doesn't endorse any store or product, and never will."

J.W., a slender middle-aged man with so much nervous energy that he twitched even while sitting down, wasn't willing to accept my decision. Born to a poor German immigrant family shortly after the so-called Revolutionary War freed the American colonies from England, he'd worked hard to earn enough money to open his own store that sold what we then called "dry goods"—mostly clothing, tools, and toys. Once he had his shop, he labored tirelessly to make it successful. J.W. sold products of good quality at reasonable prices and made a point of memorizing all his customers' names so they could be greeted warmly whenever they came in. I'd made his acquaintance when I learned that each Christmas Eve he would personally take sacks of toys and candy into the poorest neighborhoods of Philadelphia, distributing gifts to those children who never dared hope they might celebrate the holiday with presents. Of course, my companions and I had the same mission, and on a worldwide scale, but we always realized we could never brighten the Christmas of every deserving child and so welcomed those kind souls like J.W. who didn't simply sit back and assume it was only Santa's responsibility to provide holiday happiness. As was often the case with those fine people I would personally meet and thank, J.W. recognized me immediately. For almost a dozen years, he had gladly kept our friendship secret. But now, in October of 1841, he'd come up with a new way to encourage Christmas trade at his store, and it involved me making a well-publicized personal appearance there. He'd nail posters to every tree in Philadelphia, J.W. vowed, each urging parents to bring their children to J. W. Parkinson's at noon on December 18, one week before Christmas. There, the little ones would have the thrill of meeting Santa Claus, and at the same time their parents could purchase all the Christmas toys needed— J.W. would have available an especially big selection of dolls, whistles, hoops, and wooden blocks, among other playthings.

"Business has been a bit slow of late, and so I want to do something to stimulate sales," J.W. told me, his eyes flashing with excitement. He was someone who got so worked up about his own ideas that he couldn't understand it when others didn't share his enthusiasm. "I know you like to keep your presence in Cooperstown, New York, a secret"—until we moved to the North Pole in 1913, that was where my friends and I lived and made toys—"but I'll protect your privacy. The children, of course, will be meeting the real Santa, but I'll tell their parents I simply hired a stout bearded man to dress up in red-and-white robes to look like you. They'll never know they were in the same room with the actual Kris Kringle!"

I winced at the word "stout"—"burly" is so much more dignified—and held up my hand in a cautionary gesture.

"So you're not only asking me to endorse a specific store, you're also asking me to lie?" I said, keeping my tone gentle. "I never deceive anyone, J.W. Telling parents that I wasn't who I really am would be untrue."

"Think of the excitement in the eyes of the children you'd meet, Santa," he pleaded, neatly switching the topic to a safer subject. "We've spoken of how you've dedicated your life to children, and yet you never really have the opportunity to spend time with them. You regret that so much, you've said over and over. Well, here's your chance."

"And what of the children who couldn't be at your store that day?" I asked. "If their parents chose to shop somewhere else, wouldn't that mean they didn't have the same opportunity to meet Santa? No, J.W., it's out of the question. Let's not discuss it any further. I have to be leaving for Cooperstown soon, but do you suppose Mrs. Parkinson has some of her tasty home-baked cookies for us to enjoy before I go?"

In fact, she did, and for another half hour J.W. and I chatted about other things—the problems I sometimes had getting the proper feed for my reindeer, his endless efforts to find better brands of canvas work pants that would last farmers through more than one harvest—but I could sense he hadn't given up on his Christmas plan. For the next several weeks, I expected a letter from J.W. to arrive at our isolated farm property in Cooperstown, pleading with me to reconsider. But nothing of the sort came, and by early December I had completely forgotten about it.

Then one afternoon I was just going over my list of toys already in hand for Christmas Eve 1841—we had sufficient dolls crafted and stored in our massive Cooperstown barn, but there weren't half enough wooden tops; with just three weeks to go, we'd have to spend a few extra hours crafting them every day right up to December 24—When my wife, Layla, knocked on the door of my study. I was glad to see her, as always. After almost sixteen centuries of marriage, her smile still makes my heart beat faster. But on this occasion, she wasn't smiling.

"Here is something you need to see," Layla said, handing me a sheet of wrinkled paper. "Your friend J. W. Parkinson is going to have Santa at his store after all."

I put on my reading glasses and examined the paper, which turned out to be a promotional poster. In large letters, it announced *"Kris Kringle in Philadelphia! Bring the little ones to J. W. Parkinson's, 100 North Donovan Street, at noon exactly on December 18. Mr. Kringle himself will visit with the tots while Father and Mother take advantage of our store's unmatched selection of holiday toys. See him arrive down our chimney! Don't be late!"* There was also a cartoon on the poster. It depicted a *very* heavy bearded man in fur-trimmed robes, reaching into a large sack overflowing with toys. On the side of the sack was printed, *"My friends shop at Parkinson's!"*

I felt both frustrated and sad. Despite my refusal, J.W.—a good man, I believed, one who truly loved Christmas and meant no harm to anyone—was doing something that went against everything the holiday was supposed to be about. That was frustrating. The sadness came from knowing trusting children would be introduced to an impostor. Some, I knew, would believe they had truly met Santa Claus—or, in this case, Kris Kringle, a nickname by which I was known in some other parts of the world. Growing up in a German family, J.W. had undoubtedly called me Kris Kringle rather than Santa when he was a child. Now he was promising Kris Kringle to another generation of children. What if this Kringle-in-disguise was so obviously an actor rather than the real Santa that some children who'd come to meet him went away disillusioned, convinced that because he was a fraud, Santa Claus must not exist after all?

"Even though we still have a great deal to do here before Christmas, I'll go to Philadelphia at once and inform J.W. I simply forbid him to do this," I told Layla.

"I think it's too late for that," she replied. "One of our other friends in Philadelphia sent us this and added that the posters were already tacked up all over the city. Thousands of parents will have seen them by now, and many must be already making plans to take their children to J.W.'s store on the eighteenth. Perhaps you should appear as Kris Kringle after all."

"That is something I just cannot do," I said. "Santa Claus by any name does not endorse products or stores. We'll just have to hope that this promotion isn't too disastrous. We'll get the reindeer ready, and I'll fly down to Philadelphia to see what happens for myself."

I didn't go alone. Layla came along, as well as Ben Franklin, who'd lived much of his early life in Philadelphia. Felix, my oldest friend and helper, and historian Sarah Kemble Knight also decided to join us. Sarah was always a useful companion on such trips. In the early 1700s, she'd written the first book about traveling in the American colonies. Sarah had a fine memory for roads and rivers and could always suggest shortcuts that saved the reindeer considerable flying time.

So on the morning of December 18, 1841, the five of us secured ourselves in the sleigh, and our eight great sources of propulsion and flight leaped into the cold winter air and whisked us south. Dasher, Dancer, Prancer, Vixen, Comet, Cupid, Donder, and Blitzen were fine, intelligent animals who responded to my slightest tug on the reins. We flew faster than the human eye could follow and were kept warm by thick robes draped over our shoulders and across our laps. Normally on such trips, my passengers and I would talk and laugh and sing, but this time we spoke very little, and even then in hushed, worried tones. No good, we felt, could come of J.W.'s scheme.

After about fifteen minutes in the air, we spied Philadelphia far below. Though measured against modern-day Philadelphia it would have seemed a messy collection of cabins, dirt streets, and corrals, by the standards of 1841 it was a great city indeed. With almost ninety-four thousand residents, it was the fourth largest in all of America, ranking in population only behind New York City, Baltimore, and New Orleans. Still, the houses and farms on its outskirts dwindled down quickly, so it was no real problem for us to land the sleigh in an isolated area. We scattered some feed for the reindeer to enjoy while they awaited our return. We didn't have to worry about someone stumbling upon them and perhaps taking them away. The reindeer were trained to obey only those of us from the farm in Cooperstown. If any strangers approached, they would fly into the air and hover out of sight until the interlopers were gone.

J.W.'s store was on the west side of the city. Though we could have walked the three or four miles there in less than a minute—traveling much faster than ordinary humans was one of the powers granted to us in our gift-giving mission—we chose instead to stroll at a more ordinary pace. It was about eleven o'clock in the morning, a full hour before "Kris Kringle's" promised arrival.

"Philadelphia was one of the first American cities to pave some of its roads with cobblestones," Ben informed us. "That field over there was where I flew my kite in a thunderstorm to see if lightning carried electricity."

"I'll bet you were shocked to find out that it did!" Felix joked.

As soon as we reached the main part of town, we saw J.W.'s posters everywhere. They were tacked to trees and pasted on walls. No modern-day media like radio and television and the Internet existed, so posters were the accustomed means of promoting civic events. If you wanted people to know about some program or other, you put up as many posters as possible and hoped passersby would notice them.

As Layla had predicted, many people had seen J.W.'s posters. When we neared Parkinson's, we saw a crowd of several hundred all trying to get in the front door at once. Grown men and women herded ahead of them children who were shrieking with excitement. J.W.'s employees were trying in vain to get everyone lined up neatly.

"I expect they'll have to call the police to come and get this under control," Sarah said. "Some of those children may be knocked down by accident. How awful!"

Then J.W. himself emerged from the store, standing on its front porch and waving his arms to get everyone's attention. His costume alone could have accomplished that—J.W., who normally dressed quite conservatively, was wearing a long bright green coat and purple trousers, and on his head was a red stocking cap with white tassel. He must have ordered the clothes especially.

"I'm J.W., one of Kris Kringle's assistants, and I request that you all calm down," he shouted. "Our Christmas friend is on his way here"—there was loud cheering from all the assembled children and many of the grown-ups—"and if everyone will just give us some room, you'll be able to watch him arrive. Stand back, and in a few minutes keep a careful eye on the roof. Do you see the chimney there? Do you remember how Kris Kringle, or Santa if you prefer calling him that, likes to come into houses on Christmas Eve? Boys and girls, get ready to meet your hero! Mothers and fathers, prepare to purchase some of the best toy bargains in Philadelphia!" Then J.W. disappeared back into his shop. His employees were now able to convince the crowd to form a semicircle in front of the store, backed far enough away from the porch to have a good view of the roof.

"He means to have this false Kris Kringle jump down that chimney," Ben said. "He's keeping the crowd in front of the store because he's going to get him up there from the back. Let's go see."

My friends and I were always able to blend in when we visited cities. We dressed like everyone else and, without my famous red robes trimmed with white, no one ever seemed to realize this broadly built, white-bearded man was anyone other than an ordinary fellow. So the five of us edged our way along the fringes of the crowd to where J.W.'s workers stood to prevent anyone from going around to the back of the store. One of them stepped up and said, "Don't go any farther, please," but Layla calmly told her, "We're friends of Mr. Parkinson, and he invited my husband to be part of this," which was certainly true.

Behind the store, J.W. stood beside a heavy ladder that had been propped up against the back wall. A tent was pitched a few dozen feet away; inside we could hear someone grumbling about boots not fitting properly, and where was the cushion to be worn under his robes?

"No one is to come back here—wait! Santa, it's you!" J.W. blurted. "Have you decided to appear after all? The other fellow I've hired can just step aside!"

"I haven't changed my mind," I said firmly. "I'm sorry you haven't changed yours. You're about to do a terrible thing, old friend. It isn't too late to call this off."

"But it is, Santa," J.W. replied. "Did you see all the people out in front? This is going to be a great success. You'll see. Christmas and Kris Kringle will be more popular than ever!"

Layla placed her hand on my arm, a signal not to continue the debate.

"He's going to go through with this," she whispered. "All we can do now is watch what happens."

One of J.W.'s employees hustled up and informed him that it was noon: "The crowd is just *bristling* with anticipation, Mr. Parkinson," he said.

"Then let's give the people what they want!" J.W. responded, his voice cracking from excitement or a guilty conscience or some combination of the two. "Mr. Kringle! You, in the tent! It's time!"

There was rustling behind the tent's canvas walls, and then the front flap flipped open. A short, portly man in expensive red robes emerged. His hair and beard were white, but some of the talcum powder used to make them so hung in a cloud above his head. He was jamming a pillow underneath his robes to give the appearance of additional stoutness.

"If I fall off the roof, I'll take you to court," he growled at J.W. "You never told me a chimney was involved."

"It will all be fine, Kris Kringle," J.W. promised. "Remember, you must be jolly. I won't pay you the other half of your fee if you're not." He gently pushed the impostor over to the ladder. "Go tell the people that Kris Kringle is about to appear," he instructed a subordinate, who disappeared around the corner. Moments later, a huge cheer was raised by the crowd.

The false Kris Kringle gingerly climbed the ladder, hauling along a massive, toy-filled sack with *"My friends shop at Parkinson's"* printed on the side. As he did, J.W. hustled around to the front of his store. We followed.

"Boys and girls, look at the roof!" he shouted. "He's coming . . . he's coming . . . *here he is!*"

The impostor in red robes had indeed appeared. He'd evidently had some trouble transferring his own weight and the hefty sack from the ladder to the roof itself, for he teetered for a moment before regaining full balance by throwing his free arm around the wide chimney. In doing so, he almost lost his grip on the sack of toys, and in his frantic attempt to get a firm new grip on the sack he nearly let go of the chimney, which might have resulted in a spectacular fall to the ground.

But he didn't fall, and, once confident that he wasn't about to tumble, the fraudulent Kris Kringle nodded to the crowd below. The response was loud cheering, and I began to hope that things might conclude without any real damage to the image of Santa and the beliefs of children. But then J.W. shouted out again.

"Now it's time to enter the store, everyone!" he instructed loudly. "After all, when Kris Kringle slides down a chimney, he ends up inside rather than out! Hurry, now—he's about to come down!"

This encouraged a mass rush to the front door of the shop, which of course wasn't wide enough to accommodate so many people at once. There was much resulting confusion, with parents grumbling and children screeching and J.W. and his employees trying very hard to keep things as orderly as possible. At least the struggle to get inside distracted onlookers from the stumblings of the red-robed figure on the roof, but the five of us from Cooperstown had stayed back from the crush and so kept looking up at him with a sense of fascinated horror.

As I had learned over several centuries, "sliding down a chimney" is not the easiest thing to do. Even the largest fireplaces have relatively narrow chimneys through which smoke is meant to escape; they have never been built with the idea that a full-grown man—all right, a somewhat overweight man—might attempt to slide down them. Add a large sack of toys to the mix and it's quite easy to get stuck before you've dropped even a few feet. That's why I have always preferred using doors or windows. Cooperative parents usually make available to me more convenient ways than chimneys to get in and leave my gifts. But J.W. obviously wanted Kris Kringle to come into his store by the chimney route and no other, so his impostor Santa tried to slide down. He only managed to lower himself as far as his waist before getting stuck tight. Standing beside me, Layla and Sarah dissolved into helpless giggling; Felix and Ben chuckled, too, but I felt sorry for the fellow. I'd gotten stuck in a few chimneys myself over the years.

"Take a deep breath and suck in your stomach!" I called out helpfully. "Hold your toy sack over your head!"

He looked down at me, and even at that distance I could see the panic in his eyes. "I'm sucking in my stomach and I'm still stuck!" he cried, and I was glad all the children had finally gotten inside J.W.'s store so they couldn't hear the man they thought was me sounding so forlorn.

"Tell him to pull the cushion out from under his robe," Layla whispered, and that's what I did. He managed with great difficulty to push one arm down between the chimney wall and his body; we watched his shoulder twitch as he struggled to yank the cushion free. Evidently he succeeded, for suddenly his whole body dropped down out of sight, and the sack of toys fell right behind, with man and sack tumbling, I was certain, onto the hard floor of the fireplace itself. I hoped for the fraudulent Santa's sake that J. W. had remembered to put out the fire.

We hurried inside to find that he had—but he'd forgotten to provide some sort of padding to cushion "Kris Kringle's" fall, so the unfortunate fellow had the wind knocked out of him on impact. The toy sack landed on top of his head, knocking his red tassled hat askew and littering the floor by the fireplace with tin whistles and soft cloth dolls. Some of the crowd gasped in concern, but J. W. announced cheerfully, "In just a moment, Kris Kringle will sit on that bench over there and visit with the kiddies! Parents, this way to a display of the finest toys in all of Philadelphia!" All the mothers and fathers trooped off obediently, though Layla, Ben, Felix, Sarah, and I stayed behind. The poor pretend gift-giver was helped to the bench by a pair of J. W.'s employees, dragging his half-empty toy sack behind him while another of J. W.'s workers scurried to pick up the other scattered playthings. His red robes were streaked with soot—J. W. had also forgotten to have the chimney cleaned beforehand—one elbow of his costume was torn, and, without the cushion at his waist, the red robes hung loosely. White powder still smoked from his hair and beard. I was certain that none of the children could now believe he was really me.

And yet it seemed that all of them did. Later, Layla reminded me how people of all ages usually see whatever it is they expect: "Because they so badly wanted to meet you, Santa, it didn't matter that robes were dirty or a beard was obviously dark rather than white. The boys and girls were just thrilled that Santa in any form was there for them to see and talk to and perhaps touch."

The frazzled fellow pretending to be Kris Kringle slumped on the bench and eyed the children surrounding him with the same nervousness that a mouse might have exhibited in the presence of a pack of lively cats. The boys and girls, in turn, wriggled with excitement and waited for their beloved Christmas friend to say or do something.

After perhaps two full minutes of silence, one little girl asked, "Is your name Kris Kringle or Santa Claus? I've heard people call you both."

The proper answer would have been that his name was Santa to some and Kris Kringle to others, and that either name was entirely acceptable to him, but the bruised, sooty impostor was apparently not educated enough in the history of Christmas to realize this.

"Mr. Parkinson calls me Kris Kringle," he replied. "I guess that's good enough for me."

"Where are your reindeer?" a boy wanted to know.

"I came by wagon today."

"But why not fly with the reindeer?"

"One of them had a cold."

"Which one?"

"Um." The false Kris Kringle's brow furrowed. "Remind me of their names."

I was positive the children would realize the terrible fraud being perpetrated—how could Kris Kringle or Santa Claus not remember the names of his faithful reindeer friends? Instead, they laughed in delight and started calling out "Dasher!" and "Cupid!" and "Blitzen!," all eight names in every possible order, until finally the pretender said, "It's the first one."

This vague response luckily satisfied the children on the topic of reindeer, but of course they had many more questions—about where Kris Kringle lived, how he decided which children got what toys, and, over and over, what each individual child there at Parkinson's might expect to find in his or her stocking on Christmas morning. In every instance, the fellow pretending to be me had no plausible response.

"This would be the perfect time to tell them that presents are really the least important part of Christmas," I muttered to Layla. "He should explain that the real pleasure of the holiday comes from giving thanks to God for sending Jesus and from the companionship and love of family and friends!"

And perhaps he would have said something of the sort. I doubt it, but it might have happened. Instead, J.W. suddenly burst back into the room, with package-laden parents trailing behind him.

"Boys and girls, it's time for dear Kris Kringle to return to his secret toy factory!" J.W. said. "He's most pleased to have met you, and now you must bid him farewell. When you have, you may want to visit the toy displays here to make certain your mothers and fathers know exactly what you want Kris Kringle to bring you on Christmas Eve!"

Having been expertly goaded into a frenzy of greed, all but one of the youngsters galloped away to the far side of the store, where shelves groaned under the weight of almost every toy imaginable. But one boy, a rather pale child with red hair and countless freckles, stayed where he was.

"Mr. Kringle is leaving now, sonny," J.W. said. "Wave good-bye, and go help your parents look at the toys."

The youngster didn't budge. He pulled one of the wrinkled event posters out of his pocket, along with a pencil. "I want his autograph," he said. In 1841, autograph-collecting wasn't the widespread hobby it would later become, but some people did like to ask famous individuals to sign their names as keepsakes. The fake Kris Kringle tried to inch toward the door and escape, but J.W. caught him by the elbow.

"I'm sure he'd be delighted to oblige," J.W. said, and swung the reluctant fraud back toward the boy. The child held out the poster and pencil. The impostor took them, scribbled, and handed them back. Then he rushed through a back door, with J.W. right behind.

"Gosh," the freckled boy sighed. "I got his signature."

"May I see your poster?" I asked. He handed it over. Underneath the cartoon, there was scrawled "Cris Cringle," with capital *C*s where *K*s should have been.

"The fool can't even spell!" I grumbled, and the little boy looked alarmed. Layla took the poster from me and handed it back to him, saying, "How wonderful for you! Merry Christmas!" He ran off, brandishing the paper.

Layla, Ben, Felix, Sarah, and I went out the same back door where J.W. and his impostor had exited. That unfortunate fellow had already disappeared, undoubtedly hoping to make his getaway before any more children asked awkward questions. J.W. was folding up the torn, soot-stained robes.

"I suppose the costume shop will charge me extra, since these things will have to be washed and mended," he said. "Well, Santa, the children were excited and their parents are buying almost every toy in my shop. Would you agree this was a great success?"

"Absolutely not, J.W." I said, and proceeded to tell my well-meaning friend gently but firmly about the pretend Kris Kringle's foolish answers in response to the children's questions, and how he couldn't even spell his name correctly when asked for an autograph. "Is any amount of profit worth the risk of even one child having his or her belief in Santa Claus ruined forever? Even if that didn't happen today, it could have, and it will surely happen sooner or later if you host any more of these appearances by men pretending to be me."

"What if I made certain the next Kris Kringle I hired was a better actor who knew the names of all eight reindeer?" J.W. asked. "I admit I didn't choose this first one very carefully, but next time I would know better."

"He still wouldn't be the real Santa," I said. "Look into your heart instead of your wallet, old friend. Do you truly think what you did today was right?"

J.W. looked first indignant, then sorrowful. He was, as I have noted, a decent man who loved Christmas for the best of reasons.

"You're right, Santa Claus," he said. "The fellow I hired to portray you was simply disgraceful, and it's a mercy none of the children in my store today had their belief in you ruined. You have my word that until the *real* Santa agrees to appear, I'll never attempt such a thing again."

I hugged him—after all, no lasting harm had apparently been done—and then my companions and I returned to where the reindeer were waiting. Soon afterward, we were back in Cooperstown, enjoying a delicious meal of fried chicken.

"We still need a thousand more wooden tops, and Leonardo predicts there will be snowstorms along the East Coast on Christmas Eve, but at least we don't have to worry about impostor Santas any longer," I said, finishing my fourth piece of chicken and wondering if Layla would notice me reaching for a fifth.

"Don't sound so certain," my wife responded as she moved the chicken platter just beyond my reach. "Offering the chance to meet Santa is a fool-proof way for merchants to bring extra holiday customers into their shops. Some Christmas season in the future, ten stores might simultaneously present the 'real' Santa, or even a hundred. What will we do then?"

I thought for several moments before replying: "I have no idea."

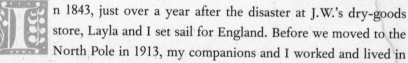n 1843, just over a year after the disaster at J.W.'s dry-goods store, Layla and I set sail for England. Before we moved to the North Pole in 1913, my companions and I worked and lived in three different locations—Cooperstown in America, Nuremberg in Germany, and London in England. Because our gift-giving mission had grown so dramatically, it was impossible for us to maintain a single gigantic toy-making facility in secret until Leonardo da Vinci designed what he accurately described as "a self-contained environment" beneath the snows of the most isolated spot on the planet.

But prior to that, we had the three separate toy factories. Arthur was in charge in London; Attila ran the operation in Nuremberg; Felix kept an eye on things in Cooperstown; and Layla and I were free to live and work in turns at each facility.

We decided to go to London for a while because Christmas in England still had not recovered from events in the 1640s, when the king was driven from his throne. The antiholiday Puritans took control of British government and banned Christmas forever. They didn't succeed—my wonderful wife Layla had much to do with that—and by 1660 the monarchy was restored and Christmas was again a legal holiday. But much of the traditional spirit had been lost. Most English business owners insisted that their employees come to work as usual on December 25. A nation that had long loved singing carols and exchanging gifts and feasting on holiday goose and pudding now hardly celebrated Christmas at all.

So in 1843 Layla and I crossed the Atlantic Ocean. In London we encouraged a fine author named Charles Dickens to write a short holiday story he called *A Christmas Carol*. The tale of how miserly, holiday-hating Ebenezer Scrooge learned to appreciate all the wonderful things Christmas stood for warmed the hearts of everyone in England. At the same time, the young English queen Victoria married Prince Albert of Germany, and Albert, like most of his countrymen, not only loved Christmas but celebrated it in public with all his heart. He introduced Christmas trees to England; this in turn encouraged people to place gifts under them and children to hang their stockings again. As Father Christmas—this is what British children called me—I was thrilled to be part of the renewed Christmas enthusiasm that spread to every part of the nation.

Of course, I didn't lose touch with my friends back in America. The reason I was able to concentrate on fully restoring Christmas in England was that belief in Santa Claus had finally taken hold in the United States. It had been quite a tussle to bring this about—the English Puritans had originally banned celebrating Christmas in their American colonies, too—but thanks in great part to the stories of Washington Irving and *A Visit from St. Nicholas* (later known as *'Twas the Night Before Christmas*) by Clement Clark Moore, in America children and their parents gradually embraced the idea of my gift-giving mission. On Christmas Eve, Felix and my other American-based companions traveled thousands of happy miles, leaving gifts for sleeping boys and girls to discover in the morning. Now, you may wonder why I was so opposed to J. W. Parkinson hiring someone to pretend to be me, yet had no problem with my friends acting in my stead. It's quite simple: they did their good deeds at night and in secret. They did not dress up in red robes and try to trick children into believing they were Santa. Any reindeer hoofbeats detected on rooftops were, however, quite real. My flying sleigh was part of Christmas tradition in America, but not yet in other parts of the world. So Dasher and the other seven reindeer stayed in Cooperstown, and on Christmas Eve they whisked Felix through the skies in my place.

Layla and I did not hurry back to America. In our many centuries of gift-giving, we had spent a considerable amount of time in England. Because of her ultimately successful efforts to prevent Christmas from being lost to that lovely green land forever, Layla had grown to love the country in a very special way. So we spent a few extra years revisiting places that had unique meaning for us, like the old barn where we had discovered the wounded Arthur around 500 A.D., and the town square in Canterbury where in 1647 Layla and ten thousand brave working-class men, women, and children defied Parliament and declared they would keep celebrating Christmas whether the Puritans in power liked it or not.

Letters from Felix back in America assured us that acceptance there of Santa Claus, as well as love for and celebration of Christmas, continued to flourish. I frowned a little when I read J. W. Parkinson was honoring the basic truth of the promise he made, but not the spirit. After 1841, he did not hire impersonators to pretend they were me. But he did annually festoon his dry-goods store with banners proclaiming that the shop was *"Kriss Kringle Headquarters"*—with the extra *s* added to "Kris," it was obvious J.W. could not spell any better than the fraud he had originally hired to portray me. I considered returning to Philadelphia to confront J.W., but I already knew how he would respond. He'd promised not to hire any more false Santas, and he hadn't. Nothing had been promised about pretending I endorsed his store by having my "headquarters" there. Such borderline deceptions are all too common, I'm afraid. Out of obligation rather than any hope he'd change his ways, I planned to see J.W. after I returned to America and ask him again to keep any form of direct or indirect Santa endorsement out of his holiday advertising, but when Layla and I finally did sail back to the United States in the spring of 1860, we were told that J.W. had recently passed away. Since then, I have remembered him with qualified affection. He loved Christmas and he generously helped poor children have happy memories of the holiday. But he also used the joy and symbols of Christmas for his own financial benefit. Of course, he was certainly not the last to do this.

Layla and I had a lovely reunion with our friends in Cooperstown. We drank hot chocolate, took the sleigh and reindeer out for lengthy spins, and caught up on all the local and national news. Some of it was very bad, and not unexpected. The young American nation was being torn apart by racial and political strife. Many white residents of Southern states owned African-American slaves. In the Northern states, slavery was not only illegal but also considered immoral. A political compromise temporarily prevented war; new states joining the Union were alternately "free" and "slave." When pressure mounted from Northern politicians to end slavery forever, Southern leaders promised they would leave the Union rather than give up their right to own slaves if they pleased. They meant it.

All of us in Cooperstown hated the concept of slavery. Felix in particular despised the idea of any human being owning another—he knew first-hand the horror of being considered property rather than a person, since he had been a Roman slave.

Civil war did break out, and the loss of lives and destruction of property was awful. It took four years for the North, which had more citizens and manufacturing plants—which meant more soldiers and weapons—to wear down the South and free slaves in America forever. It wasn't the end of slavery everywhere in the world, sad to say. In some parts of this planet, slavery still endures in various forms. But it was eradicated in America, and we were glad of it, though this came at such a terrible, bloody cost.

Curiously, public devotion to Santa increased during the war. A cartoonist had a great deal to do with it. Thomas Nast was the son of German immigrants to America; he arrived with his family in 1846, when he was six years old. From the time he was a teenager, Thomas wanted to draw cartoons for popular magazines. It took him several years to find much work, but like all talented, committed artists, Thomas simply kept trying until he succeeded. He joined the staff of *Harper's Weekly*, one of the most prominent publications, just as the Civil War commenced.

Thomas was immediately assigned to travel to battlegrounds and draw what he saw there, which mostly consisted of horrible scenes of carnage. The young man—still in his mid-twenties—was repelled, as he should have been, by the violence and blood. Feeling discouraged, in 1862 he was trying to think of some hopeful, happy theme he could work into his sketches of war.

By coincidence or fate, at exactly the same time Clement Moore and his poem *A Visit from St. Nicholas* were back in the news. At the age of eighty-two, Clement was asked by the New York Historical Society to provide them with a handwritten copy of the great work. *A Visit from St. Nicholas* had been printed in various newspapers every year since 1823, but on this particular occasion more people than ever wanted to read it and to learn about the wonderful man who had written it. There were more stories about the poem, and Thomas Nast read some of them.

So it was that in the 1862 holiday edition of *Harper's Weekly* Thomas Nast had an amazing cartoon of Santa as Moore had described him, complete with beard, pipe, robes, and a sleigh pulled by eight flying reindeer. The unique thing about the Nast cartoon was that it showed Santa passing out gifts to troops of the Union army. Some people felt this cartoon was inappropriate since it depicted me favoring one army over another—and, indeed, though I hated slavery I did not hate the young men who fought for the South. But mostly, people in the Northern states who read *Harper's Weekly*—and most of them did; remember, there was no television or radio yet, so everyone read when they wanted entertainment—fell in love with Santa as drawn by Nast. He immediately began drawing many more cartoons with Santa in them, most of them published at holiday time, and all of them generating widespread public comment. More people in America welcomed Santa into their lives than ever.

Because war limited our powers to move about at amazing speeds, my companions and I were not able to distribute as many gifts in America during the years 1861 to 1865. Though Nast depicted me handing out presents to Union soldiers, in fact I focused most of my efforts on sneaking through the Southern lines and bringing small gifts to slave children. It was a dangerous process, and I had several close calls, but the risk was acceptable;

these innocent boys and girls desperately needed proof that they were loved for themselves, and not just valued for the labor they could provide to their masters.

When the war finally ended, I wondered if the country's fascination with Santa Claus might lessen, but it didn't. Nast's cartoons remained popular, and copies of them soon hung in homes throughout the reunited land. I was pleased by that, though not with how Nast chose to present me to the world. *His* Santa Claus was an elf, though he couldn't really be blamed for thinking I was. Clement Moore's poem did describe me as "a right jolly old elf," which gave the erroneous impression that Santa and his friends were short little creatures straight out of some imaginary fairyland. I asked Felix to go to New York City, where he could find Nast and offer a private meeting with me, so the cartoonist could see I was a full-grown man. Nast also had me living and working at the North Pole, which at the time I believed would be physically impossible. I had become friends with my earlier chroniclers Washington Irving and Clement Moore, so I had no doubt Thomas Nast would prove to be a pleasant acquaintance who would correct his errors in future cartoons. But Felix reported back that Nast did not want to see me.

"He believes this would damage his artistic integrity, Santa," Felix said. "He wants you to know that he believes in you, but he says that if he met you he would lose his freedom to draw you exactly as he imagines you to be."

"Did you at least inform him I'm a man and not an elf?" I asked.

"Yes, but he said the public prefers you as an elf, and so he would continue to draw you that way."

I reluctantly accepted this. It has always been my custom to try to be whatever children wanted. That is why, in different countries, I have so many names and varying gift-giving customs. We managed to incorporate flying reindeer into our American activities because Clement Moore's poem caused so many boys and girls to believe in my sleigh and soaring steeds. But I couldn't turn into an elf. Even holiday magic has its limits.

As the nineteenth century moved along, Americans continued to love Santa, and, of course, I loved them. It was a happy time for me and my companions. One special highlight came in 1889. Layla had been an indispensable part of my mission for many centuries, but never received any credit for her efforts. Nobody who wrote about me or drew cartoons of me ever seemed to imagine that I might have a wife, let alone one who was an equal partner.

Katharine Lee Bates was a fiercely intelligent woman from the American northeast who spent much of her life proving that scholarship and writing ability was not limited to men. Miss Bates earned a master's degree in arts at a time when many women did not even have the opportunity to go to high school. She served on the faculty of several distinguished universities during a long, honorable academic career, and in the 1880s she became particularly intrigued by the whole idea of Santa Claus and Christmas gift-giving. Surely, Miss Bates thought, Santa couldn't do everything all on his own. He must have a wife, and not one who was content to stay home doing chores while her husband soared around having all the fun. So she wrote a poem about it, using some popular terms of the day, especially "goodwife." This was a way many people in the 1880s would refer to a married woman. "Goodwife" was often shortened to "goody."

The poem Miss Bates published in 1889 was titled *Goody Santa Claus on a Sleigh Ride*. It was a long, rollicking collection of verse, one that involved a great deal of colorful imagery. Taking her cue from Thomas Nast, she had my wife and me living at the North Pole, and added some whimsical details of her own. Santa and "Goody" Claus, besides making toys, presided over flocks of Thanksgiving turkeys and magical "rainbow chickens" that laid brightly colored Easter eggs. That is, Santa presided from the comfort of his favorite chair. Goody had to actually tend to the menagerie and take care of groves of Christmas trees as well.

The part Miss Bates got exactly right was that Santa's wife was not content to stay at home while her husband enjoyed the great privilege of gift-giving. How Layla laughed when she read the verse describing Goody's showdown with her husband:

You just sit there and grow chubby off the goodies in my cubby
From December to December, till your white beard sweeps your knees;
For you must allow, my Goodman, that you're but a lazy woodman
And rely on me to foster all our fruitful Christmas trees.

Goody insists that she accompany Santa on his Christmas Eve sleigh ride, and even tells him to wait once in a while on a rooftop while she goes down the chimney for a change:

> *Back so soon? No chimney-swallow dives but where his mate can follow*
> *Bend your cold ear, Sweetheart Santa, down to catch my whisper faint:*
> *Would it be so very shocking if your Goody filled a stocking*
> *Just for once? Oh, dear! Forgive me. Frowns do not become a Saint.*

When every slumbering child has had his or her stocking filled, Santa and Goody fly back to the North Pole:

> *Chirrup! Chirrup! There's a patter of soft footsteps and a clatter*
> *Of Child voices. Speed it, reindeer, up the sparkling Arctic Hill!*
> *Merry Christmas, little people! Joy-bells ring in every steeple,*
> *And Goody's gladdest of the glad. I've had my own sweet will.*

It was, and still is, a wonderful poem and caused people everywhere to start thinking of Santa as a man married to a *very* capable woman.

"Why, I believe I must meet Katharine Lee Bates," I said to Layla. "Perhaps she'd like to join our gift-giving company, though I hope she won't be too disappointed to learn we don't live at the North Pole with flocks of Easter egg–laying chickens."

"You can just stay home," Layla replied cheerfully. "Goody Claus herself is going to go see Miss Bates." She left that very day, and returned a week later to report that, though Miss Bates was a wonderful person who loved Christmas dearly, she did not want to give up writing for gift-giving.

"She says she believes she still has important work to do, Santa," Layla said, and Miss Bates was correct. Just a few years later, she felt inspired to write another poem. This one began,

> *Oh, beautiful for spacious skies, for amber waves of grain . . .*

"America the Beautiful" was first published in 1895. Miss Bates revised it several times, and in 1910 the poem was combined with music called *Ma-*

terna by Samuel A. Ward. The resulting song, of course, has become a national standard and treasure.

Looking back, I believe that 1889 might have been the last year America enjoyed a simple, heartfelt Christmas. Santa was now a permanent part of the nation's holiday tradition. On Christmas Eve children did go to bed, as Clement Moore had predicted almost seven decades earlier, "with visions of sugarplums" dancing in their heads. Choirs strolled the streets singing carols; the essence of the holiday was appreciation for the gift of Jesus and the opportunity to extend warm good wishes to family, friends, and even strangers.

In 1890, this changed. I will not say I blame J. W. Parkinson, who was by that time long gone, and who had not meant any harm to begin with. But his hiring almost half a century earlier of a fraudulent Kris Kringle suddenly had an effect on the holiday that well-intentioned J.W. would never have expected or intended.

James Edgar was a thickset Scottish immigrant who lived in Brockton, Massachusetts. He was part owner of the Boston Store, which, like J.W.'s earlier shop, sold "sundries," things like buttons and thread and shoe polish and, yes, toys. Edgar had become quite successful, with enough money to indulge himself in an expensive hobby, which was collecting old posters. He owned hundreds, including a poster from Abraham Lincoln's first presidential campaign and one of the earliest advertisements for Buffalo Bill Cody's Wild West Show.

In early 1890, Edgar visited an antique store in Philadelphia. There he found for sale one of the posters J.W. had printed to advertise "Kris Kringle's" appearance at his store on December 18, 1841. As dozens of newspapers later reported, Edgar bought the poster, paying a dollar for it, which was a considerable sum at the time. He took it back to Brockton and hung it in his office at the Boston Store.

Now, Edgar certainly enjoyed Christmas, both for the holiday's own sake and for the extra customers who came to buy Christmas gifts at his shop. The more he looked at the old Parkinson's poster, the more he thought having "Santa" greet customers was an excellent marketing strategy. Unlike J.W., Edgar didn't hire an impersonator. He had his own long white beard and considerable waistline. On December 1, 1890, Edgar put on red robes and announced Santa Claus had come to entertain holiday shoppers at the Boston Store.

Up at the Cooperstown farm, we had no advance warning, but we soon found out about it, as did much of the rest of the country. Unlike 1841, when there was very little way for news to spread rapidly, every 1890s town of any size had at least one newspaper that was widely read, and major cities like Boston, which was quite near Brockton, had as many as half a dozen. Someone tipped a reporter at one of the Boston papers that Santa Claus himself was visiting a Brockton store and would be there every day until Christmas! The reporter took the train to Brockton, watched Edgar asking children what they wanted Santa to bring them for Christmas, and wrote a long story about it that was printed the next day, along with a sketch of the scene. Well, reporters from all the other Boston papers felt obligated to come out and write about this store-visiting Santa, too. This meant that, within a few days, people all over Massachusetts and New England had read the stories. By the time newspapers in New York and Philadelphia and other major American cities picked up the story a few days later, there were already long lines in front of the Boston Store from daylight until well after dark. It was all Edgar could do to shake hands and briefly visit with every anxious child, many of whom had traveled a long way to meet with Santa. Parents in Providence, Rhode Island, even chartered a special train to bring hundreds of boys and girls from that city to Brockton.

I rushed from Cooperstown to see this latest pretender myself; Layla and Felix came along. Though we arrived early in the morning, there was already a line of waiting children that stretched for several blocks. Because we were not accompanied by youngsters, we were able to go right into the store, and what a sight it was! On one side there was Edgar, resplendent in red Santa robes, sitting on a chair placed on a high platform, shuffling children on and off his lap as each leaned forward to whisper gift requests into his ear. Mostly, the line moved briskly, though every fourth child or so had a lengthy wish list and so needed a few extra seconds of Santa's time.

On the other side of the store were long counters displaying toys of every sort, and there was frenzied activity at those counters as well. Parents were practically shoving money in the hands of clerks who tried frantically to keep up with customer demand. All this was being observed by several well-dressed men, as well as a half-dozen other fellows in less expensive suits who were scribbling in notebooks.

"I know the men with the notebooks must be newspaper reporters, but who are the men standing next to them?" I whispered to Felix. He didn't know, but Layla thought she did.

"They must be owners of other local shops," she said. "It's obvious that having Santa appear greatly boosts holiday toy sales. You know what that means, of course."

When I said I didn't, she told me: "Within the next few days, there will be a Santa greeting children in every big store in Brockton and Boston, and perhaps in shops all over the country. When one merchant has an idea that works, it's copied by competitors."

"Surely not," I scoffed. "It's working out well in this instance because Edgar looks so natural, so Santa-like, with his white beard."

"And he's fat," Felix added, perhaps intending to be helpful.

"But there can't be that many Santa impersonators who really look and act the part," I said. "No self-respecting store owner would insult Christmas and risk disappointing children with an obvious impostor." Even as I spoke, I knew I was indulging in wishful thinking.

Layla was right. In the few weeks between Edgar's first appearance as Santa and Christmas Eve 1890, stores all over America began advertising appearances by Santa Claus. It happened everywhere, not just in Brockton and Boston. I can't be more specific about how often because we stopped counting after reaching two hundred. All over the country, the number of stores with pretend Santas continued to multiply every year after that.

In a few isolated cases, the impostors were, like Edgar, at least physically appropriate to the role. Any child tugging one of their beards was rewarded with a handful of real white whiskers. A few of the false Santas at least took the time to learn Christmas history, so they could intelligently answer questions from their young admirers. But so many of these men were unsuitable. All the red robes and *ho-ho-ho*ing in the world could not make them convincing. They might wear droopy fake beards, or become cross with boys and girls who didn't act exactly as they wanted, or, worst of all, tell trusting young believers that Santa would only bring them toys from a specific store.

Within a few years, there was a predictable result. Many children began to believe that Santa Claus must not even exist. How could he, when every Christmas they saw dozens of different "Santas," all looking and acting differently, each claiming to be the real person?

Some still managed to trust their hearts rather than their eyes. In 1897, a lovely eight-year-old girl named Virginia O'Hanlon wrote to the *New York Sun* asking if there really was a Santa Claus. A wonderful editor named Francis Church replied that "Yes, Virginia, there is a Santa Claus. He exists as certainly as love and generosity and devotion exist, and you know how they abound and give to your life its highest beauty and joy." Though he did not say so specifically, I believe Mr. Church was referring to the difference between pretenders in costume and me when he added, "Nobody sees Santa Claus, but that is no sign that there is no Santa Claus. The most real things in the world are those that neither children nor men can see . . ."

It was a perfect response, one that was reprinted and repeated all over the country. Virginia was reassured, and, by reading her letter and Mr. Church's reply, countless other boys and girls were as well. But the exchange between Virginia and Mr. Church could not in any way prevent or even postpone what a few generations later would be known as "the commercialization" of Christmas. Drawings of "Santa" began to appear in product advertisements. Supposedly I was now endorsing everything from soap flakes to hand tools. It was ironic that I had spent so many years wondering if America would ever accept Santa at all, and now I was afraid that I was too much a part of holiday commerce rather than heartfelt Christmas celebration.

"I remember, during my first days with the Pilgrims at Plymouth Rock, that I hoped one day even a few people in America would know my name and allow me to be part of their Christmas happiness," I said to Layla one night as we sat together in my study. It was 1913, and we'd just moved all our operations to the North Pole. We were still adjusting to the long nights there in the winter, where the sun never comes out.

"I have heard a saying about being careful what you wish for," Layla replied. "Considering how hard you've worked so people would know about you at all, aren't you at least in some way pleased that everyone in America seems to think about you during the holidays?"

"It's not *that* they think of me, but *how* they think of me," I said. "Until now, whether I was known as Santa or Kris Kringle or Father Christmas or any of dozens of other wonderful names, my gifts were understood to be symbols of caring, gestures of love. Now children are making up long lists of things they specifically want, instead of gladly receiving whatever Santa has brought them. I don't blame the boys and girls; adults who own stores and create advertising campaigns are encouraging them to act this way. Christmas is perhaps being celebrated more enthusiastically than ever, but now there's something calculating about it. I'm afraid the sweetness of the original holiday, the innocence, is being lost."

"Well, what do you intend to do about it?" Layla asked. "Sitting here complaining won't change anything."

"I think that, beyond continuing our mission, there's very little we *can* do," I said. "Even if I came forward and presented myself as the real Santa, I'd only be taken for one more impostor. This is all very frustrating, but we'll simply carry on and hope that things change again, this time for the better."

And, for nearly another hundred years, this is what we did. I don't mean to make it sound as though Christmas in America became all bad, or even close to it. There were still many, many adults who remembered the real reason for the holiday and who taught children that Santa symbolized love and sharing rather than grabbing and getting.

Occasionally, when I believed there was cause for special concern, I did act. The best example of this came in 1931. So many poorly disguised impostors were ringing bells on street corners or pulling children onto their laps in stores that I decided it was time for everyone to at least know what Santa actually looked like. The Coca-Cola company was planning a series of holiday printed advertisements for its soft drinks featuring "Santa." Artist Haddon "Hans" Sundblom was hired to paint the portraits. I left the North Pole to find Mr. Sundblom; when I did, I volunteered to be his model.

He immediately realized who I was, and we became fast friends. He drew Coca-Cola's "Santa" ads for thirty-five years, and during that time always told anyone who asked that a retired salesman named "Les Prentice" posed for him. The Coca-Cola ads were a sensation, and, as I hoped, caused more employers to insist their pseudo-Santas at least looked the part.

There was another occasion when commercial efforts evolved into wonderful Christmas traditions. Few people today remember that "Rudolph the Red-Nosed Reindeer" was originally conceived in 1939 as a holiday advertisement for Montgomery Ward. But children and grown-ups alike fell in love with the story, and by 1949, when popular cowboy singer Gene Autry recorded a splendid Christmas carol—also titled "Rudolph the Red-Nosed Reindeer"—America had a new Christmas icon, though, unlike me, one that wasn't part of actual history. There was some consternation at the North Pole—Leonardo tried and failed to find or create a red-nosed flying reindeer—but we eventually decided Rudolph, who bravely struggled to prove himself to "all the other reindeer," was a worthy addition to Christmas lore. His never-give-up spirit was inspiring in the best holiday tradition.

There was another positive change. In the 1960s and '70s, even as so-called "shopping malls"—dozens, sometimes even hundreds of stores all located in single huge structures—began to appear, there also emerged several companies whose sole job it was to provide well-trained, more believable "Santas" to these gigantic malls during the holidays. This drastically reduced the number of pretenders who were presented to trusting children while wearing scraggly fake beards or drooping, pillow-stuffed paunches. I still wished the practice of hiring performers to portray me had never been initiated, but most of the malls had enough responsibility to ensure their fake Santas at least looked and acted authentic.

So the years passed, and it seemed, for a while, that the commercialization of the holiday in America had expanded as far as it could from its bumbling origins in 1841 at J. W. Parkinson's dry-goods store. Then, not many years after the beginning of the twenty-first century, one December day Felix returned to the North Pole from a trip to New York City and said he had to speak to me right away.

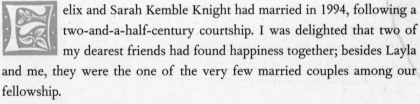elix and Sarah Kemble Knight had married in 1994, following a two-and-a-half-century courtship. I was delighted that two of my dearest friends had found happiness together; besides Layla and me, they were the one of the very few married couples among our fellowship.

Accordingly, Layla insisted afterward that each year Felix and Sarah enjoy at least one short vacation together. She told them not to do North Pole–related work while they were away. "It's good for any husband and wife," she explained to me after we waved good-bye to Felix and Sarah as they departed on a trip to Tibet to celebrate their first anniversary. "While it's wonderful that all of us have been together for so long, it's also appropriate for a couple to occasionally have some time to be away by themselves. Don't you agree?"

Having been a married man myself for some sixteen centuries, I knew when it was in my best interest to agree with my wife completely.

"Yes, dear," I said.

"Do you happen to remember the last time *we* took a vacation together?" Layla continued.

I frantically searched my memory. "Not *that* long ago," I muttered. "Surely no more than a dozen years, or perhaps twenty."

"Try almost two centuries," my wife said. She sounded exasperated. "In 1818 we went to Oberndorf in Austria to enjoy Christmas midnight mass at the Church of St. Nicholas, and while we were there we helped the priest and church organist compose 'Silent Night.'"

"And what a lovely song it was!" I exclaimed, hoping Layla's warm memory of that special moment might overcome her obvious irritation with me. It didn't.

"It would be very nice," she said, "if we had another vacation, just the two of us."

"It certainly would," I replied. "We'll have to do that."

"When?"

"Soon, I'm sure," I said, and I truly meant it. But there were always reasons I couldn't get away. Perhaps Leonardo and Ben and Willie Skokan had just invented new toys that needed thorough testing, or else I was urgently required to meet with the leader of some country whose government wanted help planning national Christmas celebrations. Layla would sigh and ask me to promise we'd definitely take a trip the next year, and meanwhile she made certain Felix and Sarah regularly enjoyed short vacations together.

On this particular trip, they'd left for New York City right after we'd finished our gift-giving in many parts of Europe on December 6, which is Saint Nicholas Day. There was an eighteen-day interim before Christmas Eve; all the necessary toys had been made, and so it was good for Felix and Sarah to relax a little in between those two special, but hectic, nights.

One of the lovely holiday traditions in New York is the display of a giant Christmas tree at Rockefeller Center. The custom had begun in 1933 and each year, it seemed, the tree was taller and decorated with more dazzling, multicolored lights. Every year the tree was at least eighty feet high, and occasionally it was a hundred. Its mighty branches extended as much as forty-one feet, and each Christmas the tree sparkled with a minimum of thirty thousand bulbs connected by five miles of wire. In all, this was a sight to gladden the heart of anyone who loved Christmas, as Felix and Sarah surely did. It had been decades since they'd last been to New York City to see the tree, so on December 7 they left the North Pole on dogsled and traveled to a railroad station hundreds of miles away. From there they continued by train into New York City, where they planned to stay for a few days to see the Rockefeller Center tree and happily stroll hand-in-hand along wide, snowy Manhattan avenues, taking in all the amazing holiday displays in store windows before returning to the North Pole and joining in final preparations for our Christmas Eve gifting-giving.

So I'd anticipated their return. It did surprise me that Felix wanted us to talk the moment he arrived. When friends have known each other for so many centuries, there usually is no hurry to catch up on each other's news.

"Surely this can wait until after dinner, Felix," I suggested. "I happen to know Lars, our chef, has prepared one of his special chocolate cakes for dessert."

"This is more important than cake, Santa," Felix replied, and I knew instantly that whatever he wanted to tell me was critical. In the seventeen hundred years we'd been together, there were very few things my overweight friend had ever considered more important than cake. It was one of the things we had in common. So I asked him to follow me to my cozy den, where a warm blaze crackled in the fireplace. Sarah came with us, and Layla, too. My wife and I settled back into chairs and waited for our friends to tell us their news. They scrunched together on the overstuffed sofa, wringing their hands and appearing rather nervous.

"Goodness, why do you look so worried?" I asked. "I can't remember the last time either of you seemed so upset!"

"It may be that there isn't any cause for concern, Santa," Sarah said. "But we had a conversation with someone we met in New York that you should know about. Something very serious might be happening."

"Something that affects you, and Christmas," Felix added. "Like J. W. Parkinson, I'm certain Bobbo Butler doesn't *mean* any harm, but still—"

"Bobo?" I interrupted. "What sort of name is that?"

"Not *BOW*-bow," Felix corrected. "It's pronounced *BAH*-bow. For

Bob O. Bob O. Butler. That's his name, and he gets upset if it's pronounced incorrectly."

"That's whose name, Felix?" Layla asked.

"Bob O. Butler is a man we met in New York City, right in front of the ice-skating rink at Rockefeller Center," Sarah said. "We went there to see the magnificent Christmas tree, of course, and they were having this special skating program at the rink beside it. The program was being sponsored by the LastLong Toy Company." Layla and I groaned when she mentioned the toy manufacturer. At the North Pole we were all completely dedicated to crafting quality toys that would hold up for years of nonstop play, but Last-Long's widely assorted products were always shoddily made and usually broke instantly upon use by children. The company spent millions of dollars each year on advertising, making their wagons and dollhouses and bicycles sound like things no child in America could do without. LastLong's promotions were every bit as catchy and effective as their products were terrible. Each year, the company sold twice as many toys as its closest competitor. In our snowbound workshops, any time we accidentally produced a substandard toy that wobbled when it should have rolled or flopped when it should have bounced, we'd cry out in unison, "Now, *there's* a LastLong toy!" But, inexplicably, the company thrived.

"It seems LastLong has a new line of ice skates," Felix explained. "There were banners everywhere advertising them. They read, *'Skate Like a Champion with LastLong,'* and some of the most famous skaters in the world like Michelle Kwan and Scott Hamilton and Kristi Yamaguchi were gliding around the Rockefeller Center rink on LastLong skates."

"What a treat for you to be there to see them!" Layla exclaimed. Ever since we'd been at the North Pole, she'd grown very fond of ice-skating, since we often needed skates or snowshoes for our occasional evening strolls outside. Without false modesty, we all believe the ice skates we make at the North Pole are the finest anywhere, and they're certainly among the gifts from us most requested by children. "Weren't you impressed with how well they could skate?"

"Actually, I felt sorry for them," Felix said. "Like all their other products, LastLong skates don't. Last long, I mean. The blades kept breaking off and all the famous skaters would fall down. And there was such a big crowd gathered around to watch, too. The whole thing was rather embarrassing. You'd think this would have convinced parents not to buy those skates for their children, but LastLong had a sales booth set up beside the rink and there were huge lines there afterward. Their advertising is so good, Santa. They know just how to make people think they have to have their products."

"Well, that's a shame, but we can't force parents to demonstrate good judgment regarding the toys and athletic gear they buy their children," I said. "Thank you for bringing this to my attention, Felix and Sarah, but we already knew LastLong toys were terrible. Shall we go in to dinner now? If we don't hurry, all the chocolate cake might be gone."

"I don't think the faulty skates were what Sarah and Felix wanted to tell us about," Layla observed. "They want to report their conversation with this man named Bobbo Butler."

Reluctantly—I could just *taste* Lars's delicious Hot Chocolate Cake, which was somehow spicy and sweet at the same time—I sat back down in my chair. "What did Bobbo—did I pronounce it right?—say that concerns you?" I asked.

Felix took a deep breath, which was always a sign that he had a great deal to say. I could forget dinner, and especially dessert, for some time.

It all started, my oldest friend explained, during the skating exhibition where the great champions took falls when their LastLong skates broke.

"They had attracted quite a big crowd, of course," Felix said. "The rink itself is not very large, and people were packed in on all sides. No one was in danger of being crushed, but everyone was jostled at least a little."

Felix had put his arm around Sarah so they wouldn't accidentally be separated. On the other side of his wife, he'd noticed an odd-looking pair who were jammed together, too. The man was of medium height, and quite wiry. He had a prominent, hooked nose and a fringe of dark hair circling an otherwise bald scalp—this hair bristled out in every direction. The woman was tall, extremely so, certainly several inches above six feet. While her companion had his eyes glued on the rink, she seemed determined to protect him from being bumped by anyone. At one point, she reached out with her left hand to gently prevent Sarah and Felix from being knocked off-balance into the short man with the wild fringe of hair. My North Pole friends nodded their thanks; the woman smiled and nodded back. Once or twice during the rest of the short program, her eyes met those of Sarah or Felix. Soon they were exchanging grins and waggling eyebrows in mock wonder at all the famous skaters who lurched on faulty skates.

The wild-haired man never looked at Felix or Sarah—or at anything or anyone else—until the program was over. Then, as the crowd thinned, he suddenly glanced at them and said, "Quite a show, don't you think? And entertaining, though not in the way the skaters wanted."

"I think it was the fault of the equipment rather than the skaters," Sarah pointed out.

"I know!" the fellow exclaimed. "LastLong Toys my, well, *foot*. They're junk, is what they are!"

"I wish they would go out of business," Felix said.

The other man's eyes widened. "Well, *I* don't," he replied. "They may make junk, but it's profitable junk, and I need them to sponsor my programs."

The tall woman looked alarmed. "We really don't need to talk about this, chief," she said hurriedly. "Program sponsors, you know, and specific company names, and . . . *junk*." She smiled at Sarah and Felix and said, "I'm so sorry if we jostled you. Happy holidays."

But the wild-haired man said, "Oh, there's no need to rush off, Miss Hathaway. We have some time before our meeting is supposed to start. Perhaps these nice people might like to join us for hot chocolate. They're selling some over there on the other side of the rink." He grasped Sarah's and Felix's arms and began steering them away. "I like to get out and talk to the public. I want to hear what you've got to say."

"Say about what?" Felix asked.

"Television, of course," the man replied. "Let's get our hot chocolate and sit down over by those tables. It's cold out, but not too cold. You'll be warm enough, won't you, if you've got the hot chocolate?"

"I'm *sure* these nice people have shopping to do, chief," Miss Hathaway protested, trailing after the other three.

"No, we're fine," Sarah said. In the centuries she and Felix had been part of our globe-spanning mission, they'd met lots of quirky, interesting people and usually enjoyed the experience.

So the man bought four cups of hot chocolate and pulled Sarah and Felix over to a nearby table, leaving Miss Hathaway to pay the vendor. When she got to the table, he discovered they had no napkins, and asked her to go find some. After that, he noticed they had no spoons to stir their drinks, and requested that she get those, too. He did not make these requests in any mean-spirited or even bossy way. His matter-of-fact tone indicated he was in the habit of asking, and expecting, her to perform these small tasks as part of an everyday routine.

"Ah, that Heather Hathaway," he said as she hurried off in search of spoons. "I can't tell her this because then she'd probably want a raise, but she's the best personal assistant any TV-network president ever had." He gave Sarah and Felix a sharp look over the top of his cardboard cup, trying to see if they were impressed.

More out of courtesy than astonishment—after all, she was close friends with such luminaries as Ben Franklin, Theodore Roosevelt, and Leonardo da Vinci, not to mention Santa Claus—Sarah politely responded, "A television-network president? Are you really?"

The fellow nodded. "Bob O. Butler. You can call me Bobbo. Not *BOW*-bow, mind. *BAH*-bow. That's how my friends know me, and I can tell you're both my friends." He said this with the same absolute certainty that a puppy demonstrates in thinking everyone he meets wants to play with him.

"We're pleased to meet you, Mr. Butler. Excuse me—I mean, Bobbo," Sarah replied. "I'm Sarah, and this is my husband Felix."

"Glad to make your acquaintance," Bobbo said. "Tell me, how old are you?"

Now, this struck my friends as odd. "I beg your pardon?" Sarah asked.

"Your ages are important to me," Bobbo replied, impatiently gesturing for his assistant to put the spoons she'd just fetched on the table, and to sit down herself. "Take out your notebook, Miss Hathaway. We may hear something important. Don't want to tell me how old you are? Can I try to guess? I'm very good at this. You, Sarah, are just about in your mid-thirties.

Right? Of course, I'm right." He mistook Sarah's sudden wide smile for corroboration. Actually, she was smiling because she had just celebrated her 342nd birthday. We all like to think we look younger than we really are, and Sarah was pleased to have this proof. Then Bobbo turned his attention to Felix. "Now, you, my friend, have a few more years on you than your wife. I'd say, what—forty-two?"

During Felix's early life no one kept exact track of when slaves were born. He had no idea how old he was, only that he was at least seventeen hundred.

"Close enough, Bobbo," he replied. "What a good guesser you are."

"I have to be, in my job," Bobbo said. "Now, I want to know more. Felix, what do you do for a living?"

In modern times, our fellowship had developed a safe, traditional answer to this inquiry. "I'm a consultant," Felix said. "I work in manufacturing. Around the holidays I'm mostly involved in distribution." This description, though vague, was certainly accurate. All of us tried never to lie.

Bobbo wasn't done asking questions. Did Sarah and Felix have children? "No." Favorite hobbies? "Crafts and world travel." Miss Hathaway jotted down all these answers. Hometown? "We've moved a lot. Right now we live up north."

"Ah," said Bobbo. "You're from Boston."

"Why are you asking us all these things, Bobbo?" Sarah asked. "I know it's natural to be curious about new friends, but this is almost more an interrogation than a conversation."

"Demographics, Sarah," Bobbo replied, tossing out the word like they must certainly be familiar with it. The puzzled expressions on their faces convinced him they weren't. "In the television business, we try to know as much about every segment of the general public as possible. Where people live, what they do to earn their livings, what their hobbies are, especially how old they are—these are the things that help us decide what programs to put on the air. Each show is specifically created to please certain types of people; we pay to produce and broadcast our programs by selling commercial time to sponsors who want to bring the attention of the same market audience to their products. I hope that isn't too complicated an explanation."

"It isn't," Felix said. "To pay for your programs, you need sponsors. To get sponsors, you have to have the right audiences watching your programs."

"Exactly!" Bobbo exclaimed. Then his grin turned into a grimace. "Recently, I'm afraid, my network hasn't been succeeding as well as it once did. Now, I'm sure you've enjoyed many of our wonderful shows over the years. You do watch FUN, don't you?"

"Fun?" Felix asked, sounding puzzled, which he was. "How do you watch *fun*?"

"No, F-U-N," Bobbo said. "That's the name of our network. FUN-TV. It stands for Family Ultimate Network. That's been our special demographic. For decades we've produced wholesome shows that families can watch together—parents, children, grandparents, different generations gathered together in front of their televisions enjoying programs that never include anything sordid or violent or what kids today call *gross*."

"That's very admirable, Bobbo," Sarah said.

"It may be admirable, but in recent years it hasn't been working very well," Bobbo sighed, and from the corner of her eye Sarah saw Heather Hathaway's eyes glisten suddenly with unshed, sympathetic tears. "Tell me, folks, what programs on FUN-TV have you seen lately?"

"None, I'm afraid," Felix said. "Don't take it personally, Bobbo. We never actually watch television."

"Of course you do," Bobbo snapped. "Everybody does. It's a fact."

"I'm sorry, but it isn't," Felix replied.

"Well, what do you do at night?"

"We enjoy visiting with old friends," Felix said. "Now, we often watch DVD movies. But we really don't watch television *shows* as such. The few times we've tried, there haven't been many programs that seemed to be worth our time."

"Exactly!" barked Bobbo. "People like you have been driven away from television by all that awful *reality* programming that's saturating the TV industry!" That wasn't precisely what Felix had told him, but Bobbo was obviously a man who heard what he wanted to hear. "The ones who watch it now want spectacle, not quality entertainment. What's involved in a modern-day hit show? Why, people pretending to be stranded on a desert island! People singing badly and being made fun of for doing it! People eating *bugs*! Yuck!" He was quite distressed; Miss Hathaway leaned over, patted him on the back, and had him take a sip of hot chocolate.

"He gets very upset when he thinks about this," she whispered.

Bobbo gulped a little more hot chocolate. "Holiday programming was always the most-watched part of our broadcast year," he said. "Our ratings doubled every other network's—heck, *tripled* 'em. Parents and children would wait all year to see whatever Christmas specials we'd have on FUN-TV. And we had some great ones, like our remake of *A Christmas Carol* starring Bob Hope as Scrooge and Bing Crosby as Marley's ghost. You must have seen that one. Millions did."

"Sorry," Felix said.

"Ah, well. Everything was fine until about ten years ago, when that so-called 'reality TV' got started. I believed it would never catch on. I mean, nobody was really going to starve on that *un*deserted island. For heaven's sake, they had a whole *camera crew* right there with them. But for some reason that kind of silly show got popular, and families stopped watching TV together because older people were disgusted with the programming. They could watch movies on DVD instead, like you two do. That left kids as the big audience, though not younger ones, because their parents wouldn't *let* them watch unsuitable shows. So it was down to the teenagers, who want to act cool and *not* watch family programming in favor of the nastier stuff, and so sponsors stopped buying many commercials on FUN-TV and things have been terrible for us since."

"That's actually why we're at Rockefeller Center today," Miss Hathaway added. "We still have commercial time to sell for our Christmas special this year, and we're hoping the LastLong Toy Company might buy some of it. They've got these new skates of theirs, though apparently they're not very good ones."

"Oh, that's because the heels of the skates above the blades are too short," Felix said. "To provide enough support for the foot and the blade, the heel on any ice skate has to be one and a half inches long. To save on production costs, I suppose, these skates of LastLong's appear to have only three-quarter-inch heels, which throws off the weight of the skater, puts too much pressure on the blade, and so the blade snaps and the skater falls. It's very obvious."

Bobbo Butler stared at Felix. "Now, how would you know a thing like that?"

"I've designed and built some ice skates in my time," Felix said. "All kinds of toys, too. The LastLong products are junk because the company cuts corners on materials, plus they're shoddily put together. They could manufacture fine toys if they wanted to, but clearly they don't."

"He's a toy expert, Miss Hathaway," Bobbo remarked. "You don't meet many of those at the Rockefeller Center skating rink. Well, it's been grand, folks, but Miss Hathaway and I have a meeting in a few minutes with Lucretia Pepper, the LastLong company president. Their headquarters is near Rockefeller Center. She hasn't bought advertising on FUN in years, but we're hoping she'll like the concept of this year's Christmas special."

"What is it about, Bobbo?" Sarah asked.

"We're calling it *Merry Monkey.* A monkey in the Central Park Zoo suddenly understands the spirit of Christmas and spends Christmas Eve distributing gifts to all the other animals there. We're using real animals, not cartoon or computer-generated ones. Do you like it?" Bobbo asked anxiously.

"It's certainly unique," Sarah said carefully.

"Well, it's the best we can do on a limited budget," Bobbo said. "The cost of renting monkeys has just skyrocketed. But maybe Lucretia Pepper will like it. I wish I had something better to tell her about."

"In the middle 1800s, toy monkeys were among the most popular Christmas gifts for children in France and Germany," Felix said. "It was one of the first times in history that material was sewn to look like animals. Before that, the stuffed toys children received for Christmas had mostly been dolls shaped like humans. Maybe you could do your special about toy monkeys in Christmas history. That would be interesting."

Bobbo had stood up, preparing to leave with Miss Hathaway for his meeting with Lucretia Pepper. Now he sat slowly down again.

"You're a toy expert *and* a Christmas expert? I wish I'd met you before we put *Merry Monkey* into production. It's too late to change the show now. But can I have your phone number, please? If FUN-TV can keep going, I'd like to have you consult on our next holiday special."

Sarah shot her husband a warning glance, but Felix had always been happy, even eager, to offer advice to anyone who asked and many who hadn't. Some years earlier Leonardo had insisted that all of us at the North Pole carry individual cell phones. It made it easier to stay in touch. Except for certain world leaders and a few other trusted friends who didn't live at the North Pole, we'd never given out the numbers before, certainly not to someone who was still almost a total stranger. Felix had taken a great liking to Bobbo Butler, though, and before Sarah could stop him he recited his cell-phone number. Without being asked, Heather Hathaway copied it down for her boss.

"If you want to start thinking about it, I've decided that next Christmas we're going to have to take a crack at reality TV ourselves," Bobbo said. "There's got to be some form of it that's family-friendly, that parents and young children *and* teenagers would all want to watch. I just need one can't-miss holiday show, one that pulls a huge demographic, and then I'm sure FUN-TV's reputation would be restored and people would start watching our wholesome programs again. Then we'll be beating sponsors off instead of going to them to practically beg, like I have to do right now at LastLong Toys. Reality TV and Christmas, though—that's a difficult combination."

Having told this much of the story, and having taken so very long doing it that every crumb of Lars's chocolate cake had certainly been gobbled up by the rest of our fellowship, Felix now began to fidget on the couch in my North Pole den. It was obvious he didn't want to tell me the rest of what happened with Bobbo Butler. We all sat for a moment in uncomfortable silence until Sarah finally said, "Go ahead, Felix. Tell Santa."

"Why don't *you* tell him?" Felix asked plaintively. But Sarah gave him a stern look. He sighed and said, "Remember, I didn't mean any harm."

"It's all right, Felix," Layla said soothingly. "I'm sure this is something we need to hear."

"Well," Felix said, looking everywhere but at me, "Bobbo said again that he had to be going to his meeting. He double-checked my cell-phone number and said he would be in touch soon. Miss Hathaway told him they had to start for Lucretia Pepper's office right away if they didn't want to be late."

"Go on," I said, though Felix so obviously didn't want to.

"Bobbo looked so sad," Felix said. "You would have pitied him, too. Anyway, he told us that he would give anything to have just one great idea for a Christmas reality-TV special, anything that would let his network survive and keep on producing programs for families. And that's when I said, well—"

I have loved Felix dearly for going on eighteen centuries, but sometimes he can be so exasperating.

"Great heavens, man, tell me what you said!" I urged. Though Layla later told me I did, I'm sure I didn't shout. I just sounded definite.

Felix grimaced. "What I said to Bobbo was, 'Well, it's Christmas. Maybe Santa Claus will bring you a wonderful reality-TV idea.' And all of a sudden his eyes lit up and he whooped out loud. Miss Hathaway jumped a foot, she was so startled. 'That might be it!' Bobbo shouted. He really yelled. People all around us were staring."

"Bobbo grabbed Felix and gave him a great big hug," Sarah added. "He said to Felix, 'You're a genius! Even if Lucretia Pepper doesn't like *Merry Monkey,* she's going to love my new plan for next Christmas!' Felix asked him, 'What plan is that?,' but Bobbo said he needed time to fine-tune the premise, whatever that means. He went racing off, dragging Miss Hathaway behind him. He called back to Felix that he'd be in touch soon, and that next Christmas FUN-TV would jump all the way back to the top of the ratings."

Layla and I exchanged glances. There was obviously the very real possibility of disaster here, though it was impossible to know what form it might take.

"Bobbo Butler didn't say anything else, Felix?" I asked. "Nothing more about Santa Claus and this reality-TV program he wants to produce for next Christmas?"

"No, not a word," Felix said, trying to sound hopeful. "He and Miss

Hathaway disappeared into the crowd. Who knows? By now he might have forgotten whatever it is he thought of."

I hoped he had. We went ahead with all our preparations for Christmas Eve, and on the night of December 24 we recorded the FUN-TV special *Merry Monkey* while we were out circling the globe and delivering gifts to boys and girls everywhere. Of course, all of us were tired when we returned to the North Pole as dawn broke on Christmas Day, and so we went to bed. It wasn't until December 26 that we gathered in front of a widescreen television to watch Bobbo Butler's holiday program. To be honest, it wasn't very good. The monkey in the starring role kept eating the wrapping paper on his gifts instead of handing them through cage bars to the other animals in the Central Park Zoo.

But at the end of the program—which had, by the way, no commercials sponsored by LastLong Toys—Bobbo Butler himself appeared to speak directly to the audience. Even before his name flashed onscreen, I knew who he must be. Felix and Sarah had very accurately described his wild fringe of dark hair, otherwise bald head, and obvious eagerness to please.

"Folks, if you've stuck around to watch the conclusion of *Merry Monkey*, all of us at FUN-TV truly appreciate it," he said. "We know that every Christmas Eve you've got a wide variety of programs to choose from. That's why we're so proud to make this announcement a whole year in advance."

Bobbo took a deep breath. So did all of us watching at the North Pole. Then he continued:

"Next year, right here on FUN-TV, we will proudly join with LastLong Toy Company to bring you the most wonderful holiday special ever, and perhaps the first reality-TV show that's really suitable for the whole family. You'll hear more details in the months ahead, but for now, plan to keep two hours on Christmas Eve reserved for the show that everyone will want to watch on December 24, the show everyone will talk about for years afterward. One year from tonight, folks, right here on FUN-TV, it will be . . ."

Bobbo paused for emphasis.

"It will be . . . *The Great Santa Search*!" And with that, FUN-TV signed off for the night.

All of us at the North Pole spent the rest of December 26 and all of December 27 wondering what *The Great Santa Search* might be about.

Then on December 28, Felix's cell phone rang. Heather Hathaway was calling. She said Bobbo Butler wanted to see him right away in New York City.

Four

eather Hathaway was a striking woman for reasons other than her great height. In her early thirties, she had dark, expressive eyebrows that were in constant motion, sometimes knitted in deep thought and at other times arched in surprise. She kept her brown hair pulled back in a long ponytail that always had some strands escaping. Being quite a busy person, and constantly preoccupied with keeping the erratic Bobbo Butler on schedule, she rarely smiled. But when she did smile, her whole face lit up, as it did when she greeted Felix on December 29 as he arrived at the FUN-TV offices in New York City.

"Thanks so much for coming!" she said, taking Felix's overcoat and hanging it neatly in a closet. "Bobbo has been excited ever since he met you, and you gave him that wonderful idea for our next Christmas special!"

"What idea was that?" Felix asked. He was very nervous. When Bobbo had summoned him the day before, Felix begged not to go to the meeting alone. He wanted me to come, too, or at least Sarah. But the rest of us agreed Bobbo was more likely to reveal everything about this mysterious *Great Santa Search* if there were fewer people around. Felix was charged with finding out everything he could and then promptly reporting back to the rest of us at the North Pole.

"Oh, I'm going to let the chief tell you the details himself," Miss Hathaway replied. "Go right through that door. They're waiting for you." Before Felix had time to ask who *they* might be, she was whisking him into a paneled conference room where Bobbo and a gargantuan woman were seated at a heavy rectangular table. Like Heather Hathaway, this woman was tall; unlike Bobbo's personal assistant, she was wide as well, with the menacing heft of a rhinoceros that might at any moment decide to charge. Her short, stiffly coiffed hair was as hard as a helmet. Makeup was caked thick on her face; it was impossible to tell her age. She might have been forty or fifty or even a well-preserved sixty. After dismissing Heather Hathaway with a curt nod, she stood and extended a heavily jeweled hand for Felix to shake. He tried not to flinch.

"I am Lucretia Pepper, president of LastLong Toys," she announced in the same self-confident tone a queen might use to identify the country she ruled. "And you must be Felix, the genius my old friend Bobbo has been telling me about!" Though her words were warm and her smile was wide, her eyes remained cold, and her voice bothered Felix most of all. It was curiously high-pitched, even childlike, not at all in keeping with her hulking appearance.

"Pleased to meet you," Felix said, grimacing as her hand squeezed his hard. "Hello, Bobbo."

Bobbo waited until Lucretia Pepper had released Felix's hand and sat down again before he stood and shook hands, too. His grip seemed almost feathery compared to hers.

"It's a treat to see you again, Felix," Bobbo said. "I think you're going to be impressed with what we've got to tell you, and we hope you'll want to be part of *The Great Santa Search* team."

"Well, I'd certainly like to hear more about it," Felix replied, and sat down himself. We had instructed him to speak as little as possible, which, for Felix, was always a challenge. But we hadn't factored in the presence of Lucretia Pepper.

"I'd first like to learn more about your own background, Felix," she said. "I'm sure you understand that Bobbo and I must know potential associates better before we share confidential plans with them." She looked pointedly at Bobbo, waiting until he nodded nervously before returning her gaze to Felix. Clearly, their partnership was not one between equals. "How did you become an expert in both toys and Christmas history?"

"I've always loved the holiday, and I tried to learn as much about it as I could," Felix said, struggling to keep his voice from shaking. Lucretia Pepper had fixed him with a steely stare, and it made my old friend even more nervous. "As far as toys, well, I've built more than my share."

"Really?" she asked, tilting her huge head forward. "What company did you build them for?"

"Oh, quite a few," Felix replied, keeping his response intentionally vague. "I've always preferred consulting to working in just one place. I've spent lots of time on the job in Europe and Asia Minor as well as in America. Really, I'd prefer to talk about this *Great Santa Search* idea. I'm sure it must be fascinating."

Just for a moment, Lucretia Pepper's smile faded. When she frowned, it was easy to imagine storm clouds puffing out of her ears and lightning shooting from her eyes. She was clearly used to controlling conversations. But then the massive woman rearranged her lips back into a smile.

"Of course, Felix," she said. "You're quite direct. I respect that. Bobbo, won't you enlighten our friend?"

Bobbo jumped to his feet. "It was what you said about Santa Claus bringing me a wonderful idea for a reality-TV show," he declared. "I immediately thought, 'Why not a Christmas Eve reality show with Santa Claus in it?' The problem, of course, is that Santa Claus *isn't* real."

"Many would disagree," Felix protested.

"Perhaps. Well, in the next instant I remembered that people watching reality TV like to suspend their disbelief. Especially on Christmas Eve, the night we always have our big FUN-TV holiday special, they might be willing to believe in Santa Claus again if we gave them a reason to." As he spoke, Bobbo was practically quivering with excitement; his enthusiasm for his plan had caused him to forget the forbidding presence of Lucretia Pepper. "Felix, now what do you suppose we could do to create a reality show involving Santa Claus that everyone in the country would want to watch?"

"I can't wait to hear," Felix replied honestly.

"The most popular reality shows let audiences vote. How's that for a clue?"

"You'll ask people to vote on whether they believe in Santa or not?"

"No, no," Bobbo scoffed, waving his hand in disdain. "We've got something much better than that. Reality-TV audiences want to see *competition*, Felix. They want to see a winner and, perhaps even more, lots of losers. Can't you guess? We're going to have a show where people vote for Santa!"

Felix rubbed his face and looked perplexed, which he was. "But how can they do that, Bobbo? There's only one Santa. What does voting have to do with it?"

Now Bobbo was actually hopping up and down with glee. "Wrong, Felix! Go to any city in America during November and December. There are Santa Clauses everywhere—posing for photos with children in malls, ringing bells on street corners, telling you to buy this product or that one on TV commercials. No two of them look or sound exactly alike. Why, we're a country *crammed* with Santas. And how do you suppose that makes people feel?"

"I'm sure you'll tell me, Bobbo."

"It makes everyone feel confused and frustrated. Parents don't know what to tell their children when the kids ask which one is the *real* Santa. Little boys and girls can't understand why there are so many. And teenagers may be the most frustrated of all. They're at an age to doubt almost everything, and Santa's one of the childhood beliefs it hurts them most to lose. But they're sharp enough to realize all these guys with fake beards and pillows stuffed down their fronts are frauds. There are too many impostors going around claiming they're Santa Claus. People of every age have had enough of it. As a culture, we've reached the point of Santa saturation."

Bobbo was echoing the same concerns we'd felt at the North Pole since James Edgar adapted J. W. Parkinson's original "Santa-in-the-store" plan back in Brockton in 1890. Felix couldn't help nodding in agreement. Bobbo's enthusiasm was infectious, and his point was irrefutable.

"So what we're going to do," Bobbo said, leaning forward confidentially and lowering his voice, "is settle this Santa thing once and for all."

"You mean you're going to have a show that reveals all the mall and street-corner Santas are pretenders in red robes?" Felix asked.

Lucretia Pepper snorted disdainfully. The force of the air exhaled through her sizable nose actually ruffled Felix's hair.

"Oh, tell him, Bobbo," she commanded. "Stop building up the suspense."

"Yes," Bobbo agreed, and although he didn't add "ma'am," the subservient word was still understood by all three in the room. It might be Bobbo's original plan, and his TV network, but Lucretia Pepper was in charge.

Bobbo collected himself for a moment, glanced nervously at Lucretia Pepper, then continued. As soon as he resumed talking, his enthusiasm once again overcame his obvious fear of the woman.

"It's just the best idea for reality TV anyone's ever had, Felix, if I say so myself. We are going to hold a Christmas Eve competition next year that lets a studio audience select the real Santa Claus! Now, what do you think of that?"

Felix thought a lot of things, many of them unfit to be spoken aloud. Fortunately, Bobbo and Lucretia Pepper mistook his inability to immediately express himself as a sign that he was stunned by the ingenuity of Bobbo's proposed program.

"Well—" Felix tried, but further words failed him. "But—" he began again, then stuttered to a sudden halt. Finally, after several deep breaths, he was able to gasp, "How are you going to get Santa Claus in your studio? He's rather busy on Christmas Eve!"

Lucretia Pepper howled with laughter, and Bobbo chuckled heartily.

"You see, Lucretia?" Bobbo asked. "Is this guy going to add authenticity to the show, or what? 'Santa's rather busy on Christmas Eve'! We'll work that right in; it'll add to the tension. Those last couple of segments, maybe we can have a clock superimposed onscreen showing time running out for the Santa vote, so the winner can get his sleigh in the air and start delivering those presents. It's magic, just *magic*!"

For the first time, there seemed to be a hint of genuine pleasure in Lucretia Pepper's otherwise gargoyle-like grin. "It's a splendid touch. Bobbo, you've made your share of mistakes in recent years. That *Merry Monkey* disaster you just put on the air is a good example. But I believe that this time you've got the right program and the right man advising you about it. Yes, be certain to show a ticking clock onscreen."

"Wait," Felix protested. "I don't understand this whole *voting* thing."

"Just amazing!" Bobbo said. "He still doesn't have the basic concept, and yet he's already tossing out great ideas. Felix, it's like this. We're going to send a scout to all the biggest shopping malls in the country, because they hire the most authentic fake Santas anywhere. We'll pick, oh, the ten best, and bring 'em to our New York studio on Christmas Eve. We'll pack the audience with kids who still believe in Santa Claus. The ten contestants will compete in different events, though I don't know what they'll be yet. Reindeer-roping, maybe. Present-wrapping. We'll think of them later. After each round, the kids in the studio vote out one of the Santas until only two are left. Then for the grand finale—oh, this is so good, you're going to *love* this—the two remaining Santas each get, what, three minutes to speak directly to the audience and explain why *he* should be voted in as the real, actual, one-and-only Santa Claus. The kids vote, we get a winner, and right there on FUN-TV we present the official Santa, case closed. It can't miss. The ratings will go through the roof."

Felix thought sadly that Bobbo might just be right. "Are you certain you want to do this, Bobbo?" he asked. "What if, for instance, the Santa who's selected is really awful? Won't you be risking millions of children watching the program being so disappointed that their belief in Santa is damaged or even lost forever?"

"We're going to do our best to see that doesn't happen, Felix," Bobbo said. "We'll work hard to get ten contestants who've got the right look and voice and, I guess, attitude. These big malls hire only good ones, usually from companies that screen potential Santas to weed out anyone unsuitable. We'll end up with a fine Santa, I promise."

"Your concern does you credit, Felix," Lucretia Pepper added. "That's all the more reason for you to be part of *The Great Santa Search* team. You'll help shape the program format, work with Bobbo to design the various competitions, and even coach our ten Santa finalists on the real history of the holiday. Of course, the winner must be a Santa Claus children can believe in. LastLong Toys will settle for nothing less in its new national spokesman."

It took Felix a minute to process what he'd just heard. Finally, he managed to croak, "I beg your pardon?"

"It's nothing we have to talk about right now, Felix," Bobbo said quickly. "Just the business end of the show. Nothing you'll be involved with."

"That's entirely incorrect, Bobbo," Lucretia Pepper snapped. "As much as you've come up with a brilliant concept, there is still going to be a financial bottom line, and the more familiar with it everyone is, the better chance we have of all of us being happy when everything's over. And I *do* want to be happy, Bobbo. LastLong Toy Company is making a considerable investment in *The Great Santa Search*. We expect to get our money's worth, including the *right* Santa Claus as our spokesman."

"Santa Claus doesn't endorse specific toys," Felix protested. "I mean, at the North Pole he and his friends *make* them. Why would he be a spokesman for *yours?*"

Bobbo Butler grimaced, and hunched his shoulders as though to avoid a blow. Lucretia Pepper briefly seemed to consider swinging her hamlike fists, but instead burst into high-pitched laughter.

"He's just *astonishing*, Bobbo," she declared. "Listen to the resentment he's able to get into his voice when he pretends to believe in Santa Claus. I could almost think he does! If we can just bring that kind of apparent sincerity to *The Great Santa Search*, you'll have your ratings blockbuster and LastLong Toy Company will have an excellent return on our investment. And," she added, the girlish note in her voice suddenly absent, "I hope you both realize how *seriously* we take investments. Felix, do you know what my company is paying to be the exclusive sponsor of this program?"

Felix shrugged.

"On a Christmas-season special, networks with high ratings can charge as much as $500,000—yes, that's *half a million dollars*—to air one thirty-second commercial," the towering woman said. "Of course, FUN-TV has had terrible ratings, but Bobbo still charges $300,000 for thirty seconds. In each sixty minutes of airtime, perhaps forty-two minutes are actually part of a program, another five or so are used by networks to advertise other shows, and thirteen are set aside for commercials. Are you good at multiplying, Felix? For the commercials that would usually air during just one hour of *The Great Santa Search*, Bobbo expects $7,800,000. But *The Great Santa Search* is two hours long, so Bobbo is charging—and LastLong Toy Company is paying—$15.6 million. That's a great deal of money, don't you think?"

"Certainly," Felix admitted.

"As our corporate Christmas gift to the millions and millions of adults and children who are watching—they'd *better* be watching—LastLong Toy Company is going to pay for two hours' worth of commercials, but we're not going to actually put any on the air. *The Great Santa Search* will be almost two consecutive hours of uninterrupted entertainment. But at the end of the program, whoever's elected Santa will be presented to everyone watching as the new spokesman for LastLong Toys. Afterward he'll be featured in all our advertising and make personal appearances on behalf of our products. Didn't Bobbo tell me he met you at our Rockefeller Center skating show? Think what a greater sensation it would have been if we'd had Santa out there hawking our ice skates—the one and only, the *official* Santa Claus!"

It made painful sense to Felix. It was, he thought, the logical if disastrous culmination of what J. W. Parkinson had started so long ago.

"Bobbo, did you think of this . . . this . . . *scheme?*" he mumbled.

Bobbo hung his head. "I thought up *The Great Santa Search*, Felix, the voting and all. When I met with Lucretia to see if she'd buy commercial time on the program, she came up with the rest of it. Santa as the LastLong spokesman, I mean."

"And what a wonderful partnership we're going to have!" Lucretia Pepper announced, her voice once again high-pitched and sinisterly cheerful. "Bobbo, I must fly. As agreed, I'll have the first few million dollars deposited in the FUN-TV account. You'll be able to pay your overdue bills after all!"

Heather Hathaway was coming in through the conference-room door as Lucretia Pepper swooped out. They collided, and the younger woman bounced off the door frame. Lucretia Pepper didn't bother apologizing. Instead, she continued on her way through the outer office and then into the corridor, waving one meaty jeweled hand in impersonal farewell. Miss Hathaway rubbed her shoulder and glared after her.

"Are you all right?" Bobbo asked her, real concern in his voice. "I hope you're not bruised. Lucretia doesn't realize her own, well, *strength*."

Miss Hathaway looked at her boss and blushed. Felix had no idea why. "I'm fine, Bobbo," she said. "I hope the meeting went well."

"I suppose it did," Bobbo said, and he looked and sounded ashamed again. "Felix, I hope you understand. *Merry Monkey* was just a ratings disaster. No one anywhere watched it."

"Some of my friends and I did," Felix said.

"Well, then, you were about the only ones. My own children didn't watch it. *The Great Santa Search* can change everything for our network, but no other potential sponsors besides LastLong have even been willing to meet with me because our ratings have been terrible for so long. Lucretia's gruff, I know, even rude sometimes, but she understood right away what size audience we'd be able to attract if we had enough money to produce the kind of quality program I was describing. So she offered me a deal. She'd sponsor the whole thing for $15.6 million, but afterward the Santa who was elected had to become the LastLong spokesman. Felix, I needed the money to produce the show and save my network."

"What about saving children's belief in Santa Claus?" Felix asked, trying hard not to sound angry. "No one's going to accept Santa Claus as a spokesman, a *shill*, for a company whose toys break the moment anyone starts to play with them."

"Actually, they might," Bobbo said, and, standing beside him and still rubbing her sore shoulder, Heather Hathaway nodded. "Lots of people rely on television to tell them what to believe. The old-fashioned idea of Santa and his helpers making the toys at the North Pole and then delivering them by whizzing around in a sleigh pulled by flying reindeer doesn't cut it these days. But Santa endorsing a certain brand of toys? That, kids might believe. They see all their other so-called heroes doing it. Why not him?"

"Because Santa Claus is *different*, Bobbo," Felix argued. "That's why he's been special to children for centuries. He represents love and sharing, not some company's products."

Bobbo sighed. "Look, Felix, I'm going to broadcast this show next Christmas Eve. LastLong Toys is going to sponsor it. I'd like you to be my consultant, on everything from real Christmas history to picking the ten candidate Santas to planning all the actual details of the program. We can work out whatever salary you want—Miss Hathaway will handle that. I know you've got some misgivings, but look at it this way: as part of *The Great Santa Search* team, you can make this as authentic as possible—throw in bits of real Christmas history, and satisfy yourself that we've got some fine Santa candidates for the kids. What do you say?"

"I need to think about this, Bobbo," Felix said. "Can you give me a few days to make up my mind?"

Bobbo agreed. "Just don't take too long, Felix. We've got lots to do." They shook hands. As Miss Hathaway reached for Felix's arm to escort him from the office, Bobbo called after him, "Felix, wait. I want you to know this. I believed in Santa Claus for a long, long time. I wish I still did. But at least more children might keep on believing, if we make *The Great Santa Search* good enough. Help me make that happen, Felix."

As she helped Felix into his coat, Miss Hathaway leaned down and whispered, "*I* still believe."

Somehow, her words comforted Felix on his long trip back to the North Pole.

Five

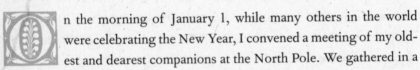

n the morning of January 1, while many others in the world were celebrating the New Year, I convened a meeting of my oldest and dearest companions at the North Pole. We gathered in a large, well-lit conference room that had its walls covered with world maps and giant computer and radar screens. This was where, on Christmas Eve, Amelia Earhart would monitor weather conditions around the globe and radio to me in my sleigh if blizzards or thunderstorms necessitated changes in air routes. There was a long, wide conference table surrounded by comfortable chairs—each year we might gather a few times to talk over gift-giving ideas and test some of the new toys that Leonardo, Ben Franklin, and Willie Skokan were constantly inventing. I'd rarely had to call a North Pole meeting for any emergency purpose. But Felix's report of Bobbo Butler's plan for *The Great Santa Search* certainly required immediate discussion.

So, after breakfast—Lars's pecan waffles, cinnamon scones, and freshsqueezed orange juice tasted delicious despite our collective concern—everyone drifted singly or in small groups to the conference room, and found places to sit around the long table. Before I called our meeting to order, I looked around and marveled at my luck in forming such a colorful, unique fellowship. At the far end of the table, Attila the Hun lounged with his wife, Dorothea. The few outsiders who knew of us were always astonished that this legendary warrior had eventually dedicated himself to the gentler task of gift-giving, but the Attila I knew was warmhearted and sincerely remorseful for the havoc he once wreaked with his sword and spear. Attila and Dorothea chatted quietly with St. Francis of Assisi, who even before joining our fellowship had been devoted to encouraging Christmas joy through the establishment of holiday traditions. In the early 1200s, Francis wrote some of the earliest carols that were specific to Christmas, and he suggested the first "manger scenes" to remind everyone that Baby Jesus came into the world as a poor, rather than wealthy, child. To Francis's left sat Leonardo da Vinci and Willie Skokan, the great painter-inventor and equally great craftsman, respectively. The two were fast friends and seldom apart; on this occasion they had spread in front of them as usual bits of paper filled with sketches and designs for toys no one else but that pair could have ever imagined. Ben Franklin sat beside them, seeming distracted by some random thought that caused his brow to furrow. Ben always appeared to be thinking, as opposed to daydreaming. There is a great difference.

Along the other side of the table were Amelia Earhart, the finest aviator of the early twentieth century, and Theodore Roosevelt, surely the most colorful American president of any era. Bill Pickett, the great African-American cowboy, was leaning toward them, no doubt telling some rip-roaring tale about wrestling steers or riding bucking broncos. Sequoyah, the brilliant Cherokee who invented a whole new alphabet for his tribe, sat calmly beside Arthur, whose exploits as a war chief somehow expanded into legends of a king with a magical sword and great castle called Camelot. Felix and Sarah looked the most concerned of anyone, but they had reason to be—they'd actually met Bobbo Butler, and Felix, of course, had made the nerve-racking acquaintance of Lucretia Pepper. Finally, Layla sat on my immediate right, looking serious but not anxious. However our discussion might proceed, I knew my beloved wife would remain calm, always preferring common sense to wild conjecture.

Layla gently nudged my arm. "We should begin," she suggested. "There's so much to talk about, and we still have to finish preparations for Epiphany."

She was right, of course. On January 6, children in Italy expected gifts from an old woman named Befana, and we would never want to disappoint them. That meant on the night of January 5 we'd transport mountains of toys and countless tons of candy across the seas, where Layla in particular would take great delight in dressing as the legendary peasant woman and distributing treats to all the Italian boys and girls who believed.

"Please, let's come to order," I suggested, and the words I used sent an unmistakable message. We're generally quite informal at the North Pole. In the eyes and imaginations of most of the world, Santa Claus is a sort of genial ruler over all his other helpers, but that was—is—simply not true. Still, someone has to chair each meeting, if only to be certain everyone has a chance to express himself or herself. A few of our number—Teddy Roosevelt and Felix, especially—are fond of their own voices, while others like Willie Skokan, St. Francis, and Dorothea are unlikely to offer opinions unless specifically asked. So I used more formal language than usual to get everyone's attention. We had urgent business to discuss; *The Great Santa Search* threatened everything we had tried to accomplish for so many centuries.

"Two days ago, Felix returned from New York City and delivered his shocking news," I reminded them. "The idea of a studio audience supposedly voting for the real Santa Claus while countless American families watch is bad enough. That LastLong Toy Company intends to use the winner as its corporate spokesman is completely unacceptable. Today, we must try to come up with some sort of plan, because if we simply sit back and let events take their course, it's possible children in America will have to choose between believing in the LastLong Toy Santa or deciding no Santa Claus exists at all."

I was surprised to see Francis immediately raise his hand, and yielded the floor to him at once.

"Santa, it has been our traditional policy not to try in any way to affect events," he said, brushing his thin hair back from his forehead. "We have always referred to ourselves as *gift-givers,* not *history-makers.* If we attempt to intercede with *The Great Santa Search,* aren't we violating our own rule? If Americans choose to embrace the winner of some silly TV contest as the real Santa, isn't that their right, foolish though it might be? Perhaps we should do nothing but observe."

Arthur stood as Francis returned to his chair.

"In most cases, old friend, I would completely agree," he told Francis. "But there are rare moments when some sort of intervention is absolutely required. Surely all of us here remember how Layla came forward in England in 1647 to lead protesters when Parliament attempted to ban the celebration of Christmas forever. If she hadn't done that, it was possible, even probable, that the holiday would have been lost there forever, and never introduced in the English colonies in the so-called New World that became America. This *Great Santa Search* may be the greatest threat to Christmas since, not because it threatens celebrating the holiday, but because it thwarts the real purpose of the celebration. Our gifts have always been meant to enhance the special time when we all should offer thanks to God for his son. We give gifts to demonstrate to children that real happiness is derived from love and generosity. All of us here realize that some will consider Christmas as nothing more than a fine opportunity to collect presents from others. That's why the presence—not the *presents*—of Santa Claus is so important. By symbolizing the act of gift-giving, he reminds children it is always better to give than to receive. It's a lesson they carry with them into their adult lives, and hopefully pass on to their own children in turn. Any declaration of an 'official Santa' whose sole purpose is to help one greedy company sell even more of its terrible toys jeopardizes the message we have spent centuries attempting, mostly successfully, to communicate." Arthur paused to take a breath, and suddenly looked embarrassed. "I'm sorry. I intended to make a brief comment, not a speech. I feel strongly about this, as you can see."

"We all do, Arthur," Ben Franklin said soothingly. "I find myself wondering, though, if the threat is as great as we fear. Isn't it true that all the recent Christmas Eve specials on FUN-TV have hardly been watched by anyone?"

Leonardo looked up from the sketches he and Willie Skokan had been studying. He, not surprisingly, was the North Pole computer expert. If requested to do so, Leonardo could log on to the Internet and track down any bit of information required, no matter how obscure. Now he reached into a voluminous pocket and withdrew a handful of crumpled papers. For all his brilliance, Leonardo was not especially organized. The rest of us had to wait while he smoothed out the papers, then peered at each one as though seeing it for the first time. Some sheets he recrumpled and jammed back into his pocket. A few others were shuffled into some sort of order. Only then did Leonardo clear his throat, glance briefly around the table, and begin speaking.

"Just over a week ago, the *Merry Monkey* Christmas Eve special on FUN-TV drew a two-tenths of one percent market share," he announced. "*Share* means the percentage of households with televisions that are tuned in to a specific program while it is on the air. Roughly translated, this two-tenths of one percent indicates approximately 219,800 households watched *Merry Monkey.*"

Bill Pickett whistled.

"More than 200,000 families! That's a whole lot of people, Leonardo."

Leonardo smiled.

"Bill, my good friend, consider this: there are some 110 *million* television households—families who watch television—in America. I'm afraid 219,800 of them is almost the tiniest market share possible."

"Then my point is well-taken," Ben Franklin said. "Why are we so worried? I admit that every child's belief in Santa is important, but at least where FUN-TV is concerned, the network's ability to damage children's beliefs appears to be quite limited."

Willie Skokan cleared his throat, and everyone else was startled. Willie *never* spoke during our meetings.

"We have to consider the *potential* viewership here," he blurted, and immediately sat down again.

Leonardo patted his best friend on the back. "Exactly, Willie. While FUN-TV currently attracts very few viewers, there is no reason the network can't reach a much wider audience the moment it has a program more people want to watch. From Felix's description, *The Great Santa Search* could attract widespread attention. If that's the case, there would be many millions of viewers instead of a few thousand."

Attila, the old Hun war chief, phrased his question in a military way.

"If this battle goes against us in the ratings, Leonardo, what's our worst-case scenario?"

Leonardo looked through the wrinkled papers on the table in front of him, frowned, dug back into his pocket, extracted the other papers he found there, peered at each, and finally exclaimed, "Ah!" as he found the one he was looking for.

"To date, Attila, the most-watched non-sports program in television history was aired in 1983. It was the final broadcast of a popular series called *M*A*S*H,* and it drew a share of just over 60 percent. About 50 million households tuned in to the show."

That figure impressed us. There were gasps all around the table.

"But remember," Leonardo cautioned, "there are many more households with televisions now than there were in 1983. Of course, they also have more programs to choose from. There was no real cable television then. These days, most people have hundreds of channels available at any given viewing moment. In recent years, no program has even approached a 60 percent market share. Bobbo Butler will have to work hard and spend a lot of money on advertising if he expects to match that, let alone set new viewing records with *The Great Santa Search*. It won't be easy."

"He has the money he needs, $15.6 million, remember?" Felix reminded us. "And though he's fallen on hard times of late, I'm convinced Bobbo knows the television industry inside out. He'll find ways to let everyone know about *The Great Santa Search*."

Theodore Roosevelt leaped to his feet. I'd been surprised he'd stayed silent this long.

"Enough of this mealymouthed discussion!" he declared. "Action is wanted here, not talk! Now, Santa Claus, have you considered the most obvious way of defusing this threat? By that I mean, going to this Bobbo person yourself and demanding he desist, at peril of being socked right in the snoot!"

"You know we never resort to violence, Theodore," Layla said calmly.

"Oh, I know, but snoot-socking can be very effective," Theodore replied, sounding sulky. "I just thought it ought to be mentioned. What I'd really recommend is this: Santa Claus, you've got a bully pulpit, perhaps the bulliest of them all. We're worried Bobbo Butler might get his silly program watched by millions of children who would then lose their faith in Santa Claus for one reason or another. Correct?"

"Yes, Theodore," I replied, wondering what was coming next.

"And Bobbo—what a silly nickname!—can do this because of modern media? Not only through his own network, but perhaps being featured on talk shows on other channels? And also articles in newspapers and online news sites and so forth?"

"Obviously," I said, hoping he'd get to the point. Theodore did love the sound of his own voice, and was never content to say something briefly and then sit down.

"Well, then, why not use your own bully pulpit and beat him to the punch, so to speak? If you, the real Santa Claus, contacted every media news outlet in the world and called a press conference to reveal yourself here at the North Pole before this so-called *Great Santa Search* ever got on the air next Christmas Eve, wouldn't that do the trick? With the one-and-only Santa already on every television screen, not to mention every magazine cover and newspaper front page, who would care about some reality program with ten fakers? No one! FUN-TV would get a zero market share, if such a thing is possible. Isn't this the simplest, most effective way of dealing with the problem?"

I heard several murmurs of assent. Theodore certainly had a point. If Bobbo was threatening us through the electronic medium of television, we could use the same means to thwart him. But that could only be done at a terrible, unacceptable cost.

"That's insightful, Theodore," I said, and the former American president nodded to acknowledge the compliment. "Unfortunately, what you suggest is the very thing we cannot do."

"Why is that?" Theodore asked.

"We must all remember why we live at the North Pole," I said. "Why have we chosen to live and work in an undetectable environment as far from civilization as remains possible in this widely traveled world? It's because privacy is important to us, and for two reasons. One is obvious. If our presence and location were common knowledge, we'd be overrun not just by the media, but by well-meaning, Christmas-loving tourists who would want to see our toy shops and feed the reindeer and pose for pictures with us and interrupt, however unintentionally, the vital nonstop work that is necessary if we're to effectively carry out our gift-giving mission. If I called a press conference to identify myself and explain what we do here, Theodore, why, afterward we'd never be left to work in peace."

"All right," Theodore grumbled. "You could leave out our exact location at the North Pole, then. But you could still announce yourself as the real Santa Claus. Fly in to the press conference on your sleigh pulled by the reindeer. That would do the trick."

"Now you touch on the second reason I can't do what you suggest," I said, making sure I sounded gentle so Theodore wouldn't feel I hadn't appreciated his comments. "We've all talked a great deal over the centuries about magic and illusion, how illusion can always be explained but magic simply *is*. Our fellowship, our mission, combines both. What some would call magic, we recognize as gifts from God—living without aging, being able to travel at speeds a hundred times faster than ordinary men and women. These are things that can't be explained, and of course they would greatly impress the public. But in trying to fit whatever Christmas expectations children might have, we've often turned to illusion, too, though only when absolutely necessary. After Clement Moore charmed American boys and girls with *A Visit from St. Nicholas,* for instance, Leonardo invented a way reindeer could *appear* to fly by rigging their harness and a sleigh with wings. When the reindeer run fast enough, air pushes under the wings and lifts the sleigh. It's the same principle that allows airplanes to fly. But the children believe it's the reindeer themselves who are soaring, and we let them believe it. If I *whooshed* down by sleigh to a press conference and some sharp-eyed reporter figured out how the reindeer really don't fly as such, that might cast doubt on the rest of our very legitimate magic and mission. In these cynical times, people look for reasons *not* to believe, Theodore.

Trying to circumvent *The Great Santa Search* by calling my own press conference would, I think, end up doing more harm than good. It's best for everyone that the real Santa remains just mysterious enough. *Believing* in me is a far better thing than actually *seeing* me."

Layla waved her hand; she had something to add. Instantly, everyone gave her their complete attention.

"In the past we've taken extraordinary measures to keep our location and methods of gift-giving secret," she said. "Surely all of you remember the Roswell incident in 1947."

We certainly did. That year, Americans seemed even more fascinated than usual with the possibility that aliens—*spacemen*—might be visiting the earth, either in friendship or else to enslave the human race. In response, Leonardo had invented a very realistic "alien" doll whose oddly shaped head, size, and greenish color reflected the images suggested in the most popular novels, comic books, movies, and radio programs (a lot of people didn't have television then).

I don't fly in my sleigh only on Christmas Eve. The reindeer are spirited, energetic animals who not only enjoy but require frequent exercise. So several times each month from January through November, I climb onto the sleigh and take my eight wonderful horned-and-hoofed steeds out for long excursions through the night sky. Just as I was preparing to take off on a July evening in 1947, Leonardo bustled up and asked if I'd load some of his new alien dolls on the sleigh. He was worried their particular shapes and weight might upset the load balance necessary for stable flight on Christmas Eve, and wanted to see in advance if they would. So I helped him load a few dozen of them, and then took off. That night I thought it would be pleasant to fly out over the American Southwest, where the scent of desert sage often wafts high up into the air. My route took me into the skies of southeastern New Mexico. As Leonardo had feared, the alien dolls somehow never settled properly in the sleigh, and just north of the little town of Roswell most of them tipped out and fell to the ground. Unfortunately, a few people in the area saw the dolls land in the distance, and by the time I'd contacted the U.S. government to retrieve them—Harry Truman, the American president at that time, was our friend, though we were always careful not to identify ourselves to any heads of state who were not absolutely trustworthy—rumors were flying around Roswell that aliens had invaded. Soldiers from the military base in Roswell found the dolls before the curious townspeople did, and locked the "aliens" away in an airplane hangar until we could secretly come and retrieve them. Afterward, the army announced that a weather balloon had crashed outside Roswell, and all that had been collected from the area was balloon debris. If they'd told the truth—that Santa Claus had accidentally spilled some dolls out of his sleigh—our gift-giving mission might have been irreparably compromised.

Not everyone believed the weather-balloon story. Ever since, a considerable number of people have been certain the government covered up the crash of an alien spaceship. I never again wanted to experience such unfortunate confusion or risk having any of our North Pole secrets revealed.

Theodore sighed. "I'd forgotten about Roswell," he admitted. "But we can't just sit back and let this *Great Santa Search* go unchallenged. Surely we can do *something*."

For the next half-hour, we tried to think what that might be. Someone would suggest something, but someone else would offer a reason it wouldn't work. Amelia Earhart wondered if Leonardo couldn't invent an electronic signal that would jam the FUN-TV broadcast, but Bill Pickett reminded her that this was essentially sabotage, and therefore something morally wrong that we could not do. Dorothea thought Bobbo Butler might be persuaded to cancel his *Great Santa Search* plans if it was demonstrated to him that the *real* Santa Claus didn't want him to do it, but Sarah made a good case for not even bothering.

"He's desperate to save his television network," she said out loud. "That is what Bobbo cares about right now. He made it clear to Felix that he's not a believer himself, so what good would it do for Santa to approach him? Bobbo would think he was just another impostor."

"What about Lucretia Pepper?" Sequoyah wanted to know. "Could Santa perhaps persuade her to pull her money out of the project?"

Felix had the answer to that one. "There are always people who care only for themselves," he said. "They have no interest in whether things they do hurt others. At least Bobbo wants FUN-TV to stay in business so families can watch wholesome programs together. Lucretia Pepper only wants to add more money to an already-considerable fortune. If *The Great Santa Search* will help LastLong sell even more toys—and it will—then the risk of innocent children losing their belief in Santa Claus means absolutely nothing to her. She'd sneer in Santa's face."

I was just ready to suggest that we'd talked enough for one meeting, that perhaps it would be best if we all took a day to reflect before continuing to debate the best response to *The Great Santa Search*. But then I happened to catch Layla's eye. She was looking at me intently, and as our gazes locked it seemed to me I understood exactly what she was thinking. This is sometimes the case with couples who have been together for a great deal of time, and to my knowledge no marriage in the history of the world has lasted longer than ours. The right action to take was suddenly clear to me. Common sense was necessary in any response, and also the observing of our fellowship's moral beliefs, which included no violence or sabotage. But sometimes daring was called for, even risk, and this was one of those occasions.

"All right," I said, standing once again. "Here is what I think we need to do. Feel free to point out any errors in my judgment, anything I might be leaving out or forgetting. Leonardo, use the Internet to get all the information you can about Bobbo Butler and Lucretia Pepper. Don't hack into any restricted sites, of course. But we want everything that's public record. The more we know about these people, the better. Then, Felix must contact Bobbo tomorrow and tell him he's ready to join *The Great Santa Search* team. Afterward, we'll always have up-to-the-minute inside information about what is going on. I know that means Felix is technically spying for us, but I'm sure he'll be certain to offer Bobbo only helpful advice. When the program goes out on the air on Christmas Eve, it *will* be broadcast live, won't it, Felix?"

"Bobbo was very clear about that," Felix said. "He wants viewers to believe Santa has to hurry to his sleigh as soon as the program is over."

"And whoever is selected as the real Santa will end the program with a short speech?"

"That's what I understand."

"All right. What I'm getting at here is that we need information from Felix to be certain the right Santa Claus gets the most votes. Then that winning contestant can use his final featured moments on the program to talk about the right reasons to celebrate Christmas, not about LastLong Toys."

"You mean we'll fix the voting so that our favorite contestant wins?" Ben Franklin asked, sounding puzzled. "I thought we didn't believe in sabotage, Santa."

"We don't, Ben," I assured him. "The members of the studio audience must vote as they think best. We'll let their own eyes and ears and hearts help them make that decision in favor of one specific contestant."

"Who will that be, Santa?" Bill Pickett asked, and out of the corner of my eye I saw Layla smiling.

"Why, me, of course, Bill," I replied. "I'm going to compete on *The Great Santa Search,* and I'm going to win it!"

Six

It's true we love nothing better than racing around the world leaving children gifts on the occasions of St. Nicholas Day, Christmas, and Epiphany. We derive great pleasure from those frantic nights, which test even our miraculous ability to travel faster than any other humans in history.

But it's also a fact that, by the time we return home, we're worn out. What we call "the mornings after" find us sleeping late, perhaps rising only in time for a tasty brunch prepared by Lars. On the mornings of December 6, December 25, and January 6, while children shriek with delight upon discovering their presents, those of us at the North Pole are probably enjoying well-earned rest.

This is what I was doing in the early morning of January 6. After our meeting where I decided I would enter and win *The Great Santa Search* competition, I put the whole thing out of my mind to prepare for Epiphany gift-giving. It is always quite complicated. As is also the case in the days leading up to St. Nicholas Day and Christmas, prior to Epiphany we must finalize our lists of boys and girls and the gifts being delivered to each, map out travel routes at the last minute to allow for unexpected storms or high winds, load the sleigh carefully so that the first gifts to be delivered are on top (no matter how carefully we plan, some always end up on the bottom, and valuable time is lost rooting through the entire load of gifts to reach them), and, just before takeoff, check to see that all the reindeer's harnesses are secure. The reindeer and sleigh whisk me from house to house only in America. They are not involved in the holiday gift-giving traditions of many other cultures, so on St. Nicholas Day and Epiphany they are used to transport us and our gifts from the North Pole to our destination countries. From there, our fellowship often delivers gifts on foot, each toting a heavy sack of toys and a list reminding us what is to be taken where. It's a challenge to get everything delivered before daylight, when the children we love so much wake up and rush to find their presents!

As always, it was exhilarating for all of us to speed around leaving Epiphany gifts. We returned to the North Pole exhausted but happy sometime after midnight. Following a snack of hot chocolate and Lars's homemade chocolate-chip cookies, still warm from the oven, we all went off to bed, planning to sleep much of the new day away. But it seemed I had scarcely turned out the light and closed my eyes when there was an insistent tapping on the door of the bedroom where Layla and I slept.

I squinted at my bedside clock—it was 6:00 a.m. Between early October and early March, we have to rely on clocks at the North Pole to know what time of day it is. That's because, for all that time, the sun never shines at all. It is always dark outside. The opposite is true from late March through late September. Then, the sun never stops shining, and we still need our clocks. There's no other way to tell morning from night.

But in this case my clock confirmed that it was *very* early morning, and right after one of our three long, tiring nights of holiday gift-giving, too! I first felt annoyed, but then wondered if there might be some sort of emergency. I stumbled up, pulled on my robe, and tried to tiptoe to the door without turning on my bedside lamp so I wouldn't wake Layla. I immediately stubbed my toe on the nightstand, and when I hopped in pain my elbow made contact with the lamp, which crashed to the floor. So I was not in the best of moods when I opened the door and found Theodore Roosevelt standing in the hall outside.

"Whatever is the matter, Theodore?" I asked. "Is there a problem of some sort?"

Theodore grinned, his large square teeth and eyeglasses glinting in the hallway light. "Nothing at all's the matter, Santa!" he boomed in a cheerful voice that was entirely inappropriate for such an early hour. "It's time for you to get up. You begin training this morning, you know!"

"No, I *don't* know, Theodore," I hissed. "It's six in the morning on Epiphany, and, if you don't mind, I'm going back to bed." I yawned, looked at him more carefully, and added, "Why are you dressed like that?"

Theodore wore a bright green New York Jets football jersey—he'd once been governor of New York and never lost his special affection for sports teams from that state—gray sweatpants, and a baseball cap with *"World's Greatest President"* emblazoned on the front. We'd given him the cap a few years earlier as a 150th birthday present. He'd since taken to wearing it everywhere. What I'd never seen him wearing until now was the silver whistle dangling from a cord around his neck.

"Don't joke, Santa Claus," Theodore said sternly. "You're planning to compete on *The Great Santa Search,* aren't you? There will be all sorts of contests, though we don't yet know what kind. But running and climbing will certainly be involved. You said we'd begin preparing right after Epiphany gift-giving. Well, that gift-giving's over. Now we've got to start getting you into decent physical shape. You're quite overweight, you know, and I can't remember the last time you had some real exercise."

I chose to ignore his reference to my weight—I'm rather big-boned and carry any extra pounds quite gracefully—and instead concentrated on his preposterous claim that I didn't exercise.

"I'm constantly getting exercise, Theodore," I argued. "All day I'm hurrying around our North Pole offices, seeing first to this and then to that. I often go hours without even sitting down."

"But when you do sit down, it's at a table," Theodore replied. "Chewing and swallowing don't count as exercise. When is the last time you did a chin-up or jogged a few miles?"

"Never," Layla called from under the warm covers of our bed. "Of course, I've only known him for sixteen centuries. He might have been a fiend for exercise before that."

"Please go back to sleep," I said to her, then returned my attention to Theodore. "Your point is well taken. I'll tell you what—come back at noon and perhaps we can take a walk."

Theodore shook his head. "This can't be put off, Santa. We're going to start every morning from now until the broadcast with hard, healthy exercise before breakfast. The combination of working up a good sweat and following a sensible diet for a change will soon have you feeling like a new man. Now, get dressed in comfortable clothes. Not good ones, mind you. Perspiration stains can be difficult to get out in the wash."

"I really don't think—" I began, but Layla, her voice still somewhat muffled by the covers, informed me I would find a sweatshirt and sweatpants in the middle drawer of our bureau. "Now, I know I don't own either of those items," I replied, and then realized what was going on. "Admit it," I demanded of the Layla-sized, covered lump swaddled so comfortably in bed while I was being rousted out by Theodore. "You two planned this. Layla, you got me workout clothes, didn't you?" Theodore, still standing in the doorway, tried and failed to look innocent. I think Layla chuckled, but her head was still hidden under the covers and she might have been snoring. She certainly didn't deny it.

Sighing, I put on the new workout clothes as well as a comfortable pair of athletic shoes that I often wear during long days at the North Pole. I know most children and many parents expect me to always be shod in high black boots, and I do wear those when I'm making my holiday gift-giving rounds, along with bright red robes trimmed in white fur. At all other times, I must admit I prefer comfort to style, especially where shoes are concerned. After more than seventeen hundred years of faithful service, my feet have earned some pampering.

No sooner had I tied my shoelaces than Theodore was urging me out the door. "It's getting on quarter past six," he nagged. "Breakfast is at eight sharp. We have lots to do before then."

"We spent last night delivering gifts, Theodore," I reminded him. "No one will even be stirring until noon, when Lars will serve brunch."

"*You* are having breakfast at eight," Theodore said, and didn't explain further.

We hustled down the hallway at a faster pace than I found comfortable. Theodore's legs were shorter than mine, but he moved them at a very rapid rate. When I began to lag behind, he looked back over his shoulder and said, "Come on, come on!" I was in no hurry because I knew where he was taking me.

It is never warm or even comfortably cool outside at the North Pole. During winter, the temperature regularly drops as low as 35 degrees below zero and even in the so-called "summer months" it rarely gets warmer than 32 degrees above zero, which is still officially designated as "freezing." Even if we could spend much time outside, there is no actual *land* to look at or walk on. The Arctic ice cap is some ten feet deep, and usually covered with thick layers of snow. During the coldest months, it can expand to a size roughly equal to the continental United States. There are no trees or other sturdy shrubbery. Everything is pale and cold. This has its own certain barren beauty, especially when the gorgeous Northern Lights—electrons and protons from the sun colliding with atoms of oxygen and nitrogen, among other things, in the earth's upper atmosphere—suddenly blaze green, red, and blue across the inky sky. But anyone standing long in the icy air would suffer frostbite.

So in designing our North Pole home, which is a dazzling array of underground buildings connected by tunnels we have come to think of as "hallways," Leonardo added a cavernous indoor gymnasium that eventually included basketball and handball courts, gymnastics equipment, an Olympic-sized swimming pool, and a quarter-mile track. The gymnasium is open to all of our fellowship. Sometimes when the holidays draw near, many of my companions work late in the toy factory and relax afterward with a friendly game on the basketball court or perhaps a rowdy session of water polo in the pool. Willie Skokan is fond of the parallel bars in the gymnastics area, and after all these centuries he is still quite lithe. Sometimes, just for the fun of it, he spends the entire day walking around on his hands. Attila loves handball, but he competes so aggressively, shouting and throwing his body wildly into every shot, that no one really likes playing with him. Layla, Sarah, Dorothea, and Amelia Earhart meet in the evenings before dinner to jog together around the track, sometimes forgetting how many laps they've completed if the conversation proves especially interesting, which it often does.

I rarely visit the gym myself. I feel obligated to spend much of my spare time reading about new or changing holiday customs around the world, and if I do this seated in a comfortable chair in my den, and if I occasionally doze off while conducting my intense research, well, what is the harm of it? I certainly don't *mind* exercise, it's just that I have other priorities.

"Here we are, Santa," Theodore announced, throwing open the double doors that led into the gymnasium. All the lights were already on; still sleepy, I blinked in the sudden glare. When my eyes adjusted, I saw Theodore opening a locker along the near wall. He took out some sort of large, heavy ball, a stopwatch, and a jump rope.

"We'll start out with some simple stretching exercises to loosen up your muscles, Santa," he said briskly. "Now, spread your feet about shoulder-width apart and begin by touching your toes a dozen times. Do it the right way, please, returning to full standing position after each time you bend down."

"Is this really necessary?" I asked.

Theodore raised the silver whistle to his lips and blew hard. The resulting loud, ear-piercing sound made my head ache.

"It's time to *exercise,* Santa!" he barked, and I suddenly understood how army recruits must feel when a grumpy drill sergeant organizes calisthenics. Glumly, I moved my feet apart as ordered and bent down to touch my toes. Unfortunately, Theodore noticed that my fingertips hovered a good dozen inches above my feet unless I bent my knees, which he immediately made clear was not allowed.

"I said to do it the right way, Santa," he commanded, and there was a certain steely note in his voice that must have harkened back to his days in the White House, when he issued orders to everyone and expected to be obeyed. "Keep your legs straight! Suck in your stomach! Get those fingers down to your toes!" I wanted badly to oblige him, if only to stop him shouting in my ear, but the lower my fingertips were able to go, the more a series of alarming crackling sounds issued from my already-aching back. I huffed and crackled and bent and strained for what seemed like a very long time before I finally made fleeting contact between fingertips and toes. Theodore blew his whistle again, and informed me I would be expected to do better tomorrow.

"By the time I'm done with you, you'll be able to touch your toes a hundred times in a row," he said. "You're going to be amazed how much progress you'll make."

"I'll be amazed if I even survive until breakfast," I replied. "Really, Theodore, my back is hurting. Haven't we done enough for the first day?"

Theodore polished his glasses on his New York Jets jersey, held them up to the gymnasium lights to check for remaining specks of dust, put them back on, and peered at me.

"I hope you're joking, Santa Claus," he said. "I've put a great deal of time into developing a workout routine for you."

"Thank you, Theodore," I told him. "What torture have you planned for me next?"

"We're going to tighten up that stomach of yours," he said ominously. "Have you ever worked out with a medicine ball before? No? Well, here is how it's done. I'll stand a few feet away, and then bounce the ball off your belly like *this*. Say, why is your face turning red? That was a *very* soft toss!"

The ball was so heavy that I suspected it had some sort of cast-iron core. When it hit my stomach, it knocked me backward and quite took my wind away. I gasped for several seconds before I was able to ask Theodore to please not ever do that again.

"But it's good for you, Santa!" he protested. "In my college days when I was on the boxing team, we worked out with medicine balls all the time. It's quite a bully exercise!"

"I doubt boxing will be one of the competitions on *The Great Santa Search*, Theodore," I said. "If it is, we'll find a way to disguise you as me and you can get in the ring."

I was being sarcastic, but Theodore didn't realize it. "Really, Santa?" he cried. "Could I? Do you promise? Boxing is such fun."

"You have my solemn oath, Theodore," I said. "Meanwhile, please put the medicine ball away. I notice a jump rope there by your feet. I'm sure that sort of exercise will be quite good for me, and pleasant, too. For centuries I've seen children skipping rope, and I always wanted to try it myself. May I?"

Theodore handed me the jump rope. I took one handle in each hand and pulled it up in an arc over my head, trying at the same time to hop off the floor so there would be room for the rope to pass under my feet. Perhaps I twirled the rope too fast, or didn't jump high enough. In any event, the rope somehow snagged around my ankles and I went toppling off-balance into Theodore, who staggered, tripped over the medicine ball, and tumbled onto his back. He immediately jumped up, placed the whistle between his lips, and blasted out a particularly harsh, ear-splitting note.

"Concentrate, Santa Claus!" he barked. "Jumping rope is not intended to be a contact sport!"

"I'm sure it won't happen again," I assured him. I untangled the jump rope from my ankles and tried again, and again. The results were no better. Every time I twirled the rope quickly and tried to jump, it hit my ankles or got snarled at my shins. If I swung it very slowly, I could take only a ponderous hop that concluded with me thumping hard back on the floor while the rope sagged behind me. Theodore impatiently snatched the jump rope from me and demonstrated how it was supposed to be done. He immediately fell into a brisk, graceful rhythm, with the rope slapping pleasantly against the floor each time it passed beneath his feet. All the jumping made the whistle on the cord around his neck flap madly up and down. After a minute he stopped and handed the jump rope back to me.

"Any little girl in the world can do this, Santa," he remarked. "Surely you can, too."

But I couldn't. It was much harder than it looked. Theodore looked more and more exasperated. Finally he waved at me to stop.

"You can't touch your toes, catch a medicine ball, or jump rope," he said. "This is going to be tougher than I thought."

"If it's too much trouble, just say so, and I'll go back to bed," I informed him. "It's not as though *I'm* having a good time, either."

Theodore immediately looked stricken. "Oh, I'm sorry, Santa," he said. "It's just that I know how important it is for you to win this *Great Santa Search*, and you really do need to be in better physical shape for it, just in case. What sort of events did Bobbo Butler mention to Felix? Stocking-stuffing was one, I think. Another was reindeer-roping. How can you lasso a reindeer if you can't even use a jump rope? Please let me help you with all this. I promise to be more patient."

I could hardly be angry with my dear old friend. He meant so well, and he was certainly right in suggesting I ought to get myself into better physical condition.

"That's fine, Theodore," I said. "All right. Obviously that's enough jump-roping, or jump-*tripping*, for one day. What do you want me to do next?"

Theodore consulted a list he drew from his pocket. "It's time to run, Santa. Well, not actually *run*. *Jog* is a more appropriate term. I don't expect you to get on the track and run for miles, at least not yet. Each time around is a quarter mile. Do you think you could go around twice? I've got a stop-watch here. Maybe you could jog two laps in, oh, five or six minutes? That would be an excellent start."

He led me to the track, and offered several suggestions about how to jog. I was to *shuffle* my feet rather than lift them up high as I went along. I should try to breathe through my nose rather than my mouth. My arms should pump gently back and forth at the same rate as my legs. These things, he promised, would improve my stamina.

"Just do your best," Theodore said as he held up the stopwatch and signaled for me to start. He sounded mournful, as though he already knew I wouldn't be able to jog even a hundred yards without stopping, let alone half a mile.

But in his excitement at designing a training regimen for me, Theodore had apparently forgotten that one of the powers granted to all of our gift-giving fellowship is the ability to move faster than is possible for normal people. In the evenings at the North Pole gymnasium when Layla and the others jogged around the track, they did not bother to run as fast as they could. The deliberately slow pace allowed them time to unwind from their workdays and chat with each other about inconsequential things. On any given St. Nicholas Day, Christmas, or Epiphany, I moved at speeds the fastest Olympic athlete could never match. So when Theodore asked me to do my best as I ran around the track, it didn't take me five or six minutes to complete two laps. I was done in five or six seconds.

"Well, *that* was easy!" I announced with a certain sense of satisfaction. Theodore looked shocked, then grinned as he realized there was one area of athletic endeavor, at least, in which I already excelled.

"I hope one of the contests on *The Great Santa Search* is a foot race," he said. "I suppose I can cross running off your daily workout list."

"Just so long as you don't cross off breakfast," I replied. "Now that I've been working out a while, I feel terribly hungry. Exercise certainly helps work up an appetite. What do you say?"

"I say, let's be off to the kitchen!" Theodore agreed. He handed me a towel to wipe off my face—I had actually gotten a bit sweaty—and we left the gym through another hallway that led to our dining area.

We eat cafeteria-style at the North Pole. The dining hall itself is filled with long tables where we sit and serve ourselves at mealtimes from great heaping platters of food prepared in a spacious, adjacent kitchen by Lars and his staff, which includes a grizzled old railroad chef named Worth who prepares some of the best fried chicken anyone has ever tasted. Now, I hardly expected fried chicken at this early morning hour, but I still had visions of fluffy scrambled eggs, thick slices of ham, and perhaps a jelly doughnut or two washed down with several tall glasses of freshly squeezed orange juice.

But when we arrived in the dining hall, there was no one there. Theodore reminded me that everyone else at the North Pole was sleeping in, even Lars.

"So I'll be preparing your breakfast myself, Santa," he announced proudly. "I like fixing a meal now and then. I used to do it all the time at the White House. Everyone loved my special pancakes with swirls of strawberry preserves."

"Now, that sounds delicious, Theodore," I replied enthusiastically. "Will you be making those pancakes for me this morning?"

"Not exactly, Santa," Theodore said. "Why don't you make yourself comfortable at that table over there, and I'll just go into the kitchen and get things going. It won't take long."

"I hope not," I called after him. "I'm starving."

I expected Theodore to be gone ten minutes at least, and more likely twenty. Cooking fine meals takes a while. But it seemed like no time at all before the swinging doors to the kitchen bumped open, and Theodore emerged carrying a tray covered by a green cloth.

"Here you are, Santa!" he said cheerfully, placing the tray on the table in front of me. "Dig in!"

Smiling with anticipation, I pulled the cloth off the tray and was puzzled to find beneath it only a medium-sized bowl of steaming oatmeal.

"Is this the first course, Theodore?" I inquired. "I believe you forgot to put butter and brown sugar on the tray. That's what I always like to put on my oatmeal."

"No butter or brown sugar for you, Santa," he said. "Too many calories. This oatmeal is your first course this morning, and also your last. Don't look so unhappy. For lunch, you'll get a nice fruit salad with yogurt dressing."

"I can't eat oatmeal without butter and brown sugar, Theodore," I protested.

"That's your decision," he said, "but it's a long time until lunch. If you're as hungry right now as you say you are, you probably want to eat that oatmeal just the way it is."

So I did, one plain, boring spoonful at a time.

"Why aren't *you* eating, Theodore?" I asked. "Aren't you hungry, too?" He was sitting at the table watching me eat and chatting ominously about push-ups and sit-ups and getting the hang of jumping rope.

"I'm going to wait until noon, Santa," Theodore said. "Lars has promised brunch will include smoked salmon and freshly baked blueberry muffins. It's going to be a memorable meal."

"When will I be allowed to enjoy blueberry muffins again?" I inquired.

The thought of Lars's delectable baked goods made the oatmeal taste that much worse.

"Why, just as soon as you've won *The Great Santa Search*!" Theodore said cheerfully. "Finish every bit of that oatmeal, Santa. You need to keep up your strength! Children all over the world are depending on you!"

"I hope next Christmas Eve some of them leave out blueberry muffins for me," I mumbled. But I did eat all of the oatmeal, because it was hours until lunch and my fruit salad with yogurt dressing.

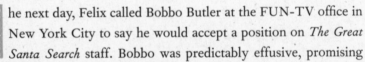he next day, Felix called Bobbo Butler at the FUN-TV office in New York City to say he would accept a position on *The Great Santa Search* staff. Bobbo was predictably effusive, promising Felix that afterward he'd be bragging about being part of the most famous broadcast in television history. When Felix repeated this to the rest of us, some wondered why Bobbo remained so certain the program would attract unprecedented public interest. Though he'd mentioned *The Great Santa Search* on Christmas Eve at the conclusion of *Merry Monkey*, there hadn't been any speculation about the show in the news media. Of course, very few people had watched *Merry Monkey*. I felt sure Bobbo had all sorts of marketing plans in mind and was glad Felix would be finding out about them.

Bobbo informed Felix his title would be "senior consultant," and that he should come to New York in another two weeks for the program's first planning meeting. Bobbo himself would be producer, but Felix also needed to meet the show's director and set designer and several other important members of "the team."

That agreed upon, Bobbo then informed Felix he was handing the phone

over to Heather Hathaway, who would discuss salary with him. She astonished Felix by telling him he would be paid several hundred thousand dollars, broken down into monthly increments. She asked for a home address
where the paychecks could be sent, and Felix supplied her with a post-office
box number in Boston, where Bobbo Butler assumed he and Sarah lived. We
had post-office boxes in a number of major cities all over the world, so on
the rare occasions when we needed to communicate with outsiders we
wouldn't have to reveal our North Pole location. Certain government officials and special friends had our North Pole e-mail addresses, but we did not
include Bobbo Butler or Heather Hathaway in this exclusive group.

"Well, my new salary means that's one less toy patent we'll have to sell
this year," Felix told me proudly. Our North Pole toy-manufacturing operation is both extensive *and* expensive; we pay for raw materials like wood
and paint and plastic by licensing some of the inventions of Leonardo, Ben,
and Willie Skokan to carefully selected toy companies who pledge to produce only the highest-quality products for children. We never do business
with manufacturers who don't adhere to the most rigorous standards—
LastLong Toys, for example, was not and would never be our partner. Some
of the income is also used to defray other expenses like food for humans and
feed for reindeer; upkeep of our electric, heating, and plumbing systems;
clothes; and assorted costs of travel. We are exceptionally fortunate not to
need health-care benefits. Everyone who lives and works at the North Pole
is blessed with apparently endless good health. And, of course, there's no
need for North Pole salaries. Everything any of us might want is supplied,
and no one is afflicted by the terrible disease of greed. Felix's considerable
Great Santa Search salary would be contributed to the general North Pole
account, to be used as needed.

We were glad there was a little time before Felix had to go to New York
to meet with Bobbo, because Leonardo was working hard to find out all he
could about him, and about Lucretia Pepper, too. A few times, Leonardo
asked me if he might not be allowed to hack into certain government files to
see if there might be any information in them about the two that might
prove useful to us. It was something my friend the famous painter-inventor
could have accomplished; there was no password he couldn't guess or fire-

wall he couldn't crack. But at the North Pole, as it should be everywhere, we respect each individual's right to privacy. Anything that was a matter of public record about Bobbo Butler and Lucretia Pepper we could and would study, but even if we were working against them regarding *The Great Santa Search* we would still observe appropriate limits.

Just before Felix was supposed to return to New York, Leonardo announced he'd completed his Internet investigations and wanted to report on what he'd discovered. It was a welcome distraction for me. Every morning at 6:00 a.m., Theodore knocked on my bedroom door to escort me to the gymnasium. There he would direct me through an increasingly difficult series of exercises that left me feeling sweaty and quite sore, often with muscles aching in body areas where I had not previously realized I even had muscles. Afterward he would escort me to the dining hall, where I would have to swallow down oatmeal or plain, tasteless cold cereal while all around me everyone else enjoyed omelets and French toast and English muffins. At lunchtime, I interrupted my workday for salad of some sort. Dinner, always a highlight of everyone's North Pole day, found me settling for broiled chicken breast or vegetable soup while the rest of our fellowship dined splendidly on pot roast or shrimp-stuffed crab cakes or the unmatchable enchiladas and tamales Lars likes to cook while wearing a massive Mexican sombrero. At times each day my stomach rumbled so loudly that anyone standing near me thought they were hearing thunder. Feeling sore and hungry at the same time is a particularly depressing combination. Theodore assured me that, after a month when I weighed myself and saw how many pounds I had lost, it would all seem worth it. I wasn't as positive. Once or twice—all right, nearly every night—I attempted to sneak out after midnight to raid the six-foot-high refrigerator in the kitchen, but my annoyingly alert wife always woke up and ordered me back to bed. I know I mentioned earlier that no one is anyone else's boss at the North Pole, but Layla has a certain air of command that makes disagreement with her difficult, if not impossible.

When we all gathered in the main conference room to listen to Leonardo's report, several in our fellowship had to muffle giggles because my stomach was rumbling at a particularly concussive rate. It was not my stomach's fault. Leonardo had chosen to call us together in mid-afternoon, and the garden salad I'd consumed just a few hours earlier hadn't come close to satisfying my appetite. Four slices of tomato, a half-dozen leaves of lettuce, a bit of radish, and some cucumber slices, plus a small pear for dessert, simply do not constitute a full meal.

Then Leonardo came in, laden with what appeared to be a dozen manila file folders that were each crammed with documents. Willie Skokan trailed after him, also carrying a pile of folders. Leonardo directed him to drop them on the long table, and, after Willie did, dropped his own folders on top. The resulting mountain of material rose nearly to Leonardo's chest, and then he had to find his reading glasses, fumbling though various pockets and becoming increasingly confused until someone told him the glasses were perched on the top of his head. Leonardo put his glasses on and then had to spend several more minutes shuffling the file folders until he had them in the right order. Finally, he cleared his throat and we all leaned forward to listen.

"We are dealing with two very interesting people," he began. "I'll begin with Bob O. Butler, who has referred to himself as 'Bobbo' ever since the fifth grade, when he was asked to produce a school Christmas play. Willie, the first picture, please." Willie Skokan pushed a button; the room darkened and a photograph of a school flashed on the screen that covered one wall. "Milligan Elementary School in Ward, Ohio, in 1961. This is where Bob O. Butler staged what was apparently a spectacular program; the local newspaper did a story afterward. Every child in the school participated. There were production numbers where dozens of children danced while all the teachers played kazoos. Young Mr. Butler's picture was included with the newspaper article—slide, Willie—and you can see he was a very cheerful-looking boy. He asked the reporter to identify him as 'Bobbo' in the story because he thought that was a good name—this is a direct quote—'for a show-business impresario.' We can see that Bobbo Butler knew early in life what he really wanted to do. In looking through his subsequent school yearbooks, it seems that every year he always organized some sort of holiday extravaganza. As a senior at Dewberry High in Ward, he gave an interview to his school newspaper and said—do we have that photo, Willie? Good—that he would always try to help everyone especially enjoy Christmas because—this is another direct quote—'Santa Claus is very real to me.'"

"What a lovely sentiment, Leonardo," Layla commented. "Tell me, what kind of record of Bobbo Butler's childhood do we have in our own North Pole archives?"

"Lights, Willie," Leonardo requested. He adjusted his glasses and fumbled with the pile of file folders on the table in front of him, picking up and discarding each in turn until he found the one he wanted. "Bobbo Butler of Ward, Ohio, was one of our most exemplary children, a maximum true believer."

Leonardo's description of young Bobbo Butler as a *maximum true believer* told us a great deal. It was one of several categories we used at the North Pole to record when and under what circumstances we no longer delivered Christmas gifts to individual children. This was and will always be a critical moment in any young person's life, and we take it very seriously.

Even Santa Claus can't do *everything*. Each Christmas, our fellowship is taxed to its physical limits by endeavoring to bring presents to every deserving, believing boy and girl. Every year, naturally, there are new children who expect and must receive our presents, so they will learn through this wonderful, traditional process how important it is to celebrate each holiday season with acts of love and generosity. But because North Pole resources, though immense, still have their limits, this also means that each Christmas a certain percentage of children must for the first time do without a gift from Santa, though hopefully this will not in any way lessen their enjoyment of the holiday.

From the moment we became organized enough to establish toy factories in certain cities, and afterward when we consolidated our operations at the North Pole, one of our greatest challenges has been to keep careful track of all the world's children who believed in and hoped for gifts on St. Nicholas Day, Christmas, and Epiphany. There were always homes where we were not welcome. In some cases, this was because the families there were not of the Christian faith. We respect all beliefs. Because our mission is intended to spread ideals of universal goodwill, we do hope our holiday gift-giving also benefits those who don't participate in "Santa" traditions.

But we're still welcome, or, I should say, *expected,* in millions of other households with children who can't wait for the one morning each year when gifts from the North Pole ought to be waiting for them. Before the advent of computers, we had to maintain thick ledgers listing the names and addresses of each deserving boy and girl. It was extremely difficult, but necessary. Much of the months of November and December were taken up just planning proper delivery routes, because the list of places where we had to stop changed each year as we added and subtracted names.

I know certain popular holiday carols (and, sometimes, exasperated parents) suggest otherwise, but we never eliminate children from our gift-giving because of bad behavior. No child is perfect; reasonable discipline from responsible adults is necessary in the life of any young person. Gift-giving is a gentler form of lesson, and one all of us at the North Pole believe is just as effective.

We stop bringing children gifts under certain specific sets of circumstances, and, over the years, we have developed code words for these. Now that the North Pole is equipped with state-of-the-art computers (usually Leonardo, Ben Franklin, and Willie Skokan are the masterminds of technological breakthroughs), we are able to enter raw data on each child as it arrives in the form of reports from parents, teachers, clergy, and so forth. As in the cases of Bobbo Butler and Lucretia Pepper, this means Leonardo can call up a report on anyone's childhood gift-giving history at the touch of a keyboard.

Some children are classified as *believers.* During their early years, they believe in Santa. They're thrilled by the thought I'll visit their homes and leave them a gift. But at some point, at age six or seven, perhaps, they stop believing. Often it's because an older sibling mocks their belief. Sometimes they're so disappointed by "department store" Santas that they decide there can't be a real one. They might have stayed up on Christmas Eve to try to see me, only to see instead their parents putting gifts under the tree. (They wouldn't realize I arrive much later, after even parents are in bed and fast asleep.) In any event, they no longer expect me in their homes. Now, this doesn't mean they no longer get Christmas gifts, but all of these will now come from parents and other caring relatives and friends. Believers don't have to lose their love of the holiday or necessarily fail to understand and practice the love and generosity exemplified by the season. When they grow up, they even tell their own children about Santa, because they think they're entertaining with stories about someone mythical. That's all right.

True believers are children who retain their faith in me much longer. They know in their hearts that I exist, and because of that, they also gradually realize even Santa can deliver only so many gifts on one night. So each of these generous boys and girls at some point—usually around the age of ten, or eleven, or twelve—makes it clear he or she no longer expects gifts from Santa, which allows me a bit more precious time on Christmas Eve to visit the home of a younger child instead. It's such a natural, generous gesture. True believers always grow up to be warmhearted, admirable adults who encourage their own children to believe in me because they know that belief offers rewards far beyond a gift to open on Christmas morning. The majority of children are true believers.

Then there are the rare, wonderful *maximum true believers*. These boys and girls reach the moment when they voluntarily give up my gifts so that others might receive them, and their love for me never wavers. Besides welcoming me into their homes forever, they find ways to personally spread Christmas generosity into their communities, often by organizing efforts to make certain the neediest children enjoy happy holidays. They become in the finest sense my most valuable companions, every bit as important to what I do as anyone at the North Pole. I have often thought that maximum true believers are God's special Christmas gift to me, and I am grateful for them.

It's almost unheard-of for a child who was a maximum true believer to reach a point in adult life where he or she no longer believes in Santa Claus. Bobbo Butler had told Felix he didn't. My curiosity was aroused.

"Leonardo, does your research give any indication when and why Bobbo stopped believing in me?" I asked.

Leonardo shuffled some papers. "I think we can tell. I've got some reports here. Now, after he grew up Bobbo always held Christmas in his heart.

When FUN-TV was dominating television, he was often quoted as saying his network's annual holiday broadcast was his favorite show of the year. He wanted everyone everywhere to love Christmas and Santa Claus as much as he did. I suppose here at the North Pole we didn't take as much notice as we should have because we seldom watch television at all. But Bobbo certainly still believed, right up until five years ago."

"What happened then?" I wondered.

"I have some of this from media reports and more from two other children's files that I'll come to in a moment. When reality TV began to snatch high ratings at the expense of more wholesome, family-oriented programming, the FUN-TV network got into terrible financial trouble. Fewer companies wanted to buy commercial time on their programs. Bobbo wanted to save his company, naturally, and so he began to put in twice as many hours on the job as he had before. Soon he was working all day and then sleeping on a cot in his office. He rarely went home to be with his wife and children."

"I think I know what happened next," Layla interjected. "Mrs. Butler became unhappy."

"That's what court documents indicate," Leonardo agreed. "Four years ago, Lily Chin Butler sued her husband for divorce. She claimed he no longer spent time with her or their two daughters, Cynthia and Diana. Apparently she had asked him to change his ways, and he promised he would, but his concern for his network overwhelmed him and he didn't shape up. So the Butlers divorced."

"This is a sad story, but not an unusual one," I noted. "How did this divorce cause Bobbo to stop believing in me?"

"We learn *that* from our North Pole records for Cynthia and Diana Butler," Leonardo replied. "Cynthia is now ten and Diana is eight. According to our files, until four years ago both girls seemed destined for classification as maximum true believers. They believed in Santa Claus with all their hearts, and it wasn't surprising, given how their father loved you and Christmas so much. But after the divorce, the girls blamed all the hours Bobbo would put in on his annual holiday specials for the breakup of their parents' marriage. Since then they have hated Christmas and—I'm sorry— they apparently despise even the idea of you. Diana more so than Cynthia.

Since the divorce, they have refused to allow their mother to put up a Christmas tree. They won't accept Christmas gifts from anyone. Apparently they are so bitter that they don't like to see or even talk to their father during the month of December. Bobbo realizes, of course, that the divorce was his fault. He put business before family, as too many grown-ups unfortunately do. He still loves Christmas, but resents the holiday at the same time because of his daughters' attitudes. That's why he says he doesn't believe in you anymore. And, having lost his daughters in part because of his devotion to the holiday, he's determined not to lose his network. Exploiting Christmas and Santa Claus might make him feel guilty deep down inside, but he's still willing to do it. At least, that's how it seems to me."

"You're undoubtedly right, Leonardo," I said. There were murmurs of agreement all around the table. "Felix, as you spend time with Bobbo, you might try to learn more about this. Since he was a maximum true believer, it might be possible that sufficient urging could persuade him to begin believing again. And now, Leonardo, what about Lucretia Pepper?"

"This fifty-year-old woman is fascinating in many unfortunate ways," Leonardo replied. "I honored your instructions not to break into any secret files. I'll tell you, though, that there are many of them for Lucretia Pepper. I suspect by the identity of the organizations that have gathered confidential information on her—the Justice Department, the U.S. Attorney General's office, and practically every Better Business Bureau in the country—that she is suspected of all sorts of questionable behavior."

"Has she ever been taken to trial on any charges?" Ben Franklin wanted to know.

Leonardo shook his head. "Lucretia Pepper retains the services of the best lawyers in the world," he said. "Once or twice, according to news reports, it was rumored she was in legal difficulty, but apparently her lawyers always got her out of trouble. We'll have to be *very* careful in dealing with her. She has sued countless individuals for slander, usually when they've complained publicly about the quality of LastLong Toys. One mother whose son's toy train broke an hour after he received it for his birthday made the mistake of complaining about it at a school gathering. Someone reported her remarks to Lucretia Pepper, and she successfully sued the woman for $100,000, claiming LastLong products were being unfairly defamed in public. This is a very dangerous lady."

"What is her personal background, Leonardo?" Amelia Earhart asked.

"She is the daughter of Delbert Pepper, founder of LastLong Toy Company," Leonardo said. "The Pepper family lived in Scarsdale, New York. As a child, young Lucretia attended the finest private schools. She had no brothers or sisters. From birth, her father trained her to succeed him as head of the family business. He is the one who taught her to spend as little as possible on raw materials, and to build toys that broke quickly so new ones would have to be purchased to replace them. She obviously learned that lesson well. She received an undergraduate business degree from Yale"—this elicited a snort from Theodore, a proud alumnus of Harvard—"and a graduate degree from Wharton. Lucretia made fine grades, all A's except in Business Ethics, which she failed several times before finally passing. I note from an article in a school newspaper that, after she finally passed, she was accused of hiring a stand-in to take the Business Ethics final exam for her. But her family's lawyers squelched that. I understand the professor making the accusation was eventually fired. Hmm. In any event, Delbert Pepper passed away ten years ago, and, as planned, his daughter succeeded him as president of LastLong Toys. Every year since, the company's profits have increased dramatically."

"To some, I'm sure her life is considered a success story," Arthur observed. "There are many people who believe making money to be the ultimate reason for living."

"She makes it, but except to invest it in ways that bring her even more riches, she doesn't spend it," Leonardo said. "There are no records whatsoever of any charitable gifts, either by her or by LastLong Toys. While she's willing to spend millions for product publicity, she won't give one cent to help the poor."

Layla wanted to know if Lucretia Pepper had a husband and children. Leonardo said she had no family at all. She'd never married, and her parents were both deceased. There was no record anywhere of her having friends or pets or hobbies.

"Well, there's at least one more source of information, Leonardo," I said. "What is Lucretia Pepper's status in the North Pole gift-giving archives?"

Leonardo nervously cleared his throat in the way people do when they're about to say something unpleasant. "Santa Claus, Lucretia Pepper was a never."

"Ah," I muttered. "I suppose I shouldn't be surprised."

Sadly, every so often we encounter children who cannot and will not accept even the possibility that Santa Claus exists. In our files, they are designated as *nevers* because they never have believed—not in Santa Claus and not in the generosity of spirit that characterizes the holiday season itself. From the time they learn to talk, they mock other children who believe in me. They do their best to embarrass others into abandoning their beliefs. At Christmas they want lots of gifts for themselves and resent anyone else receiving even a single present. Afterward, they never believe they have gotten enough. There are not many of them. I'm glad, and not because they consider me an annoying myth. Never children are inevitably unhappy and usually grow up to be adults like Lucretia Pepper who are obsessed with building their own massive fortunes and couldn't care less about anyone else. I reluctantly accept that they don't believe in me—this is their right. But I do mind that they disparage and try to ruin the beliefs of others.

"Since she's a never, I expect we can't hope Lucretia Pepper might change her mind about this *Great Santa Search*," Bill Pickett drawled. "You better keep on getting in shape, Santa Claus. You'll need to be, come December. Theodore tells me you might have to rope a reindeer or two, so sometime I expect I'll be joining you two in the gym. Ever use a lasso before?"

"I can't say that I have, Bill," I replied. "You're right. Based on what Leonardo has told us, it appears we're dealing with two people with very different reasons for trying to use Christmas for their own ends. Felix, pay careful attention to everything Bobbo says when you attend your meeting with him in New York the day after tomorrow. In fact, take notes."

"I can't read my own handwriting," Felix admitted. "Could I bring Sarah with me this time? She learned to take wonderful notes when she was writing her travel books about colonial America. I'll tell Bobbo that I always work with my wife. Perhaps he won't mind."

Sarah was willing, so it was agreed she should go to New York, too. We filed out of the conference room, talking in subdued voices about Bobbo's unhappy loss of Christmas faith and about Lucretia Pepper being a never. Everyone else returned to their places in the toy factory or in offices where they checked shipments of raw materials or maintained our correspondence with certain companies and governments. I limped back to the private quarters I shared with Layla. My back ached from Theodore's rigorous schedule of early-morning exercises, and I badly needed to soak in a hot tub. It was still a long way to December and *The Great Santa Search,* but not nearly long enough.

Eight

S arah and Felix had a great deal to report when they returned
from New York City. What they had thought would be one short
visit with Bobbo Butler stretched into several meetings spread
out over three days. There was much more involved in planning a holiday
television special than those of us at the North Pole had realized.

My friends arrived in Bobbo's office as requested at 10:00 a.m. on a Monday morning. Heather Hathaway welcomed them warmly, then escorted
them to the same conference room where Felix had met earlier with Bobbo
and Lucretia Pepper. This time, Bobbo introduced four people—sound engineer Ken Perkins, costume designer Eri Mizobe, set designer Robert Fernandez, and Mary Rogers, whom Bobbo introduced as "the best director
anywhere in television, and she's going to prove it with *The Great Santa
Search*."

"How are you folks?" Mary asked, and Sarah and Felix couldn't help but
grin at the Texas twang in her voice. "Felix, Bobbo has bragged on you no
end. And this lady is Sarah, your wife? I always like to see couples working
on a show together. That's how I met three of my own husbands."

"I hope you don't mind that I brought Sarah," Felix said. "She's a great source of ideas, and has been involved in some of my previous projects."

"Of course Sarah is welcome," Bobbo replied genially. "Miss Hathaway, I think if you'll bring coffee for everyone and then sit over there to take notes, we can get started."

When Heather came back and passed around coffee, Sarah gasped when she saw the mugs. They were red and white; the handles were painted to look like candy canes. Each had *"The Great Santa Search"* stamped on one side in lovely, flowing script.

"Where did you get these, Bobbo?" she asked.

"I know a manufacturer in New Jersey," Bobbo said. "Do you like them? We've had a thousand made up, and in another month or so when we really start promoting the program we're going to send one of these mugs to everyone who writes about television. Journalists love free gifts. Every time one of them drinks coffee from that mug, he'll think of *The Great Santa Search*. Of course, that's just the tip of our promotional iceberg. I'm sure you and Felix will think of even better gimmicks. For a change, we've got a big enough budget to pay for anything within reason. Just don't tell me we need to give away flying reindeer."

"We'd never suggest that," Felix said. "After all, there are only eight."

Felix hadn't meant to be funny, but everyone around the table except Sarah and Heather Hathaway began to laugh.

"And their names are Donder and Rudolph and Prancer and what else?" Ken Perkins asked, chuckling.

"Actually, Rudolph isn't one of Santa's eight flying reindeer," Felix said. "He was originally created as part of a sales promotion for Montgomery Ward. The idea of a red-nosed reindeer is wonderful, but that's just something made up. There's never been a red-nosed reindeer at the North Pole."

"See?" Bobbo said proudly. "We've got a real Christmas expert here. Felix, you pay close attention to everything we discuss. If something doesn't match up to official holiday history, say so right away. We want to be as authentic as possible."

"Speaking of which, let's get back to what we were talking about before

Sarah and Felix arrived," Mary said. "We've got to figure out how to find these ten men who'll be on the show competin' to become the real Santa. Does everybody still think we just need to search the malls?"

"The Santas hired by the biggest malls are usually the most authentic-looking," Robert Fernandez said. "They have the best costumes and most of the time their beards are real. That could be *very* important if some of the competitions on the show involve sudden movements. We wouldn't want beards flying off into the crowd. That would just *kill* us with the critics."

"The mall idea makes sense, but it also presents a problem," Eri Mizobe interjected. She was a slender, serious-looking young woman. "If we get the media coverage we want, some reporter is sure to ask how we can be certain one of our ten contestants is the *real* Santa. If it comes out in the press that we're getting contestants only from the mega-malls, we'll be accused of not making the competition open to anyone who claims he's Santa."

"So what do you suggest?" Mary asked. "We can't have five hundred fat men in red suits on our program."

"At some point we need to have an open audition, one that the media can come and cover," Eri said. "Maybe we can use the same theater where we'll hold the actual program. We'll invite anyone who wants to be voted the real Santa to come and audition. We'll have them go through some kind of in-terview process, and in the end probably one or two of them would be good enough to be among the ten who compete on the show."

"But one of the mall Santas will win," Ken Perkins predicted. "The companies that provide them actually train their Santas how to act before they send them out in public."

Bobbo thought the Santa open audition ought to be announced in March and then held during the late spring, perhaps May. He said that was televi-sion's "sweeps" month when every network tried especially hard to domi-nate ratings.

"If we generate media buzz with the auditions in May, that'll keep mo-mentum building right into the fall," he said. "By the time Halloween rolls around, kids all over the country will be too obsessed with finding out who the real Santa is to even think about trick-or-treating."

The Monday morning meeting continued for another two hours. Ken Perkins wanted to know if one of the events on the show might require the would-be Santas to sing Christmas carols; if so, he'd have to install extra microphones and either bring in a studio orchestra or prepare tapes of background music.

"I like the carol-singing," Mary said. "Gives it that *American Idol* feeling. Good reality-TV tradition there, besides Christmas history."

"I don't know that singing is something the real Santa Claus would necessarily be good at," Felix warned, and with good reason. He'd been listening to me warble off-key for centuries. "You wouldn't want to have some otherwise perfect Santa be eliminated because he couldn't carry a tune."

"Ah, if a few of 'em are awful singers, that'll just be comic relief," Mary replied. "We'll need some laughs. You wouldn't want this to get too serious."

By noon, when Bobbo suggested it was time for lunch, Felix and Sarah were certain everything possible had been discussed. But Heather Hathaway was sent out for sandwiches, and it took the whole afternoon for Bobbo and his non–North Pole associates to decide which theater to rent for *The Great Santa Search* (Manhattan's Ed Sullivan Theater was the eventual choice) and whether all the competing Santas had to wear traditional red-and-white costumes.

"I'm imagining more of a rainbow effect," mused Robert Fernandez, the set designer. "That whole North Pole motif is so *stark*. Let's brighten up the background—some aqua and lemon shadow effects, maybe—and Eri can put our Santas into robes of contrasting colors."

"I could do that, but I believe it would detract from the sense of authenticity we're trying to achieve," Eri said. "Felix, you're the history expert. What do you think?"

"The Santas definitely need to stick to red and white," Felix said firmly. Robert looked unhappy for a moment, but then smiled widely.

"Well, at least those red robes will look good in the dance routines," he said. "Mary, have we hired the choreographer?"

"Wait a minute," Sarah interrupted. "*Dance* routines? The ten Santas are going to *dance*?" She sounded almost as horrified as I must have looked when she and Felix informed me of this later.

"Oh, we've gotta have dancing," Mary Rogers said firmly. "Singing and dancing—it sells that spirit of entertaining competition to the audience. Haven't you ever watched a Miss America pageant?"

Before Felix or Sarah could reply, Bobbo looked at his watch and announced everyone would have to return to the conference room at ten the next morning.

"It's almost six now, and I'm supposed to pick up my daughters for dinner at seven," he explained. "They live with their mother up in Scarsdale. I'm going to take them to a restaurant there. I've got to leave now if I'm going to be on time." Bobbo shook hands with everyone and rushed out.

Felix and Sarah needed to find a hotel, and Heather Hathaway volunteered to help. She and Sarah consulted a list of hotels that Bobbo kept in the office, and soon they made a reservation at one a few blocks from the FUN-TV offices. They arranged to stay for two nights. Heather told them there were still many preliminary details of *The Great Santa Search* to talk about.

"Do you have dinner plans, Heather?" Sarah asked. "Felix and I are going to find some nice little restaurant. Perhaps you could suggest one."

Heather mentioned a place that was convenient and not too expensive— "On my salary, I can't afford fancy places," she laughed. "But the food is very good. Once in a while when we've been working late, Bobbo and I have eaten there. I think he likes it a lot, though he's never said so." These last words were spoken quite wistfully, and Sarah shot Felix a quick look that puzzled him.

Over dinner—delicious Italian lasagna with spicy tomato sauce, warm garlic bread, and spumoni for dessert—Felix and Sarah became great friends with Heather. She was a native of Langdon, North Dakota, near the Canadian border. Her family owned and operated a farm there.

"Langdon is wonderful if you like small-town life," Heather explained. "I had nothing against it, but when I was in high school I was Helen Keller in our production of *The Miracle Worker*. As you probably know, as a child Helen Keller couldn't see, speak, or hear, but because of a wonderful teacher named Annie Sullivan she learned to communicate. Afterward, I had two new ambitions. I thought sign language and lip-reading were fascinating, so I learned how to do both, and well enough to win some national competitions. I also discovered I loved being on stage in front of an audience. From then on, my dream was to live in New York so I could become a famous actress on Broadway. I moved to the city right after I graduated from college."

Heather shared some amusing stories about her early years in New York, when she auditioned for every on- and off-Broadway production but kept losing out on roles because she was always taller than the leading men.

"But I loved everything about show business," she explained, waving a lasagna-laden fork. "The creativity involved in thinking of a play or program, then doing all the things necessary to make it happen in front of an audience, is just magical to me. I really believe in magic, don't you?"

"We think there's magic in every life and certainly in both of ours," Sarah replied.

"When I was twenty-six, and after living in New York for almost five years, I finally realized I wasn't ever going to become a famous actress," Heather continued. "There were two choices. I could give up completely and go back home to help run the family farm, or I could find some other way to stay in New York and show business. About the same time, I saw an ad in a magazine for an executive assistant to the president of FUN-TV. I'd watched some of that network's shows when I was much younger and remembered how sweet they always were. I interviewed with Bobbo and he hired me. I take notes during his meetings, I'm the one who's sent out to get coffee, and three or four times a week I have to help him look for his wallet or his reading glasses, which he's constantly misplacing. He doesn't pay me much because he can't. Until we got this *Great Santa Search* deal with Last-Long Toys, every month we couldn't be sure we'd have enough to pay the office rent. But I keep things running as smoothly as possible, and once in a while Bobbo will ask me if I have any ideas for shows he's producing. Sometimes he even lets me write a scene or two."

"It sounds like you're a young woman with great potential," Felix said. "Have you thought about changing jobs and perhaps moving on to a bigger, better network than FUN-TV?"

Heather shook her head vigorously.

"Bobbo needs someone who really understands him," she said. "If I weren't there I don't know what might happen to him. He's such a good, decent guy, though you've probably noticed he doesn't have a lot of common sense. But when he thinks he has a good idea, he gets as excited as a little boy at, well, *Christmas,* and that's what I lo—"

Heather stopped in the middle of a word. Felix, spooning up his spumoni, waited for her to finish the sentence, but she didn't. Instead, she blushed and looked down at her plate.

After a few moments of uncomfortable silence, Sarah said, "Bobbo mentioned he had to leave to have dinner with his daughters and that they live with their mother. I assume he's divorced and can only see the girls at certain designated times."

"That's right," Heather confirmed. "Cynthia is ten. Diana is almost nine. Bobbo adores both of them. He and their mother divorced not long after I came to work at FUN-TV. Bobbo was miserable because he missed the girls so much. He's allowed to see them only once a week, though he can call them every day if he wants to, which he always does. He says the divorce was completely his fault because he got too wrapped up with work. Tonight he'll take them out to dinner and ask them to tell him all about what their week was like, and then he'll drop them off at home and drive back to his apartment in the city, already counting the days until he can see them again. Even so, that's much better than last month, when they didn't want to see him at all. Bobbo says he used to love Christmas, but now he dreads December."

The final factor in the breakup of Bobbo's marriage, Heather believed, was the inordinate amount of time he would devote each year to producing FUN-TV's annual Christmas Eve special. From the day after Thanksgiving to long after Cynthia and Diana had fallen asleep on the night of December 24, it wasn't unusual for Bobbo to never get home to Scarsdale at all. Instead, he'd work late and then nap for a few hours on a couch in his Manhattan office.

"After the divorce, I believe it was Diana who told Bobbo that she hated Santa Claus and Christmas because they'd taken her daddy away from her," Heather said. "She was just four. Now the girls usually won't even let their father come visit them during the whole month of December. I keep hoping they'll change their minds and realize how very much he loves them. No parent is perfect. But since the divorce, Christmas has been ruined for Cynthia and Diana, and for their father, too. That's why I'm so pleased to see him excited about *The Great Santa Search*. Deep in his heart, he knew *Merry Monkey* wasn't very good, but because he's always so sad now during the holidays, he just couldn't think of anything better. Maybe if *The Great Santa Search* is as wonderful as we think it's going to be, Bobbo will learn to love Santa Claus and Christmas again."

In their hotel room that night, Felix asked Sarah why she thought someone as capable as Heather stayed in her low-paying job at floundering FUN-TV.

"It's simple," Sarah said. "She's in love with Bobbo, and she hopes if she stays with him long enough, he'll fall in love with her."

"If he hasn't after four years, I'd guess he never will," Felix replied.

"Four years is nothing," Sarah remarked, rolling her eyes. "How long did we know each other before you realized you loved me?"

"It was only a matter of minutes," Felix assured her. "If I waited a century or two to tell you, it was only so you'd have enough time to learn to adore me completely."

"Do you really expect me to believe that?" Sarah asked sarcastically, but she gave her husband a warm hug and kiss and fell asleep hoping Heather Hathaway's romantic dreams came true, too.

Much of Tuesday's discussion at FUN-TV was focused on events in which *The Great Santa Search* contestants would compete. Mary Rogers was adamant: carol-singing would have to be included.

"The real fun here could be that the Santas won't know in advance what song they'll have to sing," she suggested. "We'll put titles on slips of paper, toss 'em in one of those funny red Santa hats, and make the competitors each pull one out. That'll keep 'em from gettin' any chance to rehearse. Plus, we won't know which ones can carry a tune and which can't. Some of 'em are bound to be horrible. That'll be funny, and it'll make the whole thing seem that much more spontaneous."

Robert and Ken liked the idea of a dance number with all ten Santas to start the show; that kind of onscreen action would encourage audiences to sit down and pay close attention, especially if not all the Santas were light on their feet.

"If one of them trips and the audience starts howling with laughter, that'll be even better," Ken said.

"I'm sure one of them will," Felix predicted gloomily.

Bobbo said that pace was important. Scenes with lots of action needed to alternate with calmer ones. All sorts of talents needed to be tested. This would give everyone watching a way to pick his or her favorite. He also wanted all the competitions—"challenges"—to have some connection with Santa's traditional Christmas Eve duties.

"No sense having them run the hundred-yard dash or anything like that," Bobbo remarked. "We need challenges that play out on a set designed to look like a living room on Christmas Eve—you know, with a fireplace that has stockings hung in front of it."

That inspired eventual agreement on two challenges, chimney-sliding and stocking-stuffing. Santa contestants would race against the clock to see who could slip down a fake chimney fastest while hauling along a heavy bag of toys. In another segment, contestants would race the clock by vying to fill the most stockings with toys within a specified time, perhaps sixty seconds.

"Lucretia Pepper will like that one," Eri Mizobe said. "We can use Last-Long Toys." Bobbo told Heather Hathaway to make a note of that and to remind him to call Lucretia Pepper later with the news.

Robert Fernandez wanted to know why there would be two "speed challenges" if the studio audience was supposed to be voting Santas out of the contest after each individual competition. Mary said it would be best to have both "clock" and "vote" challenges, so if those in the studio quickly arrived at a consensus favorite, the winner wouldn't be a foregone conclusion early in the two-hour broadcast.

"We've got to keep the viewers wonderin' who'll win," she reminded everyone.

Even without commercial breaks on behalf of LastLong Toys, it soon became clear there couldn't be more than six challenges. The first few would take longest, because there would be more competitors then. Bobbo had already decided that the final event would have the two surviving Santas each delivering a short, heartfelt speech explaining why he alone should be voted the "official" Santa Claus. Along with carol-singing, chimney-sliding, and stocking-stuffing, that made four, so two more were needed. Bobbo then remembered he'd originally considered reindeer-roping, and Mary immediately agreed. That would involve lots of *action*, she explained.

"People are used to watchin' shows where everything and everybody gets blown to smithereens," she said. "On *The Great Santa Search* we won't have that going for us. If we can't have bullets flyin', we can at least get some lassos in the air. I guess we can rent some reindeer from the Central Park Zoo."

Robert Fernandez cleared his throat and said, "I don't like to be a party pooper, but, well, *poop*. This is live television, and I doubt those reindeer from the zoo will be potty-trained."

"Okay, we'll go to a taxidermist and buy some stuffed reindeer," Ken suggested.

"That will alienate animal-rights activists," Eri argued. "We should use models of reindeer that obviously aren't real. They can look cute, with big eyes and goofy antlers. Put them on some sort of conveyor belt so they move from one side of the stage to the other while the Santas take turns trying to rope them. That would work—and no poop involved."

"That's five," Mary said. "We need one more."

It took a while to come up with the sixth challenge. Bobbo insisted that, whatever it was, it had to be something historically associated with Santa. Present-wrapping was discussed, then discarded. Ken said Santa's helpers probably did that for him. Mary thought the finalist Santas might arm-wrestle, but Sarah quickly pointed out that arm wrestling was rather violent, and Santa Claus never resorted to violence. Eri said hopefully that the Santas might participate in a Christmas quiz, having to answer questions about real events in holiday history. Felix enthusiastically endorsed that one, since it would give me a tremendous advantage. After all, I'd been present for most of it.

But Heather Hathaway, offering her opinion for once, said the quiz was a bad idea. Viewers who didn't know the answers themselves might feel they were somehow being mocked. That would make them change channels.

"We can't have that," Bobbo said emphatically. "All right, then, Felix, I think we're going to put this one on you. You're the Christmas expert here. We need one more challenge that involves Santa tradition and won't offend animal-rights advocates or viewers who don't know holiday history. What's it going to be?"

Now, here I must give my beloved old friend Felix a great deal of credit. He came up with something brilliant.

"Cookie-eating," Felix announced. "It's got everything we need. Kids always leave cookies out for Santa. We set trays of them in front of the competitors, and they each try to eat the most in, let's say, sixty or ninety seconds."

"I like it!" Mary declared. "Those fat men jammin' cookies into their mouths, and crumbs spillin' over their red coats. Clock in one corner of the screen countin' down the seconds. We can put big glasses of milk by the cookie trays so they can wash down the snacks. Bobbo, I think you need to give Felix a bonus for that one!"

"Oh, no bonus is necessary," Felix said. "I just feel certain the real Santa loves cookies, so this will be his favorite challenge on the whole show."

It took another day of meetings before preliminary planning was complete. The longest discussion involved who would make up the live studio audience. Bobbo had originally envisioned an entire crowd of children who were still young enough to all believe in Santa Claus. Ken, who had a son and daughter of his own, said it was very unlikely parents of kids that age would let them go sit in the Ed Sullivan Theater all by themselves. Eri thought it would be a good idea to have children come with their parents "so we keep that whole family theme working." Everyone liked that, and then Heather Hathaway, speaking up for the second time, suggested that grandparents be added to the mix.

"We want three generations of viewers, don't we?" she asked. "So we'll have three generations in the audience."

By late Wednesday afternoon, everyone was anxious to go home. Bobbo said he'd be in touch soon, because the first steps in the long *Great Santa Search* publicity campaign were about to begin. Sarah and Felix asked him to explain more about that, but Bobbo said he knew all of them were worn out and, besides, publicity would be handled by LastLong Toy Company's marketing department.

"We'll meet back here in April," he concluded. "I hope you'll each take some time to rest, because from April on we'll be working nonstop until Christmas Eve."

That didn't worry Sarah and Felix. They were used to that schedule, only without a few months off. What did concern them on their trip back to the North Pole was how I would react when I learned I would have to sing and dance as well as rope reindeer, slide down a chimney, eat cookies, and explain to an audience of untold millions why I should be chosen for a wonderful job that already was mine to begin with.

But when they returned, I was already in a grumpy mood. Their news only added to the gloom I'd felt since the day before, when I learned my new regimen of diet and exercise might not bring the results I had every right to expect.

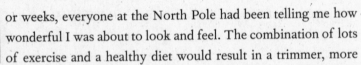or weeks, everyone at the North Pole had been telling me how wonderful I was about to look and feel. The combination of lots of exercise and a healthy diet would result in a trimmer, more energetic Santa, they promised, often as they wolfed down Lars's fabulous desserts while I made do with bran cereal or perhaps a tiny dollop of cottage cheese. I always responded that we'd have to see, wouldn't we? But deep inside I felt rather hopeful myself. After centuries of knowing I weighed a few pounds—all right, many pounds—more than I should, it would have been immensely satisfying to inform Layla I needed trousers with smaller waistlines.

Theodore had suggested that I not weigh myself during the early portion of my *Great Santa Search* training.

"Give it two weeks, or, even better, three," he'd urged. "Then you can climb on the gymnasium scale and feel thrilled at all the pounds that are gone. It will be a bully moment for you, Santa. We'll invite everyone else to come and share in the excitement."

So every morning I got up and ran and jumped and bent and stretched and sweated. Mealtimes found me eating sensibly; Lars complained that

he'd have to start stocking twice as much lettuce, broccoli, and other vegetables. I even stopped trying to sneak out of my room to raid the refrigerator in the middle of the night.

The day before Felix and Sarah returned from New York, I exercised as
usual, took a refreshing shower, and then returned to the gym instead of going into the dining hall for breakfast. Everyone else was gathered in the gym
beside a scale placed between the rows of lockers. In all the time we'd lived
at the North Pole, I had stepped on that scale only once before. Theodore
had insisted I do so just as we started my training, so we'd know what I
weighed when we began. The scale had an electronic screen that flashed the
weight of whoever stood on it. Theodore swore my initial weight would remain a secret between us. I would have been too embarrassed for anyone else
to know. But now, dressed in a T-shirt and gym shorts, I proudly stepped
back on the scale. Everyone leaned forward to stare at the screen that would
announce my new, vastly reduced weight. The night before, relaxing after
dinner, we'd all speculated how much I would prove to have lost. The consensus was at least twenty-five pounds. I was privately hoping for thirty.

So we all stared at the little screen, and after what seemed to be an eternity, a number popped up. A very disappointing number. The same number,
in fact, that had appeared when I'd first weighed myself several weeks
earlier.

"This is impossible," Theodore muttered. "Santa, I'm sure there's
something wrong with the scale. Step off it for a moment." I did, and
Theodore reached down, shook the scale a bit, and then stepped back and
gave it a firm kick. "There," he said. "Try again."

I did. Everyone leaned forward. My weight was the same.

"Will someone tell me why I haven't lost an ounce?" I asked plaintively.
My wife and friends all looked as distressed as I felt. They came over to
gently pat me on the back and offer words of encouragement. They meant
well, but I didn't feel better. After all that exercise and all that delicious food
I'd given up, I was still as stout as ever.

"Perhaps we haven't worked *hard* enough, Santa," Theodore said. "It's
my fault entirely. You've done all that I asked. Tomorrow we'll start at
5:00 a.m. instead of 6:00, and then—"

"That won't help," Leonardo da Vinci interrupted. "Where his weight is concerned, it will make no difference what time Santa starts to exercise, or how long he exercises, or what he does or doesn't eat, for that matter."

I got off the scale. "Whatever do you mean, Leonardo?" I asked.

"It's unfortunately obvious," he replied. "Now, Santa, of course you're aware that through the magic of your mission, you've stopped aging. In effect, every part of your body—your heart, your brain, your muscles and bones and nerves and digestive system—is apparently invulnerable. They stay healthy and strong."

I nodded. "Please go on."

"Well," Leonardo said, "the same is true for—please forgive me, I'm just being honest—all your, well, *fat cells*. These are impervious to being lost through exercise or diet. They are, like you, timeless, perhaps eternal. You can do nothing to get rid of them. They are part of you, and always will be."

My friends had said of me over the centuries that I was somewhat self-conscious about my weight, and they were right. No one really *likes* being heavy. Until Theodore began my training regimen, though, I'd never really dedicated myself to doing anything about it. I had my gift-giving mission to occupy most of my attention, and, besides, there was so much food that tasted good. So it was hard to accept that when I'd finally tried to get thinner, it was impossible.

My disappointment was so profound that I might easily have given up exercising and following a more sensible diet, but Layla, as always, knew exactly what to say to me.

"It's too bad about not being able to lose weight, Santa, but that wasn't the real reason you've been working so hard with Theodore," she reminded me. "The goal has been to get you into the best physical shape possible to compete in *The Great Santa Search*. Benefits from regular exercise include healthier heart rate, more physical endurance, and a greater sense of self-esteem. Tell the truth: haven't you begun to feel better? Don't you have more energy than you did before?"

Over her shoulder, I saw Theodore. He looked regretful, and my heart went out to him.

"You're right, Layla," I replied. "Theodore, my waistline might remain the same, but my determination to benefit from your expert advice is stronger than ever. Keep helping me, old friend. I may not be the slimmest Santa Claus in this television competition, but I'll surely be the best-prepared! At least until *The Great Santa Search*, I'll remain on the diet and exercise programs you developed for me." Then we all went off to breakfast, where everyone else dined on Lars's savory *huevos rancheros* with *chorizo* (a spicy egg dish accompanied by sausage) while I gulped down my usual oatmeal without butter or brown sugar.

Of course, I couldn't help feeling privately disappointed about the impossibility of my ever losing weight. That is why, when Felix and Sarah returned the next day with their news about my having to sing and dance as part of the competition, I was already not in the best of moods.

"Surely you can convince Bobbo and this program staff of his that Santa Claus doesn't have to sing and dance," I protested. But they told me about producer Mary Rogers and ratings and choreography, and I reluctantly concluded that singing and dancing were in my future.

"There's probably nothing we can do about your voice," Layla said firmly. "Don't look so offended. We've all heard you try to sing. But dancing might be different. I've never actually seen you dance. Perhaps that's one of your talents you've never told me about?"

I shook my head. "Though there were village celebrations I attended that included dancing, I never danced myself when I was a bishop in the early Christian church," I explained. "It would have been considered undignified. And I haven't danced in all the centuries since. There has never been any opportunity."

"Dancing was and remains part of many countries' holiday traditions," St. Francis of Assisi noted. "I wrote some of the first Christmas carols in the early 1200s just so people would have special holiday music to dance to. Perhaps you're a natural dancer, Santa. Let's find out right now!"

Before I could protest, Francis, Felix, Sarah, Ben Franklin, and Willie Skokan all started singing "Jingle Bells" and clapping their hands to establish a solid rhythm. Layla took my arm and pulled me out into the center of the floor.

"This isn't the kind of dancing you'll have to do on *The Great Santa Search*, but at least we can discover if you've got natural rhythm," she said. "Put your left hand in mine, right hand on my waist—one and two and *go*," and away we whirled.

Despite what some suggested afterward, I really did try my best. Layla moved her feet nimbly, and I tried to do the same. Somehow, her instep got between the floor and my foot. She grimaced with pain but gamely kept dancing.

"Sorry," I whispered.

"Concentrate!" she hissed back.

Then I stepped on her other foot—the crunching noise almost drowned out our friends singing "Jingle Bells." Layla dropped my hand and leaned down to massage her bruised toes. I bent down to assure her I was very, very sorry for injuring her twice in succession, and somehow our heads collided. Layla straightened with some difficulty and announced we'd danced enough for the first lesson.

"Francis, can you be responsible for teaching Santa to dance?" she groaned, hobbling a bit more than I thought absolutely necessary. "I'm not sure I'll be healed in time to do it myself."

He looked at me doubtfully. "I'll try my best, Layla."

My friends' news about the other competitions—*challenges*—on *The Great Santa Search* was much more welcome. Chimney-sliding would not, we all believed, present much of a problem. I had far more experience doing this than anyone else in history. Stocking-stuffing was another sure victory. If I could fill them fast enough to please every hopeful child on Christmas Eve, I could surely speed through that competition as though the other contestants were moving in slow motion.

"Perhaps I'd better train hard in the area of cookie-eating," I suggested.

"Wonderful work, Felix, in suggesting that one. I won't disappoint you, I promise." But Theodore reminded me that cookies were not included on my current diet.

"I'm sure when the time comes, you'll excel in this area," he assured me.

That left reindeer-roping. In all my time at the North Pole, and at the Cooperstown farm before that, I'd never roped one of the flying reindeer because I'd never had to. Intelligent, perceptive animals, they simply came when called. Sarah explained how *The Great Santa Search* would involve make-believe targets rather than real reindeer. She added that I was sure to win the roping challenge because I had the best possible instructor. She was right.

In his day, Bill Pickett was perhaps the most famous and talented of all rodeo performers. He could ride any bucking bronco, wrestle any snorting bull to the ground, and rope whatever target was set in front of him. He did all this in a time in America when black men and women were too often considered inferior and not allowed the same rights as white citizens. It was a tribute to Bill's skills, and his character, that he was able to overcome such crippling prejudice and become a national hero to people of all races. Since he had joined our fellowship in 1932, we always found him to be among our most valuable companions. Besides assisting with the development and crafting of toys, he was always ready to help out with the reindeer. We had a full-time handler whose job it was to feed, groom, and exercise them, but Bill had a special touch with all hoofed creatures. While I made a point of taking all eight reindeer and the sleigh out for regular training flights, Bill liked to place a halter on them individually to give extra exercise to whichever reindeer needed it. Comet and Blitzen especially liked additional runs out along the North Pole's ice and snow.

So it was natural for Bill to join Theodore and me when roping became part of our training regimen. I was surprised to see him leading one of the reindeer into the gym on the first morning I was to try my hand at tossing a lasso.

"Vixen here had a restless night," Bill explained. "She hasn't had a good run in a week or more, so she's got all that pent-up energy. I talked to her and she's proud to help you with your roping practice, Santa." As Bill spoke, Vixen watched him with wide, bright eyes. It was easy to believe she understood every word that was being spoken.

"So what we'll do is, Vixen will stand about ten feet away to start with," Bill continued. "Now, later on you can practice lassoing a reindeer on the run—Felix told me that on *The Great Santa Search* they'll have those models moving around the stage somehow—but for now you can use a stationary target. Get on over there, Vixen." She obediently trotted to the designated spot, her hooves clicking smartly on the wooden gymnasium floor. "Here's the rope, Santa. Have you ever used one before?"

I hadn't, so Bill explained the basics. One end of the braided rope was passed through a metal ring, called a *honda*, attached to the other end. A noose or loop about six feet in diameter was formed, with the rest of the rope coiled and held in the left hand. The right hand grasped the loop, with a little extra rope gathered as well. Keeping the right wrist loose, the loop was to be gently swung from right to left overhead. When enough momentum had been established and the swinging hand reached a point at the front of the right shoulder, the right arm stretched to full length, a step was taken forward, the right arm was brought down level with the shoulder, and the loop was released, with the right side of the loop a bit lower than the left.

"It's not as complicated as it sounds," Bill assured me. "Watch while I do it." He gathered up the rope, shook out a good-sized loop, whirled the loop over his head, and with a smooth, quick motion tossed it at Vixen. The loop settled around her thickly muscled neck like a loose-fitting collar. Bill walked over, took the rope from around the reindeer's neck, gave her a quick hug, and came back to where Theodore and I stood. "Now you try," he instructed.

I had some trouble at first. I couldn't make the loop the right size, and then I didn't twirl the rope fast enough and the loop slipped down over my head instead of flying smoothly to where Vixen patiently waited. Bill untangled me, and Theodore was nice enough not to laugh. The first few times I actually managed to toss the loop, it seemed to go in every direction but toward Vixen. But Bill was a patient teacher. He kept encouraging me, and on perhaps my tenth toss the loop actually did float properly through the air. It still flew several feet from where Vixen stood, but the thoughtful reindeer moved over quickly and stretched out her neck so the loop settled over it. Bill whooped, Theodore clapped, and even Vixen seemed to be smiling. After that I had more confidence and did much better. By the end of an hour, my shoulder was sore from rope-twirling and tossing, but I was consistently able to get the loop loosely around Vixen's neck from all sorts of angles and distances.

"Well done, Santa!" Bill exclaimed. "We'll practice with a stationary target for a few more days, then move up to lassoing reindeer on the run. By the time you're on that TV show, you might just be one of the best ropers in the world!"

"I just have to be the best roper among the ten would-be Santas," I replied. "But thank you, Bill—and thank you, too, Vixen. I know you're only supposed to get sugar cubes on special occasions, but I hope you'll accept some from me now." Vixen's muzzle tickled my palm as she gently ate the treats from my hand.

For the first time in North Pole history, we began keeping careful track of television news programs and many print publications. In February, Bobbo Butler and the LastLong Toy Company marketing department started the publicity campaign for *The Great Santa Search*. They began with occasional items on programs and in articles about the television business. Commentators and reporters mentioned in passing that the FUN-TV network was planning a holiday blockbuster. Though Bobbo had mentioned *The Great Santa Search* at the conclusion of *Merry Monkey*, very few people had actually been watching. These new remarks were on shows and in publications that reached much larger audiences. We wondered why until Amelia Earhart pointed out that they were inevitably programs sponsored by LastLong Toys. Lucretia Pepper was spending a lot of money to make certain *The Great Santa Search* got sufficient publicity.

By early March, there was speculation in some popular magazines about what form *The Great Santa Search* might take. Did FUN-TV network president Bobbo Butler mean that the *real* Santa Claus might host his own holiday special? Commentators were doubtful. From CNN to the Fox Network, it was widely suggested that Santa had many other things to do on Christmas Eve. But the "buzz," as Bobbo called it, kept growing stronger.

Then, during the third week in March, Bobbo held a press conference at the Ed Sullivan Theater in New York City. Every major television network and cable channel sent reporters and camera crews; so did all the important newspapers and magazines from around the country. A few days earlier, Bobbo had revealed to Felix and Sarah and the rest of *The Great Santa Search* team what he planned to say, so all of us at the North Pole knew what was coming. Still, we wanted to see the press conference for ourselves. Because the press conference was carried live on television, we gathered around one of our big-screen TVs to watch. Bobbo walked out on stage. If anything, the fringe of hair around his bald head bristled even more wildly than Sarah and Felix had described.

"I want to thank all our friends from the media for coming today," Bobbo began. "I know it's barely spring, but already there's a sense of Christmas in the air—or there will be, anyway, when you learn more about *The Great Santa Search*."

For more than 150 years, Bobbo explained, children in America had met a bewildering series of pretenders who insisted they were Santa Claus. He told about J. W. Parkinson and James Edgar and the Salvation Army—as consultants, Felix and Sarah had provided Bobbo with volumes of information about Christmas history. The result, Bobbo said, was that too many children weren't at all certain whether Santa Claus even existed. But *The Great Santa Search* would change all that.

"From 8:00 to 10:00 p.m. on Christmas Eve, right here in this very theater, FUN-TV will bring together the ten most outstanding Santas in the country," Bobbo said. "One of them will be the *real* Santa Claus. How will we know which one? Because all ten will compete in a series of challenges, with some winners established by beating the clock and others through a vote by our studio audience—an audience, incidentally, made up of three generations gathered together in the wholesome holiday spirit that typifies the best tradition of America and Christmas!"

At the end of the program, Bobbo promised, the audience—"who will represent all of you out there who love Christmas"—would select "the one, the only, the *official* Santa Claus!"

There was an excited murmur from his audience in the theater. Even jaded journalists can become enthusiastic if they think they've come upon a particularly interesting story.

"Where will you find these Santas, Bobbo?" someone cried out.

Bobbo leaned into the microphone and grinned. "Mostly, we're going to keep that part of it a secret. I can tell you that we've hired a team of experts who know exactly where to look for Santa."

"What if Santa isn't that easy to find, Bobbo?" another reporter wanted to know. "Maybe your experts won't look in the right place."

Bobbo's grin widened. "We've thought of that, and it brings me to our next announcement. We don't want to overlook anyone who might turn out to be the bona fide Santa we all want to meet so much. So on March 31, one week from today, FUN-TV invites anyone who claims to be Santa to come right here to the Ed Sullivan Theater in New York, where we'll hold open auditions for *The Great Santa Search* from noon to 6:00 p.m. We'll set up an interview process that will eliminate all but the most persuasive, and then they can meet with a panel of judges who will decide which of them, if any, should be included among the ten finalists on *The Great Santa Search* itself."

"Can we come to cover the audition, Bobbo?" one particularly famous TV newswoman wanted to know. She didn't so much ask a question as state the obvious. Everyone in the media knew exactly what Bobbo was up to—extensive coverage of the open audition would practically guarantee high ratings for *The Great Santa Search*.

"Come in red suits and white beards and audition yourselves, if you want to!" Bobbo replied.

After a few more questions—someone wanted to know what the challenges would be (Bobbo said that would be announced closer to the program itself) and someone else asked why such an important competition would take only two hours (Santa would have present-delivering business to attend to, Bobbo explained—it would be Christmas Eve, after all)—Bobbo thanked everyone for coming. Ben Franklin, looking thoughtful, reached over and switched off our television.

"There was no mention of LastLong Toys or how the winning Santa is supposed to become the company's spokesman," he said. "I wonder why there wasn't."

"Those are the kind of details that will be made public later," I said. "For now, they want to build excitement, and I think they've succeeded. Felix, Sarah, have you heard from Bobbo about any further plans for the open audition next week?"

"He called just before the press conference began," Felix replied. "There wasn't time to tell you before it started. Bobbo wants Sarah and me to fly down to New York; I'm to be one of the judges, along with Bobbo and Heather Hathaway and the rest of the program staff. Some recent college graduates who are working as FUN-TV interns will do the initial screening of whoever shows up. Bobbo thinks we might have fifty or even a hundred people claiming to be Santa. The more who audition, the more interest there is in *The Great Santa Search*, he believes."

"We already know one person who'll be showing up," I said. "We've been talking about what I must do to become one of the ten finalists on Christmas Eve. Of course, I could get hired as a Santa at some big mall; when you go around the country evaluating mall Santas you could pick me then, Felix. But we've agreed I'll go to this Ed Sullivan Theater in New York, answer the interns' questions, do whatever I have to in front of the judges, and I don't see how I won't be an obvious choice as a finalist. I mean, I'm *Santa*. How hard could this be?"

Ten

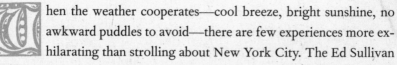hen the weather cooperates—cool breeze, bright sunshine, no awkward puddles to avoid—there are few experiences more exhilarating than strolling about New York City. The Ed Sullivan Theater is located on Broadway, one of the most famous avenues in New York. Times Square is about a dozen blocks further south; to the north is Central Park and Lincoln Center, an elegant hodgepodge of venues where symphonies and ballets are often performed. At any time of the day or night, Broadway is busy, its sidewalks thick with pedestrians and the street itself jammed bumper-to-bumper with buses, private cars, and taxis. But all the commotion is usually quite exciting. There's a definite special energy involved. On those occasions when I visit New York, I always like to take a long walk along Broadway, starting at the lower end of Central Park with its golden monument to those who fought in the Spanish-American War and concluding amid the garish neon signs that cover whole huge walls in Times Square.

So I knew exactly how to find the Ed Sullivan Theater from my hotel across from Lincoln Center on West Sixty-third Street and Broadway. I was pleased to take my usual enjoyable stroll. It was a magnificent spring day, with bright sunshine and temperatures in the very comfortable mid-seventies.

I wore a dark blue sports coat, open-necked white shirt, and charcoal gray slacks. There appeared to be no reason to wear my so-called "Santa suit" of red coat and pants with white fur trim. It seemed clear from Bobbo's comments at the previous week's press conference that costumes were not required, only the ability to convince first some FUN-TV interns and then the final panel of judges that I was well qualified to be Santa Claus. But, to be on the safe side, I brought along my "Santa" clothes in a valise. It never hurts to be prepared, I reminded myself.

As I mentioned, Broadway is always crowded. But as I neared Columbus Circle, it seemed that there were even more pedestrians than usual, all hurrying in the same direction as me. Every car on the avenue was stopped dead in place; horns were blaring. It was just after 11:00 a.m., and Bobbo had said the open audition for *The Great Santa Search* would begin at noon. Under ordinary circumstances, even walking at normal "people" pace it would have taken about fifteen minutes to walk from my hotel to the Ed Sullivan Theater, but now I began to worry that I might not make it on time. It was impossible to walk any faster—people were shoulder-to-shoulder across the sidewalks on both sides of Broadway. I couldn't flag down a cab, because none of the cars on the street were moving.

A policeman trotted by on horseback. I called out to him, "What's causing all this congestion?"

He reined in his steed, leaned down from his saddle, and replied, "There's a mob out in front of the old Sullivan Theater. Haven't you heard about that Santa Claus show? They're having auditions for it today, and at least a thousand people are trying to get inside. If I were you, I'd take a detour around Broadway."

"But I can't," I said. "I'm trying to get to the theater myself. It's very important that I do."

The policeman looked at me, taking in, I suppose, my white beard and wide waistline.

"I'll bet you want to try out to be Santa Claus!" he said, smiling. "I guess you do look a little like him. I think Santa's taller, though."

"I'm tall enough," I answered. "Please, could you help me get to the the-ater? I'd appreciate it very much."

"You may be too short to be Santa, but at least you're polite," the police-man replied. "Here, I'll pull you up behind me. Hang on tight!" With that, he reached down, took my hand, and hauled me up on the horse, which I'm sure didn't appreciate the extra burden but did not snort or buck in protest. As soon as I was settled, he nudged the horse's sides lightly with his heels, and off we trotted. It was an awkward ride. I had to hold on to my valise and the policeman's waist at the same time, and once or twice I came perilously close to falling off. But I managed to remain generally upright, and people on the sidewalk gaped and pointed at us as we passed.

The policeman pulled his mount up in front of the Ed Sullivan Theater. The name of the venue was emblazoned in yellow letters on a dark blue sign. Guards in uniform were stationed in front of the theater; my friend the policeman called to one, "I brought Santa Claus for you," as he helped me slide down from the back of the horse to the sidewalk. I waved good-bye to him as he rode off, then turned to go inside. But one of the guards gently but firmly placed his hand on my chest and said, "Where do you think you're going, pal?"

"I'm going to go in and convince the judges that I'm Santa Claus," I replied in equally friendly fashion. "Isn't there an audition here today?"

The guard rolled his eyes. "You got that right, buddy, but it's not as easy as you seem to think. There's you and about a thousand others. Take a look around."

I did. All around me, for a hundred yards down the sidewalk in both di-rections and even across Broadway, people who obviously planned to audi-tion for *The Great Santa Search* were waiting. They comprised a colorful lot. Many were older and more than half had beards, but those beards were every possible hue, from snow white like mine to all sorts of bright, dyed colors. There were stout men, certainly, but some thin ones, too. Many wore variations of "Santa suits," and more than a few were in full holiday regalia, including shiny black boots. One man led on a leash a Great Dane with fake antlers dangling from its head. A sign hanging around the dog's neck read *"Dasher."*

There were men of every race—and a few women, too. One carried a sign suggesting that the Santa Claus tradition was sexist. It made me smile, because she had obviously never met Layla. And weaving their way through the mob were cameramen from every TV network, recording the crazy scene for their evening newscasts. *That* would thrill Bobbo Butler, I knew.

"How do I get inside?" I asked the guard, who gestured toward the front theater doors with his thumb.

"The people in charge are going to send out assistants and have all of you form a line," he said. "You're lucky that cop brought you right up front. My best advice is to hold your ground. It's going to get even more nuts than it already is."

Exactly at noon, a number of young men and women emerged from the theater. I guessed they were FUN-TV's interns. One had a battery-powered megaphone. She shouted into it that everyone who wanted to audition needed to form a single line. That announcement resulted in further chaos rather than order. All the would-be Santas surged toward the theater, elbowing each other in very unseemly fashion. The guard I'd been speaking to winked, then yanked me right to the head of the line.

"Just be sure to bring me something special on Christmas Eve," he chuckled. I looked carefully at the name badge on his coat.

"I certainly will, Gary Elders," I promised. "Don't I remember that, as a boy, you especially liked baseball equipment from Santa? This year, you'll receive the finest catcher's mitt you've ever owned." And it would be, too: Jackie Robinson, who was the first black athlete to play in the major leagues, is now one of my North Pole helpers. He designs all of the sports equipment we distribute on Christmas Eve.

The guard stared at me, muttered, "Yeah, well, good luck," and moved away to help control the other Santa hopefuls trying to shove their way into line. I wish I could have seen his face on Christmas morning. Every so often, Santa Claus *does* bring gifts to special grown-ups.

I regretted the chaos. So many would-be Santas behaving badly didn't set a good example for children. But that was beyond my control. At least I was at the head of the line. It would be a simple thing, now, to get through the first round of questions and then go before the panel of judges. Felix didn't think they would ask me to sing or dance. I might have to talk a bit about life at the North Pole or something similar, he'd predicted. Mostly, Bobbo and the others would just want to get the open audition over with so they could concentrate on mall Santas, since they remained certain their eventual winner would come from that relatively small, select group.

One of the interns, a trim young woman dressed in a stylish business suit, motioned me over. She held a pen in one hand and a clipboard in the other.

"You're the first one in," she announced. "Follow me."

Now, *this* was more like it! She guided me through the theater lobby and past the entrance to the main auditorium. The doors to the auditorium were open, and I glanced in as we passed. The stage looked very small, and so did the tiers of seats. I remembered Felix telling me the Ed Sullivan Theater had an audience capacity of 461. A long table was set on the stage, and sitting behind it, chatting idly, were Felix and Bobbo Butler. I didn't know any of the others with them, but I guessed the very tall woman was Heather Hathaway and the other four must be director Mary Rogers, sound engineer Ken Perkins, set designer Robert Fernandez, and costume designer Eri Mizobe. It would be interesting to meet them in person, as I felt certain I would after my initial interview.

The FUN-TV intern and I proceeded along a lengthy corridor and then up a flight of stairs. We entered a wide room that contained perhaps a dozen square tables, with folding chairs set up by each. The young woman walked to the table farthest from the door, sat down, and motioned to me to take the seat across from her. She put her clipboard down on the table and studied it for a moment. Behind us, other interns led more Santa candidates into the room. They seated themselves at the adjacent tables. When each table was taken by an intern and a would-be Santa, the door was shut.

"My name is Emily Vance," the young woman informed me as she looked up from her clipboard. Her blond hair was pulled back in a severe bun, and her expression was properly businesslike. But there was still a sense of softness, a not-quite-disguised sweetness and even lingering childish innocence, about her. Like many young people in their early twenties,

Emily was still in the process of transitioning from youth to adulthood. It can be a difficult, even frustrating, time. "I'm going to ask you some questions from a list we're supposed to use, and I want you to answer them as completely and persuasively as you can," she said. "Got it?"

"That seems simple enough," I replied. "I'm ready to begin."

She picked up her pen. "Name, please."

"Santa Claus."

Emily rolled her eyes. "You have to take this seriously."

"I am. My name is Santa Claus."

The young woman sighed, rolled her eyes again, and then suddenly nodded. "Oh, I get it. You're doing this completely in character. That's pretty good." She made several notes on the paper attached to the clipboard. "I guess you'll tell me next that your hometown is the North Pole."

"Exactly," I said. "I've lived there since 1913. Before that, I lived on an isolated farm near Cooperstown, New York."

Emily looked up from her clipboard. "If you don't mind my saying, try not to add too many unnecessary details. Stick to the real Santa story. You're from the North Pole, period."

"I just thought you might want to know," I said. "All right, I'm from the North Pole."

"What's in your bag?" Emily wanted to know.

"I didn't know if I would need my red-and-white clothes," I told her. "I brought them just in case. Would you like to see them?" When she nodded, I opened the valise and took out my red coat with fur trim and red trousers. I hadn't brought my hat or boots.

Emily rubbed one of the coat's sleeves between her fingertips.

"Gee, real wool!" she exclaimed. "Where'd you buy this? It must have cost a fortune."

"I like wool," I replied. "It keeps me quite warm, and that's important when I'm flying my sleigh through freezing winter snowstorms."

"That's not bad," Emily said approvingly. "The part about keeping warm while flying through snowstorms is a nice little detail. You were smart to think of it." She consulted the list of questions again. "Okay, when and why did you first give presents?"

"Oh, that goes back a very long way," I told her. "In 292 A.D. I was twelve years old and living in the little town of Patara in the country of Lycia, which is known today as Turkey. A merchant named Shem had three daughters who wanted to get married, but their father had lost his fortune and could not provide them with dowries. I quietly went into their home one night and left coins for each in stockings they had hung to dry by the fire." I smiled at this very happy early memory, but Emily was not equally pleased. In fact, she seemed irritated.

"I told you, stick to the real Santa story."

"I am," I protested.

Emily sighed again. She had very expressive sighs. This one clearly indicated she was quickly losing patience with a foolish old man who was wasting her valuable time.

"Look," she said, "At first I had some hopes for you. You've got the right look, you know? Fat, but not too fat. Old, but not decrepit. I think that beard is real, isn't it? And actually white, not just dyed that color? But you've got to do better with these answers. Think about it. Santa Claus is American, and you're telling me you're an Arab."

"I have no specific nationality because Santa Claus loves all children and nations," I explained. "By birth, I suppose I am Turkish, which, by the way, is not the same thing as an Arab, which itself is a catchall term for natives of a vast region."

"Oh, please," Emily scoffed. "On *The Great Santa Search*, nobody's going to vote for you if you're not American. Are you trying to make me eliminate you? You seem like a nice man. I'd like you to do well—it'll look good on my résumé if I'm the one who processes the guy who wins. But you've got to work with me."

"How do I do that?" I inquired politely.

"By sticking to the actual facts about Santa Claus."

"And what are those?"

Emily put the clipboard down on the table and looked around the room, probably feeling jealous because all the other interns appeared to be flying through the interviews with *their* Santas.

"It's really simple," she said. "Santa Claus is American. He lives at the North Pole. He started giving his presents, I think, after the Revolutionary War when we won our freedom from the British. He gives toys as gifts, not money to girls who want to get married. Are you with me so far?"

"The North Pole isn't in America," I pointed out. "If I live there, how can I be an American?"

Emily's shoulders shook with the force of her latest sigh.

"The North Pole is American if we want it to be. Are you going to argue about everything?"

"Not at all," I assured her. "Technically, I suppose you're right that Santa Claus is American, because that is the name by which I'm known to American children. Of course, in Britain I'm Father Christmas, in France I'm Père Noel, in—"

Emily waved her hand to cut me off in mid-sentence. She made several notes, looked at me doubtfully, and said, "Enough about that. Let's keep going. Tell me about the North Pole."

"That would be a pleasure," I replied. "I live in a large self-contained environment with some dear friends who help me in every phase of my gift-giving mission. These very special men and women—"

Emily waved her hand again. "Don't say men and women. Say *elves.*"

"Why would I say that?"

"Because Santa Claus lives at the North Pole with his elves. Everybody knows that."

Now it was my turn to sigh.

"Thomas Nast, why did you ever have to draw those cartoons?" I muttered.

"What?" Emily asked. "Thomas who?"

"Thomas Nast was a cartoonist for *Harper's Weekly* and other publications during and after the Civil War," I said. "He was very talented, and his drawings encouraged belief in Santa Claus, which I appreciated. But what I didn't appreciate was him drawing me as an elf and surrounding me with elf helpers. That's where this whole silly elf business comes from. My friends who work with me are real human beings, not mythical creatures."

"Legolas the elf is my very favorite character in *Lord of the Rings*," Emily snapped. "Don't make fun of elves."

"I didn't mean to offend you," I assured her. "All three books in the *Lord of the Rings* trilogy are wonderful."

"Are they books, too?" Emily asked. "I thought they were just movies. The guy who played Legolas was really cute. Anyway, let's get back to my questions. I don't think we need much more. Now: why do you want to be Santa Claus?"

"I already *am* Santa Claus. Perhaps you should ask why I love *being* Santa."

Emily looked around again. Already, most of the other interns were shaking hands with their first Santa candidates, ushering them out the door, and sitting down with their next round of applicants.

"Okay, whatever. Why do you love being Santa?"

"It is a privilege to help children learn the true meaning of Christmas, which is gratitude to God for sending us his son Jesus, and gaining from that gratitude a sense of love and generosity of spirit toward others," I said. "It is always my goal for Santa Claus to be part of the holiday celebration, but never mistaken for the reason for the holiday itself."

Emily put down the clipboard and pen.

"I think that's all I need to hear. Mister, you can't bring God and Jesus into a Christmas Eve TV special. Do you know how many viewers would change channels? Do you have any idea what would happen to *The Great Santa Search* ratings? The last thing people want to think about on Christmas Eve is something *serious*. Santa Claus isn't about Jesus. He's about toys under the tree on Christmas morning. Jeez, don't you know *anything* about Christmas?" She stood up and extended her hand. "Thanks for coming in. You can go out through that door; somebody will escort you back to the street."

"Are you eliminating me from the audition?"

"You're just not Santa Claus material," Emily declared. "All that Arab stuff, and the North Pole isn't America, and no elves. And then bringing Jesus into it. You need to learn your Christmas history better. Next!"

I stood up and shook hands.

"You did believe in Santa Claus once, didn't you?" I asked gently.

Something briefly flashed in Emily's eyes—surprise at my question, certainly, but also the joy of some childhood Christmas memory, and finally regret for innocence lost.

"I guess," she said. "But then I grew up."

Another young intern guided me back down the corridor and toward the theater lobby. As I passed the open door leading into the main auditorium, I could see Felix and the other judges down on the stage. They were talking with the first few candidates who'd passed the initial interview process. One was the man with the Great Dane.

Eleven

t least we didn't choose the man with the Great Dane as a *Great Santa Search* finalist," Felix said soothingly. "Almost nine hundred Santas tried out at the open audition, and we ended up picking just two of them. It's no disgrace that you didn't get through the first round."

Felix and all my other friends were trying hard to lift my spirits, but without much success. I'd been so sure I would go to New York, sail through the audition, be chosen as a finalist, and then not have to worry anymore about getting the opportunity to compete on the Christmas Eve program. There, of course, I'd win easily and then thwart Lucretia Pepper's plan to have the "official" Santa serve as spokesman for LastLong Toy Company. Now, nothing seemed certain. What if I never had the chance to be on *The Great Santa Search* at all?

But when I expressed my concern to everyone at the North Pole on the day after my disastrous trip to New York, they took turns telling me not to worry.

"After all, only two places out of ten are taken so far," Amelia Earhart noted. "You'll get one of the other eight. Remember, Felix is one of the people who'll be making those selections. Just get a job as Santa at a big mall. It's not going to be that hard."

"That's what I thought about the open audition, and I was wrong," I reminded her.

"But becoming a mall Santa is entirely different," Leonardo said. He and Willie Skokan had barged through the door to my den, carrying more of their manila file folders. "There's a specific process to be followed, Santa Claus. May I tell you about it?"

I was sitting in my favorite easy chair, a pot of steaming chamomile tea on a small table in front of me. I waved Leonardo and Willie to seats on the other side of the table, and poured them each a cup. Layla, Felix, Sarah, Amelia, Bill Pickett, and Teddy Roosevelt were already in the room. I have a rather large den.

"I thought I'd have to simply fly the sleigh to some city or other, go to its largest mall, find the mall's employment office, and apply for its holiday position of Santa," I said. "I hope I'll do better with some mall personnel manager than I did with young Emily, the FUN-TV intern. I'm afraid she found me to be quite unqualified."

Leonardo shook his head, which made his long white beard waggle. He and Willie dropped their folders on the table.

"It no longer works that way, at least at most of the larger, more popular malls," Leonardo told me. "Mall management considers it crucial to have highly believable Santas working during the Christmas season. Someone like J. W. Parkinson's silly Kris Kringle would never be hired today. Willie and I have done considerable research on this. The malls work with what I suppose you might call 'Santa search firms,' companies that hire and train prospective Santas before they ever interact with trusting children. These companies provide Santas to the malls, guaranteeing their ability to help boys and girls enjoy the holidays without endangering their belief in, well, *you*. So what we must do is select one of these companies, have you hired by it, and then placed in some prominent mall where Felix can 'discover' you and recommend you as a finalist on *The Great Santa Search*."

I sipped my tea and nodded. "I'm pleased that there's some procedure in place to ensure competent Santa imitators. Still, Leonardo, you seem to take it for granted that one or another of these Santa companies will hire me. It simply isn't enough to be the *real* Santa. If it was, I'd already have been picked as a finalist in yesterday's audition."

"You have to consider the circumstances," Layla said in the slightly sharp tone she sometimes used when she felt I was missing an obvious point. "Bobbo Butler allowed interns to ask superficial questions and make their own snap judgments. While I'm sure those young people did their best, if Emily is an example then they clearly knew very little real Santa history, or even cared about it. If these search firms are as committed to high Santa quality as Leonardo obviously believes, then they will recognize how qualified you are. Until you're given reason to think otherwise, give them the benefit of the doubt."

I finished my tea and set down the cup. Leonardo immediately pushed a dozen sheets of paper into my hand.

"I contacted one of the search companies and asked them to send an application," he explained. "The Noel Program is based in Golden, Colorado. They provide Santas to malls around the country every holiday season. They really want to hire only the most qualified people, Santa. You can tell from the questions they require applicants to answer."

There was a letter stapled to the application form. I adjusted my glasses and read it out loud:

"Dear Santa," it began. *"Thank you so much for your interest in The Noel Program. We are delighted you have contacted us!"*

"Already, they're friendlier than Emily!" Layla observed. "Please keep reading, Santa."

"We serve more than 175 malls nationwide," the letter continued. *"Our Santa Team always welcomes cheery and enthusiastic gentlemen with natural white beards to perform the role of the lovable character Santa Claus during the holiday season."*

"Ah, I see that they realize I'm lovable," I said to Layla.

"Some of the time," she replied. "Go on with the letter."

So I did. It requested that I completely fill out the application forms provided, then send them on to the company office in Colorado. When they were received, I would be contacted by telephone. If I was considered a prospective Santa candidate, a personal interview would be arranged.

"I suppose I ought to get this application filled out," I suggested. "Does anyone have a pen?"

Amelia lent me hers, and I turned to the first page of the application form. The first request was for basic personal information—name, address, and employment background.

"I suppose I can't put down my name as 'Santa Claus,'" I said. "Like Emily at yesterday's audition, they'd think I was joking."

"Well, you can certainly say your first name is Nicholas," Sarah reminded me. "But a last name is necessary, too. Have you ever had one?"

Actually, I hadn't. When I was born in 280 A.D., people were generally known only by one name. I was simply called "Nicholas" then. So Theodore suggested it might be great fun to think up a new last name for me, and the suggestions flew—"North," from Amelia, alluding to my home at the North Pole, and "Priest," from Sarah, since that had been my original profession. Layla thought "Grinch" might be a delightful possibility—we all loved that fanciful Christmas story written by Dr. Seuss.

But it was quiet Willie Skokan who came up with the best one.

"Why not call yourself 'Nicholas Holiday'?" he asked. "It's in keeping with the spirit of the Christmas season, and 'Holiday' is quite a common last name."

Everyone agreed, and that was the name I wrote at the top of the application.

I next had to supply a home address, social security number, and telephone number. That part was easy. Leonardo's wizardry with computers and electronic data systems allows us to create satisfactory personal backgrounds when necessary. Felix and Sarah, for instance, had to supply an address and other data to FUN-TV before officially becoming employed there. I used one of our North Pole cell phones as my contact number.

"Employment history" was a bit more difficult. I almost put "bishop," which was factual but liable to result in additional scrutiny by the Noel Program staff. I did not want to mislead anyone, though—after some discussion we finally settled on "self-employed toy consultant," adding Willie Skokan's name and North Pole cell phone number if Noel decided to check references.

"I'll only tell them good things about you, Santa," Willie assured me.

Next came something labeled "Data Sheet." The questions were quite curious—Did I have a natural beard? ("Yes.") Did I have my own black Santa boots? ("Of course.") Did I have my own tiny round gold Santa glasses? ("Actually, they have silver frames.")

"These Noel people are very thorough," Bill Pickett observed. "Are you sure you shouldn't just get some gold-framed glasses?"

"I will if they insist," I said. "But I don't see why it would make any difference."

I noted on the Data Sheet that I hoped for full-time holiday employment and that I was willing to travel from my home (which we'd said was in Half Moon Bay, California, an hour's drive south of San Francisco; Layla and I were particularly fond of a seafood restaurant there called the Fish Trap, and it just seemed like a nice town to be from) to any mall in the country where I might be assigned.

A section called "Special Notes" asked if I spoke any languages other than English. Now, *there* I felt certain I would surpass any of Noel's other prospective Santas. I'd been born and grew up in Lycia, where I learned to speak Turkish, Greek, Latin, and Aramaic. In the centuries since, I'd spent considerable time in Spain, Italy, France, and Germany; I spoke those countries' languages perfectly. I proudly listed them all.

Then came the final page: "Frequently Asked Questions for Santa Claus." I was instructed to write down the answers I would give if children happened to ask me such things as how I knew the name of every boy and girl; how I was able to leave presents for every child in the world in just one night; how I prepared for my Christmas Eve flight; what I liked to do on the day after Christmas; and why I chose to live at the North Pole.

"I think I should answer them all truthfully," I said. "For instance, I believe it should be explained to children that Santa *doesn't* deliver gifts to every child in the world on Christmas Eve. There's St. Nicholas Day and Epiphany, too."

"Perhaps you should only give the answers they expect," Amelia Earhart cautioned. "All these malls are in America, after all, and American children care only about Santa Claus and Christmas Eve."

"I just don't think that's correct," I replied. "That is, I believe children are naturally curious and like to learn new things. If they hear about holiday customs in other parts of the world, it will enrich their enjoyment of the season. Differences in cultures should be interesting rather than threatening, Amelia."

When every question was answered on the application form, I posed for the snapshot Noel required. I wore my full Christmas Eve costume. It felt odd to be wearing those clothes in April. I sealed the application form and photo in an envelope, added sufficient stamps for delivery, and then hopped in the sleigh and flew to Half Moon Bay. We had to mail the application from there so the postmark on the envelope would be from the appropriate place. Layla came along, and we enjoyed dinner afterward—seafood at the Fish Trap. I had my fish grilled rather than fried. Theodore had me in the habit of eating healthier food, though I assured Layla I would allow myself occasional treats once *The Great Santa Search* competition was over.

"For instance, I'll enjoy Lars's delicious desserts perhaps one night each week," I predicted.

"I'll believe it when I see it," she replied. After sixteen centuries, Layla knew me all too well.

Then I spent several increasingly anxious weeks back at the North Pole, training with Theodore in the mornings, going about my usual planning process for the next cycle of holiday gift-giving in the afternoons, and worrying every waking minute whether the Noel Program would hire me as a mall Santa or not. If they didn't, how would Felix ever be able to include me as one of the ten *Great Santa Search* finalists? Layla insisted there was no cause for concern. If the company really sought out only the best possible Santas, it was certain to hire me, she said. But as the days passed and April turned into May, the cell phone I kept in my pocket remained silent.

Then one afternoon as I was testing some new remote-controlled toy race cars with Bill Pickett and Ben Franklin, the cell phone buzzed. It took me a moment to realize what was happening, but then my heart leaped. Only the Noel Program had that number. They were finally contacting me!

Motioning for my friends to stop racing the cars around the room—they made loud noises when they crashed into the walls—I snapped the phone open and said hello.

"May I speak to Mr. Nicholas Holiday?" a woman inquired.

I almost blurted, "Who?" before remembering that was the name I'd used on the application.

"This is Nicholas Holiday," I replied, trying to sound calmer than I felt.

"Mr. Holiday, my name is Stephanie Owen and I'm a vice president of the Noel Program," she said. "Thank you for your application. It's one of the most interesting we've received so far this year. And from your photograph, you certainly look the part. The beard in particular is just lovely, almost too perfect to be real."

"It's real, I promise," I told her, feeling more hopeful by the second. "And please call me Nicholas." She laughed, said I should call her Stephanie, and asked a few more questions—Did I really speak all those languages? Had I lived in many other countries before settling in California?—before confirming what I'd hoped.

"We'd like to arrange a meeting with you," Stephanie said. "Could you come to our offices in Colorado?"

I said I'd be glad to do so. Stephanie said I should arrive at the Noel offices the following Monday at 10:00 a.m. She added that her company would reimburse me for my travel costs, but I said that would not be necessary.

"They wouldn't ask you to meet with them if they didn't plan to hire you," Theodore said after I'd gathered everyone together to announce the good news. "You're as good as on *The Great Santa Search*. Bully!" (This was Theodore's favorite word to express great pleasure.)

I arrived for my appointment promptly at ten, wearing the same sport coat, dress shirt, and slacks I had worn to the FUN-TV audition. After dropping me off a block or two from the Noel Program office, Bill Pickett took the delighted reindeer for a long, energetic flight. He promised to come back and pick me up in about two hours. I didn't think my meeting at

Noel would last longer than that. If it did, Bill and the reindeer would gladly log additional flying time until I was ready to return to the North Pole.

Stephanie Owen was a pleasant-looking woman with very broad shoulders and straw-blond hair. She greeted me with a handshake and escorted me into a comfortable office. I was startled to see a large framed photograph of Santa Claus on one wall—startled because I had difficulty believing it wasn't me. This actor—he looked so genuine it seemed rude to think of him as an *impostor*—had a fine white beard, genial smile, and husky physique. The white trim on the cuffs of his red suit was spotless. His arms were wrapped around a quintet of beaming children, who gazed up at him adoringly. If anything, I thought, he looked more like me than I did.

Stephanie saw me staring at the photo.

"That's Jimmy Lee from Leeds, Alabama, and he's perhaps the greatest Santa in the entire history of mall Christmases," she explained. "From the moment fifteen years ago when he first sat down and invited a child to sit on his lap, he *was* Santa Claus. He knows all about the history of the season. He loves the children just as much as they love him. We feel it's an honor to be associated with Jimmy Lee. Every year, the managers of all the biggest malls in the country beg us to assign him to theirs. Why, a few have even offered us bribes!"

"How do you decide which mall will be blessed with Jimmy Lee's presence?" I asked carefully. I admit I was just a bit annoyed by Stephanie's claim this fellow was such a superior Santa. Though, I had to admit ruefully to myself, he certainly *looked* perfect.

"He likes to be somewhere different each year," Stephanie said. "So we pick a region—the northwest, perhaps, or maybe mid-America, and put the names of all our mall clients in that area in a hat. Jimmy Lee comes here to our office in October—that's when our Santas get their assignments—and draws the winning name. It's very exciting. Last year he was in Seattle, the year before in Houston, and so on. After he's been a mall's Santa for one Christmas, he doesn't go back to that mall again. When a Santa's as special as Jimmy Lee, as many malls as possible should have the opportunity to be his holiday headquarters. Someone so wonderful has to be shared."

"That's very generous of you and Jimmy Lee," I said.

Stephanie gazed fondly at the photograph.

"This Christmas we think we'll *really* have to share him," she said. "You've heard about *The Great Santa Search* competition on Christmas Eve, of course. Someone from FUN-TV has already contacted us to say they'll be visiting all the big malls where our Santas work. It's a foregone conclusion, to us at least, that Jimmy Lee will win. Who else?"

"Why, *I* might," I suggested.

Stephanie chuckled. "Nicholas Holiday, I like a Santa who is optimistic! Now, why don't you sit down and we'll have a chat. We've talked enough about Jimmy Lee. I'd like to know more about *you*."

For the next half-hour, Stephanie asked me all sorts of questions. As much as possible, I told her the absolute truth. I was born in Turkey, lived all over the world, and had loved the holiday season for as long as I could remember. She wanted to know how I had become a "self-employed toy consultant," and I replied that I very much enjoyed tinkering with toys and discovering ways they could be improved.

"Why, at this point in your life, do you want to work as Santa Claus?" she inquired.

"Because nothing is better than being Santa," I replied. "I believe that with all my heart."

"We were particularly intrigued by one of your responses on the application," Stephanie continued. "You wrote that if children asked how you took presents to every boy and girl in the world on the same night, you'd tell them you actually do your gift-giving on three nights. None of our other Santas have ever mentioned St. Nicholas Day and Epiphany on their applications. Why do you think American children should know about those celebrations?"

"Children have far more sense than most grown-ups give them credit for," I replied. "It's a fact that many boys and girls who don't live in America expect to receive their holiday gifts on December 6 or January 6. In telling them this, I'm respecting rather than insulting their intelligence. And there's another reason for sharing this information. May I tell you what it is?"

"Please," Stephanie said.

"The more we understand the holiday traditions of other cultures, the more we can share in a universal spirit of goodwill," I replied. "That's true for people of all ages. I believe that the more everyone knows about the real history of Christmas, the more they will love it. And, after all, Santa Claus should be part of the Christmas celebration without being mistaken as the reason for it. I would hope people love Santa because of what my gifts truly represent—reminders of the greatest gift ever given."

Stephanie sat back and rubbed her chin.

"Well," she said. She seemed deep in thought.

"Have I offended you?" I asked, remembering how young Emily from FUN-TV chastised me for bringing religion into Christmas.

"Not at all," Stephanie replied. "You expressed yourself beautifully. While we ask our Santas not to bring up personal religious faith—it's for parents to discuss such things with their children, we believe—we never think it's wrong for a Santa to reinforce the inspiration for Christmas *if* the child mentions it first."

"I feel quite relieved," I told her, and it was true. "If I may, I'd like to ask about something else. You may think it's unimportant, but it has troubled me ever since I first read your application form."

Stephanie looked concerned.

"Please, ask whatever you'd like."

"Well," I said, "it has to do with spectacles, or glasses, if you prefer. You asked whether I had 'tiny round gold Santa glasses,' and mine, as you can see"—I took them from my coat pocket—"actually have silver frames. Do you require gold frames, and, if so, why?"

Stephanie opened a desk drawer and took out several dozen small photographs. Each was of a mall Santa, who had smiled at the camera. Each wore an identical pair of small, round, gold-framed spectacles.

"Many boys and girls visit more than one mall and speak to more than one of our Santas during the same Christmas season," she explained. "Now, our Santas don't look exactly alike, but we try to have them appear as similar as possible so young children in particular aren't confused. We'll gladly furnish you a pair of gold-rimmed glasses so you can match all the others. We don't consider even the smallest detail to be unimportant, and we do expect outstanding performances by our Santas. I hope, this Christmas, you'll be one of them."

"Are you offering me a job?" I asked.

Stephanie laughed.

"Yes, I am," she said. "I can tell you're going to be a fine Santa. Maybe you'll even be another Jimmy Lee. Now, let's discuss some details. First, I'm sure, you'll want to know about salary."

"Actually, the salary doesn't matter," I said. "I'll accept whatever you think is fair."

"You really *are* unique," Stephanie declared. She explained that her company paid their Santas based on a combination of experience and performance. Since I'd never worked as a mall Santa before, I would have to start at minimum pay, but if I did good work, there would be merit raises. I would be assigned to a specific mall, Stephanie continued, and would work there full-time for about forty-five days beginning in early November and up through Christmas Eve. I would be notified of my mall assignment sometime in October.

"If you prefer a specific region we'll try to accommodate you," she added. "And if you do have to temporarily move somewhere, we help with travel costs and rent."

"I have friends in most major cities," I informed her. "I'm sure I'll be able to stay with them. Assign me wherever you like." Actually, I could commute by sleigh from the North Pole to any city in America. I'd sleep in my own bed every night no matter where I was assigned.

Stephanie had me fill out a few more forms. I remembered to say I was sixty-three, my age back in the year 343 A.D., when I gave up being a priest and embarked on a full-time gift-giving mission. I hadn't grown physically older since.

"By the way," I said, "you mentioned I'd work through Christmas Eve. But if I happen to be selected for *The Great Santa Search*, I would have to be in a New York City theater that night."

"You *are* optimistic," Stephanie said. "We've already decided that if any of our Santas become *Great Santa Search* finalists, and we expect several will, then we'll send substitute Santas to replace them in their malls on Christmas Eve. We always have some 'floaters,' as we call them, available in case a Santa becomes ill or can't report to work for some reason."

"You do seem to think of everything," I told her. I was thinking of something, too—specifically, how much I was going to enjoy proving to Jimmy Lee that he wasn't the best Santa anywhere. It wasn't the nicest thought, but no one is perfect, the real Santa Claus included. Now that I was going to be a mall Santa I was once again certain I would compete on *The Great Santa Search*, where I would win. I had to. The possibility of a false Santa Claus acting as the spokesman for LastLong Toy Company was absolutely unacceptable.

Twelve

he months seemed to rush by. I practiced roping with Bill Pickett until we wore out all the lariats at the North Pole. Every day, Theodore directed me through a series of increasingly difficult exercises. At mealtimes, I dined sensibly. Sometime in August, I realized I hadn't consumed any sugar since the beginning of my training on the morning of January 6, Epiphany. Though I hadn't lost a pound, I'd gained considerable energy. In all my seventeen centuries, I could not recall feeling better.

During these same months, *The Great Santa Search* became one of the most talked-about topics in America. Just as Bobbo Butler predicted, his Christmas Eve competition had captured the ongoing attention of the media. As a result, it was virtually impossible for anyone to read a magazine, listen to the radio, or watch television without some daily reminder of FUN-TV's holiday special on December 24. Most of the coverage resulted from the unceasing efforts of publicists hired by the LastLong Toy Company, but not all of it. A supermarket tabloid revealed that Rick Press, one of the two open-audition winners, was actually wanted by police in Florida for selling "prime beachfront property" to unsuspecting senior citizens. Only after giving him all their money did these unfortunate people discover they owned swampland instead. Immediately, every major television network and print publication began covering "the Santa scandal." After Press was arrested, Bobbo announced that he could only compete on *The Great Santa Search* if he was innocent of all criminal charges against him. Instead, Press loudly declared his guilt, adding he had hoped to be voted the "real" Santa on Christmas Eve so he could spend the rest of his life atoning for his crimes by inspiring children to love the holidays. He was then kicked off *The Great Santa Search*, but within a week signed a publishing contract for a tell-all book, and not long afterward a major network paid him millions for the right to produce a made-for-television movie about his life: *From Sinner to Santa*. That undoubtedly made the three years he was sentenced to spend in prison easier to endure.

"At least there are nine places available on *The Great Santa Search* now instead of eight," Felix reminded me. "That improves your chances of getting selected."

"I hope you're joking, Felix," I said. "Now that I'm going to work as a mall Santa, you're going to see to it that I'm picked for the program. We're agreed on that, aren't we?"

"I haven't seen you working in a mall yet," he joked. At least, I hoped he was joking. "If I come to observe and you're not doing a good job, I might have to leave you off my list. We want only the very best for *The Great Santa Search*, you know!"

"I'm going to be the best," I assured him. "I really am Santa, after all. I just wish Stephanie Owen would call and tell me where I'm going to work. It's nearly October."

All the publicity for *The Great Santa Search* made me especially anxious to get started. Media commentators were speculating endlessly on where the program competitors might be found. Already, most of them assumed malls would be logical locations. Several veteran mall Santas were tracked down and interviewed about their interest in competing. All of them were, and each promised he would be the winner.

Whole weeks of media coverage focused on who would serve as *The Great Santa Search*'s master of ceremonies. The names of three ex-presidents were mentioned, as well as the star of a late-night TV talk show, a comedian who regularly hosted the Academy Awards broadcast, the reigning Miss America, and several famous athletes. One columnist made headlines by suggesting the Easter Bunny be selected "in the spirit of crossover holiday collaboration, and proof to all Americans that spokespersons for opposing groups or causes can still work together for the common good." Just as speculation reached fever pitch, Bobbo announced *he* would be the host. Heather Hathaway privately told Sarah and Felix that Bobbo had intended to be master of ceremonies all along.

"He couldn't stand not being on the program that makes FUN-TV one of the major networks again," Heather said. "I think, sometimes, that Bobbo forgets the star of the show is going to be the winning Santa."

"Heather is an exceptionally perceptive woman," Sarah told Felix later. "Have you noticed? She studies people carefully and seems to have considerable insight into their motives. It's so sad Bobbo Butler doesn't appreciate her properly."

"He's told us she's the best executive assistant in the television business," Felix reminded her.

"That's just it—he thinks of her as an *assistant*."

Eventually, Lucretia Pepper was interviewed on a weekly television prime-time news program after reports surfaced that LastLong Toy Company would be the sole sponsor of *The Great Santa Search*. She refused to confirm that the winning Santa would become her company's year-round spokesman, saying only that various possibilities were under consideration. She did say that LastLong toys were the most popular choice for Christmas gifts, and announced that there would be a brand-new set of action figures based on the various *Great Santa Search* challenges available in stores right after the program aired.

"But won't that be too late to sell toys associated with Santa?" she was asked by one of the most famous TV reporters of all. "On December 26, Christmas will be over for another year."

Lucretia Pepper looked directly at the camera and smiled.

"After watching *The Great Santa Search*, children in America will be obsessed with Santa Claus all year long," she predicted. "They'll be asking for Christmas presents, especially the new LastLong Santa action figure, from

January through December. The simplest way to say it is that Christmas presents won't just be for Christmas anymore."

"Won't that make December 25 itself much less special?" the reporter wanted to know. "That would be terrible."

"But as a result, LastLong Toy Company will create more than one thousand new jobs to meet increased demand for our products," she replied. "We're not hurting Christmas, we're helping the American economy. I certainly hope you're not questioning our patriotic motives or our corporate love for the holiday."

On several occasions, Felix and Sarah were summoned to New York for meetings with Bobbo and the rest of *The Great Santa Search* staff. There were discussions about how the stage sets should look, and how tall the chimneys for the sliding competition should be, and how Bobbo, as host, should dress. It was finally agreed that he would wear a special red tuxedo with white fur cuffs and collar trim.

Sarah and Felix said that the attention to smallest details was incredible. The appropriate length of the antlers on fake reindeer took hours to determine. A *Great Santa Search* theme song had been commissioned, and everyone had to listen to every possible variation of it, from waltz to rap. Motown-style, with a good beat for the audience to clap along with, was the eventual choice. Newly hired choreographer Lauren Devoe cast the deciding vote.

"She says we'll need a strong beat to disguise the simple steps for the dance routine she's developing," Felix reported. "She feels the ten Santas may be limited in their dancing ability."

At the end of the first week in October, there was still no word about my mall assignment. I fretted that perhaps Stephanie Owen had forgotten me, but on October 10 my cell phone vibrated and she was finally in touch.

"I have some wonderful news for you, Nicholas Holiday!" she began. "Usually our first-time Santas start out in smaller towns and malls, but we've decided you're right for one of the biggest and best. You're assigned to the Galaxy Mall in Cleveland, Ohio! Have you ever been to it?"

"I've certainly been to Cleveland," I said. "I don't believe I've gone to a mall there."

"Well, this one is absolutely fabulous," Stephanie assured me. "There are four stories and over five hundred shops, many of them quite up-scale. Your Santa set is going to be one of the most spectacular anywhere. I don't want to describe it ahead of time. You'll see for yourself. Now, you'll officially start work on the second Saturday in November, but we're asking that you actually visit the mall one or two days before that, so you can meet the Galaxy manager, make sure its Santa suit fits, and get settled in."

"I have my own Santa suit," I replied. "It fits perfectly. I'll bring it with me."

"We're really committed to our Santas wearing authentic-looking suits," Stephanie cautioned.

"I give you my word that no Santa suit is more authentic than mine," I promised.

Stephanie provided additional information. The manager of Galaxy Mall was named Lester Sneed. She warned me that he was rather gruff. But his mall attracted some of the largest crowds of Christmas shoppers in the entire country.

"In fact, Jimmy Lee was the Galaxy Mall Santa four Christmases ago," Stephanie added. "You know we wouldn't let Jimmy Lee go to a mall that wasn't one of the very best!"

"And where will Jimmy Lee be spending this particular Christmas?" I inquired. It is always good to keep track of the competition.

"We just drew his location this morning," she said. "He'll be right there in New York City! Isn't that just *perfect* for *The Great Santa Search*?"

"How convenient," I replied. "Well, I hope the program talent scouts find their way to Cleveland, too."

"I'm sure they will," Stephanie agreed. "Meanwhile, can we help at all with Cleveland logistics? Housing, transportation, that sort of thing?"

I told her I'd be able to make my own arrangements, and thanked her for the call.

"I'll try to live up to your expectations," I said. "Should I get in touch with Lester Sneed, the Galaxy Mall manager, right away?"

"We've sent him your file," Stephanie said. "I think if you call in a few weeks and make an appointment to see him just before you officially go to work, that would be fine. Good luck!"

But I couldn't wait to see the mall where I was to work. Within the hour, Layla, Willie Skokan, Arthur, and I were in the sleigh and speeding through the cool fall skies to Cleveland. We found the Galaxy Mall close to the shores of Lake Erie. Arthur was particularly excited because the Rock and Roll Hall of Fame was not far away.

"I might just visit there while the rest of you inspect the mall," he said. "Do you think the Hall of Fame might have a Beach Boys exhibit?" Arthur was quite fond of the Beach Boys, and would make his way about the North Pole humming "Help Me, Rhonda" or "I Get Around" at any hour of the day or night. Over the years, all of us had developed unfathomable attachments to various musical groups, books, or films. Theodore couldn't get enough of travel books written by Bill Bryson. Amelia Earhart joked that any movie was wonderful if Sean Connery was in it. I, myself, have never succumbed to fandom of any sort, though I will admit to a limited, sensible fondness for SpongeBob. Besides sports and occasional news programs, we had never watched television until *The Great Santa Search* forced it on us. Now, we had to pry Lars from in front of the widescreen set every night when it was time for him to begin preparing dinner. If he'd had his way, he would have watched the Food Network every waking minute. He'd already sent off several fan letters to Rachael Ray and Emeril Lagasse.

We assured Arthur that the Beach Boys would be well-represented in the Hall, and when I discreetly set the sleigh down near Galaxy Mall he hurried off. After instructing the reindeer to hover out of sight until we returned, Willie Skokan, Layla, and I made our way to the mall. There was no chance we'd be unable to locate it. Galaxy Mall was a massive structure that dwarfed every other building around it. The parking lot alone seemed to exceed the size of America's smaller states. When we stepped inside we were overwhelmed by the sheer immensity of the place. Glass elevators delivered shoppers to each of four levels; the pungent aroma of curry and barbecue and pizza wafted from the food court. The array of shops was bewildering. Every hundred feet or so there was a giant map indicating what was where, and each had a helpful arrow accompanied by the assurance *"YOU ARE HERE."*

"This is amazing!" Layla observed. "How can anyone know where to go or what to do? There's just too much of everything!"

But a flood of other mall visitors felt otherwise. Men, women, and children of all ages poured into and out of stores, jostling one another and shouting to companions and, in more cases than I could count, chattering into cell phones. Above the din came regular announcements over some massive public-address system—there was a ten-minute sale in *this* store, a half-day "shopper's special" in *that* one. Willie Skokan, Layla, and I were swept up in the irresistible flow of humanity. We tried frantically to hang on to one another. Finally we found ourselves stumbling past the food court where, with considerable effort, we separated ourselves from the rampaging herd and caught our breaths.

"It can't be like this all the time," I said hopefully.

"I think it can," Willie Skokan replied. "Leonardo and I have done some research, and we found that—"

Layla and I never heard what they had found, because another blaring announcement was being made on the mall's public-address system:

"Remember, customers, that in only three weeks, that's twenty-one days, Santa Claus arrives at Galaxy Mall! We're busily building our own Santa Land on the first floor of the west wing. Be on hand for our traditional welcoming ceremony there at 4:00 p.m. on Santa Saturday, and then bring the children often so they can sit on Santa's lap and tell the jolly old elf everything they want for Christmas! Of course, anything made by Santa and his helpers will be on sale in our shops! We've already got the holiday spirit at Galaxy Mall!"

"Let's go see what this Santa Land is going to be like," Layla suggested. We inched our way back into the mob. It took us almost half an hour to finally arrive on the first floor of the mall's west wing, where it was instantly clear we'd come for nothing. Huge plywood barriers had been erected around an area fully ten thousand feet square, with a massive plywood sheet fixed over the top to thwart anyone from ascending two or three stories to try to peek from above. The protective barrier only added to the mystery of the sounds coming from within. Hammers pounded, chainsaws buzzed, and the muffled shouts of workers combined in a tantalizing cacophony.

"Obviously, this mall takes Santa seriously," I said. "It will be interesting to see what they've done when I officially arrive in three weeks. Meanwhile, let's collect the reindeer and Arthur and get back to the North Pole, where it's quieter."

The three of us who'd been to the mall were mostly silent on the sleigh ride home. Arthur sang "Good Vibrations" until we asked him, please, to stop, and then he hummed the tune to himself all the rest of the way.

I returned to the Galaxy Mall on the day before "Santa Saturday." I was dressed in a gray business suit, and I had my Santa costume with me in the same valise I'd brought to the audition in New York City. The mall was still crowded, but this time I knew what to expect. A woman at an information kiosk gave me directions to the mall manager's office, which was on the second level, tucked behind the men's and women's restrooms. The office was surprisingly small; I later learned that, in malls, prime floor space is always reserved for stores and crowd-attracting exhibits. The manager's office is built wherever it can be wedged in.

There was barely room in Lester Sneed's office for a tiny desk, two uncomfortable chairs, a phone, and the man himself. He did not stand up to greet me, instead shoving out his hand and briefly clasping mine.

"Lester Sneed," he growled.

"I'm Nicholas Holiday. Please call me Nicholas."

He didn't invite me to call him Lester.

"I don't like a Santa without experience," he declared, and I was taken aback. There was no welcome in his voice, only exasperation. "For what we pay those Noel people, I expect the best Santa they've got. Instead they send me a rookie. What's going on?"

"I don't consider myself a rookie," I replied, trying to remain polite. "It's true I've never worked as a mall Santa before, but I know what's required and I'm perfectly qualified."

"I decide that, pal, not you." Mr. Sneed leaned back in his chair as far as he could. It wasn't far, because the back of his chair immediately bumped against the wall. He silently stared at me for several long moments. Not knowing what else to do, I stared back, using the time to study him. Lester Sneed was a gray-haired, sour-faced man of perhaps fifty. His gray beard was scraggly and grew thicker in some places on his chin and cheeks than others. He wore a rumpled blue suit and white shirt with a faded maroon tie. There was about him the air of a man who found little to enjoy in life. There were no photos of family or friends on his desk, only piles of paper with "Priority" stamped on almost every sheet. As he sat, he drummed his long, thin fingers on the top of his desk.

"Okay," he said suddenly. "You're here. Show me the Santa suit."

I opened the valise and pulled out the red coat and trousers and hat, all with white fur trim. Mr. Sneed yanked them from my hands and inspected them, turning the garments over in his hands to check, I suppose, for worn places.

"Looks okay," he announced, and tossed the garments back to me. "Custom-made? I didn't see any brand labels."

"I have a fine tailor," I said. "This suit was made exclusively for me."

"With what you people charge me, I guess you can afford it," Mr. Sneed snapped. "Okay. Let's go look at the Santa Land set."

"You say 'okay' a lot, don't you?" I asked, trying to make friendly conversation. I wanted to get along with Mr. Sneed, who was, after all, my boss. I hadn't ever really had one of those before.

"What's it to you, buddy?"

"I meant no offense," I told him. "And, please, call me Nicholas."

"Let's get moving, buddy."

Mr. Sneed did not say another word to me as we made our way from his office to Santa Land. Helped by long experience, he expertly weaved his way through the crowds. I did my best to keep up.

The plywood barriers still blocked every view of Santa Land, but there was a door cut in one wall, and Mr. Sneed and I went through it. As I stepped inside, I gasped. I couldn't help it.

The boundary of Santa Land was circled by a miniature railroad track, and a lovely little steam engine with a dozen open cars attached stood ready to offer a merry ride. A wrought-iron bridge rose over one section of the track—this, obviously, was where visitors would enter Santa Land. The bridge was bedecked with holly that had to be plastic but certainly looked quite real. And in the center of Santa Land was an incredible structure. Red-and-white candy canes fully twenty feet high supported a rotunda of sparkling icicles. I realized the candy canes were plaster and the icicles were plastic, but they were so skillfully crafted that they in no sense seemed artificial. Underneath the rotunda was nothing less than a throne, a high-backed seat seemingly made from toy blocks, with a ten-foot-tall Raggedy Ann doll on one side and an equally giant wooden soldier standing at attention on the other. A series of brightly colored steps led to the throne, and along the steps plastic-limbed Christmas trees gleamed with thousands of colored lights.

"This is astonishing," I said to Mr. Sneed.

"Expensive, is what it is," he replied. "Okay. Sit in your seat. Got to make sure you fit. You're pretty broad across the beam."

I gingerly went up the steps and settled myself on the throne. Though it appeared to be constructed of wood blocks, in fact the portion on which I sat was cushioned. It was very comfortable, and I told Mr. Sneed so.

"Okay, then, got some people for you to meet," he said, and waved over a group I hadn't previously noticed, since I'd been so overwhelmed by Santa Land itself. Four young men and three young women walked up.

"These are the helpers," barked Mr. Sneed. "Dave, Scott, Xander, Seiler, and Yelena are your elves. Jill's the photographer; most parents'll pay extra to have their kids' pictures taken on your lap. Ralphie's her assistant. Okay with all that?"

"I actually don't have elves," I protested, more out of habit than any hope someone would believe me. "My North Pole friends are real people."

"You're Santa, but I'm the boss," Mr. Sneed said. "I want elves, so you get elves. Okay?"

"Okay," I replied.

"I got things to do, so you people get acquainted. Santa, Holiday, whatever your name is, these people did the same jobs here last year, so they know what they're doing, even if maybe you don't. Jill, make sure this new guy knows where the dressing room is. I want all of you in costume and ready to go tomorrow at 3:00 p.m. Opening arrival ceremony's at four. I want it to be perfect. Okay?"

"Okay," the others chorused. That seemed to be the response Mr. Sneed preferred. He nodded, though he didn't smile, and walked off without another word, leaving me with seven strangers in the middle of Santa Land.

"How do you like Old O.K.?" the helper named Dave asked me.

"Who?" I asked.

"Old O.K. You know, Mr. Sneed. That's what we call him. Friendly guy, eh?"

"Don't get started, Dave," Jill the photographer said. "Your name is Nicholas, isn't it? We're all pleased to meet you. Let's go over to the dressing room and we'll fill you in on everything else."

All seven proved to be delightful people. They each loved Christmas and told me they derived great pleasure from helping children enjoy it. With the exceptions of Jill and Ralphie, who were both professional photographers, the others went to college in the area and worked at Galaxy Mall over the holidays to earn extra money. They asked about my background, and I told them the usual story of being a freelance toy consultant who had decided, at age sixty-three, to spend more time with the children who played with toys.

"The main thing to remember is, smile and be jolly no matter what the kids on your lap do or say," Jill cautioned me. "I know you probably think they'll all act fine, but you're going to be surprised at some of the things that happen. Two years ago, a little girl yanked part of Santa's beard off, and it wasn't a fake beard."

"Really," I mumbled, instinctively placing a protective hand over my own whiskers.

"Do you have lots of pairs of those gold-framed little glasses?" Jill continued. "Toddlers especially like to grab at those, and I've seen Santas lose a half dozen in one day. Most kids will want a hug, but every so often one may throw a punch, especially if you don't promise to bring whatever present you've just been asked for. That's another thing: lots of times you need to be vague when they ask what you're bringing them. Tell them their parents will help make that decision."

"That's actually the way it works," I said. "With input from teachers, ministers, and other caring adult friends, of course."

"My," said Jill, "you really do get into the role, don't you?"

She next explained the jobs each of the seven played in what was termed "the production." Seiler and Yelena were "greeters." They met adults and children at the bottom of the bridge and escorted them into line, chatting in friendly fashion and trying to make them feel comfortable. Xander and Dave served as "hosts." They brought children from the head of the line to where Santa sat, even as they quietly conferred with parents to get some idea of what should and shouldn't be promised to boys and girls in the way of Christmas gifts. Scott was cashier. If parents asked Jill and Ralphie to photograph their children with me, they were charged for the snapshot. When Scott had extra time, he picked up litter so Santa Land remained sparkling clean. Jill herself was "production coordinator" in addition to taking photos. As such, she was the senior member of the group and could give special instructions to any of the others.

While the rest of the crew was occupied checking their costumes in the dressing room (Ralphie inspected the cameras), Jill also mentioned that Mr. Sneed had a special reason for being so grouchy.

"Up until four years ago, he was the mall's Santa himself," she said. "Then the owners decided they wanted to use a Santa search company instead. Mr. Sneed loved playing Santa. That's when he grew his silly-looking beard. The kids seemed to like him. But then they brought in an outside Santa, and he was just better at it than Mr. Sneed. Everything about him was perfect."

"Jimmy Lee," I mumbled.

"Yes, Jimmy Lee. He was such a hit that we've used the Noel Program to supply our Santas ever since, and Mr. Sneed has never been allowed to do it again. So don't take it personally if he's unfriendly to you. He actually loves Christmas and wants all the children who come to Galaxy Mall to have a great time with Santa. He just wishes that he was the one in the red suit."

After I'd hung my own red suit on a hook in the dressing room, Jill reminded me to be in costume the next day no later than 3:00 p.m.

"Mr. Sneed will want to inspect us before we go out," she said. "Don't be nervous. You're going to have a wonderful time."

"I think I will," I replied. I felt very excited. After long months of planning and preparation, tomorrow I would actually start working in a mall!

Thirteen

he next afternoon I waited anxiously in the dressing room. Outside the plywood walls of the dressing room I could hear the muffled sounds of thousands of excited voices and shuffling feet. The children of Cleveland were ready to greet Santa Claus!

"Okay, then," Mr. Sneed barked. "It's 4:00 p.m. Time to get rolling. All of you remember, this is a special experience for these kids! Make it perfect for them. Smile no matter what. Greeters, get 'em in as fast as you can. Get 'em on Santa's lap, push the parents to buy the pictures, thank 'em for coming, and always keep the line moving. Nothing worse than frustrated parents who have to wait two hours for their kid to meet Santa. Think they'll stay and shop in our mall afterward? Okay, let's—wait a minute. Ralphie, where are your elf ears? What's the matter with you, buddy?"

Ralphie, who already looked rather silly—grown men shouldn't wear candy-striped leotards—hung his head and reached in his pocket. He extracted two flesh-colored, plastic points, which he stuck on the tops of his ears. The other six helpers already had theirs on.

"All elves have pointed ears," Mr. Sneed lectured. "I don't want to have to remind anybody of that again. Okay, let's go."

Mr. Sneed reached for a cordless microphone resting on the dressing-room table. Motioning for the rest of us to remain completely silent, he flipped a switch on the microphone and declared in a surprisingly deep, dramatic voice, *"Ladies and gentlemen, and children of all ages. Everyone who loves Christmas, welcome to Santa Land in Galaxy Mall. Our favorite holiday friend has arrived from the North Pole. But first, let's greet Santa's elves!"*

Jill, Ralphie, Yelena, Xander, Seiler, Scott, and Dave hurried out the door. There was loud applause and cheering. The atmosphere was simply electric.

Mr. Sneed looked at me quite sternly, then spoke into the microphone again.

"And now, direct from the North Pole, here's the star of the season—Santa Claus!"

As I'd been instructed earlier, I walked slowly from the dressing room. Children and parents were packed tight on all four levels of the mall, leaning forward and straining to see me. The cheers were deafening. Boys and girls and more than a few grown men and women were shouting, "Santa! Santa!" and I was somewhat blinded by what seemed to be thousands of cameras flashing. I raised my white-gloved hand in greeting, and the din grew more intense. I couldn't stop smiling. How wonderful to be among so many Christmas-loving people! Yes, I'd spent centuries bringing gifts to millions like them, but that was always in the dark of night when they were asleep. This was my first opportunity to be in direct, wide-awake contact with any of them while wearing my traditional Santa costume, and if they were excited, I was thrilled. I paused in my walk to the wooden block throne and waved energetically with both hands, turning around slowly so that I would be able to at least momentarily face everyone. I have rarely experienced a more gratifying moment.

Then I approached the throne and, after one final wave, took my seat. As I did, Seiler and Yelena ushered the first breathless children and their parents across the wrought-iron bridge into Santa Land. Xander and Dave went forward to meet this initial group, taking charge of them while the two young women returned to the bridge to guide in the next contingent. Jill and

Ralphie readied their cameras, and Scott took his place by the photo-table cash register.

A bright-eyed little boy, followed by his beaming mother and father, was first in line. Just before the child was brought up to me, Xander leaned forward and briefly whispered with the parents. Then Xander looked at me and nodded discreetly. This was the agreed-upon signal that the present the youngster was about to request from Santa would, in fact, be under his tree on Christmas morning. I did feel a qualm about making what would be a very brief visit with this child all about some toy or other he hoped to receive from me. What a joy it would have been to regale him and every child in line with stories about the joy of Christmas gift-*giving* rather than *getting*. But I nodded back at Xander, and he gently led the child up to me on my wooden block throne. I reached down, picked him up, and settled him on my knee, noting to myself that he was a fine, healthy-looking youngster with thick hair and sparkling eyes.

"Merry Christmas!" I told him. "And how are you today?"

He grinned, and replied, "Hi, Santa. My name is Harper Cummings. I'm seven."

While I'm able to remember the names of many children present and past, I can't recall every one. But Harper's enthusiasm assured me that he was at least a believer, and perhaps a true believer. What fun to actually talk to a Santa-loving child!

"It's a pleasure to meet you, Harper," I said, and meant every word. "What shall we talk about?"

Harper giggled. "My little sister Andrea flushed her doll down the toilet."

"I'm sure it was an accident," I said. "Where is Andrea this afternoon?"

Harper wrinkled his brow. "She's over at her friend Marcia's house. She's coming to see you next weekend."

"I'll look forward to that," I replied. Looking over Harper's head, I could see Xander and Paul already gesturing for me to hurry. I couldn't blame them—there were *lots* of other children waiting in line.

"Can I tell you what I want you to bring me?" Harper asked.

"Please do," I replied, and actually felt a sense of anticipation. After all the gifts I'd given to so many children for so many centuries, this would be the first time I'd ever received a direct request from a child in person. What fun! Perhaps Harper would want a toy truck. I knew Willie Skokan had just crafted some wonderful ones with horns that really honked. Or maybe he'd ask for a basketball. We'd recently manufactured several thousand of them, and they all bounced beautifully.

Harper ducked his head as though telling me a secret. "Here's what I want," he whispered.

"What?" I whispered back.

"I want a PS3 with its Blu-ray disk drive and Cell processor chip."

"I beg your pardon?" I had no idea what Harper was talking about.

"You know, Santa. PlayStation 3. The Cell processor runs at 3.2 gigahertz, and that whole system will have two teraflops of overall performance."

"Teraflops," I said hesitantly.

"Yep," Harper agreed, looking happy at the prospect. "My friend Charles has the PS2 and thinks it's really cool, but wait 'til you bring me the PS3. Hey, you're not going to bring him one, too, are you?"

"Who knows?" I muttered.

Xander walked up and carefully began to lift Harper off my lap.

"More kids are waiting, Santa," he reminded me.

Harper hopped down, but whirled around as Xander began leading him away.

"You *are* bringing my PS3 and everything, aren't you?" he called back anxiously.

"With teraflops," I promised. After all, I'd received the signal from Xander that Harper's parents intended to give him the gift he wanted.

"Thanks, Santa. You're the greatest!" Harper called, and scooted back to where his parents were waiting. They handed money over to Scott. Apparently, Jill or Ralphie had snapped a photograph of Harper sitting on my lap.

I hissed to Xander, "What's a teraflop?" but he was busy bringing twin girls over to me, again nodding to indicate their parents wanted me to tell them they'd be getting whatever it was they were about to ask me for.

Nora and Carol were nine. I could tell they both were teetering on the edge of Christmas disbelief. Probably some of their friends at school were telling them Santa really didn't exist. But they still seemed to be believers, at least marginally.

Unlike Harper, they didn't volunteer their names and ages. I had to ask. But they were ready, in fact eager, to tell what they wanted from me for Christmas.

"CD burners!" they said in unison.

Now, I did know that things called CDs, an abbreviation for compact discs, had replaced vinyl record albums. I was not entirely ignorant of current technology. But I certainly did not think it was appropriate for children to burn them.

"Are you certain?" I asked. The twins nodded their heads vigorously.

"Excuse me for a moment," I said. I had one twin sitting on each leg, so I gently set them down. Then I walked over to where their parents were waiting. They were a pleasant-looking couple, and I knew they would be appalled to learn what their daughters had just requested from Santa.

"I think there's a problem," I whispered.

The girls' mother stamped her foot.

"I *told* them they're too young for tattoos!" she exclaimed. "When they said they each wanted one for Christmas, I said absolutely not. Didn't I, Harold?"

"You bet, Susie," her husband agreed. "That's exactly what you told them."

"I was actually more concerned about pyromania," I said. The parents looked puzzled. "Burning things," I added. "Apparently, compact discs."

Now Susie laughed.

"Oh, *that's* all right," she told me. "They're each getting a CD burner from us. Or we can say they're from you, if you want."

"Certainly not!" I replied. "Santa Claus would never condone something so potentially dangerous!"

Susie and Harold looked at me incredulously, as though I were the one saying something foolish.

"Where'd you people get this Santa?" Susie asked Xander. He shrugged, and seemed embarrassed.

"CD burners don't set fire to anything, dude," Xander whispered to me harshly. "They copy CDs, that's all. Burning's just a term. Don't you know anything?"

"Apparently not," I said. Modern technology has, for the most part, passed me by because I usually don't need to know much about it. Leonardo is in charge of our North Pole operations concerned with computer programs and video games and the like. Though we develop prototypes for computers themselves, we license these to outside manufacturers and use the proceeds to underwrite all our operational expenses. Reindeer feed isn't cheap.

My own manufacturing involvement is usually limited to the traditional sorts of toys I've given as gifts down through the centuries—dolls and wagons and balls and other simple yet pleasure-giving things. You could say, as Layla often does, that I'm deliberately old-fashioned. I don't disagree. I have no quarrel with technological breakthroughs that have resulted in more complex playthings. But I could tell just from these first few youngsters I'd met at Galaxy Mall that I had a great deal of catching up to do.

From that moment on, so long as their parents approved, I told children I would bring them the gifts they wanted whether I knew what those gifts were or not. I went back to the building-block throne and informed Nora and Carol that they could look forward to many happy hours of CD-burning. They hugged me while Jill, beaming, stepped forward to snap a picture.

After that, things seemed to happen in a blur. As soon as one child jumped off my lap, another hopped up onto it. Almost all of them were quite specific about what they wanted me to bring them for Christmas.

Barry wanted a chemistry set so he could mix up a potion that would turn his teacher's teeth "a really sick green."

"I don't think that's a good idea," I said.

"That's only 'cause you don't know my teacher," he replied.

Alison asked for a tennis racquet, which was fine. But she also wanted me to give her the ability to win her school's tennis championship.

"If you practice hard enough, perhaps you'll become good enough to be champion," I suggested.

"If I have to practice, I'll get all sweaty."

"Well, I'll bring you the racquet, but you'll have to provide the sweat."

There were occasional youngsters who became so excited about meeting Santa that they forgot completely whatever gifts they meant to ask me for. Six-year-old Byron sat tongue-tied on my lap for several minutes while his mother urged him to "tell Santa what you want! Hurry up! Other kids are waiting!"

"Ummm," Byron said.

"Would you like a toy truck, Byron?" I asked, trying to be helpful. I was also suggesting a truck because we'd made thousands at the North Pole and no child had asked for one yet.

"Hmmm," said Byron.

"Perhaps a basketball?" I inquired. We had plenty of those at the North Pole, too.

"He wants a PS3," his mother said sharply. "Don't you, Byron?"

Byron managed to nod.

"With a Blu-ray disk drive and Cell processor chip?" I added, remembering Harper Cummings's request.

"Yeah!" Byron blurted.

"It will give you two teraflops of overall performance," I assured him. I still didn't know what that meant, but it seemed like the right thing to say.

From the mall's standpoint, I suppose, my first day as Santa was an acceptable one. At the end of my six-hour shift, 4:00 p.m. until 10:00 p.m., when Galaxy Mall closed for the night, I had visited with just over eight hundred children. I say "children" in a general sense. Most of my lap-sitters were between three and ten years old. Some parents had brought infants for me to hold, and I enjoyed that. I also was pleased by visits from grown men and women who, to judge by the delighted smiles on their faces, remained maximum true believers. A few teenagers waited in line to see me for the sole purpose of saying unkind things about Santa Claus being make-believe, and stupid besides. I wasn't angry. I felt sorry for them. They had to be very sad themselves, I knew, to make such an effort to hurt the feelings of someone else. I wished them a Merry Christmas anyway, and meant it.

My frustration came from a different source. I was asked many more times for presents I knew nothing about. Besides PS3s and Xboxes and Blu-ray disk drives and teraflops, there were multiple requests for things called MP3 players and iPods. Other children asked for extravagant things I knew about, but could never bring—ponies and designer clothes and visits from famous rock musicians or professional athletes or movie stars.

There were times each Christmas Eve—and St. Nicholas Day, and Epiphany—that whatever simple gift we would bring from the North Pole for a boy or girl might be the only gift that child received. More often, whatever present we left would be one among several or even dozens of others from the child's family and friends. Extravagant items were beyond our ability to provide.

"Sometime, somewhere, too many people got the wrong idea about Santa Claus and his gifts," I said to Layla and several of my other longtime companions after I'd made my weary way back to the North Pole that night. "The greed of some of these boys and girls is troubling. We work hard to give presents that enhance holiday celebrations for children, but we could never bring anyone a pony, for goodness' sake. When I told one boy named Robert that I couldn't promise to bring him a fire-engine-red Mustang convertible, he actually jumped off my lap and kicked my shin. I think he might have been eight."

"But most of the children weren't like that, were they?" Amelia Earhart wanted to know.

"No, of course not," I assured her. "Hundreds gave me warm hugs, and I couldn't begin to tell you how many said they loved me and would leave out cookies and milk on Christmas Eve."

"Well, then, you have to decide whether to become discouraged by the actions of a few or encouraged by the responses of many," said Layla in her no-nonsense way. "If part of your problem is not being familiar with newer sorts of toys and gadgets, we can fix that. Perhaps Leonardo could prepare a few study sheets."

"I'd be glad to," Leonardo said.

"Please remember to include something called teraflops," I requested. "And now, if you'll all excuse me, I must go to bed. It's been quite a tiring day, and I have to be back at the mall at eleven tomorrow morning. Santa Land is open from noon until ten p.m. on Sundays."

It took the better part of a month, but I gradually grew more comfortable in my mall Santa role. Leonardo coached me in modern toy terminology. (A "teraflop" is a way of measuring the speed at which a computer or computer game operates; a single teraflop can represent *one trillion* numbers being processed, which is apparently something a modern-day seven-year-old might know but someone born in 280 A.D. like me wouldn't.) I learned about digital music players and the difference between DVD-R and DVD+R. And when an eleven-year-old boy requested a Blackberry for Christmas, I even knew he wasn't asking me for fruit.

I mastered the art of giving each child on my lap my full attention without forgetting how many more children were waiting for their turns with Santa. I happily answered thousands of questions about what it was like living at the North Pole and how I could visit the home of every child in just one night ("Three nights, not one!") and whether the reindeer *liked* pulling my sleigh. I even began to enjoy the challenge of responding to children who, for one reason or another, were hostile. The more unpleasant they acted, the harder I tried to make them feel welcome. It didn't always work, but sometimes their frowns would turn to smiles. Above all, I was warmed by the sense of how many people, children and grown-ups alike, truly loved Christmas.

"You're just the most fantastic Santa ever," Jill enthused one early December evening as we prepared to shut down Santa Land for the night. Most of my "elves" were helping Scott clear away scattered trash, while I waved good-bye to several children and their parents who were obviously reluctant to bid Santa Claus farewell.

"It's great fun for me," I replied. "Look at that little girl just crossing the bridge. She gave me the most wonderful hug, and told me if my sleigh got too crowded I should bring presents for her brothers but not her. Well, I won't forget young Christina Weeks on Christmas Eve, I can promise you that!"

"You sound like you plan to personally bring her a present!" Jill exclaimed.

"I just might; after all, I'm Santa Claus," I said. In fact, I was already imagining the doll I'd leave for little Christina to discover on Christmas morning. That was what she had asked for.

"I just wish Mr. Sneed didn't look so unhappy," Jill continued, gesturing toward the top floor of the mall. Mr. Sneed was slumped against the rail, watching forlornly as Christina and her parents and the other lingerers who hated leaving Santa finally made their ways out into the parking lot. I wasn't surprised to see him there. Often, each day, I glimpsed him watching enviously as children paraded one after another to sit on my lap and whisper their requests into my ear.

"Did he really love playing Santa so much?" I asked.

"I remember that when he played Santa, he never took a dinner break," Jill said. "He told me that he didn't want even one child to miss seeing Santa because Santa had gone off duty for a while. But I can understand why the mall owners decided to hire an outside Santa. Mr. Sneed's gray beard was too scraggly. He wasn't fat enough to be Santa, and he wouldn't put a cushion under his costume because he said the children might notice it was fake instead of a real belly. When I first saw Jimmy Lee looking perfect in his Santa costume, I realized Mr. Sneed just couldn't compare to him."

I hadn't thought of Jimmy Lee for a while. I'd been having too much fun.

"I guess no Santa could compare to Jimmy Lee," I said.

"You might," Jill replied, which surprised and pleased me. "He always says just the right thing. He looks like everyone imagines Santa ought to look. But you, well, you're sort of *real*. Say, I heard something interesting this morning. I was in Mr. Sneed's office, reminding him we need replacement lights for some of the trees in Santa Land. His phone rang. It was somebody from that *Great Santa Search* program that's going to be on FUN-TV. They're going to come here to the mall next week to check you out. I think they might pick you to be on their program! Wouldn't that be something?"

"It certainly would," I said. Jill hadn't surprised me. Felix already mentioned a few days earlier that he would be coming to Galaxy Mall soon to observe me in action. Already, another half-dozen Santas from malls around the country had been selected as *Great Santa Search* finalists. They didn't know themselves that they'd been picked. Bobbo Butler wanted to keep the names of the finalists secret at least until mid-December, to reduce the chances of nosy members of the media writing about them too far in advance of the program itself. About a week before Christmas Eve, Felix said, all ten finalists would be notified and brought to the FUN-TV offices for a briefing on the show. I was eager to compete against them. My experiences at Galaxy Mall had reinforced my belief that being Santa Claus was an honor—and a responsibility I took very seriously. It was unacceptable that some false "Santa" would use my name and image to promote the shoddy products of LastLong Toy Company.

"Do you want to be on *The Great Santa Search*?" Jill asked.

"Oh, yes," I confirmed. "Definitely."

Fourteen

hile I was perfecting my skills as a mall Santa, program-planning continued at the FUN-TV offices in New York City. On the same day that Jill the photographer told me about someone from *The Great Santa Search* coming to the Galaxy Mall, Bobbo Butler convened a meeting.

"Eight Santa finalists down, two to go," he reminded Felix, Sarah, and Heather Hathaway. The four of them were in the FUN-TV conference room. It was late afternoon, and they'd spent the last several hours deciding how to distribute tickets for *The Great Santa Search,* which was now only two weeks away. The Ed Sullivan Theater had 461 seats. Eleven of these would go to hand-picked members of the media, men and women who represented the very biggest newspapers and television programs. (Oprah Winfrey, Katie Couric, Jon Stewart, and David Letterman were among those whose attendance was already confirmed.) Another 150 were promised to executives of LastLong Toy Company and their families. That left only three hundred for the general public. Bobbo originally suggested that these simply be made available on the morning of December 24 "on a first-come, first-served basis; they'll be lining up for 'em a week in advance, and that line will stretch all the way from the box office back to Central Park. That story will headline every TV news program for days. What a lead-in to the broadcast itself! Ratings magic, I tell you!"

But Heather tactfully reminded her boss that they hoped the audience would include small children and grandparents. It would be very cold in New York City during the week before Christmas; there probably would be snow. It would look like FUN-TV didn't mind that very young and very old people lined up for *Great Santa Search* tickets were suffering from the winter weather, she suggested. That sort of bad publicity might hurt the show's ratings rather than boost them.

"You're right, Miss Hathaway," Bobbo reluctantly agreed. "Can you think of something better?"

"What about an online ticket giveaway, chief?" Heather asked. "Our www.thegreatsantasearch.com website is averaging more than two hundred thousand hits an hour. We could put out a press release tomorrow morning that, say, this Saturday we'll make the tickets available for free. Anyone interested can log on and apply. The FUN-TV computer system can pick one hundred fifty winners of two tickets each at random. They'll be notified electronically, and those who live out of town will have enough time to make travel arrangements to New York."

Bobbo thought the idea was wonderful, and Felix and Sarah liked it, too. Bobbo instructed Heather to write and send out the press release the next morning, though he added that three hundred wasn't the actual number of tickets that would be available to the public. Everyone on the program staff would each receive two, he said. Felix asked if he and Sarah could have a few more for special friends, but Bobbo said all the rest had to be distributed in the online lottery.

"You and Sarah are going to be backstage anyway," he said. "So you'll have four to give away, and I'll even let you bring one of your friends backstage with you during the program. Will that do?"

Felix thought it was quite generous, and told Bobbo so. Heather did some quick mental arithmetic and said that meant 288 tickets would be available to the public.

"Not quite," Bobbo said, a wide smile splitting his face. "I need two myself. Diana and Cynthia are coming to the program!"

"I thought your daughters weren't fond of Christmas anymore," Sarah said.

Bobbo's grin grew even wider.

"All these months, I've been telling them about *The Great Santa Search*, and promising that when it made Daddy's network successful again I would have more time to spend with them," he explained. "The girls have really been warming up to me lately. It's just wonderful. In fact, their mother is letting them have dinner with me in the city tonight, as long as I get them home by ten since it's a school night. Say, Sarah and Felix, why don't you join us? And you, too, Miss Hathaway."

Felix, Sarah, and Heather said they had too much work to do to go out to dinner—they planned to stay at the FUN-TV office and order in pizza.

"Then after I've taken the girls to dinner, I'll bring them here," Bobbo said. "I'm planning a special treat for them after we eat, and I'd like the three of you to be part of it. And by the way, Miss Hathaway, make sure you use our network credit card to pay for the pizza. Order all the extra toppings you want. Thanks to *The Great Santa Search*, it's good times again for FUN-TV!"

After Bobbo had left, Heather, Felix, and Sarah poured themselves cups of coffee and settled back in the conference room's comfortable chairs. It had been a hectic day. During the morning, Lauren Devoe had gone over the opening dance routine, Ken had talked about sound checks, and Eri had final sketches of costumes for everyone to look at. Mary discussed how long each show segment would take. Everything had to be calculated down to split seconds. Then the afternoon found Felix, Sarah, Bobbo, and Heather having to plan for ticket distribution. With December 24 looming, there was a real sense of urgency to *The Great Santa Search* meetings now.

"I don't think many people realize how complicated it is to put together a television program," Felix said, slouching down in his chair until it almost appeared he was sitting on his neck. "Heather, I don't see how you and Bobbo can do this all the time."

"We really don't," Heather admitted. "In the last few years when FUN-TV ratings were so bad, sometimes Bobbo hardly put any planning into shows at all because he was so discouraged. I've never seen him work as hard as he has for *The Great Santa Search*. Of course, we're all working hard. You're flying to Cleveland tomorrow, aren't you, Felix? You think you're going to find our ninth Santa finalist there."

"I've heard good things about the Santa at Cleveland's Galaxy Mall," Felix said carefully. "His name is Nicholas. We've actually got a great regional mix of finalists among the eight we have so far. There's Luis from a mall in Miami, and Buck from Kansas City, and Andy from Chicago. We have some Santas from smaller cities and malls, too. Brian from Missoula, Dillard from College Station in Texas, and Zonk from Rutland, Vermont. Wesley wasn't a mall Santa at all; he was starring as Santa in a Christmas play in St. Paul. And Joe is the finalist who made it through that open audition. I think he's from Bloomington, Indiana."

"If the Cleveland Santa is picked, that makes nine finalists," Sarah said. "There's not much time left. Where will you find the tenth?"

Felix sighed.

"Right from the beginning, there was one name that everyone kept mentioning," he said. "He's Jimmy Lee, and this Christmas he's working right here in New York at the Manhattan Mega-Mall just east of Central Park. The people from the Noel Program told us he's the inevitable *Great Santa Search* winner because there's no mall Santa, or any other kind of Santa, who's half as good. It's odd—I was already going to go see him sometime this week, but Bobbo mentioned him to me today, too. I wonder how Bobbo heard about him."

"I can tell you," Heather said. "He got a call this morning from Lucretia Pepper. She told him some LastLong Toy people had been to Manhattan Mega-Mall and saw Jimmy Lee there. They thought he was wonderful, and she insists that he ought to be a finalist."

"How did they find out his name?" Sarah asked.

"I have no idea," Heather replied. "But Lucretia Pepper knew it. If he's any good at all, Felix, please pick him as a finalist. We want to keep our sponsor happy."

Around 7:00 p.m., the pizza arrived. By mutual consent, they decided to talk about anything but *The Great Santa Search* while they ate.

"Have you and Felix done all your Christmas shopping, Sarah?" Heather asked as she carefully raised a drippy slice of double-cheese-and-Italian-sausage pizza to her mouth.

"No, but we usually wait until the last minute," Sarah said. "Late on Christmas Eve, in fact."

"Really?" Heather replied. "Where do you find a good store open then?"

"We're lucky; where we live, there's a wonderful place that has all the presents anyone reasonable could want," Sarah laughed. "What about you, Heather? Is your shopping done?"

Heather said she'd purchased gifts for her parents and mailed them to North Dakota almost a month earlier.

"And I found some nice bracelets for Diana and Cynthia," she added. "Bobbo's so excited about *The Great Santa Search* that I'm afraid he might forget to buy them Christmas presents. That would be terrible, especially since the girls seem to be getting along better with him. Wait—I think I hear them coming in."

Bobbo bustled into the conference room accompanied by two young girls. Ten-year-old Cynthia seemed quite gentle and very funny. Her eight-year-old sister Diana was rather outspoken. She informed her father that he had to get them back home to Scarsdale by ten.

"Mom says to keep reminding you it's a school night, because you're going to forget," she said. "Last time we had dinner with you on a school night we didn't get home until after midnight, and Cyn fell asleep the next day in class. Her teacher got *real* mad."

"But I had a nice dream," Cynthia said cheerfully. "There was a spaceship in it. Maybe I was flying to the moon."

"Or possibly the North Pole," Heather suggested. "Your father is so excited you'll both be coming to the studio for his Christmas Eve show. You'll help pick the real Santa Claus, and maybe afterward he'll take both of you to the North Pole for a visit. Wouldn't that be fun?"

Cynthia thought it would be, but Diana said Heather was being silly.

"There's no Santa Claus, and Christmas stinks, anyway," she declared. "People talk about time for families and being together for the holiday, but all they really care about are their stupid *jobs*." She glared at Bobbo as she said this.

Her father looked guilty, and reminded Diana that just as soon as *The Great Santa Search* was over, he'd start spending more time with his daughters.

Diana sneered.

"You always say you're going to spend more time with us, but then you never do."

"I really mean it this time," Bobbo promised.

"That would be nice, Daddy," Cynthia said. "Are we really going to pick Santa Claus on your show?"

"Definitely," Bobbo said. "There are going to be all sorts of contests for the ten finalists. They're going to sing and rope reindeer—not real ones—and climb down chimneys and put toys in stockings and even eat cookies. It will be great. The audience is going to vote twice during the program for their favorites, and the other times we'll eliminate Santas who finish last in the competitions. You and Diana might cast the deciding votes!"

"There's no Santa Claus, and you're just going to make people pick from a bunch of actors," Diana said, managing to sound bored and hostile at the same time. "Cyn and I don't believe in Santa Claus anymore, Daddy. Why do you keep acting like we do?"

"I sort of believe in him," Cynthia said. "I remember he brought me a bicycle when I was seven."

"Mom and Daddy got you that," Diana declared. "They just told you Santa brought it."

"Well, maybe he did," Cynthia muttered.

For several very long moments, no one at the table spoke. Then Heather said cheerfully, "We ordered too much pizza and there's a lot left over. Cyn, Diana, would you like some?" Cyn did. Diana said grumpily that she was full already, and maybe it was time for Daddy to bring them home. But Heather praised the nice earrings Diana was wearing and asked her questions about school until the little girl relaxed and began chattering comfortably. She even ate two slices of pizza while Heather turned the conversation back to *The Great Santa Search*, emphasizing how pleased Bobbo was that his daughters would be in the audience.

"Why does she keep mentioning that?" Felix whispered to his wife.

"Heather knows it would break Bobbo's heart if Cynthia and Diana decided not to be there," Sarah whispered back. "At the same time, she's reminding the girls how much their father loves them. Heather just has an amazing ability to understand how people think."

So while the last slices of pizza were eaten, the Butler girls heard about Eri Mizobe's plan for Santa costumes—all the finalists would be dressed in gorgeous red velvet robes with snow-white fur trim—and how Robert Fernandez's crew was building a whole herd of wooden reindeer for the roping competition.

Then Felix talked about the eight *Great Santa Search* finalists he'd found so far. He mentioned flying to Cleveland the next day to scout a promising candidate. That was when Bobbo announced his surprise.

"It's not much after eight, so there's a little time before I have to take the girls back to Scarsdale," he said. "Somebody told me today about a great Santa at the Manhattan Mega-Mall. What do you say that we all pile in my car and go over there to take a look at him? From everything I hear, he ought to be one of our finalists, Felix."

Diana didn't want to go to the mall. She said she had homework and was tired. But Cynthia wanted to, and Felix said he had to go see this Jimmy Lee sometime. Heather and Sarah coaxed Diana until she finally said fine, she'd come, but nobody had better ask her to sit on some phony Santa's lap. Cynthia said she'd sit on Santa's lap for both of them.

Bobbo drove an SUV, so there was plenty of room in it for all six people. They soon reached the high-rise parking garage for Manhattan Mega-Mall, and then took an elevator and two escalators to enter the mall itself. They set out to find Jimmy Lee, and it wasn't hard.

Felix told me later that Santa Land at Galaxy Mall in Cleveland was impressive, but didn't remotely compare to "Clausville" at Manhattan Mega-Mall. To begin with, at my mall I had seven "elf" helpers; Clausville boasted forty. A whole army of men and women in leotards and fake pointed ears bustled around a roped-off area easily three or four times as large as Galaxy Mall's Santa Land. Besides photographers selling pictures, Clausville had booths offering Christmas candy and cookies, holiday-themed books, bright sweaters and T-shirts decorated with Christmas sayings and symbols, and literally mountains of toys, many of which, Felix and Sarah noted, were shoddy LastLong products.

In the middle of Clausville, high on a raised platform, was a gleaming throne apparently made from giant candy canes. Seated on that throne was a red-robed, white-bearded fellow who simply glowed with happy holiday spirit. His charming smile was mirrored on the faces of hundreds of children and adults lined up waiting to briefly meet him. Everything about Clausville was spectacular, but the Santa in the center of it all effortlessly held everyone's attention.

"Wow," Felix breathed. He couldn't help himself. Then he looked at the others standing beside him. They appeared equally impressed. Even Diana Butler's eyes were wide with astonishment.

"Now, *that's* a Santa," Bobbo Butler declared, and Felix, even though he knew I was the real one and not Jimmy Lee, found himself nodding in agreement.

Heather suggested that they all join "the Santa line" so Felix could see and hear Jimmy Lee in action. It took almost twenty minutes just to maneuver themselves down to the lowest mall level and then fight through the crowds to the entrance of Clausville, where two lovely young women in elf costumes informed them there would be about a sixty-minute wait in line.

"That's too long, Daddy," Diana insisted. "Remember Cyn and I have school tomorrow."

Bobbo reluctantly agreed.

"I bet he's perfect, though," he said. "Felix, make sure you get this guy for the show. I mean, maybe he *is* Santa Claus."

"Told you there might really be one," Cynthia whispered to Diana.

They turned to leave, but as they reached the Clausville entrance they were stopped by a medium-sized, balding man.

"Are you Mr. Butler?" he inquired. "Mr. Bobbo Butler of *The Great Santa Search?*"

"Why, yes, I am," Bobbo replied, beaming. He was always happy when he was recognized, and the advance publicity for *The Great Santa Search* had kept his face on the news and his picture in the papers for months.

"Well, it's an honor to have you visiting Clausville, sir," the bald man assured him. "I'm Mr. Fuquay, the mall manager, and it's such a pleasure to meet you. My whole family is going to be watching your program on Christmas Eve—my wife, our four children, and our seventeen grandchildren!"

"Imagine that," Bobbo said. "Why, your family alone is a bigger audience than we drew last year with *Merry Monkey*."

Mr. Fuquay looked confused. He was quite good at it. His forehead rippled with sudden, deep furrows, and his eyebrows knitted together.

"I'm afraid I don't know about any *Merry Monkey* program, sir," he said.

"You and the rest of America," Bobbo laughed. "Well, I'm glad this time we've got a show you want to watch. We hoped to meet your mall Santa tonight, but unfortunately we can't stand in line for an hour. My girls need to get home to Scarsdale. It's a school night." He looked over at Diana. "See? I remembered."

Mr. Fuquay's expression changed from concern to joy.

"Please, Mr. Butler, you don't have to worry about standing in line! A celebrity like you, sir, well—would these lovely girls be your daughters?" He gestured toward Cynthia, Diana, and, unfortunately, Heather, who shook her head emphatically.

"I'm Mr. Butler's executive assistant," she said.

"I do beg your pardon," said Mr. Fuquay. "Well, then, these two young ladies certainly want to meet Santa Claus!"

Cynthia nodded so hard that her bangs flopped up and down. Diana made a face, but she didn't disagree.

"All right," Mr. Fuquay announced. "I expect all the grown-ups want to meet him, too. Follow me, please." He guided the four adults and two girls past the winding line. The people in front, who'd been waiting a long time for their turns with Santa, grumbled when they saw newcomers being escorted in front of them, but Mr. Fuquay explained that this was Mr. Butler's party, Mr. Butler of *The Great Santa Search* that everyone in America would be watching on Christmas Eve.

"You've got to have Mega-Mall's Santa on your show, Mr. Butler," a father being displaced at the front of the line told Bobbo. "I've brought my boy here eight straight nights to see him. He's the best Santa ever!" His son, a strapping six-year-old, shouted "Yeah!" in agreement.

"Watch *The Great Santa Search* on Christmas Eve and see," Bobbo suggested.

Mr. Fuquay led the way up steep stairs to the candy-cane throne, and there the group was greeted with a hearty "Merry Christmas!" by a man whose beaming face was framed by the most perfect of snow-white beards. Genuine pleasure emanated in his pleasantly deep voice. Blue eyes twinkled behind his gold-rimmed spectacles, and when he stood his belly protruded just the right amount from his spotless, shining red suit.

"Santa Claus, may I present Mr. Bobbo Butler," Mr. Fuquay announced. "Mr. Bobbo Butler of *The Great Santa Search*, you know."

Mega-Mall Santa laughed.

"Of course!" he exclaimed. "Mr. Butler of *my* show! I'm glad to meet you and your friends"—he nodded to Felix, Sarah, and Heather—"but I'm especially pleased to see these two wonderful people." He gestured toward the little girls. "Now, then, remind me of your names."

"I'm Cynthia," said one. When her younger sister didn't speak up, Cyn added, "That's Diana. She says she doesn't believe in you, but sometimes I still do."

"Really?" Mega-Mall Santa inquired. Felix knew the man's real name was Jimmy Lee, but somehow it was hard to think of him as anyone other than Santa Claus. "Well, that's too bad. Perhaps you'll believe in me again," he said to Diana, who didn't say anything, but at least didn't make a face.

"My daughters are going to be in the studio audience on Christmas Eve, Santa Claus," Bobbo said. "So they'll see you again there. If, of course, you're one of our finalists," he added, glancing meaningfully at Felix.

"Just let me know soon; I already have a lot to do on Christmas Eve!" he replied. "Now, Cynthia and Diana, get a good night's sleep so you'll do well in school tomorrow. Try to believe in me again. I have some very special gifts to leave under your tree this year!"

"I wonder if he'll bring me an MP3 player," Cynthia mused as they made their way back to the parking garage. "Diana, you should have told him what you wanted, too." Diana didn't reply, but she also didn't say anything more about Santa being stupid or not existing.

Bobbo dropped Heather, Sarah, and Felix back at the FUN-TV offices before returning his daughters to Scarsdale.

"That fellow was amazing," he whispered to them, keeping his voice low so the girls wouldn't hear. "Felix, I think we've found our winner."

"We'll find out on Christmas Eve," Felix replied. "Well, I'll go to Galaxy Mall in Cleveland tomorrow. If I select the Santa there, and then if I pick Jimmy Lee—"

"Of *course* you're picking Jimmy Lee," Bobbo interrupted.

"Well, that will make up our ten finalists," Felix said. "I'll see you when I get back from Cleveland, Bobbo."

While they got ready for bed in their New York City hotel room, Felix and Sarah discussed Jimmy Lee.

"If I hadn't known the real one for so long, I could certainly believe he was Santa Claus," Sarah admitted. "His voice, and his smile, and, well, everything about him is just right. Even little Diana was impressed by him."

"True, but do you remember what he said to the girls?" Felix asked. "He told them he hoped they'd believe in him again, but right afterward he promised them special presents. That's bribery. The *real* Santa would never stoop to that."

"I wonder if he was good at playing Santa from the beginning, or if he really had to work hard at it," Sarah said, ignoring her husband's criticism of Jimmy Lee. "You can tell he's someone who's loved Christmas all his life. I'm sure he's at least a true believer, or even a maximum true believer. Has Leonardo checked into his background at all?"

"No, but he certainly should," Felix replied. He picked up his cell phone and called the North Pole. This late in December, in the time between St. Nicholas Day and Christmas, he knew everyone would be up working very late. When he was connected with Leonardo, he asked him to do a background check on Jimmy Lee.

"I have to fly to Cleveland tomorrow to see the real Santa at Galaxy Mall," Felix told Leonardo. "So could you run your check before you go to bed tonight, then call me early in the morning before I leave for the airport if there's anything you find out that I should know?"

Leonardo agreed. Felix soon was asleep. The next morning he was in a taxi heading to LaGuardia Airport in New York when his cell phone rang. It was Leonardo.

"The Jimmy Lee you're asking about is from Leeds, Alabama, correct?" he asked. "Not the Jimmy Lee from Birmingham or the one from Tuscaloosa?"

"I'm sure the real Santa said this Jimmy Lee is from Leeds."

"Well, then," Leonardo said, "I have interesting news. This man is supposed to be a great mall Santa?"

"I have to admit, he *is* great."

"Odd," Leonardo mumbled.

"What's odd about it?" Felix demanded.

"Jimmy Lee from Leeds, Alabama, is a never."

Fifteen

I t was clear Mr. Sneed was not pleased by the possibility I would be selected for *The Great Santa Search*. That added to his other concerns. With eight days left until Christmas, the crowds of shoppers had swelled to the point that there was sometimes an hour wait just to be admitted to the mall parking lot. The crush made Mr. Sneed especially nervous. He fretted about small children becoming separated from their parents in crowds, and the mall food court running out of French fries. Now he also had *The Great Santa Search* to worry about.

"Okay, some guy from that program's coming today," Mr. Sneed informed me when I arrived in the Santa Land dressing room. "Even if he asks you to be on it, you don't have to say yes. We're going to have mobs of kids all the way up through Christmas Eve. You've done okay for a beginner. If you're on that show, your company might send me a real loser to fill in for you."

"If I'm picked, perhaps you could step in as Galaxy Mall Santa," I suggested. "Jill has told me you're very good at it."

For a single fleeting second, it seemed that Mr. Sneed might smile. But he fought the impulse, and his lips remained in their usual pursed position.

"Ah, that was a while ago," he muttered. "I really haven't got the beard for it, I guess, or the belly." He ran his fingers through his scraggly whiskers. "Guys like you with the white beards and the big bellies are better. Well, the *Great Santa Search* guy wants to meet me in my office right at ten. You just do everything like usual with the kids. No showing off, okay? Remember, this is all about them having a great time with Santa, not you getting to be on some TV show. The kids here at the mall come first. Promise?"

I promised, and then, dressed in my Santa costume, I made my way out into Santa Land, where an agreeably long line of children and their parents was already stretched from my wooden block throne to the wrought-iron bridge. By the time Mr. Sneed and Felix appeared a half-hour later, I'd already greeted some forty-five children. Their gift requests had ranged from an electric race-car set to a donkey. The girl who wanted the donkey said she'd always thought they looked interesting. I assured her they were, but added that they rarely made good house pets.

"Could you bring me a PS2, then?" she wanted to know.

"A PS3 might be better," I suggested. "Two teraflops of performance, you know." I was beginning to love all this new toy- and game-related jargon.

From the corner of my eye, I saw Felix and Mr. Sneed maneuvering so they could clearly see and hear me. Felix looked distinguished in a pinstripe suit. Sarah had bought him a whole new wardrobe in New York City stores. It was hard to believe this was my same old dear friend who'd been dressed in a filthy tunic when I'd first met him in a Roman alley nearly seventeen centuries earlier.

As he and Mr. Sneed watched closely, I pulled a lovely little boy with curly golden hair up onto my lap and asked him his name.

"I'm Nathan!" he crowed. "I'm going to be six!"

"That's a wonderful age, Nathan," I replied. "My name is Santa Claus." Nathan giggled.

"I know. Mommy says you might bring me a toy truck if I'm good."

I glanced over at Nathan's parents, who stood with Xander. Xander was nodding.

"I'm sure you will be good, and I think there might be a fine toy truck at the North Pole for me to bring you," I said. "And please, Nathan, always remember that Christmas is about more than you getting a present from Santa."

"I know that, too. Daddy wants it to be about you bringing him a bowling ball, but Mommy says you're going to bring him a new lawn mower, and he better use it."

I noticed Nathan's father did not look particularly cheerful.

"Well, please tell your daddy that Santa loves him even if he does happen to receive a lawn mower instead of a bowling ball," I said. "We don't always get every Christmas present we want, but the thought behind the gift is what's most important. In this case, that thought might involve a nice-looking lawn. Merry Christmas, Nathan. I can't wait to come to your home on Christmas Eve."

"I'll leave out milk and cookies, Santa," he promised, and gave me a big hug as Jill and Ralphie snapped their photographs.

"Okay, Santa, I've got somebody here who wants to meet you," Mr. Sneed called around noon as I prepared to take my forty-five-minute break for lunch. "Guy's name is Felix, uh—guess I forgot his last name."

"Felix *North*," said my old friend, grinning and extending his hand. "And your name is Nicholas Holiday, I think. It's a pleasure to meet you."

"Likewise," I said, enjoying the chance to pretend we hadn't been greeting each other on a regular basis for almost seventeen centuries. "I understand you're an executive with *The Great Santa Search*."

"I am," Felix replied, "and based on my observation of you this morning, I'd like to invite you to compete as one of ten finalists on our Christmas Eve broadcast. I guess you know about the program, what's going to happen at the end and so forth."

"Someone will be elected as the official Santa Claus," I said. "It sounds very exciting. I'd like to participate, if that's all right with Mr. Sneed. I'm under contract to work for him right up through Christmas Eve, and, of course, Santa Claus never breaks his word."

"I'm *sure* Mr. Sneed won't mind," Felix said, though he didn't really sound sure. Obviously, his conversation with Mr. Sneed had indicated my boss wasn't the most agreeable of employers. "Can Nicholas Holiday, here, be excused on Christmas Eve to compete on *The Great Santa Search*?"

"That might be tough," Mr. Sneed suggested. "The mall owners pay this guy's placement agency a ton of money, and they sure wouldn't like it if that Santa Land seat of his got filled by some replacement on one of our biggest holiday-shopping nights. I'm going to have to think about this."

Felix looked at me over Mr. Sneed's shoulder, and rolled his eyes.

"The Santa placement agency you use is the Noel Program, correct?" he asked. "Well, I've been in touch with Ms. Stephanie Owen there, and she assures me Noel will provide substitute Santas as needed for any of their employees who are selected for *The Great Santa Search*. You'll have a satisfactory white-bearded man in a red suit here on Christmas Eve, I promise."

Mr. Sneed rubbed his face with his hand.

"Well, that sounds okay, but maybe the bozo they send for that night won't be any good," he said. "This guy here has done okay with the kids. I don't want any of 'em disappointed by a second-rate Santa. We couldn't have that."

"There's a simple solution, Mr. Sneed," I said. "I'm told that you make an excellent Santa Claus. I'd consider it a personal favor if you would step in to be Santa in my place on Christmas Eve. The children will love you."

Now Mr. Sneed did grin. He couldn't help himself.

"That's nice of you," he said. "But I really shouldn't."

"Why not?" I asked.

"Like I said before, I don't have the beard for it. Or the belly. Look at you, that big gut, and it's all real. I hate using pillows. They're too fake. The kids catch on."

"Now, Mr. Sneed," I said. "We both know that Santa is more than his beard and a few extra pounds. Please agree to take my place on Christmas Eve. I'm asking for my own sake as well as the children's. I'll be a better competitor on *The Great Santa Search* if I don't have to worry about the boys and girls back at the Galaxy Mall suffering with an unsuitable Santa."

Mr. Sneed pretended to think it over.

"Okay, buddy, I guess I can do it. For you, that is. I'll get my red-and-white outfit over to the dry cleaners today and tell 'em it's a rush job, 'cause I'll need it on Christmas Eve."

"Actually, you'll need it sooner than that," Felix noted. "Tomorrow we want to get all ten *Great Santa Search* finalists together at the FUN-TV offices in New York, so we can go over the program schedule with them, fit them for their costumes, and so on. That means you'll need to substitute for Nicholas Holiday tomorrow and on Christmas Eve both, Mr. Sneed. I hope that won't be a problem."

Mr. Sneed had a dreamy look on his face. I could tell he was already imagining himself in full Santa regalia, perched on the wooden block throne and helping hundreds of children enjoy the happiest of holidays.

"We'll manage," he said. "Okay, buddy, good luck to you. I hope you win this thing. Mr. North, by any chance is a guy named Jimmy Lee one of your other finalists?"

"We're not supposed to say anything about that," Felix replied. "But if you'll keep it to yourself, Mr. Sneed, then, yes, he is."

"Ah, well, second place is no disgrace," Mr. Sneed told me. He clapped me on the back and hurried off to fetch his Santa suit and take it to the dry cleaners.

Felix flew back to New York that afternoon, and I took the sleigh to the North Pole when my day's work at Galaxy Mall was complete. I felt quite excited. For months I'd thought about competing on *The Great Santa Search,* and now it was certain I would. The next day, I would meet the other nine would-be Santas, including Jimmy Lee. Then Sarah, who was back at the North Pole, too, told me about him being a never. This was shocking news.

"But you say he seems so right in the Santa role," I told her. "How can he possibly appear to love Christmas so much if he doesn't personally believe in me or the spirit of the holiday at all?"

"He's obviously a talented performer," Sarah replied. "Leonardo insists that there's no mistake. Jimmy Lee never believed in Santa Claus. He was raised by parents who mocked the whole history of the holiday, Santa included. He learned from their unfortunate example. Worse, he never outgrew his disdain for Christmas. But he never disdained money. He's spent his whole life involved in all sorts of get-rich-quick schemes, though none ever worked out as he'd hoped. It's unfortunate that he found a way to use the holiday he otherwise hates as a means of filling his bank account."

"Go on," I said.

"Jimmy Lee is fifty-five now," Leonardo continued. "When he was forty, he applied to the Noel Program and was an instant success as a mall Santa. They pay based on both experience and excellence, you know. According to their company records—we hope you don't mind that Leonardo hacked into their files—Jimmy Lee earns almost $75,000 each year just during November and December when he's Santa in a mall."

"That's awful," said Theodore Roosevelt, who'd been eavesdropping. "This fellow hates Christmas and loathes the concept of Santa Claus, but he'll pretend to be him anyway because he makes so much doing it. I'd be wary of him during this broadcast, Santa. If Jimmy Lee makes $75,000 now as one among many mall Santas, can you imagine the fortune he could wring out of being the one and only *official* Santa Claus from *The Great Santa Search*?"

"Well, it's not going to come to that," I promised. "I admit, though, that I'm curious to meet him. And I will tomorrow, at the FUN-TV office. It may be that he's not as bad as you imagine, Theodore. Anyone who makes fun of the beliefs of others is obviously unhappy himself. Who knows? During the course of the competition, the true spirit of Christmas might touch even Jimmy Lee!"

The next morning, I hitched up the reindeer and flew to New York City. I landed the sleigh in a discreet corner of Central Park, used hand signals to instruct the reindeer to hover out of sight until I returned, and then took a pleasant stroll to the FUN-TV meeting at Rockefeller Center. The December air was bitingly cold, but I wore a warm coat. Besides, compared to weather conditions at the North Pole, New York City seemed tropical.

I recognized Heather Hathaway right away, as much for the warm smile that Felix and Sarah had described as her great height. She greeted me in formal though friendly fashion, informing me I was the last of the ten finalists to arrive and that everyone else was waiting in the conference room. I followed her inside and was greeted by a quite stunning sight. The nine individuals seated around a long table composed one of the most amazing groups of human beings I'd ever encountered.

All but two had beards of varying lengths and shades, mostly to mid-chest and white, though one had dark brown whiskers. Collectively, they defined the possible degrees of *stout*, running the gamut from a slightly bulging tummy to a fellow whose belly actually protruded so far forward that the front of it rested on the conference table. No two wore the same sort of clothing. There were blue jeans and expensive, tapered slacks, flannel shirts, and plush cashmere sweaters. One man had a cowboy hat jammed on his head, even though he was indoors.

Though it was difficult to tear my eyes away, I glanced at the others in the room. Felix was at one end of the table, and Sarah was on his right. On Felix's left was Bobbo Butler—I recognized the bristly rim of hair around his otherwise bald scalp from watching him so often on TV. The rest of the *Great Santa Search* staff was present—Mary the director, Ken the sound engineer, Eri the costume designer, Robert the set designer, and the woman in the black leotard had to be Lauren the choreographer.

Then there was a large, formidable-looking woman with makeup caked thick on her sharp-featured face—Lucretia Pepper, of course. I wondered why the LastLong Toy Company president found it necessary to attend.

"Well, now we're all here," Bobbo Butler announced. "Welcome, everyone. I hope you realize you're part of television history, and part of Christmas history, too. Exactly one week from tonight, we're going to work together and give America the official Santa Claus that it deserves. Think of it!"

After a moment, Heather Hathaway clapped. Then everyone else did, too. Bobbo nodded to acknowledge the applause.

"Everybody needs to know everybody else, so let me get it started. I'm Bobbo Butler, president of the FUN-TV network. The tall woman over there is my assistant, Heather Hathaway. Does anybody want her to bring coffee? No? Well, I'm sure we'll want some later. Stay to take notes for now, Miss Hathaway. Here to my left is Mary Rogers, who'll be our director next week, and Ken Perkins, the sound engineer who'll make you all sound perfect, and Eri Mizobe, who you'll get to know *very* well in a bit when she measures you for the Santa costumes you'll wear on the show. Robert Fernandez has designed the sets, and they're gorgeous. Lauren Devoe is our choreographer—yes, you're going to dance and do lots of other things. We'll be getting to that. On my right, this is Sarah North, who's an assistant to her husband, Felix North. All of you know Felix. He's the one who picked you. I think he's the greatest Christmas historian in America. Any questions you have about Christmas history, just ask him."

Bobbo paused to clear his throat.

"Last but not least, this lady beside me is Lucretia Pepper, who has generously taken time away from her job as owner and chief operating officer of LastLong Toy Company to be with us today. LastLong is the sole sponsor of *The Great Santa Search*. She has made this broadcast possible. I know we'd all like her to say a few words."

Lucretia Pepper uncoiled and coolly fixed each of us finalists with a brief, penetrating stare.

"What an honor to be among so many potential Santas," she said. "I'm sure any of you would make an outstanding spokesman for my company's equally outstanding toys. I hope you are already aware that the winner of *The Great Santa Search* will be obligated to spend the next full year exclusively representing LastLong Toy products, and we will have a company option binding you to us for an additional five years if we choose to exercise it. Please us and we will. My attorneys have drawn up contracts for the winner to sign immediately following the program. You might like to know that there is a generous salary involved. One million dollars per year, to be specific. Is one of you ready to become rich as well as famous?"

There was a chorus of "Yesses" and "You bets" from most of the finalists. The man in the cowboy hat whistled shrilly. I said nothing. I saw Lucretia Pepper's eyes briefly dart in my direction; she had noticed my lack of enthusiasm for her announcement.

"I think, Bobbo, that it would be appropriate now to learn the names of our ten finalists," she suggested.

"Of course, Lucretia," Bobbo replied. "Felix, you're the one who made the selections. Will you do the honors?"

Felix stood up and fiddled nervously with his tie.

"Right from the beginning, let's be sure you all understand some things," he said. "We want to keep an air of mystery about you. The less the public knows in advance, the more their curiosity will make them watch *The Great Santa Search*. As the first condition of you becoming our official finalists, you each must agree that you will not speak or communicate in any way with the media between now and the program on Christmas Eve. That means granting no interviews, making no phone or e-mail contact with reporters, or anything like that. Got it?"

We did.

"For now, we're going to identify each of you by your first name and the city where we found you," Felix continued. "On the program itself, you'll each be identified by number—Santa 1, Santa 2, and so on. We don't want children watching our program to wonder how Santa got some other name. When I picked you, I told each of you that you were not to tell even your family or closest friends. If any of you just couldn't resist—and I'm sure some of you couldn't—then make sure they know they're under the same rule not to talk to the media as you are."

Felix hadn't told *me* this in Cleveland, but of course he didn't have to. My wife and friends knew everything about *The Great Santa Search* and its selection process already.

"But there's no reason the ten of you can't get to know one another a little better," Felix said. "I'm going to introduce each of you. Remember that on Christmas Eve we want to project a spirit of friendly competition. We believe you are the best Santas in America. Act like it. Now, here we go. This is Andy from Chicago." Andy was one of the two beardless finalists. "Luis from Miami." He was the most slender among us. "Dillard from College Station." This was the fellow wearing the cowboy hat. "Brian from Missoula." He had the dark brown beard. "Zonk from Rutland." Zonk was the other beardless competitor, and, by the looks of him, the oldest—except for me, of course. "Nicholas from Cleveland." It felt odd being described as from Cleveland rather than the North Pole. "Wesley from St. Paul." I knew he had been in some sort of Christmas play there, rather than working as Santa in a mall. "Joe from Bloomington." He had the huge belly. "Buck from Kansas City." I liked his warm smile. "Jimmy Lee from right here in New York City."

Jimmy Lee appeared very much at ease. He wore tailored slacks and a baby-blue cashmere sweater. When Felix called his name, he waved languidly in response. His snow-white locks curled in an engaging way around his ears and the nape of his neck. His equally snow-white beard rested in fluffy splendor on his chest. The rest of the finalists, I felt, seemed somewhat ill at ease. The pressure of knowing they would soon appear on a television program watched by millions was affecting them, as it would almost anyone. But Jimmy Lee showed no signs of nervousness. His relaxed posture reflected an attitude of complete self-confidence bordering on arrogance. He did nothing blatantly offensive, but there was no mistaking that he believed, and expected everyone else to believe, that the actual *Great Santa Search* competition was a formality. Lucretia Pepper certainly seemed to agree. When the other nine of us were introduced, she stared hard. But when Felix announced Jimmy Lee's name, she looked at the man from Leeds, Alabama, and actually smiled.

"Thank you, Felix," Bobbo Butler said. "Now I'm going to tell you about what you'll be doing on the program—keep it all in confidence, remember. We're letting you know ahead of time so you can practice some things a little, if you want. After I do that, we'll need you to go with Eri Mizobe for your costume fittings. You are not to bring your own Santa suits to the Ed Sullivan Theater on Christmas Eve. Everybody wears the same things. We don't want to give any of you an unfair advantage over the others. Miss Hathaway, do you have the list of challenges?"

"Right here, chief," Heather said, handing a printed sheet of paper to her boss. Bobbo fumbled in his shirt pocket for his reading glasses, couldn't find them there, poked around in all his other pockets, still couldn't find them, and finally looked up to see Heather holding them out to him. He put them on and pretended to study the sheet for a moment. Ever the showman, Bobbo did this to build tension; obviously, he'd memorized the six challenges long ago.

"All right, then," Bobbo finally said. "You heard we're going to have a dance number to begin the show. It starts at eight p.m., and we're going to ask you to be in the studio at three that afternoon. Don't worry, Lauren is keeping things simple for you. After you get measured for your Santa costumes today, she's going to go over the basics of the dance routine with you. Now, on *The Great Santa Search* the challenges will follow the opening dance in roughly the same order that Santa would probably follow on Christmas Eve. First is reindeer-roping, though we won't be using real reindeer. Wooden reindeer will be pulled across the back of the stage by conveyor belt. I guess you Western boys from Montana and Texas might have an advantage there. The two Santas who rope the fewest in—what, Miss Hathaway, forty-five seconds?—those two are eliminated. So we've got eight of you left for the second challenge, which will be Christmas carol–singing. There's going to be a big surprise then. Don't ask, because we're not going to tell you what it is. After you all sing, the audience votes. One Santa is eliminated."

"To vote, the audience'll use little devices mounted on their armrests of their seats," Mary Rogers interjected. "They'll push buttons marked one through ten for their favorite. Whoever gets the fewest votes is out."

"Exactly," Bobbo agreed. "Miss Hathway, could you bring me some coffee? Next comes chimney-sliding with seven Santas left competing. You'll have to get up on the roof of a fake house and slide down the chimney, and do it while carrying a big sack of toys. The two slowest are eliminated. Now there'll be five left."

Bobbo paused as Heather handed him a steaming cup of coffee. He took a slow, deliberate sip.

"Then the set will switch to a living room decorated for Christmas," he said. "You know—Christmas tree, mistletoe, stockings hung by the chimney with care. The five remaining Santas each get sixty seconds to fill as many stockings with toys as possible. The three Santas who can cram toys into the most stockings get to go on."

Lucretia Pepper had something to add.

"I think that only stockings full of *unbroken* toys should count," she said. "If finalists place any damaged toys in stockings, then those stockings would not be included in the final total. After all, on Christmas Eve Santa doesn't leave broken toys for children."

Bobbo seemed puzzled.

"Well, fine, Lucretia," he said. "You're paying for the program, so you can certainly suggest a rule. We'll do it that way. Now, after stocking-stuffing comes a fun challenge, cookie-eating. Simple as it sounds. Cookies get eaten. The Santa who eats—and that means chewing up and completely swallowing—the fewest cookies in sixty seconds is gone from the competition. That leaves two."

Bobbo paused again, milking the moment. All around the table, would-be Santas leaned forward, hanging on his every word, except for Jimmy Lee, who slouched comfortably in his seat, and me, because Felix and I had discussed all these details many times before.

"Now, the last two Santas have to appeal directly to the studio audience," he finally explained. "Each one has to tell why he and not the other one deserves to be elected America's official Santa. They'll both have three minutes to do it in. The audience votes, and we've got our winner."

Lucretia Pepper cleared her throat.

"The winner is then presented as the spokesman for LastLong Toy Company, and for the duration of his contract with us cannot work for anyone else," she declared. "I don't want anyone to forget that."

"We won't, Lucretia," Bobbo promised.

For the first time, Jimmy Lee sat up straight.

"It would be an honor," he said. "An *exceptional* honor."

No one else seemed to have anything to say, so we finalists trooped off to be measured for our *Great Santa Search* costumes. I couldn't help noticing how magnificent Jimmy Lee looked in his.

Sixteen

On December 20, four days before *The Great Santa Search* broadcast, Sarah and Heather Hathaway decided to go out for lunch. The ten finalists had been chosen. All the tickets were distributed. The day of the show itself would be tremendously hectic, but until then there was a little time for the staff to rest. After lunch, Sarah and Heather thought, they might even find something else relaxing and interesting to do, and perhaps not go back to the office at all. They'd become good friends over the past months, and had promised to stay in touch after the program was over.

Over a meal of miso soup and sushi, though, they found themselves talking about the show. Heather predicted *The Great Santa Search* would achieve record ratings, and FUN-TV would be saved. She disliked Lucretia Pepper and couldn't bring herself to think well of Jimmy Lee, saying there was something about him that bothered her even though she was certain he'd win.

"I guess mostly I'm happy for Bobbo," she added. "I wish he could have found a different sponsor. I know he feels terrible about what Lucretia Pepper is going to do. But the FUN-TV ratings have been so bad, Sarah, and nobody else would even consider buying advertising time with us. It was Lucretia Pepper or no *Great Santa Search*. Please don't hate Bobbo for selling out to LastLong Toys. He was only doing what he had to."

Sarah finished her soup and pushed the bowl away.

"I certainly don't hate Bobbo," she said. "I think that in his desperation to save his television network, he's chosen to risk the belief millions of children have in Santa Claus. That belief is precious. Much more than gifts, Santa Claus represents generosity of spirit, something Lucretia Pepper obviously lacks."

"Bobbo has a generous spirit and he's special," Heather said wistfully. "I just wish he'd, well, I guess you know."

"I do," Sarah assured her. "Someday he's going to understand just how special you are, too. But in the meantime, you can't focus your whole life on him. Maybe if you weren't always right there for Bobbo, available at his every beck and call, he'd realize he really needs and cares for you."

Heather sighed. "As far as he's concerned, I'm just the assistant who works for him."

"Well, you're not going to work for him this afternoon," Sarah said briskly. "I'm told there's a wonderful new exhibit at the American Museum of Natural History. Would you like to come with me to see it?"

"I love that museum," Heather said enthusiastically. "Did you know Theodore Roosevelt was one of its greatest supporters? There's even a statue of him in front of it."

"You don't say," Sarah replied. Up at the North Pole, Theodore constantly bragged about "his" museum.

"I'll just call Bobbo and tell him I won't be back today," Heather said. She took her cell phone from her purse. When she reached Bobbo, he said it was fine for her to take a few hours off, but then he had questions about some minor things and Heather ended up spending almost ten minutes talking to him.

Sarah didn't want to appear to be eavesdropping on their conversation, so she idly looked around the congested streets. Her eye was suddenly caught by a bulky man making his way through the crowd. He had a floppy hat pulled low on his head, and a muffler obscured the lower portion of his face. But there was something about his eyes and the way he moved, languidly yet deliberately, that seemed familiar. Then a gust of wind blew off his hat, which skittered along the sidewalk, and the man stalked over to where it lay. As he bent down to retrieve it, the muffler briefly fell away from his face.

It was Jimmy Lee.

At first, Sarah simply wondered why he wasn't at Manhattan Mega-Mall, dressed as Santa and greeting adoring children. All the *Great Santa Search* finalists were back at their mall jobs, except for Wesley from St. Paul, and he was in Minnesota starring in his holiday play. None of them were supposed to deviate from their previous routines, for fear someone in the media might notice and publicly identify a competitor in advance of the program.

Yet here was Jimmy Lee, swaddled in so many winter clothes that he was virtually unrecognizable. Sarah found this odd, but then the situation became odder still, for Jimmy Lee raised an arm and waved briefly to catch the eye of someone walking toward him. It was Lucretia Pepper. She stalked up to Jimmy Lee, whispered in his ear, and accompanied him down the sidewalk.

Sarah tugged at the sleeve of Heather's coat.

"Look at that!" she hissed.

Heather was still talking to Bobbo. She waved impatiently at Sarah and said into her cell phone, "I'm sure your wallet is somewhere on your desk. Just move some of the papers around. You'll see it."

"*Heather,*" Sarah whispered urgently. "Get off the phone." Jimmy Lee and Lucretia Pepper were about to disappear into the crowd. When Heather didn't conclude her call, Sarah simply yanked her along as she hurried after them.

"Just look on your desk, please, Bobbo," Heather pleaded, and snapped her cell phone shut. "Sarah, why are you dragging me like this? What's your problem?"

"Jimmy Lee has met Lucretia Pepper, and they're walking right ahead of us," Sarah explained. "Don't you think that's odd?"

Heather stared.

"Maybe they just bumped into each other by accident," she said.

"Hardly," Sarah replied. "I saw him wave at her. She went right to him, even though he had most of his face covered by a hat and muffler. She was expecting him. They had an appointment."

"I wonder why they'd do that," Heather mused. She and Sarah had to maintain a brisk pace. A few dozen yards ahead of them, Lucretia Pepper and Jimmy Lee were scuttling along rapidly. The sidewalks were crowded, but they made good progress because Lucretia Pepper simply lowered her shoulder and knocked aside anyone in her path. It was difficult to keep up with them.

"I don't know, but it can't be anything good," Sarah said. "We need to see where they're going."

"It's not against the law for people to meet," Heather pointed out. "Do we have the right to spy on them?"

"Heather, this is Lucretia Pepper and Jimmy Lee," Sarah retorted. "*The Great Santa Search* is in four days. The Christmas beliefs of millions of children are at stake, and these two are having some sort of secret meeting. Look at how he's got his face covered up, and how fast she's making them walk. They don't want anyone to know what they're doing. If it was innocent, they could talk at the FUN-TV offices or at the theater on Christmas Eve. No, they're up to something."

"You're right," Heather said. "Come on, we've got to cross the street before the light changes. We can't let them get away!"

Jimmy Lee and Lucretia Pepper hurried down Madison Avenue past Grand Central Terminal and the Pierpont Morgan Library. Just beyond Madison Square Park and the Flatiron building, they ducked into a coffee shop.

"They certainly wanted to get as far away as they could from Manhattan Mega-Mall and the LastLong Toy Company offices," Sarah remarked, puffing. She and Heather were out of breath from their frantic, lengthy walk. "That coffee shop is fairly large. Let's see if we can go in and sit down without them noticing us."

The shop was teeming with customers, who were packed around dozens of small tables. The buzz of general conversation was quite loud. When Heather and Sarah went in, they soon spotted Lucretia Pepper and Jimmy

Lee huddled together at a table toward the rear. None of the other tables around them was vacant; the only place for the two women to sit was a table on the far side of the room.

"Well, we can see them, and we're far enough away that they shouldn't notice us," Sarah said. "But we can't hear what they're saying, and that's what we need to do."

Heather didn't reply. Her eyes were locked on the far table where Jimmy Lee and Lucretia Pepper sat with their heads close together, talking.

"Heather?" Sarah queried. "Heather, did you hear me? Because we can't hear *them*."

"Maybe we can't hear them, but we can still know what they're talking about," Heather muttered. "Give me a minute, Sarah. I'm trying to concentrate."

"What do you mean?"

"I can read lips, remember?" Heather replied. "Quiet, please. She's asking him—oh! How awful!"

Sarah couldn't help herself.

"What? What are they saying?"

Without taking her eyes off the pair, Heather muttered, "I'll tell you if you'll just keep quiet."

"I will," Sarah promised.

"All right. She just asked if he really understood what he was supposed to do during the show. He said he did. He said he knows he's supposed to mention LastLong Toys any time he can, and especially during his speech in the final challenge. But he's worried the stupid audience might vote against him earlier so he won't make it to the final challenge."

"It's awful that he's going to talk about LastLong Toys during the program," Sarah declared.

"No, what's really horrible is that he's calling the audience stupid. In television, we have to respect our audiences, even when it's hard. Hush, Sarah. She's telling him something about—what's she saying?—oh, all right. She said he doesn't have to worry about the audience vote. He's so much better than all the others that everyone will vote for him, and besides, there are 150 seats reserved for LastLong executives and their families.

They've been told they all have to vote for Jimmy Lee or they'll be fired immediately. So he's got 150 solid votes to start with. Only about three hundred other people will be in the theater and voting. With that kind of built-in advantage, he's bound to win."

"What cheaters!" Sarah blurted. "Sorry, Heather. I'll keep quiet."

"Now they're talking about the challenges that don't have audience votes. She says he shouldn't have trouble with the reindeer-roping because she hired the world-champion rodeo cowboy to give him lessons. He says he quit at the Manhattan Mega-Mall so he'd have time for the lessons, and he's gotten pretty good. Carol-singing won't be a problem, he says. He's got a great voice. Modest, isn't he? I don't know what she just said. She had her coffee cup in front of her mouth. Now they're talking about stocking-stuffing. She's reminding him only unbroken toys will count. She's going to be backstage to make sure when it's his turn, he gets the right kind of well-manufactured toys. All the other Santas will get regular LastLong toys, and most of them break the moment anyone touches them, let alone tries to shove them in a stocking. So that's why she made up that rule the other day during our meeting with the finalists. This is all so *evil*! And she says don't worry, she'll take care of the cookie-eating contest. *Oh!* That—that— *witch*!"

"What? What?" Sarah demanded.

"She says Bobbo will probably ask that ugly, gawky girl Heather to get the cookies, but Jimmy Lee shouldn't worry. She'll fix things. Lucretia Pepper's got some nerve calling *me* ugly! Has she looked in a mirror lately?"

"Perhaps you should pay attention to what else they're saying," Sarah suggested gently.

"Fine. So far as the final speech goes, he doesn't care which of the other Santas is left. Jimmy Lee says he personally will sound sincere and look wonderful, and he'll fool the studio audience just like he's fooled kids for fifteen years since he started playing Santa in malls. He says she shouldn't worry. He may hate Christmas, but he loves the money he's going to win."

Now Lucretia Pepper set down her coffee cup, stared intently into Jimmy Lee's eyes, and shook her finger at him as she spoke.

"She's telling him to remember the bottom line. For that million dollars, it's his job to make children all over America believe that Santa will bring them only LastLong toys," Heather reported. "She says if he doesn't do that, she'll make him regret it for the rest of his life. He says she can count on him."

Lucretia Pepper and Jimmy Lee stood up and left the coffee shop. Heather and Sarah ducked their heads as they passed, then got up themselves and followed the conniving pair outside.

Jimmy Lee pulled his hat down over his forehead and wrapped his muffler around his face. He shook hands with Lucretia Pepper and disappeared into the crowd. She turned and began walking north, to the LastLong Toy Company office.

"Well, that was just horrifying," Heather said. "I guess we have to go back to FUN-TV now and tell Bobbo. It's going to break his heart. *The Great Santa Search* was going to save his network, and now it's not going to happen after all."

"Why not?" Sarah asked.

"We just found out the sponsor and one of the contestants are planning to cheat," Heather said. "They've packed the audience with Jimmy Lee voters, and they're going to fix the stocking-stuffing and cookie-eating challenges so he's sure to win them. It's not going to be an honest contest. Bobbo will have to call it off."

"And what would happen then?" inquired Sarah.

"We'll have to broadcast some other program in place of *The Great Santa Search*," Heather predicted with a sigh. "Maybe it'll be a rerun of *Merry Monkey*. Everybody will switch channels. The media will tear Bobbo apart. He could explain about Lucretia Pepper and her cheating, but she'd be sure to sue him and without the LastLong money Bobbo can't afford to pay office rent, let alone a lawyer. So he'll be ruined and FUN-TV will shut down. I'll lose my job. Probably I'll have to go home to North Dakota and live on the farm again. And instead I'd hoped that Bobbo and I—well, I guess it doesn't matter anymore what I hoped."

"Don't give up on those hopes just yet," Sarah said. "In fact, I don't think you should tell Bobbo about any of this. You know what people say about the best-laid plans often going wrong. That's also true for evil schemes. Let me deal with this, Heather. The best thing you can do is wait. On Christmas Eve, I may need your help. But for now, try to go on as you usually would."

"What are you going to do?" Heather asked.

Sarah couldn't tell her friend about how she and Felix had been providing inside information about *The Great Santa Search* to me long before the LastLong Toy Company president had even known Jimmy Lee existed. She certainly couldn't tell Heather how some of the smartest individuals in human history would soon gather together at the North Pole and come up with ways to ruin Lucretia Pepper's plot.

"I don't know, yet," Sarah answered honestly. "But I promise to think of something. Say, you're going to have to go on to the museum without me. I just remembered an appointment."

She waited until Heather was out of sight before taking out her own cell phone and calling me at Galaxy Mall in Cleveland.

Seventeen

left Galaxy Mall in Cleveland for the last time on December 23. Even though Santa Land was scheduled to be open until 10:00 p.m., my personal work shift ended at noon, when we closed for an hour so Santa could eat lunch and rest his lap. I was able to leave early because Lester Sneed, the mall manager, was so eager to fill in for me.

"Okay, glad to do it," he said enthusiastically when I asked if he would take my place after lunch. We'd already arranged for me to be gone the next day, of course—I was due at the Ed Sullivan Theater in New York City at 3:00 p.m. on Christmas Eve. But I had some errands to run before then, and I needed extra time. Mr. Sneed had apparently substituted for me quite adequately when I'd made my one-day trip to New York for the *Great Santa Search* finalists meeting almost a week earlier. Jill the photographer told me she couldn't tell who was having more fun, "Santa" Sneed or the children clamoring to tell him what they wanted for Christmas. Even Xander agreed that "Old O.K." did well.

"Will you need to go home to get your costume?" I asked.

"Nope," Mr. Sneed replied. "Got it right in my office. Hey, if you've got a lot of errands, I could step in for you all day, okay? Be a pleasure."

"I think it would be fine if you just took over for me after lunch," I assured him. Privately, I was somewhat concerned. Though Mr. Sneed had the best of intentions, it was also true his gray beard was rather scraggly and his waistline was not of full Clausian proportions. Children who'd waited in line to see a completely authentic-looking Santa—and I believed I fit that description—might feel let down to see a less-convincing version take over for the afternoon and evening.

But it had to be that way. I had important things to do. Ever since Sarah contacted me with the news of Lucretia Pepper and Jimmy Lee plotting to fix *The Great Santa Search* competition, all of us from the North Pole had been devising ways to thwart them. Many possibilities had been considered and for a while it seemed we would ask Leonardo to come up with some sort of electronic device to divert audience votes from Jimmy Lee to me. Leonardo is such a genius that he would surely have developed an invention to do just that. But Layla eventually pointed out that this ploy would never work. The moment Lucretia Pepper saw that her "rock solid" 150 LastLong employee votes weren't being credited to Jimmy Lee as intended, she'd assume the vote controls on the studio seats were somehow faulty and demand on the spot that some other means of voting—perhaps raising hands—be used instead.

"Anyway, you have to beat Jimmy Lee without lowering yourself to his level," my wife insisted. "So what if he gets 150 fixed votes? That's still not a majority. You just have to convince all the honest voters to pick you."

But the two nonvoting challenges that Lucretia Pepper and Jimmy Lee planned to win through cheating were another matter entirely. Stocking-stuffing and cookie-eating were events that I intended to win decisively. We felt we had come up with ways to do just that—and one of them required me to abandon my Galaxy Mall Santa duties earlier than scheduled on December 23.

After I changed into everyday clothes in the dressing room and carefully packed my Santa regalia in a suitcase, which I then took with me, I made my way to a large toy store on the second level of the mall. There, I spent several hours selecting and purchasing a considerable number of small Last-Long toys—plastic action figures, sports cars, dolls with jointed limbs, and so forth. The clerk recognized me as the mall Santa and joked, "You going to load up your sleigh with these tomorrow night?" I assured him Santa Claus delivered only North Pole–manufactured toys on Christmas Eve.

As I left the store, I happened to look down at Santa Land below me. There was, as usual, a long line of children waiting for their turns with Santa. I was struck by how excited they all seemed—their smiles were visible and their happy laughter quite audible, even though I was certainly fifty or more yards away. What I noticed most, though, was the obvious joy apparent in both parties when each boy or girl joined the bearded man wearing the red suit and sitting on the wooden block throne. I could tell from Mr. Sneed's every gesture that he loved the experience of greeting them and that his pleasure was completely reciprocated. The children hopped eagerly up on his lap, and when they left, almost all of them offered him warm farewell hugs. I wasn't jealous. It was a wonderful sight.

Then I took my hefty sack of LastLong toys outside to the remote corner of the mall parking lot where I knew the reindeer hovered overhead. It took the briefest of moments for Dasher and the other seven to swoop down, pause while I loaded the toy sack and valise in the sleigh, took up my seat in front, picked up the reins, and gave the signal to swoop into the sky. Any normal human beings in the lot would not have noticed anything except, possibly, an infinitesimal flicker of movement out of the corners of their eyes. In two minutes, we were sailing above the clouds far beyond Cleveland, and in another half hour I was guiding the sleigh in for a North Pole landing.

Willie Skokan and Leonardo da Vinci were waiting in the barn. While I unharnessed the reindeer and fed them some extra treats, my two friends lifted the sack of LastLong toys from the sleigh and hurried off with it to their workshop.

"It won't take them long to do what they have to," I observed to Layla when she joined me in my study. "It did feel quite odd to fly *back* to the North Pole with toys loaded in the sleigh. It has always been the other way around."

"Well, tomorrow is going to be a Christmas Eve unlike any other," she reminded me. "While Willie and Leonardo are working, there's really nothing more for you to do. Why not take a nap? You'll need all your energy for the competitions."

"I'm not a bit tired," I informed her. "I think I'll just spend the afternoon studying Amelia Earhart's tentative flight plan for tomorrow night. After I win *The Great Santa Search*, I'll still have my full Christmas Eve delivery schedule to complete."

"Study away," Layla said cheerfully, and left me alone with Amelia's voluminous charts and maps. I must have remained awake reading them at least thirty seconds after my wife had gone.

After dinner that evening—Lars prepared his delicious *pollo de Portugal*, a chicken dish with red and green peppers that Francis discovered centuries earlier while traveling in that country—we gathered to review our plans for the next night. Everyone had something important to do, but not all of these tasks were related to *The Great Santa Search*. Christmas Eve is, of course, one of our three busiest nights of the year. Even as I was onstage, routine last-minute preparations for global gift-giving would be underway at the North Pole and most of our beloved companions would have to be occupied with these. Felix and Sarah were not at this meeting, because they were in New York City fulfilling their own last-minute obligations as part of *The Great Santa Search* staff; they would, of course, remain there until the program was over. Layla, Arthur, St. Francis, and Bill Pickett would use the four "friends" tickets granted by Bobbo Butler to Sarah and Felix. Willie Skokan would be the additional friend they were allowed to bring backstage during the show. His presence there would be critical. All my other gift-giving associates would remain at the North Pole, keeping our Christmas Eve operation there in full, effective swing.

A few were particularly unhappy to miss *The Great Santa Search* events. I explained to Amelia Earhart that she must be on hand at our headquarters to monitor the weather; changes in flying conditions are a constant on Christmas Eve, and if, after I was done with television and back in my sleigh, I encountered an unexpected snowstorm, the delay might result in children somewhere not receiving their well-deserved gifts from Santa. She reluctantly agreed.

Theodore Roosevelt was harder to convince. He loved New York

City—he had once lived there and later served as police commissioner, after all—and argued that, as former president and commander in chief, it was important for him to be "where the action is. What will you do, for instance, if fisticuffs are required?"

"They won't be, Theodore," I assured him. "Brute force is not the most effective way to defeat evil."

"But sometimes a good poke in the belly comes in handy, Santa Claus," he argued. "I've trained you in lifting weights and jumping rope and so forth, but never in boxing."

I finally persuaded my enthusiastic friend to remain behind because, if he appeared at the Ed Sullivan Theater, too many people might recognize him.

"Yours is one of the most familiar faces in American history, Theodore," I explained. "Your presence might very well cause considerable speculation."

Theodore always liked the fact he had been and remained quite famous.

"Well, perhaps you're right," he agreed. "All right, I'll stay behind. But do you promise to throw a manly punch or two if the situation calls for it?"

"I'm sure that won't be necessary," I said hopefully.

The morning of December 24 came as it always does at the North Pole—in complete darkness and with freezing winds whipping over the ice and accumulated drifts of snow. I dressed in warm street clothes and spent most of the morning visiting all the North Pole workshops, making certain all was in readiness for that night's gift-giving. This is always a day of particular excitement for us, and my imminent participation on *The Great Santa Search* only added to everyone's high-spirited mood.

By lunchtime, I admit I had begun feeling nervous. It was an unusual sensation for me. My life's work is devoted to service to others and spiritual faith; these things enrich and calm rather than disturb the mind. I didn't doubt I was going to win *The Great Santa Search*. We knew exactly what Lucretia Pepper and Jimmy Lee were up to and had planned accordingly. And, despite anything they might attempt, I had one insurmountable advantage—I really *was* Santa Claus.

Still, I was a bit jumpy, and Layla suggested I lie down for a bit before we had to get in the sleigh and fly to New York City. Instead, I sat quietly in my study, remembering all the challenges of the past centuries and how things had somehow always worked out for the best. In particular, I remembered myself as a boy back in the long-forgotten country of Lycia, when I yearned to give gifts and survived a rough beginning to eventually be honored by centuries of doing exactly what I loved best. I was—I am—so lucky, so blessed. And realizing this, my nerves were calmed, and by the time Layla knocked gently on the door to inform me it was time to leave I was eager to experience what I knew would be a memorable evening.

Layla, Bill, Francis, Arthur, Willie, and Attila all climbed in the sleigh with me. Attila was coming because someone had to fly the reindeer back to the North Pole after the rest of us had been dropped off in New York City. Once it had been returned to our snowy headquarters, the sleigh would be carefully loaded with just the right amount of toys. Then, at the appropriate time, Attila would fly it back to an alley behind the Ed Sullivan Theater. The moment that *The Great Santa Search* was over, I would hurry out to the alley, greet my beloved reindeer, and instruct them to whirl me up into the winter sky so my Christmas Eve gift-giving could begin. Attila would join my other friends as they returned to the North Pole via train and, eventually, dogsled.

We landed in the alley behind the theater just before 3:00 p.m. Felix was waiting for us there. He informed Bill, Layla, Arthur, and Francis that they would find their tickets at the box office around 7:00 p.m. Those four all wished me luck, then trooped off to enjoy a few hours of strolling amid the colorful sights and sounds of New York City on Christmas Eve. Felix told me I was expected in the theater lobby and instructed Willie to come with him through a backstage door. Willie did, carrying with him the big sack of LastLong toys I'd purchased at Galaxy Mall the day before.

I went around to the front of the theater and was greeted by the same security guard I'd met on the day of *The Great Santa Search* open audition. Gary Elders didn't recognize me, but a yelping crowd of reporters and cameramen did. Apparently they'd been outside the theater all day, waiting for the finalists to arrive. My white beard and impressive waistline clearly identified me; there were shouts of "Look at the cameras!" and "Where are you from?" and "Are you the real Santa?"

"Hurry up inside," Gary urged me, and he called back, "You'll have to watch the program to see if he's the one," to the media mob.

Several FUN-TV interns were in the lobby, ready to escort finalists to wherever we were supposed to go next. It was too perfect: the young woman greeting me was the same one who'd dismissed me from the open audition.

"Hello, Emily Vance," I remarked.

She looked startled.

"How did you know my name? Oh, you must have read it on my badge. Which one are you?" Clearly, all Santas looked alike to young Emily.

"Nicholas Holiday, from the Galaxy Mall in Cleveland."

Emily consulted a list.

"Fine, you're in Dressing Room D. Follow me."

I was surprised by how cramped it was behind the main theater stage. There was a virtual warren of small, square dressing rooms. Mine was quite plain. There was a table with a mirror, a small bathroom, two chairs, and a clothes rack that had a half-dozen empty wire hangers dangling from it. On two more hangers were dazzling red velvet Santa costumes. Accessories— white gloves, black boots, the famous red "Santa hats" with white fur trim and pom-pom—were stacked on the chairs.

"You're in here with Zonk from Green Mountain Mall in Rutland, Vermont," Emily said. "There's a meeting about the opening dance routine in ten minutes on the main stage. You're supposed to be in full costume but not makeup. I'll be back for you."

"Makeup?" I asked, horrified. But Emily was already out the door. She seemed to be a young person who was always in a hurry.

Sighing, I took off my street clothes. The Santa suits were tagged *"Cleveland"* and *"Rutland,"* so I knew which was mine. As I pulled on the red trousers, Emily reappeared with my dressing-room partner. Being an old-fashioned, modest sort of fellow, I tried to hide behind a chair, but I tripped and nearly went sprawling, though I still managed to hold up my pants. Emily left without comment, but Zonk made one.

"Jeez, how can you dance if you can't even get your pants on without falling over?" he asked, laughing. But his tone and laughter were quite good-natured, and I knew he was being friendly, not insulting.

"I'm really not sure," I replied, clambering up. "We don't dance too much at the North Pole."

"Nah, 'cause we're too busy tripping over penguins," Zonk said. I considered telling him penguins lived at the South rather than the North Pole, but thought better of it. Instead, as we dressed we chatted about Christmas and our experiences with children while serving as mall Santas. Zonk did most of the talking. He was quite an outgoing, gregarious sort. I learned that he first began dressing up as Santa to delight his small grandchildren on Christmas Eve and had been so good at it that friends of the family began asking if they could bring their little ones over to meet "Santa," too. Then the Santa working at the Rutland mall quit unexpectedly, and Zonk was asked to fill in until a new one was sent by the Noel Program. But he was so popular that Noel's Stephanie Owen asked if he'd like to keep the job himself. That had been six years ago; ever since, he was the mall's Santa. Stephanie had offered to send him to more prestigious malls in bigger cities, but Zonk was perfectly happy to stay in Rutland.

He kept up a constant stream of chatter even when Emily returned to take us to the dance session. I learned Zonk had once been in the Navy, and that he got his nickname from the sound he made when he tackled rival players in high school football games.

"There was this loud *zonk!*" he claimed. "Nobody else's tackles sounded like that. I've always been real unusual. Like, I've got ageusia."

That stopped me short: "What?"

"Ay-GOO-see-uh. I can't taste things. Which is good, considering my wife's cooking."

Lauren Devoe was waiting onstage. The other Santa finalists came trailing in. Everyone was in proper costume. Brian from Missoula looked a little odd with his dark beard. Zonk and Andy from Chicago had no beards at all. False whiskers, I presumed, would be provided to them later. We all milled around for a moment, shaking hands and wishing one another luck. Jimmy Lee stood apart from the rest of us. He clearly was not interested in being sociable.

"Everybody gather 'round," Lauren instructed. "We tried some basic dance moves back when we met at FUN-TV. I know it didn't go very well, but like I told you then, don't worry about being great dancers. You don't have to be. And we've already taped the vocals with a hired choir, so you won't have to sing. You'll be doing that later in one of the challenges anyway. In this first number, concentrate on getting the steps right. Show some energy. Act like you're having fun, even if you aren't. The idea is, this dance will give the audience at home and in the studio a chance to see all of you. It lasts only two minutes, and then you're offstage while Bobbo Butler talks and things get set up behind the curtain for the first challenge. Now, we're going to hear the theme song." She gestured toward the control booth and recorded music began to play:

Searching for Santa, searching for Santa,
We must find the bringer of toys.
Searching for Santa, searching for Santa,
A magical evening for all girls and boys!
And so we're searching for Santa, searching for Santa,
What better way to spend Christmas Eve?
We'll all just glow by the end of the show
Because we'll finally know who Santa is and all can believe!
We hope that you know Santa loves you too
You make his days seem merry and bright.
So by your leave on Christmas Eve
We'll be searching for Santa tonight!

Lauren demonstrated the various dance steps she'd tried to teach us at the FUN-TV offices—step-step-*slide*-step-pirouette-turn-*slide*-step.

"Just remember to move to the beat," she added. "We decided it would be better not to run through the dance before the actual show. Let's just be, well, natural." I emitted a quiet snort. Dancing, I knew, was anything but natural for me.

Then show director Mary Rogers bustled up, explaining it was past 5:00 p.m. and there was still a lot of stage setup to be done.

"These Santas need to get back to their dressing rooms for makeup," she added.

"All right," Lauren said cheerfully. "This is supposed to be entertainment tonight, not ballet. Just do your best. From what I remember at FUN-TV, you two"—she gestured to Joe and Jimmy Lee—"need to be in the middle of the front row. You'll line up in two rows of five tonight. If you fall down while you're dancing, anybody, just grin, get up, and keep going. It's live TV. We're going to give them something amazing to look at, one way or the other."

Emily and the other FUN-TV interns led us back to our dressing rooms. While we were gone, someone had placed boxed meals on the tables. There was a chicken-salad sandwich in each, along with an apple, a chocolate-chip cookie, and an eight-ounce plastic bottle of water. Zonk and I sat down to eat.

Just after 6:30 p.m., a man and woman knocked on our dressing-room door and said they had come to "make us up." This involved rouge and powder and eyeliner. The process was rather embarrassing.

"Now, you don't want all those wrinkles around your eyes to show on camera, do you?" the makeup man coaxed.

"I earned every one of those wrinkles," I responded. "I have no problem with them being visible."

But the makeup couple did. Zonk's makeup process was even more excruciating. They had brought with them a fake white beard, which they attached strand by strand to his cheeks and chin. It did look quite real, and they warned Zonk it would be necessary to let the adhesive wear off gradually.

"Don't try to pull the beard off," he was informed. "You'll take skin with it."

At 7:00 p.m. we could hear rumblings from the theater itself; the audience was beginning to be seated. Members of the backstage crew scurried frantically about. The tension made Zonk even chattier. I learned the names and ages of his grandchildren and the location of every birthmark on his body. Just as he was beginning to describe his recent root-canal surgery, our dressing-room door opened and Felix came in.

"It's time to pick your numbers," he said rather formally, and I knew he was being careful not to acknowledge me in any special way. "Take turns reaching in this box; take out one slip of paper. There will be a number on it from one to ten. That's how you'll be identified during the program—no other names at all, remember. It will be Santa 1, Santa 2, and so forth."

Zonk went first, and picked number 8. I took my turn, and became Santa 6.

At 7:45 all the finalists were gathered just offstage. We could hear the audience but couldn't see it. The curtains were drawn. But behind the curtains was a spectacular stage set, with cutouts of snowy mountaintops and towering fir trees glowing with colorful Christmas lights. Lauren showed us where we were to take our places in the two lines of five, and then Mary Rogers came down from the control booth to wish us all luck.

"Just remember, this is live television," she reminded us. "No matter what happens, keep goin'. And remember to smile."

Then a larger group approached us. I could see Sarah, and also Robert the set designer and Eri the costume designer and Ken the sound engineer and nasty Lucretia Pepper and, lingering just behind everyone else, Willie Skokan, who grinned at me and furtively offered the "thumbs up" sign that all was well. Bobbo Butler stepped up in front of us, with Heather Hathway standing to his right.

"This is it," Bobbo said, sounding nervous and excited, certainly an understandable combination for a network president who was about to gamble his company's future on a live television program. "Do your best. If you're eliminated, act like a good sport. Each challenge has a time limit. Don't dawdle. Get on- and offstage promptly when it's your turn. You may be wondering how we're going to handle some of the challenges—what order you'll go in and so forth. We deliberately haven't told you. We want to keep as much spontaneity as possible. That's what reality TV is all about. Last questions?"

No one had any.

Bobbo glanced at his watch.

"All right, then," he said. "Seven fifty-nine." He was dressed in his red velvet tuxedo with white trim on the cuffs of his coat and pants. Perhaps it should have looked ridiculous, but somehow it seemed impressive. So did Bobbo. His fringe of hair was neatly combed for once, and he looked alert but not frantic.

He looked at his watch again. I could see Mary Rogers in the control booth; it had large glass windows. She said something into a microphone on the console in front of her. A stagehand standing just to the side of the curtains waved at Bobbo.

"This is it," Bobbo said. He pushed past the curtains and walked on-stage.

The Great Santa Search was on the air.

Eighteen

ost ballyhooed television holiday specials kick off with flashy production numbers, which include loud music and lots of action to capture the audience's attention. But Felix had told me Bobbo Butler wanted something simpler and far more dramatic.

So instead of drumrolls or trumpet fanfares, *The Great Santa Search* got underway with Bobbo walking out onstage. Those of us backstage were able to watch on monitors. The theater was dark; he was illuminated by a single spotlight. The crowd applauded enthusiastically, and Bobbo gestured for silence.

"We're here to make television and Christmas history," he said solemnly. "We're going to have fun, but there's serious business involved, too. My name is Robert O. Butler. Call me Bobbo. I have the privilege of being president of the FUN-TV network. Backstage we have ten men in red-and-white suits. Each claims he's Santa Claus. But there's only one. Tonight, this studio audience will help decide who that really is. If you'll look at that clock on the studio wall, it reads 8:01 p.m. Eastern Standard Time. By 10:00 p.m., the one and only Santa will have been identified. We'll have seen him, heard him, and none of us will ever again have to wonder, 'Is there really a Santa Claus?' That's what *The Great Santa Search* is all about."

Bobbo paused, and the audience applauded again, heartily but briefly. They, and certainly the millions of others watching at home, were anxious to hear more.

"During the next two hours, I'll occasionally come onstage to visit with you," Bobbo continued. "After all, this is live television, and we'll need to change some sets and let our Santas get in place for some of the competitions that will help decide which one of them is who he claims to be. But there will be no commercial breaks. Thanks to our generous sponsor, the LastLong Toy Company, this program will run uninterrupted, and that's a good thing, too. Because there's a lot we have to do before 10:00 p.m. Remember, we can't run late: it's Christmas Eve, and Santa's going to be a busy man after we're off the air!"

Bobbo paused again; backstage, Lauren and other crew members pulled the ten Santa finalists into two lines of five. As she'd instructed, Joe from Bloomington and Jimmy Lee were in the center of the front row. I was on the far right in the second row.

"Are you ready to select Santa?" Bobbo asked the studio audience.

"Yes!" they chorused.

Bobbo looked concerned.

"That didn't sound very enthusiastic," he chided. "Are you ready?"

"*Yes!*"

"The real Santa Claus is backstage. Let's make sure he hears you. Are you ready?"

"*YES!!!*"

Bobbo spread his arms theatrically and shouted, "Ladies and gentlemen, children of all ages, meet—*our Santas!*" The curtains opened incredibly quickly. *The Great Santa Search* theme blared out:

Searching for Santa, searching for Santa,
We must find the bringer of toys! . . .

And we ten finalists were dancing.

For a very few seconds, it seemed that something miraculous was happening. We stepped and slid in something very close to unison. Brian from Missoula, whose dark beard was now thickly colored to look pure white, was next to me in line. His eyes were squinched tight with concentration. In front of me was Wesley from St. Paul. The back of his neck was a brighter red than his costume. I noted these small things with a sense of wonder, because my feet seemed to be operating without any direct connection to my brain. My boots stepped and shuffled exactly as they were supposed to be doing. The same seemed true for everyone. Then we had to pirouette.

Critics wrote later that the resulting carnage was among the most entertaining moments ever broadcast on television. Perhaps it was. One of the main goals of so-called "reality" TV is to let audiences observe people looking foolish, and in this instance that goal was served well. I believe the main culprit was my new friend Zonk, who spun out of control on the end of the front line and smacked into Buck from Kansas City, who was directly behind him. At least that's what Buck claimed two weeks later, when he sold his "*Great Santa Search* inside story" to a publication called the *National Enquirer.* No matter who was originally at fault, Buck lurched sideways into Luis from Miami, who went sprawling and tripped Dillard from College Station, and I staggered when Dillard caromed into me, and we all ended up falling. The only two finalists who remained on their feet were Joe from Bloomington, whose bulk was impervious to flailing bodies, and Jimmy Lee, who coolly stepped to one side and continued making minimal movements to the theme music.

From the side of the stage, I thought I heard someone, probably Lauren, hissing, *"Keep going!"* and that was what we did. We picked ourselves up and tried to form some semblance of the original two lines. The song was up to *"We hope that you know Santa loves you too, You make his days seem merry and bright"* by the time all ten of us were back on our feet, and it was hard to hear the final lines because the audience, too, was standing, applauding and cheering and laughing at such a concussive level that it seemed our dance number had been a great success. The music ended, we stood panting and nursing various injuries, and the crowd kept roaring. Bobbo came back onstage, laughing as he, too, clapped heartily.

"Maybe they can't dance, but next we're going to find out whether they can rope some reindeer!" he announced. "Our Santas are going to head backstage to put Band-Aids on their bruises"—the audience chuckled as one—"but before they do, we're going to very briefly let them say hi." He pulled Andy from Chicago to his side. "Here's Santa 1!"

No one had mentioned being introduced. Andy, his Santa hat drooping over his eyes after various dance collisions, stood mutely by Bobbo, perhaps trying to think of what to say.

"Hi," he finally muttered. Santa 2 (Dillard) could only manage, "Hello." But Jimmy Lee was No. 3.

He strolled comfortably up to Bobbo, looked out at the audience, waved genially, and declared, "Merry Christmas, and may your holiday joy Last-Long!" I found this unsubtle mention of the program sponsor quite offensive, but Sarah told me later that Lucretia Pepper, standing backstage, beamed with ill-concealed satisfaction.

Santas 4 and 5 (Luis and Buck) awkwardly mumbled greetings. Then it was my turn, and I smiled and said simply, "Hello. I'm Santa Claus." Now, *that* elicited audience reaction, mostly cheers and whoops. From the corner of my eye, it seemed that Jimmy Lee was glowering, but I might have imagined it.

Santa 7 (Brian) tried saying exactly the same thing, but I'd said it first so the audience reaction was far less enthusiastic for him. Besides, his nose was bleeding. When we all fell over one another, someone's elbow or knee had apparently smashed into his face during the melee. Earlier, the makeup experts must have put some sort of coloring on his beard to make it white instead of dark brown, but now his whiskers appeared to be spattered with crimson polka dots.

"Better get that nose taken care of, Santa 7," Bobbo quipped. "Your suit is supposed to be red and white, not your beard. But say, folks, aren't all of our Santas great sports? Let's give them another hand."

As Santa 8, I thought Zonk made a fine impression by casually saying, "Hey, there," as though he were greeting old, familiar friends. Santa 9 (Wesley), having had time to think about it, launched into a lovely speech about how everyone watching was certain to have a Merry Christmas if they voted for him. He might have said more, but Bobbo cut him off.

"It's Christmas Eve, Santa 9," he cautioned. "Not much time, and lots yet to do."

Santa 10 (massive Joe) contented himself with a quick "Merry Christmas," and then we finalists were ushered offstage while the curtains closed behind Bobbo.

"First challenge in two minutes, at 8:12," one of the stagehands announced. Behind the closed curtains and to my right, I could see the crew frantically hauling what appeared to be hundreds of coiled ropes to one side. Part of the floor toward the rear of the stage was lowered, and new flooring hydraulically replaced it. Placed on that new flooring was a conveyor belt stretched out in perhaps a thirty-foot oval. On this belt were a dozen wooden full-body reindeer silhouettes, the animals apparently frozen in graceful mid-leap. Their forelegs extended, and their antlers were tall and majestic, much more elaborate than the lovely stubs on the heads of my real reindeer.

"One at a time, you'll be called onstage," said Felix, who had walked up while I was looking at the stage set. We finalists gave him our full attention. It was one thing to fail as dancers; those who performed worst in the challenges would be eliminated from the competition.

"You'll each have forty-five seconds to rope as many reindeer as you can," Felix continued. "You'll see a mark on the stage where you're supposed to stand. Don't worry if you step over it just a little. You won't be disqualified for that. If you rope one of the reindeer—I mean, *when* you do—drop your end of the rope and let it just be pulled along with the wooden reindeer on the conveyor. Pick up a new rope and keep going. The two Santas who rope the fewest get eliminated. In case of a tie, audience applause level decides who stays and who goes. Got it?"

We did. Onstage, Bobbo Butler was telling the studio and television audiences much the same things. In the extra half-minute between Felix concluding his instructions and the curtains opening again, I listened as Bobbo went on to explain how the evening's challenges would roughly simulate the order of Santa's usual activities on Christmas Eve.

"In this first event, our Santas will be racing the clock," Bobbo said. "In the next event, plus one other, we're going to ask our studio audience to determine the results by their votes. More on that later. Right now, we begin our series of challenges the same way Santa begins his Christmas Eve—by roping the reindeer!"

Of course, I never had to rope the reindeer. None of us at the North Pole did. They came when we called them. Reality TV, I mused, actually had very little real about it. But there was no time for further philosophizing. The curtains opened, and the audience *oohed* and *aahed* to see the wooden reindeer whirling on the conveyor belt. They were quite attractive reindeer models, I had to admit. We Santas were sent out in a line determined in order by number—Santa 1 was first, and so on. As Santa 6, I was comfortably in the middle. Just in front of me, I heard Buck, as Santa 5, mutter, "Am I supposed to be Santa or a cowboy?" The answer, evidently, was "both."

Bobbo welcomed us back. He reminded everyone that time was flying, and soon, so would Santa and his reindeer, "but you've got to catch them first, and there's forty-five seconds for each of our Santas to do it in." The studio audience was encouraged to keep an eye on the clock; at home, viewers were informed, they should keep track of two small clocks superimposed on opposite corners of their television screens. The one on the left would keep track of the time left in each Santa's individual attempt; the one on the right indicated how much time was left before the conclusion of *The Great Santa Search* and "the beginning of the real Santa's long night's work!"

Forty-five seconds can seem very long if you just sit still or if you're listening to or watching something boring. But when that's the time you have to accomplish something quite complicated in front of an audience of millions, forty-five seconds seem to expire in a single short instant. Santa 1, Andy from Chicago, was called forward by Bobbo. He picked up a rope from the pile on the floor, took his place at the line marked on the stage, and Bobbo shouted, "Go!"

Santa 1 frantically made a loop, spun it briefly over his head, and threw it in the general direction of the circling wooden reindeer. The loop plopped perhaps a yard in front of him—the reindeer spun unroped another dozen feet away. The audience hooted. Andy tried again. He was inadvertently offering a lesson in how not to use a lasso: you *cast* rather than *throw* it, as Bill Pickett had constantly reminded me at the North Pole. *Casting* allows the loop to retain its shape as it floats through the air. It goes farther and can then drop over its target. It took Santa 1 quite a bit to figure this out, and just before a buzzer blared to note the passage of forty-five seconds, one of his casts managed to snare a single reindeer antler. Bobbo solemnly announced, "One reindeer for Santa 1. I hope if he's the real Santa, he starts trying to catch the reindeer *very* early in the morning of December 24. Otherwise, poor old Dasher will have a tough time pulling the sleigh all by himself!"

Santa 1 shuffled offstage, and Santa 2, who was Dillard, took his place by the pile of lassos. I had thought he would probably do well, being from Texas, but it quickly became obvious that not every Texan knows how to use a rope. Dillard didn't snare a single wooden reindeer.

Jimmy Lee was Santa 3. He'd had, as Sarah and Heather learned, private lessons from a champion rodeo cowboy who was paid by Lucretia Pepper to instruct him. He calmly shook out a nice loop, twirled it properly, cast it perfectly, and smiled as it settled neatly around a wooden reindeer neck. There was applause from the audience, which obviously appreciated not only the roping success but the elegance with which it was accomplished. Never seeming to hurry, Jimmy Lee made eight more casts in his forty-five seconds, succeeding with seven. The eighth looked just as perfect, but somehow the loop slipped off the reindeer's head. Jimmy Lee shrugged gracefully, and the buzzer sounded.

"That's eight reindeer for Santa 3," Bobbo bellowed. "Why, he roped the whole herd!"

There was some grumbling among the other finalists who had yet to try.

"That Number 3 is going to blow us away," somebody muttered. Jimmy Lee walked offstage without acknowledging the rest of us.

But there is some advantage in watching others try before you have to, and Santa 4, Luis, had obviously benefited from Jimmy Lee's example. He cast rather than threw, and though his results were not as impressive he still managed to rope three reindeer before his time was up. Santa 5, Buck, also roped three.

Then it was my turn. The seating area of the theater was darkened so I couldn't actually see him, but I was certain that somewhere in the studio audience Bill Pickett was leaning forward, hoping I would remember everything he'd spent so many months trying to teach me. And I did.

With a minimum of fuss, I cast at and lassoed eight reindeer in a row. Unlike Jimmy Lee, I didn't even have any near-misses. I just imagined I was back in the North Pole gym, with Theodore and Bill by my side and lovely little Vixen volunteering as my target. I could have made many more than eight casts in the allotted forty-five seconds, but I saw no reason to use my special power to move faster than normal humans. It was clear eight would be more than enough to ensure my continuing in the competition.

"Amazing," Bobbo declared. "We've got another Santa who's caught the whole herd!"

I wished I could have seen Bill's expression, but I still knew he was pleased.

Santa 7, Brian, seemed intimidated by my performance. On his first try, the rope slipped out of his hand and went flying offstage far from the wooden reindeer. There was much audience laughter. He never succeeded in snagging a single target.

Zonk, Santa 8, roped four. I noticed that on every cast he moved a little farther in front of the clearly marked line. Whether he did this on purpose or by accident I don't know.

Santa 9, Wesley, roped two, and massive Joe, Santa 10, managed only one. But that was still enough.

"Santas 2 and 7 roped zero reindeer, and they are eliminated," Bobbo announced. "Say good-bye, 2 and 7!" Dillard and Brian waved at the audience, which responded with a friendly cheer, and then were whisked away.

Bobbo talked about the inspiration for *The Great Santa Search*, how he and his assistant had been watching a skating exhibition at Rockefeller Center "sponsored by our wonderful friends at the LastLong Toy Company, who are also the generous sponsors of this program," and how the crisp winter air and the sight of so many people enjoying the massive Christmas tree there made him think of how fine it would be for Santa Claus, the real Santa Claus, to suddenly appear and make the whole moment absolutely perfect. He didn't mention meeting Sarah and Felix, or how Felix's chance remark actually initiated the whole *Great Santa Search* business.

At that moment, Emily the FUN-TV intern instructed me to join the other finalists gathered backstage with Felix.

"Carol-singing is the next competition," he said. "When it's your turn, you'll walk out onstage, take a slip of paper from the big drum on a table on Bobbo's right, and hand the slip to Bobbo. He'll read it and announce the Christmas carol you'll sing. We've got taped instrumental accompaniment. When the music begins, start singing. Some of the songs are longer than others. That's why, after Bobbo reads the slip you draw, he'll take the correct lyrics sheet from the table on his left and hand it to you. If you don't know the words to your carol, there they'll be. But sing only the verses on the sheet. We're trying to limit each singer to ninety seconds."

"What are the names of the songs in the drum?" asked Santa 9, Wesley from St. Paul.

"I can't tell you that," Felix said. It was true. He didn't know which carols they were himself. He knew which they *weren't*—Bobbo had explicitly instructed Heather Hathaway to research famous songs that were not under current copyright, so he and FUN-TV could avoid paying performance royalties to their owners. Even with the money from LastLong Toy Company in the bank, Bobbo couldn't break many of the penurious habits he'd developed during FUN-TV's recent tough financial times.

"Do we have to stand around while the other Santas are singing?" my pal Zonk asked. "I have to go to the Little Santa's room, if you know what I mean." There were murmurs of agreement from the rest of us.

"If you hurry," Felix said. "Now, we drew the singing order at random. It'll be Santa 4 first, then 8, 6, 3, 5, 1, 10, and 9. It's posted right over there on that blackboard if you forget."

Backstage, there was a sudden flurry of activity as stagehands hauled out a long table and three immense padded chairs.

"What are those for?" one of the Santas asked.

"Never mind," Felix said quickly. "It's the surprise Bobbo's been promising since he first announced *The Great Santa Search*. None of us knew what it was until a minute ago. You'll find out soon enough." I knew my old friend very well, and could sense a certain apologetic tone. "Just remember this is *reality* TV," he added, and hurried away without elaborating further.

"One minute to the first singing Santa," a stagehand said, and Luis from Miami began frantically clearing his throat. I was scheduled to be third. Zonk had hurried off to our dressing room, so I knew the bathroom there would be in use. Besides, I was curious to see how the other Santas performed, so I stayed just offstage to watch. I had little hope my own singing would be much more than adequate. This challenge would, I thought, be my closest call.

Onstage, Bobbo was explaining the rules of the singing challenge, and how audience members would vote.

"You'll find a small console built into the right armrest of your seat," he said. "For this challenge, and for the last one when you'll also vote, these consoles will be activated and a small light will appear up at the top. See it?" Apparently they did. "Now, there are ten clearly numbered buttons on the console. As Santas are eliminated, their individual buttons are deactivated. Right now, you can no longer vote for Santa 2 or Santa 7, because they're already out. After our eight remaining Santas have sung the carols that they will select completely at random, we'll ask each member of the studio audience to vote in support of one Santa by pressing his numbered button on their consoles. Just push *one* button for the Santa whose performance you think was best. Then, if the folks in the studio will watch the monitors on their right, and everyone at home watches the bottom on their television screens, the vote totals will appear in seconds. The Santa with the fewest votes is eliminated. The other seven go on. Got it?"

They did; there was a burst of applause.

"And now, just before our first singing Santa comes out, we've got a big surprise," Bobbo announced. "You're going to be amazed at what's happening next."

Based on the audience's reaction, he wasn't exaggerating.

Nineteen

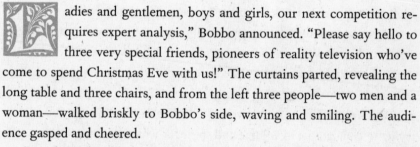adies and gentlemen, boys and girls, our next competition re-
quires expert analysis," Bobbo announced. "Please say hello to
three very special friends, pioneers of reality television who've
come to spend Christmas Eve with us!" The curtains parted, revealing the
long table and three chairs, and from the left three people—two men and a
woman—walked briskly to Bobbo's side, waving and smiling. The audience gasped and cheered.

"Yes!" Bobbo shouted. "Our Santas are going to sing. And if they
are, who better to critique their performances for you than, straight from
American Idol, none other than Randy Jackson, Paula Abdul, and Simon
Cowell!"

I'd heard of *American Idol,* though I'd never actually watched the program. I knew it involved young would-be singing stars who performed
popular songs and were periodically eliminated by viewer vote until one
winner remained.

Bobbo traded a few quips with his guests. Randy, a rangy fellow wearing glasses and a diamond stud in one earlobe, said he couldn't wait "to hear
Santa gettin' down, 'cause he's gonna be da bomb!" I had no idea what that

meant. Paula, who I felt had a lovely smile, remarked that when she was a little girl, she couldn't wait to get up on Christmas morning to see what Santa had brought her.

"And I still can't," she added breathlessly. "Maybe this year, he'll bring me a doll!" She was obviously a true believer, at the very least.

I was puzzled by the audience's reaction when Simon, who seemed pleasant enough, commented that "Santa will get a fair chance to prove himself. I'm prepared to be convinced—or not." They booed, and I thought some of the booing sounded less than good-natured.

"If you'll take your seats," Bobbo suggested, and they sat behind the table. Randy was on the left, Paula in the middle, and Simon on the right.

Bobbo quickly reiterated how audience members should vote.

"Please wait to select the best singing Santa until *all* our finalists have performed," he stressed. "And I should note that all eight songs have been selected at random from among the most popular Christmas tunes of all time."

Backstage, Santa 1—Andy from Chicago—tugged at Felix's sleeve.

"What *key* will the backing tapes be in?" he asked. "Can you at least give us some idea of *tempo?*"

"Bobbo wants spontaneity," Felix replied. "All I can tell you is, just do your best."

I was, frankly, nervous. I have never been able to sing very well, always trying to compensate in volume and spirit for whatever I might lack in talent. At least most of the other finalists seemed equally worried. Jimmy Lee, still standing somewhat apart, was the only one who appeared unconcerned.

"Let's go," Bobbo commanded. "Again, our finalists are performing in the order determined by a backstage draw. Here's Santa 4!" Luis from Miami walked onstage. Small tables had been set on either side of where Bobbo stood. Luis reached into a colorful drum resting on the first one and took out a slip of paper, which he handed to Bobbo, who then picked up a lyric sheet from the other table and handed it to Luis.

"Santa 4 will sing 'Up On the Housetop'!" Bobbo announced. He walked quickly offstage. Behind the table, the three *American Idol* judges leaned forward.

The moment Bobbo was offstage, recorded music began to play. Taking a deep, desperate breath, Luis started singing, his eyes frantically darting across the lyric sheet clutched in his hand:

"Up on the housetop reindeer pause, out jumps good old Santa Claus,
Down through the chimney with lots of toys,
All for the little ones' Christmas joys.
Ho, ho, ho, who wouldn't go
Ho, ho, ho, who wouldn't go
Up on the housetop, click, click, click,
Down through the chimney with good Saint Nick?"

Halfway through his song, Luis managed to tear his eyes away from the lyric sheet. He looked out at the audience and began to move awkwardly to the music, and as he did Paula Abdul jumped up from her chair and began to dance, too. As she did, the audience began to clap, and Luis, who was staring out at them and didn't see Paula, assumed the applause was for him. He began singing much louder, and when he finished the second verse the music abruptly cut off. Luis bowed and grinned.

Bobbo came back onstage.

"*American Idol* judges, what did you think?" he asked.

Randy went first.

"Well, Mr. Claus Number 4 sure was *feeling* the music," he remarked. "Gotta give the ol' guy that. But it's one thing to move and another to dance, you know? Props more for effort than performance."

"I think Santa 4 sounded very genuine and sweet," Paula enthused. "Bravo."

Then Simon cleared his throat.

"That was absolutely awful," he declared. "The reindeer would have done better."

Luis looked shocked.

"Thank you, Santa 4," Bobbo said hastily. "And now, Santa 8."

Zonk walked onstage as Luis was walking off. He plucked a slip of paper from the drum and handed it to Bobbo.

"Santa 8 is singing 'Deck the Halls,'" Bobbo said. He tried to hand Zonk a lyric sheet, but my dressing-room friend waved it off.

"We sing this all the time at the North Pole," he explained, and the comment earned him considerable applause from the audience.

When the music started, Zonk began singing:

"Deck the halls with boughs of holly
Fa-la-la-la-la, la-la-la-la
'Tis the season to be jolly
Fa-la-la-la-la, la-la-la-la"

I thought he sang quite well. His enthusiasm was obvious. When he was through, Randy pronounced him "a little pitchy, but still *alllll* right." Paula said he deserved a hug, and scampered over to give him one. Simon grumbled that "it was nothing special, but still a vast improvement over that first incompetent."

Then it was my turn. I took a slip of paper from the drum and handed it to Bobbo. He glanced at it, grinned, and said, "Santa 6 is going to sing one of the most traditional holiday favorites—'Jingle Bells'!" He handed me a lyric sheet.

I felt slightly better. At least this was a carol I knew by heart. I moved to the center of the stage. A single hot spotlight shone on me. The music began.

Then I forgot the words.

That in itself was no cause for panic. After all, I had the lyric sheet in my hand. But as I tried to read it, the spotlight was directly in my eyes and I couldn't. So the music blared out and not one sound came from me. I frantically tried to shade my eyes so I could read the lyrics. I sensed as much as heard concerned murmuring from the audience. It was an awful moment.

"Wait," Bobbo Butler snapped. "Can we dim that spotlight a little? It's blinding Santa 6." The light switched off. After a moment, my eyes could focus again. "This is what happens on live television, folks," Bobbo explained. "Is it all right if we start Santa 6's music again and give him another chance?" There were scattered shouts of agreement. I looked at the lyrics, and they were instantly familiar.

The music began to play for the second time, and I was ready:

"Dashing through the snow
In a one-horse open sleigh,
Over the fields we go
Laughing all the way;
Bells on bobtail ring,
Making spirits bright,
What fun it is to ride and sing
A sleighing song tonight!
Oh, jingle bells, jingle bells,
Jingle all the way!
Oh, what fun it is to ride
In a one-horse open sleigh!"

Now the problem was that I was singing spectacularly off-key, and knew it. For centuries all my dear North Pole companions routinely suggested I *hum* rather than sing whenever we gathered by the fire to enjoy performing Christmas carols. But that wasn't an option on the Ed Sullivan Theater stage. The harder I tried to sing well, the worse I sounded.

I thought about simply quitting in mid-song, but then I would have been disqualified. So I sang the second verse about the sleigh driver and Miss Fanny Bright getting dumped in a snowbank, and even though they "got all sot," or wet, they still were singing "Jingle Bells" at the top of their lungs, and so was I. As I sang, I acted out the sleigh's overturning, and when I hit some particularly unpleasant notes I rolled my eyes to indicate to the audience that I was fully aware of my abysmal vocalizing.

After what seemed like hours, I finished the second chorus and the music stopped. The audience applauded—a lovely gesture, I felt, after what they'd just had to listen to. I tried to smile, but I felt certain I had just eliminated myself from the competition.

"*American Idol* judges?" Bobbo inquired.

Randy looked at me, his lips pursed sympathetically.

"It takes some guts to keep on going," he mused. "Good for you, dawg. But if Santa's gotta sing well, we all know you're not him. Maybe you got other more important talents. Just don't ever sing again when I gotta listen, okay?"

Paula blew me a kiss.

"I don't care if he was on-key or not," she told the audience. "It was like listening to your grandpa or favorite uncle when the whole family is gathered 'round the tree. Everybody knows he can't sing on-key and nobody cares. Santa 6, you can sing Christmas carols to me anytime."

Then it was Simon's turn.

"That was totally pathetic," he declared. "The horrible off-key yowling aside, I didn't even detect any genuine Christmas spirit. In no way did you convince me that you might be Santa Claus. The bloody Easter Bunny could have done better." He waved his hand dismissively.

The audience began to boo—at Simon, I felt, not at me. He, in turn, grinned and informed them, "I'm just being honest."

I was still looking at Simon when I was bumped from behind.

"Out of my way," Jimmy Lee hissed as he brushed by me. His nasty tone was in direct contrast to the wide smile on his face, which he had turned toward the audience. I made my slow, sad way offstage, where Zonk clapped me on the shoulder and several of my other fellow competitors muttered encouraging things. I could tell, though, that they were also relieved after my awful showing. It seemed obvious which Santa finalist would soon be eliminated.

Jimmy Lee drew his slip, handed it to Bobbo, and beamed when informed he would sing "O Christmas Tree." Strolling confidently to center stage, he placed a hand over his heart and sang in an undeniably wonderful baritone voice:

> "*O Christmas tree, O Christmas tree,*
> *How steadfast are your branches!*
> *Your boughs are green in summer's clime,*

And through the snows of wintertime.
O Christmas tree, O Christmas tree,
How steadfast are your branches!"

It wasn't just that Jimmy Lee sang perfectly on-key. His voice throbbed with great emotion. He made it clear he unapologetically *loved* his Christmas tree. I knew all the bad things about him, and still his singing moved me deeply.

And then, beginning the second verse, Jimmy Lee did something unexpected. He switched from English to German:

"O Tannenbaum, O Tannenbaum,
Wie treu sind deine blätter!
Du grünst nicht nur zur Sommerzeit,
Nein auch im winter, wenn es schneit.
O Tannenbaum, O Tannenbaum,
Wie treu sind deine blätter!"

The music stopped. Jimmy Lee was no longer singing, but Bobbo seemed spellbound. So did the audience. It was Jimmy Lee himself who finally broke the silence.

"I repeated the first verse in German rather than singing the second in English," he explained. "I hope that was all right. I especially wanted all the little ones to remember that Christmas is a holiday celebrated all over the world, not just in America. 'O Christmas Tree' was originally written and sung in German. So I tried to pay tribute to that."

Everyone seated in the theater rose as one. Their applause and cheers were deafening.

The *American Idol* judges were on their feet, too.

"That's it, get the sleigh and let the Big Dawg ride!" Randy shouted. "We got international Santa excellence here!"

Paula appeared to be wiping tears from her eyes.

"You took my breath away," she gushed. "Wow. That's all I can say. Wow."

As for Simon, he dashed across the stage to shake Jimmy Lee's hand.

"You are the one to beat in this contest," he declared. "You made me believe every word you sang, and I swear you made me believe in *you*."

Jimmy Lee was the picture of modesty as he smiled, waved to the audience, and walked offstage. He brushed past the rest of us finalists. Lucretia Pepper, not even feigning neutrality, hurried over to embrace him.

"Wonderful," she cooed. "Just *wonderful!*"

"Somebody get me some water," Jimmy Lee demanded, and a half dozen different stagehands scampered off to do his bidding. When the first one returned with a frosty plastic bottle, Jimmy Lee took a huge swig and handed the bottle back without a word of thanks. Then he marched off toward his dressing room, Lucretia Pepper at his side.

Onstage, Santa 5—Buck from Kansas City—was performing a credible rendition of "The Holly and the Ivy," but the audience's attention seemed listless at best. The *American Idol* judges tried to act enthusiastic with him and the other remaining contestants. But they, too, clearly believed they'd already heard the best performance. Standing offstage, I was extremely discouraged and expected the upcoming vote to go against me.

I felt a light tap on my shoulder and turned to see Felix.

"He was something, wasn't he?" my old friend remarked.

"It's bad enough I'm about to be eliminated, but it's worse that Jimmy Lee was so good," I replied. "The audience loves him. After this, who else has a chance to win?"

"The next three events don't involve voting," Felix reminded me. "They're skill competitions. Maybe he'll be terrible at chimney-sliding or stocking-stuffing or cookie-eating and eliminate himself."

"Remember, he and Lucretia Pepper are going to cheat in stocking-stuffing and cookie-eating," I reminded him.

Felix grinned.

"Maybe they think they are, but we're going to stop them," he said. "Willie Skokan and Heather Hathaway are ready to go. Say, those two have become instant friends. It turns out Heather likes to build and repair things. They have a lot in common."

Meanwhile, Santa 1, Andy from Chicago, sang "We Wish You a Merry

Christmas." Santa 10, Joe from Bloomington, his bulging belly vibrating visibly, charmed everyone with "Jolly Old St. Nicholas." If Jimmy Lee's performance hadn't been so spectacular, Santa 10 might have earned a standing ovation.

"That does it," I muttered to Felix. "Nobody will sing as badly as me. I'm gone."

"We haven't heard the last Santa yet," Felix cautioned. "He might be worse than you."

"Hardly," I grumbled. "It's Santa 9, Wesley from St. Paul. You found him in a play there, remember? He probably sings as well as Jimmy Lee."

Santa 9 practically bounded out onstage. He clapped his hands when Bobbo said he'd be singing "The Twelve Days of Christmas"—"but only the first five days, actually! It's already almost nine o'clock!" Clearly, this Santa finalist's experience in theater was helping him avoid the stage fright that the rest of us, except for Jimmy Lee, were suffering.

The music began. Santa 9 sang.

"On the first day of Christmas my true love sent to me,
A partridge in a pear tree.
On the second day of Christmas my true love sent to me,
Two turtle doves,
And a partridge in a pear tree."

I have never actually heard fingernails being scraped across a chalkboard. But I am willing to wager that Santa 9's singing ranked high among the most noxious, horrible sounds ever emitted in human history. Members of the audience cringed and covered their ears. From his place at the *American Idol* judges' table, Simon Cowell yelped, "Stop! Please! I'll pay anything!" But Santa 9 seemed oblivious. He kept right on, putting special, if ear-splitting, emphasis on the drawn-out *"Five . . . golden . . . riiiiiiings!"*

When he was finally finished, all Randy had to say was, "Huh." Paula seemed lost in thought, apparently trying to come up with any sort of positive comment. She settled for, "I'll remember that as long as I live." Simon commented, "You have just made Santa what's-his-name, Santa 6, seem tuneful by comparison."

Bobbo called all eight remaining finalists back onstage. The applause was loudest by far for Jimmy Lee. The audience was reminded how to vote, pushing just one button whose number corresponded with the number of their favorite singing Santa. The results were almost instantly flashed on monitors all around the theater. Those of us onstage could see the totals clearly. There were 461 possible votes, since there were that many seats in the theater. Jimmy Lee, Santa 3, got 410. Joe, Santa 10, was second with twenty-seven. Santas 4, 8, 5, and 1 each had five. I received four—not coincidentally, the number of North Pole friends I had in the audience—and Wesley, Santa 9, got none. He was eliminated.

"Did you know he was such a terrible singer?" I asked Felix as Bobbo called Wesley back for a farewell bow. The same audience whose vote had just eliminated him responded with a rousing ovation. "Was that why you picked him?"

"Not really," my old friend replied. "Look, the play he was in wasn't a musical. How was I supposed to know he was a worse singer than you? Although, I guess there had to be one somewhere."

I had my doubts, and would have pressed Felix further, but he loudly announced to everyone backstage that it was time to get ready for the chimney-sliding challenge. With *The Great Santa Search* almost half over, I still had a chance to keep the name Santa Claus from becoming synonymous with "terrible toys." Jimmy Lee and Lucretia Pepper hadn't won yet!

ary Rogers sent someone down from the control booth to tell the remaining Santa finalists there would be approximately a five-minute break before the next challenge commenced. That much time would be needed to prepare the elaborate chimney-sliding set. We could go back to our dressing rooms for a brief bathroom break or just to sit down and catch our breaths. The FUN-TV interns would fetch us when we were needed.

As I made my way toward the dressing room I shared with Zonk, I passed Willie Skokan and tall, serious-looking Heather Hathaway. They were bent over a large canvas sack full of toys—a sack, I knew, that contained all the LastLong products I'd purchased the day before at the Galaxy Mall in Cleveland. It rested among six other sacks that looked exactly the same.

"We're making sure you get the right one," Willie whispered. "After the chimney-sliding, you'll keep the same sack for stocking-stuffing." Beside him, Heather looked momentarily puzzled.

"I still don't understand why Santa 6 needs *this* sack," she said to Willie. He smiled at her, and I wondered why I'd never realized for so many centuries that Willie Skokan was, in his sweet, simple way, a rather good-looking fellow.

"I'll explain after the program is over," he replied. "For now, trust me."

Heather smiled back. Before, I'd thought she looked pleasant enough. But now it seemed to me that she was quite pretty.

"For some reason, I do," she assured Willie. As I continued toward my dressing room I wondered if the pressure of competing on *The Great Santa Search* was somehow causing me to find everyone attractive, but then I passed Lucretia Pepper and knew that wasn't the case. The expression on her broad, blunt-featured face was ferocious. I had the impression of a particularly savage lioness about to devour her prey.

As I walked into our dressing room, Zonk was in the process of eating my unfinished chicken-salad sandwich.

"You don't mind, do you?" he mumbled, his mouth full. "All this competing business made me hungry."

"Maybe you ought to remain hungry," I suggested. "We've got that cookie-eating challenge coming up."

Zonk shrugged and took another huge bite of sandwich.

"Nah, I'm one of those people who can eat all day," he said. "It's crazy, I know, especially since I can't taste anything."

It seemed it hadn't even been a few moments, let alone five minutes, before we were summoned by Emily the intern. Bobbo had filled the time needed for changing the set by introducing various celebrities in the audience—Oprah Winfrey got the most applause, which seemed to annoy David Letterman—and reminding everyone about the generous decision by sponsor LastLong Toys to let the program be broadcast without commercial interruption.

We remaining Santa candidates clustered around Felix. He announced the random order in which the seven remaining finalists would participate in the chimney-sliding challenge: 5, 3, 10, 8, 4, 6, 1. Jimmy Lee would be second, and I would be sixth.

"You can see how it's all set up behind the curtain," Felix said. "The idea is to simulate actually getting out of the sleigh, carrying a sack of toys across a rooftop, then holding the sack as you slide down the chimney. So, each in turn, you'll take a sack of toys—they're right over there—and climb that ladder up to where the sleigh is suspended. Put the sack of toys in the back of the sleigh and climb on the seat in front. You won't be on camera until you're actually in the sleigh, which will then seem to float onstage to the roof of the set. As the sleigh reaches the roof, get off and take the sack of toys. Walk across the roof—you can see it's just going to be a few feet—and, making sure to hang on to the toy sack, position yourself in the chimney and slide down. Don't worry about falling straight down and hurting yourself. We've got the inside of the chimney curved, like the slide on a playground. The clock will start timing you as soon as the sleigh appears by the roof. You're done when you come out of the chimney into the part of the set that looks like a living room. The side of the chimney facing the studio audience is Plexiglas, so they can see you the whole way down. So will the TV audience. When you're done, come offstage with your toy sack. You'll need it for the next challenge, which is stocking-stuffing. The two slowest Santas in chimney-sliding will be eliminated. Questions?"

There weren't any. Santa 5, Buck from Kansas City, went first. Someone took him over to where the seven canvas sacks of toys had been piled. Heather Hathaway stood over my special one, while Willie Skokan helpfully picked up a different sack and handed it to him. I noticed that Lucretia Pepper had placed herself by the toy sacks, too. Just as Willie and Heather were making sure I got the right one, she was there to see Jimmy Lee took possession of his special sack.

"All right, on to our third challenge," Bobbo announced. "We've told you this competition is designed to roughly parallel Santa's actual schedule on Christmas Eve. So far he's roped the reindeer and sung some carols. Now it's time for him to get down to work. Santa's loaded his sleigh, and he's flying through the cold winter sky, all ready to land on that first roof and slide down its chimney. Why, I think he's coming now!"

The curtains parted, and the crowd gasped. Their reaction was appropriate, because they were looking at one of the most dazzling sets ever created. The high roof looked absolutely real, extending two-thirds of the way from one side of the stage to the other. Its chimney was high and wide. Beneath was a wonderful living room, where the mouth of the fireplace stretched fully six feet. The Plexiglas chimney wall extended above to the rooftop. Empty stockings dangled in front of the fireplace. On one side of the room was a large green Christmas tree festooned with colorful lights. It was all quite lovely.

High above the left-hand side of the stage, a golden sleigh with sparkling side panels was hydraulically pulled to the roof.

"It's Santa 5," Bobbo announced, and monitors began to record passing seconds as Buck from Kansas City gingerly eased himself off the front seat. I couldn't blame him for feeling uncomfortable. Even faux roofs can seem very high if you're trying to balance on them.

As the audience cheered, Santa 5 carefully inched to the back of the sleigh, where he picked up the sack of toys. He tried slinging the sack over his shoulder, but the sudden weight shift made him wobble. For a moment it looked like he might tumble off the roof completely—Robert, the set designer, had placed thick, pillowy cushions all around in case of just such an accident—but then regained his balance. Moving very deliberately, he tiptoed to the chimney and laboriously settled himself over the opening. He then made the mistake of lowering the toy sack ahead of him as he slid. As a result, the sack hit the bottom of the fireplace first, followed by Santa 5's seat smacking squarely onto the sack, crushing most of the toys in it. The sound of cracking plastic echoed through the theater.

"Santa 5's time in the chimney-slide is one minute, forty-eight seconds," Bobbo announced. Santa 5 got to his feet and remembered to take the sack of smashed toys with him as he limped off the set.

While Santa 5 had been sliding and smashing, the sleigh had been hydraulically pulled back offstage. Jimmy Lee walked over to the toy sacks. Lucretia Pepper pointed to one, which he picked up. Then he climbed the ladder, carefully placed the sack in the sleigh, and took his seat in front just as Santa 5 made his shamefaced way backstage.

"It's Santa 3," Bobbo shouted, and as Jimmy Lee came into view there was prolonged cheering. This time, though, he was competent rather than memorable. He got out of the sleigh, picked up his sack of toys, eased his cautious but steady way across the roof, made certain to hold the toy sack over his head as he slid, and recorded a time of 1:25. The only flaw in his performance involved his hat, which had been jarred slightly during his chimney descent and flopped comically over his left eye. Jimmy Lee impatiently straightened it, smiling all the while.

Things did not go as smoothly for Santa 10. Joe from Bloomington was severely overweight. He had trouble just climbing the backstage ladder to the sleigh, and when he took his seat in the front his bulk caused the conveyance to tip precariously forward. When the sleigh creaked into view, its front end pointed almost directly down, many of the audience members began to laugh.

Santa 10 had trouble just extricating himself from the front seat. When he finally did, he successfully retrieved his sack of toys, but had tremendous difficulty balancing as he tried to cross the roof to the chimney. When he settled his bulk over the opening of the chimney, his legs and seat slid down but the rest of him didn't. I knew what had happened. He was stuck. He wriggled frantically as perhaps thirty seconds passed, and then finally threw up his hands in surrender.

"Santa 10 is, I think, resigning from the competition," Bobbo announced. "Let's go ahead and close the curtain for a moment so we can help Santa 10 out of the chimney." The curtains shut, and while Bobbo reminded viewers that live television will have its unexpected moments, members of the stage crew tugged until Santa 10 was unwedged. He stumbled down the ladder and went directly to his dressing room.

My friend Zonk was next. He was a theatrical chimney-slider, to the point of pausing on the edge of the chimney, facing the TV cameras, and deliberately placing his finger beside his nose before sliding down. It was a slight mistake; in my old friend Clement Moore's epic poem, St. Nicholas placed his finger beside his nose before soaring back *up* the chimney after delivering his gifts. But Zonk's intended tribute to the epic Christmas poem was clear, and there was considerable applause when Bobbo announced that Santa 8's time was 1:19, the best so far.

It was certainly better than Santa 4 could do. Luis from Miami was able to climb out of the sleigh and take up his sack of toys without much trouble, but when he approached the chimney he circled it, examining it from all possible angles, while the clock ticked away. His overall time was two minutes exactly.

"Why were you moving so slowly?" Zonk demanded when Luis came backstage.

"I'm from Florida," he replied. "We don't have chimneys there."

Now it was my turn.

I walked over to the pair of remaining toy sacks. Willie Skokan gestured toward one and winked. I picked up the sack Willie had indicated and went to the ladder. Some of the other finalists had trouble climbing the ladder while holding on to their sacks of toys, but I didn't. Once I reached the top, I put the sack in the back of the sleigh. Despite its glittering gold side panels, the sleigh would not have impressed Leonardo. He would have pointed out that the bed of the sleigh was too wide (bad aerodynamics), the runners underneath were too short (insufficient traction), and the front bench had no seat belt (Santa never flies without his seat belt being securely fastened). But I climbed on the front bench and immediately there was a slight lurch as the hydraulic system was engaged to pull the sleigh over to the roof. I blinked in the sudden harsh light; once over the stage, the spotlights held me in their beam.

Below me Bobbo said, "And now, here's Santa 6." There was a reasonably warm crowd response. Though they all clapped for every finalist, the majority clearly reserved their highest regard for Jimmy Lee. A moment later the sled bumped onto the false roof. Without hesitation I hopped out. I knew exactly how to keep my balance. In one sure, confident motion I pulled the toy sack from the sleigh, hoisted it over my shoulder, and turned. From there it took only three quick steps to reach the chimney. Shifting the toy sack higher on my back, I swung my legs over the side of the chimney, made certain to bring my heels together so my feet wouldn't separate and slow my progress (a typical mistake by novices), and slid down smoothly. I had a brief, distorted glimpse of the theater audience through the Plexiglas; then my boots thumped comfortably down on the floor of the fireplace. I stepped out onto the living-room set with the toy sack in perfect position on my shoulder and my long tassled cap perched at a jaunty angle on my head. I couldn't help peeking offstage. Jimmy Lee was staring intently. I allowed myself a slight nod in his direction, then waved to the cheering audience.

"And Santa 6 is down the chimney in twenty-four seconds!" Bobbo enthused. "If there was a previous world record, I believe Santa 6 may have broken it!"

Layla later suggested that I strutted as I left the stage. I'm sure I didn't, but I admit it felt uplifting to have performed so well. Of course, I had an advantage the other six finalists didn't. I'd been sliding down chimneys since they were first invented almost five hundred years earlier.

Emily the intern greeted me backstage.

"That was totally awesome," she declared. "You can put your toy sack over there until the next challenge."

"Thank you, but I think I'll just hold on to it," I replied. I noticed that Jimmy Lee was also carefully clutching his bag, which Lucretia Pepper had undoubtedly made certain was full of sturdily constructed toys. He glared at me. I smiled in return.

While Santa 1, Andy from Chicago, took the last turn in the chimney-sliding challenge, I noticed Felix, Buck from Kansas City, and Lucretia Pepper engaged in a hushed but heated debate. I edged over to listen.

"Santa 5 has to keep his chimney-sliding sack of toys for use in the stocking-stuffing competition," Lucretia Pepper snapped. "Those are the rules."

"But a lot of them broke when I sat on them coming down the chimney," Buck protested. "Broken toys will count against me in stocking-stuffing. Unless I substitute unbroken ones for these, I'm going to lose."

"Surely it won't hurt to let him use unbroken toys," Felix said. "That's only fair."

"Following the rules is fair," Lucretia Pepper replied. "It's too bad Santa 5 broke some of his toys. But he's going to follow the rules. If he loses in stocking-stuffing because of a mistake in chimney-sliding, that's the way the Christmas cookie crumbles. I'm sorry." She didn't sound sorry at all.

Santa 1 completed his chimney-sliding in 1:41. Bobbo declared that Santa 4 and Santa 10 had been eliminated, and asked them to come back out onstage for a final bow. Santa 4, Luis, did, but rotund Santa 10 never emerged from backstage. Joe had changed clothes and left immediately for Bloomington, and I never saw him again. I regretted that, because he seemed to love Christmas very much, and he sang "Jolly Old St. Nicholas" quite well.

"We're down to our last five Santas," Bobbo announced. "Let's ask them to all come back out onstage." We trooped out, each carrying a toy sack. "The real Mr. Claus is either Santa 1, Santa 3"—there was another ovation for Jimmy Lee, but not quite as enthusiastic as before—"Santa 5, Santa 6"—there was another chorus of cheers, which thrilled me; the cheers weren't quite as loud as Jimmy Lee's, but I was certainly making up ground in popularity with the voters in the theater—"and Santa 8."

Bobbo looked meaningfully at the clock on the theater wall.

"It's now ten minutes after nine, so we have less than an hour to identify the real Santa Claus and send him on his Christmas Eve way. Fortunately, we can start our next challenge almost immediately. Can you guess what it is? Santa's come down the chimney, and now he's got to fill stockings in a hurry so he can move on to the next house. So, remaining Santa finalists, get ready. It's time for . . . *stocking-stuffing!*"

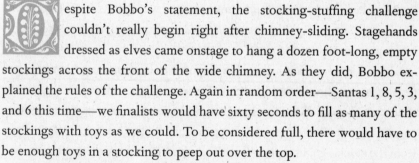 espite Bobbo's statement, the stocking-stuffing challenge couldn't really begin right after chimney-sliding. Stagehands dressed as elves came onstage to hang a dozen foot-long, empty stockings across the front of the wide chimney. As they did, Bobbo explained the rules of the challenge. Again in random order—Santas 1, 8, 5, 3, and 6 this time—we finalists would have sixty seconds to fill as many of the stockings with toys as we could. To be considered full, there would have to be enough toys in a stocking to peep out over the top.

"There's one more catch," Bobbo said. "If any stocking contains a broken toy, it will not count toward that Santa's final total. Even one broken item disqualifies its stocking. So our Santas need to be very careful. At the conclusion of each finalist's turn, the toys in his filled stockings will be examined by none other than . . . the president of LastLong Toy Company herself, Lucretia Pepper!" That large, unpleasant woman made her way onstage.

"I'll keep everything absolutely fair and square, Bobbo," she promised, and I reflected how liars frequently claim they are doing one thing while doing exactly the opposite. With Lucretia Pepper as judge, Jimmy Lee didn't have to worry about succeeding in this fourth challenge.

He knew that, of course. As Santa 1, Andy from Chicago, carried his toy sack onstage and waited for Bobbo's signal to begin, Jimmy Lee actually sidled up to where I stood watching in the wings.

"You're a pretty good chimney slider," he remarked. In group meetings and onstage, his voice had been clear and unaccented. But I noticed that, with no audience other than me, he had a pronounced southern drawl. "Not bad on the reindeer-roping, either. It's a real shame you can't sing."

"At least I managed well enough so that I wasn't eliminated," I replied, watching as Bobbo snapped out a command to start the clock and Santa 1 began frantically pulling LastLong toys out of his sack and stuffing them in the first stocking. It was difficult if not impossible to keep them from breaking. The toys in the sack were comprised of tiny LastLong dolls and so-called "action figures." As was typical with that company's products, their spindly arms and legs were not securely joined to their bodies. The slightest pressure could detach plastic limbs in much the same way the dried wishbone of a roast chicken or turkey can be snapped with very little effort.

"You heard how much louder my applause was than yours," Jimmy Lee continued. "Even if you're the other one left at the end, no way you're going to get more votes than me."

I shook my head slightly, not in response to his comment but in sympathy for the onstage plight of Santa 1. Try as he might, it was proving impossible to stuff more than a few LastLong items in a stocking without breaking part of one off. Every time that happened, he had to extract the broken toy from the stocking and replace it with another. The clock on the theater wall included a prominent second hand, and as the end of his sixty-second turn approached, the audience began to chant, *"Ten—nine—eight—seven—"* which only ratcheted the tension higher. When Santa 1's time was up, loud jingle-bell chimes sounded.

"Thank you, Santa 1," Bobbo cried. "Lucretia Pepper of LastLong Toys, please take a close look and tell us Santa 1's stocking total."

While Santa 1 looked on unhappily, she removed and inspected in turn each of the stockings in which he had placed toys.

"Santa 1's total is three stockings, Bobbo," she announced. "No, wait.

There's a leg missing from a doll in this one. Santa 1 was clumsy. His final total is two."

"Who knows, Santa 1? That might be good enough to win," Bobbo said cheerfully. "All right, then. You wait offstage. It's time for Santa 8."

My dressing-room friend Zonk was one of those husky men who is actually quite nimble. I consider myself much the same. In any event, he literally bounded onstage with his sack of toys and waited for Bobbo to give the signal to start.

"This guy's a showman," Jimmy Lee observed as Bobbo barked out the command to begin and Zonk hustled over to where the stockings were hung by the false fireplace. "If he didn't have to go up against me, he might convince the voters *he* was Santa. But that's not going to happen."

"You have your reasons for feeling so confident," I responded, and Jimmy Lee's eyes narrowed. I could tell he was wondering what I meant by that. "But don't underestimate Santa 8."

Santa 1 had broken too many flimsy LastLong toys by cramming them in the stockings as fast as he could. Zonk had watched and learned. His stocking-stuffing pace was much more deliberate. He extracted one small doll or action figure at a time from his sack of toys, and inserted them very gently until a stocking was just full enough to be counted.

"I'll go faster than that," Jimmy Lee boasted. "None of my toys will break, either. Don't get your hopes up, pal. That million dollars from Last-Long Toys is going to be mine."

"You're really going to settle for just a million dollars?" someone asked, and Jimmy Lee and I, both startled, whirled around to see Heather Hathaway standing beside us, with Willie Skokan just behind her. I'd been so preoccupied with watching Zonk, and Jimmy Lee had been so intent on trying to intimidate me, that we hadn't noticed them.

Heather's question had been posed in a very conversational tone. When Jimmy Lee looked puzzled, she continued matter-of-factly, "If somebody smart wins *The Great Santa Search*, a million dollars from LastLong Toys would be nothing, compared to what he could have made. But I guess you've thought of that."

"What are you talking about?" Jimmy Lee demanded.

Heather shrugged.

"Oh, I just meant that for a million dollars, LastLong Toys would be getting the winner cheap," she said. "That Lucretia Pepper is sure to insist on a contract that doesn't let him appear as Santa Claus for anyone else. He'll be stuck doing commercials and appearances for her company. Too bad."

"Stuck?" Jimmy Lee asked. "What do you mean, 'stuck'?"

Onstage, the seconds ticked down and the audience shouted, "Ten—nine—eight—seven" as Zonk placed toys in a final stocking. The jingle-bell chimes sounded, Bobbo called in Lucretia Pepper to inspect Zonk's work, and Jimmy Lee was oblivious to anything other than his conversation with Heather. She, in turn, seemed quite fascinated by everything onstage, and Jimmy Lee had to ask several more times what she meant by "stuck" before she turned her attention back to him.

"It's just that there would be so many other opportunities to make a lot more than a million dollars," Heather said. "Whoever wins here is going to instantly be one of the most famous people in America. *Everybody*'s going to want to hire him to make appearances and give speeches. He could even count on a movie deal."

"*Movies?*" Jimmy Lee gasped. "There could be movies?"

"Sure," Heather replied. "Oh, look! They say Santa 8 filled five stockings! That's great!"

"What about the movies?" Jimmy Lee persisted, but Heather now seemed occupied with whispering encouraging things to Santa 5, Buck from Kansas City, as he prepared to take his turn.

"Just concentrate on not breaking the toys, and don't think about anything else!" she advised. Santa 5 nodded nervously and went onstage just as Zonk, Santa 8, hustled off. Heather patted his shoulder and told him he'd done wonderfully well. Jimmy Lee twitched impatiently.

"Get back to the movies," he insisted.

"Isn't it obvious?" Heather said. "Don't you think a hundred producers are watching *The Great Santa Search* right now and telling themselves that whoever wins needs to star in a movie about Santa's life? Wouldn't that be natural? And they'd have to pay the winner a *ton* of money to do it, because he could just tell all of them to start bidding at two million dollars, or five million, or ten million, who knows? That is, he could tell them that if he wasn't already under contract to appear as Santa exclusively for LastLong Toys. I don't think Lucretia Pepper is someone who likes to share, do you?"

"No, she wouldn't share," Jimmy Lee said thoughtfully. "Ten million dollars to star in a movie, you say?"

"Oh, at least," Heather replied carelessly. "And that might be only the beginning. Eventually there could be a TV series. Look! Poor Santa 5's toys are all broken even before he's putting them in the stockings!"

Sadly, this was true. Santa 5 had squashed most of his toys when he sat on his sack during the chimney-sliding. He had no chance to stuff even one stocking full of unbroken items. The crowd counted down, and in the end Lucretia Pepper declared that Santa 5's total was none at all.

"But you've been a great competitor and we wish you all the best, Santa 5," Bobbo assured him as he made his sorrowful way offstage. "With two more finalists to go, Santa 8's five stuffed stockings is the total to beat, and Santa 1 hopes his total of two is good enough to squeak through. We'll have to see. And now, here's Santa 3!"

The rest of us shifted aside so Jimmy Lee could have an unobstructed path onstage, but he didn't move. He seemed lost in thought. After a few moments, Bobbo repeated, "Santa 3 is the next finalist. Let's go, Santa 3!"

"They're calling you," I whispered, and nudged Jimmy Lee in the ribs with perhaps a bit more emphasis than necessary. He blinked, looked out at Bobbo, snatched his bag of toys, and waved at the audience as he walked out.

I looked at Heather Hathaway, whose expression was one of exaggerated innocence.

"Those were some very interesting comments," I said. "I wonder how you thought of them."

Heather smiled.

"I've negotiated with lots of performers while I've worked for Bobbo," she said. "I just thought Santa 3 might want to consider a few things."

"He certainly seemed to be considering them," I said, and thought Sarah and Felix were exactly right—Heather Hathaway was an extremely intelligent, capable young woman.

Onstage, Jimmy Lee's sixty-second time limit had commenced. As he began to fill his first stocking, I saw that he had a different advantage than we'd suspected. It had been our belief that Lucretia Pepper would provide Jimmy Lee with dolls and action figures whose limbs were much more securely attached than those of typical LastLong toys. That would keep them from breaking as he stuffed them in the stockings at the fastest rate he could manage.

Instead, the toys Jimmy Lee extracted from his sack were larger, one-piece items—plastic cars and flutes and shovels. Not only were they virtually unbreakable, they were bulky as well. Three or four could and did easily fill a single stocking. Jimmy Lee sailed down the line of stockings along the fireplace mantel, and by the time the crowd counted down, Bobbo called a halt, and Lucretia Pepper inspected, Santa 3's final total was eleven.

"We had only twelve stockings available," Bobbo observed. "If Santa 3 had a few more seconds, we would have had to bring out another dozen! Now we know how Santa can fill all the stockings in the world in just one night!"

Felix walked up. He told me not to be nervous, but that wasn't necessary. I wasn't nervous at all.

Jimmy Lee came offstage and immediately looked for Heather, who was nowhere to be seen. I knew she had gone with Willie Skokan to fetch the cookies to be used in the next competition.

"Where did that tall woman go?" Jimmy Lee asked me.

"I'm not sure," I replied. "And, if you'll excuse me, I think they want me onstage."

"Santa 3 was a stocking-stuffing machine," Bobbo said by way of greeting. "Do you think you can even come close to what he did, Santa 6?"

"I hope so, Bobbo," I replied. "Of course, I've had many more centuries of practice than Santa 3." This accurate comment earned cheers from the audience.

"Then let's see what you can do, Santa 6," Bobbo said. "Ready . . . set . . . *go*!"

There was never any question that in sixty seconds I could fill more stockings than Jimmy Lee or anyone else. As I'd learned seventeen centuries earlier, time was different for me than normal humans. Jimmy Lee had filled eleven stockings in one minute. If necessary I could have filled eleven *hundred* in the same period.

But that wasn't necessary on *The Great Santa Search*. Since two of the five remaining finalists would be eliminated, and the low totals so far were Santa 1 with two filled stockings and Santa 5 with none, all I had to do in my own minute was fill three with unbroken toys, or twelve if I wanted to win the challenge outright. The fragility of LastLong toys didn't have to be factored in. Back at the North Pole, Willie Skokan and Leonardo had taken the items I'd bought at Galaxy Mall and secured every leg, arm, and head tightly to plastic bodies. That was why Willie and Heather Hathaway had been instructed to see I took the right bag of toys onstage.

So my real challenge in stocking-stuffing was to make a statement strong enough to impress the theater audience members who'd be voting soon, without demonstrating so much of my special power that they and the vast television audience would realize real magic was on display. I'd thought carefully about how to proceed and had a plan.

To all those watching in the theater or in their homes, it must have seemed that I rushed to the stockings. I actually had to remind myself to keep my usual Christmas Eve speed almost completely in check. As I'd done untold millions of times over the centuries, I opened my bag, took an empty stocking in my left hand, reached down and pulled out a toy, and then in one smooth motion eased it down into the very bottom of the stocking. I repeated this action five more times—you can fit a lot more into any Christmas stocking if you put in only one thing at a time—until the first stocking was stuffed. I returned it to its hook over the fireplace and took down the second. I filled it in turn, replaced it, did the same with the third, and kept going until all twelve were overflowing with toys and hung back in place. Then I turned to Bobbo, smiled, and gestured to indicate there were no stockings left to be filled.

"I'm sure your special judge won't find any broken toys in these," I said helpfully.

The crowd in the theater just went wild. Bobbo pointed to the clock.

"That took you only thirty seconds, Santa 6!" he announced. "Stupendous! Mind-boggling!"

"I haven't inspected the stockings yet," Lucretia Pepper snapped, and she stalked over to the fireplace, favoring me with an especially nasty glare on the way. I nodded pleasantly in return and strolled over to stand by Bobbo as she frantically pawed through the dozen stockings, looking for any reason to reduce my final total. I believe she might even have stooped to trying sneakily to break a toy or two in each, but the TV cameras were recording her every move and she couldn't.

"Twelve stockings," she finally acknowledged. More cheering erupted.

"Fantastic, Santa 6," Bobbo enthused. "Can we have all our finalists back onstage? Here they come. Well, we have to say good-bye to two more of you, and with no filled stockings and two, respectively, Santas 1 and 5 are eliminated. We've enjoyed meeting you, friends, and Merry Christmas."

Zonk, Jimmy Lee, and I were left standing there. Zonk leaned over and whacked me on the back.

"Great job!" he said. There were microphones placed everywhere, so his compliment was audible to the theater audience and the TV viewers. The crowd in the theater responded with applause because Zonk was being such a good sport. Jimmy Lee, mindful of the pending vote after the final challenge, had no choice but to congratulate me too.

"Well done," he remarked, and his voice was warm even though his expression wasn't.

"How about that?" Bobbo asked. "Our Santas are not only intense competitors, but friendly ones, too! Now, *that's* the real Christmas spirit!" There was more applause. I suspected everyone in the Ed Sullivan Theater would wake up on Christmas morning to find their palms sore and swollen from so much clapping.

"It's twenty-five minutes after nine, and time is flying," Bobbo continued. "We've got to hurry if the real Santa is going to have time to climb in his sleigh and get his Christmas Eve rounds completed tonight. Santas 3, 6, and 8 square off next in a contest that the true Mr. Claus is bound to love. Gentlemen, if you'll just wait offstage for a moment, we'll get set up for the fifth and next-to-last challenge."

The three of us made our way to the wings. Behind him, Bobbo left the curtains open so everyone could see the elf-costumed stagehands hauling three comfortable overstuffed chairs and a trio of long, low coffee tables out in front of the fireplace. As they did, Bobbo began explaining that Santa had roped his reindeer, sung his carols, slid down chimneys, and stuffed every available stocking. Now, his night's work mostly complete, it was time to relax and enjoy a snack. Well, not *relax*, especially, because countless children left out cookies for Santa and he didn't want to hurt any feelings by leaving even a crumb behind anywhere.

I didn't hear the rest of what Bobbo said. I was distracted because Willie Skokan and Heather Hathaway were approaching me with bewildered expressions, and I could tell instantly that something had gone very, very wrong in our plans to keep Lucretia Pepper and Jimmy Lee from cheating in the cookie-eating competition.

Twenty-two

e had thought it would be simple to thwart any attempt by Lucretia Pepper to somehow cheat in the cookie-eating contest so Jimmy Lee would win. On the morning of December 24, Heather Hathaway went to a bakery near Central Park and bought ten dozen round sugar cookies decorated with bright red sparkles. No one on *The Great Santa Search* staff thought it would be possible for anyone to gulp down more than thirty or so in the allotted sixty seconds, so 120 were plenty. Forty would be placed on each of three trays, and the trio of Santa finalists remaining would be served their mountains of cookies onstage.

The way Lucretia Pepper would try to cheat, we were certain, was to somehow get her hands on the cookies backstage before the competition and sprinkle something bad-tasting on those to be eaten by the two finalists matched against Jimmy Lee. So during the program, Willie Skokan kept a careful eye on the cookie trays. Lucretia Pepper never came near them.

While the stocking-stuffing competition wrapped up, Heather and Willie gathered the three trays of round sugar cookies and started taking them behind the curtain where three easy chairs had been set up by stagehands. There were low tables in front of the chairs, and resting on the tables were three tall glasses of delicious cold milk. But before my friends could place their trays of cookies on the tables, Lucretia Pepper ordered them to stop.

"Those cookies are just too drab to use on this wonderful program," she announced. "We'll use *these* instead." She gestured behind her, where three stagehands stood holding heaping trays of much bigger cookies festooned with a rainbow of colored sprinkles and cut into holiday-themed shapes—Christmas trees and bells and leaping reindeer. Truthfully, they were considerably more eye-catching than those Heather and Willie carried.

"But we already have these other ones," Heather argued. "It's all arranged."

Lucretia Pepper glowered.

"I am the sole sponsor of this program," she said. "You'll use the cookies I tell you to, and you'll do it without arguing."

"Well, I *will* argue," Heather replied, but just then Mary Rogers came bustling down from her director's booth.

"What's the holdup with the cookies?" she demanded. "The last Santa's stuffing the stockings. We've got to keep moving back here."

"This young woman is causing a commotion," Lucretia Pepper said smoothly. "We have these lovely, very attractive cookies to put on the tables and she is selfishly insisting we use plain ones just because she brought them."

Mary looked at both sets of trays.

"We're usin' the pretty ones," she said briskly. Heather started to object, but Mary waved her hand and added, "Look, I've got to get back to the booth. Put Lucretia's cookies on the tables. That's it."

It was at that moment that Zonk, Jimmy Lee, and I came offstage. We were immediately instructed to follow the stagehands to the chairs and tables set up behind the curtain. Lucretia Pepper held back Jimmy Lee and one of the stagehands, who didn't put his cookie tray down on the table in front of Jimmy Lee until Zonk and I were already seated with the other two trays in front of us. Short of shoving Jimmy Lee out of his chair so I could eat cookies from the tray on the table in front of him, there was nothing to be done. Something was going to be very wrong with the cookies Zonk and I were about to try to eat.

Perhaps if I'd had more time I could have come up with something, but on the other side of the curtain Bobbo Butler was addressing the audience.

"What I have to say almost defies belief," Bobbo declared. "Some ninety minutes ago I promised you that tonight we would be creating television history. That was guaranteed, of course, by the purpose of *The Great Santa Search*—identifying once and for all the real Santa Claus. And we're having fun doing that here at the Ed Sullivan Theater, aren't we? But something else just as amazing is happening all across America. Families in every city and town, in every neighborhood and on every block and street, have gathered together to spend their Christmas Eve watching *The Great Santa Search*—so many that we can announce this. There are approximately 110 million families in America watching television at this moment. Of those, eighty-five million are tuned in to *The Great Santa Search*. The biggest previous audience for any single program was just over fifty million. On behalf of FUN-TV and everyone associated with *The Great Santa Search*, I thank you for setting a new viewing record that may last as long as the television industry itself! Now, how's *that* for Christmas cheer?"

Behind the curtain, I settled in my chair and mournfully contemplated the plate of cookies in front of me. Zonk, sitting in the middle of the three chairs, turned to me, winked, and whispered, "Hope you worked up an appetite. Me, I'm starving!" I looked past Zonk and saw that Jimmy Lee seemed lost in thought.

"Okay, folks," Bobbo continued on the other side of the curtain. "Here comes our next-to-last challenge. We're close to identifying the real Santa Claus. Now, at this point in his night, he's filled all the stockings and it's time for a snack. Kids in America love to leave out cookies and milk for Santa to enjoy. So be it!"

The curtains opened, and there we three Santa finalists were in our chairs, with trays of cookies and glasses of milk on the tables before us.

"This is going to be very simple," Bobbo said. "You can see each of our finalists—from left to right they're Santa 3, Santa 8, and Santa 6—has a heaping tray of delicious cookies to enjoy. We're going to ask three elves to take their places behind the chairs."

Stagehands in elf regalia stood behind us. Each held a large electronic sign.

"The two Santas who eat the most cookies in sixty seconds will advance to the finals," Bobbo explained. "By eat, I mean chew up and completely swallow. The Santa who eats the fewest cookies is eliminated. There are forty cookies on each tray. The elves will keep track of how many cookies each Santa has eaten. At the end of sixty seconds, they'll enter the amounts on their electronic signs and hold them up one at a time until we see who was eliminated. Santas 3, 8, and 6, are you ready?"

Jimmy Lee jerked his head up. He'd been thinking hard about something. He waved at Bobbo to indicate he was ready. I nodded resignedly. I thought I would be able to choke down a few more bad-tasting cookies than poor, unsuspecting Zonk, but I wasn't looking forward to the experience.

Zonk picked up a cookie and brandished it toward the cameras.

"They look great!" he enthused. "I know it won't count, but I can't wait. I've got to eat one now!" And he crammed the cookie in his mouth.

Afterward, when we'd brought a few back to the North Pole for testing, Leonardo reported that the cookies placed in front of Zonk and me had been dusted by Lucretia Pepper with a nasty combination of crushed dill seed and onion powder. The colorful candy sprinkles on top effectively hid the vicious mixture.

I thought, as Lucretia Pepper and Jimmy Lee must have, that Zonk would immediately grimace and spit out the cookie. But he didn't. Instead, he swallowed, grinned, and smacked his lips.

"Let's start eating!" he suggested.

Then I remembered—Zonk had ageusia. He couldn't taste anything, so he wasn't able to tell that the cookies were supposed to be too horrible to eat. He and Jimmy Lee could both munch away happily, while I had to suffer through every foul bite.

"Keep a close eye on your favorite Santa finalist, folks," Bobbo commanded. "All right, then. Ready . . . set . . . *eat!*"

Jimmy Lee ate his untainted cookies at a steady, calculated pace. You could tell he'd studied how to consume the most in a limited time. He took big but not gigantic bites, chewing just thoroughly enough so that he wouldn't choke when he swallowed.

Zonk was more erratic. His plan, if he had one at all, was to quickly stuff cookies in his mouth until there wasn't room for one more crumb, somehow chew up and swallow it all, and repeat the pattern until time was up. So he got off to a good start, but within fifteen seconds he already had to stop and take several swallows of milk to wash down his massive mouthful. At least he didn't taste what he was eating.

My first bite of cookie was almost my last. Lucretia Pepper had planned well. The combination of crushed dill and onion powder burned my tongue and made my eyes water. I wanted to spit the nasty cookie out—and almost did. But then two things happened.

First, I remembered the millions of children who had left out cookies for me over the centuries. In many cases they'd baked the cookies themselves, and sometimes the results were not exactly delicious. But I ate those cookies anyway, because they had been prepared with love, and knowing that helped me ignore the less-than-pleasant taste. (One boy named Wilson loved licorice so much he actually put that in the cookies he prepared and left for me. Have you ever tasted baked licorice? Oh, I hope not!) So, in the past, I had been able to consume cookies regardless of how terrible they might taste.

Second, I'd just spent a whole year on the first diet of my life. For several centuries before that, I hadn't gone a day without cookies. I loved eating them. The batch of cookies in front of me might taste horrible, but they were still *cookies*. They had that wonderful, comforting cookie consistency that feels so right in your mouth when your teeth crunch everything up. Every dessertless day of my diet, I'd dreamed of the moment when I could once again enjoy all the cookies I wanted. Now it had arrived.

So I swallowed that first bite of cookie and took another, then another. Gradually the terrible taste seemed less important than the act of eating itself; it seemed I could almost hear my stomach joyfully shouting, "Finally! Cookies!" And the next thing I knew the jingle bells had sounded to end the sixty-second challenge, and the tray in front of me was quite empty. Jimmy Lee and Zonk each had cookies left on theirs.

For a moment, there was complete silence. Then Bobbo said in a voice filled with wonder, "Wow, Santa 6, you sure can eat a lot of cookies."

There were a few crumbs on my beard, so I brushed them off. I wasn't quite sure how to respond, and finally settled for, "Thank you."

Zonk was laughing, but Jimmy Lee's eyes bulged with shock. Somewhere offstage, I knew Lucretia Pepper was stunned, too.

"Well, we know Santa 6 goes on to the final challenge," Bobbo said. "Let's ask the elves standing behind the other two Santas to take turns showing us the total number of cookies eaten by each of them. Let's hear from the elf behind Santa 3."

Jimmy Lee's "elf" punched some buttons on his sign, then held it up. The number on the screen was *29*.

"Twenty-nine cookies in sixty seconds is quite impressive, Santa 3," Bobbo said. "I wonder if Santa 8 did better?"

Jimmy Lee never even glanced back at the electronic screen behind his chair. He'd obviously kept careful track of his cookie count, and knew it was twenty-nine. He'd expected Zonk and me not to be able to manage more than a few of the tainted cookies, so twenty-nine should have won easily.

But I'd polished off all forty of mine, and Zonk had certainly crammed down a considerable number of his. How fine it would be, I thought, if his total surpassed Jimmy Lee's, preventing the cheater from even advancing to the final challenge.

"Now, the total for Santa 8," Bobbo commanded, and Zonk's elf pushed buttons and held up his sign:

28.

"By one cookie, Santa 8 is eliminated," Bobbo announced, and the audience in the Ed Sullivan Theater gave my new friend a warm ovation as he waved, took one more cookie off his tray, stuffed it in his mouth, and walked offstage.

The most-watched program in all of television history had fifteen minutes left to go. The camera crews moved in for close-ups of Jimmy Lee and me.

Bobbo lowered his voice dramatically.

"And now, the final challenge," he said. "For the children of all ages in America who love and believe in him, you in our studio audience are about to choose the real Santa Claus."

He turned to Jimmy Lee and me.

"Santas 3 and 6, you can step offstage for just a moment. But don't go far. We'll be hearing from each of you very soon."

As soon as I was safely off-camera, Heather and Willie greeted me enthusiastically.

"How did you *do* that?" Heather wanted to know.

Willie answered for me.

"Santa Claus can do almost anything," he told her.

A few yards away, Lucretia Pepper and Jimmy Lee stood together, and it was obvious things weren't right between them. He said something and she shook her head emphatically while pointing her finger in his face. Whatever she said next made him angry, because his back straightened and his own finger shot out to point at her. Just then, she glanced in our direction and saw me watching. She said something else briefly to Jimmy Lee. He nodded and moved away, watching intently as she walked over to me.

"Well done, Santa 6," Lucretia Pepper said. "You certainly surprised me."

"The cookies you provided were quite interesting," I replied, trying to match her overly sincere tone. "Of course, I know you prepared them from your own special recipe."

She blinked, and I realized this woman was not used to anyone standing up to her. Her forcefulness, or, perhaps I should say, her nastiness, had intimidated everyone she dealt with—until now.

"You're not going to win," she declared. "Let's not pretend. I've seen to that. Jimmy Lee already has the votes. Be a good sport when you lose, don't mention anything that might embarrass either of us, and there'll be something in it for you afterward. I have deep pockets."

"Let's wait and see what happens," I suggested. "Perhaps in the next few minutes, you might learn something about the true spirit of Christmas. That's always possible, even for nevers."

"Nevers?" Lucretia Pepper responded. "What do you mean by *nevers?*"

I smiled at her.

"That's one of the things I'm going to talk about," I said. "And because I'll have to rush off after we're done here, I'll say this now in case I don't have the opportunity later: Merry Christmas, Lucretia Pepper. It's my sincere wish that somehow, some day, the joy of Christmas touches your heart."

Before she could reply, Felix tugged at my sleeve.

"It's time, Santa 6," he said. "Bobbo Butler is explaining the final challenge."

Twenty-three

I t's quarter of ten," Bobbo Butler reminded the 461 people in the Ed Sullivan Theater and the eighty-five million families watching *The Great Santa Search* at home. "Very soon, the one and only real, official Santa Claus will climb in his sleigh and fly through the Christmas Eve sky to bring presents to good boys and girls everywhere. But who *is* the real, official Santa? We've spent one hundred five minutes so far trying to find out. Christmas experts from *The Great Santa Search* staff spent months combing the country, and through their efforts we've presented ten Santa finalists to you tonight. Now it's down to the last two. Through reindeer-roping and carol-singing, from chimney-sliding to stocking-stuffing and just minutes ago during cookie-eating, these two individuals have proven they have all the necessary skills to be the undisputed Santa. But which one truly deserves your trust, your belief—I'll even say, your love? To know that, we have to know *them,* and this brings us to the final challenge of *The Great Santa Search.* First Santa 3, and then Santa 6, will have three minutes to tell our studio audience why he deserves their votes. Though all you wonderful, Christmas-loving viewers at home can't physically vote, we ask that you vote with your hearts."

Bobbo paused to take a breath—and, I think, to build tension.

"After each of our two *Great Santa Search* finalists has made his presentation, our studio audience will vote by pushing either the 3 or 6 button on the voting devices by their seats," he said. "Within seconds, you'll see the final totals flash on the studio monitors. At home, they'll be displayed on the lower part of your television screen. Then the official, the one and only elected Santa Claus, will be presented with a check for one million dollars to become the spokesman for LastLong Toy Company, which has so generously sponsored *The Great Santa Search* as a commercial-free broadcast."

It seemed to me, as I watched from the wings, that there was a sudden undercurrent of grumbling from the people in the theater. At least some of them found it disagreeable for Santa Claus to sell his services to LastLong and Lucretia Pepper.

Bobbo must have heard it, too, for he hastily added, "And, of course, our officially elected Santa Claus will undoubtedly have a few last words for us before he has to jump in his sleigh and start delivering presents. Let's begin. The studio monitors and a clock on the TV screens for you at home will count down the three minutes of each finalist's presentation. And so, let's hear first from Santa 3!"

Jimmy Lee had been huddled with Lucretia Pepper, who now seemed to be coaxing rather than threatening him. Instead of pointing a red-nailed finger in his face, she patted him soothingly on the shoulder. She did this in full view of everyone backstage. She was not trying to give even the slightest appearance of impartiality.

"Remember, you *are* Santa Claus," she told him loudly enough for all of us to hear. Jimmy Lee nodded and walked out onstage. Bobbo shook his hand and walked off. As soon as he was out of camera range he turned and, like the rest of us, watched and listened intently to Jimmy Lee.

I had to give Jimmy Lee credit. He must have been badly shaken when, despite his and Lucretia Pepper's best cheating efforts, I won the cookie-eating competition. He certainly had been distracted ever since Heather Hathaway had explained to him how he might make even more money by betraying Lucretia Pepper and refusing LastLong Toy Company's million dollars to become its corporate spokesman. And, of course, there was the tremendous pressure of knowing so many people were watching him in person and on television as he stood in his red-and-white Santa costume, the hot stage lights glaring in his eyes and burning on his skin. It would have been natural for him to not only feel but look nervous, perhaps with the added discomfort of sweating profusely while words he wanted to say somehow stuck in his throat.

But instead he appeared calm, even happy. And though his three minutes had begun as soon as Bobbo Butler walked offstage and he walked on, Jimmy Lee didn't start talking right away. Instead, he stood for a moment with his hands folded comfortably in front of him, smiling and looking at the studio audience and then directly into the TV cameras so his gaze could seem to touch on everyone watching at home, too.

"Well, Merry Christmas to you all," he finally began. "We've had a wonderful evening, haven't we? Good manners are as important for Santa Claus as they are for everyone else, so let me begin by recognizing the FUN-TV network and especially its president, Mr. Bobbo Butler, for making all this possible. Please, Mr. Butler, come out and let us thank you."

Bobbo, thrilled with the record audience *The Great Santa Search* had attracted, came beaming out from the wings. He waved his arms over his head in response to the warm applause from the studio audience, then theatrically looked at his watch, tapped it to indicate time was passing, and hurried off.

"There's someone else special," Jimmy Lee continued. "She would not really want anyone to know how responsible she is for this moment. No words exist to honestly describe her goodness and generosity. The owner and president of LastLong Toy Company, Lucretia Pepper."

It was only at this moment, I realized, that Lucretia Pepper completely believed everything would turn out as she wanted. Her chosen finalist, Jimmy Lee, was going to win *The Great Santa Search,* and he was going to be a loyal, effective company spokesman, which might eventually destroy many children's belief in Santa Claus but would also earn her untold millions of dollars, which was all she really cared about.

"Thank you, Santa, thank you," she cooed as she blew kisses to the studio audience whose token clapping for her was far less enthusiastic than their genuine ovation for Bobbo Butler.

Only then did Jimmy Lee begin his plea for the studio audience's votes.

"*I* am Santa Claus," he declared. "I think most of you know that already. We know each other, you and I, because I've been in your homes each Christmas Eve as a most welcome, if not visible, guest. You've written letters to me, and I've read them. We do read your letters at the North Pole, by the way. How else would my elves know what toys to make, and how many of each?"

Elves again, I thought. *If only I could have talked to Thomas Nast and convinced him to do away with the elf business altogether!*

Jimmy Lee smiled warmly.

"So that's our bond, isn't it? The gifts I bring. They are the connection between us. When you hold that special toy in your hand, you believe in me and love me with all your heart. I can feel that love now. It's coming from everyone here tonight in New York City's Ed Sullivan Theater, and from all of you watching at home."

He waved his hand toward the wings.

"Backstage tonight I made nine new friends. I don't resent that they tried to convince you they were Santa Claus instead of me. You weren't deceived. You're about to prove it when you vote. But once you make it official, no one else should ever pretend to be me again. You won't need pretenders. You'll have the real Santa Claus. And what will that mean?"

Now Jimmy Lee hunched slightly forward, as though he was about to confide a secret.

"It will mean that from now on, you'll know for certain that I'm the one hearing which presents you want. It won't be some imitation Santa with his fake beard falling off. I know that all these years I've mostly been up at the North Pole, but after tonight I expect to be out and about much more. Don't worry—we'll still be making toys back in the North Pole shop! My elves are very efficient. And what they can't make, other companies can, like Last-Long Toy Company. If you get the toys you want, I don't think you care too much who actually made them. You see, I understand that, because I understand you."

He paused again, and adopted a serious expression.

"And I understand something else. We should speak about it. We live in a terrifying world. Awful things sometimes happen. They frighten you. You don't feel safe. And then, every year for a little while, Christmas comes. And so do I, to help you forget all the other terrible things. That's what my presents are for. This is why you must vote carefully tonight. Earlier, I sang to you in English and in German. I did it so you would realize that Christmas is important all over the world. I'm needed all over the world. When you vote for me, you are doing something wonderful not only for yourselves but for others in many foreign countries who are looking to you tonight for leadership, for wisdom. Don't let them down."

Jimmy Lee craned his neck to peek at the studio clock.

"Time is precious on Christmas Eve," he said. "I won't say good-bye, because before the sun comes up in the morning I'll have been to all your houses. Now that we've officially met, we'll see much more of each other, I promise. And tonight, I know exactly what presents you want, and soon I'll be on my way to deliver them. Good night."

The applause was loud and extended. I knew that 150 members of the audience were controlled by Lucretia Pepper. They had to support and vote for Jimmy Lee to keep their jobs. That left 311 voters who were available to be persuaded by one of us. Judging from the crowd's reaction to his speech, Jimmy Lee had made a good impression on them.

Bobbo Butler hustled out onstage, clapping along with the audience as Jimmy Lee took several deep bows.

"Just wonderful, Santa 3!" he commented. "Well done indeed!"

Jimmy Lee took a final bow and walked to the wings, where he was embraced by a leering Lucretia Pepper.

I took a deep breath. Willie Skokan shook my hand. So did Felix; if Lucretia Pepper was making it obvious which finalist she favored, so could he.

Heather Hathaway hugged me, and whispered in my ear, "I think I know. I'm sure I do. I believe in you."

Those words rather than the hot studio lights warmed me as Bobbo Butler called me out onstage.

"Santa 6, take it away!" he commanded, and shook my hand on his way off. It was a firm, friendly handshake. Unlike Lucretia Pepper, Bobbo Butler would be happy with whoever won *The Great Santa Search*.

I stood onstage. Perhaps I should have felt nervous. I didn't. Thanks to Lucretia Pepper's duplicity, Jimmy Lee already had 150 votes out of a possible 461. But he wasn't Santa Claus. I was.

And that is why I began my own remarks by saying, "Good evening. It's less important for you to know *who* Santa Claus is than *why* Santa Claus is. Perhaps that sounds rather confusing. Let's talk about it."

I rubbed my chin, gently untangling white strands of beard with my fingers. I didn't try to think of words before I spoke them. I just let them come from my heart.

"By many different names—Santa Claus, St. Nicholas, Father Christmas, Kris Kringle, Père Noel, Grandfather Frost, and others—there has been widespread if not universal belief in a special holiday gift-giver for centuries," I explained. "When the legends began, like most tales they were based on some truth. If we had more time, I would tell you of my early days as a simple young boy named Nicholas, when I lived in a country called Lycia and gave my first gifts to young girls who desperately needed dowries to be married. You can find these things in history books. I promise you, the information is there.

"But in time the gift-giving was linked to me, and people began to speculate what this St. Nicholas looked like. There were paintings of me with a white beard, wearing a red cloak trimmed with white fur. In the 1860s, a very talented American artist named Thomas Nast suggested in his drawings that I lived at the North Pole, which was eventually true, and that I was helped in my gift-giving mission by elves, which wasn't. As I said, most legends begin with truth, but the tale-tellers add colorful details that have more basis in imagination than fact. And another important fact is that Dutch settlers brought their beliefs in me to America, and when their children told English-speaking children about me, the way they pronounced St. Nicholas was 'sintnicklass,' which the English children heard first as 'sinter klass' and eventually as 'Santa Claus.' That's how I got the name most of you here and watching at home tonight call me. And, over time, my friends and I—I have very special companions, though they're certainly not elves—became welcome in homes all over the world. In different places and by different names, we are expected on December 25 or December 6 or January 6. And we are glad to oblige."

I paused, not to collect my thoughts but to allow my listeners to gather theirs.

"The present confusion over who is Santa began, I believe, in 1841, when a friend of mine who owned a general store in Philadelphia hired someone to impersonate me one Christmas season. He thought having a pretend Santa in his store would boost holiday sales, and he was right. It took some time, but others eventually followed his example. Soon there were so-called Santas everywhere. How very confusing for everyone! But, always, there was really only one Santa, and that was me.

"So that's the history of who Santa is, but I mentioned earlier it is more important to know *why* Santa is. I began giving gifts in times when most people didn't have enough to eat, or sandals to wear, or blankets to keep them warm at night. So I gave these things for hundreds of years, until it was explained to me by wise friends that it was just not possible to give something to everyone. Children needed most to know they were loved, so I must concentrate on them. Something lasting and joyful was required, because food would be quickly eaten and clothes outgrown—that was how I came to bring toys."

The audience in the Ed Sullivan Theater listened in perfect silence. I hoped it was because my words touched them.

"I come to many of your homes on Christmas Eve, December 24, because on Christmas Day you celebrate the greatest gift of all, God's gift of his son," I continued. "Jesus was sent to give us comfort and hope. He was proof of God's love. There are some who do not believe in that, or in me. This is your right. But I do hope you at least believe in giving comfort to those who need it. I hope you believe in love.

"As Santa 3 has told you, this can be a terrifying world. It would be wrong to ignore its faults and its dangers. But there is no greater gift than caring for others and making sure they know you care. Yes, I bring toys, but I want you to understand that those toys are a symbol of love. They are not meant to make you forget the bad things in your lives. They are intended to remind you that goodness exists, too, and hope. My gifts are not supposed to be distractions from evil. They are proof of the goodness that exists, of the hope that is always possible, and of the dreams which might still come true. This is *why* there is Santa Claus."

Now it was my turn to peek at the studio clock. I had one minute remaining.

"Will someone please turn up the lights so I can see the audience?" I asked. "What I say next is more about you than me."

Everyone in the theater was instantly illuminated. I could see Layla and Arthur and Francis and Bill in their middle-row seats, and the various television stars much closer to the stage, and in the center of the front row Cynthia and Diana, Bobbo Butler's daughters.

"Some people believe in Santa Claus all their lives, some believe for a while, and some never believe in me at all," I said. "What few ever realize is that no matter what you do or don't believe, each of you has the ability to *be* Santa Claus. At Christmas or any other time of year, if you take it upon yourself to give a gift with the intention of reminding the recipient that someone cares, that happiness as well as sorrow can be part of each life, then you and I are the same. You, too, are extending the loving, gift-giving tradition that goes back to the original time when the Wise Men brought their gifts to the baby Jesus. The bond between us is not the gifts I give you, but the love and caring that is extended from one person to another."

I found myself gazing at ten-year-old Cynthia and eight-year-old Diana Butler. Seeing them, I knew how to conclude.

"In any of your lives, the time has come, or will come, when for one reason or another you're no longer sure that I exist," I said. "At that moment, you'll have to make your own decisions about Santa Claus. But I hope you'll remember one thing. Whether you remain a true believer, or believe for a while, or never believe at all, so long as you do your best to be a kind and caring person, Santa Claus will always believe in *you*.

"Merry Christmas."

There was total silence for one second, two seconds, three. Then, slowly at first, hands began to clap, and the clapping got louder and then there were cheers and with all the theater lights on I could see many people had tears running down their cheeks. I stood there while Bobbo raced back onstage, his own eyes shining with tears, and called a suddenly surly-looking Jimmy Lee out to stand beside me while the audience voted.

Then, by a margin of some half-dozen votes, Jimmy Lee won *The Great Santa Search*.

Twenty-four

ackstage, Lucretia Pepper shrieked in triumph when the voting totals were announced. The unnerving sound reverberated through the Ed Sullivan Theater and must have been heard by all the viewers at home. A moment later *The Great Santa Search* theme song blared out instead. Jimmy Lee embraced Bobbo Butler, then walked to the front of the stage, waving at the crowd. Everyone in the theater was standing and applauding. Almost half of them would have preferred the winner to be me, but they were being good sports and showing appreciation for the victor. I could do no less.

I walked to where Jimmy Lee stood waving and tapped him on the shoulder. He'd been quite lost in his moment of triumph; he flinched as I touched him, but when he turned and saw me he threw his arms wide and we hugged.

"You can still do the right thing," I whispered in his ear.

"Watch," he whispered back.

Then, after a quick wave toward Layla and my North Pole friends in the audience, I made my way offstage.

"Let's hear it for Santa 6, a great competitor," Bobbo Butler urged, and the crowd responded with a fine ovation. Then I was off-camera in the wings, and Felix, Sarah, Heather Hathaway, and Willie Skokan greeted me with hugs and assurances that they were proud of me.

"What a lovely speech," Sarah declared. "I don't understand why Santa 3 got even one vote."

"*I* do," Heather grumbled. "He and Lucretia Pepper are such cheaters!"

"We're also *winners,*" someone snarled. Lucretia Pepper was standing beside us, and the expression of evil joy on her face was frightening in its intensity. "And I'd better not read or hear suggestions from any of you that this contest wasn't on the up-and-up. If I do, you'll be hearing from my lawyers. And now, the *real* Santa Claus is about to become part of the team at LastLong Toys!"

Jimmy Lee stood with Bobbo Butler at the center of the stage. Two of the stagehands dressed as elves carried out a long, rectangular cardboard check. The amount on it was $1,000,000.00, and it was made out to Santa Claus. The LastLong Toy Company logo was prominently plastered on the upper left-hand corner.

Felix, Sarah, Heather, Willie, and I watched from the wings as Bobbo Butler raised his hand to request silence. The audience finally stopped applauding and sat back down. As they did, Oprah Winfrey shouted, "You're coming on my show first, Santa honey!" and everyone laughed.

"Just before he leaves to spend the rest of the night delivering gifts, we have a gift for Santa himself," Bobbo said. "To present our winner, the real and only official Santa Claus, with this million-dollar check is the president of LastLong Toy Company, Lucretia Pepper!"

Sarah, who has a way with words, later remarked that Lucretia Pepper slithered rather than walked out on the stage. The hulking woman rudely pulled the cardboard check away from the stagehands.

"Santa Claus, it is with the utmost pleasure that I present you with this check for one million dollars," she said. "And along with it you have my very warmest welcome as the new, year-round spokesperson for LastLong Toy Company. Santa Claus and LastLong Toys—names that as of now are linked together."

She extended her arms to present the check to Jimmy Lee. He took a step back.

"Here's your check, Santa," Lucretia Pepper said.

"Thank you, but no," Jimmy Lee replied. He turned to Bobbo. "Mr. Butler, may I have a few moments for concluding remarks?"

"Of course, Santa," Bobbo said. "But don't you want your check?"

"Actually, no," Jimmy Lee repeated. "I'll explain. Perhaps you'd escort Ms. Pepper offstage while I do."

Bobbo tried to take Lucretia Pepper's arm, but she yanked it away. Her face was twisted with rage. I'm sure she thought about attacking Jimmy Lee on the spot, but the largest audience in television history was watching, so she stormed off after leaning toward Jimmy Lee and muttering undoubtedly horrible threats that the studio microphones thankfully did not pick up and broadcast.

"What's he up to?" Felix asked me.

"Let's listen," I suggested. "I think someone's stony heart may have finally been touched by true Christmas spirit."

Jimmy Lee faced the audience, smiling warmly at them. He reached up, removed his tassled cap, and held it in front of him with both hands.

"My friends, I'm so profoundly grateful to you," he said. "I feel your love for Santa Claus, and I promise you it is mutual. My unwavering belief is that Santa Claus belongs to everyone, not just one company, and so I'm afraid I can't accept money, even such a magnificent sum, to become the spokesman for LastLong Toy Company products. But here's good news. You may have noticed Ms. Lucretia Pepper whispering to me just before she left the stage. She's too modest to make it public, so I will. She has just promised to donate the million dollars to charities that provide Christmas comfort to homeless children right here in New York City. Isn't that wonderful? Won't you please join me in thanking her?"

Lucretia Pepper had no choice but to briefly emerge from the wings and make a jerky, waving motion in the direction of the audience. She was trying to twist her furious expression into some semblance of a smile, but didn't succeed. Then, glowering at Jimmy Lee, she whirled and left the stage.

"Even Santa Claus can always learn things," Jimmy Lee continued. "I've learned a great deal tonight. If I didn't before, I know now that Santa Claus *does* belong to everyone, every girl and boy and father and mother and also to grandparents and everyone else in the world. Truly, Santa must not be affiliated with one toy company—he should share his wisdom and experience with many of them, and perhaps with other creative artists in the movie and television and book industries. Santa Claus loves them all equally."

"He means *this* Santa Claus loves everybody's *money* equally," Heather grumbled.

"Jimmy Lee doesn't completely understand Christmas and generosity of spirit yet," I agreed. "He's still anxious for the book and movie deals you suggested to him. But he's making a start, Heather. Sometimes it takes a while for holiday magic to complete its wonderful work."

Felix leaned over to me.

"Attila's brought the sleigh and reindeer out in the alley, Santa," he whispered. "All the toys are packed in it. You're ready to go."

"In a moment, Felix," I replied. "Just like Jimmy Lee, I may be learning something."

Jimmy Lee concluded his speech. He thanked everyone again, and made the audience laugh when he noted he'd be bringing toys to all of them, "even the ones who didn't vote for me." After I'd asked that the theater lights be turned up, no one in the control booth had ever turned them down again, so everyone in the audience was visible. My North Pole companions—Layla, Arthur, Francis, and Bill—were listening politely to Jimmy Lee, and everyone else, including the famous TV personalities, were simply rapt. They gazed adoringly at the man who'd just become the official Santa Claus. They were hanging on his every word.

Watching Jimmy Lee charm the crowd, I remembered how, back at Galaxy Mall, all the children were thrilled to meet Lester Sneed dressed as Santa, even though Mr. Sneed's beard was scraggly and his belly clearly wasn't of Santa-like proportions.

"Oh, why do they like him so much?" Heather murmured.

And at that moment I understood it completely. Just a few moments before, Jimmy Lee had said that even Santa Claus can always learn, and he was right.

"They like him because they truly believe in the *idea* of Santa Claus," I told Sarah. "In all these years of worrying about impostors ruining belief in me, I'd never realized that. When they see Jimmy Lee, or when anyone sees a Santa in a mall or ringing a bell on a street corner, what they're really seeing is a reminder that love and generosity still exist in this imperfect world of ours. Look at Bobbo Butler's daughters!"

Cynthia and Diana were leaning so far forward in their front-row seats that they were in danger of banging their chins on the front edge of the stage. Cynthia had her usual wide-eyed look of pleased wonder, but the previously doubting Diana appeared even more enthralled. Her smile was so wide it seemed the edges of her mouth were about to touch her ears.

"You see, it really doesn't matter which Santa Claus children believe in, so long as they believe in him at all," I continued. "If they do, then they'll eventually realize that Christmas is about caring and love and hope rather than toys, and they'll teach that to *their* children, and we'll continue to have believers and true believers and maximum true believers. Jimmy Lee is only beginning to realize that even though he's not Santa, he's still an important Santa's helper. He's going to be on television shows and in movies and have books written about him, and perhaps for a while he'll think he's doing it only for the money. But eventually he'll understand he's also doing it for me, and for Christmas."

Up in the control booth, Mary Rogers was calling out last-second instructions. Listening on his headphones, a backstage worker held out his hand to signal Jimmy Lee—three, two, one.

"Merry Christmas!" shouted Jimmy Lee, and with that the program's theme music blared again. The hands on the studio clock read 10:00 p.m, the red lights on the cameras blinked off, and *The Great Santa Search* was now a permanent part of television history.

The curtains closed in front of the stage. Behind them, Bobbo Butler raised his arms over his head in triumph. Jimmy Lee hurried toward his dressing room, no doubt hoping there would already be messages there offering him roles in movies or publishing contracts for the *official* Santa's memoirs. But as he passed me he whispered, "I may want to talk to you soon. Where can I reach you?"

"I'll be glad to talk with you, and don't worry about reaching me," I whispered back. "When the time is right, I'll know where you are."

Jimmy Lee smiled. We shook hands. Then he disappeared into his dressing room.

"Where are you, Miss Hathaway?" Bobbo called. "Get me my girls! I want Cynthia and Diana!"

Heather rolled her eyes.

"The chief calls," she said. "I'll be back in a minute."

She darted down in front of the stage and collected Diana and Cynthia. They ran backstage and scampered into their father's arms.

"You were great, Daddy!" Cynthia gushed.

Diana said she wanted to talk to Santa Claus.

"I need to make sure he's got my present on his sleigh," she said.

"I thought you didn't believe in Santa Claus anymore," Bobbo pointed out.

"I do now," Diana declared.

Bobbo took both his daughters by the hand.

"Well, I think we can arrange—" he began, and then Lucretia Pepper made a bull-like charge in his direction.

"You *tricked* me!" she howled, which made no sense. Bobbo had nothing to do with Jimmy Lee's renunciation. But people like Lucretia Pepper must always take their anger out on someone, and she'd chosen Bobbo Butler. I really believe she intended to physically attack him right in front of his children. She rushed at Bobbo, ham-like hands extended to grab or pinch or punch, but she never reached him. Heather Hathaway stepped in front of Bobbo. The tall, rangy young woman lowered her shoulder, and Lucretia Pepper rammed her own midsection into it. The owner of LastLong Toys went sprawling.

Heather calmly walked over to where she lay gasping for air.

"You just assaulted me in front of dozens of witnesses," she said. "If you ever try to say anything different, you'll be hearing from my lawyers. Oh, and Merry Christmas."

Lucretia Pepper got slowly to her feet. She glared at everyone and left.

Bobbo, an awestruck expression on his face, walked up to Heather.

"Miss Hathaway," he began. "Um, Heather. You know, I've just realized something. You're very, well, *special*. It's been such an exciting night. I think I'd like to go out for a late meal after I take the girls home. I wonder, will you join me?"

Heather shook her head.

"I appreciate the invitation, Bobbo, but I can't. Willie Skokan is taking me to dinner."

"Who?" Bobbo asked.

"Someone I met tonight," Heather said. Bobbo looked panic-stricken, so she added, "Don't worry, Bobbo. It's only dinner. I'll see you at work next week, and you can ask me out then. Merry Christmas, Cynthia and Diana. I'm glad you believe in Santa Claus again." Heather and Willie walked away, while Bobbo stared after them.

"I swore I'd save my network, and I've done it," he muttered. "I promised I'd get the highest ratings for any show in television history, and it happened. Now I give my word that someday I'll convince Heather Hathaway to marry me. I'm going to do it. I am."

"I'm sure you will, Bobbo," said Sarah, patting the lovestruck man's arm. "Just don't take her for granted anymore. When someone is as wonderful as Heather, you can't expect that nobody else will notice."

"Well, *I've* finally noticed," Bobbo agreed. He sighed, and then remembered that his daughters were still standing at his side.

"Time to go home," he told them.

"Hurry up, Daddy," Diana urged. "Cyn and I need to get to sleep so Santa can come."

"Oh, so you and your sister do believe in me?" someone asked. Jimmy Lee had emerged from his dressing room. He still wore his costume and seemed every bit a warm, benevolent Santa. The little girls ran to him and received big hugs.

"Are *you* free for dinner after I get my girls home, Santa?" Bobbo asked.

Jimmy Lee shook his head.

"I'm afraid not, because I still have so much to do," he said. "It's Christmas Eve, don't forget, and there were also some messages in my dressing room that I need to return as soon as possible. But before I leave, I would love one last time for these pretty girls to tell me exactly what they want Santa to bring them tonight." He sat down on one of the big chairs we'd used during the cookie-eating challenge, and Cynthia and Diana scrambled up in his lap.

Turned down by Heather and Jimmy Lee, Bobbo still wanted company.

"What about you, Santa 6?" he asked. "I hope you're not too disappointed about losing. Let me buy you a consolation meal. I promise, we'll have the best food in New York City."

I declined, too. When my long night of work was done, I'd enjoy a North Pole feast prepared by Lars, and no New York City chef could match his abilities in the kitchen. With my diet now over, I hoped Lars would serve his fluffy pecan waffles, and also *huevos rancheros,* and perhaps some delicious blueberry muffins. I'd go back to eating sensibly after Epiphany—perhaps. Gift-giving is hungry work. And even before I returned home tonight, I'd also snack on cookies and milk left for me at so many houses by loving boys and girls. None of those cookies would be of the dill-and-onion variety, I was certain.

"Perhaps another time, Bobbo," I said. "Congratulations on your record-breaking program, and Merry Christmas to you."

"Merry Christmas, Santa 6," Bobbo replied. "I really don't understand why you're in such a hurry."

I told him the truth: "The reindeer are waiting."

Hot Chocolate Cake

This is one of our favorite cakes here at the North Pole, and is especially welcome on those really cold nights we have here from time to time. It's easy to make, and absolutely delicious.

DRY INGREDIENTS

1½ cups all-purpose flour
1 cup sugar
½ cup unsweetened cocoa
   (We use Ghirardelli.)
1 teaspoon baking soda

¼ teaspoon cayenne pepper (Use a
   little more if your family loves it
hot, but please keep it well under
1 teaspoon.)
¼ teaspoon salt

WET INGREDIENTS

1 cup cold water
¼ cup vegetable oil

1 tablespoon balsamic vinegar
1 tablespoon vanilla extract

Glaze ingredients follow baking instructions, below.

PREPARATION

1. Preheat the oven to 350°F.
2. Lightly grease a bundt cake pan, then lightly dust it with cocoa, and set it aside.
3. Combine all of the dry ingredients in a mixing bowl and stir until everything is well blended. We usually don't sift the cocoa and the flour, but do break up any large clumps before they're mixed in.
4. Add the wet ingredients, and stir until smooth.
5. Pour the batter into the cake pan and bake for 25 to 35 minutes. (When it's ready, a toothpick inserted deep into the ring will come out clean.)
6. Leave the cake in the pan for 10 minutes, on a wire rack.
7. Remove the cake from the pan and let it cool completely.
8. After the cake has completely cooled, prepare the glaze you prefer as directed below.

CHOOSE YOUR GLAZE

Chocolate Lovers' Glaze

1 cup confectioners sugar
½ cup cocoa (We use Ghirardelli.)
2 tablespoons melted butter
5 tablespoons water
1 teaspoon vanilla extract

In a small bowl, whisk together all the ingredients until smooth. Pour the glaze over the top of the cake and let it dry (about 30 minutes).

Holiday Glaze

1½ cups confectioners sugar
2 tablespoons water
2 tablespoons melted butter
1 teaspoon vanilla extract
¼ cup dried cranberries

In a small bowl, whisk together the first 4 ingredients until smooth. Pour the glaze over the top of the cake. Sprinkle the dried cranberries on top for a tasty holiday look. Let the glaze dry (about 30 minutes).

For the Chocolate Lovers' Glaze: Just before serving, dust the slices with some powdered confectioners sugar—it will look like a light snowfall! And for more color, serve it with strawberries or raspberries.

Acknowledgments

THANKS ABOVE ALL to three special people involved in this project: Sara Carder, the brilliant senior editor at Tarcher/Penguin; Andrea Ahles Koos, the best researcher in modern-day publishing; and Jim Donovan, a literary agent who combines intelligence, heart, and unerring common sense.

I'm also grateful to Joel Fotinos, Mark McDiarmid, and Ken Siman at Tarcher/Penguin; Wes Turner, Scott Nishimura, Stephanie Owen, Paul Bourgeois, Melinda Mason, Charles and Mary Rogers, Charles Caple and Marcia Melton, Rick Press, Broc Sears, Mark Hoffer, Nancy Burford, Cynthia Wahl, Diana Andro, and Heather Landy at the *Star-Telegram;* and Felix Higgins, Robert Fernandez, Larry "Lars" Wilson, Robert Olen Butler, Zonk Lanzillo, Eri Mizobe, James Ward Lee, Carlton Stowers, Doug Perry, Mary Arendes, Del Hillen, Elizabeth Hayes, and Brian McLendon.

I found inspiration in the memories of Dot and Frank Lauden, Marie and Louis Renz, Jim Firth, Jerry Flemmons, Jack B. Tinsley, Max Lale, and Iris Chang.

Special thanks for information and cooperation from the Noerr Program.

Everything I write is always for Nora, Adam, and Grant.